Language

Its Structure and Use

musician : mʊzɪsɪn
palm: pʰalm
ready: rɛdi
teacher: tiʧr

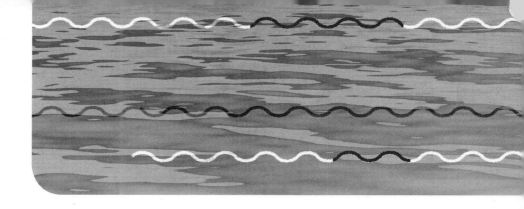

Language
Its Structure and Use

| SIXTH EDITION

Edward Finegan
University of Southern California

 WADSWORTH
CENGAGE Learning

Australia • Brazil • Japan • Korea • Mexico • Singapore • Spain • United Kingdom • United States

WADSWORTH
CENGAGE Learning™

Language: Its Structure and Use, Sixth Edition
Edward Finegan

Senior Publisher: Lyn Uhl

Publisher: Michael Rosenberg

Development Editor: Joan M. Flaherty

Assistant Editor: Erin Bosco

Editorial Assistant: Rebecca Donahue

Media Editor: Janine Tangney

Marketing Manager: Melissa Holt

Marketing Coordinator: Brittany Blais

Marketing Communications Manager:
Glenn McGibbon

Senior Content Project Manager:
Michael Lepera

Art Director: Marissa Falco

Senior Print Buyer: Betsy Donaghey

Senior Image Rights Specialist: Jennifer
Meyer Dare

Senior Rights Acquisition Specialist, Text:
Katie Huha

Production Service/Compositor:
PreMediaGlobal

Text Designer: Brian Salisbury

Cover Designer: Kathleen Kemp

Cover Image: © Veer

For product information and technology assistance, contact us at
Cengage Learning Customer & Sales Support, 1-800-354-9706

For permission to use material from this text or product,
submit all requests online at **cengage.com/permissions**
Further permissions questions can be emailed to
permissionrequest@cengage.com

Library of Congress Control Number: 2010942527

ISBN-13: 978-0-495-90041-2

ISBN-10: 0-495-90041-9

Wadsworth
20 Channel Center Street
Boston, MA 02210
USA

Cengage Learning is a leading provider of customized learning solutions with office locations around the globe, including Singapore, the United Kingdom, Australia, Mexico, Brazil, and Japan. Locate your local office at:
international.cengage.com/region

Cengage Learning products are represented in Canada by Nelson Education, Ltd.

For your course and learning solutions, visit **www.cengage.com**

Purchase any of our products at your local college store or at our preferred online store **www.cengagebrain.com**

Printed in the United States of America
1 2 3 4 5 6 7 15 14 13 12 11

Contents in Brief

Contents in Detail

Contents in Detail

Chapter 3 | The Sounds of Languages: Phonetics   81

Chapter 4 | Sound Systems of Language: Phonology   111

Chapter 5 | The Structure and Function of Phrases and Sentences: Syntax 151

Chapter 6 | The Study of Meaning: Semantics   187

Chapter 7 | Language Universals and Language Typology   231

Part Two
Language Use   267

Chapter 8 | Information Structure and Pragmatics   268

Chapter 9 | Speech Acts and Conversation   301

Chapter 10 | Language Variation Across Situations of Use: Registers and Styles   335

Chapter 14 | Acquiring First and Second Languages   499

A Special Word to Students

For century upon century, philosophers, rhetoricians, and grammarians have analyzed the uses to which people put language in their everyday lives and the linguistic structures and social structures supporting that use. The nineteenth and twentieth centuries proved rich in linguistic insight as philologists at first and then linguists and cognitive scientists broadened and deepened our understanding of the singularly human trait that is language. As with the life sciences and space exploration in recent decades, language scientists have also generated a burst of insight into the representation of language in the brain and the interactions between language use and social structures.

Despite the impressive pace at which investigators have gained insight into human language, significant questions remain unanswered and many arenas remain underexplored. Far more remains to be discovered about language than is now known, and an abundance of intellectually challenging and socially important work remains to be achieved by today's college and university students, who will become tomorrow's researchers. For those of you aiming to contribute to our understanding of the human brain or human social interaction, rest assured that what we know now about language will be dwarfed by what you and your peers discover during your careers. For you and for those wishing simply to grasp what we now know, this book offers an invitation to think about and raise your own questions about language and its role in your life and the lives of everyone around you.

Among the proverbs I have found to be generally true since my school days, one says, "A stitch in time saves nine," while another warns, "Look before you leap." Proving false, however, was the proverb claiming, "Sticks and stones may break my bones, but words will never hurt me." Most of us learn early in life how powerful an instrument for good and ill language can be. A powerful tool of enlightenment with extraordinary potential to delight us, language can also inflict injury and cause harm. Given that language is as central to our social interactions as it is to our cognitive endeavors, the ability to accomplish so much good or inflict such harm should not be surprising. Irrespective of your college major or your career goals, every student will benefit from knowing as much about language—its structure and use—as you can succeed at learning.

In reading *Language: Its Structure and Use*—LISU for short—you'll see some words in **boldface** type even when they are not examples or captions. When an important concept is first discussed (not necessarily when first mentioned), the term for it is set in boldface to highlight its significance and alert you to its appearance in the glossary. To learn more about topics that catch your fancy, the "Suggestions for Further Reading" at the end of each chapter will guide you. You'll also find website addresses at the end of most chapters and descriptions of interesting videos. For further leads and other valuable discussion, go to **http://www.CengageBrain.com** and click your way through to the LISU pages. Once there, be sure to bookmark the site for easy return visits without having to click through. At that site you'll also find answers to the Practice Exercises.

A Word to Instructors

LISU includes more chapters than can be covered in a one-semester course. Typically, instructors cover the first six chapters and then select among the others. As ordered here, the chapter on morphology appears before the chapters treating phonetics and phonology. Partly because novices find words more tangible and accessible than sounds and partly because morphology can be discussed without phonetic symbols, whose appearance at the gateway may be daunting, many instructors find that beginning the discussion of language structure with words is more appealing for students. The sequence in LISU invites teaching morphology before phonology, but if you prefer to teach phonetics and phonology first, simply postpone the section titled "Morphology and Phonology Interaction: Allomorphy" from Chapter 4 until after you've completed Chapter 2 on morphology (the order of chapters taught would then be 1, 3, 4, 2). In an effort to contain costs, the chapter titled "Writing" does not appear in the printed pages of this edition, but it remains available on the LISU website for instructors with time to teach it and for interested students; the boldfaced terms in that chapter are included in the printed glossary at the end of this text.

Each chapter contains sections on computers and a particular aspect of language such as phonology or dialects. Each chapter also offers separate exercises for English and for other languages. Under the rubric "What Do You Think?" at the head of each chapter are a few puzzlers aiming to engage students with quotidian situations in which the chapter's contents play a role, and preceding the exercises at the end of the chapter students will find brief responses. Many instructors have praised these questions, but if you or your students prefer to skip them, you should of course feel free to do so.

In other ways I've endeavored to make LISU interactive. The "Try It Yourself" sections straightforwardly apply what has just been explained in the text and encourage students to check their understanding. Although of particular interest for the designated audiences, the exercises in "Especially for Educators and Future Teachers" will usually prove helpful to all students and can be framed as for parents and parents-to-be, peering through the eyes of teachers.

This edition of LISU has been expanded in some respects, condensed in others, updated throughout, and recast thoroughly for greater clarity. In response to suggestions from instructors, Chapter 1 has been reorganized and trimmed. To clarify the treatment of morphology in Chapter 2, additional tree diagrams appear and the discussion of morphological types is expanded, with examples from Swahili and Gikuyu; I have included discussion of new words like the verbs *tweet* and *google*. Chapters 3 and 4 on phonetics and phonology have been revised for greater clarity and more explicit descriptions of manners of articulation;

Chapter 4 has additional trees, representing words of one, two, and three syllables. Chapter 5 on syntax has additional tree diagrams and more explicit trees, minimizing the abbreviated triangles; a new section on testing for constituency by movement, substitution, and coordination has been added. While Chapters 6 through 9 have benefited chiefly from improved clarity and updated examples, a new section titled "Language Universals, Universal Grammar, and Language Acquisition" has been added to Chapter 7. Chapter 10, on registers, replaces the longer passage of legalese and its analysis with a biographical passage that complements the contrasting style of the interview of President Harry Truman. In Chapter 11, on dialects, the number of maps has been reduced and a clearer and lengthier discussion of the Northern Cities Shift and Southern Shift provided. The chapters on historical linguistics and the history of English are updated, with added discussion about the use of nonsexist pronouns in Chapter 13. To balance the treatment of first-language acquisition, Chapter 14 contains expanded discussion of second-language acquisition, a subject closer to home for students who may be studying a foreign language as they read LISU. In addition, new sidebars appear, exploring subjects like foreign accent, spoonerisms and other speech errors, and a lawsuit involving the prefix *Mc* in the name of a hotel chain called *McSleep*; the sidebars aim to relate chapter content to real-world applications. Most chapters have additional "Try It Yourself" challenges, and all have updated references to print materials and websites. The sections titled "Computers and . . ." at the end of chapters have been shortened and given sharper focus, enhancing appeal and accessibility. I have endeavored to accommodate the guidance of reviewers, and it is my hope that this sixth edition will prove well adapted to students' needs and instructors' aims in the wide variety of courses for which LISU serves as the basic text.

A Word about Phonetic Transcription

Custom in the United States favors a modified version of the International Phonetic Alphabet, and the considerable variation in published sources makes it desirable for students to appreciate that in any given treatment they must determine what the symbols stand for. To minimize differences across treatments in textbooks, dictionaries, and elsewhere, many linguists favor the IPA, more or less strictly. As in all matters linguistic, prescription must yield to practice. While generally preferring IPA symbols once they have been introduced in Chapter 3, I occasionally use alternative symbols after that, hoping that in this fashion students will be better prepared for real-world practice, including the ordinary use of dictionaries; nevertheless, IPA symbols predominate throughout this edition.

Workbook and Answer Keys

Accompanying this sixth edition of LISU is a new edition of *Looking at Languages: A Workbook in Elementary Linguistics* by Paul Frommer and me. Among other additions and enhancements, it contains two problems on Na'vi, the language created by Paul Frommer and spoken by the inhabitants of Pandora in the film *Avatar*. The workbook (nicknamed LOLA) is useful in helping students review, apply, and extend basic concepts. Spoken-language files to accompany many of the workbook exercises are available on the LISU website via **http:// www.CengageBrain.com**. I encourage instructors to urge students to bookmark the LISU and LOLA websites once they click their way through to them the first time. Answer keys for LISU and LOLA are available to instructors from the publisher.

Acknowledgments

I have relied on many scholars whose work provided a footing from which to address topics in LISU. References in each chapter hint at the range of scholarship I've invoked, and I am also indebted to the many whose work has influenced me but cannot be cited conveniently or realistically in an introductory book. I am grateful to readers of earlier editions for helpful comments and suggestions: Michael Adams and his students, John Algeo, Joseph Aoun, Anthony Aristar, Dwight Atkinson, Robin Belvin, Douglas Biber, Betty Birner, Dede Boden, Larry Bouton, Leger Brosnahan, William Brown, Paul Bruthiaux, Ronald Butters and his students, Dani Byrd, Steve Chandler, Bernard Comrie, Jeff Connor-Linton, Janet Cowal, Marianne Cooley, Carlo Coppola, Katherine Crosswhite, Nicole Dehé, Jakob Dempsey, John Dienhart, David Dineen, Alessandro Duranti, Paul Fallon, Geoff Finch, Andreas Fischer, Zygmunt Frajzyngier, Paul Frommer, John B. Gatewood, Peter Gingiss, John Hagge, Jim Hlavac, John Hedgcock, Kaoru Horie, José Hualde, Larry Hyman, Yamuna Kachru, Christine Kakava, William A. Kretzschmar, Juliet Langman, Peter Lazar, Audrey Li, Ronald Macaulay and his students, Joseph L. Malone, Erica McClure, Sam Mchombo, David Mortensen, James Nattinger, Emily Nava, Michael Newman, Thomas Nunnally, John Oller, Ingo Plag, Timothy J. Pulju, Doug Pulleyblank, Vai Ramanathan, Angela Reyes, Gregory C. Richter, La Vergne Rosow, Johanna Rubba, Robert Seward, Trevor Shanklin, Harold F. Schiffman, Deborah Schmidt, Barbara Speicher, Giedrius Subacius, Chad Thompson, Gunnel Tottie, Edward Vajda, Robert R. van Oirsouw, Heidi Waltz, Charlotte Webb, Rebecca Wheeler, Roger Woodard, Anthony Woodbury, Thomas E. Young, and Rüdiger Zimmermann. I appreciate data provided by Marwan Aoun, Zeina el-Imad Aoun, Dwight Atkinson, Makela Brizuela, Liou Hsien-Chin, Yeon-Hee Choi, Du Tsai-Chwun, Nan-hsin Du, Jin Hong Gang, José Hualde, Yumiko Kiguchi, Yong-Jin Kim, Won-Pyo Lee, Christopher Long, Mohammed Mohammed, Phil Morrow, Masagara Ndinzi, Charles Paus, Minako Seki, Don Stilo, and Bob Wu.

I received thoughtful and much appreciated recommendations from the commissioned reviewers for this edition: Susan Garrett of Goucher College, Peter Gingiss of the University of Houston, Joseph J. Lee of Georgia State University, Thomas E. Nunnally of Auburn University, Caroline Payant of Georgia State University, and Christopher D. Sapp of the University of Mississippi.

Julian Smalley contributed the photograph in Chapter 2 and Eric Du the one in Chapter 3. William Labov contributed the map in Figure 11-11. My appreciation to them for those graphics and to Jenny Ladefoged for sharing the photograph in Chapter 1, permission for which comes from CBS Broadcasting. The photograph in Chapter 14, taken by me, shows Joanne Smalley talking with her 4-month-old daughter Anya Smalley Lowe.

Publishers increasingly acknowledge their staff and the freelancers who contribute centrally to making a textbook all that it can be. I applaud that acknowledgment. Under the leadership of Michael Rosenberg, the publisher, Michael Lepera of Cengage and Beth Kluckhohn of PreMedia Global have been the consummate book production professionals; Marissa Falco, as the art director at Cengage, coordinated the creation of the beautiful cover; Janine Tangney, media editor at Cengage, developed the website content and eBook; and Erin Bosco was the ever-efficient and accommodating assistant editor.

A special word of thanks to Joan M. Flaherty, whose patience and guidance in her role as development editor for this edition are greatly appreciated.

For countless technical contributions and beams of solid support over the years, I am grateful to Julian Smalley, my spouse.

A Word to All

From any student, instructor, or interested reader I welcome comments at Finegan@USC.edu.

—Edward Finegan
Los Angeles

Language

Its Structure and Use

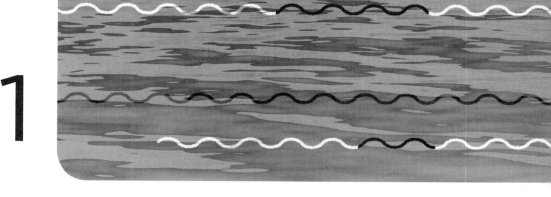

1

Languages and Linguistics

What Do You Think?

- Two college roommates who'll argue over anything are debating the number of languages in the world. One says thousands. The other says there's no way to count 'em. What do you say?
- A friend in Los Angeles opens her utility bill and, glancing at an insert, says with alarm, "Look at this—five different languages—Spanish and Chinese and who knows what! Isn't English supposed to be the official language of the USA?" Is it?
- Reading a magazine, sixth-grade Suze looks up and asks what *note* means. Figuring she knows its meaning in expressions like *thank-you note* and *musical note*, you ask her to read the sentence aloud. She reads it, and you say *note* means 'bill,' as in "$20 bill." She asks how hearing the whole sentence helped you. Your explanation?
- Grumpy Gretchen grouches that her history instructor corrected the word *snuck* to *sneaked* on her term paper. "Everyone I know says *snuck*," she says, and she wonders what planet the prof lives on! What sources can students (and profs) rely on for authoritative information in deciding what's right and wrong in English usage, and where can Gretchen find reliable guidance about using *sneaked* and *snuck*?
- At a family picnic, fifteen-year-old Felix is teasing seven-year-old Seth and asks, "Do you know when your birthday is?" When Seth says, "May ninth," Felix retorts, "I didn't ask *when* your birthday is, dude! I asked if you *knew* when it is!" What does Seth understand about the question that Felix pretends not to?

How Many Languages Are There in the World?

Some dictionaries include language names among their entries, and you've probably seen lists that provide information about the number of speakers of various languages. When the U.S. Census Bureau compiles its data each decade, it records which languages residents speak and publishes that information. At the United Nations, most countries are represented, and their ambassadors would know which languages are spoken in their home countries. With all that information, it should be easy to answer this question: *How many languages are there in the world?*

Actually, enumerating the languages of the world is not a straightforward task. First, it's not always clear whether to call two language varieties *dialects* of the same language or *different languages* altogether. Then, too, languages previously unknown to outsiders are sometimes discovered in the Amazon, Papua New Guinea, and other remote parts of the world. Some compilations of languages may be limited to spoken tongues, while others include signed languages. Finally, languages die when their last speaker dies, and that happens more often than you'd think.

Even when criteria are established for inclusion on a language list, compiling the information may be tough. For one thing, a given language may have different names, as with *Hebrew* and *Ivrit* or *Irish*, *Erse*, *Gaeilge*, and *Irish Gaelic*. For another, a name may be spelled in different ways. One language spoken mainly in China (but not related to Chinese) can be spelled *Uyghur*, *Uighur*, *Uighar*, *Uygur*, *Uigur*, *Uighuir*, *Uiguir*, *Weiwuer*, and *Wiga*. By its speakers, Uyghur isn't spelled with the Roman alphabet but with Arabic script, and it is also represented sometimes in Cyrillic and in Chinese characters.

In the course of a century, many languages die and a few may be born. Occasionally, a dead language may be revived, as Hebrew has been. Similarly, the last speaker of Cornish, a Celtic language, died in 1777, but in the southwest of England it is being revived and is in use now among 500 speakers, including some native speakers under 20 years of age. Manx, also Celtic and formerly spoken on the Isle of Man, is now extinct as a first language, but some second-language speakers are endeavoring to revive it. In Worcester, Massachusetts, Red Thunder Cloud died in 1996—and with him died Catawba, a Siouan language. In 2010, Boa Sr., the last native speaker of Bo, died in the Andaman Islands in the Bay of Bengal, and with her died her language. Estimates are that a natural language dies every couple of weeks.

New languages can also be born. Pidgins are spoken in some places as a second language, usually for limited functions such as bartering or commerce between speakers of different languages, but when circumstances in those places allow children to acquire a pidgin as their first language it will undergo a process called **creolization**, through which it develops into a full-blown language. Creoles such as Nigerian Pidgin and Saramaccan must be counted among the world's languages (even when their speakers call them pidgins).

One useful source of information, *The Ethnologue*, lists 6,909 languages. But don't take that to be an exact number. Consider that in this book we sometimes refer to "Chinese" and that the U.S. Census Bureau allows residents to identify themselves as speaking "Chinese," whereas *The Ethnologue* cites Chinese only as a "macrolanguage," with thirteen distinct language members carrying names such as Hakka Chinese, Mandarin Chinese, Wu Chinese, Xiang Chinese, and Yue Chinese, each of which may have dialects of its own. In the English-speaking world, Mandarin Chinese is known simply as Mandarin and Yue Chinese as Cantonese. Included among the 6,909 languages are sign languages. Except for their channel of expression, sign languages are like spoken languages and share with them the challenges of being identified and counted. In the city of Chiangmai in Thailand, Chiangmai Sign Language is known only among older signers in the deaf community, while younger signers use a distinct language called Thai Sign Language.

It seems safe to stick with the conventional wisdom that there are close to 7,000 languages in use in the world. Of those, only Arabic, Chinese, English, French, Russian, and Spanish have official status at the United Nations, and French does not rank among the top ten languages in number of speakers, while Hindi, Bengali, Portuguese, German, and Indonesian-Malay have greater numbers of speakers than some official U.N. languages. For the year 2000 the U.S. Census Bureau named 30 individual languages in use in the United States—but many more unnamed languages are included under broad labels like "African languages," "other Indic languages," "other Native North American languages," and "other Asian languages." Given the 30 named languages (with all varieties of Chinese counted as a single language and with no sign languages included) and given those other broad categories, how could you be confident estimating the number of languages spoken even in the United States? *The New York Times* reported in 2010 that New York City's public schools were home to speakers of 176 languages and that residents of Queens, one of the city's five boroughs, spoke 138 languages. In all, it estimated that the Big Apple was home to some 800 languages! Consider, too, that *The Ethnologue* lists 41,186 primary names, alternate names, and dialect names for language varieties. The challenge of determining an exact number of languages in the entire world is not insignificant!

Does the United States Have an Official Language?

Many Americans think English is the official language of the United States. It is not. In fact, the United States does *not* have an official language—and has never had one. Some states have official languages: Spanish in New Mexico and English and Hawaiian in Hawaii, but not the nation as a whole.

Some Americans also tend to think of the United States as essentially a monolingual nation, albeit with large numbers of Spanish speakers in the Southwest, Southeast, and Northeast. Actually, nearly 47 million U.S. residents over the age of 5 speak a home language other than English (that's almost 18 percent). Twenty-eight million of those speak Spanish, and more than half of these Spanish speakers report that they also speak English very well. Youngsters between the ages of 5 and 17 who speak a home language other than English number close to 10 million, and the vast majority are reported to speak English very well. In seven heavily populated states, at least one of every four residents over the age of 5 speaks a home language other than English. All 50 states have speakers of Arabic, Hindi, Hungarian, Korean, Tagalog, Thai, Urdu, and Vietnamese. All 50 states also have Native American speakers of indigenous North American languages. Navajo, with about 150,000 speakers, is used in homes in half a dozen states. According to figures in *The Ethnologue*, 176 living languages are used in the United States today. They range from Achumawi, Alabama, and Louisiana Creole French to Hawaiian, Lakota, Maricopa, Uyghur, Vietnamese, and Yatzachi Zapoteco. The California Department of Motor Vehicles administers its written driver's license exam in no fewer than 31 languages, including Amharic, Armenian, Cambodian, Hindi, Hmong, Hungarian, Indonesian, Laotian, Punjabi, Samoan, Tongan, and Turkish. At the 2010 U.S. Census website, instructions for filling out the census form were available in 59 languages, including Cebuano, Chamorro, Chuukese, Dinka, Haitian Creole, Marshallese, Navajo, Nepali, Swahili, Tamil, and Telugu. Wherever useful, even election ballots may be printed in multiple languages.

Los Angeles, California. Voter information pamphlets are available in English, Spanish, Tagalog, Korean, Vietnamese, Chinese, and Japanese.

For General Election Information, please call 1-888-873-1000

Under federal law, voter information pamphlets are available in English as well as in the following languages:

Si Ud. desea obtener una copia de la pamfleto en español por favor llame al teléfono 1-800-994-VOTE (8683)

Kung kailangang ninyo ang kopya ng pamplet sa Tagalog, tumawag po lamang sa 1-800-994-VOTE (8683)

이 팸플릿을 한국어로 원하시면 다음 전화번호로 연락하십시오. 1-800-994-VOTE (8683)

Nếu quý vị muốn có tập sách bằng tiếng Việt xin gọi cho số điện thoại này. 1-800-994-VOTE (8683)

若您希望索取本手冊的中文譯本，請撥此電話號碼。 1-800-994-VOTE (8683)

このパンフレットの日本語版をご希望の方は、お電話ください。 1-800-994-VOTE (8683)

Federal Election Commission

Still, the linguistic richness of the United States is not stable. The survival of most Native American languages is threatened, both because speakers tend to be older and because insufficient resources support these heritage languages, which yield to English among younger Native Americans. After English, no language spoken in the United States comes close to Spanish in number of speakers. Its 28 million U.S. speakers far exceed the 2 million who speak Chinese and the 1.6 million who speak French. With few exceptions, the children or grandchildren of immigrants cannot comfortably speak or readily understand the language of their grandparents, and this is true even of Spanish. Moreover, for all the richness of languages other than English throughout the United States, 215 million U.S. residents above the age of 5 speak English at home— a whopping 80 percent.

Try It Yourself Using your knowledge about current and past immigration patterns, identify the eight most popular non-English languages spoken among U.S. residents aged 5 and older. Spanish, Chinese, and French fill the first three slots, and Polish and Arabic are ranked ninth and tenth. Which languages are in between?

What Is Human Language?

The modern study of language is rooted in questions first asked millennia ago. As old as speculation on any subject, inquiry into the nature of language occupied Plato and Aristotle, as well as other Greek and Indian philosophers. In some areas of grammatical analysis, the ancients made contributions that have remained useful for 2,000 years and established some of the categories still used today. In the nineteenth and twentieth centuries, the field of linguistics emerged to address certain age-old questions, including these:

- What is the nature of the relationship between signs and what they signify?
- What are the elements of a language, and how are they organized within words, sentences, and discourse?
- What enables us to produce and understand countless sentences we have never heard before?
- How do languages achieve their communicative goals?
- What is the origin of language?
- In what ways do languages change and develop?
- What does it mean to say two languages are related?
- What is the relationship between a language and a dialect?
- What enables a young child to learn a language so efficiently?
- What makes it so challenging for an adult to learn a language?
- Are there right and wrong ways to express things, and—if so—who decides?

This book provides a modern context for asking and addressing those questions.

Three Faces of a Language System

The fundamental function of every language system is to link meaning and expression—to provide verbal expression for thought and feeling and for that expression to be comprehensible to others. A grammar can be viewed as a coin whose two sides are *expression* and *meaning* and whose function is to systematically link the two. But language is not simply a two-sided coin; it has a third face, so important in producing and interpreting utterances that it can override almost all else. That face is *context,* and only in context can an expression convey a speaker's intended meaning and be correctly interpreted by a hearer.

Imagine a New England dinner-table conversation about, say, the cost of living. In the course of the conversation, a guest asks the host, "Is there a state income tax in Connecticut?" This question could elicit replies of "Yes," "No," and "I don't know," because in this context the question is likely to be taken as a request for information. But consider an equally straightforward inquiry made of the host on the same occasion: "Is there any salt on the table?" In this

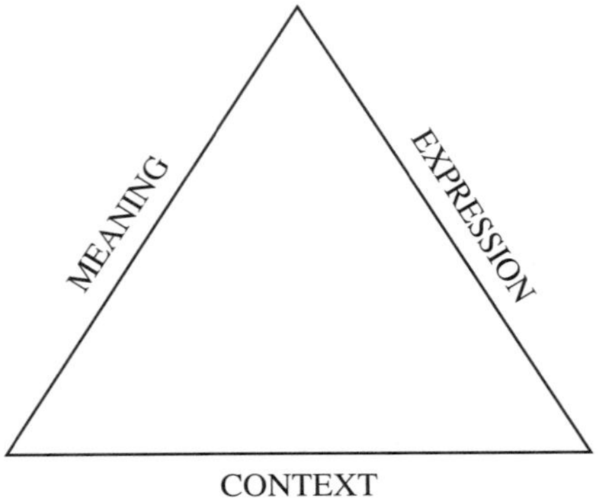

Figure 1.1 Three Faces of Language

instance, an earnest reply of "Yes," "No," or "I don't know" would mark the host as inconsiderate.

Is there a state income tax in Connecticut?

Is there any salt on the table?

The form of the salt question resembles the form of the income tax question, but the *point* of the questions—their *intended* meaning—and the expected responses could scarcely be more different. At a dinner table, a guest inquiring about salt expects a host to recognize that it's *salt* that's wanted, not *information*! By contrast, in a related context—with the host in the kitchen, pepper mill in hand, and facing a guest who's just come from the dining room—the question, "Is there any salt on the table?" is likely to be understood as seeking information even though *the form of the question* is exactly the same as the one asked by the guest at the table. In answer to the question asked in the dining room, a reply of "Yes" or "No" or "I don't know" would seem bizarre. In the kitchen, it would be altogether appropriate.

You can see, then, that conversationalists can't interpret the point of an utterance from expression alone. To grasp the intended meaning of an expression, hearers must consider it *in its context*. And speakers routinely rely on a hearer's ability to recognize their intentions in uttering an expression in a specific context.

Besides meaning and expression, then, at the base of language use is *context*, and language can be best viewed as a three-sided triangle of expression, meaning, and context, as shown in Figure 1.1.

Expression encompasses words, phrases, and sentences, including intonation and stress. **Meaning** refers to the senses and referents of these elements of expression. **Context** refers to the social situation in which expression is uttered and includes whatever has been expressed earlier in that situation and on shared knowledge between speaker and hearer. What links expression and meaning is grammar. What links grammar and interpretation is context. Without attention to both grammar and context, language utterances cannot be understood.

Language: Mental and Social

Language is often viewed as a vehicle of thought, a system of expression that mediates the transfer of thought from one person to another. In everyday life, language also serves equally important social and emotional functions.

Linguists are interested in models of how language is organized in the mind and how it is shaped by the social structures of human communities, reflecting those structures in expression and interpretation.

Signs: Arbitrary and Nonarbitrary

In everyday conversation, we talk about *signs* of trouble with the economy, no *sign* of a train arriving at a railway station, a person's vital *signs*, and so forth. **Signs** are indicators of something else. In the examples mentioned, the indicator is inherently related to the thing indicated. Nonarbitrary signs have a direct, usually causal relationship to the things they indicate. Smoke is a nonarbitrary sign of fire, clouds a nonarbitrary sign of impending rain.

Arbitrary Signs

Nonarbitrary signs such as clouds and smoke differ from partly or wholly arbitrary signs. With arbitrary signs like traffic lights, railroad crossing indicators, wedding rings, and national flags, there is no causal or inherent connection between the sign and what it signifies or indicates. Arbitrary indicators can be present even when the thing indicated is absent (as with a bachelor wearing a wedding ring). Because they are conventional representations, arbitrary signs can be changed. If a national transportation department decided to use the color blue as the signal to stop traffic, it could do so. The relationship between words and what they represent is generally arbitrary, and we say that language is a system of *arbitrary* signs.

Representational Signs

Some essentially arbitrary signs are not entirely arbitrary and may suggest their meaning. Poison may be suggested by a skull and crossbones ☠, while an icon such as ☼ may suggest the sun, and the roman numerals II and III, with two and three strokes respectively, represent the numbers two and three. Because these signs suggest what they indicate, they are partly iconic. Signs that are basically arbitrary but partly iconic are called **representational**. Linguistic examples include the English *meow* and *boom*, insofar as those words suggest what they signify, but even words that mimic natural noises are cross-linguistically distinct.

Iconic expression can also appear spontaneously in ordinary speech. I once telephoned the home of a friend, and her four-year-old son answered. He reported that his mother was showering, and when I said I'd call back in a few minutes he indicated that calling back soon would do no good. His explanation was this: *My mother is taking a long, loong, looong shower.* By stretching out his pronunciation of the vowel sound in *long*, the boy demonstrated the potential for iconicity in human language. By making his vowels longer, he directly signaled length of time and thus iconically emphasized the salient part of his meaning. Representational (or iconic) language is expression that in any fashion mimics or directly suggests its content.

Try It Yourself Besides the boy's stretching out the vowel in *long* to represent length of time, can you identify a second way in which his utterance was iconic? Now, identify another very, very common example in English in which this second way conveys a meaning different from extended length. (Hint: Examine the preceding sentence attentively.)

Iconicity can also be expressed in grammar. Consider that English has two ways of organizing conditional sentences. The condition (the "if" part) can precede the consequence or follow it.

> *If you behave, I'll give you some M&Ms.* (condition precedes consequence)
>
> *I'll give you some M&Ms if you behave.* (condition follows consequence)

English permits placing the condition (*if you behave*) before or after the consequence (*I'll give you some M&Ms*). While contextual factors can influence the choice, speakers and writers show a strong preference for the condition to precede the consequence, a preference found in many languages. The reason has to do with the order of occurrence of real-world events described by conditional sentences. In our example, the addressee must *first* behave, and *after that* the speaker will provide some M&Ms. These real-world events are ordered in time, and the real-world order is reflected in the preferred linguistic order of condition preceding consequence. With condition preceding consequence, the expression iconically mimics the sequencing of real-world events. Some languages allow *only* the condition-preceding-consequence pattern; others permit both. But no language appears to limit conditional sentences to the noniconic order, consequence before condition.

Language—A System of Arbitrary Signs

Despite occasional iconic characteristics, human language is essentially arbitrary. The form of an expression is generally independent of its meaning except for the associations established by convention. Imagine a parent trying to catch a few minutes of the televised evening news while preparing dinner. Suddenly a strong aroma of burning rice wafts into the TV room. This *nonarbitrary sign* will send the parent scurrying to salvage dinner. The aroma is *caused* by the burning rice and will convey its message to speakers of any language. There is nothing conventionalized about the message. Now consider the words of a youngster who sees the smoke in the kitchen and shouts, "The rice is burning!" That utterance is just as likely to send the parent hurtling to the kitchen, but the words are arbitrary. It is a set of facts about *English* (not about burning rice) that enables the utterance to alert the parent. The utterance is thus an arbitrary sign.

Other languages express the same meaning differently: Korean by *pap tʰanda*, Swahili by *wali inaunguwu*, Arabic by *yaḥtariqu alruzzu*. The forms of these utterances have nothing to do with rice or the manner in which it is cooking; they are not iconic. Instead, they reflect only the language systems of Korean, Swahili, or Arabic. As you see, a central characteristic of human language is that the connection between words and what they mean—between signifier and signified—is largely arbitrary.

Languages as Patterned Structures: Grammatical Competence

Given the arbitrary relationship between linguistic signs and what they represent, languages must be highly organized systems in order to function as reliable vehicles of communication.

What underlies the observable patterns that languages follow are called "rules." Not rules imposed from the outside like traffic regulations, they do not specify how something *should* be done. Instead, the rules described in this book are based on the observed regularities of language behavior and the underlying linguistic systems that can be inferred from that behavior and certain kinds of intuitions. They are the rules that even children acquire unconsciously and put to use when they display mastery of their native tongue.

A language is a set of elements and a system of rules for combining those elements into patterned expressions that serve to accomplish specific tasks in specific contexts. Utterances report news, greet relatives, invite friends to lunch, request the time of day from strangers. With language, we make wisecracks, poke fun, argue for a course of action, express admiration, propose marriage, create fictional worlds, and so on. And a language accomplishes its work with a finite system that a child masters in a few years. The mental capacity that enables speakers to form grammatical sentences such as *My mother is taking a long shower* rather than "A taking long my shower is mother" (or thousands of other possible ill-formed strings of exactly those seven words) is **grammatical competence**. It enables speakers to produce and understand an infinite number of sentences they haven't heard before. Besides arbitrariness, then, four other hallmarks of human language systems deserve highlighting.

Discreteness

Speakers can identify the sound segments in the words of their language. English speakers recognize the sounds in *cat* as the three represented by the letters *c*, *a*, and *t*. Likewise for the sounds in *though*, which are recognized as only two: the initial consonant sound represented by *th* and the following vowel sound represented by *ough*. It is a structural feature of language that words are made up of discrete (separate) elemental sounds.

Duality

Human languages can be analyzed on two levels, and this fact leads us to say it has the hallmark called duality. At one level, a language can be viewed as having meaningful parts. For example, *tabletop* has two meaningful parts—*table* and *top*. At a lower level the elements that make up the meaningful parts do *not* themselves carry meaning. The three sounds of *top* don't individually have meaning; they form a meaningful unit only when combined. And it's precisely because the individual sounds in *top* don't carry meaning that they can be formed into other combinations with different meanings, as in *pot*, *opt*, *topped*, and *popped*.

Displacement

Human languages are capable of representing things and events that are not present but are spatially or temporally distant, and we call this feature **displacement**. Speakers aren't confined to discussing events of the here and now but can talk of faraway places and events of yesterday or yesteryear and even of events yet—or never—to occur. When asked whether tool use or language had contributed most to human development, primatologist Jane Goodall identified our development of sophisticated spoken language as "the biggest difference between us and the chimpanzees and the other apes. . . . We can teach our children about things that aren't present, events in the distant past, [and] we can plan for the distant future!"

Recursion and Productivity

From relatively few elements and rules in a language system, humans can produce and understand a limitless number of sentences by combining and recombining the same relatively few elements in relatively few patterns. Even a single week's issues of, say, *Time, Newsweek*, and *The Economist* are unlikely to repeat any sentences (other than quoted utterances), and the same is true over years and years of publication. The human capacity for linguistic inventiveness makes repeated sentences unlikely, and an ordinary speaker of English is capable of understanding the countless English sentences in a lifetime of reading. Consider that to any sentence, no matter how long, one can add "I said" at the beginning. That property of incorporating existing sentences and parts of sentences within similar linguistic frames (e.g., other sentences) is known as **recursion** and underlies the phenomenon of **productivity**. For many observers this productivity—this ability to generate and understand an infinite number of sentences by combining and recombining the same few elements and structures—is the singular hallmark of human language, the characteristic that linguistic theory centrally addresses.

Speech as Patterned Language Use: Communicative Competence

Knowing the elements of a language and the rules for putting them together into well-formed sentences still falls short of knowing how to accomplish the work that speakers can accomplish with language. That requires mastery of grammatical rules, and it also requires competence in the appropriate use of the sentences produced by the rules. Among other things, accomplishing the work of language in use requires knowing how to link sentences appropriately in conversations and rely appropriately on context to shape and interpret utterances.

The capacity to use language appropriately is called **communicative competence**. It enables us to weave utterances together into narratives, apologies, requests, directions, recipes, sermons, scoldings, jokes, prayers, and all the other things we do with language. Being a fluent speaker presumes both communicative competence and grammatical competence.

Grammatical competence is the language user's unconscious, or implicit, knowledge of vocabulary, pronunciation, sentence structure, and meaning. *Communicative competence* is the implicit knowledge that underlies the appropriate use of grammatical competence in communicative situations. Because the patterns that govern the appropriate use of language differ from one speech community to the next, even a shared grammatical competence in a language such as English may not be adequate to make you a fluent speaker across other English-speaking communities. For example, members of one culture may find jokes about other people's misadventures funny, whereas members of another culture may find them offensive. In fact, the very concept of telling jokes (*Did you hear the one about . . . ?*) as distinct from telling "funny stories" seems not to exist in certain societies. Likewise, what is considered impolite in one place might be routine interaction elsewhere. Differences in interactional customs explain why even some American visitors to the Big Apple judge New Yorkers brusque or impolite when giving directions, though the same directions may be interpreted by a fellow New Yorker as routine or routinely polite.

Languages and Dialects

Along with physical appearance and cultural characteristics, language contributes to defining nationality. But even within a nation's borders, people may speak different languages. In Quebec, ethnic French-Canadians maintain allegiance to the French language, while ethnic Anglos maintain loyalty to English. Citizens of Switzerland may speak French, German, Italian, or Romansch. Across India, scores and scores of languages are spoken, some confined to villages, others used regionally or nationally. In Papua New Guinea one may hear hundreds of languages, and an English-based language called Tok Pisin is used for communication across groups.

Wherever speakers of a language become separated by geographical or social distance, linguistic variation is likely to arise. Striking differences can be noted between the French varieties of Quebec and Paris, between the Spanish varieties of Madrid and Mexico City, and between the English varieties in Sydney, London, Dublin, and Chicago. Every language variety reflects the social identity of those who speak it.

Try It Yourself Identify a characteristic of your *pronunciation* that others have commented about when you've traveled outside your region. What about a *vocabulary* item that others have found unusual? Do the same for a roommate or classmate whose speech differs from yours in pronunciation or vocabulary.

Some people seem to believe that only *other* people speak a **dialect** but that *they themselves* don't. Instead, they think of themselves as speaking a *language* or even *the* language. The truth is, everyone speaks a dialect and speaking a dialect means speaking a language. American English, Australian English, and British English are national dialects, and speakers of those national dialects also speak a regional dialect. Anyone who speaks a dialect of English speaks the English language, and anyone who speaks the English language does so only by using one of its dialects. When we speak of a "language"—Chinese, Spanish, Arabic, Navajo, or any other—we are speaking simply of a set of dialects. Languages do not exist independently of their dialects.

What Are Social Dialects?

Besides differing from nation to nation and region to region within a nation, languages may differ across gender, age, ethnicity, and socioeconomic status. In the United States, communities of white Americans and communities of black

Americans may speak differently even when they live in the same city. Similarly, middle-class and working-class speakers may be distinguished from one another by their characteristic speech.

The characteristic linguistic practices of ethnic groups, socioeconomic groups, and gender and age groups also constitute dialects. You speak a dialect characteristic of your nationality, region, gender, and socioeconomic status. The classic film *My Fair Lady*, based on George Bernard Shaw's play *Pygmalion*, tells the story of phonetics professor Henry Higgins (played by Rex Harrison) making good on a bet to teach London street vendor Eliza Doolittle (Audrey Hepburn) to speak "correctly." Eliza says, "I want to be a lady in a flower shop 'stead of sellin' at the corner o' Tottenham Court Road. But they won't take me unless I can talk more genteel." Determined to win his wager, the professor threatens, "You'll say your vowels correctly before this day is out or there'll be no lunch, no dinner, and no chocolates." One's dialect is an important part of one's persona, and changing it, as some people want to do for themselves (and many want to do for someone else), is by no means as inconsequential as changing a sweater or hairstyle. "I'll make a duchess of this draggle-tailed guttersnipe," Professor Higgins predicts of Eliza. In real life, things are more complicated.

UCLA Professor Peter Ladefoged, second from right, coaches Rex Harrison, left, on the set of *My Fair Lady*. Ladefoged later became president of the International Phonetic Association and the Linguistic Society of America.

© Courtesy of CBS Broadcasting Inc.

Different Dialects or Different Languages?

The Romance languages developed from the regional dialects of Latin spoken in different parts of the Roman empire. Those dialects eventually gave rise to Italian, French, Spanish, Portuguese, and Romanian, now the distinct languages of independent nations. While these tongues share certain inherited features of grammar, pronunciation, and vocabulary, the nationalistic pride taken by the Italians, French, Spaniards, Portuguese, and Romanians supports the view that they speak distinct languages rather than dialects of a single language.

The opposite situation characterizes Chinese. Not all Chinese dialects are mutually intelligible (for example, speakers of Cantonese and Mandarin can't understand one another), but speakers regard themselves as sharing a single language and highlight that unity with a shared writing system.

Whether two varieties are called dialects of one language or distinct languages is a social matter as much as a linguistic one, and the call may be influenced by nationalistic and religious attitudes. Hindus in northern India speak Hindi, while Muslims there and in neighboring Pakistan speak Urdu. Opinions differ as to how well the groups understand one another. Until a few decades ago, Hindi and Urdu constituted a single language called Hindustani, and the fact that professional linguists wrote grammars of "Hindi-Urdu" reflects a judgment that the two varieties required only a single grammatical description. Naturally, with the passage of time, Hindi and Urdu—whose different names proclaim that their speakers choose to belong to different social, political, and religious groups—will become increasingly differentiated, as did the Romance languages.

What Is a Standard Variety?

No single variety of English can be called *the* standard. After all, different national standards exist for British, American, Australian, and Canadian English, among others. Furthermore, at least with respect to pronunciation there may be several standard varieties of a national variety. The simple fact is that what is called "standard English" comes in many varieties.

What then is meant by a **standard variety**? We could identify as standard the variety used by a group of people in their public discourse—newspapers, radio broadcasts, political speeches, college and university lectures, and so on. In other words, we could identify as standard the variety used for certain activities or in certain situations. Alternatively, we could identify as standard the variety that has undergone a process of *standardization*, by which it is organized for description in grammars and dictionaries and encoded in such reference works.

An important point about any standard or standardized variety is that it does not differ in linguistic character from nonstandard varieties. It isn't more logical or more grammatical or better (or worse). On the other hand, for some purposes a standardized variety may be more useful than another variety. For example, this book is written in a variety of English that has been standardized, and that makes it possible to be read in many parts of the world. Instead of using spellings that would reflect my own pronunciation, I use standardized American spellings, which differ from British spellings in familiar ways.

Typically, varieties that become standardized are the local dialects spoken in centers of commerce and government. In those centers a need arises for a variety that will serve more than local needs, such as in distributing technical and medical information, propagating laws, and producing newspapers and books. The centers are also where dictionary makers and publishers—those engaged in the process of standardization—are likely to be located. Samuel Johnson (1709–1784) published his great dictionary in London in 1755. Noah Webster (1758–1843) lived in Connecticut and in 1828 published his two-volume *American Dictionary of the English Language* in New York.

Try It Yourself In II—the second of the points his dictionary was intended to exhibit—Webster speaks of "the genuine orthography and pronunciation of words" and in III of "accurate . . . definitions, with numerous authorities . . . ." If you used the words *genuine*, *accurate*, and *authorities* in connection with writing a dictionary, what would you mean by them? If you had to guess, what would you think Webster meant by them? If you set out to uncover what Webster actually meant by them, how would you go about the endeavor?

Had circumstances been different, the varieties of English represented in their dictionaries might well represent the dialects of other groups. Dictionaries serve first to describe and then to enshrine a variety of the language that can be used for public discourse across social groups, regions, even countries. You can't discern it fully in the accompanying photograph, but the subtitle to Webster's dictionary highlights that it is "Intended to Exhibit, I. The origin, affinities and primary signification of English words . . . . II. The genuine orthography and pronunciation of words, according to general usage, or to just principles of analogy. III. Accurate and discriminating definitions, with numerous authorities and illustrations."

Noah Webster, a patriot and the best-known American lexicographer, spent decades preparing *An American Dictionary of the English Language*. That two-volume work helped make his name synonymous with *dictionary* in the United States.

AN

AMERICAN DICTIONARY

OF THE

ENGLISH LANGUAGE:

INTENDED TO EXHIBIT,

I. The origin, affinities and primary signification of English words, as far as they have been ascertained.
II. The genuine orthography and pronunciation of words, according to general usage, or to just principles of analogy.
III. Accurate and discriminating definitions, with numerous authorities and illustrations.

TO WHICH ARE PREFIXED,

AN INTRODUCTORY DISSERTATION

ON THE

ORIGIN, HISTORY AND CONNECTION OF THE

LANGUAGES OF WESTERN ASIA AND OF EUROPE,

AND A CONCISE GRAMMAR

OF THE

ENGLISH LANGUAGE.

BY NOAH WEBSTER, LL. D.

IN TWO VOLUMES.

VOL. I.

He that wishes to be counted among the benefactors of posterity, must add, by his own toil, to the acquisitions of his ancestors.—*Rambler.*

NEW YORK:
PUBLISHED BY S. CONVERSE.
PRINTED BY HEZEKIAH HOWE—NEW HAVEN.
1828.

Bettmann/Corbis

Not all standardizing situations follow a single pattern. With Basque (spoken chiefly in the Basque Country of Spain), the regulatory authorities in the Royal Academy of the Basque Language during the 1960s combined forms from different regions into a single standardized variety, aiming for manifest social and regional inclusiveness. Likewise with the process of standardizing Somali in the 1970s, where social and regional variants were incorporated in the standard language variety as represented in dictionaries and grammars in an effort to make standard Somali more inclusive of a range of Somali speakers.

Is There Right and Wrong in English Usage?

All the variation we've been speaking of raises the question of whether there are right and wrong ways of saying things and writing them? In particular, are only standard varieties correct and all others incorrect?

Let's begin by considering the spellings *honor* and *honour*—which is correct? In pronouncing *schedule*, which is right—the Canadian "shedule" or the American "skedule"? Is the break between theater acts rightly called an *intermission* (as on Broadway) or an *interval* (as in London's West End)? Americans, Canadians, and Britons may prefer their own expressions and pronunciations, but depending on who and where you are and what you want to accomplish, any of these alternatives may be appropriate and correct. If you say "shedule" in Detroit, you'll likely identify yourself as Canadian. If you say "skedule" in Toronto, you may be judged a Yankee. Similar differences exist within a country.

What about matters of vocabulary and grammar? Are *sneaked* and *snuck* both okay? Aren't some language forms (like those on posted signs that say *Drive Slow* instead of *Drive Slowly*) just wrong? Does *beg the question* mean 'raise the question' or 'take the answer for granted'? To answer those questions, it helps to think of grammar as a *description* of how language is organized and behaves. In that case, ungrammatical sentences of English would include these:

> *Experience different something allergy season this.*
>
> *Season experience something different allergy this.*

Both are *ungrammatical* arrangements of the words in the grammatical sentence *Experience something different this allergy season* (taken from a print ad for an allergy medicine). No one who speaks English would normally say or write either of them, and in that sense they are ungrammatical.

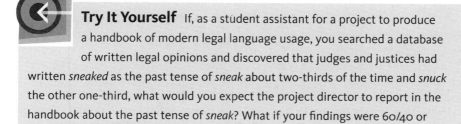

Try It Yourself If, as a student assistant for a project to produce a handbook of modern legal language usage, you searched a database of written legal opinions and discovered that judges and justices had written *sneaked* as the past tense of *sneak* about two-thirds of the time and *snuck* the other one-third, what would you expect the project director to report in the handbook about the past tense of *sneak*? What if your findings were 60/40 or 50/50 instead of 66/33?

Another view would count as ungrammatical any violation of a relatively small set of prescriptive "rules" such as these:

♦ Don't end a sentence with a preposition (e.g., *Which one did you work at?*).

♦ Don't split an infinitive (e.g., *to boldly go*).

♦ Don't use double negatives (e.g., *I don't want none*).

♦ *It's me* is ungrammatical; *it is I* is correct.

Such prescriptions arose in the eighteenth and nineteenth centuries, and of course they would not have arisen had the condemned language features not been widely used. Commentators in the prescriptive tradition formulated rules for what they regarded as the "proper" use of *shall* and *will* and condemned phrases like *between you and I*; they tried as well to ban the use of *ain't* and other negative contractions (*don't, didn't, wouldn't*, etc.) More recently, they've poked fun at *like* when it marks quoted speech or thought (*And I'm like, "Do I really wanna do this?"*).

Partly from this prescriptive tradition, judgments became widespread that some common expressions are ungrammatical, as with *Me and him would sit and talk all day* and *He don't like to cook* or *It don't matter*. These sentences are not standard English, but they are used ordinarily by millions of English speakers—and in that sense they're perfectly grammatical in some varieties of English. It isn't reasonable to judge the sentences permitted by the rules of one variety as ungrammatical simply because they don't follow the rules of another variety. By that logic, any expression permitted in British English but not in American English would be ungrammatical—and vice versa. In American English, "England hold the advantage in the World Cup final" would be ungrammatical, even though it is a perfectly acceptable sentence in British English. In American English, a team name like "England" would require the singular verb form *holds*.

Try It Yourself Given the premise that, say, Japanese and Italian are grammatical, Parisian French and Montreal French are grammatical, and American English and British English are grammatical, make an argument that it is equally logical to regard Brooklynese, Bostonese, and African-American English as grammatical.

Because languages rely essentially on arbitrary signs to accomplish their work, no linguistic justification exists for claiming there is only one right way of saying something or that the structure of one language variety is better than that of another. Judgments of "illogical" and "impure" are imported from outside the realm of language and represent attitudes to particular varieties or forms of expression within particular varieties. Sometimes, rather than representing judgments about speech itself, they represent judgments about the speakers of those varieties.

In this book we describe an utterance as "ungrammatical" only if the utterance *cannot* be said by native speakers of that variety. We limit the term to an utterance like *Book that reading am I right now* (compare *I am reading that book right now*) because it does not occur in the speech of those who know English (except as an example of an ill-formed sentence for use in textbooks like this). We do not regard an expression such as *Him and me are friends* as "ungrammatical," although we acknowledge it is not standard.

Modes of Linguistic Communication

There are three basic **modes** of linguistic communication, corresponding to different modes of perception: oral communication, relying on the use of speech and hearing organs; writing, a visual representation; and signing, a visual or tactile representation.

Speaking

The most common vehicle of linguistic communication is the voice, and speech is thus a primary mode of human language, with some advantages over other modes. Because it does not need to be viewed, speech can accomplish its work effectively in darkness and in light, straight ahead and around corners. During the development of the human species, with hands and eyes occupied in hunting, fishing, and food gathering, speakers remained free to report, ask for and give directions, explain, promise, apologize, bargain, warn, and flirt.

Speaking has other advantages. For one thing, the human voice is complex and has many channels. It has variable volume, pitch, rhythm, and speed; it's capable of wide-ranging modulation. Besides a set of sounds, speech takes advantage of the organization of those sounds, their sequencing into words and sentences. Like writing and signing, speech can take advantage of word choice and word order. In its natural state, of course, speech evaporates and cannot span time, but modern technologies are making it possible to preserve speech indefinitely.

Writing

Long before the invention of writing, people painted stories on cave walls and exploited other visual signs to record events. Such *pictograms* were independent of language—a kind of cartoon world in which anyone with knowledge of the lives of people but without specific linguistic knowledge could reconstruct the depicted story. When shown to adult speakers, depicted stories can be told in any language. Pictograms (☠ ☼ ♀) can be understood by speakers of any language because they are a direct, nonlinguistic symbolization, like a silent film or road signs used internationally to indicate a curved roadway or the availability of food and lodging. Of course, some things are more difficult than others to convey using pictograms, as the photograph below indicates. Among icons common in email correspondence and able to be made with a standard keyboard are the emoticons :) and :(. But, increasingly, they are replaced by ☺ and ☹, which can't be made with a standard keyboard.

© Edward Finegan

Signs on a wall at the sea, outside Dublin, Ireland, where fishing and nude bathing are forbidden. The fishing prohibition is communicated iconically; for obvious reasons, the prohibition of nude swimming relies on arbitrary linguistic signs.

If icons come to be associated not with the entities they represent but with the words that refer to the entities, we have a more sophisticated system. Written representation becomes *linguistic* when it relies on language for its organization and communicative success. For example, while it is difficult to use pictograms to express a message about abstractions (such as hunger or fairness), the task becomes manageable if the graphic signs represent existing words. The moment some imaginative person first recognized that the written sign ☼ could represent not only the sun itself but also the word for 'sun' in his or her spoken language, the initial step was taken toward the development of writing. Writing was invented about 5,000 years ago by ingenious people who chanced upon an occasion to use pictograms to represent spoken words instead of the objects they usually represented. Recent scholarship suggests that writing may have had multiple origins, and the social, economic, cultural, and historical circumstances of the invention in each case are important to an overall understanding of its origins.

Speech and writing are not related to the world they symbolize in the same way. Speech directly represents entities in the world—things such as the sun, the moon, my car, that book, fresh fish, and today's weather. Writing represents the physical world only indirectly. A written sentence such as *Meg hates rainy weather* is a secondary symbolization: the written words represent the spoken words, not the entities and activities themselves.

Writing has certain advantages over speech. Although it generally takes longer to produce than speech, it can be read and understood much more quickly than speech. Writing (in correspondence or books or on cave walls) endures longer than nonrecorded speech, and publications have a greater reach. A message on a blackboard can be read after its author has left the room; not so for an unrecorded spoken utterance.

Signing

The third mode of linguistic communication is signing, the use of visible gestures to communicate. To accompany their talk, speakers often use gestures and facial expressions to convey meaning in support of oral communication, but signing can be used as the sole means of accomplishing the work of language. American Sign Language, the principal sign language of North America, is used by somewhere between half a million and 2 million signers, not all of them deaf.

ASL, as it's called, and similar sign languages use manual signs and facial and bodily gestures, combining them under a system of grammatical rules to create an infinite number of sentences. The linguistic character of sign languages and the linguistic character of spoken languages such as Japanese and English are alike, except for the channel of expression, but such sign languages are fundamentally independent of any spoken language.

Manual signs in a language like ASL have three main components:

- *hand shape* and *orientation* (which fingers are open or closed and how the palm is facing)
- *hand location* with respect to the signer's body
- *hand movement*

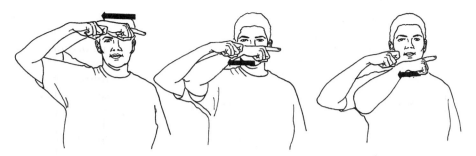

Figure 1.2 ASL signs for SUMMER, UGLY, and DRY

Source: Lucas and Valli 2004

Signs differ from one another in one or more of those components. As shown in Figure 1.2, the manual ASL signs SUMMER, UGLY, and DRY are identical in hand movement and in hand shape and orientation. For all three, the right hand, with index finger extended but the others closed, is drawn across and in front of the signer, the index finger closing in the process. The three signs are identical except in hand location. For SUMMER, the sign is drawn across the front of the signer's forehead; for UGLY, across the nose; and for DRY, across the chin. Note that you cannot guess the meanings of these signs, and that would be the case for most signs. But some other signs do show a resemblance to what they represent. For example, in ASL the sign TREE can be viewed as resembling a tree, and the sign CAT suggests a cat's whiskers, as you can see in Figure 1.3. As with spoken languages, then, sign languages like ASL are basically arbitrary, although some signs are representational, with meanings that can be guessed.

We've focused our discussion of sign language on vocabulary, but sign languages also have grammars for combining vocabulary into phrases and sentences. Spoken languages don't construct sentences by stringing words together like beads on a string, and neither do sign languages. Both signed and spoken languages observe complex systems of grammatical rules, and the rules for ASL differ from the rules for American English in ways akin to those that

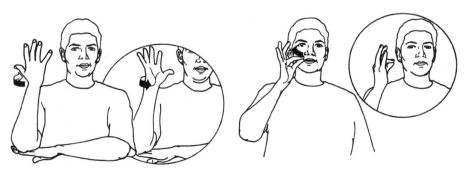

Figure 1.3 ASL signs for TREE and CAT

Source: Lucas and Valli 2004

differentiate the rules for German, say, from those for Spanish. Knowing even a long list of ASL signs and knowing English or French grammar, but not ASL grammar, would not allow a person to communicate effectively in ASL or understand a conversation between signers using ASL.

Given the way languages and dialects develop historically, it shouldn't surprise us that ASL has regional and ethnic varieties, but it's not so obvious that sign language dialects need not parallel spoken language dialects in the same locations. Spoken American English, for example, derives chiefly from spoken British English, but ASL does not derive from British Sign Language, and ASL and BSL aren't mutually intelligible. Thomas Hopkins Gallaudet, the founder of the first American school for the deaf, had studied French Sign Language in Paris and returned to Connecticut with a teacher of French Sign Language, so ASL developed from a combination particularly of FSL and a sign language used on Martha's Vineyard, in Massachusetts, at the time Gallaudet started his school.

Another kind of signing, the one used by Helen Keller, differs fundamentally from ASL because Keller was blind as well as deaf. Her signing was a kind of manual spelling system and, unlike ASL, relied on an existing spoken language. Her signing consisted of spelling out words by "drawing" *with* the hands and *in* the hands the shape of written signs that are used to represent sounds (as with letters of the alphabet). Helen Keller's sign language depended on the prior existence of a spoken language and on a written form of that language. Signing systems that rely on the modeling of letters are two steps removed from the linguistic system acquired by hearing and seeing children. In a minor way ASL also relies on finger spelling—for example, to represent people's names and other words that lack signs of their own. Unlike Helen Keller's manual system, the finger spelling of names and some other words in ASL is carried out to be seen rather than by drawing in the hand, which is designed to be felt.

In this book, we focus on language as represented in spoken and written communication. Keep in mind that, both historically and developmentally, writing is a secondary mode of linguistic communication. Speaking is the primary mode. This priority can be a challenge to students, whose principal focus and context for discussing language in academic settings has been reading and writing.

Do Humans Alone Have Language?

When you observe animals in groups, it's obvious that they interact—that they communicate with one another. Dogs display fangs to communicate displeasure or aggression; male frogs attract female frogs by croaking. It's only natural to wonder how the forms of communication used by animals differ from human language.

We sometimes speak of porpoises, chimpanzees, gorillas, dolphins, whales, bees, and other animals as though they had language systems similar to those of humans. Doubtless, all species of animals have developed systems of communication with which they can signal such things as danger and fear, and we know a good deal about how and what bees communicate. In recent decades, chimpanzees have been taught to use signs.

How Animals Communicate in Their Natural Environment

For a long time people wondered how bees were able to tell one another the exact location of a nectar source and speculated about a "language" of bees. After years of observation and hypothesizing, Karl von Frisch claimed that honeybees have an elaborate system of dancing by which they communicate the whereabouts of a honey supply. Various aspects of the dance of a bee returning to a hive indicate the distance and direction of a nectar source. The quality of the source can be gauged by sniffing the discoverer bee. Although some of von Frisch's interpretations have been questioned, his careful analysis demonstrated that the kind of creativity characteristic of a child's speech is lacking in the bee's dance. Bees do not use their communicative system to convey anything beyond a limited range of meanings (such as 'There's a pretty good source of nectar in this direction'), so analogies between bee dancing and a child's language are fundamentally misleading.

The same lack of creativity characterizes communication between other animals. Beyond a highly limited repertoire of meanings, even intelligent mammals such as dogs lack the mental capacity to be communicatively creative. For one thing, much of the communication between animals relies on nonarbitrary signs. When gazelles sense potential danger, their fleeing sends a signal to nearby gazelles that danger is lurking, and the communicative function of the act is incidental to its survival function. Similarly, a dog signals the possibility that it might bite by displaying its fangs. These acts are nonarbitrary signs that accompany desires and possibilities.

Whatever animals express through sounds seems to reflect not a logical sequence of thoughts but a sequence accompanying a series of emotional states. The communicative activities of most animals thus differ from human language in that they do not consist essentially of arbitrary signs.

Can Chimpanzees Learn a Human Language?

But what about chimpanzees? In the wild, they use a limited nonlinguistic communicative system similar to that of other mammals, though it is generally more sophisticated. Relying on the fact that the intelligence of chimps comes closest among other mammals to the intelligence of humans, researchers have attempted to teach them human language in ways that do not depend on vocal articulation.

The earliest chimp to gain notoriety for her communicative prowess was Vicki. After being raised for about seven years by psychologists Keith and Catherine Hayes, she could utter only four words—*mama, papa, up,* and *cup*—and she managed them only with considerable physical strain. Chimps are simply not equipped with suitable mouth and throat organs to speak.

Granted, then, that chimps lacked the *physiological* capacity to speak, the question remained whether they had the *mental* capacity to learn language. After viewing a film of Vicki trying to vocalize human language, psychologists Allen and

Beatrix Gardner gave a home to a ten-month-old chimp named Washoe, whom they raised as a human child in as many ways as possible. Eventually, Washoe ate with a fork and spoon, sat at a table and drank from a cup, and even washed dishes after a fashion. She wore diapers and became toilet trained; she played with dolls and showed them affection. Like human children her age, she was fond of picture books and enjoyed having her human friends tell her stories about the pictures in them.

Ingeniously, the Gardners arranged to conduct all communication with Washoe in American Sign Language (ASL), which they also used to communicate between themselves and with members of their research team whenever Washoe was present. Noting the kinds of simplified communication that human parents provide for children in some societies, the Gardners used repetition and simplified signing with Washoe, who in her first seven months in this very human environment learned four signs and in the next 14 months an additional 30 signs. After 51 months, she had acquired 132 signs describing objects and notions, and she understood three times that many. She used the signs to designate particular objects and classes of objects. She used the sign for 'shoe' to mean shoes in general; she used the 'flower' sign for flowers in general, and even for aromas like the smell of tobacco. She signed even to dogs and trees. She asked questions about the world of objects and events around her. After mastering only eight signs, she started combining them to make complex utterances: YOU ME HIDE; YOU ME GO OUT HURRY LISTEN DOG (when a dog barked); BABY MINE (referring to her doll); and so on. After just 10 months in her foster home, she made scores of combinations of three or more signs, such as ROGER WASHOE TICKLE and YOU TICKLE ME WASHOE.

In subsequent work with four other chimps (Moja, Pili, Tatu, and Dar) who arrived at their laboratory within days of birth, the Gardners demonstrated that chimps who are cross-fostered by human adults replicate some of the basic aspects of language acquisition characteristic of human children, including the use of signs to refer to natural language categories such as DOG, FLOWER, and SHOE. Remarkably, when these chimps subsequently took up residence in another laboratory, an infant chimp named Loulis acquired at least 47 signs that had no source other than the signing of his fellow chimps.

In cross-fostering Washoe and her chimpanzee playmates, the Gardners made the pivotal assumptions that human language is acquired by children in a rich social and intellectual environment and that such richness contributes to the child's cognitive and linguistic life. In other laboratories, the language activities of other celebrity chimps were not vocal like Vicki's nor gestural like Washoe's but visual. Sarah used plastic chips as symbols for words and showed considerable ability putting them in sequence. Lana used an appropriately marked computer terminal to create series of symbols similar to the plastic ones used by Sarah. As a result of the kinds of success enjoyed by the Gardners and other researchers working with chimps, some observers, especially among psychologists, came to believe there might be a continuum between human and non-human communication. But by no means was everyone persuaded.

Project Nim

Indeed, some psychologists have voiced skepticism about the various projects to teach chimps human-style language. They believe the individual words selected by the chimps in the various modes could have been triggered in some instances by inadvertent clues from the researchers. As a result, they claim, the sequences of strings produced by chimps are not productive sentences that parallel those created by human children. Other critics doubt that chimps have the ability to use language to make comments, ask questions, and express feelings as humans do.

In an attempt to provide more control on the effort to teach language to a chimp, a rigorous experiment sought to avoid many of the objections to previous research (though, inevitably, it introduced problems of its own). This chimp was named Nim Chimpsky, and in the course of his education Nim had several linguistic accomplishments, in part repeating the achievements of his predecessors. But after five years of work with Nim, psychologist Herbert Terrace concluded that chimps are incapable of learning language as children do. Even with elaborate training, Nim produced very few longer utterances and displayed little creativity and spontaneity in his use of signs. Unlike Washoe, Nim signed only when researchers prompted him, and he never initiated interactions. These characteristics, Terrace contends, clearly distinguish what Nim could learn from what children can do with language.

Critics of Project Nim note that Terrace employed more than 60 research assistants over five years and suspect that fact may have contributed significantly to the limitations in Nim's linguistic achievements. Moreover, the assistants were instructed to treat Nim in a detached fashion and were forbidden to comfort him even if he cried during the night. Critics questioned how similar Nim's learning environment was to the environment in which a normal human child acquires language and maintained that the research conditions of Project Nim had a crippling impact on the chimp's emotional and linguistic education.

We see, then, that some researchers claim that human and animal language fall along a continuum, while others conclude that chimps cannot learn language as children do. To help reconcile these views, it is useful to consider the assessment of the distinguished primatologist Jane Goodall, who identified "talking" as the biggest difference between humans and chimps, "because we can discuss ideas, we can teach about things that aren't present. We can draw from the distant past and teach each other from it and we can plan the distant future. Mostly it is this discussion of ideas" that distinguishes humans from chimps. The consensus among psychologists and linguists seems to be that animal language, including that of chimpanzees, does not exhibit all the hallmark features of human language we laid out above. While there are some similarities between human language and the sign and other visual languages taught to chimps, several criterial features of human language appear to be lacking, notably displacement and recursion and productivity.

The Origin of Human Languages: Babel to Babble

Many people are persuaded that language originated in a paradise where its form was logical and perfectly grammatical. Even beyond that, the belief is widespread that, with the passage of time, pristine languages have become contaminated with impurities, illogicalities, and ungrammaticalities.

As examples of *impurities*, subscribers to this worried view cite borrowed words such as the American *OK* and the French *disco*, which have spread into many other languages and made them less "pure." Among alleged *illogicalities*, double negatives are a commonly cited English example. The claim is that, just as two negatives yield a positive in algebra or logic (*It is not untrue* means 'It is true'), the double negative in a sentence like *I don't want none* should logically mean 'I do want some,' and the double negative in *He didn't do nothing wrong* should mean 'He did something wrong.' Of course, they don't. Putative *ungrammaticalities* include the personal pronoun *I* in *just between you and I* and the pronouns *him and me* as subject in the sentence *Him and me were friends in the Army*. The argument offered is that objects of a preposition *should* be in the objective case (*just between you and me*) and subjects of a sentence *should* be in the common (or subject) case (*He and I were friends in the Army*). Another alleged ungrammaticality is the word *snuck*, which many regard as an illegitimate form of *sneaked*. Of course, millions of speakers around the globe use these and other allegedly impure, illogical, and ungrammatical expressions—and the sun rises over them each morning and sets each evening, just as it does over those whose language is regarded as more pure, logical, and grammatical.

As well as having different views on the origins of languages, people have different ways of explaining why languages differ from one another and why they change. The Old Testament relates that before the Tower of Babel all men and women spoke the same language and could understand one another. Eventually human pride provoked God into confounding their communication with mutually unintelligible tongues. In this view, language differences among people can be seen as a penalty for pride or misbehavior. Similarly, Muslims believe that Allah spoke to Mohammed in pure and perfect Arabic, as represented in the Koran. By contrast, the varieties of present-day Arabic spoken in the Persian Gulf, North Africa, and elsewhere are seen as deriving later from human weakness and culpability.

Professional linguists take a different approach. They see the multiplicity of languages as resulting from natural change over time, the inevitable product of reshaping speech to meet changing social and intellectual needs and reflecting contact with people speaking other languages. When people move to new places and mix with speakers of different tongues or settle areas with unfamiliar plants and animals, their language must adapt to new circumstances. Encountering unfamiliar aspects of nature and meeting others who engage in different cultural practices and hold different views prompts accommodation in one's language. As a result, languages evolve differently around the globe.

Still, compared to linguistic differences, what is equally striking is the extent of similarity across languages around the globe. The differences are all too apparent, the similarities sometimes too subtle to recognize. But similarities should not be surprising because, after all, every language must conform to the character and abilities of the human vocal apparatus, which must produce all spoken language, and to the character and abilities of the human brain, where everyone's language system resides. As it happens, of many conceivable language structures, only a relatively narrow band exists across the languages of the world. (Chapter 7 examines universals of language structure.)

Still, the question persists: When and how did human language arise? The question has been of interest for millennia. You may know the story of the

Egyptian king Psammetichus, who entrusted two children to mute shepherds so the children would hear no language and whose first words, it was thought, would therefore indicate the original language. When the first spoken word, recorded as *bekos,* was judged to be Phrygian for 'bread,' Psammetichus decided Phrygian must be the original language. Experimentation and wild speculation took a particularly vigorous turn in the mid-nineteenth century around the time Darwin published his *Origin of Species* (1859). Speculation grew so fantastical that in 1866 the Linguistic Society of Paris banned the offering of papers on the origins of language, and the spirit of that prohibition—coupled with a lack of sufficient knowledge in the necessary fields—kept the question on the back burner until very late in the twentieth century. In the past 20 or 25 years, though, language origin has become a hot topic and has engaged researchers from several disciplines, including biology, neuroscience, anthropology, and computer science, as well as linguistics. Unfortunately, while some of the issues have been clarified, answers have remained elusive.

Suffice it to say that one of the principal challenges in determining the origin of language is the fact that three vastly different timelines are involved, and the computer modeling needed to help determine when and how language evolved is hampered by the greatly different scope of these timelines and our incomplete knowledge about them. For example, while a human being develops a language over a period of a decade or so, languages themselves develop over centuries or millennia, and the human brain and vocal apparatus developed over hundreds of thousands of years. Thus, anything we know about language evolution along each of these dimensions is very difficult to combine in a single model. But there are still more fundamental questions—for example, about the degree to which and manner in which human language differs from animal communication, as we have just seen; even about precisely what human language is—which aspects of what we regard broadly as human language are characteristic of language per se and which belong to more general cognitive, sensory-motor, or cultural functions. Fascinating as they are, even detailing these questions would take us well beyond our scope. To learn more about language origins, check the references at the end of the chapter.

What Is Linguistics?

Linguistics can be defined as the systematic inquiry into human language—into its structures and uses and the relationship between them, as well as into its development through history and its acquisition by children and adults. The scope of linguistics includes both language structure (and its underlying *grammatical competence*) and language use (and its underlying *communicative competence*).

Language is often defined as an arbitrary vocal system used by human beings to communicate with one another. This definition is useful as far as it goes although it downplays writing and signing. It also downplays an important fact that philosophers have emphasized about language, namely, that it is more than communication. It is social action, with work to perform. Language is a system that speakers, writers, and signers exploit purposefully. It is used to *do* things, not just *report* them or *describe* them or *discuss* them. "That shirt looks terrific on you!" is not a mere report (whereas "Halloween falls on a Tuesday this year" might well be). More likely, it is a compliment. "Out!" is a mere opinion or conjecture when a fan behind home plate shouts it during a baseball game, but when it is said by the umpire, "Out!" is a *call* and as such can end an inning or a game.

As we said earlier, people have been interested in analyzing language for millennia. Plato and Aristotle discussed language in the fourth and third centuries B.C., and we have inherited several categories of grammatical analysis from them. More than a century earlier, Pāṇini wrote a description of Sanskrit that is one of the finest grammars ever produced for any language. Today, the empirical study of language has taken on additional importance in an age in which communication is critical to social, intellectual, political, economic, and ethical concerns. Now augmented by insights from cognitive science and neuroscience, from computer science, psychology, sociology, anthropology, philosophy, and rhetoric, as well as from communications engineering and other sciences, linguistics has become a prominent academic discipline in universities and research centers throughout the world.

What Are the Branches of Linguistics?

Historically, the central focus of language study has been *grammar*—patterns of speech sounds, word structure, sentence formation, and meaning. More recently, attention has also focused on the relationship between expression and meaning, on the one hand, and context and interpretation, on the other. This field is called *pragmatics*. Some linguists describe particular languages; others examine universal patterns across languages and aim to explain them in cognitive or social terms.

Some linguists focus on *language variation* across speech communities or within a single community, across time, or across situations of use, such as conversation and sports announcer talk. Linguists studying variation seek two kinds of explanation—cognitive ones having to do with constraints on the human language-processing capacities and social ones having to do with human interaction and the organization of societies.

A third group of linguists applies the findings of the discipline to real-world problems in *educational* matters, to the acquisition of literacy (reading and writing) and of second languages and foreign languages; in *clinical* matters, to understanding aspects of Alzheimer's disease and aphasia; in *forensic* settings, to analysis of conversation for evidence of conspiracy, threats, defamation, and other matters of legal concern, to interpretation of contracts (from rental agreements and insurance policies to agreements for manufacturing airplanes), to clarification of public safety instructions (such as medical labels and dosage directions), and to identification of voices and the authorship of documents. Some applied linguists address problems in *language policy* at national and local levels: what languages to designate for use in schools, courts, voting booths, and so on; what kind of writing system to employ in a culturally diverse modern nation; what regulation of existing language is needed, as in the Plain English movement in the United States or in the development and production of the tools of standardization, such as dictionaries and grammars. As the world shrinks and cultures mix together, linguists are also applying their skills to the challenges of cross-cultural communication.

COMPUTERS AND LINGUISTICS

At the end of each chapter in this book, you'll find a section that discusses some aspects of computers and language related to the topics in the chapter. You don't have to be a sophisticated computer user to understand these sections and benefit from them. Seeing the substance of a chapter from a different perspective will help you grasp it. The section below serves as an introduction to the parallel sections in later chapters.

Computers and Machine-Readable Texts

In the eighteenth century, Samuel Johnson's dictionary provided illustrative citations taken from books to exemplify how words were used. During his own reading, Dr. Johnson marked sentences whose context made a word's meaning or use especially clear. His assistants then transcribed the passages onto sheets of paper, and he organized them in the entries of the dictionary. In the nineteenth century, essentially the same process was used by Noah Webster in preparing his two-volume *American Dictionary of the English Language*. Later again the same practice was followed when others compiled the multi-volume *Oxford English Dictionary*, which was so large that the project required thousands of readers and consumed half a century to complete. In the twentieth century, the makers of *Webster's Third New International Dictionary* also mined a collection of several million citations to uncover different word senses. Dictionary making today is undergoing dramatic change, owing to advances in computers and the availability of machine-readable collections of texts known as *corpora*.

Corpus linguistics is the term used for compiling collections of texts and using them to probe language use. In this context a **corpus** is a representative body of texts (*corpus* is the Latin word for 'body'). You're familiar with the kinds of machine-readable texts created by word processors, and it is the fact that they are machine-readable that enables you to search for a particular word or phrase. The first computerized corpus—the Brown University Corpus—included 500 texts from U.S. books, newspapers, and magazines. The texts were selected to represent 15 genres, including science fiction, romance fiction, press reportage, and scholarly and scientific writing. Each text contains 2,000 words, and the total collection contains a million words. Researchers later compiled a parallel corpus of British English called the London–Oslo/Bergen Corpus, or LOB for short. These two corpora are parallel collections of American and British writing that appeared in print in 1961.

More recent corpora contain over 100 million words, and corpora of texts in many languages are being compiled. Corpora are proving essential for twenty-first-century dictionary making and in many other ways, including speech recognition and artificial intelligence. ∎

Summary

- The total number of spoken and signed languages in the world is almost 7,000.
- In the year 2000, according to U.S. Census data, 47 million United States residents over the age of 5 spoke a home language other than English.
- The United States does *not* have an official language and has *never* had one.
- Human language is an enormously complex system that is easily mastered by children in a remarkably short time.
- Natural processes of linguistic change affect all languages over time, and linguistic change is not linguistic decay.
- All languages are equally logical (or equally illogical).
- A human language is primarily a system of arbitrary signs, but some linguistic signs are representational.

- Grammar is a system of elements and patterns that organizes linguistic expression.
- Five hallmarks of human language systems are arbitrariness, discreteness, duality, displacement, and recursion/productivity.
- Rather than being a two-sided coin, a language system is better viewed as a triangle whose faces are meaning and expression and whose base is context.
- Linguistic communication can operate in three modes: speaking, writing, and signing.
- Everyone speaks a dialect, and languages do not exist independently of their dialects.
- Chimpanzees do not have a suitable vocal apparatus for speaking, but in limited ways they are capable of putting together several signs to form meaningful strings.
- The degree to which the language of chimps and that of very young children are alike remains under investigation, but they appear fundamentally different at least in displacement and recursion and productivity.
- In the field of corpus linguistics, large bodies of computerized texts called corpora are used to explore natural language use in all its contexts.

What Do You Think? REVISITED

- *How many languages?* The question can't be answered exactly, but there are in the world about 7,000 languages, including sign languages.
- *Multilingual utility bill.* The United States has never had an official language. Utility bills need to be understood by customers, and one can successfully communicate with people only in a language they understand. We all feel relieved when confronted with an important piece of text in a language we don't understand and then find a translation in a familiar language. The United States accepts large numbers of immigrants, and when they cluster in urban or suburban areas it makes sense for commercial and government establishments to communicate with them in a familiar language.
- *Sixth-grade Suze. Note* carries different senses in *musical note, bank note*, and the metaphorical *discordant note*. And besides its senses as a noun, *note* may be a verb. So knowing the context of use may be essential in recognizing the appropriate sense of a word in an utterance, and a sentence such as, "The U.S. Treasury issued new $20 notes in 2003 to help stem the tide of counterfeiting," makes clear that "notes" is a synonym for "bills."
- *Snuck or sneaked?* Traditionally, *sneaked* has been the past-tense form of *sneak*. But English speakers increasingly say and write *snuck*. Languages change and what's "right" for one generation may not be right for the next generation. When usage changes, judgments about right and wrong also change. People often cite "the dictionary" as authority for one usage or another, and some dictionaries tout themselves as "authoritative." But even dictionaries differ in their views of right and wrong usage. Lexicographers understand that any authoritative

position they hold rests on their ability to track actual usage—what is being said and written at a particular time.

- *Seth's birthday.* Seth understands that utterances must be interpreted in context. Felix pretends that utterances have only a literal meaning, irrespective of context. Because everyone knows his or her own birthday, Felix's question ("Do you know when your birthday is?") would appear silly if taken at face value, so Seth figures out an interpretation that makes sense of it. "May ninth" is information Seth presumes Felix doesn't have: Why else would Felix ask the question?

Exercises

1-1. Here's a set of questions that could constitute a basis for your linguistic autobiography. Jot down your answers in bulleted form. (1) When did you first become aware that people judge certain linguistic expressions to be naughty or nice, and what do you think the basis for those judgments must have been? (2) When did you first become aware that some people judge certain linguistic expressions to be grammatically correct or incorrect, and what do you think the basis for their judgments would have been? (3) Do you think of speech as more fundamental than writing—and, if so, for how long have you thought that? (4) Was there ever a time when you judged writing to be the basis for speech, and, if so, what gave you that impression? For example, have you ever thought that *palm* or *salmon* are best *pronounced* with an *l* because they're spelled with an *l*? What about *herb:* would it be more correct to pronounce it with an *h*? (5) Can you identify two aspects of your current views about language that place writing in a superior position to speaking?

1-2. Over the course of a single day, write down every instance you hear (on radio or television programs, in class lectures, or in talk among your acquaintances) of representational expressions (representing length, loudness, speed, repetition, emphasis, ordering, etc.). (You may find it easier to gather examples from sitcoms or programs for children.) Compare your examples with those collected by your classmates to see how many kinds you have uncovered.

1-3. Below is a list of characteristics that describe linguistic communication through speaking, writing, and signing. Decide which modes of linguistic communication the characteristic applies to, and provide an example to illustrate your claim. Pay particular attention to the different types of spoken, written, and signed communication because certain of these characteristics might apply to some but not other types of communication. Also note the impact of modern communication technology on these characteristics.

    a. A linguistic message is ephemeral—that is, it cannot be made to endure.

    b. A linguistic message can be revised once it has been produced.

    c. A linguistic message has the potential of reaching large audiences.

    d. A linguistic message can be transmitted over great distances.

e. A linguistic message can rely on the context in which it is produced; the producer can refer to the time and place in which the message is produced without fearing misunderstanding.

f. A linguistic message relies on the senses of hearing, touching, and seeing.

g. The ability to produce linguistic messages is innate; it does not have to be learned consciously.

h. A linguistic message must be planned carefully before it is produced.

i. The production of a linguistic message can be accomplished simultaneously with another activity.

1-4. Consider the following quotation from a mid-twentieth-century dictionary (*A Pronouncing Dictionary of American English* by John S. Kenyon and Thomas A. Knott, Springfield, MA: Merriam, 1953, p. vi).

> As in all trustworthy dictionaries, the editors have endeavored to base the pronunciations on actual cultivated usage. No other standard has, in point of fact, ever finally settled pronunciation. This book can be taken as a safe guide to pronunciation only insofar as we have succeeded in doing this. According to this standard, no words are, as is often said, "almost universally mispronounced," for that is self-contradictory. For an editor the temptation is often strong to prefer what he thinks "ought to be" the right pronunciation; but it has to be resisted.

a. Make an argument supporting the view that editors should resist the temptation to record their own personal pronunciation preferences in a dictionary. Explain whether your argument also applies to an editor's expressing personal preferences for other aspects of language, such as spelling or usage.

b. Make an argument supporting the view that the phrase "almost universally mispronounced" is self-contradictory.

c. What do you understand by the phrase "cultivated usage"? How would you determine whose usage is "cultivated"? How do you imagine a dictionary editor would determine whose usage is "cultivated"? Given that different social groups pronounce some words differently from one another, whose pronunciations do you think a dictionary should describe? Explain and justify your view.

1-5. In papers and exams comparing natural conversation with written varieties of English, students sometimes claim that conversation is filled with errors such as those given below. Offer an alternative explanation to the claim that they are errors.

> I was, like, "Hi," and she goes, "Hi."
>
> I said, "Hi Pat," I went, she goes, "Hi Chris."

1-6. Consider the following, said by John Simon (*Paradigms Lost*, New York: Penguin, 1980, pp. 58–59) concerning Edwin Newman's book, *A Civil Tongue*:

> With demonic acumen, Newman adduces 196 pages' worth of grammatical errors. Clichés, jargon, malapropisms, mixed metaphors,

monstrous neologisms, unholy ambiguities, and parasitic redundancies, interspersed with his own mocking comments . . . and exhortations to do better. . . .Worse than a nation of shop-keepers, we have become a nation of wordmongers or word-butchers, and abuse of language, whether from ignorance or obfuscation, leads, as Newman persuasively argues, to a deterioration of moral values and standards of living.

a. Simon seems to equate "grammatical errors" with clichés, jargon, malapropisms, and so on. Which of these can legitimately be called errors of grammar in the linguistic sense? What would be a more appropriate way to characterize the others?

b. Cite two ungrammatical structures that you have heard from nonnative speakers of English. Have you heard similar errors of grammar from native speakers? What reason underlies your findings about native-speaker errors and nonnative-speaker errors?

c. The point that Newman and Simon make about "abuse of language" leading to a deterioration of moral values and standards of living is a common claim of language guardians. What kinds of abuse does Simon seem to have in mind when he makes that claim? Are he and Newman correct in claiming that such abuses lead to a deterioration of moral values? Could it be the other way around? Could they be entirely independent of one another? What stake could anyone have in advancing the Newman/Simon claim? To put it differently, who are the winners and losers if that view prevails?

d. Do you think that genuine grammatical errors (such as those made by nonnative speakers) could lead to a deterioration of moral values? Explain your position.

1-7. Writing and gesture are visual modes of linguistic communication. What is the relationship between writing and Braille (the writing system used for blind readers)? Is Braille a mode of linguistic communication? How many modes of linguistic communication are there?

1-8. When there is a choice between linguistic modes, as in telephoning a distant friend or sending a letter or email note, what are the advantages and disadvantages of each mode? What about instant messaging and texting? List some of the circumstances in which each mode of linguistic communication would be preferred over the others.

Especially for Educators and Future Teachers

1-9. For students whose home language matches the language of instruction in school, do you regard the primary focus of teaching language arts to be reading and writing or speaking and listening? Explain your position.

1-10. For the same group of students, do you think the emphasis of the curriculum is actually on reading and writing, or is it on speaking and listening? Explain the basis for your view.

1-11. For students whose home language differs from that of school instruction (for example, for students who speak Spanish at home but attend an English-language school), would your answers to the previous two questions be different? If so, how?

1-12. For students whose home language is a different dialect from that of school instruction, would your answers to questions 1-9 and 1-10 be different (focus on your local situation or the situation in a district you are likely to work in). If so, how?

1-13. In your early years in school, did your teachers speak the same language you spoke? The same dialect? If they didn't, did they convey different attitudes toward their speech and yours? Was there any discussion of other language varieties, and can you reconstruct what attitudes your teachers fostered toward the language varieties of other students? Can you remember anything a teacher might have said about another language or dialect? Did you feel comfortable speaking up in class? Did other students? Did any teacher discuss the importance of language in a child's life and how central an aspect of a child's personal identity his or her speech is?

1-14. During your school and college years, did anyone convey an impression of what they thought of your speech? Of your writing? If so, what were their attitudes, and do you think teachers are wise to correct your writing and your speech?

Other Resources

Internet

Information and the results of considerable laboratory research are available on the Internet. In this section of each chapter you will find Internet addresses that will help you understand the contents of the chapter and provide a laboratory unlike any previously available to students of linguistics at even the best-equipped universities. Because Internet addresses can change unexpectedly, the ones given below may no longer be accurate by the time you try them. If an address has changed, you may find yourself automatically linked to a new address. Updated addresses can also be found at the first website given below. There, too, you may find links to new sites that may interest you.

 LISU Website: http://www.CengageBrain.com For users of this textbook. Provides updated Internet links as well as supplemental material for students and instructors. Here you will find chapter-specific interactive learning tools in your English CourseMate, accessed through the URL above.

 The Domain of Linguistics: http://www.lsadc.org/info/ling-fields.cfm For general information, the website of the Linguistic Society of America. Here you will find brief treatments on a wide variety of topics, including language and brain, language and thought, computers and language, endangered languages, prescriptivism, writing, slips of the tongue, linguistics and literature, and a dozen other topics.

An Animated ASL Dictionary: http://commtechlab.msu.edu/sites/ aslweb/browser.htm You can see animated representations of ASL signs.

 James Crawford's Language Policy Website & Emporium: http://www.languagepolicy.net/ Bilingual education and bilingual policy are important matters in the United States, as they are around the world. In the United States, the subject of bilingual education is a tender one. This website is a rich source of information and interpretation of language policy in the United States. Much of what is of value at the site can be reached through the "Archives" tab or at **http://www.languagepolicy.net/archives/ home.htm** directly.

 The Ethnologue: http://www.ethnologue.com/ This reference database offers a wealth of information about the distribution of languages, numbers of speakers, dialects, and so on. Organized by country and by language name.

 Census 2000 Gateway: http://www.census.gov/main/www/cen2000. html At the official site of the U.S. Census Bureau, you can see which languages are spoken by how many people in every state and the entire United States, with easy-to-read tables. At **http://www.census.gov/2010census** you will find information gathered in the 2010 U.S. Census.

 Endangered Language Alliance: http://endangeredlanguagealliance. org/main/ Established by Daniel Kaufman, who calls New York City "an endangered language hot spot," this alliance fosters recording of endangered languages that, in some cases, have more speakers in NYC than in their original homelands.

Films and Videos

- **UNESCO Endangered Languages: http://www.unesco.org/culture/en/ endangeredlanguages** A rich site, with maps documenting the state of endangered languages around the globe.
- **The Linguists: http://thelinguists.com/** *The Linguists* is a riveting story of two linguists' efforts to record endangered languages around the globe. Supported by the National Science Foundation, the film had its world premier at the Sundance Film Festival in 2008. At the website you can see a trailer and find ordering information.
- **Student Productions** Inspired in part by *The Linguists* (see preceding bullet), two undergraduate students at the University of Southern California produced videos about remote and endangered languages. Focusing on the language Central Alaskan Yup'ik, Lydia Green's project at **http://www.lydiajewlgreen/yupik.com/** shows how involved a college junior can become and how much firsthand information and insight she can gain. At **http://www. archive.org/details/SouthernCaliforniaIndigenousLanguagesPilotFilm** you can also "hit the road" with college senior Joseph Henderer on his journey to find the last fluent speakers of Southern California's indigenous languages.
- **The Human Languages Project** An award-winning set of informative and entertaining videos, originally broadcast on PBS in 1995: *Discovering the Human Language: "Colorless Green Ideas"; Acquiring the Human Language: "Playing the Language Game";* and *The Human Language Evolves: "With and without Words."* 55-minutes each. Produced by Equinox Films, Inc.
- **Sound and Fury** Nominated in 2001 for an Academy Award as a documentary feature, *Sound and Fury* tells the story of two families grappling with the complicated and controversial decision about whether to have a deaf child receive a cochlear implant. You can see a trailer at **http://www.pbs.org/wnet/soundandfury/**. There you'll also find links

to information about Deaf culture, cochlear implants, American Sign Language, and related topics. The documentary's director, Josh Aronson, has made two follow-up films, *Sound and Fury: Six Years Later* and *Twins*; they can be ordered by writing to aronsonfilms@aol.com.

Suggestions for Further Reading

- **Jean Aitchison. 2000.** *The Seeds of Speech: Language Origin and Evolution* (Cambridge, UK: Cambridge University Press). A basic treatment of language beginnings.
- **Douglas Biber, Susan Conrad & Randi Reppen. 1998.** *Corpus Linguistics: Investigating Language Structure and Use* (Cambridge, UK: Cambridge University Press). An accessible introduction to corpus linguistics.
- **David Crystal. 2010.** *Cambridge Encyclopedia of Language*, **3rd ed.** (Cambridge, UK: Cambridge University Press). Treats topics in a few pages each, with illustrations.
- **Edward Finegan & John R. Rickford, eds. 2004.** *Language in the USA: Themes for the Twenty-first Century* (Cambridge, UK: Cambridge University Press). Twenty-six essays treat such topics as multilingualism, Spanish in the Southwest and the Northeast, African-American English, Asian-American voices, Ebonics controversy, language and education, language of cyberspace, rap and hip-hop, and slang.
- **Ray Jackendoff. 1994.** *Patterns in the Mind: Language and Human Nature* (New York: Basic Books). Accessible, fascinating discussion of the cognitive aspects of language structure and language acquisition.
- **Donna Jo Napoli. 2003.** *Language Matters: A Guide to Everyday Thinking about Language* (New York: Oxford University Press). An enjoyable introduction to most topics treated in this chapter.
- **Edward Sapir. 1921.** *Language: An Introduction to the Study of Speech* (New York: Harvest). This accessible classic continues to yield insight, and that's why it's still in print.
- **Simon Winchester. 2003.** *The Meaning of Everything: The Story of the Oxford English Dictionary* (Oxford: Oxford University Press). An engaging introduction to the making of the OED and to lexicography more generally.

Advanced Reading

Crystal's (2008) *Dictionary of Linguistics and Phonetics* is a useful reference work for a wide set of terms and concepts. For discussion of the relationship between arbitrary and nonarbitrary signs, consult de Saussure (1959). The papers in Haiman (1985) touch on iconic elements in syntax and intonation. For speaking and writing, see "Suggestions for Further Reading" in Chapter 15 (available at the LISU website). On standard varieties and attitudes to correctness in English usage, see Finegan (1998) with an emphasis on British and Finegan (2001) with an emphasis on American, as well as Milroy and Milroy (1999) and Wardhaugh (1999). For information on American Sign Language, see Lucas and Valli (2004) upon which we have relied in our exposition here, and for a survey of sign languages among Native Americans and Australian Aborigines, see Umiker-Sebeok and Sebeok (1978). On the origins of language, see Lieberman (2006). For corpus linguistics, see McEnery et al. (2006) or Meyer (2002); for computers and language, see Lawler and Dry (1998). Articles reviewing the state of knowledge about language evolution include the excellent and accessible Christiansen and Kirby (2003) and the even more accessible Croom (2003).

References

Christiansen, Morten H. & Simon Kirby. 2003. "Language Evolution: Consensus and Controversies." *Trends in Cognitive Sciences* 7 (7): 300–307.

Croom, Christopher. 2003. "Language Origins: Did Language Evolve Like the Vertebrate Eye, or Was It More Like Bird Feathers?" Available at http://www.csa.com/discoveryguides/lang/overview.php.

Crystal, David. 2008. *A Dictionary of Linguistics and Phonetics*, 6th ed. (Oxford: Wiley-Blackwell).

de Saussure, Ferdinand. 1959. *Course in General Linguistics*, trans. from French by Wade Baskin (New York: Philosophic Library).

Finegan, Edward. 1998. "English Grammar and Usage." In S. Romaine, ed. *Cambridge History of the English Language*, Vol. 4 (Cambridge, UK: Cambridge University Press), pp. 536–88.

Finegan, Edward. 2001. "Usage." In J. Algeo, ed. *Cambridge History of the English Language*, Vol. 6 (Cambridge, UK: Cambridge University Press), pp. 358–421.

Haiman, John, ed. 1985. *Iconicity in Syntax* (Amsterdam: Benjamins).

Lawler, John M. & Helen Aristar Dry, eds. 1998. *Using Computers in Linguistics: A Practical Guide* (London: Routledge).

Lieberman, Philip. 2006. *Toward an Evolutionary Biology of Language* (Cambridge, MA: Harvard University Press).

Lucas, Ceil & Clayton Valli. 2004. "American Sign Language." In Edward Finegan & John R. Rickford, eds. *Language in the USA* (Cambridge, UK: Cambridge University Press), pp. 230–44.

McEnery, Tony, Richard Xiao & Yukio Tono. 2006. *Corpus-Based Language Studies: An Advanced Resource Book* (London: Routledge).

Meyer, Charles F. 2002. *English Corpus Linguistics: An Introduction* (Cambridge, UK: Cambridge University Press).

Milroy, James & Lesley Milroy. 1999. *Authority in Language: Investigating Language Prescription and Standardization*, 3rd ed. (London: Routledge).

Umiker-Sebeok, Jean D. & Thomas A. Sebeok, eds. 1978. *Aboriginal Sign Languages of the Americas and Australia*, 2 vols. (New York: Plenum).

Wardhaugh, Ronald. 1999. *Proper English: Myths and Misunderstandings about Language* (Malden, MA: Blackwell).

Part One

Language Structures

When you think about languages at all you are likely to think about words. In this book, we begin our investigation of language structure by looking at words, and we look at them from several perspectives:

- their meaningful parts
- the sounds and syllables that make them up
- the principles that organize them into phrases and sentences
- the semantic relationships that link them in sets.

In the first part of this book, you'll see how just a few elements combine into speech sounds, how just a few speech sounds combine to form a larger number of syllables, how syllables combine to produce word parts that carry meaning, and how languages package these word parts into a finite vocabulary and an infinite number of phrases and sentences. You'll also see how the systematic principles underlying language structure help you understand countless utterances that you've never heard or read before. Finally, you'll examine the semantic relationships among sets of words.

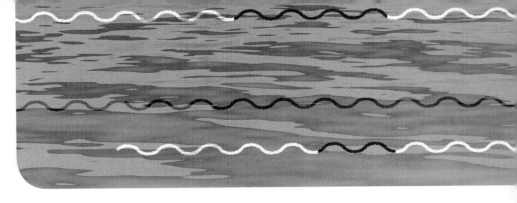

2

Words and Their Parts: Lexicon and Morphology

What Do You Think?

- If you were the parent of a 3-year-old daughter who asked if you "maked" a cake and "telled" your friends about it, how would you describe the pattern your daughter uses to mark past time on these verbs?
- You've agreed to make a list of foods and drinks that volunteers can contribute to a fundraiser for a college choir undertaking an international tour. All the items must bear a name that English borrowed from another language. You think of *sushi* from Japanese, *chop suey* from Chinese, *tortilla* from Spanish, *pâté* and *champagne* from French, and *curry* from a language of India (Tamil). Can you identify several other food names from these languages? From any other languages?
- If you were to speculate about the top ten most frequently used words in printed English, what would they be? Why did you choose those particular ones?
- Spouting the obvious, Nerdy Ned mentions that the state of Washington is named after a famous person and that he knows at least three other states named after famous people. He challenges you to identify them. Can you?

Introduction: Words Are Tangible

The most tangible elements of a language are its words. You've heard people say "There's no such word!" or ask "What does the word *lollapalooza* mean?" Someone doing a crossword puzzle may ask you, "What's a three-letter word for *excessively*?" We say one person likes to use "two-bit" words and another has a preference for "four-letter" words. In these instances people have clear notions of what a word is. When it comes to meaningful parts smaller than a word, we readily understand that *bookstore, laptop,* and *headset* have two each, but our intuitions may be less confident about *bookkeeper, sneakers, women's, sang,* and *impracticality*. This chapter examines words and their meaningful parts, as well as the principles that govern the composition of words and their functions in sentences. You'll learn what it means to know a word and how languages increase their store of words.

What Does It Mean to Know a Word?

Consider what a child must know in order to use a word. The child who asks "Can you take off my shoes?" knows a good deal more about the word *shoes* than what it refers to. She knows the sounds in *shoes* and the sequence in which they occur. She knows that the word can be used in the plural (unlike, say, *milk* or *sugar*) and that the plural is formed regularly (it isn't irregular like *teeth* or *children*). She also knows how to use the word in a sentence.

Using a word requires four kinds of information:

- its sounds and their sequencing (this is called *phonological* information, the topic of Chapters 3 and 4)

- its meanings (*semantic* information, discussed in Chapter 6)

- its category (e.g., noun or verb) and how to use it in a sentence (*syntactic* information, discussed here and in Chapter 5)

- how related words such as the plural (for nouns) and past tense (for verbs) are formed (*morphological* information, treated in this chapter)

For children and adults, using any word requires information about sounds, meanings, related words, and use in sentences, and that information is stored in the brain's dictionary, which is called the *mental lexicon*, or simply *lexicon*.

There are some parallels between the kinds of information stored in the metal lexicon and those found in a desk dictionary. Both contain information about pronunciation, meaning, related words, and sentence use. But a desk dictionary also contains information that is not needed for speaking—for example, a word's spelling and historical development (its *etymology*). Dictionary entries also provide illustrative phrases or sentences, showing how a word has been used by writers or speakers. A mental lexicon does not normally contain etymological, illustrative, or spelling information.

Lexical Categories (Parts of Speech)

The ability to use any word in a sentence requires knowledge of its **lexical category**. Even young children must know the category of every word they use—whether it is a verb, noun, or adjective. To be able to say, "I need some help" and "Can you help me?" requires knowing that *help* can be a noun (the first sentence) or a verb. Of course, a child's knowledge is unconscious, and even a grammarian's child wouldn't ordinarily know the *names* of the categories.

How to Identify Lexical Categories

There are several ways to help identify the lexical category of a word, and to some extent they rely on principles similar to those children must use in figuring out that same information. One way focuses on closely related forms of a word. *Spoon* and *spoons*, *book* and *books*, *frog* and *frogs* show parallel patterns of related forms, and words with parallel forms belong to the same category—in this case, noun. The words *old*, *tall*, and *bright* have a different pattern. Their related forms have *-er* and *-est* endings: *older/oldest, taller/tallest, brighter/brightest*. *Old*, *tall*, and *bright* are members of a category called adjective. Words such as *jump*, *kick*, and *laugh* appear with a different set of parallel endings, including *-ed* (*jumped, kicked, laughed*), *-ing* (*jumping, kicking, laughing*), and *-s* (*jumps, kicks, laughs*); they belong to the verb category.

Another way to identify categories focuses on which words and categories can occur together in phrases. For example, the nouns above can be preceded by *the* and *a* (or *an*): *a spoon/the book*, and the plural forms ending in *-s* can be preceded by *the*. Basic adjectives can be preceded by *very* or *too*, as in *very old* and *too bright*. Basic verbs can be preceded by *can, must,* or *will*: *will laugh*. Below are examples of these patterns for the three lexical categories we've mentioned.

Nouns

bike	bikes	a bike	the bike(s)
aunt	aunts	an aunt	the aunt(s)
camp	camps	a camp	the camp(s)

Adjectives

old	older	oldest	very old	too old
new	newer	newest	very new	too new
red	redder	reddest	very red	too red

Verbs

look	looks	looked	looking	can look	will look
play	plays	played	playing	can play	will play
camp	camps	camped	camping	can camp	will camp

Knowing the typical related forms in each category enables you to gauge that a word like *sharper* is related to the adjective *sharp* (note *too sharp* and *very sharp*), whereas a word like *shaver* is related to the noun *shavers* ("shavest" isn't a word, and you can't say *too* or *very shave* or *shaver*). A word like *missed* can be related to the verb *miss*, with its related forms *missing/misses*, *can miss*, and *will miss*. From an early age, children recognize that words belonging to different categories have characteristic endings or forms and characteristic distributions in phrases.

Relying on meaning is a third way to identify a word's lexical category. While it is a less reliable method than those we've just examined, it is useful at least in forming an initial hypothesis about a word's category. From the perspective of meaning, nouns refer to (or name) entities: persons, places, or things. Thus, *swimmer, sugar, city,* and *trees* are nouns, as in the phrases *that swimmer, some sugar, the city,* and *these trees.* Adjectives identify, refer to, or name qualities or properties of nouns, as with *tall* and *impressive* in the phrases *tall trees* or *an impressive swimmer.* Verbs identify or name actions, as with *jump* and *sings,* or states of being, as with *remain* or *seem.*

Verbs

English-speaking children know that **verbs** have a set of related forms (*talk, talks, talked, talking*) and that the base form—without one of the endings *–s, -ed, -ing*—can be preceded by *can* or *will.* Such knowledge is implicit: children know it but are not consciously aware of that knowledge.

Subcategories of Verbs A child knows more about a word than its category. To use a particular verb a child must implicitly know the kinds of sentence structures it allows, and such knowledge is stored in the child's mental lexicon. Consider items 1 through 6, where the asterisks preceding 2, 3, and 5 mark those sentences as ill-formed.

1. Sarah told a joke.
2. *Sarah laughed a joke.
3. *Sarah told at a joke.
4. Sarah laughed at a joke.
5. *Sarah told.
6. Sarah laughed.

You can see that the verbs *told* and *laughed* don't permit the same structures after them. Sentences with *tell/told* require a noun after the verb, as the ill-formed 5 demonstrates; if they didn't require a noun, 5 would not be marked with an asterisk. But 6 demonstrates that not all verbs require a noun after them. In fact, *laugh/laughed* does not permit a noun to follow directly, as 2 shows, but *laugh* permits the phrase *at a joke* to follow. Still other verbs permit—but don't require—a following noun, as shown in 7 and 8:

7. The diva played.
8. The diva played the piano.

Sentences 1 through 8 illustrate that words such as *tell, laugh,* and *play* belong to the *category* verb but do not permit the same sentence structures. They are said to belong to the same category but different *subcategories,* and even children possess implicit information about verb **subcategorization**; if they didn't, they couldn't avoid uttering sentences like 2, 3, and 5.

To introduce a bit of terminology, verbs that take a noun after them (*told a joke, caught the train*) are called **transitive** verbs. Those that do not require a noun are called **intransitive** (*lie, pray, shower*). In a child's mental lexicon, each verb is categorized as a verb and subcategorized as transitive or intransitive.

Nouns

Nouns constitute another lexical category. You have already seen that English nouns share a set of endings, technically called inflections. The inflection at the end of *spoons* represents information about *number*. **Number** is the term used to cover *singular* and *plural*. Nearly all English nouns have distinct singular and plural forms, as with the "regular" *cat/cats* and *dish/dishes* or the "irregular" *tooth/teeth* and *child/children*. A few exceptions like *deer* and *sheep* have the same form for singular and plural. Not all languages mark number on nouns. Chinese is one that does not.

Adjectives

Many **adjectives** can be recognized by the pattern of their related forms, namely, the endings -*er* and -*est*, as in *larger* and *largest*. But others, especially those whose basic form contains more than two syllables, do not permit these endings; **beautifuller* and **beautifullest* are not well-formed English words (hence the asterisks). But *beautiful* does share what are called co-occurrence patterns with other adjectives. In particular, it can be preceded by *very* or *too* (*very beautiful*) and can precede nouns (*beautiful flowers*). (Not all words preceding nouns and seeming to modify them are adjectives. In particular, nouns often precede other nouns, as with *summer fun, graduation party, egg industry*, and *California governor*. The pre-nominal position of such nouns does not make them adjectives.) As a third frame, the only single words that fit into "it seems __" or "he/she seems __" would be adjectives: *odd, able, sure, funny, sweet, beautiful*. Later in this chapter we'll discuss suffixes that transform words of one lexical class into words of another lexical class. As a consequence of their ability to form adjectives from certain other lexical classes, some suffixes may also be helpful in identifying adjectives, as with -*able* (*breakable, changeable, debatable*), -*ful* (*peaceful, wishful, thoughtful*), -*ish* (*Spanish, childish, thirtyish*), -*ous* (*dangerous, joyous, odorous*), -*al* (*fictional, parental, global*), -*ic* (*allergic, scientific, academic*), -*less* (*harmless, priceless, odorless*), and -*y* (*slimey, creepy, bloody*).

Pronouns

Pronouns constitute a category of relatively few words, and they fall into several subcategories. Generally speaking, we can say that pronouns substitute for noun phrases in specific kinds of contexts. They function independently, taking the place of noun phrases and not as modifiers of other words. Below are listed some of the subcategories of pronouns.

Personal Pronouns The most familiar pronouns are **personal pronouns**, such as *I, me, she, him, they,* and *theirs.* Primarily, personal pronouns are distinguished from one another by representing different parties to a conversation or other social interaction. This aspect of pronouns is called *person,* and the first person is the speaker or speakers; the second person is the person or persons spoken *to* (the addressee); and any persons or things spoken *about* are called third persons.

> First person—speaker: *I, me, mine, we, us, ours*
>
> Second person—addressee: *you, yours*
>
> Third person—spoken about: *she, her, hers, he, him, his, it, its, they, them, theirs*

Interrogative Pronouns *Who* in *Who played the role of Neytiri?* and *what* in *You told Rosie what?* and *What did you tell Rosie?* are interrogative pronouns. **Interrogative pronouns** are used to ask questions.

Try It Yourself The sentence *Whose are those?* contains two pronouns. Which words are pronouns and what kind of pronoun is each?

Relative Pronouns In form, **relative pronouns** resemble other kinds of pronouns, but they're used differently. In sentences 1, 2, and 3 below, examples include *who* (in 1), *that* (in 2), and *which* (in 3). Other relative pronouns include *whose* and *whom.* Notice that relative pronouns are related to some preceding noun phrase. In the examples, the relative pronoun and the related noun phrase are italicized, with the relative pronoun underlined.

1. Ellen's *a doctor <u>who</u>* specializes in gerontology.
2. *The show <u>that</u>* won the most awards is *60 Minutes.*
3. She's *a licensed masseur, <u>which</u>* I am not.

Indefinite Pronouns Pronouns whose referents can't be specifically identified are called **indefinite**, as in *<u>Somebody</u> ate my pizza!* Other indefinite pronouns are: *some, someone, anyone, everyone, one, no one, somebody, anybody, everybody, nobody, something, anything, everything, nothing.*

Demonstrative Pronouns To refer to things relatively near (*this, these*) or, by contrast, relatively far away (*that, those*) when the referent can be identified by pointing or from the context of a discussion, we use a subcategory of pronouns called **demonstrative pronouns**. Examples include *that* in *That really bothers Dana* and *those* in *Those are Dana's.* The forms *this and that* and *these and those* are pronouns when they are used independently of a noun, but they aren't always pronouns, as we'll discuss below in the section on determiners.

Determiners

Determiners precede nouns (*a book, an orchestra, the players, this problem, those guys, which film, whose iPad*), although words in some other categories can intervene (*a great book, an acclaimed orchestra, the very best players*). Unlike adjectives and verbs, determiners do not have endings. Despite its being a small category, with few members, determiners fall into several subcategories:

- definite and indefinite articles as in the underscored parts of these phrases: _the_ book, _a_ film, _an_ iPad
- demonstratives: _this, that, these, those_
- possessives: _my, our, your, her, his, its, their_
- interrogatives: _which, what, whose_

Unlike nouns, adjectives, and verbs, categories whose members cannot be fully enumerated, determiners can be enumerated, as in the subcategories just listed. Categories whose members can be fully enumerated are called "closed" classes. Note that some determiners are identical in form to pronouns, but determiners introduce nouns or noun phrases, whereas pronouns substitute for nouns or noun phrases. In _Whose is this? whose_ and _this_ are pronouns. In _Whose book is this red one? whose_ and _this_ are determiners.

Prepositions and Postpositions

Prepositions constitute a class with few enough members that they can be enumerated. They are invariant in form—no endings. They typically precede a noun phrase, as in _at a concert, on Tuesday,_ or _under the table_. Prepositions indicate a semantic relationship between other entities. The preposition in _The book is on_ (or _under_ or _near_) _the table_ indicates the _location_ of the book with respect to the table. Notice the underlined prepositions in _Tina rode to_ (or _from_) _Athens_ (indicating _direction_ with respect to Athens) _with_ (or _without_) _Daniel_ (indicating _accompaniment_) _at_ (or _near_ or _by_) _her side_ (indicating _location_ of Daniel with respect to Tina).

Instead of prepositions, Japanese and some other languages have **postpositions**, which function like prepositions in that they indicate a semantic relationship between other entities but follow the noun phrase instead of preceding it. Compare the Japanese-English pairs below:

Japanese Postpositions	English Prepositions
Taroo _no_	_of_ Taro
hasi _de_	_with_ chopsticks
Tookyoo _e_	_to_ Tokyo

The placement of prepositions before a noun, which seems natural to speakers of English (and French, Spanish, Russian, and many other languages), would seem unnatural to speakers of Japanese, Turkish, Hindi, and many other languages that **post**pose rather than **pre**pose this category.

Adverbs

Adverbs have been called "the most nebulous and puzzling of the traditional word classes," and indeed the category doesn't suit English very well. For one thing, adverbs can't be identified solely by their form and don't generally have related forms. Many adverbs are derived from adjectives by adding *-ly*, as with *swiftly, oddly, brightly,* and *possibly* (from *swift, odd, bright, possible*). But other adverbs, including the most common ones, carry no distinctive marker, as with *then, now, here, soon,* and *away.* Besides that, not all words ending in *-ly* are adverbs (*manly* and *lonely* are adjectives). The most reliable way of identifying adverbs is by their patterns of distribution in sentences—where they occur and with which other categories. The meaning of a word can also hint at its being an adverb insofar as adverbs often indicate something about the action of the verb—for example, when (*now, then, often, soon*), where (*here, there*), how (*quickly, suddenly, fiercely*), or to what degree (*very, too*). Some grammarians include the word *not* as an adverb. Grammatically, adverbs display a wide range of functions: they can modify verbs, adjectives, other adverbs, and even whole sentences.

Adverbs Modifying Verbs (Sentences with related adjectives in parentheses)

He talked *loudly*. (He was a *loud* talker.)

She slept *soundly*. (She was a *sound* sleeper.)

She thought *quickly*. (She was a *quick* thinker.)

They studied *diligently*. (They were *diligent* students.)

Adverbs Modifying Verbs

She spoke *often*.

She studied *here*.

It *suddenly* stopped.

She *fiercely* believes it.

Below, the modifying adverbs are italicized, and the modified adjectives or adverbs are underlined.

Adverbs Modifying Adjectives
a *very* tall tree

a *bitterly* cold winter

a *truly* splendid evening

Adverbs Modifying Adverbs
very soon

unbelievably quickly

truly unbelievably fast

Adverbs Modifying Sentences
Actually, it was Danielle who said it.

I don't know why I'm here, *frankly*.

Unfortunately, the remark wasn't funny.

Conjunctions

There are two principal kinds of **conjunctions**. **Coordinating conjunctions** such as *and, but,* and *or* serve to conjoin expressions of the same category or status—for example, noun phrases (*fish and wildlife, tea or coffee*), verbs (*sing and dance, trip and fall*), adjectives (*slow and painful, hot and cold*), and clauses (*she sang and he danced*).

Subordinating conjunctions serve to link one clause to one another in a noncoordinate role, as in *She visited Montreal* twice <u>while</u> *she attended Bates College* or *He said <u>that</u> she was tired* or *They spoke quietly <u>because</u> he was sleeping.* (Clauses and some kinds of subordinate clauses are discussed in Chapter 5.)

Subordinating conjunctions may be referred to simply as *subordinators* and coordinating conjunctions as *conjunctions* or *coordinators*.

Morphemes Are Word Parts That Carry Meaning

You know that words such as *girl, ask, tall, uncle,* and *orange* cannot be divided into smaller meaningful units. *Orange* is not made up of *o* + *range* or *or* + *ange*. Neither is *uncle* composed of *un* and *cle*. But most words do have more than one meaningful part. You can find two elements each in *grandmother, bookshelf, homemade, asked, taller, oranges,* and *uncles. Beautiful, supermarkets,* and *decomposing* also have more than one meaningful element. A set of words can be built up by adding elements to a core element. All the following have *true* as their core, or root, element:

truer	untrue	truthfully
truest	truth	untruthfully
truly	truthful	untruthfulness

These words share a root whose meaning or lexical category has been modified by the addition of elements. The meaningful elements in a word are called **morphemes**. Thus, *true* is a word with a single morpheme, while *untrue* and *truly* contain two morphemes each, and *untruthfulness* contains five (UN- + TRUE + -TH + -FUL + -NESS). *Truer* has the elements TRUE and -ER (meaning 'more'). The morphemes in *truly* are TRUE and -LY; in *untrue,* TRUE and UN-; in *truthful,* TRUE + -TH + -FUL.

Most morphemes have what linguists call lexical meaning, as with *look, kite,* and *tall.* Other morphemes represent a grammatical category or semantic notion such as past tense (*-ed* in *looked*) or plural (*-s* in *kites*) or comparative degree (*-er* in *taller*).

Don't be tempted to equate morphemes with syllables. Consider that *harvest, grammar,* and *river* contain two syllables but only one morpheme each. *Gorilla* contains three syllables, *Connecticut* four, and *hippopotamus* five, but each of those words comprises only a single morpheme: they are **monomorphemic.** The other way around, a single syllable can represent more than one morpheme: *kissed* is a monosyllabic word that contains two morphemes (KISS + 'PAST TENSE'); *dogs* (DOG + 'PLURAL') and *feet* (FOOT + 'PLURAL'), also monosyllabic, contain two morphemes each. In a single syllable, *men's* contains three morphemes (MAN + 'PLURAL' + 'POSSESSIVE').

Try It Yourself Identify all the morphemes in these words and whether they're free or bound: *bakery, baseball, borderlands, cider, dusty, fried, outlaw, prayer, prefabs, these.*

Morphemes Can Be Free or Bound

Some morphemes can stand alone as words: TRUE, MOTHER, ORANGE. Others function only as part of a word: UN-,

TELE-, -NESS, and -ER. Morphemes that can stand alone as words are known as **free morphemes**. Those that cannot are **bound morphemes**.

Morphemes That Derive Other Words

Certain bound morphemes change the category of the word to which they are attached, as with the underlined parts of *doubtful*, *sweetly*, *establishment*, *teacher*, *darken*, and *frighten*. When added to the noun *doubt*, -FUL derives the adjective *doubtful*, as in Figure 2.1. When added to the adjective sweet, -LY derives the adverb *sweetly*; when added to the verb *establish*, -MENT derives the noun *establishment*. *Dark* is an adjective, *darken* a verb; *teach* is a verb, *teacher* a noun; *sane* is an adjective, *sanity* a noun; *fright* is a noun, *frighten* a verb. English has many more derivational affixes, and derivational morphemes in English (but not all languages) tend to be added to the ends of words (as suffixes). We can represent these relationships in the following rules of derivation:

Noun + -FUL   →   Adjective (*doubtful, beautiful, bountiful, careful*)
Adjective + -LY   →   Adverb (*sweetly, really, slowly, responsibly*)
Verb + -MENT   →   Noun (*establishment, advancement, amazement*)
Verb + -ER   →   Noun (*teacher, rider, banker, glider*)
Adjective + -ITY →   Noun (*sanity, abnormality, reality, frugality*)
Adjective + -EN   →   Verb (*darken, sweeten, brighten, harden*)
Noun + - EN   →   Verb (*frighten, lengthen, hasten, christen*)

A similar process adds a morpheme at the beginning of a word—as a prefix. English prefixes typically change the meaning of a word but *not* its lexical category. Thus, *align* and *realign* are both verbs; *kind* and *unkind* are both adjectives; *spell* and *misspell* are both verbs. The derivation of *realign* is illustrated graphically in Figure 2.2.

RE- + Verb   →   Verb (*realign, repaint, rephrase, rewrite, reassess, retake*)
MIS- + Verb   →   Verb (*misspell, misstep, miscalculate, misfire, misclassify*)
UN - + Adjective   →   Adjective (*unkind, uncool, unfair, unreal, untrue*)
UN- + Verb   →   Verb (*undo, uncover, undress, uninstall, untag*)
UNDER- + Verb   →   Verb (*underbid, undercount, undercut, underrate, underscore*)
EX- + Noun   →   Noun (*ex-cop, ex-nun, ex-husband, ex-convict*)

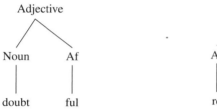

Figure 2.1

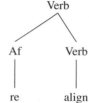

Figure 2.2

Processes of **derivation** that transform a word into another word with a related meaning but belonging to a different lexical category are common in the languages of the world. Here's an example from Persian. (Note: æ is pronounced like the *a* in English *hat*, x like the *ch* in German *Bach*.)

dærd 'pain'	dærdnak 'painful'
næm 'dampness'	næmnak 'damp'
xætær 'danger'	xætærnak 'dangerous'

The suffix -*nak* can be added to certain nouns to derive adjectives. Thus Persian has the following derivational rule:

Noun X + -NAK → Adjective 'the quality of being or having X'

Another derivational suffix of Persian creates abstract nouns from adjectives, as illustrated in these word pairs:

gærm 'warm'	gærma 'heat'
pæhn 'wide'	pæhna 'width'

This process of derivational morphology can be expressed by this rule:

Adjective + -A → Noun

Try It Yourself Using as models the derivational rules given above, write the rule by which *rusty* is derived from *rust*, and cite two examples of words formed by that rule. Write the rule by which *bookish* is derived from *book*, and cite two examples of words formed by that rule.

Not every word belonging to the lexical category specified in a rule can undergo a given derivational process. In English, the nouns *doubt* and *beauty* become adjectives by addition of the suffix -FUL, but the adjective related to *rust* is formed by addition of the suffix -Y, and to make *book* an adjective requires the suffix -ISH. Thus, words are marked in the mental lexicon for particular derivational processes, yielding the grammatical *rusty* and *bookish* rather than the ungrammatical forms *rustful* and *bookful*.

In Fijian, *vaka-*, meaning 'in the manner of,' is a derivational morpheme that can be prefixed to adjectives and nouns to derive adverbs according to these two rules:

VAKA- + Adjective → Adverb
VAKA- + Noun → Adverb

The following adverbs exhibit the morpheme VAKA-: *vaka-Viti* 'in the Fijian fashion' (from *Viti* 'Fijian'), *vakatotolo* 'in a rapid manner, rapidly' (from *totolo* 'fast, rapid'); to illustrate the derivation from a noun, consider *vakamaarama* 'ladylike' (formed by prefixing *vaka-* to *maarama* 'lady').

Not all bound morphemes change the lexical category of words. Adding the bound morphemes DIS-, RE-, and UN- (*disappear, repaint, unfavorable*) to a verb changes its meaning but not its lexical category. For example, *appear* and *disappear* are both verbs, as are *paint* and *repaint*; *favorable* and *unfavorable* are both adjectives. There is a notable tendency in English for morphemes that change meaning without altering the lexical category to be added to the front of words as prefixes, but this is not true of all languages (and some languages lack prefixes altogether, as Turkish does).

The two types of morpheme we have just examined are **derivational morphemes**. That is, they produce new words from existing words. They can do that by changing the meaning of a word (*true* versus *untrue*; *align* versus *realign*) or by changing a word's lexical category (*doubt* is a noun, *doubtful* an adjective).

Inflectional Morphemes

Another type of bound morpheme is represented in the underlined parts of the words *cats, collected, sleeps,* and *louder*. These **inflectional morphemes** change the form of a word but not its lexical category or its central meaning. Inflectional morphemes create variant forms of a word to conform to different roles in a sentence or in discourse. On nouns and pronouns, inflectional morphemes serve to mark semantic notions such as *number* or grammatical categories such as *case*. On verbs, they can mark categories such as *tense* or *number*. On adjectives they can indicate *degree*. They shape the "related forms" we used earlier in the chapter to help identify lexical categories. We return to inflectional morphology later in the chapter.

How Are Morphemes Organized Within Words?

Morphemes Are Ordered in Sequence

Within a word, morphemes aren't randomly arranged, but instead they have a strict and systematic linear sequence.

Affixes Some morphemes, called **suffixes**, always follow the stems they attach to, such as 'PLURAL' in *girls* and -MENT in *commitment*: both **sgirl* and **mentcommit* would be ill-formed. **Prefixes** attach to the front of a stem, as in *untrue, disappear,* and *repaint.* (Compare the ill-formed **trueun, *appeardis,* and **paintre*.)

Derivational morphemes can be prefixes (*unhappy, disappear*) or suffixes (*happiness, appearance*), and some words have both: *unhappiness* and *disappearance*. Generally, inflectional morphemes are added to the outermost parts of words. Taken together, prefixes and suffixes are called **affixes**.

Infixes Besides affixes, some languages have infixes. An **infix** is a morpheme inserted within another morpheme. In Tagalog (a language of the Philippines), you can see infixing, for example, by comparing the word *gulay* meaning 'greenish vegetables' with the word *ginulay*, meaning 'greenish blue,' which contains the infix -IN-.

Morphemes Can Be Discontinuous

Not all morphological processes can be viewed as joining or concatenating morphemes to one another by adding a continuous sequence of sounds (or letters) to a stem. In other words, not all morphological processes involve prefixes, suffixes, or infixes. The technical term for discontinuous morphology is *nonconcatenative*.

Circumfixes Some languages combine a prefix and a suffix into a **circumfix**—a morpheme that occurs in two parts, one on each side of a stem. Samoan has a morpheme FE-/-AʔI, meaning 'reciprocal': the verb 'to quarrel' is *finau*, and the verb 'to quarrel with each other' is *fefinauaʔi*—FE + FINAU + AʔI. Malay-Indonesian has a circumfix KE-/-AN that derives an abstract noun from a concrete one; thus, *baik* 'good, kind' yields *kebaikan*—KE-BAIK-AN—'kindness.' As another example, the circumfix SE-/-NYA derives an adverb from an adjective, as in *benar* 'true' and *sebenarnya*—SE-BENAR-NYA—'actually.'

Interweaving Morphemes Semitic languages, such as Arabic and Hebrew, can have **interweaving morphemes**. Arabic nouns and verbs generally have a root consisting of three consonants, such as KTB. The Arabic word for 'book' is *kitaab*. By interweaving K-T-B and various other morphemes, Arabic creates a great many nouns, verbs, and adjectives from this single root. All the nouns and verbs in Table 2.1 contain the same KTB root, with other morphemes interwoven.

Incidentally, the English words *Muslim, Islam,* and *salaam* all contain the Arabic root SLM, with its core meaning of 'peace, submission.'

Portmanteau Words Contain Merged Morphemes

Another phenomenon joins several morphemes in such a way that the sounds in the word cannot be assigned tidily to each of its morphemes. A classic example is the French word *du*, which combines the two morphemes DE 'of' and LE 'the.' You can see the difficulty of assigning the sounds to one morpheme or the other. Some analysts call blends like *smog* (from *smoke* and *fog*) **portmanteau words**.

Morphemes Are Layered Within Words

Morphemes are organized in highly patterned ways. Typically they display an obvious linear order, but they also have a not so obvious hierarchical or **layered structure**. Take the word *untrue*: it has the obvious linear order UN- followed

Table 2.1 *Derivational Morphology in Arabic*

kitaaba	'writing'	kataba	'he wrote'
kaatib	'writer'	kaataba	'he corresponded with'
maktab	'office'	ʔaktaba	'he dictated'
maktaba	'library'	ʔiktataba	'he was registered'
maktuub	'letter'	takaataba	'he exchanged letters with'
miktaab	'typewriter'	inkataba	'he subscribed'
kutubii	'bookseller'	iktataba	'he had a copy made'

by TRUE. But in terms of layers TRUE is the root, to which UN- is prefixed; *untrue* isn't UN- with TRUE suffixed but TRUE with UN- prefixed. *Truthful* comprises a stem *truth* with -FUL suffixed to it (*truth* itself is TRUE with -TH suffixed). The morphemes in *untruthful* have the obvious linear order UN- + TRUE + -TH + -FUL. But in terms of layers, TRUE is the root to which -TH is added, creating the stem *truth* to which -FUL is added, creating the stem *truthful* to which UN- is added. In other words, the layering for *untruthful* proceeds this way: *true* > *truth* > *truthful* > *untruthful*.

Now consider *uncontrollably*. It's helpful to picture the sequence of layering from the root morpheme CONTROL, built up by a set of derivational rules that also apply widely to other words:

control (Verb)

              Verb + -ABLE → Adjective (Fig. 2.3)

controllable (Adjective)

              UN- + Adjective → Adjective (Fig. 2.4)

uncontrollable (Adjective)

              Adjective + -LY → Adverb (Fig. 2.5)

uncontrollably (Adverb)

The root of *uncontrollably* is *control*, which functions as the stem for -ABLE; in turn, *controllable* functions as the stem for *uncontrollable*; finally, *uncontrollable* functions as the stem to which is added the derivational suffix -LY to derive the adverb *uncontrollably*.

Its structure can be graphically represented in two ways. One uses labeled brackets as in [[un[[control$_{Verb}$]able$_{Adj}$]$_{Adj}$]ly$_{Adv}$]. The other is a tree diagram, as in Figure 2.5. In that figure, begin with the lowest category node, which is labeled Verb. Because the lowest category node identifies the root morpheme, the verb *control* is the root of the entire word, which is built up layer by layer as follows. To the root verb is added the affix -ABLE, yielding the adjective *controllable* (as in Figure 2.3). Note that if you added UN- prior to adding -ABLE, you'd produce "uncontrol," which is not an English word. The adjective *controllable* then serves as a stem to which can be added the affix UN-, producing *uncontrollable*, also an adjective but with the opposite meaning (see Figure 2.4). The final step in the derivation adds the affix -LY to the adjective *uncontrollable*, yielding the adverb *uncontrollably*. Looking at Figure 2.5 from the top down, you can see that the Adverb node encompasses the entire word *uncontrollably* and has two branches, one labeled Adjective (encompassing *un-control-able*) and one labeled Af (for Affix) and leading to the suffix -LY; in turn, the label Adjective has two branches—one leading to the affix UN- and the other to the Adjective node *controllable*; finally, the Adjective node that encompasses *controllable* has two branches—one labeled Verb and leading to *control* and the other leading to the affix –ABLE. The lowermost node for a lexical category (Verb) leads to the base form CONTROL, so *control* is the root of the word *uncontrollably*.

Figure 2.3

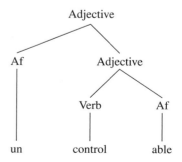

Figure 2.4

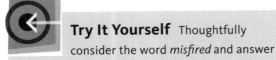

Try It Yourself Thoughtfully consider the word *misfired* and answer these questions: What is the linear order of its morphemes? What is its root morpheme and how many affixes does it have? Which affix is first added to the root, thus creating the stem for the next affixation? Is the final morpheme added derivational or inflectional? Now answer the same questions for *ex-teachers*.

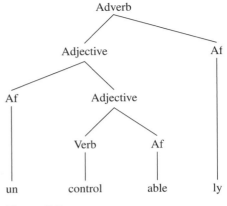

Figure 2.5

How Does a Language Increase Its Vocabulary?

Languages have three principal ways of extending their vocabulary:

- ◆ New words can be formed from existing words and word parts.
- ◆ Words can be "borrowed" from another language.
- ◆ New words can be made up, created from scratch.

Some Word Classes Are Open, Some Closed

In some societies, the need for new nouns, adjectives, and verbs may arise frequently, and additions to these lexical categories occur freely. It is for this reason that nouns, adjectives, and verbs are called *open classes*. By contrast, prepositions, pronouns, and determiners are *closed classes*, and new words in these lexical categories are seldom added. Century after century, English speakers have added thousands of new words, borrowing many from other languages and constructing others from elements already available.

How to Derive New Words

Affixes Adding morphemes to a word is a common way of creating new words. English has added the agentive suffix -ER to the prepositions *up* and *down* to create the nouns *upper* and *downer* to refer to phenomena that lift or dampen your spirits. More commonly, -ER is added to a verb (V) to create a word with the sense 'one who Vs': *singer* 'one who sings'; *campaigner* 'one who campaigns'; *designer* 'one who designs'; *blogger* 'one who blogs'; *twitterer* 'one who twitters or tweets (on Twitter.com).'

English adds new words principally by prefixing or suffixing. Prefixes like UN-, PRE-, and DIS- alter the meaning of words but not usually their lexical category, as we saw earlier. Added to the adjectives *true, popular, successful*, and *favorable*, the

McSleep Inn or Out?

In the late 1980s Quality Inns wanted to launch a chain of inexpensive, standardized inns under the name *McSleep Inn*. When McDonald's Corporation objected, the case went to court (*Quality Inns Int'l. v. McDonald's Corp.*). Linguist Roger W. Shuy helped Quality Inns determine whether the Mc prefix had become part of everyday English, with a meaning independent of its association with McDonald's. He cited journalistic sources that, without making any reference to McDonald's, appeared to use *Mc* in a general way to mean 'basic, convenient, inexpensive, and standardized.' Among his examples were *McFood, McFashion, McFuneral, McLaw, McMedicine, McMovies, McLube, McMail, McArt,* and even *McPaper* (referring to *USA Today*, "Fast News for the Fast Food Generation"). The judge in the case quipped that "A news report . . . referred to the trial . . . as taking place in the McCourt, which . . . would make [him] the McJudge," and in his "McPinion" he quoted an article that captured the situation: "This is the era of instant gratification, of poptops, quick wash, fast fix, frozen foods, McEverything." Linguist David W. Lightfoot was retained by McDonald's, and he disputed any claim that *Mc* had become a generic prefix, used without reference to McDonald's and therefore available for anyone to use. He testified that the meanings Dr. Shuy uncovered were characteristics of McDonald's and its reputation, and he concluded, according to the judge, that "in every case the allusion [in Shuy's examples] was to McDonald's and its family of marks [and] intended to be cute and playful." In the end, the McJudge decided that *McSleep* would infringe on McDonald's legitimate family of trademarks, and he ruled out naming the new chain *McSleep Inn*.

prefix UN- creates new adjectives with the opposite meanings: *untrue, unpopular, unsuccessful, unfavorable*. Prefixed to verbs, UN- creates new verbs with the opposite meaning: *undo, untie, unplug, unbutton, uninstall*. DIS- prefixed to a verb creates a verb with an opposite meaning: *disobey, disapprove, disappear, displease, dishonor*. PRE- serves as a prefix to several categories: verbs (*preplan, preregister, premix, preallot, preconceive, predecease*), adjectives (*pre-Copernican, precollegiate, preconscious, prenatal, prenuptial, presurgical*), and nouns (*precaution, precalculus, preadult, precancer*). PRE- has roughly the same sense in each case, and from an existing word it creates a new word of the same lexical category. Recently productive prefixes include CYBER- (*cyberspace, cyberpal, cybercafé, cybersex*), BIO- (*biochip, bioethics, bioterrorism, biotechnology, bioweapons*), NANO- (*nanotube, nanosecond, nanotechnology, nanoworld, nanogram*), and E- (*email, ebook, ecard, ebuddy, eshop*), none of which changes the lexical category of the stem it attaches to.

English derivational **suffixes** are added to the tail end of a stem. Unlike prefixes, derivational suffixes usually change the lexical category of the stem—from, say, a verb to a noun. For example, adding -MENT to a verb makes it a noun: *agreement, assignment, establishment*. Likewise, the suffix -ATION derives a noun from a verb: *resignation, organization, implementation, observation, reformation*.

Suffixes are widely exploited in the languages of the world. The Indonesian suffix -KAN changes a noun to a verb, and among the various meanings it can produce are: 'to cause to become X' (*rajakan* 'to crown' from *raja* 'king') and 'to put in X' (as in *penjarakan* 'imprison' from *penjara* 'prison' + -KAN).

Reduplication The process by which a morpheme or part of a morpheme is repeated to create a new word with a different meaning or different category is called reduplication. The Mandarin Chinese word *sànsànbu* 'to take a leisurely walk' is formed by reduplicating the first syllable of *sànbu* 'to walk'; *hónghóng* 'bright red' is formed by reduplicating *hóng* 'red.' Partial reduplication repeats only part of the morpheme, while full reduplication reduplicates the entire morpheme. In the Papua New Guinea language Motu, the verb *mahuta* 'to sleep' reduplicates fully as *mahutamahuta* 'to sleep constantly' and reduplicates partially as *mamahuta* 'to sleep' (when agreeing with a plural subject). In Turkish, adjectives like *açik* 'open,' *ayri* 'separate,' and *uzun* 'long' are reduplicated (by prefixing the initial vowel followed by a consonant) as *apaçik* 'wide open,' *apayri* 'entirely separate,' and *upuzun* 'very long.' Reduplication is *not* repetition: repetition does not create a new word but simply reiterates the same word, as in English *very, very* (*tired*), *night-night*, and *long, long, long* (*shower*). English does not have a productive process like the reduplication of Chinese, Motu, or Turkish.

Reduplication can have various functions. It can moderate or intensify the meaning of a word, as illustrated by the Chinese, Motu, and Turkish examples just given. Alternatively, it can mark grammatical categories, as in Indonesian, where certain kinds of noun plurals are formed by reduplication: *babibabi* 'an assortment of pigs' is a reduplicated form of *babi* 'pig.'

Compounds

English speakers show a disposition for putting words together to create new words in a process called compounding. Relatively recent compounds include *air kiss, moon shot, waterbed, upfront, color code, computerlike, dust bunny, gut-buster, plastic wrap, speed dating, strip mall,* and *radiopharmaceutical,* as well as *V-chip, email, online, web page, website, download, Facebook,* and *ringtone.* (Notice that these compounds have heavier stress or emphasis on the first element than on the second element.) To gauge the popularity of compounding, consider that one relatively short piece in an issue of the *Los Angeles Times* contained the following examples.

Nouns	Nouns	Nouns	Adjectives
petroleum engineer	whistle-blower	pay phone	whistle-blowing
government documents	troublemaker	phone call	baby-faced
government witness	debt ceiling	storerooms	high-ranking
subcommittee hearing	brain cancer	cover-up	overzealous
aircraft carrier	reserve account	kickbacks	born-again
training course	sea power	breakup	middle-aged

Compounding is widespread in the languages of the world. Mandarin, for example, has numerous compounds, such as *fàn-wǎn* 'rice bowl,' *diàn-nǎo* ('electric' + 'brain') 'computer,' *tái-bù* 'tablecloth,' *fēi -jī* ('fly' + 'machine') 'airplane,' and *hēi-bǎn* ('black' + 'board') 'blackboard.' German is famous for its compounding.

The word *Fernsprecher* (literally 'far speaker') was for a long time the preferred word for what is now usually called *Telefon*. A ballpoint pen is called *Kugelschreiber* ('ball' + 'writer'); a glove *Handschuh* ('hand' + 'shoe'); mayor is *Bürgermeister* ('citizen' + 'master'). Indonesian has exploited compounding in a word made familiar to Westerners from its use as the assumed name of a well-known World War I socialite and spy: *matahari*, meaning 'sun,' comes from *mata* 'eye' and *hari* 'day.' The word for 'eyeglasses' is *kacamata*, a compound of *kaca* 'glass' and *mata* 'eye' (similar to the English compound *eyeglasses* but with a different order of elements).

Bear Encounters at Yosemite National Park. A warning in four languages, including German. Can you spot any likely compounds in the German version? *Lebensmittel machen Bären angriffslustig. Schützen Sie Lebensmittel vor allen Tieren im Park.*

Shortening

Shortenings of various kinds are a popular means of multiplying the words of a language. Besides ordinary shortenings, we'll examine acronyms, initialisms, and blends.

Ordinary shortenings are common. In shortenings like *radials* for radial tires, *feds* for federal agents, *jet* for jet airplane, *indie* for independent film, and *narc* for narcotics agent, the first element of a compound or a shortened version of it remains and the second element is omitted altogether. We can see a variant on that in *app* for computer application program, where one of the words is shortened, the others omitted. In shortenings like *info* for information, *obits* for obituaries, *dorm* for dormitory, and *poli-sci* for political science, a word or parts of words in a compound are shortened. In shortenings like *rec room* 'recreation room' and *comp time* 'compensatory time,' the first (and multisyllabic) word is shortened and the second (often monosyllabic) word retained. Note that the shortened forms need not be morphemes in the full expression: *jet* is a morpheme, but *narc, fed, indie, obit, rec,* and *comp* are not morphemes in the words from which they have been formed.

Acronyms Shortenings in which the initial letters of the words in an expression are joined and pronounced as a word are **acronyms**:

UNESCO	*NATO*	*radar* (radio detecting and ranging)
WASP	*NASA*	*yuppy* (young urban professional + -Y)
WI-FI		*nimby* (not in my backyard)
ASCII (American standard code for information interchange, pronounced "as-kee")		

Initialisms Some shortenings resemble acronyms but are pronounced as a sequence of letters. At *U-S-C* (University of Southern California) and *N-Y-U* (New York University), a student's grade point average may be called a *G-P-A*. *PC* carries two meanings— 'politically correct' and 'personal computer.' Given their pronunciation as a series of letters, these are called *initialisms*. Many initialisms (*AI, CD, DNA, DVD, fMRI, FTC, MTV, NHL, PDA, IED, GPS, LCD*) could not easily be pronounced as ordinary words, while others could but aren't: *COO* for chief operating officer, *ADD* for attention deficit disorder, *SUV* for sport utility vehicle, and *m.o.* for modus operandi. Perhaps the most popular initialism in the world is *OK*, often spelled *okay*.

Try It Yourself Among these, which are acronyms? EU, USA, FBI, CIA, WMD, GI, SARS, NYPD, ER, DARPA, FWB, MBA, VIP, DJ, ATM, IT, IM, iPod, SNAFU, TGIF, TMI.

Blends Blends are words created by combining usually the first sounds of one word with the final sounds of another. *Smog* (from *smoke* and *fog*), *glob* (*gob* and *blob*), and *motel* (*motor* and *hotel*) are well-established examples. Newer ones include *fanzine* (*fan* and *magazine*), *punkumentary* (*punk* and *documentary*), *infomercial* (*information* and *commercial*), *agribot* (*agriculture* and *robot*), *glitterati* (*glitter* and *literati*), and *celanthropist* (*celebrity* and *philanthropist*). *Netizens* and *netiquette* blend *net* (a shortened form of *Internet*) with *citizens* and *etiquette*. Combining the existing blend *smog* with the tail end of *metropolis* forms *smogopolis*. Blends like *Spanglish, Franglais, Chinglish,* and *Yinglish* suggest how heavily some varieties of English have borrowed words and other elements from other languages. Some blends combine the beginning sounds or syllables of two words, as with *modem*, which is well known although its elements are not (*modulator* and *demodulator*) and *biotech* (*biology* and *technology*). Blends frequently serve as trade names and names of related products: *Amtrak, Eurailpass, Eurorail, Eurotrip,* and *Flexipass*. Blends often combine two nouns, but *Flexipass* combines the adjective *flexible* with the noun *pass*, and other blends combine other categories, as in *whatchamacallit*.

Try It Yourself Identify the words whose parts have been combined into these blends: affluential, andropause, automagically, beefalo, Bollywood, botel, brainiac, Chunnel, cremains, cybrarian, digicam, emoticon, gasohol, gaydar, gimmes, guesstimate, himbo, murderabilia, prebuttal, sexpert, wannabes.

Back Formation

Another type of word formation is exemplified by "pronunciate," which an occasional college student can be heard to say when searching for the verb corresponding to the noun *pronunciation*. The new verb they have "back formed" from the noun may not be sufficiently established to be entered in dictionaries, but some other back formations are well established, including the verbs *typewrite*, *baby-sit*, *spectate*, and *edit*, back formed from the nouns *typewriter*, *baby-sitter*, *spectator*, and *editor*.

Conversion or Functional Shift

In some languages, a word belonging to one category can be converted to another category without any changes to the form of the word. This is called conversion or functional shift. We request someone to *update* (verb) a report and then call the revised report an *update* (noun). We ask a fellow worker to *email* or *fax* the report, both of which are verbs converted from shortened forms of nouns (*electronic mail*, *facsimile*). Companies *hire* (verb) a group of employees and call them new *hires* (a noun). To promote a product in the *market* we *market* it. Conversion of this type commonly leads to noun/verb and noun/adjective pairs, as in Table 2.2, which also illustrates that in some instances the same form can serve as noun, verb, and adjective. Once a form has been shifted to a new lexical category, it conforms to the inflectional morphology of that category: an *update*, several *updates*, she's *updating* the report now, he *updated* it last month.

Semantic Shift

Words can take on new meanings by extending or shrinking the scope of their reference. Two well-known examples of semantic shift have remained popular since the Vietnam War, when *hawk* came to be used frequently for supporters of the war and *dove* for its opponents, extending the meaning of these words from the combative nature of hawks and the symbolically peaceful role of doves. Today, computer users utilize a *mouse* and *bookmark* Internet addresses. These new meanings did not replace earlier ones but extended the range of application for the words *mouse* and *bookmark*. Called *semantic shift* or *metaphorical extension*, this phenomenon creates *metaphors*. Over time the metaphorical origins of words can fade, as in the meanings of the underlined parts of these phrases: *to derail congressional*

Table 2.2 *Some English Forms Belonging to More Than One Lexical Category*

Noun	Verb	Adjective
email	email	
bookmark	bookmark	
bust	bust	
outrage	outrage	
market	market	
delay	delay	
plot	plot	
blog	blog	
text	text	
tweet	tweet	
local		local
inaugural		inaugural
illegal		illegal
average	average	average
model	model	model
blanket	blanket	blanket
brick	brick	brick
prime	prime	prime

Try It Yourself The *Oxford English Dictionary* recently added extended meanings for the nouns *coyote, crack,* and *thumbnail* and for the verb *zone (out).* Can you identify the recent meanings of these terms as compared to such traditional meanings as 'wolflike animal,' 'fissure or break,' 'nail of the thumb,' and 'divide into zones'?

legislation, a <u>buoyant</u> spokesman, an <u>abrasive</u> chief of staff, to <u>sweeten</u> the farm bill with several billion dollars to <u>skirt</u> a veto fight.

Borrowed Words

"Neither a borrower nor a lender be," Shakespeare advised, but speakers pay little heed when it comes to language. English has been extraordinarily receptive to *borrowed words,* accepting words from about a hundred languages in the last hundred years. As in most of its history, English borrowed more from French during the twentieth century than from any other language. Following French at some distance were Japanese and Spanish, Italian and Latin and Greek, German, and Yiddish. In smaller numbers, English is now host to words borrowed from Russian, Chinese, Arabic, Portuguese, and Hindi, as well as from numerous languages of Africa and some Native American languages.

In turn, many languages have welcomed English words into their stock, although some cultures resist borrowings. The Japanese have drafted the words *beesubooru* 'baseball,' *futtobooru* 'football' and *booringu* 'bowling' along with the sports they name, trading them for *judo, jujitsu,* and *karate,* which have joined the English-language team. Officially at least, the French are not open to borrowings, especially from English, and have banned the use of words like *weekend, drugstore, brainstorming,* and *countdown.* For using the borrowed term *jumbo jet,* Air France was given a stiff fine by the French government, which had insisted that *gros porteur* was the proper French name for, well, for the jumbo jet. The Americanism *OK* is now in use virtually everywhere, as are terms such as *jeans* and *discos,* which accompanied the named items as they spread around the globe. More recently, the terms *Internet, web,* and *tweet* have likewise circled the globe.

You can readily recognize as borrowings such popular words as *paparazzi, karaoke,* and *résumé.* Among borrowed nouns having to do with food and drink are *hummus* (from Arabic), *aioli* (from Provençal), *mai tai* (from Tahitian), *calzone, focaccia,* and *pizzetta* (from Italian), and *burrito, enchilada, fajita,* and *taco* (from Spanish). Yiddish has given us the more general term *nosh.* Other popular borrowings include the Cantonese *wok,* German *glitch,* Italian *ciao,* Spanish *macho, pronto,* and *mañana,* and Yiddish *chutzpah, klutz, nebbish, schlep,* and *schlepper.* As is true of other languages, most borrowings into English have been nouns, but some adjectives and a few verbs, adverbs, and interjections have been borrowed.

Borrowed words sooner or later conform to the pronunciation patterns and grammatical rules of the borrowing language. They undergo the same processes that affect native words. *Nosh* was borrowed as a verb that could not take an object (*I feel like noshing*) but has since taken on new use as a transitive verb—one that can take an object (*Let's nosh some hot dogs*). The verb *nosh* with the suffix -ER produces the noun *nosher* 'one who noshes,' and *nosh* itself can be used as a noun meaning 'a snack.' In Britain, *nosh* has

Jeans and Discos

The *jean* in your favorite blue jeans is a form of the word *Genoa* borrowed into Middle English (around the time of Chaucer). *Jeans* is a shortening of *jean fustian* 'Genoa fustian,' referring to a coarse cloth once produced in Genoa, Italy. The word *denim*, for the cloth from which jeans are made, evolved from *serge de Nîmes*, a cloth product from the French city of Nîmes. You might wear your favorite *jeans* to a *disco*. The French word *discothèque* 'record library' is a compound of two French morphemes, DISQUE meaning 'disk' or 'record' and the suffix -THÈQUE, as in *bibliothèque* 'library.' *Discothèque* appears to have been first used in English in 1954, and as an abbreviation, *disco*, ten years later. The noun *disco* underwent a functional shift to a verb, meaning 'dance to disco music,' a use first noted in 1979. Both noun and verb can be heard around the world in cities whose inhabitants speak neither English nor French.

been compounded into the noun *nosh-up*, meaning 'a large or elaborate meal.' In Los Angeles, a sign draped across a restaurant undergoing a change of cuisine announced "BURRITOFICATION IN PROGRESS," signaling the opening of a Mexican restaurant by punning on *beautification* and mimicking the morphological processes that created it.

Inventing Words

The advantages of using familiar elements in forming new words and the ease of borrowing from other languages are obvious. As a result, inventing words from scratch is not common. Invention has contributed such words as *granola*, *zap*, and *quark* to the English word stock. *Nerd* appears to have been invented by Dr. Seuss and *bandersnatch*, *galumph*, and *snark* by Lewis Carroll. *Gizmo*, *pizzazz*, and *lollapalooza*, whose origins are unknown, may also be invented words. Some names like *Pyrex*, *Kodak*, and *Xerox* are invented precisely to serve as trademarks for particular products or companies. But speakers and writers feel free to extend the use of brand names beyond reference to the brands themselves. As a result, *xerox* is sometimes used to mean 'photocopy,' not necessarily using a machine made by Xerox. Likewise, when students *google* something on the Internet, they are not necessarily using Google's search engine to do it. By 2010 the verb *google*, meaning 'to search the Internet,' had become so popular that members of the American Dialect Society voted it the word of the decade. As their word of the year, they chose *tweet* (noun 'a short message sent via the Twitter.com service' and verb 'the act of sending such a message').

Try It Yourself In 1995, Britain's Prince Charles fretted about a threat to "proper English" (by which he meant *English* English) from the spread of American English around the globe. Referring to American English, he said, "People tend to invent all sorts of nouns and verbs, and make words that shouldn't be." What's your assessment of the claim that some invented nouns and verbs "shouldn't be"?

What Types of Morphological Systems Do Languages Have?

You have now seen examples of derivational morphology and inflectional morphology in several languages. But not all languages have inflectional morphology, and some have little or no morphology at all. Still others have complex words with distinct parts, each part representing a morpheme. These three types of morphological systems have been called isolating, agglutinating, and inflectional. Some languages are mixed in the kinds of morphology they use.

Isolating Morphology

Chinese is a language with isolating morphology—in which each word tends to be a single isolated morpheme. An isolating language lacks both derivational and inflectional morphology. Using separate words, Chinese expresses certain content that an inflecting language might express with inflectional affixes. For example, whereas English has an inflectional possessive (*the boy's hat*) and what's called an analytical possessive (*hat of the boy*), Chinese permits only *hat of the boy* possessives. Chinese also does not have tense markers, and on pronouns it does not mark distinctions of gender (*he/she*), number (*she/they*), or case (*they/them*). Where English has six words—*he, she, him, her, they,* and *them*—Chinese uses only a single word, though it can indicate plurality with a separate word. The sentence below illustrates the one-morpheme-per-word pattern typical of Chinese:

wǒ gāng yào gěi nǐ nà yì bēi chá
I   just will give you that one cup tea
'I am about to bring you a cup of tea.'

Even more than Chinese, Vietnamese approximates the one-morpheme-per-word model that characterizes isolating languages. Each word in the sentence below has only one form. You can see that the word *tôi* is translated as *I, my,* and *we*. Note that to say 'we,' Vietnamese pairs *chúng* and *tôi* (the words for 'PLURAL' and 'I'). Like Chinese, Vietnamese lacks tense markers on verbs and case markers on nouns and pronouns, as well as number distinctions (though it can indicate plurality with a separate word).

khi tôi đến nhà bạn tôi, chúng tôi bắt đầu làm bài
when I   come house friend I   PLURAL I begin do   lesson
'When I came to my friend's house, we began to do lessons.'

Some languages that tend to minimize inflectional morphology nevertheless exploit derivational morphology to extend their word stocks in economical ways. Indonesian, for example, has only two inflectional affixes, but it utilizes about two dozen derivational morphemes, some of which we've seen in this chapter.

Agglutinating Morphology

Another type of morphology is called *agglutinating*. In agglutinating languages, words can have several prefixes and suffixes, but they are characteristically distinct and readily segmented into their parts—like English *announce-ment-s* or *pre-affirm-ed* but unlike *sang* (SING + 'PAST') or *men* (MAN + 'PLURAL'). Among other languages, Turkish (an Altaic language) and Swahili and Gikuyu (both Bantu languages) have agglutinating morphology, as shown in these examples. (Hyphens represent morpheme boundaries *within* a word.)

Turkish:

herkes	ben	üniversite-ye bašla-yacaǧ-im	san-iyor
everyone	I	university-to start-FUTURE-I	believe-PRESENT

'Everyone believes that I will start university.'

Swahili (a Bantu language of eastern Africa):

h-a-fany-i
NEG-he-do-PRES
's/he isn't doing (it)'

a-si-fany-e
he-NEG-do-SUBJUNC
's/he shouldn't do (it)'

a-me-fanya
he-PERF-do
's/he has done (it)'

a-ta-fanya
he-FUT-do
's/he will do (it)'

a-fany-e
he-do-SUBJUNC
's/he should do (it)'

h-a-ta-fanya
NEG-he-FUT-do
's/he won't do (it)'

Gikuyu (a Bantu language of Kenya):
ĩ-ngĩ-ka-na-endia
I-HYPOTHETICAL-FUTURE-INDEFINITE TIME-SELL
'if I should ever sell (it)'

Inflectional Morphology

Many languages have large inventories of inflectional morphemes. Finnish, Russian, and German maintain elaborate inflectional systems. By contrast, over the centuries English has shed most of its inflections, until today it has only eight remaining ones—two on nouns, four on verbs, and two on adjectives, as shown in Table 2.3. When new nouns, verbs, and adjectives are added to English or when a child learns new words, the words are extremely likely to be inflected like the examples listed, and the eight inflectional morphemes of English are thus said to be *productive*.

Compare this inflectional system of English with the examples from the Russian noun *žena* 'wife' and verb *pisat'* 'to write' in Tables 2.4 and 2.5.

Grammatical Functions of Inflections Consider the sentences below. They contain exactly the same words, but they express different meanings.

1. The farmer saw the wolf.

2. The wolf saw the farmer.

These sentences illustrate how English exploits word order to express meaning: different orders communicate different scenarios about *who* did what to

Table 2.3 *Inflectional Morphemes of English*

Lexical Category	Grammatical Category	Examples
Noun	Plural	cars, churches
Noun	Possessive	car's, children's
Verb	Third person	(she) swims, (it) seems
Verb	Past tense	wanted, showed
Verb	Past participle	wanted, shown (or showed)
Verb	Present participle	wanting, showing
Adjective	Comparative	taller, sweeter
Adjective	Superlative	tallest, sweetest

Table 2.4 *Russian Noun Inflections: žena 'wife'*

Case	Singular	Plural
Nominative	žena	žëny
Accusative	ženu	žën
Genitive	ženy	žën
Dative	žene	žënam
Instrumental	ženoy	žënami
After some prepositions	žene	žënax

Table 2.5 *Russian Present-Tense Verb Inflections: pisat' 'write'*

Person	Singular	Plural
First person	pišu	pišem
Second person	pišeš	pišete
Third person	pišet	pišut

whom. When semantic facts such as *who* did what to *whom* are expressed by word order rather than by inflection, it is not a morphological matter but a syntactic one, and syntax is the subject of Chapter 5.

A comparison with Latin is enlightening because Latin has relatively free word order. Given that *agricola* means 'farmer' and *lupum* 'wolf,' a Latin speaker could arrange sentence 1 ('The farmer saw the wolf') in these two ways (among others):

Agricola vīdit lupum.

Lupum vīdit agricola.

Latin does not rely on word order to signal *who* is seeing *whom*. Instead, inflections on the nouns signal such information. The following three sentences all mean 'The farmer saw the wolf'; the different word orders do not alter that meaning.

Agricola	vīdit	lupum.	
FARMER	SAW	WOLF	
Lupum	vīdit	agricola.	'The farmer saw the wolf.'
WOLF	SAW	FARMER	
Agricola	lupum	vīdit.	
FARMER	WOLF	SAW	

To say, instead, 'The wolf saw the farmer' required different inflections:

Agrico<u>lam</u>	vīdit	lup<u>us</u>.
FARMER	SAW	WOLF

Lup<u>us</u>	vīdit	agrico<u>lam</u>.
WOLF	SAW	FARMER

Agrico<u>lam</u>	lup<u>us</u>	vīdit.
FARMER	WOLF	SAW

'The wolf saw the farmer.'

The inflectional suffixes -*a* on *agricola* and -*us* on *lupus* identify them as subjects. The inflections -*am* and -*um* on *agricolam* and *lupum* make them direct objects.

A loose English parallel to Latin noun inflections can be seen in certain pronoun uses, where the form of the pronouns and the order of the words reinforce one another:

She praised him. (*She* is the subject, *him* the object.)

He praised her. (*He* is the subject, *her* the object.)

English and Latin nouns have inflections for number and case. English nouns exhibit only two cases, called possessive and common. The possessive case (sometimes called genitive) is marked by a suffix (*cat's, robot's*). The common case is unmarked (*cat, robot*) and is used for all grammatical functions except possession: subject, direct object, indirect object, and object of a preposition.

Latin, too, had a genitive case, and inflections for several other cases, notably nominative (principally for subjects), dative (indirect objects), accusative (direct objects and objects of some prepositions), and ablative (objects of some prepositions). Latin generally had five or six case inflections in the singular and in the plural, although some inflectional forms were pronounced alike, as can be seen in Table 2.6.

The set of forms constituting the inflectional variants of a word is known as a **paradigm**, and paradigms for nouns are called **declensions**. Latin had several declensions, such as the two given for *agricola* and *hortus* in Table 2.6. The paradigms for the equivalent English words *farmer* and *garden* appear in Table 2.7.

You'll notice that the four written forms in the English paradigms represent only two distinct pronunciations because *farmers, farmer's,* and *farmers'* are pronounced alike, and so are *gardens, garden's,* and *gardens'*. Spoken English usually has only two forms of a regular noun, but irregularly formed plurals may have four spoken and four written forms: *man, man's, men, men's; child, child's, children, children's*.

Some English pronouns have a third form for the objective case. In Table 2.8, you can compare the paradigms for first-person and third-person pronouns. First-person pronouns

Table 2.6 *Paradigms for Two Latin Nouns*

Singular	'Farmer'	'Garden'
Nominative	agricola	hortus
Accusative	agricolam	hortum
Genitive	agricolae	hortī
Dative	agricolae	hortō
Ablative/instrumental	agricolā	hortō
Plural	**'Farmer'**	**'Garden'**
Nominative	agricolae	hortī
Accusative	agricolās	hortōs
Genitive	agricolārum	hortōrum
Dative	agricolīs	hortīs
Ablative/instrumental	agricolīs	hortīs

Table 2.7 *Paradigms for Two English Nouns*

Singular

Common	farmer	garden
Possessive	farmer's	garden's

Plural

Common	farmers	gardens
Possessive	farmers'	gardens'

show three distinct case forms in the singular and three in the plural. Third-person pronouns have distinct masculine, feminine, and neuter forms in the singular but make no distinction for gender in the plural.

The second-person pronoun (*you*) and third-person singular neuter pronoun (*it*) do not have distinct objective forms, as can be seen in Table 2.9. Instead, they have only two forms, just like regular nouns.

Gender and Agreement In English, gender distinctions in pronouns are based on biological sex: reference to males requires the masculine pronouns *he*, *his*, or *him*, while reference to females requires the feminine pronouns *she*, *hers*, or *her*. To refer to something neither male nor female, English speakers use *it*. In German, French, Spanish, Russian, Old English, and many other languages, nouns do not have biological gender but grammatical gender. In these languages, certain other word categories such as determiners and adjectives that occur within a noun phrase carry inflections that *agree* with the noun in gender, number, and case.

In contrast to the English definite article *the* (with a single written form representing the two pronunciations "thuh" and "thee"), the German definite

Table 2.8 *Paradigms for First- and Third-Person Pronouns in English*

	FIRST PERSON	THIRD PERSON		
		Masculine	Feminine	Neuter
Singular				
Common	I	he	she	it
Possessive	mine	his	hers	its
Objective	me	him	her	it
Plural				
Common	we	they		
Possessive	ours	theirs		
Objective	us	them		

Table 2.9 *Second-Person and Third-Person Pronouns Compared to Nouns in English*

	PRONOUNS		NOUNS
Singular	Second	Third	
Common	you	it	farmer
Possessive	yours	its	farmer's
Plural			
Common	you		farmers
Possessive	yours		farmers'

Table 2.10 *Paradigm for German Definite Article*

	Masculine	SINGULAR Feminine	Neuter	PLURAL All Genders
Nominative	der	die	das	die
Accusative	den	die	das	die
Genitive	des	der	des	der
Dative	dem	der	dem	den

Table 2.11 *French and Spanish Definite Articles with Nouns*

	French	Spanish	
Masculine	le chat	el gato	'the cat'
	les chats	los gatos	'the cats'
Feminine	la maison	la casa	'the house'
	les maisons	las casas	'the houses'

article has forms for three genders and four cases in the singular, though there are no distinct gender markers in the plural, as Table 2.10 illustrates.

French and Spanish also exhibit variant forms of the definite article, though neither is as varied as German. French distinguishes only two noun genders; it marks masculine nouns with the definite article *le* or the indefinite *un* and feminine nouns with the definite article *la* or indefinite *une*; the plural form of the definite article for both genders is *les*. Gender in Spanish is marked in both the singular and the plural. Table 2.11 gives examples in French and Spanish.

There is not always a strict demarcation between agglutinating and inflectional languages, and some languages are difficult to classify. Still, the distinction among inflectional, isolating, and agglutinating is useful in characterizing languages with respect to their morphological systems.

Variant Pronunciations of a Morpheme: Allomorphy

A given morpheme may not be pronounced the same in all its occurrences. For example, the morpheme METAL is pronounced one way in "a dark *metallic* silver" and another way in "the clang of *metal*." The pronunciation of the vowel represented by <a> differs in *metallic* and *metal*, and in American English so does the sound represented by <t>. Consider that the final sound in *house* is [s] and in *wife* is [f], but in *houses* the HOUSE morpheme ends in [z], and in *wives* the WIFE morpheme ends in [v]. Alternate pronunciations of a morpheme are called **allomorphs**, and allomorphic variation is widespread in English and some other languages. (English spelling seldom represents allomorphic variation; although it captures the alternate pronunciations in *wife/wives*, it doesn't in *metal/metallic* or *house/houses*.)

Variation in the pronunciation of morphemes isn't limited to free morphemes like METAL, WIFE, and HOUSE. It can affect any morpheme, including affixes.

The English past-tense morpheme is pronounced [t] in *pick-ed,* [d] in *play-ed,* and a third way in *twist-ed.* Which pronunciation goes with which verb is rule governed, depending on the final sound of the verb stem (a matter we explore in Chapter 4). Children unconsciously learn the rules of allomorphic variation at an early age. If you taught English-speaking children a set of fictitious verbs they'd never heard before such as "plick" and "tevin," they'd pronounce the past-tense forms by adding [t] to "plick" and [d] to "tevin" in compliance with those unconscious rules.

The English plural morpheme on nouns also varies. In *cups* and *cats,* the plural morpheme is pronounced [s], but in *pads* and *rags* it's [z], and in *churches* and *dishes* and *bridges* still another way. These rule-governed pronunciations of the plural morpheme depend systematically on the final sound of the noun stem, and children who were taught imaginary nouns (like "wuck," "lutt," "mub," and "wug") would all add the correct plural allomorph to the invented words; they'd add [s] to "wuck" and "lutt" and [z] to "mub" and "wug." Of course, not all English nouns form their plural in these "regular" ways. Besides the rule-governed allomorphs, some nouns form their plurals irregularly. The plural allomorphs of *deer* and *fish* and of *man, ox,* and *tooth* are irregular and must be learned specifically. (Such irregular forms typically have an explanation in a word's history, as discussed in Chapter 13.)

Most English verbs form their past tense by rule, and new verbs tend to be "regular" in forming past-tense forms as well. But many common verbs don't follow regular patterns and must be learned, as with *teach* and *taught, make* and *made, speak* and *spoke, sleep* and *slept, tell* and *told,* and *go* and *went.* Children too young to have mastered the irregular past-tense forms are likely to produce "teached," "maked," "speaked," "sleeped," "telled," and "goed," treating them as though they were rule governed.

 Try It Yourself Identify which verbs have an irregular past-tense allomorph: *swim, head up, read, reach, break, bake, melt, say, see, meet, repeat, lead, eat, try, shave, bleed.* Identify which nouns have an irregular plural allomorph: *mouse, house, hen, egg, boy, girl, woman.* Identify which nouns have more than one allomorph: *moth, calf, child, woman, music.*

Table 2.12 *Frequency of Four Widely Distributed Words in the Brown Corpus*

Word	Occurrences	Genres	Texts
establishment	52	12	43
careful	62	14	56
powerful	63	14	54
unusual	63	15	52

Table 2.13 *Frequency of Five Narrowly Distributed Words in the Brown Corpus*

Word	Occurrences	Genres	Texts
artery	51	3	5
budget	53	7	23
dictionary	55	3	5
anode	75	1	2
fiscal	115	5	26

Using Computers to Study Words

In a corpus like the Brown Corpus (described in the "Computers and Linguistics" feature in Chapter 1), the most frequent and least frequent word forms can be identified in the whole corpus or any genre, such as science fiction or press editorials. Not surprisingly, three of the four most frequent words are *the*, *of*, and *and*. By contrast, words such as *oblong*, *obstinate*, *narcosis*, and *mystification* occur only once.

As you would guess, *the*, *and*, and *of* occur in all 500 texts of the Brown Corpus. By contrast, a proper name might occur multiple times but all in a single text. For example, the name *Mussorgsky* occurs seven times, all in the same 2,000-word text. Likewise for specialized words: *dialysis* occurs 12 times, all in one text; *radiosterilization* six times, all in one text. Contrast such specialized ranges of use with a word like *moreover*, whose 88 occurrences in the corpus are spread across 63 texts in 13 of the 15 genres. The frequency is not exceptionally high but the distribution is wide.

Table 2.12 provides examples of information you can derive from the Brown Corpus. Next to each listed word is given the total number of times it occurs and the number of genres (out of 15) and texts (out of 500) in which it occurs. These four words occur fewer than 65 times each in this million-word corpus, and those occurrences are spread across at least 12 genres, indicating that they are not specialized vocabulary items.

By contrast, the words in Table 2.13 occur in fewer than half the genres. That narrower distribution identifies more specialized words that appear in few contexts despite their overall frequency. *Anode* appears 75 times but in only two texts, both in the same genre. *Anode* illustrates that specialized words may occur in only a few genres but may be used frequently when they are on topic. This is particularly true of technical and scientific writing. You may have noticed that the word *corpus* appears only in this section (15 times) but nowhere else in the chapter.

The words in a corpus are often "tagged" with information such as their lexical category: *noun*, *verb*, *adjective*, and so on. Tagging makes it possible to study shared characteristics of words carrying a particular tag. Because tagging a corpus manually (inspecting each word and keyboarding the tag into the corpus) can be costly, researchers have devised ways to automate the process. The most direct way is to have a computerized reference dictionary that lists the lexical category of as many words as possible. Words in a corpus can be automatically assigned the tag of the corresponding word in the dictionary. In that way, if the forms *information* and *distribution* appeared in both the corpus and the dictionary, the *noun* tag assigned to them in the dictionary would be transferred to them in the corpus. Likewise, the forms *lexical* and *frequent* would be tagged "adjective," *the* and *a* "determiner" or "article," *identify* and *weigh* "verb," and so on.

This process of matching word forms in a corpus to those in a dictionary won't succeed completely because some forms may belong to more than one category (as illustrated in Table 2.2). In the paragraph you're reading now, you can find several words whose form does not uniquely identify them with a particular lexical category. For example, *forms*, *can*, *use*, *present*, and *process* could be nouns or verbs. But, in a particular context of use, word forms belong to only one category, so accurate tagging can be helped by identifying the category of words immediately surrounding ambiguous ones.

Suppose the corpus contained the expression *a big deal*; the automatic matching to the tagged dictionary would assign the tag "adjective" to *big*, but the dictionary would indicate that *deal* could be noun or verb. If *big* is tagged "adjective," however, any word following it is much more likely to be a noun than a verb because English adjectives precede nouns far more often than they precede verbs. After unambiguous tags are assigned, those tags can help determine the best tag for word forms that could belong to more than one category.

Information about which genres (press reportage or scientific writing or financial news, for example) have frequent adjectives or nouns or any other lexical category as compared with other genres can be helpful in designing language-teaching materials and creating automatic speech recognition systems. ■

Summary

- A morpheme is a minimal linguistic unit that has a meaning or grammatical function associated with it.
- Words can contain a single morpheme (*camel, swim*) or several (*bookshops, premeditation*).
- In the mental lexicon, each morpheme contains information about sounds, related words, phrasal co-occurrence patterns, and meaning.
- Free morphemes are those that can occur as independent words: CAR, HOUSE, FOR.
- Bound morphemes cannot occur as independent words but must be attached to another morpheme: CAR + -S, LOOK + -ED, ESTABLISH + -MENT.
- Bound morphemes can mark nouns for number (e.g., 'PLURAL') and case (e.g., 'POSSESSIVE') and verbs for tense (e.g., 'PAST') or person (e.g., 'THIRD PERSON').
- Bound morphemes can derive different words from existing morphemes; for example, UN- (*untrue*), DIS- (*displease*), and -MENT (*commitment*).
- Bound morphemes can be affixes (prefixes or suffixes), infixes, or circumfixes.
- In words, morphemes have significant linear and hierarchical structures.
- The array of morphological processes for increasing a language's word stock may include compounding, reduplication, affixation, and shortening.
- Languages borrow words from other languages and sooner or later submit the borrowed words to their own pronunciation patterns and morphological processes.
- Among the types of morphological systems are inflectional, isolating, and agglutinating systems.
- Isolating systems (e.g., Vietnamese) tend to have one morpheme per word.
- Agglutinating systems (e.g., Turkish) tend to have distinct affixes.
- Corpus study is useful in showing the distribution of categories of words and morphemes as well as particular words and morphemes in different genres of text, information that can be helpful in designing automatic speech recognition systems.
- *Collocation* is the term used to refer to co-occurrences of a word with other words.
- Words in a corpus can be automatically tagged for lexical category, although several rounds of tagging that rely successively on unambiguous tags may be needed to tag all words.

What Do You Think? REVISITED

- *Maked a cake.* Most English verbs form the past tense by rule, but some of the most common ones have irregular past-tense forms. Relatively early, children learn the rule for forming past tenses of regular verbs (see Chapter 14) and tend to form all verbs the same way. Instead of using the irregular past-tense forms *made* and *told,* the three-year-old forms past tenses by the general rule, as though *make* and *tell* formed past tenses like *baked* and *spelled.*

- *Food terms.* From Japanese come *sashimi, wasabi, miso, sake, sukiyaki, teriyaki, ramen,* and *tofu*; from Chinese, *dim sum, bok choy,* and *wonton*; from Spanish, *alfalfa, salsa, guacamole, tostada,* and *anchovy*; from the languages of India, *mulligatawny, chutney,* and *samosa*; from French, *beef, bouillon, chowder, cutlet, mackerel, mutton, mustard, quiche,* and the more obvious *crepe* and *croque monsieur* (as well as *du jour, au jus,* and *a la mode*). English has borrowed food names from many other languages, among them Arabic (*falafel, hummus*), Greek (*gyro, pita*), Turkish (*dolma, yogurt*), German (*bratwurst, pretzel*).

- *Top ten words.* According to the Brown Corpus, the top ten words in printed American English are *the, be, of, and, a, in, he, to* (the infinitive marker), *have,* and *to* (the preposition) and the next three are *it, for,* and *I.* There are no nouns, adjectives, or adverbs on the list and the only verbs are *be* and *have.*

- *Nerdy Ned's state names.* Carolina is named after King Charles II; Virginia after Queen Elizabeth I, who was known as the Virgin Queen; Louisiana after Louis XIV; Georgia after King George II of England; Maryland in honor of Henrietta Maria, wife of England's King Charles I. In addition, New York is named after the Duke of York, later King Charles II, and Pennsylvania is named after the English Quaker William Penn or his father, Admiral Sir William Penn.   ■

Exercises

Practice Exercise

A. For the words with more than one morpheme, identify (sometimes approximately) where the morpheme boundaries exist.

Example: governments: govern - ment - s

1. human	11. token	21. remodeling
2. tasteless	12. breadwinners	22. inexpensive
3. watching	13. turmoil	23. child's
4. undisclosed	14. heartstrings	24. illegality
5. impolitely	15. underdog	25. supermarkets
6. troublesome	16. biggest	26. globalization
7. dispassionate	17. automakers	27. antiterrorism
8. respectfully	18. indirectly	28. interdependence
9. mudslinging	19. higher	29. antiunemployment
10. indelicate	20. outpaces	30. bouncebackability

B. In the numbered list above, identify by number three words that contain a prefix.

C. By number, identify three that contain a suffix (each suffix should differ from the others).

D. By number, identify three that contain both a prefix and a suffix.

E. By number, identify three compound words.

F. By number, identify three words containing an inflectional suffix.

G. By number, identify three words containing a derivational suffix.

Based on English

2-1. Identify the category of the underscored words in the following sentences. Use the abbreviations *N* for noun, *V* for verb, *Adj* for adjective, *Adv* for adverb, *Prep* for preposition, *Pro* for pronoun.

a. People who rarely read in bedrooms can feel abnormal.

b. Nobody really knows what normal reading is.

c. The market for audiobooks is very large.

2-2. For three of the five words that belong to three lexical categories in Table 2.2 provide a sentence illustrating their use in each category. Examples for *average* might be: Is there a difference between an *average* and a median? (noun); A guide can *average* $75 a day in tips. (verb); He earned only *average* grades. (adjective)

2-3. a. Identify *the lexical category* of each word in the following *list*.

b. List all the morphemes (each word contains more than one) and indicate whether they are free or bound.

c. Indicate for each affix whether it is derivational or inflectional.

heard	tinier	unproductive
toys	saw	bookshops
listened	reassessment	children's
fixer-upper	fatherly	improbable
improbability	repayment	unamusing
tidiest	realignments	calculating
disarms	unremarkable	forewarned
untidiness	realigned	unpretentiousness

2-4. a. The three sentences below contain capitalized DEMONSTRATIVE PRONOUNS and italicized *demonstrative determiners*. Characterize the difference in how they are used. (*Hint:* Consider the lexical categories of any words they precede.)

1) THIS is the last time I'm doing THAT.

2) *This* time I'm not going to make one of *those* fancy pizzas.

3) I've had enough of THESE; give me one of *those* red ones.

b. List each pronoun in the passage below and identify its kind (personal, demonstrative, interrogative, relative). For personal pronouns, also indicate the person (first, second, third).

What about those books? Whose are they? They look like they come from the library, so they should be returned. If you want, you can put them into a shopping bag and I'll return them for you if I can get Ashley to take me in her car. It's been in the shop for a few days. I hope it's ready now.

2-5. Consider two popular compounds. *Convenience food* 'food that is convenient to buy, cook, or eat' comprises a noun and a noun. *Natural food* 'food made with natural ingredients, free of chemical preservatives and pesticides' is an adjective + noun compound. As a whole, each compound functions as a noun. List six compound nouns that combine two nouns and six that are unmistakably a combination of adjective + noun. (Note that not all adjectives preceding nouns are compounds, so it is helpful to pay attention to the stress pattern. In the following sentences, the compounds are italicized; say them aloud to see the pattern. Not every white house is the *White House*! Not every black bird is a *blackbird.*)

2-6. From a passage of about 500 words in a weekly newsmagazine like *Time, Newsweek,* or *The Economist* make a list of 20 compounds, marking the lexical category of each constituent word of the compound and of the compound as a whole. Thus, given *telephone tag* you would identify *telephone* as noun (or N), *tag* as noun, and the compound *telephone tag* as noun.

Category Of:	1st Element	2nd Element	Compound
telephone tag	N	N	N
software	Adj	N	N
bozo filter	N	N	N

2-7. *Cyber-* became a popular prefix in the 1990s. It was attached principally to nouns to form new nouns, as in *cyberlove, cyberland, cyberspace,* and *cybercowboy.* List eight words that use the prefix *cyber-*, identifying any examples of *cyber-* prefixed to a lexical category other than noun. What about the increasingly popular *eco-*? List eight words that use the prefix *eco-*, identifying any examples of *eco-* prefixed to a lexical category other than noun.

2-8. a. Write rules like those given in the section on "Morphemes That Derive Other Words" for the underscored affixes in the words below. Example: *disqualify*: DIS- + Verb → Verb

b. Draw trees similar to the one in Figure 2.3 for these words:

appear<u>ance</u>   <u>up</u>root   <u>un</u>worthy   <u>pre</u>heat

redo<u>able</u>   bright<u>ness</u>   <u>dis</u>appearance   recapital<u>ize</u>

2-9. Consider the two analyses of *untruthful* given below. Give arguments for preferring one analysis over the other.

a. $[[[un[true_{Adj}]_{Adj}]th_N]ful_{Adj}]$

b. $[un[[[true_{Adj}]th_N]ful_{Adj}]_{Adj}]$

2-10. The following terms are associated with computer or Internet use. For each one, identify the kind of formation (compound, shortening, acronym, conversion, and so on) and its lexical category.

Example: chatgroup—compound, noun

client-server	YouTube	FAQ	source code
mouse	cyberspace	PC	news feed
a flame	to flame out	IMHO	to download
info pike	to surf	to email	code writer

Internetter	I-way	to lurk	newbee or newbie
info superpike	netiquette	netter	dotcom
webcam	a remailer	smileys	browser
spamming	a sysop	a thread	cyberenthusiast
a twit filter	WYSIWYG	software	PayPal

2-11. a. From the list that follows, identify four acronyms and four initialisms: DNA, STD, AIDS, SIDS, NBA, HIV, HDTV, NHL, UNESCO, UN, UK, BBC, NATO.

b. What's interesting about the words *CD-ROM* and *JPEG*?

2-12. a. As determined by their frequency in a million-word corpus of texts (the Brown Corpus), the 26 most common words in printed American English are listed below. The category of a few of these words is already specified. For each of the others, specify its category and then answer the questions that follow. Choose your categories from this list: N (noun), V (verb), Adj (adjective), Prep (preposition), Det (determiners, including articles), Pro (pronoun).

the	——————	they	——————
be	——————	with	——————
of	——————	not	adverb
and	——————	that	conjunction
a	——————	on	——————
in	——————	she	——————
he	——————	as	conjunction
to	infinitive marker	at	——————
have	——————	by	——————
to	——————	this	——————
it	——————	we	——————
for	——————	you	——————
I	——————	from	——————

1) List the pronouns that fall among the 26 most frequent words of written English: _____

2) List the prepositions: _____

3) List the determiners: _____

4) List the verbs: _____

5) List the adjectives: _____

6) List the nouns: _____

b. The words listed in the two columns are found so frequently in print that one of every four words in the Brown Corpus ranks among the first eight words on the list (*the* through the infinitive marker *to*). To put it another way, over 250,000 of the million words in the Brown Corpus are the same eight words used repeatedly. With that in mind, answer the following questions.

1) Which two lexical categories are strikingly absent from the list? What explanation can you offer for their infrequency?

2) What explanation can you offer for the frequency of prepositions in the Brown Corpus? (*Hint:* It may help to think about what prepositions do.)

3) What explanation can you offer for the frequency of pronouns as compared to nouns?

4) The verbs *be* and *have* appear on the list. If you knew that the 27th word on the list was a verb, which verb would you guess it to be? Why?

5) Of the 21 words whose lexical category you were asked to identify in part a, how many belong to closed classes of words and how many to open classes?

2-13. The expressions below come from an article discussing new telecommuting policies for county employees in San Luis Obispo, California (*New Times*, April 22–29, 2010, p. 7). Next to each expression write the name of the process by which the italicized word has come to have its use in this discussion, drawing the terms from this list: compounding, affixation, invention, shortening, conversion, derivation, semantic shift, borrowing, blend.

a. *SLO* County 'San Luis Obispo' _____

b. *won't* _____

c. a *telecommuting* policy _____

d. the *groundwork* _____

e. *infrastructure* _____

f. *greenhouse* gas emissions _____

g. to *curb* the main source of pollution _____

h. staffers *crafted* the schedule _____

i. *municipalities* _____

j. *pollution* _____

k. allow employees to *patch* into the network _____

l. *PJs* 'pajamas' _____

Based on Languages Other Than English

2-14. Consider the following pairs of singular and plural nouns for human beings in Persian. How does Persian form these noun plurals? (*Note:* æ represents a vowel sound like the one in English *hat*, and x represents a sound like the final consonant of the German *Bach*.)

zæn	'woman'	zænan	'women'
mærd	'man'	mærdan	'men'
bæradær	'brother'	bæradæran	'brothers'
pesær	'boy'	pesæran	'boys'
xahær	'sister'	xahæran	'sisters'
doxtær	'daughter'	doxtæran	'daughters'

2-15. Spanish nouns have grammatical gender; for example, *coche* 'car' and *viento* 'wind' are masculine; *manzana* 'apple' and *sopa* 'soup' are feminine. Examine the expressions below to uncover patterns of agreement among noun, article, and adjective.

a. el coche rojo 'the red car'

b. el viento frio 'the cold wind'

c. el camino corto 'the short road'

d. la manzana roja 'the red apple'

e. la sopa fria 'the cold soup'

f. la falda corta 'the short skirt'

In those expressions, what is the masculine form of the Spanish definite article 'the' and what is the feminine form? Given the masculine form of an adjective, state the rule for forming the feminine singular for these adjectives and then provide the missing adjective in items i and j.

g. el libro amarillo 'the yellow book'

h. el hombre alto 'the tall man'

i. la flor _____ 'the yellow flower'

j. la mujer _____ 'the tall woman'

Identify how the adjectives in the following examples differ from the preceding ones. Given the masculine form of the adjectives below, state the rule for forming the feminine singular forms, and apply the rule to provide the missing adjectives in items s and t.

k. el niño feliz 'the happy boy'

l. el gato grande 'the big cat'

m. el pan caliente 'the hot bread'

n. el caballo fuerte 'the strong horse'

o. el examen fácil 'the easy exam'

p. la niña feliz 'the happy girl'

q. la casa grande 'the big house'

r. la estufa caliente 'the hot stove'

s. la persona _____ 'the strong person'

t. la tarea _____ 'the easy homework'

2-16. Consider the following Persian word pairs with their English glosses. Note the lexical category of the words in column A, and give the complete rule for forming the words of column B from those in column A. (*Note:* x represents a sound like the final consonant of the German *Bach.*)

A		B	
dana	'wise'	danai	'wisdom'
xub	'good'	xubi	'goodness'
darosht	'thick'	daroshti	'thickness'
bozorg	'big'	bozorgi	'size'
shirin	'sweet'	shirini	'sweetness'

2-17. a. Analyze the Turkish nouns below and provide a list of their constituent morphemes, along with a gloss for each. (*Note:* i represents a vowel similar to u.)

kitap	'book'	elmalar	'apples'	saplar	'stalks'
at	'horse'	masa	'table'	adamlar	'men'
oda	'room'	odalar	'rooms'	masalar	'tables'
sap	'stalk'	atlar	'horses'	sonlar	'ends'
elma	'apple'	kiz	'girl'	meyvar	'fruit' (SINGULAR)

b. On the basis of your analysis, provide the Turkish words for the following English ones: *books, man, girls, end, fruit* (PLURAL).

c. Given Turkish *odalarda* 'in the rooms' and *masalarda* 'on the tables,' provide the Turkish words that mean 'in the books' and 'on the horse.'

2-18. In the Niutao dialect of the Polynesian language Tuvaluan, some verbs and adjectives have different forms with singular and plural subjects, as in these examples:

Singular	**Plural**	
mafuli	mafufuli	'turned around'
fepaki	fepapaki	'collide'
apulu	apupulu	'capsize'
nofo	nonofo	'stay'
maasei	maasesei	'bad'
takato	takakato	'lie down'
valea	valelea	'stupid'
kai	kakai	'eat'

a. Describe the rule of morphology that derives the plural forms of these verbs and adjectives from the singular forms.

b. In the Funaafuti dialect of the same language the process is slightly different, as the following plural forms of the same verbs and adjectives show. (Double consonants indicate that the sound is held for a longer period of time.) How are plurals formed from singular forms in this dialect? How does that process differ from the process of plural formation in the Niutao dialect described in the first part of this exercise?

vallea	nnofo
maffuli	maassei
feppaki	takkato
appulu	kkai

2-19. On the basis of the examples given below, determine whether the following languages have an isolating, inflectional, or agglutinating morphology, and justify your answer.

SAMOAN

?ua	maalamalama	a?u	i	le	mataa?upu
PRESENT	understand	I	OBJECT	the	topic

'I understand the topic.'

FINNISH

tyttö	silitti	paidat
girl-SUBJECT-SING.	iron-PAST-SING.	shirt-OBJECT-PLURAL

'The girl ironed the shirts.'

JAPANESE

akiko-ga	haruko-ni	mainiti	tegamio	kaku
Akiko SUBJECT	Haruko to	everyday	letter OBJECT	write

'Akiko writes a letter to Haruko every day.'

MOHAWK

t-en-s-hon-te-rist-a-wenrat-e?

DUAL-FUTURE-REPETITIVE-PLURAL-REFLEXIVE-metal-cross-PUNCTUAL

'They will cross over the railroad track.'

THAI

kʰruu	hây	sàmùt	nákrian	săam	lêm
teacher	give	notebook	student	three	ARTICLE

'The teacher gave the students three notebooks.'

2-20. Examine the following sentences of Tok Pisin (New Guinea Pidgin English) to identify the morphemes needed to translate the seven English sentences given at the end of this exercise.

a.
manmeri	ol	wokabaut	long	rot
people	they	stroll	on	road

'People are strolling on the road.'

b.
mi	harim	toktok	bilong	yupela
I	listen	speech	of	you-PLURAL

'I listen to your (PLURAL) speech.'

c.
mi	harim	toktok	bilong	yu
I	listen	speech	of	you-SING.

'I listen to your (SING.) speech.'

d.
em	no	brata	bilong	em	ol	harim	toktok	bilong	mi
he	and	brother	of	he	they	listen	speech	of	me

'He and his brother listen to my speech.'

e. mi   laikim   dispela   manmeri   long   rot
    I   like   these   people   on   road
    'I like these people (who are) on the road.'

f. dispela man no prend bilong mi ol   laikim dispela   toktok
    this   man and friend of   me they like   this   speech
    'This man and my friend like this speech.'

Now, relying on the meaning of the morphemes you can identify in the Tok Pisin sentences above, translate the following sentences into Tok Pisin:

1) These people like my speech.

2) I am strolling on the road.

3) I like my friend's speech.

4) I like my brother and these people.

5) These people on the road and my friend like his speech.

6) You (SING.) and my brother like the speech of these people.

7) These people listen to my friend's and my brother's speech.

Especially for Educators and Future Teachers

2-21. Assume you are teaching young ESL students to change verbs into their "opposites"—for example, *appear* into *disappear*. How would you get them to provide as many different English-language prefixes to turn verbs into other verbs with an opposite meaning?

2-22. **a.** Suppose you are teaching a middle school English class how to figure out the lexical category (part of speech) of the words *newer, books, played,* and *surprise?* Would it be better to present them in isolation or in sentences? Why?

b. Now reconsider *books* and *surprise,* and try putting them into two sentences each, used as a verb in one and as a noun in the other. Any further observations about which way of presenting them is better? What else could you do to provide your students useful tools for deciding the part of speech of these words? How did you determine their part of speech for yourself?

2-23. Imagine you and your students are looking at a map of the United States, examining place names and river names. Concentrating on one side or the other of the Mississippi River, can you anticipate six names your students would rightly guess are borrowed from Native American languages? Examining the whole map, which states or state capitals could they identify as being named after some person? After another country? As using words borrowed from Spanish? French? Dutch?

2-24. How could you encourage your students to identify the names of food items that English has borrowed from the languages of the students' respective ethnic heritages?

2-25. How would you determine which words to include in the vocabulary of a textbook for international students learning basic English?

2-26. What would you tell students who thought English had infixes because in the film *My Fair Lady* they heard Eliza Doolittle use the word "abso-bloomin'-lutely" in these lyrics: "Oh wouldn't it be loverly? Oh, so loverly sittin' abso-bloomin'-lutely still! I would never budge 'til spring crept over my window sill"? Does English have other examples similar to this one?

Other Resources

Internet

The Internet addresses listed in this section will be helpful in understanding this chapter and exploring related aspects of language. Because Internet addresses often change, the ones given here may go out of date; using your detective skills will lead you to others.

 LISU Website: http://www.CengageBrain.com For users of this textbook. Provides updated Internet links as well as supplemental material for students and instructors. Here you will find chapter-specific interactive learning tools in your English CourseMate, accessed through the URL above.

 UCREL Links: http://ucrel.lancs.ac.uk/links.html The University Centre for Computer Corpus Research on Language at Lancaster University in England supports a website that provides links to a wide range of other resources.

 Merriam-Webster OnLine: http://www.m-w.com Entry to the world of dictionaries produced by the Merriam-Webster Company. Well worth bookmarking for its online definitions.

 American Dialect Society: http://www.americandialect.org/ Interesting especially for its lists of nominated and winning words of the year over the past and for its links to other fascinating websites.

 Corpus Linguistics: http://www.athel.com/corpus_introduction.html Maintained by Michael Barlow, this website is a goldmine of information and guidance about corpora and corpus linguistics.

 Bookmarks for Corpus-Based Linguistics: http://tiny.cc/corpora This excellent source for beginners and others is maintained by David Lee and provides a wealth of information about corpora and corpus-based linguistics, chiefly for English but including other languages.

 Corpus of Contemporary American English: http://www.americancorpus.org/ A 400-million-word corpus of American English, comprising five genres in equal measure (spoken, fiction, popular magazines, newspapers, and academic texts) and representing several subgenres (movie scripts, sports magazines, scientific journals, and more). COCA contains 20 million words from each year since 1990. At the website, a five-minute hands-on introduction to using COCA will greatly repay your effort. You'll learn to search for individual words and other expressions and to exploit wildcards and other tools in exploring authentic spoken and written texts lexically, semantically, and grammatically.

 phpSyntaxTree: http://code.google.com/p/phpsyntaxtree/ At this site, a bracketed representation of a word will produce a labeled tree diagram. Some experimenting and practice should enable you to produce trees akin to those in this chapter. Take care to ensure that you have the same number of open and closed brackets.

Suggestions for Further Reading

- **Jean Aitchison. 2003.** *Words in the Mind: An Introduction to the Mental Lexicon,* **3rd ed.** (Malden, MA: Blackwell). An entertaining and accessible treatment.
- **Andrew Carstairs-McCarthy. 2002.** *An Introduction to English Morphology* (Edinburgh: Edinburgh University Press). A brief, accessible treatment of English words and their structure, including a chapter on the historical sources of English word formation.
- **Rochelle Lieber. 2010.** *Introducing Morphology* **(Cambridge, UK: Cambridge University Press).** Appearing in the new Cambridge Introductions to Language and Linguistics series, this hands-on approach will appeal to students.
- **Ronald W. Langacker. 1972.** *Fundamentals of Linguistic Analysis* (New York: Harcourt). An excellent introduction to linguistic analysis and problem solving. Chapter 2 discusses morphological analysis, with illustrations from many languages, including Native American languages. Model solutions are provided for some problems.
- **Donka Minkova & Robert Stockwell. 2009.** *English Words: Structure and History*, **2nd ed.** (Cambridge, UK: Cambridge University Press). Easy to use and rich in examples.
- **"Among the New Words."** A regular column in *American Speech* (the journal of the American Dialect Society) that defines the most recent additions to the English word stock. You'll be surprised at how many words in your everyday life are brand-new to English. Look up the most recent "Among the New Words" next time you're in the periodicals room of your library or have online access to *American Speech*.
- *The Merriam-Webster New Book of Word Histories*. **1991.** (Springfield, MA: Merriam). This exciting book provides word histories for thousands of English words from *assassin* to *zombie* and all sorts of words in between, such as *jeep* and *OK*.

Advanced Reading

A good general treatment of morphological processes can be found in Katamba and Stonham (2006). Bauer (2003) is more advanced and contains a brief chapter on morphology in the mind and another on the historical development and disappearance of morphology in languages. Our examples of reduplication in Turkish come from Underhill (1976). Good treatments of morphology can be found in Shopen (1985), especially the chapters by Stephen R. Anderson on "Typological Distinctions in Word Formation" and "Inflectional Morphology," by Bernard Comrie on "Causative Verb Formation and Other Verb-Deriving Morphology," and by Comrie and Sandra A. Thompson on "Lexical Nominalization." Comrie (2009), from which several examples in this chapter are taken, provides valuable descriptions of more than 40 major languages, including treatment of morphology. The Vietnamese example comes from Comrie (1989).

References

Bauer, Laurie. 2003. *Introducing Linguistic Morphology,* 2nd ed. (Washington, D.C.: Georgetown University Press).

Comrie, Bernard. 1989. *Language Universals and Linguistic Typology,* 2nd ed. (Chicago: University of Chicago Press).

Comrie, Bernard, ed. 2009. *The World's Major Languages,* 2nd ed. (London: Routledge).

Katamba, Francis & John Stonham. 2006. *Morphology,* 2nd ed. (Basingstoke: Palgrave Macmillan).

Shopen, Timothy, ed. 1985. *Grammatical Categories and the Lexicon,* vol. 3 of *Language Typology and Syntactic Description.* (Cambridge, UK: Cambridge University Press).

Underhill, Robert. 1976. *Turkish Grammar.* (Cambridge, MA: MIT Press).

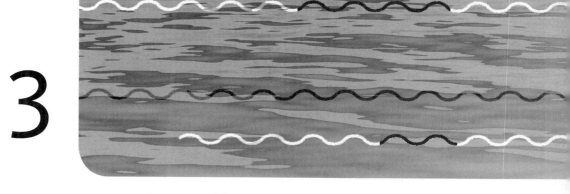

3

The Sounds of Languages: Phonetics

What Do You Think?

- A whiz at reading, your third-grade niece Nina reports one day that English has five vowels—*a, e, i, o,* and *u.* You think English must have more than five different vowel sounds. How would you figure out just how many vowel sounds English actually has?
- Your pal Penny says George Bernard Shaw claimed English spelling is so chaotic that *ghoti* could be pronounced *fish,* and she challenges you to identify words whose pronunciation and spelling could have led Shaw to his seemingly preposterous conclusion. What words can you cite in which <gh> is pronounced "f"? Can you cite any in which <gh> appears at the beginning, as in Shaw's *ghoti*?
- Roommate Ron wants to know whether English has 26 sounds to match the 26 letters of the alphabet. You know English has more than 26 sounds and point out there's no single letter to represent the initial sound in *thus* so English uses two letters. Ron then asks for other examples where two letters represent a single sound. What examples can you provide?
- Citing *put* and *putt* as a pair of English words that are pronounced and spelled differently but whose spelling difference doesn't correspond to the pronunciation difference, friend Fred claims English has many similar pairs and challenges you to name just one. Can you do it?

Sounds and Spellings: Not the Same Thing

As a reader of English, you are accustomed to seeing language written down as a series of words set off by spaces, with each word consisting of a sequence of separate letters that are also separated by spaces. You readily recognize that words exist as separate entities made up of a relatively small number of discrete sounds. The words *spat* and *post*, for example, are readily judged by English speakers to have four sounds each, while *upset* has five and *sat* has three. Somewhat less obvious is the number of sounds in *speakers*, *series*, *letters*, and *sequence*, which do not have the same number of letters and sounds. This lack of correspondence is common in English. *Cough* has three sounds but is spelled with five letters; *freight* uses seven letters to represent only four sounds.

Through with seven letters and *thru* with four are alternative spellings for a word with three sounds. *Phone* and *laugh* have three sounds each, represented by five letters. *Delicacy*, with an equal number of sounds and letters, uses the letter <c> to represent two sounds—one a *k*-like sound, the other an *s*-like sound.

Because of the close association between writing and speaking in the minds of literate people, it is important to stress that in this chapter we are interested in the *sounds* of spoken language, not in the letters of the alphabet that represent those sounds in writing.

Same Spelling, Different Pronunciations

Observe the variety of pronunciations represented by the same letter or series of letters in different words. Consider the pronunciations of the following words, all of which are represented in part by the letters <ough>:

cough	"ko__ff__"
tough	"tu__ff__"
bough	"__bow__"
through	"thr__u__"
though	"th__o__"
thoroughfare	"thurr__a__fare"

Though the precise sounds in these words may vary among English speakers, still the lesson of the distant relationship between sounds and letters is clear. The <ough> spelling represents at least six pronunciations in English, as indicated in Figure 3.1.

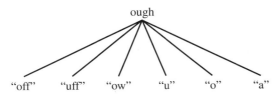

Figure 3.1 Same Spelling, Different Sounds

Same Pronunciation, Different Spellings

Other sets of English words are pronounced alike but spelled differently, as schoolchildren learn when they are taught sets of homophones (or homonyms) like *there/their*, *bear/bare*, *led/lead*, and *to/two/too*.

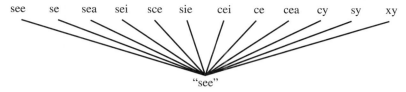

Figure 3.2 Different Spelling, Same Sounds

Consider the words in Figure 3.2, where nine different spellings represent the sounds of the word *see*, and *situ* and *cee* (the name of the letter) could be added to the list. Notice that the letter <x>, as in *sexy* and *foxy*, stands for the two sounds [k] and [s] as represented in *folksy*.

Compare the sound and spelling of *woman* and *women* and you'll note that the difference in the letters <a> and <e> does not represent a difference in pronunciation because the second syllables of these words are pronounced alike. On the other hand, <o>—the letter that does not change—represents two sounds (in *woman* like the <oo> of *wood* and in *women* like the <i> of *win*). The pair *Satan* (the devil) and *satin* (the cloth) illustrates the same point: the <a> of the first syllable represents two sounds, but the <a> and <i> spellings of the second syllable represent the same sound. The same point can be made with *loose* and *lose*, where the only pronunciation difference is in the final sound ([s] vs. [z]), while the only spelling difference is in the identically pronounced vowels.

The playwright George Bernard Shaw was a keen advocate of spelling reform and highlighted the problems in establishing correspondences between English sounds and spelling when he provocatively alleged that *fish* could be spelled <ghoti>: the <gh> as in *cough*, the <o> as in *women*, and the <ti> as in *nation*. Despite the efforts of Shaw and other reformers, English spelling has remained basically unchanged. You can see very modest success at simplification in such isolated spellings as *thru*, *nite*, and *foto*, though not even these examples have been widely adopted for the more traditional *through*, *night*, and *photo*.

Whys and Wherefores of Sound/Spelling Discrepancies

Here are five reasons for the discrepancy between pronunciations and written representations for many English words.

1. Written English has diverse origins with different spelling conventions:

   ◆ *Anglo-Saxon* The system that evolved in Anglo-Saxon England before the Norman Invasion of 1066 gave us such spellings as *ee* for the sound in words like *deed* and *seen*.

   ◆ *Norman French* The system that was overlaid on the Old English system by the Normans, with their French writing customs, gave us such spellings as *queen* (for the earlier *cwene*) and *thief* (for the earlier *theef*).

◆ *Dutch* Caxton, the first English printer, who was born in England but lived in Holland for 30 years, gave us such spellings as *ghost* (which replaced *gost*) and *ghastly* (which replaced *gastlic*).

◆ *Spelling reform* During the Renaissance, attempts to reform spelling along etymological (that is, historically earlier) lines gave us *debt* for the earlier *det* or *dette* and *salmon* for the earlier *samon*.

2. A spelling system established several hundred years ago is still being used to represent a language that continued—and continues—to change its spoken form. For example, the initial <k> in words like *knock, knot, know,* and *knee* was once pronounced, and so was the <gh> in *night* and *thought*. As to vowels, pronunciation changes in progress when the writing system was developing, along with later ones, have led to such discrepancies as those represented in *beat* vs. *great* and *food* vs. *foot*, where different vowel sounds are represented by the same spellings.

3. English is spoken differently around the world (and in different regions of a nation), despite relatively uniform standards for spellings. Such spelling uniformity facilitates international communication but also increases the disparity between the way English is written and spoken.

4. A given word part may be pronounced differently depending on its adjacent sounds and stress patterns. In *electric*, the final <c> represents the sound [k] as in *kiss*, but in *electricity* it represents [s] as in *sit*. In *senile*, <i> represents the sound of <i> in *island*, but in *senility* the sound of <i> in *ill*.

5. Spoken forms may differ across social situations. The writing system incorporates some degree of variation (*do not* vs. *don't* and *it was* vs. *'twas*), but there is less tolerance for spellings like *gonna* ('going to'), *wanna* ('want to'), and *gotcha* ('got you') and still less or none at all for *j'eat* ('did you eat?') and *woncha* ('won't you?'). Variable spellings for the same expression would force readers to determine the idiosyncratic key of the represented speech before arriving at meaning instead of relying directly on a familiar spelling, as adult readers normally do.

Advantages of Fixed Spellings Some disadvantages of an inconsistent set of sound-spelling correspondences are obvious, but the advantages are also substantial. Consider Chinese, in which many written characters make little or no reference to sounds but directly symbolize meanings—much as numerals like 3 and 7 and symbols like + and % do for European languages. Using such characters, groups of people whose spoken languages are mutually unintelligible can nevertheless communicate well in writing, as is the case between speakers of Cantonese and Mandarin Chinese. As a parallel, consider that the symbol 7 has a uniform meaning across European languages, even though the word for the concept is pronounced and spelled differently: *seven* in English, *sept* in French, *sette* in Italian, *sieben* in German, and so on. Similarly, the fact that English spelling is somewhat independent of pronunciation is not altogether a bad thing when you consider that English has exceptionally varied dialects from New Zealand to Jamaica to India, as well as in places where English is used in official capacities alongside indigenous native tongues or as a second language for scientific and other international enterprises. Despite diverse pronunciations around the globe, a uniform written word is associated with a single set of meanings. More-over, in a language with different pronunciations for the same element of mean-ing, stable spellings can contribute to reading comprehensibility—as in *musical/musician, electrical/electricity*, and even the <s> of *cats* and *dogs* (pronounced [s] and [z], respectively).

Independence of Script and Speech It's important to distinguish between the sounds of a language and the way they are represented in writing. To empha-size the independence of sounds and spellings, remember that a given language may be represented by more than one writing system. For instance, the language widely known as Hindi-Urdu is written by Hindus living in India in Devanāgarī, an Indic script that derives from Sanskrit, but it is written in Arabic script by Muslims living in Pakistan and parts of India. Sometimes, too, people adopt a new writing system for their language. Early in the twentieth century, the government of Turkey changed the orthography (the technical name for a writing system) for representing Turkish from an Arabic script to one based on the Roman alphabet.

Sometimes languages use different scripts for different purposes. Imagine sending an international telegram in a language that uses a script other than the Roman alphabet—Japanese, Korean, Greek, Russian, Persian, Thai, or Arabic, for example. Rather than using their customary orthographies, speakers of these languages use the Roman alphabet to send telegrams internationally. Even within a country, an alternative writing system may be needed: In China, each character has a four-digit numeral assigned to it and these numerals are sent telegraphically and then "translated" back into Chinese characters. Sometimes a language uses more than one writing system for different aspects of writing. Japanese draws upon three kinds of writing: *kanji*, based on the Chinese charac-ter system, in which a symbol represents a word independent of its pronuncia-tion, and two syllabaries. A *syllabary* is a writing system in which each symbol represents a spoken syllable. Throughout the world there are discrepancies between sounds as spoken and as represented in writing.

Bilingual Sign, Xinjiang Autonomous Region, China. Written alternately in Arabic script (for Uyghur) and Chinese characters (for Chinese), with Arabic numerals in both. Neither language is related to Arabic. Supplied by the author.

© Edward Finegan

In this chapter, we focus on the human vocal apparatus and the sounds it produces; Chapter 4 examines the nature of sound systems in human language.

Phonetics: The Study of Sounds

Phonetics is the study of the sounds made in the production of human languages. It has two principal branches.

- *Articulatory phonetics* focuses on the human vocal apparatus and describes sounds in terms of their articulation in the vocal tract; it has been central to the discipline of linguistics.

- *Acoustic phonetics* uses the tools of physics to study the nature of sound waves produced in human language; it is increasingly important in linguistics with attempts to use machines for interpreting speech patterns in voice identification and voice-initiated mechanical operations.

Our discussion will be limited almost exclusively to articulatory phonetics—the nature of human sounds as they are produced by the vocal apparatus.

Phonetic Alphabets

To refer to the sounds of human language in terms of their articulation, phoneticians have evolved descriptive techniques that avoid the difficulties of describing sounds in terms of customary writing systems. You already know it is impossible to use customary written representations to analyze sound structure because, even within a single language, some sounds correspond to more than one letter, and some letters to more than one sound. Besides that, a single letter can be used to represent different sounds in different languages. So we need an independent system to represent the actual sounds of human languages.

In scientific discussion, the requisite characteristics of symbols for representing sounds are clarity and consistency. The best tool is a phonetic alphabet, and the most widely used one is the International Phonetic Alphabet (IPA). The IPA provides a unique written representation of every sound in every language.

A list of symbols used to represent the consonant sounds of English is given in Table 3.1. It provides the phonetic symbol for each sound and emphases for the relevant parts of the words included. Taking advantage of an option allowed by the International Phonetic Association, we use an ordinary printed <r> to represent the initial sound of *ride*, but you should know that the association assigns the symbol [r] to a different sound. (We've indicated the standard IPA symbol for the initial sound of *ride* in parentheses.) The words illustrate word-initial, word-medial, and word-final occurrences of the sounds.

The Vocal Tract

The processes the vocal tract uses in creating a multitude of sounds are similar to those of wind instruments and organ pipes, which produce different musical sounds by varying the shape, size, and acoustic character of the cavities through

Table 3.1 *English Consonants Arranged by Position in Word*

Phonetic Symbol	Initial	Medial	Final
p	pick	caper	tap
b	bit	labor	tab
t	tick	meter	bat
d	dish	medal	pad
k	kiss	sicker	lick
g	geek	dagger	bag
f	fit	beefy	chief
v	vim	saving	grave
θ	thin	author	breath
ð	then	leather	breathe
s	sit	mason	kiss
z	zest	posit	shoes
ʃ	shed	rashes	rush
ʒ	———	measure	rouge
tʃ	chip	kitchen	pitch
ʤ	jet	bludgeon	fudge
m	mitt	dummy	broom
n	nip	sunny	spoon
ŋ	———	singer	sing
h	hit	ahoy	———
j	yes	beyond	toy
r (ɹ)	rest	berry	deer
l	last	silly	mill
w	wish	away	———

which air passes once it leaves its source. Every speech sound you make sounds different from every other speech sound because of a unique combination of features in the way you shape your mouth and tongue and move parts of the vocal apparatus while making it. Examine the simplified drawing of the vocal tract in Figure 3.3. Here we will look at the parts of the vocal tract and show how they work together to produce sounds.

How are speech sounds made? First, air coming from the lungs passes through the vocal tract, which shapes it into different speech sounds. The air then exits the vocal tract through the mouth or nose or both.

Despite the fact that speakers of all languages have the same vocal apparatus, no language takes advantage of all the possibilities for forming different sounds, and there are striking differences in the sounds that occur in different languages. For example, Japanese and Thai lack the [v] sound of English *van*, and Japanese lacks the [f] sound of *fan*. Thai lacks the sounds represented

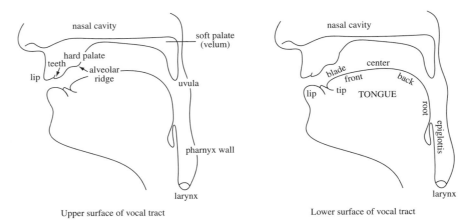

Figure 3.3 The Vocal Tract

Adapted from Ladefoged 2006.

by <g> in *gill*, <z> in *zebra*, <sh> in *shell*, <s> in *measure*, and <j> and <dg> in *judge*. French, Japanese, and Thai lack the quite different <th> sounds in *ether* and *either*.

Just as some languages lack sounds that English has, other languages have sounds that English does not have, and some languages that may share a sound may not share its distribution in words. You probably know that English lacks the trilled *r* of Spanish and Italian and that German has a sound at the end of words like *Bach* 'stream' and *hoch* 'high' that does not occur in the inventory of English sounds. Arabic has a sound similar to the German <ch> of *Bach*, but in Arabic it can occur word initially. A similar (but not identical) sound occurring word finally in the German word *ich* occurs in English (for those dialects that pronounce the <h>) in the initial sound of *human* and *huge*. Still, it can be

The Vocal Cords and Voicing

Human beings have no organs that are used only for speech. The organs that produce speech sounds have evolved principally to serve the life-sustaining processes of breathing and eating. Speech is a secondary function of the human "vocal apparatus" and is sometimes said to be parasitic on these organs. The vocal cords offer an illustration of the "parasitic" nature of speech: the primary function of these two folds is to keep food from going down the wrong tube and entering the lungs.

With respect to speech, vibration of the vocal cords is what distinguishes voiced and voiceless sounds. You can perceive the difference between voiced and voiceless consonants by alternating between the pronunciations of [s] and [z] or [f] and [v] while holding your hands clapped over your ears. You should be able to tell from pronouncing the words *thin* and *thirty* (which begin with [θ]) and *then* and *those* (which begin with [ð]) which of the two sounds—[θ] or [ð]—is voiced. Check your conclusions against Table 3.7.

tough for English speakers learning German to pronounce the sound in a word like *ich* because English doesn't permit that sound at the end of a word.

As you explore the inventory of sounds in the sections below, use your vocal tract to produce the sounds that are described. It's important to pronounce them aloud, noting the shape of your mouth and the position of your tongue for each sound. That experience will familiarize you with the reference points of phonetics, make the discussion easier to follow, and give you confidence as you master articulatory phonetics.

We will continue to use square brackets to enclose the symbols representing sounds. Thus [t] will symbolize the initial and final sounds in *tot*, [d] the initial and final sounds in *did*, and [z] the initial sound in *zebra*, the medial consonant in *busy*, and the final sound of *buzz* and *dogs*.

Describing Consonant Sounds

A **consonant** is a speech sound produced by a partial or complete closure of part of the vocal tract, thus obstructing the airflow and creating audible friction. Speech sounds can be characterized in terms of their *articulatory* properties—by *where* in the mouth and *how* they are produced, and consonants can be described in terms of three properties:

- ◆ **Voicing** (whether the vocal cords are vibrating or not)
- ◆ **Place of articulation** (where the airstream is most obstructed)
- ◆ **Manner of articulation** (the particular way the airstream is obstructed)

Voicing

Begin by pronouncing a long, continuous [zzzzz] sound and alternating it with a long, continuous [sssss] sound. You'll notice that the position of your tongue within your mouth remains exactly the same, even though the sounds are noticeably different. You can feel the difference by touching your throat at the **larynx** (voice box) while saying [zzzzz sssss zzzzz sssss]. The vibration you feel from your larynx when you utter [zzzzz] but not [sssss] is called **voicing**; it is the result of air being forced through a narrow aperture (called the **glottis**) between two mucosal folds (the vocal cords) in the larynx. When the vocal cords are held together, the air forced through them from the lungs causes them to vibrate. It is this vibration, or "voicing," that distinguishes [z] from [s] and enables speakers to differentiate between these two otherwise identical sounds. Using these highly similar but distinct sounds enables us to create words that differ by only a single feature of voicing on a single sound but carry quite different meanings, as in *bus* and *buzz*, *peace* and *peas*, *sip* and *zip*, and *sane* and *Zane*.

Other pairs of sounds are likewise characterized by a voiced versus voiceless contrast. Consider [f] and [v], as in *fine* and *vine* or *proof* and *prove*: both sounds are produced by forcing air through a narrow aperture between the upper teeth and the lower lip. The difference is that [f] is voiceless and [v] is voiced. Other voiceless/voiced pairs include [p] and [b] as in *pet* and *bet* or *rope* and *robe* and [t] and [d] as in *ten* and *den* or *net* and *Ned*.

Manner of Articulation

Besides having a voicing feature, [s] and [z] (and all other consonants) can be characterized as to their **manner of articulation**. In pronouncing [s] and [z], air is *continuously* forced through a narrow opening at a place behind the upper teeth. Compare the pronunciation of [s] and [z] with the sounds [t] and [d]. Unlike [s] and [z], [t] and [d] are not pronounced by a continuous stream of air passing through the mouth. Instead, the air stream is completely stopped behind and above the upper teeth and then released in a small burst of air. For this reason, [t] and [d] are called *stops*, and because the air is released through the mouth (and not the nose), they may be called *oral stops*. Sounds like [s] and [z] that are made by a continuous stream of air passing through a narrowed passage in the vocal tract are called *fricatives*.

Try It Yourself Pronounce the sounds [p], [b], [f], [v], [θ], and [ð] to determine which are stops and which are fricatives.

Place of Articulation

Of the sounds analyzed so far, [s] and [t] are voiceless, [z] and [d] voiced. All four are pronounced with the point of greatest closure immediately behind and just above the upper teeth. Pronounce *ten* and *den* aloud, feeling where the tip of your tongue touches the top of your mouth for the initial and final consonants. Both words start and finish at the alveolar ridge. Because [t], [d], and [n] are articulated at the alveolar ridge, they are called **alveolars**. Also articulated at the alveolar ridge are [s] and [z], as you can notice by pronouncing the words *bus* and *buzz*. ([s] and [z] are fricatives, as you should be able readily to tell, whereas [t] and [d] are stops.)

Try It Yourself Compare your pronunciation of [p] and [t]. Both are voiceless, so what is the difference between them? Pronounce word pairs like *pin* and *tin* or *tripe* and *trite* as other examples.

There are three major **places of articulation** for English stops: the lips, the alveolar ridge, and the soft palate (or velum). If you say *pin* and *bin*, you'll notice that for the initial sound in each word air is built up behind the lips and then released. Thus the point of greatest closure is at the lips, and for that reason [p] and [b] are called **bilabial** stops (*bilabial* means 'two lips').

Attend to the pronunciation of the first sound of *kin*, and you'll notice that [k], like [p] in *pill* and [t] in *till*, is a voiceless stop, but it differs from [p] and [t] in its place of articulation: [k] is a **velar** because it is pronounced with the back of the tongue touching the roof of the mouth at the velum (the soft palate); [k] is a voiceless velar stop.

Corresponding to the voiceless stops [p], [t], and [k] are three voiced stops: [b] as in *blab* is a voiced bilabial stop; [d] as in *dude* is a voiced alveolar

Try It Yourself Identify the pairs of stops pronounced at the lips, the alveolar ridge, and the velum.

stop; and [g] as in *gig* is a voiced velar stop. English has three pairs of stops, with each pair pronounced at a given place of articulation, one member of the pair voiced and the other voiceless.

Besides lips, alveolar ridge, and velum, English takes advantage of other articulators to produce consonant sounds. The <th> of *thin* is a fricative pronounced with the tongue between the teeth. It is a voiceless **interdental** fricative, represented by the Greek letter theta [θ]. [ʃ] (the sound represented by <sh> in *shoot* and *wish*) and [ʒ] (the final sound in *beige* and the middle consonant in *measure*) are pronounced between the alveolar ridge and the velum (or palate) and are called **alveo-palatals**. [ʃ] is a voiceless alveo-palatal fricative, [ʒ] a voiced alveo-palatal fricative.

Kinds of Consonant Sounds

To repeat what was said above, consonants are produced by partially or completely blocking air in its passage from the lungs through the vocal tract. If you review the inventory of English consonants given in Table 3.1 and pronounce the sounds aloud while concentrating on the place and manner of articulation, you'll perceive how the tables represent the distribution of English consonants according to their voicing, place of articulation, and manner of articulation. Below we describe these consonants, grouped according to their manner of articulation and characterized in terms of voicing and place of articulation. We concentrate on the consonant sounds of English and mention selected consonants in other languages.

Stops

Stops are formed when air is built up at a point in the vocal tract and released suddenly through the mouth. The principal stops of English are [p] and [b], [t] and [d], and [k] and [g]. By pronouncing words with these sounds in them (see Table 3.1), you can recognize that [p] and [b] are bilabial stops, [t] and [d] alveolar stops, and [k] and [g] velar stops.

English Stops

	PLACE OF ARTICULATION			
	Bilabial	**Alveolar**	**Velar**	**Glottal**
Voiceless	p	t	k	?
Voiced	b	d	g	

In addition, many languages have a glottal stop, represented by [ʔ]. It is pronounced by using the glottis to completely but briefly block the air from passing in the throat. In English, the glottal stop occurs only as a marginal sound—for example, in American English between the two parts of the exclamation *Uh-oh!* and in Cockney English as the medial consonant of words like *butter* and *bottle*, for example. In Hawaiian and some other languages, the glottal stop is not a marginal sound but an ordinary consonant that can distinguish between words: *paʔu* 'smudge' and *pau* 'finished.' (Represented by an apostrophe in its spelled name, the constructed language Na'vi, spoken in the film *Avatar*, is pronounced [nɑʔvi].)

Fricatives

Fricatives are characterized by forcing air in a continuous stream through a narrow opening at some point in the vocal tract. To pronounce the alveolar **fricatives** [s] and [z], air is forced through a narrow opening between the tip of the tongue and the alveolar ridge. In pronouncing the first sound in the words *thin*, *three*, and *theta* and the final sound in *teeth* and *bath*, the tongue tip is placed between the upper and lower teeth, where the airstream is most constricted and makes its articulation. Represented by [θ], the sound in these words is a voiceless interdental fricative. The voiced counterpart is the initial sound in the words *there* and *then* and the middle consonant sound in *either*. In English the spelling <th> is used for two distinct sounds: [θ] as in *thin* and *ether* and [ð] as in *then* and *either* or *leather*.

Try It Yourself Pronounce the following words to discover other fricatives and become aware of their common properties and their different places of articulation:

fine/vine; beefish/peevish	[f]	[v]	labio-dental fricatives
thigh/thy; ether/either	[θ]	[ð]	interdental fricatives
sink/zinc; bus/buzz	[s]	[z]	alveolar fricatives
rush/rouge; fishin'/vision	[ʃ]	[ʒ]	alveo-palatal fricatives
here; ahoy	[h]		glottal fricative

English Fricatives

	PLACE OF ARTICULATION				
	Labio-Dental	**Interdental**	**Alveolar**	**Alveo-Palatal**	**Glottal**
Voiceless	f	θ	s	ʃ	h
Voiced	v	ð	z	ʒ	

Some languages have other fricatives. Spanish has a voiced bilabial fricative (represented by [β]), as in the <b> of *cabo* 'end.' Japanese has a voiceless bilabial fricative, represented by [ɸ] and pronounced somewhat like [f] but by bringing together both lips instead of the lower lip and the upper front teeth. The West African language Ewe has voiced [β] and voiceless [ɸ] bilabial fricatives. Spanish and many other languages have a voiceless velar fricative [x] and a voiced velar fricative [ɣ]. Pronounce [x] as if you were gently clearing your throat. The sound occurs initially in the Spanish word *joya* 'jewel' and the personal name *José* (when borrowed into English, *José* is pronounced with [h], the closest sound to [x] in English). [ɣ] is represented by <g> in Spanish *lago* 'lake.' German, Irish, and Mandarin Chinese have a voiceless palatal fricative [ç], as in the German word *Reich* 'empire.'

You may have noticed that the physical distance in the mouth between the places of articulation for the English fricatives is not as great as for the stops. The bilabial, alveolar, and velar places of articulation for stop consonants are spaced farther apart than are the labio-dental, interdental, alveolar, and alveo-palatal fricatives. This closer spacing of the fricatives can cause difficulty in perceiving them as distinct, especially for speakers of languages with fewer fricatives than English or with fricatives spaced at greater distance from one another. For example, French does not have the interdental fricatives [θ] and [ð], so French speakers tend to perceive (and pronounce) English words like *thin* and *this* as though they were "sin" and "zis." One French fricative familiar to English speakers, even though English doesn't have it, is the voiced uvular *r*-sound (as in *Paris* or *rue* 'street'), which is represented by [ʁ].

Affricates

Two consonant sounds of English are more complex than its stops and fricatives. These more complex sounds combine a stop consonant and a fricative to produce an **affricate**. In the pronunciation of an affricate, air is built up by a complete closure of the oral tract at some place of articulation and then released (like a stop) and continued (like a fricative). The consonant sound at the beginning and end of *church* is a combination of the stop [t] and the fricative [ʃ] and is represented as [t͡ʃ] or [tʃ]. The consonant sound at the beginning and end of *judge* is a combination of the stop [d] and the fricative [ʒ] and is represented as [d͡ʒ]. English has only one pair of affricates, and to identify their place of articulation they are called alveo-palatal affricates (alveo for [t] and [d] and palatal for [ʃ] and [ʒ]).

Some languages have other affricates. The most common are the alveolar affricates [ts] and [d͡z], which occur at the beginning of the Italian words *zucchero* 'sugar' and *zona* 'zone,' respectively.

 Try It Yourself Focusing on the initial consonant sounds in *chin* and *gin* and the final consonant sounds in *batch* and *badge*, pronounce these words slowly until you recognize that they begin or end with stop-fricatives (that is, affricates).

English Affricates

	PLACE OF ARTICULATION
	Alveo-Palatal
Voiceless	t͡ʃ
Voiced	d͡ʒ

Obstruents

Fricatives, stops, and affricates are called **obstruents** because they share the phonetic property of constricting or obstructing the airflow through the vocal tract.

Approximants

Approximants are produced by two articulators approaching one another almost like fricatives but not coming close enough to produce friction. English has four approximants: [j], [r] (IPA [ɹ]), [l], and [w]. The sound that begins the word *you* is the palatal approximant [j], while *cute* begins with the consonant cluster [kj]. Because [r] is pronounced by channeling air through the central part of the mouth, it is called a central approximant. To pronounce [l], air is channeled on one or both sides of the tongue to make a lateral approximant. To distinguish them from the other approximants, [r] and [l] are sometimes called **liquids**. (In some Asian languages, [r] and [l] are not contrastive sounds, so native speakers of those languages may find it challenging to distinguish them in speaking or perceiving them in English speech. This is a matter to which we return in the following chapter.)

In pronouncing the approximant [w], the lips are rounded, as in *wild*. In certain dialects, [h] precedes [w] in words such as *which, whether,* or *when*. When [w] is the second element of a consonant cluster (as in *twine* or *quick*), the initial sound (in these cases, [t] or [k]) is rounded in anticipation of the [w], as you can appreciate by pronouncing *twine* and *time* and *quick* and *kick*, while focusing on the shape of your lips.

English Approximants

	PLACE OF ARTICULATION		
	Bilabial	Alveolar	Palatal
Voiced (Central)	w	r (ɹ)	j
Voiced (Lateral)		l	

Nasals

Nasal consonants are pronounced by lowering the velum, thus allowing the stream of air to pass out through the nasal cavity instead of through the oral cavity. English has three nasal stops: [m] as in *mad, drummer, cram*; [n] as in *new, sinner, ten*; and a third, symbolized by [ŋ] and pronounced as in the words *sing* and *singer*.

English Nasals

PLACE OF ARTICULATION		
Bilabial	Alveolar	Velar
m	n	ŋ

Because of the way it is usually spelled in English, English speakers may think of [ŋ] as a combination of [n] and [g], but it is actually a single sound. Test this for yourself by comparing your pronunciation of *singer* and *finger*. Ignoring the initial sounds [s] and [f], if your pronunciation of *singer* and *finger* differs (for some speakers of English it does not), then you have [ŋ] in *singer* and [ŋg] in *finger* (notice that if you had [ng] in *finger*, you'd pronounce it like "finn-ger"). Most American English speakers have a three-way contrast among *simmer*, *sinner*, and *singer*, depending on whether the middle consonant is [m], [n], or [ŋ]. By noticing whether and where your tongue touches the upper part of your mouth in articulating these nasal consonants (and by comparing their place of articulation with other sounds), you can determine that [m] is a bilabial nasal, [n] an alveolar nasal, and [ŋ] a velar nasal.

If you have successfully identified the places of articulation for nasals and understood why they fit in their slots in the consonant table, you may have noticed that English has three

Try It Yourself While you are saying [mmmm] or [nnnn], cut off the airstream passing through your nose by pinching it closed. You'll notice that the sound stops abruptly, thus demonstrating that air passes through the nose when you produce a nasal stop. Compare what happens when you cut off the air passing through your nose while saying [nnnnn] and [sssss]. You'll quickly understand one way in which the nasal and oral cavities function in producing sounds. When you cut off air passing through the nose, there is virtually no difference in the sound quality for oral consonants like [s], but for a nasal consonant like [n] or [m] the effect couldn't be more noticeable!

sets of consonants articulated in the same places and differing only in their manner of articulation: the oral stops [p] and [b] and the nasal stop [m] are bilabials; the oral stops [t] and [d] and the nasal stop [n] are articulated at the alveolar ridge and called alveolars; [k], [g], and [ŋ] are articulated at the velum and called velars.

English, as we've seen, has three nasal consonants: [m], [n], and [ŋ]. The sound inventory of other languages may contain other nasals. French, Spanish, and Italian have a palatal nasal [ɲ]. You can recognize it in the French word *mignon* 'cute' (which English has borrowed in the phrase *filet mignon*), in the Spanish words *mañana*, *señor*, and *cañón* (borrowed into English as *canyon*), and the Italian *bagno* 'bath' and *lasagna* (also borrowed into English).

Clicks, Flaps, Trills

Some languages of southern Africa have among their stop consonants certain **click** sounds that function as an integral part of their sound system. One example is the lateral click, made on the side of the tongue. Although the lateral click is not part of the inventory of English speech sounds, it does occur when English speakers urge a horse to move on. As a speech sound, its IPA symbol is [||]. Another click sound that occurs in some languages can be represented in English writing by the reproach *tsk-tsk*. This click is made with the tip of the tongue at the teeth or the alveolar ridge and is described as a dental click [|] or (post)alveolar click [!].

A few consonant sounds are not stops, fricatives, affricates, approximants, or nasals. The middle consonant sound in the words *butter* and *metal* is commonly pronounced in American English as an alveolar **flap**, which is a high-velocity short stop produced by tapping the tongue against the alveolar ridge.

We represent this flap, or tap, by [ɾ] (a sound discussed further in Chapter 4). Spanish, Italian, and Fijian have an alveolar **trill** *r*, as in Spanish *correr* 'to run.' In order to reserve the familiar symbol [r] to represent the "r" of English, North American books represent the alveolar trill by [r̃] (instead of the IPA symbol [r]).

Vowel Sounds

Try It Yourself You've heard people say that English has five vowels—a, e, i, o, and u. But that number better reflects written English than spoken English. By way of determining a more accurate count, pronounce the following words aloud, noting how many distinct vowels of spoken English they represent: *peat, pit, pate, pet, pat, put, putt, pot, port, poke,* and *pool.*

Vowel sounds are articulated without complete closure in the oral cavity and without sufficient narrowing to create the friction characteristic of consonants. They are produced by passing air through different shapes of the mouth, with different positions of the tongue and of the lips, and—unlike consonants—with the air stream relatively unobstructed by narrow passages except at the glottis. Some languages have as few as three distinct vowels; others have more than a dozen.

Vowel Height and Frontness

Try It Yourself You can get a feel for these descriptors by alternately saying *feed* and *food*—the first contains a front vowel, the second a back vowel. For tongue height, alternate saying *feet* and *fat*. If you don't feel the difference between high and low vowels with this pair of sounds, look at yourself in the mirror (or at a classmate saying them); the mouth is open wider for the vowel of *fat* than for the vowel of feet. The reason? The tongue is lower for *fat*.

Vowels are characterized by the position of the tongue and the relative rounding of the lips. Partly on the basis of auditory perception, we refer to vowels as *high* or *low* and *front* or *back*. We also consider whether the lips are *rounded* (as for *boot*) or *nonrounded* (as for *bit*).

Figure 3.4 indicates the relationship of the English vowels to one another and the approximate positions of the tongue during their articulation.

Here are English words for each of the vowel symbols shown in the figure. Note that these words are chosen on the basis of North American English; British English pronunciations may differ for some:

i	Pete, beat			u	stoop, boot
ɪ	pit, bit			ʊ	put, foot
e	late, bait	ə	about, sof<u>a</u>	o	poke, boat
ɛ	pet, bet	ʌ	putt, but	ɔ	port, bought
æ	pat, bat	a	park (in Boston)	ɑ	pot, father

The symbols [ə] (called *schwa*) and [ʌ] (called *caret* or *wedge*) represent similar sounds. Both occur in the word *above* [əbʌv]. We use [ə] to represent a

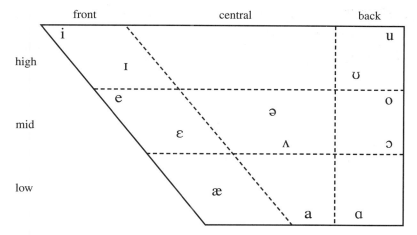

Figure 3.4 The Vowels of English

mid central vowel in unstressed syllables, such as the second syllable of *buses* [bʌsəz] and the second and third syllables of *capable* [kepəbəl]. We also use it before [r] in the same syllable, whether stressed as in *person* [pərsən] and *sir* [sər] or unstressed as in *pertain* [pərten] and *tender* [tɛndər]. We use [ʌ] to represent mid central vowels in other stressed syllables, such as *suds* [sʌdz] and the first syllable of *flooded* [flʌɾəd]. (Some books use [ɚ] to represent a mid central vowel with *r* coloring. In systems using the [ɚ] notation, *person* would be transcribed [pɚsən], *sir* [sɚ], and *pertain* [pɚten].)

Diphthongs

English also has **diphthongs**, represented by pairs of symbols to capture the fact that a diphthong is a vowel sound for which the tongue starts in one place and glides to another. Say these slowly to get a sense of what a diphthong is: [aj] (as in *ride*); [aw] (as in *loud*); [ɔj] (as in *boy, toy*). (Some books transcribe these diphthongs as [ay] or [aɪ], [au] or [aʊ], and [ɔy] or [ɔɪ], respectively.) Diphthongs change in quality while being pronounced, as you can notice by slowly pronouncing the words *buy, boy, bough*. Thus American English dialects have up to thirteen distinctive vowel sounds (plus three diphthongs). In England and certain parts of the United States, including metropolitan New York City, sixteen distinct vowels and diphthongs exist. In other parts of the United States, fewer distinct vowel sounds exist because no distinction is made between the vowels of *hawk* and *hock*.

Other Articulatory Features of Vowels

To create differences among vowels, languages can exploit other possibilities besides tongue height and frontness or backness. Vowels can have tenseness, rounding, lengthening, nasalization, and tone.

Tenseness Languages can make a distinction between *tense* and *lax* vowels. These labels represent a set of characteristics that distinguish one set of vowels from another. For example, lax vowels do not occur at the end of a stressed syllable, and they tend to be shorter; they also tend to be more centralized than the nearest tense vowel. The contrast between [i] of *peat* and [ɪ] of *pit* is in part a tense/lax contrast; likewise for the vowels in *bait/bet* and *cooed/could*. The lax vowels don't end a syllable (we have [pi] 'pea' but not [pɪ] except preceding a consonant, as in [pɪk] or [pɪt]); they are shorter than their corresponding tense vowels and more centralized in the mouth. Thus, English has the lax vowels [ɪ ɛ ʊ] as in *pit, pet, put*. The corresponding tense vowels are [i e u] as in *beat, bait, boot*. The lax vowels [æ ʌ] do not have corresponding tense vowels.

Rounding Whereas in English high front vowels tend automatically to be unrounded (and high back vowels to be rounded), some languages have *rounded* and *unrounded* front vowels. French and German have high front and mid front rounded vowels as well as unrounded ones. French has a high front unrounded [i] in words such as *dire* 'to say' and *dix* 'ten' and a high front rounded vowel [ü], as in *rue* 'street'; it also has a contrast between upper mid front unrounded [e] (as in *fée* 'fairy') and upper mid front rounded [ø] (*feu* 'fire'); and between lower mid front unrounded [ɛ] (*serre* 'hothouse') and lower mid front rounded [œ] (*soeur* 'sister'). German has similar contrasts.

Length Vowels can be of varying lengths. For each of its vowels, German has one *long* and one *short*. Long vowels are held longer when pronounced than short vowels. In phonetic transcriptions a special colon or doubled vowel symbol are commonly used to indicate a long vowel. (In dictionaries and some writing systems, a macron (̄) may be used above the vowel symbol.) Thus, in addition to the short vowels [i] and [ü], as in *bitten* 'to request' and *müssen* 'must,' German has words with high front long vowels: unrounded [i:] in *bieten* 'to wish' and rounded [ü:] in *Mühle* 'mill.' These examples illustrate how languages can multiply vowel differences by exploiting long and short varieties. English vowels may also vary in length but, unlike German, English has no two words that differ only in vowel length (see Chapter 4). To sense differences in the duration of vowels, pronounce the English words *bit, beat,* and *bead*. You should be able to hear that the vowel of *bead* is longer than the vowel of *beat*, and that both are longer than the vowel of *bit*.

Nasalization All vowel types can be *nasalized* by pronouncing the vowel while passing air through the nose (as for nasal stops) and through the mouth. Nasal vowels are indicated by a tilde (~) placed above the vowel symbol. French has several nasal vowels paralleling its oral vowels:

lin [lɛ̃] 'flax'	*lait* [lɛ] 'milk'
ment [mã] '(he) is lying'	*ma* [ma] 'my' (feminine)
honte [ɔ̃t] 'shame'	*hotte* [ɔt] 'hutch'

Other languages with nasal vowels include Irish, Hindi, and the Native American languages Delaware, Navaho, and Seneca.

Tone In many languages of Asia, Africa, and North America, a vowel may be pronounced on several pitches and be perceived by native speakers of these languages as different sounds. Typically, a vowel pronounced on a low pitch contrasts with the same vowel pronounced on a higher pitch. In Hausa, spoken in West Africa, the word for 'bamboo' is *górà*, with high tone (´) on the first syllable and low tone (`) on the second syllable. The word *gòrá*, in which the sequence of tones is reversed, has the meaning 'large gourd.' Some tone languages have more complex systems. The Beijing dialect of Chinese has a high level tone (symbolized with ¯); a rising tone (´); a falling-rising tone (ˇ), in which the pitch begins to fall and then rises sharply; and a falling tone (`), in which the pitch falls sharply. There is a four-way tone contrast among the following vowels, which happen to be distinct words.

ī (high level)	'one'
í (rising)	'proper'
ǐ (falling-rising)	'already'
ì (falling)	'thought'

A given **diacritic**, or accent mark, can be used to represent different tones in different languages. Thus, ´ represents a high tone in Hausa but a rising tone in Chinese, while ` represents a low tone in Hausa but a falling tone in Chinese.

Thai has five tones; the standard dialect of Vietnamese has six tones; and the Guangzhou (Canton) dialect of Chinese has nine different tones. Tone is a widespread and diverse phenomenon.

Tables 3.2 through 3.5 are vowel charts illustrating the sound patterns of four languages—French, Spanish, German, and Japanese.

Table 3.2 *French Vowels with Illustrative Words*

	Front Unrounded	Front Rounded	Central Unrounded	Back Rounded
Oral				
high	i	ü		u
upper mid	e	ø		o
mid			ə	
lower mid	ɛ	œ		ɔ
low			a	
Nasal				
lower mid	ɛ̃	œ̃		ɔ̃
low				ã

i gr<u>i</u>s 'gray'	ü m<u>û</u>r 'ripe'	ə ch<u>e</u>min 'path'	u f<u>ou</u> 'crazy'
e ferm<u>é</u> 'shut'	ø j<u>eû</u>ne 'fasts'	a p<u>a</u>r 'by'	o m<u>o</u>t 'word'
ɛ fr<u>ai</u>s 'fresh'	œ j<u>eu</u>ne 'young'		ɔ f<u>or</u>t 'strong'
ɛ̃ br<u>in</u> 'sprig'	œ̃ br<u>un</u> 'brown'		ɔ̃ f<u>on</u>d 'bottom'
			ã f<u>aon</u> 'fawn'

Table 3.3 *Spanish Vowels with Illustrative Words*

	Front Unrounded	Central Unrounded	Back Rounded
High	i		u
Mid	e		o
Low		a	

i ch<u>i</u>ste 'joke'	a m<u>a</u>r 'sea'	u s<u>u</u>r 'south'
e f<u>e</u> 'faith'		o b<u>o</u>ca 'mouth'

Table 3.4 *German Vowels with Illustrative Words*

	Front Unrounded	Front Rounded	Central Unrounded	Back Rounded
High				
long	iː	üː		uː
short	i	ü		u
Upper Mid				
long	eː	øː		oː
short	e			o
Mid				
short			ə	
Lower Mid				
long	ɛː			
short		œ		
Low				
long			aː	
short			a	

iː b<u>ie</u>ten 'to wish'	üː M<u>üh</u>le 'mill'	ə lieb<u>e</u> 'dear'	uː H<u>uh</u>n 'hen'
i b<u>i</u>tten 'to request'	ü m<u>ü</u>ssen 'must'	a R<u>a</u>be 'raven'	u M<u>u</u>tter 'mother'
eː w<u>e</u>n 'whom'	ø <u>ö</u>lig 'oily'	a R<u>a</u>tte 'rat'	o <u>O</u>fen 'oven'
e w<u>e</u>nn 'when'	œ R<u>ö</u>ntgen 'X-ray'		o <u>O</u>chs 'ox'
ɛː K<u>ä</u>se 'cheese'			

Table 3.5 *Japanese Vowels with Illustrative Words*

	Front Unrounded	Central Unrounded	Back Unrounded	Back Rounded
High	i		ɯ	
Mid	ɛ			ɔ
Low		a		

i <u>i</u>ma 'now'	a <u>a</u>ki 'autumn'	ɯ b<u>u</u>ji 'safe'	ɔ y<u>o</u>ru 'to approach'
ɛ s<u>e</u>nsei 'teacher'			

Tables 3.6 and 3.7 summarize all the vowels and consonants introduced in this chapter.

Table 3.6 *Vowels Discussed in Chapter 3*

(All vowels can be nasalized and either short or long.)

	Front Unrounded	Front Rounded	Central Unrounded	Back Unrounded	Back Rounded
high					
tense	i	ü		ɯ	u
lax	ɪ				ʊ
upper mid	e	ø			o
mid			ə		
lower mid	ɛ	œ	ʌ		ɔ
low	æ		a	ɑ	

Table 3.7 *Consonants Discussed in Chapter 3*

Manner of Articulation and Voicing	PLACE OF ARTICULATION								
	Bila-bial	Labio-Dental	Inter-Dental	Alve-Olar	Alveo-Palatal	Pala-tal	Velar	Uvu-Lar	Glot-Tal
Stops									
voiceless	p			t			k		ʔ
voiced	b			d			g		
Nasals									
	m			n		ɲ	ŋ		
Fricatives									
voiceless	ɸ	f	θ	s	ʃ	ç	x		h
voiced	ß	v	ð	z	ʒ		ɣ	ʁ	
Affricates									
voiceless				ts	tʃ				
voiced				ʣ	ʤ				
Approximants									
voiced central	w			r (ɹ)		j			
voiced lateral				l					
Others									
voiced trill				r̃ (r)					
voiced flap/tap				ɾ					

COMPUTERS AND PHONETICS

Alphabetic writing systems rely on the notion of discrete sounds, and it has proved useful to think of speech sounds as discrete. But in natural speech, sounds are not discrete and don't occur separately. Instead each sound touches the next sound in a word (and in an utterance), and sounds and words merge into one another.

Imagine a computer that could create discrete sounds that seem natural when spoken in isolation — it could produce the sounds [ɪ], [n], [k], [l], [u], [d], [ə], and [d]. If it put these sounds together in the sequence [ɪnkludəd], you might expect a pronunciation that resembled the word *included*. But as it is usually pronounced, *included* does not have the same [ɪ] sound that occurs in *sit*, and the [n] of *included* is often pronounced more like the [ŋ] of *sing*. So if natural-sounding words are the goal, their production cannot rely on a simple sequence of discrete individual sounds.

Suppose instead that the computer put together the sounds [ī], [ŋ], [k], [l], [u], [d], [ə], and [d]. That sequence would sound more natural but still be stiff. For one thing, the first and second [d] sounds of *included* differ from one another, and both of them differ from the [d] sound of *dig*. Even further refinement wouldn't go far enough, for the individual sounds would have to run into one another as in natural speech. They couldn't be separated as in print or a phonetic transcription. As a further complication, consider that a word like *photo* could be represented phonetically as [foɾo], but the same morpheme in *photograph* would be pronounced [foɾə] and in *photographer* [fəˈtʰɑ]. In other words, without some general principles of pronunciation, a computer could not simply combine the sounds represented in spelling and produce synthesized speech that sounded remotely like natural speech. We return to this matter in the following chapter. ■

Summary

- Sounds must be distinguished from letters and other visual representations of language.
- Phonetic alphabets represent sounds in a way that is consistent and comparable across different languages; each sound is assigned a distinct representation, independently of the customary writing system used to represent a particular language.
- This chapter uses the International Phonetic Alphabet (IPA).
- All languages contain consonants and vowels.
- Consonants are produced by obstructing the flow of air as it passes from the lungs through the vocal tract and out through the mouth or nose.
- For fricative consonants, air forced through a narrow opening forms a continuous noise, as in the initial and final sounds of *says* [sɛz] and *fish* [fɪʃ].
- For stop consonants, the air passage is completely blocked and then released, as in the initial and final sounds of the words *tap* and *cat*.
- Affricates are produced by combining a stop and a fricative, as in the final sound of the word *peach* or the initial and final sounds of *judge*.
- As a group, fricatives, stops, and affricates are called obstruents.
- An approximant is produced when one articulator approaches another but the vocal tract is not sufficiently narrowed to create the audible friction of a consonant. Examples are the initial sounds of *west* [wɛst], *yes* [jɛs], *rest* [rɛst], *lest* [lɛst].

- "Liquid" is a cover term for [r] and [l] sounds.
- Consonant sounds can be described as a combination of articulatory features: voicing, place of articulation, and manner of articulation. For example: [t] is a voiceless alveolar stop; [v] is a voiced labio-dental fricative.
- Vowels are produced by positioning the tongue and mouth to form differently shaped passages.
- The airstream for oral vowels passes through the mouth; for nasal vowels, the airstream passes through the nose and mouth.
- Vowels are described by relative height and frontness. For example: [æ] is a low front vowel; [u] is a high back vowel.
- Secondary features of vowel production—such as tenseness, nasality, lengthening, or rounding—are sometimes specified, as in "long vowel" or "nasal vowel."
- In many languages vowels (and nasals) can be pronounced on different pitches, or tones.
- Languages differ from one another in the number of speech sounds they have.
- Although linguists find it useful to conceptualize the sounds of speech as separate and discrete from one another, the sounds of natural speech are connected and overlapping.

What Do You Think? REVISITED

- *How many vowels?* An easy way to figure out which vowels exist in English is to take a simple word frame like b_t and see how many different vowels you can set inside to produce a different word: *bit, beet, bet, bait, bat, but, boot, boat, bought, bot, bite, bout.* One vowel that doesn't occur in that frame but does occur in the p_t frame is *put.* That's already thirteen vowels, far more than the five suggested by those in the alphabet.
- *Shaw's "ghoti."* Words in which <gh> is pronounced as [f] include *cough, tough,* and *rough.* A word in which <gh> appears at the beginning is *ghost,* but the pronunciation is not as [f]. No English word beginning with <gh> (there are only a few such as *ghetto, Ghana, gherkin,* and *ghee*) is pronounced like [f]. Shaw was exaggerating.
- *Sounds and letters.* <gh> for the initial sound in *ghost;* <th> initial sound in *thin* and final sound in *path;* <th> initial sound in *then* and final sound in *smooth;* <ph> initial sound in *physics* or *philosophy;* <sh> initial sound in *shoot* and final sound in *wish;* <pn> initial sound in *pneumonia;* <ps> initial sound in *psalm;* <ch> initial sound in *cheese* and *choir;* some of these sounds can be spelled with one letter.
- *Put and putt.* English words that are pronounced and spelled differently but whose spelling difference doesn't correspond to the pronunciation difference include *satin/Satan; bit/bite; lit/light; woman/women.* ∎

Exercises

Practice Exercise

The words in each pair below differ from one another in only a single consonant, and within each pair the different consonant sounds differ in only one or two properties (voicing, manner of articulation, or place of articulation). For each pair, give the IPA symbols for the contrasting consonant sounds and then identify the properties that differentiate the consonants.

Examples: i) fat/vat: f/v (voicing); ii) vat/that: v/ð (place of articulation) iii) wren/red: n/d (manner of articulation)

sin/sing	either/ether
pit/bit	arrive/arise
pit/pick	thief/fief
dig/gig	chief/sheaf
ten/den	rung/young
Dan/Nan	rung/rum
shirk/jerk	climb/crime
many/penny	Sadie/shady

Based on English

3-1. Refer to Tables 3.6 and 3.7 or the inside back cover, and give a phonetic description of the following sounds. For consonants, include voicing and place and manner of articulation. For vowels, include height, a frontness/backness dimension, and (where needed) a tense/lax distinction. *Examples*: [s]—voiceless alveolar fricative; [i]—high front tense vowel

Consonants: [z] [t] [b] [n] [ŋ] [r] [j] [ʃ] [θ] [ð]
Vowels: [ɛ] [æ] [ɔ] [ɪ] [ʊ] [o] [ə] [ɑ] [e] [aj]

3-2. A minimal pair is a set of two words that have the same sounds in the same order, except that one sound differs: *pit* [pɪt] / *bit* [bɪt]; *bell* [bɛl] / *bill* [bɪl]; and *either* [iðər] / *ether* [iθər].

a. For each of the following pairs of English consonants, provide minimal pairs that illustrate their occurrence in initial, medial, and final position. (Examples are given for the first pair.)

		Initial	**Medial**	**Final**
[s]	[z]	sue/zoo	buses/buzzes	peace/peas
[k]	[b]	_____	_____	_____
[t]	[b]	_____	_____	_____
[s]	[t]	_____	_____	_____
[r]	[l]	_____	_____	_____
[m]	[n]	_____	_____	_____

b. For each of these pairs of vowels, cite a minimal pair of words illustrating the contrast.
Example: [u] [æ] *boot/bat.*

[i] [ɪ]; [ɔj] [aj]; [u] [ʊ]; [æ] [e]

3-3. Write out in ordinary spelling the words represented by the following transcriptions. *Examples*: [pɛn] *pen*; [smok] *smoke*; [bənænə] *banana*

[ton] *tone*	[plærər]	[læŋgwəʤ]	[træpt]	[spawts] *pots*
[tʃip] *sheep*	[prɛpəreʃən]	[θwɔrt]	[ðiz] *these*	[ðɪs] *this*
[ʤerəd]	[ʌðərwajz]	[lʌvd] *loved*	[plɛʒər]	[kwɪkli]
[anər]	[ferəlɪstək]	[mənɑrənəs] *means*	[frənɛrək]	[ɛntərprajzɪŋ]

3-4. Below are phonetic transcriptions of the names of popular movies. Write the names using ordinary English spellings. *Example*: for bʌɾi you would write Buddy; for əvitə, Evita; for et majəl, 8 Mile.

ævətar
kəpoɾi
kɪŋ kɑŋ
nɔrθ kʌntri
bætmæn bigɪnz
prajd ən prɛʤədəs
brokbæk mawntən
gʊd najt ən gʊd lʌk
ɪnglɔriəs bæstərds
slʌmdɔg mɪljənɛr
spajɾər mæn *Pla uhr*
hæri paɾər ən ðə hæf blʌd prɪns
ɛnran ðə smartəst gajz ɪn ðə rum
tʃarli ən ðə tʃaklət fæktri / tʃɔklət
ðə kjuriəs kes əv bɛnʤəmən bʌʔən
prɛʃəs best ɑn ðə navəl pʊʃ baj sæfajr
ðə kranəkəlz əv narniə ðə lajən ðə wɪtʃ ən ðə wardrob

3-5. For each word below a broad phonetic transcription is provided, each transcription containing at least one clear error. Identify the mistakes and correct them.

spitting	[spɪtiŋ]
trees	[tris]
Spain	[spajn]
scientific	[sajəntifək]
cutting	[kʊrɪng]
sketchy	[sketʃi]
women	[wɪmɛn]
psychological	[psajkəlɑʤəkəl]
cuddle	[kudəl]
television	[tɛləvɪʒən]

3-6. The transcription below represents one person's reading of a passage about the actor Will Smith (adapted from *Newsweek*, July 7, 1997). The transcription does not represent secondary features such as vowel length or consonant aspiration, and capitalization and punctuation are not represented. Write out the passage using ordinary English spellings, as indicated in the first few lines and the last line.

wɪl smɪθ hæz ə dɑrk ferəl flɔ	Will Smith has a dark, fatal flaw.
ɪts ən əbsɛʃən əv sɔrts	It's an obsession of sorts,
ðə kajnd əv θɪŋ ðæt kən drajv lʌvd	the kind of thing that can drive loved
wʊnz krezi	ones crazy.
ən majt ivən ɪf əlawd tə rʌn əmʌk	
direl ən dəbɪlətet ən ʌðərwajz praməsɪŋ kərir	
hi hets bæd græmər	
prənʌnsieʃən ɛrərz mɪsteks əv ɛni lɪŋgwɪstək sɔrt	
ðe mek hɪm nʌts	
hɪz gərlfrɛnd ði æktrəs ʤedə pɪŋkət noz ət	
əkeʒənəli ɪn ðɛr ʤɛntləst most kærɪŋ we	
ðe traj tə kɔʃən hɪm əbawt ðə sɪriəsnəs əv hɪz əflɪkʃən	
sɪrɪŋ dawn ovər brɛkfəst wʊn mɔrnɪŋ	
ɪn ðɛr spæɪʃ stajəl vɪlə awtsajd ɛle	
pɪŋkət kæsts ə tɛnərəv glæns ɪn hɪz dərɛkʃən	
wat wər jə tɛlɪŋ mi ði ʌðər de ʃi sɛz	
ðæt pipəl se ðə wərd ɔfən lajk ɔf fən wɛn ɪts rili prənawnst ɔf tən	
smɪθ lʊkɪŋ spɔrri ən prapər ɪn ə wajt rælf lɔrɛn polo ʃərt	
wajt swɛtpænts ən najki ɛr ʌp tɛmpoz	
sɛts dawn ə plærər əv bənænə pænkeks wɪθ ə dɪsəpruvɪŋ θʌd	
no no hi sɛz	
ðə rajt we ɪz ɔfən	
pipəl hu prənawns ðə ti ar trajɪŋ tə sawn səfɪstəkerəd	
bət ðe ʤʌst sawn rɔŋ	
pɪŋkət gɪgəlz ðɛn əfɛks ə supərmæn ton əv vɔjs	
ɪts ə nawn ɪts ə vərb	
no ɪts kæptən kərɛkʃən	No, it's Captain Correction.

3-7. The following transcription represents one person's reading of a passage about love potions (adapted from *The Encyclopedia of Things That Never Were*, p. 159). Write out the passage using ordinary English spellings.

æz ðə nem ɪndəkets	As the name indicates,
ðiz poʃənz ar kampawndəd	these potions are compounded
spəsɪfəkli	specifically
tu ətrækt ə sʌbʤɛkt	to attract a subject
hu ɪz rilʌktənt tə sərendər	who is reluctant...
tə wʊnz karnəl dəzajərz	
ðə poʃən me bi hæd ærə prajs frəm ɛni ælkəmɪst	
ɔr ʌðər pərsən skɪld ɪn ðə prɛpəreʃən əv majn tʃɛnʤɪŋ kampawnz	
wɪtʃəz wɪzərdz ən sɔrsərərz	
hu ar ʤɛnrəli nat ɪntrəstəd ɪn lʌv	

ar sʌmtajmz ənwɪlɪŋ tə mænjəfæktʃər ðə poʃənz

ðə pərtʃəsərz onli prabləm me bi ðæt əv pərswerɪŋ

ði abdʒɛkt əv hɪz ɔr hər dəzajər

tə swalo ɛni əv ðə poʃən

ə risənt rɛsəpi fɔr ə lʌv poʃən ɪŋklurəd

dʒɪndʒər sɪnəmən drajd ən grawnd grep sidz

ɔjstər ɛlk æntlər ən tel her frəm ə mel ænəməl

ænd ɛni surəbəl abdʒɛkt frəm ðə pərsən

sʌtʃ æz hɪz ɔr hər nel klɪpɪŋz

3-8. Transcribe each of the following words as you say them in casual speech. (Don't be misled by the spelling; it could be helpful to have someone else pronounce them for you.) *Examples: bed* [bɛd]; *rancid* [rænsəd]; *shnook* [ʃnʊk]

changes	mostly	very	friend	teacher
semantics	system	ready	more	musician
crackers	peanuts	palm	music	photographer
pneumonia	attitude	psalm	fuel	photograph

3-9. Examine the following list of consonants as they are represented in four popular dictionaries (the first three are American, the COD British), and compare the dictionary symbols with the IPA symbols. The abbreviation MWCD stands for *Merriam-Webster's Collegiate Dictionary,* eleventh edition; WNWCD for *Webster's New World College Dictionary,* fourth edition; AHD for *The American Heritage Dictionary of the English Language,* third edition; COD for *The Concise Oxford Dictionary of Current English,* tenth edition.

IPA Symbol	MWCD	WNWCD	AHD	COD
p	p	p	p	p
k	k	k	k	k
θ	th	th	th	θ
ð	<u>th</u>	*th*	*th*	ð
s	s	s	s	s
ʃ	sh	sh	sh	ʃ
ʒ	zh	zh	zh	ʒ
tʃ	ch	ch	ch	tʃ
dʒ	j	j	j	dʒ
ŋ	ŋ	ŋ	ng	ŋ
h	h	h	h	h
j	y	y	y	j

Some symbols used by dictionaries are the IPA symbols, but not all. North American dictionaries tend to prefer their own symbols, while the British dictionary leans strongly toward the IPA. Choose three sounds for which at least one dictionary uses a different symbol from the IPA symbol, and discuss why it might have been chosen.

3-10. Examine the following list of vowels as they are represented in three dictionaries; compare the dictionary symbols with the IPA symbols. (See Exercise 3-9 for identification of the dictionaries.)

IPA Symbol	Words	MWCD	WNWCD	AHD	COD
i	peat, feet	ē	ē	ē	iː
ɪ	pit, bit	i	i	ĭ	ɪ
ɛ	pet, bet	e	e	ĕ	ɛ
e	wait, late	ā	ā	ā	eɪ
æ	pat, bat	a	a	ă	a
ə	soda, it<u>e</u>m	ə	ə	ə	ə
ʌ	putt, love	ə	u	ŭ	ʌ
u	pool, boot	ü	o͞o	o͞o	uː
ʊ	push, put	u̇	oo	o͞o	ʊ
o	boat, sold	ō	o	ō	əʊ
ɔ	port, or	ȯ	ô	ô	ɔː
ɑ	pot, bottle	ä	ä	ŏ	ɒ
aw	cow, pout	au̇	ou	ou	aʊ
aj	buy, tight	ī	ī	ī	ʌɪ
ɔj	boy, toil	ȯi	oi	oi	ɔɪ

In contrast to their practice with consonants, desk dictionaries differ from one another and from the IPA in transcribing vowels. Cite three instances of a difference from the transcription in this book, and discuss the advantages and disadvantages of the dictionary's representation as compared to ours.

3-11. George Bernard Shaw's tongue-in-cheek claim that English spelling is so chaotic that *ghoti* could be pronounced [fɪʃ] 'fish' has been called misleading. That judgment is based on observations like these: <gh> can occur word initially in only a few words (for example, *ghost* and *ghastly*), and then it is always pronounced [g]; only following a vowel in the same syllable (as in *cough* and *tough*) can <gh> be pronounced as [f]; thus, *ghoti* could not be pronounced with an initial [f]. What other generalizations about the English spelling patterns of <gh>, <o>, and <ti> can be used to argue that Shaw's claim is exaggerated?

Especially for Educators and Future Teachers

3-12. Your ESL class complains that English spelling is chaotic. Reading would be easier, they say, if spelling reflected pronunciation. As examples, they claim that *electricity* should be spelled <elektrisity> or <alektrisatee> and *electrical* <elektrikal> or <alektrakal>; likewise, they say, *cats* should be spelled <kats> and *dogs* <dogz>. In what sense could your students' claim be right? On the other hand, what arguments could you offer in support of the view that reading is easier with little or no variation in the spelling of the ELECTRIC morpheme and the 'PLURAL' morpheme even when the pronunciation differs? In other words, what good arguments can you offer for keeping traditional spellings in such cases?

3-13. As a follow-up to the discussion about consistent spelling of the same morpheme in different words even when the pronunciation of that morpheme differs in the words, you realize that native speakers from different regions have different vowel pronunciations. Some have the same pronunciation for *talk* and *tock* (and *walk* and *wok*), while others do not pronounce these pairs alike. What would your student spelling reformers propose to accommodate these pronunciation differences across different groups of speakers?

3-14. Your ESL class notices that you pronounce words like *later*, *fatter*, and *metal* as though they were spelled with <d> instead of <t>—you pronounce them as in *lady*, *ladder*, and *medal*. They ask why you don't pronounce them with the [t] sound of the spelling. What's your explanation?

Other Resources

Internet

 LISU Website: http://www.CengageBrain.com For users of this textbook. Provides updated Internet links as well as supplemental material for students and instructors. Here you will find interactive learning tools.

 International Phonetic Association: http://www.langsci.ucl.ac.uk/ipa/ Here you'll find the most up-to-date version of the IPA, including vowels, consonants, diacritics, suprasegmentals, tones and word accents. You'll also find links to sites where you can download IPA fonts for your word processing programs, as well as information about recordings of the sounds of the IPA.

 UCLA Phonetics Lab Data: http://www.phonetics.ucla.edu/course/chapter1/chapter1.html Here you'll be able to hear all the speech sounds represented in the IPA charts.

 The Sounds of the IPA: http://www.phon.ucl.ac.uk/home/wells/cassette.htm A cassette and CD of the sounds of the International Phonetic Alphabet are available. For ordering information, use the link at the IPA home page or go directly to this website.

 Signal Analysis and Interpretation Laboratory: http://sail.usc.edu/index.php At this site, click on SPAN (Speech Production and Articulation kNowledge Group) for fascinating clips of people pronouncing many sounds of English in American and Indian English. Be sure to click on "Videos" or **http://sail.usc.edu/span/video.php** for images of the tongue and its movement, as well as other features of the vocal tract pronouncing various sounds.

Suggestions for Further Reading

- **Michael Ashby & John Maidment. 2005. *Introducing Phonetic Science*** (Cambridge, UK: Cambridge University Press). A basic treatment with separate chapters on voice, place of articulation, manner of articulation, suprasegmentals, and speaker and hearer, as well as good introductory treatment of instrumental phonetics.
- **Dani Byrd & Toben H. Mintz. 2010. *Discovering Speech, Words, and Mind*** (Chichester: Wiley-Blackwell). An accessible, richly illustrated, and accessible book exploring the speech production and perception and the relationship of speech to language and mind.
- **David Crystal. 2008. *A Dictionary of Linguistics and Phonetics*, 6th ed.** (Oxford: Wiley-Blackwell). A rich source of information about the meanings of terms.
- **Peter B. Denes & Elliot N. Pinson. 1993. *The Speech Chain*, 2nd ed.** (New York: Freeman). An accessible account of the physics and biology of spoken language; includes chapters on

acoustic phonetics, digital processing of speech sounds, speech synthesis, and automatic speech recognition.

- **Peter Ladefoged & Keith Johnson. 2010.** *A Course in Phonetics*, **6th ed**. (Boston: Wadsworth). An excellent introduction to the production mechanisms of speech and the variety of sounds in languages.

- **Peter Ladefoged & Ian Maddieson. 1996.** *The Sounds of the World's Languages* (Malden, MA: Blackwell). An advanced treatment of the articulatory and acoustic phonetics of the various sounds in the languages of the world.

- **Ian R. A. MacKay. 1991.** *Phonetics: The Science of Speech Production*, **2nd ed**. (Boston: Allyn and Bacon). The most complete elementary treatment of all aspects of phonetics; accessible and with excellent illustrations.

- **Ian Maddieson. 1984.** *Patterns of Sound* (Cambridge, UK: Cambridge University Press). An inventory of the sounds in a representative sample of the world's languages; the inventories vary from a low of 11 to a high of 141 sounds.

- **Geoffrey K. Pullum & William A. Ladusaw. 1996.** *Phonetic Symbol Guide*, **2nd ed**. (Chicago: University of Chicago Press). Discusses the various symbols used in the International Phonetic Alphabet (IPA) and by other writers in their treatments of phonetics and phonology; arranged like a dictionary, with each symbol clearly illustrated.

- **Michael Stubbs. 1980.** *Language and Literacy: The Sociolinguistics of Reading and Writing* (London: Routledge). Contains an excellent discussion of the relationship between sounds and spelling in English and other languages; offers insights into the problems facing spelling reform.

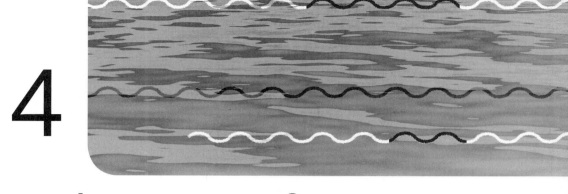

4

Sound Systems of Language: Phonology

What Do You Think?

- You're visiting Paris with your cousin Karen, who takes pride in her mastery of the French language. She's fluent enough to carry on an energetic conversation with a taxi driver taking you to your hotel one evening. You're impressed, and Karen seems delighted. Then, as you arrive at your hotel, the cabbie inquires of Karen whether she's Canadian or American. Crestfallen, she later asks you which characteristics of her pronunciation identified her as an English speaker and why she hasn't been able to eliminate them. What do you say?
- At work you get a message that reads "Call Jules Biker," but you don't know anyone by that name. Trying to remember, you say it aloud and then recognize that it must refer to your friend Jewel Spiker. When you tell Jewel about the misspelling, she can't imagine what accounts for the secretary's perceiving *p* as *b*. Can you explain it?
- Your techie friend Ted claims machines can synthesize speech so well that you can't tell whether you're listening to a real person or not. But you're skeptical and determine to explore the subject. After 15 minutes on the Internet, what can you report to Ted about the quality of speech synthesis?

Introduction: **Sounds in the Mind**

This chapter focuses on the systematic structuring of speech sounds in a language. It examines which phonetic distinctions are significant enough to signal differences in meaning, the relationship between how sounds are stored in the brain and how they are pronounced, and the ways in which sounds are organized within words.

Throughout the chapter, you will find it useful to bear in mind two seemingly obvious points that may help you appreciate the phenomena analyzed here. The first is that, given the human vocal apparatus, words need to be readily pronounceable. The second is that listeners need to perceive different words as different. Unless words and utterances are heard as distinct from one another, understanding another speaker would require mental telepathy. As we'll see, much of what happens in a language's sound patterns seems to be influenced by those simple facts.

It's useful to approach sound systems from the point of view of children acquiring a native language. Imagine the task of an infant listening to utterances made by parents, siblings, and others. From the barrage of utterances encountered in early life, a child must decipher a code of language and learn to speak his or her mother tongue. In addressing children, caregivers in some cultures use slow and careful speech, sometimes called "baby talk," but they don't do it consistently, and not all cultures follow that practice. To make matters more difficult, the utterances children hear are often incomplete, interrupted, or flawed in other ways.

In Chapter 3 we distinguished between the number of letters in a written word and the number of sound segments in its pronunciation. We have taken it for granted that words have a specific number of sound segments. But in their early months children would seem to have no ready access to that information. Attempting to count the number of words in even a few seconds of a conversation or radio broadcast in an unfamiliar language will quickly demonstrate how difficult that task is because words run together in an utterance of any language.

Ifwordswereprintedwithoutspacesbetweenthemtheywouldbeprettytoughtoread.

As you recognize, sorting out the individual words would not be easy. Actually, the task is even more difficult than the run-together words in the printed sentence might suggest because the letters in the sentence above are discrete and separated from one another, but the individual sound segments in spoken words blend together into a continuous stream. To take our writing analogy a step further, imagine attempting to spot the beginning and end points of each letter in a handwritten sample: this challenge would more closely capture the one that infants face in deciphering the code of distinctive sounds in their language. Consider the following:

In cursive writing, the letters of each word are joined.

Although anyone who knows English and can decipher this handwriting could count the letters in each word, there is no clear separation in their visual representation. The letters within a word blend into one another. The same is true of speech; there is no separation between the individual sounds of a word, no beginning or end for most of the individual sounds in the speech stream. Children nevertheless learn the words and sounds of their language quickly and efficiently, a remarkable feat.

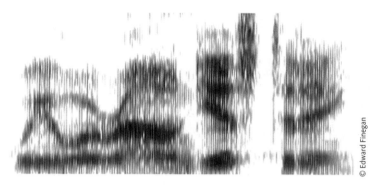

© Edward Finegan

Figure 4.1 Sound Spectrogram of Utterance: Weren't you here yesterday?

If you examine a physical "picture" of a word as made by a sound spectrogram, you can see that there is no separation between the sounds. One reason for the continuity between sound segments is that a segment's phonetic features—for example, voicing and nasalization—do not all begin or end simultaneously. To say the word *twin*, you don't say [t]; then [w]; then [ɪ]; then [n]. Instead, individual phonetic features of one segment may continue into the next segment, and features of an upcoming segment may be anticipated in pronouncing a preceding segment. For example, the rounded lips that characterize the pronunciation of [w] affect the character of the preceding [t] in *twin* (you need only say the words *tin* and *twin* to see that *twin* shows lip rounding for [t], but *tin* doesn't). Note, too, that the nasal character of [n] is anticipated in the vowel [ɪ]. Similarly, the voicing of a voiced sound may be discontinued in anticipation of a following voiceless sound—in saying *lint*, for example, the tail end of [n] will be devoiced in anticipation of the following voiceless [t]. Figure 4.1 presents a spectrogram that illustrates how the utterance *Weren't you here yesterday?* appears acoustically. There isn't any separation between sounds within a word or between one word and the next. In the same way, the acoustic signal picked up by an infant's ears is continuous, and part of a child's task is to sort out words within sentences and sound segments within a word.

Children pass through stages in learning words. Some children appear to take up phrases and clauses in utterances as whole units and later to dissect them into parts (a gestalt approach). Others manage a more analytic approach from the start, taking up words directly and constructing phrases and clauses from them as necessary. All children eventually sort utterances into distinct units of meaning.

We can ask what kind of information a child must learn about the sounds of a word. What is needed just to recognize a word? For one thing, a child must recognize pronunciations of a given word by different people as the same word. To understand speech it is essential to disregard certain voice characteristics and personal particularities of volume, speed, and pitch. For another, a child must observe a word's sound segments and the order in which they occur—for example, that *cat* contains the three sound segments [k, æ, t] in that order. And, of course, in some fashion a child must know the phonological features that characterize each segment—for example, that [k] is a stop and voiceless and velar.

Phonemes and Allophones

Eventually every child also learns that sounds are pronounced differently in different contexts—in other words, that the "same sound" can have more than one pronunciation, or realization. Without being aware of it, English speakers pronounce the words *cop* [kɑp] and *keep* [kip] with different [k] sounds. If you alternately pronounce the two words, focusing on where your tongue touches the roof of your mouth at the very beginning, you'll feel that it touches the velum farther back for *cop* than for *keep*. The reason is simple: [ɑ] in *cop* is a back vowel and [i] in *keep* is a front vowel; in anticipation of the back vowel, [k] is pronounced farther back than when it precedes the front vowel in *keep*.

> **Try It Yourself** Prepare to say *keep*. Then, once your tongue is in position for the initial sound of *keep*, say *cop* instead. You'll find that you must reposition your tongue to do it. If you say *cop* from the initial position for *keep*, it will sound peculiar or foreign. The need to reposition the back of your tongue to achieve a natural pronunciation demonstrates that the initial sounds of *keep* and *cop* are not identical.

As a second example of a sound being pronounced differently in different environments, note the sounds represented by <p> in *pot* and *spot* or *poke* and *spoke*. Hold the back of your hand up to your mouth when saying these word pairs and you'll feel a difference in the puff of air that accompanies the sounds represented by <p>. In *pot* and *poke* it's aspirated, and we represent it as [pʰ]. But after [s], the sound represented by the <p> of *spot* and *spoke* is not aspirated, and we represent it as [p].

> **Try It Yourself** The aspiration accompanying the [pʰ] sound in *pot* and *poke* is strong enough to blow out a lighted match held in front of the mouth. Be careful! The [p] sound following [s] in *spot* and *spoke* is not aspirated and will not blow out a match. Try saying *spot*, *spot*, *spot*, followed by a single *pot*. If everything is positioned correctly, saying *spot* will leave the match burning, but saying *pot* will blow it out.

In discussing [pʰ] and [p], we've noted that they occur in different positions within a word. The list of words below highlights the positions in which aspirated [pʰ] and unaspirated [p] occur.

pot	[pʰɑt]
poker	[pʰokər]
plate	[pʰlet]
spot	[spɑt]
spine	[spajn]
split	[splɪt]

Aspirated [pʰ] occurs at the beginning of words (*pot, poker, plate*) and unaspirated [p] only after [s] (*spot, spine, split*). When you have two sounds and neither can occur where the other one occurs in a word, we say they are in **complementary distribution**.

In the words listed above, aspirated [pʰ] occurs only word initially, unaspirated [p] only after [s]. In all of English, there is no word with an initial unaspirated [p] and no word with [pʰ] after [s] in the same syllable. By definition, then, [pʰ] and [p] are in complementary distribution. And because [pʰ] and [p] do not occur in the same position in a word, they cannot contrast: they cannot be the basis for distinguishing one word from another. In order for [pʰ] and [p] to contrast, there would have to be a pair of words like [pʰɑt] and [pɑt] or [spʰɑt] and [spɑt] with different meanings, but there isn't. English has only [pʰɑt] 'pot' and [spɑt] 'spot.' We conclude that [pʰ] and [p] cannot signal a contrast between English words. Instead, they constitute different realizations of a single unit of the sound system: they are *allophones* of that single unit—the *phoneme* /p/.

Note: To enclose phonemes we have started using slanted lines / / and to enclose allophones we use square brackets [ ]. We will continue this practice, but sometimes we will need to choose one representation or the other when either one would serve. Angled brackets < > enclose letters, not sounds.

A **phoneme** is a structural unit in the sound system of a language, and the set of phonemes in a language is the set of distinctive, or contrastive, sounds it exploits. **Allophones** of a phoneme are realizations of a single structural unit. They cannot create different words, so they are noncontrastive. Native speakers perceive allophones of a phoneme as the same sound despite physical differences in pronunciation. Thus, English speakers regard [pʰ] and [p] as the same sound segment, namely /p/. Likewise for the two [k] sounds of *cop* and *keep*—they appear in complementary distribution (the first before back vowels and the second before front vowels) and could not make contrasting words: they are therefore allophones of the phoneme /k/.

Besides the aspirated and unaspirated allophones of /p/, there is a third voiceless bilabial stop in English, which can occur in words like *mop* and *stop*. This allophone can occur at the end of a word at the end of an utterance, as in *Don't stop!* or *Where's the map?* In this position, the lips may remain closed, resulting in a sound with no audible release; we represent this allophone of /p/ as [p̚]. You may have noted that this fact slightly complicates what we have said because both unaspirated [p] and unreleased [p̚] can occur word finally. They are *not* in complementary distribution. When two phonetically similar sounds such as [p] and [p̚] *can* occur in the same position in a word but cannot form contrasting words, they are said to occur in **free variation**. At the end of an utterance, English speakers can pronounce *map* as [mæp] or [mæp̚] and *stop* as [stɑp] or [stɑp̚]. Both unaspirated [p] and unreleased [p̚] are allophones of /p/, and /p/ therefore has three allophones, all of them voiceless bilabial stops: aspirated [pʰ], as in *pot*; unaspirated [p], as in *map* or *spot*; and unreleased [p̚], as in *Don't stop!* Ditto for aspirated, unaspirated, and unreleased voiceless *alveolar* stops: they are allophones of /t/. Likewise, aspirated, unaspirated, and unreleased *velar* stops are allophones of /k/. To recapitulate, the allophones of a phoneme occur in complementary distribution or free variation; in no case can a change of meaning be signaled by different allophones of the same phoneme.

Distribution of Allophones

It is helpful to view a phoneme as an abstract element in the sound system of a language—a skeletal unit with bones but not a fleshed out pronunciation. How a phoneme will be fleshed out, or realized, depends on its environment. For example, the phoneme /p/ would have the skeletal features *voiceless bilabial stop*, but it would be aspirated in some environments (*pot, pill*), unaspirated in others (*sport, spell*), and sometimes unreleased (*flop, blip*). Its realization can be fully specified only when its position in a word or utterance is known.

We have just seen that particular allophones are determined by where they occur in a word. If you examine the sets of words in Table 4.1, you'll see that the picture is even more interesting. In these words the accent mark (´) indicates the syllable that bears the primary stress (as in *rídicule* versus *ridículous*).

All the words in Table 4.1 have a syllable-initial /p/. In column A primary stress falls on the first syllable, and /p/ is aspirated. In column B, although primary stress does *not* fall on the first syllable, word-initial /p/ is also aspirated. Columns A and B thus demonstrate that /p/ is aspirated *word initially* and elsewhere in a word. In the words of column C, /p/ initiates a stressed non-initial syllable and is aspirated. Thus, /p/ is aspirated [pʰ] when it is word initial or initiates a stressed syllable. The words in column D demonstrate that /p/ is not aspirated when it initiates an unstressed syllable word internally. In sum, the English phoneme /p/ is always aspirated word initially (that is, in both stressed and unstressed syllables—*pérfect* and *perféction*) and within a word when it initiates a stressed syllable (*compúter* and *topógrapher* but not *táper* or *cópious*).

Given these observations, we can be more precise in describing the distribution of the allophones of /p/, taking account of stress patterns. This we do in Table 4.2.

Table 4.1 *Allophones of /p/ in English Words*

A	B	C	D
[pʰ]	[pʰ]	[pʰ]	[p]
pédigree	petúnia	empórium	rápid
pérsonal	patérnal	compúter	émpathy
pérsecute	península	rapídity	competítion
pílgrimage	pecúliar	compétitive	computátional

Table 4.2 *Two Allophones of English /p/*

Phoneme	Allophones	Distribution
/p/	[pʰ]	In syllable-initial position in a stressed syllable and in word-initial position
	[p]	Elsewhere

Contrast the facts about aspirated [pʰ] and unaspirated [p] with the facts about /p/ and /s/. A child aiming to say the word *sat* but saying *pat* instead would fail to observe one of the significant differences in English pronunciation. That's because /p/ and /s/ are distinct phonemes and, as such, can distinguish words, as in these pairs:

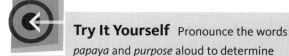

Try It Yourself Pronounce the words *papaya* and *purpose* aloud to determine which of the four occurrences of /p/ are aspirated and which are not. Using the information about the distribution of /p/ allophones as described in Table 4.2, explain their distribution in these two words.

A	B	C	D
/pɪt/ pit	/pʌn/ pun	/læpt/ lapped	/sip/ seep
/sɪt/ sit	/sʌn/ sun	/læst/ last	/sis/ cease

The words in each pair have different meanings but differ by only a single sound. Two words that differ by only a single sound constitute a **minimal pair**. (Note that the distinction depends on *sounds*, not *spelling*.) Minimal pairs are valuable in identifying the contrastive sounds of a language—its phonemes. Each minimal pair above demonstrates that /s/ and /p/ are distinct phonemes of English and not variants of a single phoneme. The articulatory descriptions of /s/ and /p/ show that they differ in both place and manner of articulation.

	/s/	**/p/**
Voicing	-voice	-voice
Place of Articulation	alveolar	bilabial
Manner of Articulation	fricative	stop

To take another example, /s/ and /b/ differ from one another in place and manner of articulation and also in voicing.

	/s/	**/b/**
Voicing	-voice	+voice
Place of Articulation	alveolar	bilabial
Manner of Articulation	fricative	stop

The fact that /s/ (a voiceless alveolar fricative) and /b/ (a voiced bilabial stop) contrast in English (as in the minimal pairs *sat/bat* and *lass/lab*) proves they are distinct phonemes.

Realizations (that is, allophones) of a single phoneme share some phonetic features but differ in at least one feature—for example, voicing (voiced vs. voiceless), aspiration (aspirated vs. unaspirated), manner of articulation (e.g., stop vs. fricative), or place of articulation (e.g., dental vs. alveolar). Consider the words *tap* [tʰæp] and *tab* [tʰæb]. They mean different things, and the difference must be signaled by the only difference in sound, namely, the voicing that differentiates [p] and [b]. In fact, the [p]/[b] distinction serves to differentiate hundreds of English word pairs, including *pat/bat*; *lap/lab*; *cap/cab*; *pit/bit*; and *rope/robe*. And in other sounds of English the voicing feature serves to differentiate thousands more.

The English phonemes /p/ and /b/ contrast in word-initial (*pit/bit*) and word-final (*tap/tab*) position, as we've seen. But sometimes two sounds contrast in some positions but not all. Two sounds are distinctive if they contrast in *any* position. The minimal pair *pit/bit* demonstrates that /p/ and /b/ are distinct English phonemes. The fact that English does not have a /p, b/ contrast in the position following /s/ as in *s_at* or *s_ill* does not undercut the distinctiveness of /p/ and /b/ as separate phonemes. The contrast between them happens not to be exploited in the position following /s/. In other words, there is no pair of words in English like *spat/sbat* or *spill/sbill*. (We return to this point later.)

Now consider the situation of bilabial stops in another language. Korean, like English, has three bilabial stops [pʰ], [p], and [b], as in these words:

[pʰul]	'grass'
[pul]	'fire'
[pəp]	'law'
[mubəp]	'lawlessness'

The minimal pair [pʰul] 'grass' and [pul] 'fire' demonstrates that [pʰ] and [p] contrast in Korean and therefore belong to different phonemes. (In English, as we've seen, they are allophones of a single phoneme.) On the other hand, Korean does *not* have a minimal pair in which [p] contrasts with [b]. In fact, [p] and [b] are in complementary distribution: [b] occurs only between vowels and other voiced segments, as in [mubəp], and [p] never occurs in that environment. This demonstrates that [p] and [b] are allophones of a single phoneme. (Note that the same morpheme meaning 'law' occurs in both [pəp] and [mubəp].)

The diagram in Table 4.3 captures the difference in the phonological systems of English and Korean with respect to these sounds. The same three sounds occur in both languages, but the systematic relationships among them in those languages are different. In English, [pʰ] and [p] are noncontrastive allophones of a single phoneme and therefore cannot signal a meaning difference, but in Korean [pʰ] and [p] are contrastively different sounds—distinct phonemes—and *can* distinguish one word from another (as in [pʰul] 'grass' and [pul] 'fire'). We say

Table 4.3 *Three Sounds of English and Korean Compared*

English Phonemes	Sounds: English and Korean	Korean Phonemes
/p/	[pʰ]	/pʰ/
	[p]	
/b/	[b]	/p/

that voicing is phonemic in English (the *voiced* bilabial stop [b] contrasts with the *voiceless* bilabial stop [p]). Aspiration, however, is *not* phonemic in English (no two English words—and therefore no two English phonemes—differ solely in aspiration). In Korean, on the other hand, the voiced bilabial stop [b] is an allophone of /p/ and occurs regularly and predictably between voiced sounds (as in [mubəp]); hence [b] and [p] cannot distinguish Korean words.

To summarize: in Korean, voicing is not contrastive but aspiration is; in English, voicing is contrastive but aspiration is not.

Phonological Rules and Their Structure

You may be aware that French has nasal vowels, and you may think English lacks them. In fact, English does have nasal vowels, as in the words of column B in Table 4.4. The vowels in those words are pronounced with air passing through the nose, as well as through the mouth, whereas the words in column A have oral vowels (pronounced through the mouth). When you pronounce the words of column B, air from the lungs exits through the nasal passage; when that passage is blocked, the sound of the vowel changes perceptibly.

Try It Yourself Pinch your nose closed while saying the words in Table 4.4. You'll discover that for the words in column A it will make no perceptible difference; for those in column B it will make a striking difference.

If you search out nasal vowels in English words, you'll discover that *all* of them precede a nasal consonant, /m, n, ŋ/. That's another way of saying that the distribution of nasal vowels in English is rule-governed and predictable: English vowels are nasalized before a nasal consonant. Since the distribution is rule-governed, the occurrence of nasal vowels cannot signal a meaning distinction. There is no pair of English words distinguished solely by virtue of one having a nasalized vowel and the other having the same vowel not nasalized. (By contrast, in French and some other languages, nasalization can signal a difference in meaning because its distribution is not predictable by rule.) Two phonetically similar sounds whose distribution with respect to one another is predictable by rule constitute allophones of a single phoneme.

Phonological rules have this general form:

A → B / C ___ D

You can read a rule like this as "A becomes B in the environment following C and preceding D" or, more simply, "A becomes B following C and preceding D." The dash on the right side of the arrow indicates where what is on the left side of the arrow would occur. A, B, C, and D can be specified informally or in terms of phonological features. In cases where it is unnecessary to specify both

Table 4.4 *Oral and Nasal Vowels in English*

A	B
sit	sin
pet	pen
light	lime
brute	broom
sitter	singer

C and D, one of them will be missing. For example, the phonological process of nasalization in English can be represented as follows:

Nasalization Rule
vowel → nasal / ___ nasal
(Vowels are nasalized when they precede nasals.)

As we said earlier, in acquiring a word a child must learn the number of phonemes it contains, what those phonemes are, and the order in which they occur. As the English *cop/keep* alternation shows for the allophones of /k/, and as the *poke/spoke* alternation shows for the allophones of /p/, a child must also learn the rules that determine the particular allophones of a phoneme depending on its position in a word and the character of nearby phonological features such as nasal or voicing or position in a word or syllable. For example, for each word in Table 4.4, a child doesn't have to learn whether its vowel is nasalized or not: the nasalization rule will apply only to the words in Column B because only those words meet the structural conditions specified by the nasalization rule.

The situation for a child acquiring Korean [p] and [b] is parallel to that of an English-speaking child acquiring nasal vowels. Since [p] and [b] never contrast in Korean, they are allophones of a single phoneme and have only a single representation in the lexicon. Of course, speakers must also know the phonological rule that specifies the distribution of the allophones: [b] between vowels (and other voiced sounds) and [p] elsewhere. The alternative to having a single representation in the lexicon for [p] and [b] would require a specific differentiation between these sounds in every word that contains either of them. For example, *pəp* 'law' and *mubəp* 'lawlessness' would have different specifications for [p] and [b]. But to have different specifications for [p] and [b] in the lexicon of a Korean speaker would be equivalent to an English speaker's having different specifications for the different /k/ sounds of *cop* and *keep*, the different /p/ sounds of *poke* and *spoke*, and the different /i/ sounds of *seat* and *seen*. Instead, each phoneme in a language is represented in the lexicon by a single form (called an underlying form, to be discussed shortly). Native speakers internalize the phonological rules specifying the distribution of allophones and automatically apply them wherever the conditions for rule application are satisfied.

Generalizing Phonological Rules

Until now we have considered phonological rules as though they were formulated to apply to particular sound segments. But they are much more general than that. Let's revisit aspiration as it accompanies the realization of /p/ in English words like *poke* and *oppose*:

1. Aspiration Rule for /p/:
   -voice
   bilabial   → aspirated / word initially and initially in stressed syllables
   stop

This rule says that a voiceless bilabial stop is aspirated in specific environments. In *poke* it would prompt aspiration because /p/ occurs word initially, and in *oppose* it would prompt aspiration because /p/ initiates a stressed syllable.

Why a Foreign Accent? Part I

Consider a native speaker of English who knows no French and has been introduced by a French speaker to a neighbor named Pierre. Unlike English speakers, French speakers do not aspirate initial voiceless stops like /p/. So the French speaker introducing Pierre will pronounce his name without aspiration. Despite the fact that the English speaker has *not* heard aspiration in the pronunciation of *Pierre*, he or she will tend to pronounce the name with an aspirated [pʰ] in conformity with the phonological rules of English (but in violation of the French rules). The subconscious application of one's native phonological rules to words in a foreign language contributes significantly to creating a foreign accent and marking someone as a nonnative speaker.

On the flip side, when speaking a foreign language you may fail to make a necessary distinction. English speakers don't have to learn separately for *cop* and *keep* which *k* sound to use because English distinguishes these sounds by rule. But in other languages these two sounds may be distinct phonemes; they may contrast. The IPA represents the initial sound of *cop* by [k] and of *keep* by [c]. In languages like Basque, Malay, and Vietnamese, it is critical to know which velar stop occurs in a word, just as English speakers must know whether /p/ or /t/ occurs: in those languages, [k] and [c] are not distributed by rule and are not predictable. They must be learned for every word that has either one of them.

If, besides words like *poke* and *oppose*, you examine English words with other stop consonants, you'll discover that /t/ and /k/ are aspirated in precisely the same environments in which /p/ is aspirated. Since /p, t, k/ have parallel distributions of aspirated allophones, English would appear to need two additional rules as parallels to the Aspiration Rule for /p/: one for /t/ and another for /k/.

2. Aspiration Rule for /t/:
   -voice
   alveolar → aspirated / word initially and initially in stressed syllables
   stop
3. Aspiration Rule for /k/:
   -voice
   velar → aspirated / word initially and initially in stressed syllables
   stop

But in fact English doesn't need these three parallel rules because the application of these rules exhausts the list of voiceless stops in English. That allows the three processes of aspiration to be captured in a single, more general rule covering /p, t, k/:

English Aspiration Rule
-voice
        → aspirated / word initially and initially in stressed syllables
stop
(Voiceless stops are aspirated in word-initial position and initially in a stressed syllable.)

The English aspiration rule omits place of articulation (bilabial, alveolar, and velar) but maintains the voiceless and stop features. Because the English aspiration rule specifies voiceless stop but not place of articulation, it will apply to all voiceless stops irrespective of their place of articulation. It is thus a more general rule.

The more general a rule, the simpler it is to state using feature notation. Using the features voiceless bilabial stop (instead of /p/) seemed initially to complicate the statement of the Aspiration Rule for /p/. But using features also allowed us eventually to recognize that the Aspiration Rule for /t/ and the Aspiration Rule for /k/ were essentially the same rule as the Aspiration Rule for /p/ and to collapse the three of them into a single—and simpler—rule that any of the individual rules for /p, t, k/. For this reason and others, linguists regard internalized phonological rules as being specified not in terms of phonemes like /p/ and /k/ or allophones such as [p] and [pʰ] but in terms of feature sets such as [-voice] and [stop].

Natural Classes of Sounds

A set of phonemes such as /p, t, k/ (voiceless stops) that can be described using fewer features than would be needed to describe any single member individually is called a **natural class** of sounds. A natural class contains all (and only) the sounds that share a particular set of features. For example, /p, t, k/ constitutes the natural class of voiceless stops in English. These three sounds share the features [-voice] and [stop], and no other sounds in English have only those features. The importance of natural classes is that phonological processes in the world's languages do not operate on individual sounds but on natural classes. As we have just seen, there are not three aspiration rules in English, one each for /p/, /t/, and /k/. Instead, there is an English aspiration rule that applies to the natural class of voiceless stops.

Now consider the set /p, t, k, b, d, g/. This is the natural class of stops. There are no other stops in English, and all the sounds in the set share the feature [stop]. By contrast, the sounds /p, t, k, b, d/ do not constitute a natural class because they share the feature stop, but so does /g/, which is not included. Likewise, /p, t, k, m/ does not constitute a natural class because any feature introduced to specify /m/ would also characterize sounds other than /p, t, k, m/. Adding "nasal" to the description would entail the nasals /n/ and /ŋ/. Adding "bilabial" would entail /b/. Notice, too, that in order to characterize the set /p, t, k, m, n, ŋ/, which includes the voiceless stops and the nasals, we would need an either/or description: either "voiceless stop" *or* "nasal." Because no combination of features uniquely specifies just those six sounds, /p, t, k, m, n, ŋ/ is not a natural class. Thinking about phonological processes, then, we would not expect to find a rule in any language that applies to /p, t, k, b, d/ (which is not a natural class) or /p, t, k, m, n, ŋ/ (which is not a natural class) or any other set of sounds that do not constitute a natural class. Phonological rules operate on natural classes of sounds.

Underlying Forms

Thanks to internalized rules that yield the correct realizations for the phonemes in a given word, children eventually produce entries in their lexicons like those in Table 4.5. Such representations are called **underlying forms**, and we write

Table 4.5 *Underlying and Surface Forms for Six English Words*

Underlying Form	Rule	Surface Form	Written Form
/kʌlər/	aspiration	[kʰʌlər]	color
/bʊk/	none	[bʊk]	book
/bit/	none	[bit]	beet
/ʌp/	none	[ʌp]	up
/spɪn/	nasalization	[spĩn]	spin
/pɪn/	aspiration, nasalization	[pʰĩn]	pin

them between slanted lines, using the notation for phonemes. A **surface form** results from the application of phonological rules to the underlying form and underlies a word's pronunciation. In some examples in Table 4.5, the surface form is the same as the underlying form because no phonological rule (of those discussed in this chapter) is applicable, and we have indicated "none" in the Rule column.

Rule Ordering

One additional rule will illustrate a point about the organization of phonological rules in the internal grammar. Consider the following words:

A	B	A	B
glop	glob	mop	mob
write	ride	treat	treed
rope	robe	clout	cloud
tap	tab	root	rude
lock	log	sack	sag
flack	flag	clock	clog

If you listen attentively while pronouncing these words aloud, you'll notice that the vowels in column B are longer in duration than those in the corresponding words of column A. We represent long vowels with a colon after them, as in [u:]. Since English has no minimal pair such as [pi:t]/[pit] or [bæt]/[bæ:t], vowel length cannot be contrastive in English. Instead, it is predictable, specified by rule. If you look past the spelling, you'll notice that all the words of column A end with a voiceless consonant /p, t, k/, and all the words of column B end in a voiced consonant /b, d, g/. English vowels are lengthened when they precede voiced consonants. Using V to represent vowel, we can state the rule as follows:

Vowel Lengthening Rule (first approximation)
V → V: / ___ stop
                  + voice
(Vowels are lengthened preceding voiced stops.)

As a result of this rule, the following processes take place in English:

æ → æ: / ___ /b/ (as in *tab* versus *tap*)
ɛ → ɛ: / ___ /d/ (as in *bed* versus *bet*)
o → o: / ___ /g/ (as in *brogue* versus *broke*)
aj → a:j   / ___ /d/ (as in *slide* versus *slight*)

(Note that this rule applies to diphthongs like /aj/; in fact, it applies to all English vowels.)

Try It Yourself You may suspect that if a following voiced *stop* lengthens a vowel in English, a following voiced fricative or affricate might have the same effect. Find out by saying these word pairs aloud: *proof/prove*; *ether/either*; *Bruce/bruise*; *fishin'/fission*; *batch/badge*. Does that list illustrate all voiced/voiceless pairs of fricatives and affricates in English? What did you discover about whether vowels are lengthened before voiced fricatives and affricates?

If, besides stops, you examined fricatives and affricates in word pairs such as those given immediately above in Try It Yourself, you'd discover that English vowels are lengthened preceding stops and fricatives and affricates. In fact, English vowels are lengthened before *all* voiced consonants. That means that the vowel lengthening rule can be generalized as follows, where V represents vowel and C represents consonant:

English Vowel Lengthening Rule
V → V: / ___ C
            + voice
(Vowels are lengthened preceding voiced consonants.)

Because English vowel length can be specified by rule, it is predictable and need not be learned individually for each word.

In some languages, vowel length is *not* predictable. It must be learned word by word. For example, Fijian has minimal pairs distinguished only by vowel length. Compare the members of these pairs (in which long vowels are represented by doubling): *oya* meaning 'he, she,' *oyaa* meaning 'that (thing)'; *dredre* 'to laugh,' *dreedree* 'difficult'; *vakariri* 'to boil,' *vakaririi* 'speedily.' Because vowel length in Fijian words cannot be assigned by a phonological rule, it is contrastive, distinctive, phonemic in that language.

Now consider the following pairs of words, paying attention to how the column A pronunciations differ from the corresponding ones in column B. You'll note that the difference is not the one suggested by the spellings <t> and <d>; rather, the difference between the corresponding words is in the length of their vowels. In some varieties of American English, the first vowel in each word of column B is longer than the corresponding vowel of column A.

A	B
writer	rider
bleater	bleeder
rooter	ruder

The medial consonants <t> and <d> in the words above do not represent different pronunciations, and the reason is that in words like those with /t/ and /d/ between vowels, Americans tend to use a tap (or flap) allophone (see Chapter 3). In the pronunciation of medial /t/ and /d/, the tip of the tongue rapidly taps the alveolar ridge. (Go on. Try it!) Because the tap realizations of /t/ and /d/ are identical to one another (and are represented by IPA [ɾ]), the difference of pronunciation that might have resulted from the distinction between /t/ and /d/ is lost, or **neutralized**. The distinction is maintained in *write* [rajt] and *ride* [ra:jd], *bleat* [blit] and *bleed* [bli:d], and *root* [rut] and *rude* [ru:d] but lost when underlying /t/ and /d/ meet the conditions of the tapping rule (as in the examples above). Using V to represent any vowel, the tapping rule for American English can be represented as here:

Tapping Rule

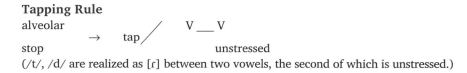

alveolar stop → tap / V __ V unstressed

(/t/, /d/ are realized as [ɾ] between two vowels, the second of which is unstressed.)

An interesting observation to be made here is that, despite the fact that the tapping rule neutralizes the distinction between /t/ and /d/ in this environment, some Americans nevertheless pronounce the column B words differently from those in column A. By applying the tapping rule and the lengthening rule, speakers of American English pronounce the words in column B with a vowel of longer duration even though there is no difference in the pronunciation of the medial consonant, the tap. Here's an explanation for how it may work.

We've described tapping and lengthening rules that may operate on the same words. Let's examine how the rules interact to produce a surface form. Assume that the underlying forms in the lexicon are /rajtər/ for *writer* and /rajdər/ for *rider*. We can represent the derivation of the surface forms as in Table 4.6. (When the form of a word does not meet the requirements of a rule, the rule is not applicable, so we write NA.) From the underlying forms and the application of the two rules in the order shown (first lengthening, then tapping), the surface forms [rajɾər] and [ra:jɾər] are produced. These are the correct realizations of these words for some speakers. Let's call them speakers of dialect A.

If we apply the same rules in the reverse order (first tapping, then lengthening), the realizations will be different. Here's how it works: because the tap sound is voiced, the vowel preceding it is lengthened in both words. As Table 4.7 shows, this is precisely what happens for speakers of another variety of English. Call it dialect B.

The identical surface forms [ra:jɾər] 'writer' and [ra:jɾər] 'rider' that are derived by applying the tapping rule prior to the lengthening rule would not be correct for dialect A. In dialect A, *writer* and *rider* are not pronounced alike. Instead, *rider* has a longer vowel than *writer*. Beginning with the same underlying forms and the

Table 4.6 *Derivation of* Writer *and* Rider *in Dialect A*

	Writer	Rider	
Underlying form	/rajtər/	/rajdər/	(input)
Lengthening rule	NA	applies	
		↓	
Derived form	[rajtər]	[raːjdər]	(output/input)
Tapping rule	applies	applies	
	↓	↓	
Surface form	[rajɾər]	[raːjɾər]	(output)

Table 4.7 *Derivation of* Writer *and* Rider *in Dialect B*

	Writer	Rider	
Underlying form	/rajtər/	/rajdər/	(input)
Tapping rule	applies	applies	
	↓	↓	
Derived form	[rajɾər]	[rajɾər]	(output/input)
Lengthening rule	applies	applies	
	↓	↓	
Surface form	[raːjɾər]	[raːjɾər]	(output)

same two phonological rules, applying them in one order produces correct surface realizations for a specific dialect, and applying them in the other order produces correct surface realizations for a different dialect. Evidence such as this has led some researchers to hypothesize that rule ordering (or an equivalent process) is part of the organization of phonological rules.

Note that the forms resulting from the derivation in Table 4.7, though incorrect in dialect A, are correct in dialect B. This illustrates how speakers of different dialects can share underlying forms and rules but produce different surface forms as a result of applying the rules in different orders. Dialects with lengthening before tapping exhibit different forms of *writer* and *rider* (Table 4.6). Dialects with tapping before lengthening exhibit identical forms with a long vowel (Table 4.7).

Syllables and Syllable Structure

So far we've said little about how sounds are organized within words (although our analyses have presumed a certain organization, as you'll see). We've relied on the obvious fact that segments in a word occur as a sequence *abcdef*, but by no means is that the whole story. When we discussed aspiration, we also relied on the fact that words consist of one or more syllables. We now analyze the structure of syllables, and we'll see that the sounds within a syllable are organized not merely sequentially but also hierarchically.

Syllable isn't a tough notion to grasp intuitively, and there is considerable agreement in counting syllables within words. Probably most readers of this book would agree that *cod* has one syllable, *ahi* two, and *halibut* three. But technical definitions are challenging. Still, there is agreement that a **syllable** is a phonological unit consisting of one or more sounds and that syllables are divided into two parts— an onset and a rhyme. The **rhyme** consists of a peak, or nucleus, and any consonants following it. The **nucleus** is typically a vowel, although certain consonants called sonorants may function as a nucleus. **Sonorants** include nasals ([m, n, ŋ]) and liquids ([r, l]). Consonants that precede the rhyme in a syllable constitute the **onset**. Any consonants following the nucleus as part of the rhyme are the **coda**.

The tree below represents the structure of a syllable as just described.

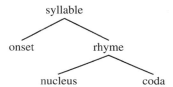

Not every syllable has an onset, and not every rhyme has a coda. That means the only essential element of a syllable is a nucleus. Because a single sound can constitute a syllable and a single syllable can constitute a word, a word can consist of a single vowel—but you already knew that from knowing the words *a* and *I*.

Try It Yourself First, in the lines below from a Shakespearean sonnet, determine whether the rhymed parts of the rhymed words meet the definition of rhyme formulated above. In other words, do these Shakespearean rhymes consist solely of the nucleus and coda of a syllable? *Sometime too hot the eye of heaven shines, / And often is his gold complexion dimm'd; / And every fair from fair sometime declines, / By chance or nature's changing course untrimm'd.*

Table 4.8 gives some English words with one, two, three, and four syllables.

Table 4.8 *English Words Divided into Syllables*

1 Syllable	2 Syllables	3 Syllables	4 Syllables
fat	even	loveliest	respectively
[fæt]	[i-vən]	[lʌv-li-əst]	[ri-spɛk-təv-li]
spin	although	potato	accumulate
[spɪn]	[ɔl-ðo]	[pʰə-tʰe-ɾo]	[ə-kʰjum-jə-let]
through	consists	computer	algebraic
[θru]	[kʰən-sɪsts]	[kʰəm-pʰju-ɾər]	[æl-dʒə-bre-ək]

The trees in the table illustrate the linear and hierarchical syllable structure of the words *fat, even,* and *loveliest*. As an exercise, you are invited to formulate the tree representing the word *respectively*.

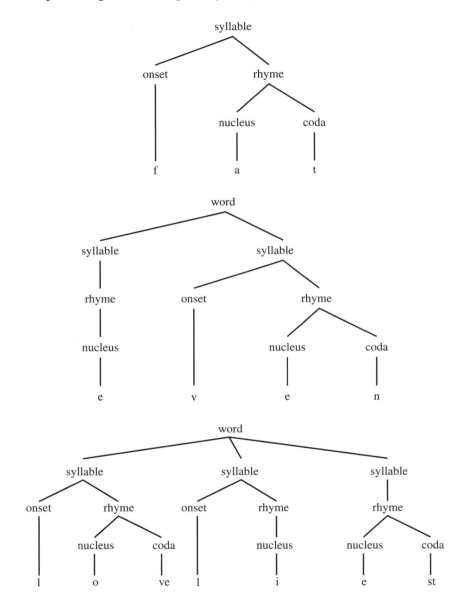

Sequence Constraints

The sequences of sounds permitted in a syllable differ from language to language. Notice in the phrase below that English allows several patterns of consonants (C) and vowels (V) in its syllables. (We use dashes to separate syllables within a word.)

in	a	pre-vi-ous cap-tion
ɪn	ə	pri vi əs kæp ʃən
VC	V	CCV-CV-VC CVC-CVC

In that expression, you can see that English permits VC, V, CCV, CV, and CVC syllable types, and other permissible types occur in monosyllabic words like these:

past	/pæst/	CVCC	queen	/kwin/	CCVC
turned	/tərnd/	CVCCC	squirts	/skwərts/	CCCVCCC

Within a multisyllabic word (e.g., at the end of a syllable that is not word final), fewer coda types are permitted.

Not every language allows so wide a variety of syllable types as English does. The preferred syllable type among the world's languages is a single consonant followed by a single vowel: CV. Other common types are CVC and V. (All three types occur in the illustrative phrase above.) Polynesian languages like Samoan, Tahitian, and Hawaiian have only CV and V syllables. Japanese also allows CV and V syllable types, but it also permits CVC if the second C, the coda, is a nasal. Korean permits V, CV, and CVC syllables. Mandarin permits syllables of the forms V, CV, and (if the coda is [n] or [ŋ]) CVC.

It is not common in the languages of the world to have onset consonant clusters—CC—as in English *try*, *twin*, and *stop*, and it is very uncommon to have onset consonant clusters of more than two consonants—CCC—as in *scream*, *splint*, and *stress*. English itself has a limited range of consonants that can occur as C_1 and C_2 in a two-consonant onset cluster (C_1C_2) and a narrower range in each position of a three-consonant onset cluster. It is no coincidence that all three illustrations (*scream*, *splint*, *stress*) of onset CCC begin with /s/. Furthermore, English three-consonant onset clusters have different constraints from clusters that constitute a coda. Notice, for example, that the word *squirts* /skwərts/ has a three-consonant cluster as the onset and another as the coda. But the onset cluster /skw/ could not occur as a coda, and the coda /rts/ could not occur as an onset; in those syllable roles, they would be impermissible clusters.

The rules that characterize permissible syllable structures in a language are called **sequence constraints** (or **phonotactic constraints**), and they determine what constitutes a possible syllable. As a result of such constraints, there are—besides the words that do exist in a language—thousands more that *do not* exist but could, and thousands upon thousands that *could*

Try It Yourself Cite three English words that have onset clusters of three consonants. What consonant sound do they all begin with? Which sounds occur as C_2? What about C_3? Can you think of any onset clusters that have a different C_2 or C_3? What are they?

Try It Yourself The following forms violate the sequence constraints of English and could not serve as English words: *ptlin*, *brkop*, *tsmot*, *ngam*. Add three more impossible words to the list.

Why a Foreign Accent? Part II

When learning a foreign language whose syllable structure differs from our native tongue, we tend to impose the sequence constraints of our native syllables onto the foreign words. For example, neither Spanish nor Persian permits onset clusters such as /st/ and /sp/, and that makes it a serious challenge for native speakers of Spanish and Persian to say English words like *study* and *speech* as an English speaker would say them. Instead of /stʌdi/ and /spitʃ/, speakers of Spanish and Persian are often heard to say /ɛs-tʌdi/ and /ɛs-pitʃ/, pronunciations that conform to the sequence constraints of their native languages. Similarly, as noted in Chapter 2, the words *baseball* and *strike* have been borrowed into Japanese, and here we note that Japanese speakers pronounce them *beesubooru* and *sutoraiku* in conformity with the CV sequence constraint of their language.

not exist because their syllable structures are not permissible sequences of consonants and vowels in that language. The following would be impossible words in Hawaiian and Japanese because they violate the sequence constraints of those languages: *pat* (CVC), *pleat* (CCVC), and *spa* (CCV).

Stress

An aphorism among American linguists points out that "Not every white house is the White House, and not every black bird is a blackbird." The point is that *stress* patterns can be significant. In pronouncing the phrase *every white house*, relatively strong stress is given to both *white* and *house*: *whíte hóuse*. In referring to the official residence of the U.S. president, relatively strong stress is assigned to *White* but only secondary stress to *House*: *Whíte Hòuse*. The stress pattern assigned to the name of the president's residence matches that in the word *téachèr*: *Whíte Hòuse*. The stress pattern of the same words in the phrase *(every) white hóuse* does not. From the fact that stress can vary and that the meanings of the two expressions differ, it follows that stress can be contrastive in English. Below is a list of several other word pairs. The pairs in column A are distinct words—they constitute noun phrases, comprising an adjective and a noun (as well as an article); the stress patterns of the pairs in column B match the pattern of *téachèr*—they constitute compound nouns.

A	B
a bláck bóard	a bláckbòard
a blúe bírd	a blúebìrd
a hígh cháir	a híghchàir
a réd néck	a rédnèck
a jét pláne	a jétstrèam
an íced téa	an íce crèam
a yéllow jácket (clothing)	a yéllow jàcket (a kind of wasp)

> **Sniglets**
>
> Comedian Rich Hall has compiled lists of "sniglets" for English—words that do not appear in the dictionary but should. Here are a few sniglets and Hall's proposed definitions. Note that sniglets conform to the sequence constraints of English.
>
> *charp* 'the green mutant potato chip found in every bag'
>
> *elbonics* 'the actions of two people maneuvering for one armrest in a movie theater'
>
> *glarpo* 'the juncture of the ear and skull where pencils are stored'
>
> *hozone* 'the place where one sock in every laundry disappears to'
>
> *spibble* 'the metal barrier on a rotary telephone that prevents you from dialing past O'

English has variable stress, not fixed stress, and so do some other languages, including German. Many other languages have fixed stress, with stress assigned regularly to a particular location in words. In Polish and Swahili, stress typically falls on a word's next-to-last syllable (called the penultimate syllable). Czech words carry stress on the first syllable. French words usually carry stress on the last syllable.

> **Try It Yourself** Identify three additional examples of phrase and compound noun pairs like *blúe bírd* and *blúebìrd* in the preceding columns.

Syllables and Stress in Phonological Processes

We saw above that certain phonological rules depend for their formulation on the syllable (aspiration), on stress (tapping), or on both. English aspiration of the voiceless stops /p, t, k/ occurs "word initially and initially in stressed syllables." Such a formulation assumes that in the brain words are organized by syllable. In turn, that means children must have some grasp of how words are organized into syllables. The tapping rule that produces [rajɾər] for *writer* and [mɛɾəl] for *metal* also relies on stress, and by now you can probably imagine that the tapping rule could be formulated in terms of syllables instead of vowel segments, which is how we formulated it in the section on "Rule Ordering" above. Current models of word structure use multiple tiers to accommodate phonologically significant levels, including segments, syllables, and stress, but analyses of that kind lie beyond the scope of this book.

Morphology and Phonology Interaction: Allomorphy

Before leaving the subject of phonology, let's return to the pronunciation of the most productive inflectional suffixes of English, which we briefly introduced at the end of Chapter 2. Some striking regularities in the patterns are worthy of further exploration.

English Plural, Possessive, and Third-Person Singular Morphemes

Regular nouns exhibit several realizations of the plural morpheme, as in *lips* [lɪps], *seeds* [sidz], and *fuses* [fjuzəz]. The surface forms for these realizations of the plural morpheme are called its **allomorphs**. As the following three lists demonstrate, the allomorphs of the plural morpheme are determined by the character of the final sound of the singular stem to which it is attached.

Allomorphs of the English 'Plural' Morpheme

[əz]	[s]	[z]
bus-es	tip-s	tab-s
fus-es	cat-s	seed-s
bush-es	book-s	fig-s
peach-es	whiff-s	car-s
judg-es	birth-s	ray-s

These lists indicate the distributional pattern of the plural realizations in English:

1. [əz] after nouns ending in /s, z, ʃ, ʒ, tʃ, dʒ/ (a natural class called *sibilants*)
2. [s] following all other *voiceless* segments
3. [z] following all other *voiced* segments

We will assume that the underlying form of the plural morpheme is /z/. From this underlying form, all three allomorphs must be derivable by general rules that apply to all regular nouns. From an underlying /z/, a rule such as the following would derive the [əz] allomorph that follows sibilants. (*Note:* + marks a morpheme boundary and # marks a word boundary.)

Schwa Insertion Rule A
/z/ → [əz] / sibilant + __#
(Schwa is inserted before a word-final /z/ that follows a morpheme ending in a sibilant.)

In order to derive the allomorph [s] from the underlying /z/ after voiceless sounds, a rule would be needed that changes the voiced /z/ to [s], reflecting the voiceless final consonant sound of the stem. The process of a sound becoming more like an adjacent sound is called **assimilation**.

Table 4.9 *Derivation of English Plural Nouns*

	Coops	Pieces	Weeds
Underlying forms	/kup+z/	/pis+z/	/wid+z/
Schwa insertion	NA	applies	NA
		↓	
Derived form	[kup+z]	[pis+əz]	[wid+z]
Assimilation	applies	NA	NA
	↓		
Surface form	[kups]	[pisəz]	[widz]

Assimilation Rule A

/z/ → -voice / -voice + __#

(Word-final /z/ is devoiced following a morpheme that ends in a voiceless sound.)

In order to derive the correct forms of all regular plural nouns, the schwa insertion and assimilation rules must have considerable generality, and Table 4.9 illustrates the application of these rules in the nouns *coops, pieces,* and *weeds.* (NA means a rule is not applicable because a condition necessary for it to apply is missing; slanted lines / / represent underlying forms; square brackets [ ] represent forms derived by application of one or more phonological rules.)

These rules for deriving the plural forms of regular nouns have even wider applicability. It turns out that for two other extremely common inflectional morphemes of English—the possessive marker on nouns (*church's, cat's, dog's*) and the third-person singular marker on verbs (*teaches, laughs, swims*)—the distribution of allomorphs parallels the distribution of plural allomorphs.

Possessive Morpheme on Nouns

[s]	for *ship, cat, Jack, puff* . . .
[z]	for *bag, pad, dog, John, arm* . . .
[əz]	for *church, judge, fish* . . .

Third-Person Singular Morpheme on Verbs

[s]	for *laugh, leap, eat, kick* . . .
[z]	for *swim, hurry, lean, crave, see* . . .
[əz]	for *teach, tease, judge, buzz, rush* . . .

We posited /z/ as the underlying form of the plural morpheme, and if we posit /z/ as the underlying phonological form of the possessive morpheme and the third-person singular morpheme, the very same rules that derive the correct allomorphic realizations of the plural morpheme will derive the correct realizations of the possessive morpheme on nouns and of the third-person sin-gular morpheme on verbs. (Unlike plurals, some of which are irregular, all nouns have regular possessive morpheme realizations, and all verbs—except *is, has, says,* and *does*—are regular with respect to the third-person singular morpheme.)

English Past-Tense Morpheme

Going beyond the plural, possessive, and third-person singular morphemes just examined, we see a further parallel for another extremely common English mor-pheme. As you can readily determine, the inflectional morpheme that marks the past tense of regular verbs in English has three realizations:

[t]	for *wish, kiss, talk, strip, preach* . . .
[d]	for *wave, bathe, play, lie, stir, tease, roam, ruin* . . .
[əd]	for *want, wade, wait, hoot, plant, need* . . .

If we posit /d/ as the underlying phonological form of the past-tense mor-pheme, only two rules are needed to derive the past-tense realizations of *all* regular verbs.

Schwa Insertion Rule B
/d/ → [əd] / alveolar stop + __#
(Schwa is inserted preceding a word-final /d/ that follows a morpheme ending in an alveolar stop.)

Assimilation Rule B
/d/ → -voice / -voice + __#
(Word-final /d/ is devoiced following a morpheme that ends in a voiceless segment.)

Notice that, just like the rules for deriving plurals, possessives, and third-person singular allomorphs, the rules for deriving past-tense allomorphs involve schwa insertion and assimilation. Table 4.10 provides derivations of the past-tense forms of the verbs *wave, wish,* and *want* as examples.

Table 4.10 *Derivation of English Past-Tense Verbs*

	Waved	Wished	Wanted
Underlying form	/wev + d/	/wɪʃ + d/	/want + d/
Schwa insertion	NA	NA	applies
			↓
Derived form	[wev + d]	[wɪʃ + d]	[want + əd]
Assimilation	NA	applies	NA
		↓	
Surface form	[wevd]	[wɪʃt]	[wantəd]

Underlying Phonological Form of Morphemes in the Lexicon

A word's phonological shape in the lexicon is called its *underlying form*, and generally speaking it is not the same as the surface or realized form, as we've seen. This section explores the phonological form of words as they are thought to exist in a speaker's mental lexicon.

Consonants The same kinds of phonological processes that operate between a stem and an inflectional suffix (for example, between /trɪp/ and /d/ to produce [tʰrɪpt] 'tripped') also operate between a stem and a derivational morpheme. Think about a child who knows the words *metal* and *medal*. In North American English, the sound that occurs in the middle of both words is not [t] or [d] but [ɾ] (an alveolar tap, created when the tip of the tongue taps quickly against the alveolar ridge as in *pity, later, bladder*).

A child hearing *metal* and *medal* would have entered exactly what he or she heard into the lexicon—for a speaker of American English that would be /mɛɾəl/ (with a tap) in both cases. But after the child had heard someone say a new car was painted *metallic* [mətʰælək] *red* and recognized that *metallic* contains the morpheme METAL and the derivational suffix -IC (as in *atomic* and *sulfuric)*, then the alternate pronunciations of the METAL morpheme ([mɛɾəl] and [mətʰæl]) would have to be reconciled. One task of a language learner is to posit an underlying form that will efficiently yield the right surface forms as output from general phonological rules.

Next consider what happens when the child subsequently hears someone report that the metallic red car's *medallion* is missing from the hood. For *medal*, [mɛɾəl] is heard and for *medallion*, [mədæljən]. What underlying form must be posited once the child recognizes that the morpheme MEDAL occurs in both words?

Assuming the child has recognized METAL as a common element in *metal* and *metallic* and MEDAL as a common element in *medal* and *medallion*, here are the pronunciations that have been observed:

Metal		Medal	
[mɛɾəl]	[mətʰælək]	[mɛɾəl]	[mədæljən]
metal	metallic	medal	medallion

The child could account for the different pronunciations of the morpheme METAL by positing /mɛtæl/ in the lexicon and applying rules that change this underlying form into the realized surface forms. Focusing first on the consonants, an underlying form /mɛtæl/ would require a phonological process that changed /t/ into [ɾ] to yield [mɛɾəl]. (Below you'll see why we've used underlying /æ/.)

For the word *medal* /mɛdæl/, this same rule will be needed to change /d/ into [ɾ] in [mɛɾəl]. The tapping rule formulated earlier would change underlying /t/ and /d/ into [ɾ] between a stressed vowel and an unstressed vowel. Using a somewhat more formal notation, the rule would be:

Tapping Rule

alveolar stop $\rightarrow$ tap / V (+stress) ___ V (-stress)

Slips of the Tongue

In a tribute to England's Queen Victoria, the warden of one of Oxford's colleges aimed to toast "our dear old queen" but is reputed instead to have offered "Three cheers for our queer old dean!" That and many another slip of the tongue ascribed to the Reverend William Archibald Spooner falls into a kettle of speech errors, or slips of the tongue, that have amused and fascinated professional and lay observers for centuries. Accidentally calling the "dear old queen" a "queer old dean" makes clear that the brain/tongue combination has access not just to whole words but separate sound segments—and that's not surprising. In "queer old dean," [kw] and [d] have been interchanged. The onset of the syllable [diːr] 'dear' has been exchanged with the onset of the syllable [kwiːr]. You won't have failed to note that both syllables have the same rhyme, probably helping to prompt the confusion and suggesting that syllable rhymes are also be available to the brain. Other speech errors offer insight into which parts of words besides segments and onsets are accessible to the brain/tongue and therefore susceptible to slips.

In the 1970s, linguist Victoria A. Fromkin analyzed a sizeable collection of speech errors she'd gathered. It is interesting to consider her examples to see what they suggest about which word elements the brain can access in producing speech. Fromkin's examples point definitively to anticipated sound *segments*, as you can see in an example like "alsho share" [ɔlʃo ʃɛr] for *also share* and "reek-long race" for *week-long race*, where an anticipated segment is substituted for a preceding one. Other examples also point to the psychological reality of whole segments, as in "teep a cape" for *keep a tape* and "the nipper is zarrow" for *the zipper is narrow*. Whole segments need not be consonants; they may be vowels, as in *Wang's bibliography* mistakenly called "Wing's babliography" and *dissertation topic* mistakenly pronounced [dɪsərtaʃən tepək]. Strong evidence pointing to the availability of segments comes from examples like "frish gotto" for *fish grotto* and "blake fruid" for *brake fluid*. In "frish gotto," [r] has been extracted from the [gr] cluster and inserted after [f] to create a cluster, while in "blake fruid" the second segment in each cluster has been exchanged for the other.

Beyond individual segments, evidence for access to onsets can be surmised from "brittle island in litany" for *little island in Brittany* and "coat thrutting" for *throat cutting*. The onset of the first syllable in *Brittany* has been interchanged with the onset of the first syllable in *little* ([br] and [l]), and the onset of *throat* has been exchanged with the onset of *cutting* ([θr] and [k]). Evidence for the reality of elements smaller than a segment comes from examples like "glear plue sky" for *clear blue sky*, where only a single feature of the segments is interchanged, while other features remain unchanged. In particular, voicing is interchanged, while place of articulation and manner of articulation remain unaffected. Thus, [p] in "plue" (like [b] in *blue*) remains a bilabial stop but assumes the voicelessness of [k] in *clear*, while [k] in *clear* assumes the voiced feature of [b] in *blue*. In another example, "pig and vat" instead of *big and fat*, only the voicing values of the segments [b] and [f] are interchanged, while their respective places and manners of articulation remain unaltered; thus *big* becomes "pig" and *fat* becomes "vat." Note that in all the speech errors cited here from Professor Fromkin's collection—and this is true more generally—the sequence constraints of the language are honored and segments that don't exist in the language are not produced in error. Speech errors don't create nonpermissible sounds or sound sequences.

It's not surprising that phonological rules that account for one set of facts may also account for other facts. After all, phonological rules apply to *all* morphemes and words that meet the structural description unless they have been specifically blocked from applying. For instance, nouns like *tooth* and *foot* that have irregular plural forms are specifically blocked from taking the regular plural morpheme. If *tooth* and *foot* weren't marked as irregular, adults would say *tooths* and *foots* just as children do before they learn to exempt these morphemes from the regular processes.

Thus, the relationship between the phonological representation of morphemes in the lexicon and their actual realization in speech is mediated by a set of processes that can be represented in phonological rules of significant generality. Not only will *metal* and *medal* be affected by the tapping rule, but so will every word that meets the conditions specified in the rule, including single-morpheme words like *butter*, *city*, *meter*, and *lady*; two-morpheme words like *writer*, *rider*, *raider*, *rooter*; and so on.

Vowels Consider a youngster who knows the words *photograph* and *photographer* ([forəgræf] and [fətʰɑgrəfər]). At some point the youngster posits the entry PHOTOGRAPH in the lexicon to represent the core of these two words. A moment's thought will suggest that an underlying form /fotɑgræf/ would represent the baseline knowledge needed for the pair of alternate realizations. Given the underlying representation /fotɑgræf/ and the surface forms [forəgræf] and [fətʰɑgrəfər] and the recognition that [ə] occurs only in unstressed syllables, a rule that changes unstressed vowels into [ə] would produce the correct vowels.

On the other hand, if /ə/ appeared in the underlying form, no rule could produce the correct surface forms, and here's why. In order to produce the [ɑ] in [fətʰɑgrəfər] from an underlying form /fətəgrəfər/, a rule would need to produce [ɑ] from underlying /ə/. But for the word *photograph*, different rules would be needed to produce [o] from underlying /ə/ in the first syllable and [æ] from underlying /ə/ in the third syllable. This amounts to knowing which vowels exist in the surface realizations and encoding that knowledge in the underlying form along with /ə/, but that is exactly what we assume does not happen. Instead, if we postulate different vowels in the underlying forms, a single rule can derive [ə] from any underlying vowel when it occurs in an unstressed syllable. We can now derive the pronunciations for these words by formulating the rule as follows:

$$
\begin{bmatrix} V \\ \text{-stress} \end{bmatrix} \rightarrow [\text{ə}]
$$

(An unstressed vowel is realized as schwa.)

Of course, a rule that relies on information about stress would require prior assignment of stress, a matter that lies beyond the scope of this chapter.

Until now, we've represented underlying forms essentially as a sequence of phonological segments—for example, /kæt/ for *cat* and /kæt + z/ for *cats*. As some of our rules have suggested, though, representations in terms of segments like /k/ and /t/ are shorthand for a set of phonological *features*, akin to the sequence of bracketed columns below, whose columns represent the segments /k, æ, t/. Entries in the mental lexicon embody information equivalent to that in a feature matrix. (Many treatments of phonology employ a partly different and more abstract set of features from those we use here.) In addition, as we saw earlier, they include information about syllable structure, in this case that /æt/ (shorthand for the features) constitutes the rhyme, /t/ the coda, and /k/ the syllable onset. In producing and comprehending speech, the brain is able to access several levels of phonological representation—not only segments and the features they comprise but syllable structure and more.

$$
\begin{bmatrix} \text{-voice} \\ \text{velar} \\ \text{stop} \end{bmatrix} \quad \begin{bmatrix} \text{low} \\ \text{front} \\ \text{vowel} \end{bmatrix} \quad \begin{bmatrix} \text{-voice} \\ \text{alveolar} \\ \text{stop} \end{bmatrix}
$$

What the Brain Knows in Going from Lexical Entries to Surface Realizations

Let's reexamine the phonological processes from this and an earlier chapter in order to determine which phonological units the brain must access for those processes to operate. For assimilation (e.g., of the plural morpheme /z/ to a stem ending in a voiceless consonant as in *cats* [kæts] or *peaks* [piks]), the relevant phonological unit is the *feature* voice. Likewise for nasalization, aspiration, and lengthening, where the relevant unit again is the phonological *feature*—in these cases, the set of features that constitute a *natural class* (nasals, voiceless stops, voiced consonants). For reduplication (discussed in Chapter 2), the relevant unit is the *syllable*. For rhyming, as in poems, the relevant phonological unit is the *rhyme*, a structural part of the syllable. (For alliteration, as mentioned earlier in the chapter in the section "Syllables and Syllable Structure," the relevant unit is the *onset*, another structural part of the syllable.) In sum, ordinary phonological processes indicate that the brain can access segments, features, syllables, and structural parts of syllables. And there are still other phonological units that the brain can access.

COMPUTERS AND PHONOLOGY

Several decades ago researchers thought it would be a matter of only a few years until computers would be able to recognize speech and synthesize it. (Think of *speech recognition* as turning speech into print and of *speech synthesis* as turning print into speech.) The process is taking longer than anticipated, and the reasons don't lie in limitations of computing power or technology. Despite the fact that children master the phonology of their language at a very young age, researchers have not yet nailed down the extraordinary complexity of the phonological processes that characterize human languages. Phoneticians, phonologists, psycholinguists, and others have not yet sufficiently modeled what humans do when we produce and understand utterances. Natural speech occurs in a continuous stream and cannot be segmented without knowledge of the particular language involved. Just how human beings segment a stream of spoken language into distinct words and recognize the sound segments in those words is not fully understood.

The synthesis of speech by machine has also proved challenging. To understand why, consider the string of sounds that occur in a simple word like *sand*. It might appear straightforward to put together a machine-generated form of /sænd/: produce a voiceless alveolar fricative /s/, then the vowel /æ/, then an alveolar nasal /n/, and finally an alveolar stop /d/. That's overly simple. Notice, to begin with, that the vowel of *sand* differs markedly from the "same" vowel in *hat*: the first is nasalized, the second isn't. If a synthesizer produced the vowel of *hat* in the word *sand*, it would sound artificial. Therein lies one challenge for speech synthesis: how to blend sounds into one another as people do. In ordinary human speech, there is no separation between the sound segments of a word.

But the situation is more complicated. A sound is a bundle of features. The phonological form of *sand* isn't just the segments /s, æ, n, d/ but also the features characterizing each segment:

/s/	/æ/	/n/	/d/
-voice	+voice	+voice	+voice
alveolar	low front	alveolar	alveolar
fricative	vowel	nasal	stop

It's important to recall that the articulation of each feature in a segment does not start and end at the same time as all the other features in that segment. The voicelessness of /s/ doesn't abruptly end and the voicing of /æ/ start at exactly the same split second as the fricative character of /s/ stops and the vowel character of /æ/ begins. The systems of the vocal tract move continuously in the production of even the simplest words, and it is useful to conceptualize a word as a series of vocal gestures in continuous movement from one to the next.

To make artificial speech sound natural, a good deal more about the nature of underlying phonological forms, their surface realizations, and their pronunciations, as well as about how to get from the brain to vocal articulation (and from perceived speech to the brain), must be understood. ■

Summary

- Phonology is the study of the sound systems of languages.
- A phoneme is a unit in the sound system of a language. It is an abstract element, a set of phonological features (e.g., bilabial, stop) having several language-specific predictable realizations (called allophones).
- Two words can differ minimally by virtue of having a single pair of different phonemes (as in *pin/bin* or *tap/tab*).
- Each phoneme comprises a set of allophones. Each allophone is the specific rule-governed and therefore predictable realization of the phoneme in a particular linguistic environment.

- The allophones of a phoneme never contrast but occur in complementary distribution or free variation. Allophones of the same phoneme cannot signal the sole difference in a minimal pair of words with different meanings.
- Two languages can have the same sounds but structure them differently within their systems. Both Korean and English have the sounds [p, pʰ, b]. In English, unaspirated [p] and aspirated [pʰ] are allophones of a single phoneme, while [b] belongs to a different phoneme. In Korean, [pʰ] and [p] are separate phonemes (they contrast), while [b] is the allophone of the phoneme /p/ that occurs between voiced sounds.
- Each simple word in a speaker's lexicon consists of a sequence of phonemes that constitutes the underlying phonological representation of the word. Underlying forms differ from pronunciations and cannot generally be observed in speech directly.
- From the underlying form of a word, the phonological rules of a language specify the allophonic realizations of an underlying segment in accordance with its linguistic environment.
- In acquiring a language, children must uncover the phonological rules of their language and infer efficient, economical underlying forms for lexical entries. Given these underlying forms, the phonological rules of a language will specify the rule-governed features of the surface form.
- Phonological rules may be ordered with respect to one another, with the first applicable rule applying to the underlying form to produce a derived form and the subsequent rules applying in turn to successive derived forms, until the last applicable rule produces a surface form. Two dialects of a language may contain some of the same rules but apply them in a different order, thereby producing different surface forms and different pronunciations.
- The sounds within a word are organized in syllables, and syllables have constituent parts, including a rhyme and an onset. Every syllable must have at least a rhyme, and the rhyme must have at least a nucleus.
- Languages have sequence constraints on the structure of permissible syllable types and the occurrence of particular consonants and vowels within syllable types.
- CV is the most common syllable type in the world's languages. English has an unusually large range of syllable types, including clusters of two and three consonants. The particular consonants that can appear in each position of a cluster are limited or constrained.
- Stress is contrastive in English: "Not every white house is the White House."
- Phonological processes (for example, aspiration and tapping in English) can depend on syllable structure and stress, as well as on a sequence of sound segments.

What Do You Think? REVISITED

- *French cabbie.* Part of the answer to why the cabbie knows Karen is an English speaker probably lies in her use of English allophones instead of French ones.

By general rules, English aspirates initial /p/ sounds, but French doesn't. Ditto for other voiceless stops. Given how many common French words begin with a voiceless stop (*par, pas, pour, tout, très, tu, comme, croire, que*), there's plenty of opportunity for Karen to cue her nonnative status by aspiration. Other rules that are even more subtle and often operate below the level of conscious awareness include those for the length of vowels and consonants, stress patterns, and intonation patterns.

- *Jules Biker.* One explanation is that the /p/ in Jewel Spiker's family name is neutralized in the environment following /s/. In other words, because English does not exploit the /p/-/b/ contrast in that environment, the sounds are pronounced more alike there than elsewhere. While initial /p/ in English is aspirated, initial /b/ is not. In the environment following /s/, as in *Spiker*, /p/ is not aspirated, and the absence of aspiration contributes to easy confusion of /p/ and /b/ in that environment.

- *Techie Ted.* On the Internet, you can quickly discover that speech can be readily synthesized sound for sound, but it is not nearly so easy to achieve a natural connection between sounds within a word or across words, or to create natural-sounding intonation patterns. ■

Exercises

Practice Exercise

A. The words below are given in standard spelling and a broad phonetic transcription. Examine the allomorphic variation in the pronunciation of the underlined morpheme, and provide an underlying form from which the allomorphic variants could be derived by rule. Attend only to the *pronunciation* represented in the transcription, and ignore the spelling. (For this exercise, nasalization has been ignored.)

Example: metal [mɛɾəl]   metallic [mətʰælək] Underlying form: /mɛtæl/

human	[hjumən]	humanity [hjumænəɾi]
courage	[kʰʌrəʤ]	courageous [kʰəreʤəs]
industry	[ɪndəstri]	industrial [ɪndʌstriəl]
medicine	[mɛɾəsən]	medicinal [mədɪsənəl]

B. Transcribe these monosyllabic words and underscore the rhyme in your transcription; then, in order, identify the nucleus, and (if they are present) the onset and coda; if any element is absent, write ∅.

Examples: rest: [r̲ɛst̲] ɛ, r, st   clinched [kl̲ɪntʃt̲] ɪ, kl, ntʃt

sit	spent	squirts
sin	squash	scrunched
scent	sprint	scratched

Based on English

4-1. Consider the following words of English with respect to how the sound represented by <t> is pronounced. For each column, specify the phonetic character of the allophone (how it is pronounced). Is it aspirated? Tapped? Then, as was done in this chapter for the allophones of English /p/, describe the allophones of /t/ and specify their distribution.

A	B	C	D
tougher	standing	later	petunia
talker	still	data	potato
teller	story	petal	return

4-2. Using the monosyllabic English words below, provide a list of ten ordered pairs whose stress pattern indicates they are compounds—that is, with stress as in the examples. It will be helpful to mark the stress pattern on the vowel of each element, using ´ for primary and ` for secondary stress.

Examples: tímezòne, shówhòrse

ball	beam	court	face	fall	free	gear	hand	hat
heart	hold	horse	house	kick	lance	land	lap	life
light	paint	port	rein	ride	road	show	style	table
throw	tide	time	top	way	weight	year	zone	

4-3. Apparently, the following words do not exist in English. Some are "sniglet" candidates (they could exist), but others violate the sequence constraints of English. Identify the potential sniglets, and explain why the others are not permitted. For the potential sniglets, provide an appropriate spelling in the standard orthography.

pɛtribɑr	twɪntʃ	rizənənt
pʌpkəss	blɪbjulə	læktomæŋgjuleʃən
pæŋgəkt	spret	spwənt

4-4.   **a.** Make a list of as many monosyllabic words as you can, each of which represents a different onset of three consonants. *Example*: *spr* in *spread*

   b. Examine the initial clusters you listed in (a) and answer these questions about English:

   Which consonants can occur first in a three-consonant cluster onset?

   Which consonants can occur second in a three-consonant cluster onset?

   Which consonants can occur third in a three-consonant cluster onset?

   Examine your three lists to decide whether or not they constitute natural classes, and provide the name for any that do constitute a natural class.

4-5. Although English makes a contrast between /p/ and /b/ (*pill* versus *bill*), it doesn't exploit the contrast in the environment following /s/ (as in *spell* and *spin*). Hence, there is no pair of words such as /sbɪn/ and /spɪn/.

When a language exploits a distinction in some environments but not all, the potential contrast tends to be neutralized where it isn't exploited. As a consequence, the /p/ of *pill* differs more from the /b/ of *bill* than does the /p/ of *spin* (try distinguishing "spin" from "sbin"). For one thing, the /p/ of *spin* (but not the /p/ of *pill*) lacks aspiration, like the /b/ of *bill*. Thus, a feature that distinguishes /p/ and /b/ elsewhere is not exploited following /s/.

Below are two sets of words. Those in column I contain a contrast that English exploits in that environment but not in the environment of column II. In other words, for the words in column II there cannot be a contrast based on the sound difference represented in the pair of words in the same line in column I.

I	II
i. sit seat	sing ring king
ii. bit beat	here beer peer
iii. hat hate	hang sang rang
iv. tad dad	sting star study
v. cad gad	skill score scam

a. Identify the segment that is likely to prompt different phonetic transcriptions and specify what those transcriptions would be.

b. Characterize the environment (in column II) that supports the neutralization.

c. Based on your knowledge of English phonology (such as its sequence constraints), provide reasons for preferring one of the transcriptions over the other.

4-6. We noted earlier that the English tapping rule could be reformulated in terms of syllables instead of vowel segments. Formulate the tapping rule in terms of syllables and their parts.

4-7. For the words below, identify each syllable's rhyme and nucleus and (where appropriate) onset and coda. *Example*: for *past*, rhyme: *ast*; nucleus: *a*; onset: *p*; coda: *st*

   twin   turned   e-vil   love-lorn   a-tro-cious   re-spec-tive   na-sa-lize

4-8. a. The nasalization rule (in the section on "Phonological Rules and Their Structure") and the assimilation rules A and B (in the "Morphology and Phonology Interaction" section) have the effect of making nearby sounds more alike. In the nasalization rule, which feature spreads from one sound to another sound? Which feature spreads in the assimilation rules?

   b. One way to characterize schwa insertion rules A and B (in the "Morphology and Phonology Interaction" section) is to say they make neighboring sounds dissimilar. Another way to characterize schwa insertion is to say it separates sounds that are very similar. What features do the neighboring sounds share before schwa insertion A? What about schwa insertion B?

c. In light of the rules mentioned in (a) and (b), we can see that some English rules make neighboring sounds more alike, while others make them more dissimilar. Examine these rules carefully and propose an explanation of these competing tendencies. *Hint*: Think about how hard or easy it might be to pronounce these sequences without the rules; think about how hard or easy it might be to perceive these sequences without the rules.

Based on Languages Other Than English

4-9. Fijian has prenasalized stops among its inventory of phonemes. The prenasalized stop [ⁿd] consists of a nasal pronounced immediately before the stop, with which it forms a single sound unit. Consider the following Fijian words as pronounced in fast speech:

vi^{n}di	'to spring up'	dina	'true'
ke^{n}da	'we'	dalo	'taro plant'
tiko	'to stay'	vu^{n}di	'plantain banana'
tutu	'grandfather'	ma^{n}da	'first'
viti	'Fiji'	tina	'mother'
dovu	'sugarcane'	mata	'eye'
do^{n}do	'to stretch out one's hand'	mokiti	'round'
		veve^{n}du	(a type of plant)

On the basis of these data, determine whether [d], [ⁿd], and [t] are allophones of a single phoneme or constitute two or three separate phonemes. If you find that two of them (or all of them) are allophones of a single phoneme, give the rule that describes the distribution of each allophone. If you analyze all three as separate phonemes, justify your answer. (*Note*: In Fijian all syllables end in a vowel.)

4-10. Examine the following words of Tongan, a Polynesian language. (*Note*: In Tongan all syllables end in a vowel.)

tauhi	'to take care'	sino	'body'
sisi	'garland'	totonu	'correct'
motu	'island'	pasi	'to clap'
mosimosi	'to drizzle'	fata	'shelf'
motomoto	'unripe'	movete	'to come apart'
fesi	'to break'	misi	'to dream'

a. On the basis of these data, determine whether [s] and [t] are allophones of a single phoneme in Tongan or are separate phonemes. If you find that they are allophones of the same phoneme, state the rule that describes where each allophone occurs. If you conclude that they are different phonemes, justify your answer.

b. In each of the following Tongan words, one sound has been replaced by a blank. This sound is either [s] or [t]. Without more knowledge of Tongan than you could figure out from the preceding question, is it possible to make an educated guess as to which of these two sounds fits in the blank? If so, provide the sound; if not, explain why.

| _s_ ili | 'fishing net' | fe _t_ e | 'lump' |
| _t_ uku | 'to place' | lama _s_ i | 'to ambush' |

c. In the course of the last century, Tongan borrowed many words from English and adapted them to fit the phonological structure of its words.

kaasete	'gazette'	suu	'shoe'
tisi	'dish'	koniseti	'concert'
sosaieti	'society'	pata	'butter'
salati	'salad'	suka	'sugar'
maasolo	'marshall'	sikaa	'cigar'
sekoni	'second'	taimani	'diamond'

How does the phonemic status of [s] and [t] differ in borrowed words and in native Tongan words? In other words, is the situation the same in these borrowed words? Write an integrated statement about the status of [s] and [t] in Tongan. (*Hint*: Your statement will have to include information about which area of the Tongan vocabulary each part of the rule applies to.)

4-11. The distribution of the sounds [s] and [z] in colloquial Spanish is represented by the following examples in phonetic transcription:

izla	'island'	tʃiste	'joke'
fuersa	'force'	eski	'ski'
peskado	'fish'	riezgo	'risk'
muskulo	'muscle'	fiskal	'fiscal'
sin	'without'	rezvalar	'to slip'
rasko	'I scratch'	dezde	'since'
resto	'remainder'	razgo	'feature'
mizmo	'same'	beizbɔl	'baseball'
espalda	'back'	mas	'more'

Are [s] and [z] distinct phonemes of Spanish or allophones of a single phoneme? If they are distinct phonemes, support your answer. If they are allophones of the same phoneme, specify their distribution.

4-12. Consider the following Russian words. On the basis of this limited list, where does Russian appear to have a contrast between [t] and [d] and where does it appear not to have one? (*Note*: An apostrophe marks a palatalized consonant.)

pərʌxot	'steamboat'	t'ɛlə	'body'
gʌz'ɛtə	'newspaper'	pot	'perspiration'
zapət	'west'	dərʌgoj	'dear'
rat	'glad'	d'ɛlə	'business'
zdan'ijə	'building'	ʃtat	'state'
most	'bridge'	pot	'under'

4-13. In Samoan, words may have two forms, one called "bad speech" (used in informal oratory when addressing peers or kin) and another called "good speech" (used in literary and religious situations and with foreigners). The difference between the two forms can be described by phonological rules. (*Note*: The Samoan words for "good" and "bad" do not carry the same connotations in this case as the English words.)

"bad"	"good"	
taatou	kaakou	'us all'
teine	keiŋe	'girl'
taŋata	kaŋaka	'man'
ŋaŋana	ŋaŋaŋa	'language'
totoŋi	kokoŋi	'price'
nofo	ŋofo	'to stay'
ŋaalue	ŋaalue	'to work'
fono	foŋo	'meeting'

a. Describe the phonological difference between the "bad" and "good" forms. Which is more basic—the "good" form or the "bad" form? (In other words, which one can serve as the underlying form for both forms?)

b. Wherever possible, fill in the blanks in the following table. If it is impossible to know the form of a missing word, explain why.

"bad"	"good"	
manu	_____	'bird'
mate	_____	'dead'
_____	maŋoo	'shark'
_____	kili	'fishing net'
tonu	_____	'correct'
_____	kaŋi	'to cry'

4-14. In German, the sequence of letters <ch> can represent (among other things) either of two sounds: [ç] (a voiceless palatal fricative) or [x] (a voiceless velar fricative). On the basis of the following data, determine whether these two sounds are distinct phonemes or allophones of a single phoneme.

kɛlç	*Kelch*	'cup'
fiçtə	*Fichte*	'fir tree'
knœçl	*Knöchel*	'knuckle'
kɔx	*Koch*	'cook'
tsurɛçt	*zurecht*	'in good order'
vʊxt	*Wucht*	'weight'
çɪrʊrk	*Chirurg*	'surgeon'
nüçtʊrn	*nüchtern*	'sober'
bux	*Buch*	'book'
bərajç	*Bereich*	'scope'
hɛkçən	*Häkchen*	'apostrophe'
bax	*Bach*	'brook'

If [ç] and [x] are distinct phonemes, justify your answer. If they are allophones of the same phoneme, specify their distribution.

4-15. In this chapter you learned that Japanese sequence constraints allow syllables of the forms CV, V, and (when the second C is a nasal) CVC. Using that information, divide the words given in the Japanese vowel chart (Table 3–5) into syllables: *ima* 'now'; *aki* 'autumn'; *buji* 'safe'; *yoru* 'to approach'; *sensei* 'teacher.' Now do the same for the borrowed words *beesubooru* 'baseball' and *sutoraiku* 'strike,' where <ee> and <oo> represent long vowels, not doubled vowels.

4-16. In light of our discussions in this chapter and your experience with some of the preceding exercises, discuss the following quote from Halle and Clements (1983).

> The perception of intelligible speech is . . . determined only in part by the physical signal that strikes our ears. Of equal significance . . . is the contribution made by the perceiver's knowledge of the language in which the utterance is framed. Acts of perception that heavily depend on active contributions from the perceiver's mind are often described as illusions, and the perception of intelligible speech seems . . . to qualify for this description. A central problem of phonetics and phonology is . . . to provide a scientific characterization of this illusion which is at the heart of all human existence.

Especially for Educators and Future Teachers

4-17. As an exercise for a class of middle-school international students studying English, you've asked them to draw up a list of English names for games, and they offer these: *skokey, skwinty, twint, stwink, plopo, splopt, sprats, skretsht, spretched, skwickt, spwint, stwirl, tprash, stpop, frash, quirt, splast, plsats.* You recognize that a few names are not legitimate because they have sequences of *sounds* (not letters) that English doesn't permit. Which are impossible, and what explanation can you give the students about why they are impossible?

4-18. Using phonological terms from this and the previous chapter, identify two characteristic features of "foreign accent" for students represented in the schools of your community. Aim to account for the differences between the way native and nonnative speakers of English pronounce certain accented words. It may help to reflect on (a) inventory of sounds, (b) phonological rules for the distribution of allophones, (c) sequence constraints for sounds.

4-19. Recall from Chapter 3—and perhaps your own experience—that French speakers tend to pronounce the English word *thin* as "sin" and *this* as "zis." From this observation, what can you say about (a) the inventory of French consonants as compared to English ones; and (b) whether or not French uses voicing as a contrastive feature? Finally, what would you predict about how a French student might tend to pronounce the English words *then* and *thick*?

4-20. Focusing on high front vowels, carefully compare the Spanish vowel chart in Table 3.3 with the English vowel chart (inside front cover or Figure 3.4). Relying on those charts and any relevant experience of yours, identify with IPA symbols which pair of distinctive vowels in English you would predict to be challenging for Spanish-speaking students learning English, and explain why. Then cite two minimal pairs of English words (words that are identical except for those vowels) that could prove challenging for those students to perceive and produce.

4-21. In listening to your Spanish-speaking students talking among themselves, you notice among the words borrowed from English that their pronunciation in Spanish differs systematically from their pronunciation in English. For example, the word *scanner* has been borrowed as *escaner* and *slogans* as *eslóganes*. What do these pronunciations suggest about phonotactic constraints on some word-initial consonant clusters in Spanish?

4-22. One of your students returns from a summer visit to Berlin, Paris, and Madrid and tells you that when she listened to the local radio in those cities she could not separate the stream of speech into separate words: it all seemed a blur. She thinks English is different because English words are separate from one another and easy to identify. What would you tell her about the difference she experienced between her ability to hear English words and her inability to sort out those of German, French, and Spanish?

Other Resources

Internet

LISU Website: http://www.CengageBrain.com For users of this textbook. Provides updated Internet links as well as supplemental material for students and instructors. Here you will find interactive learning tools.

Speech on the Web: http://www.acoustics.hut.fi/~slemmett/speech. html If you're interested in hearing synthesized speech, several websites provide examples. The site above is a "jump station," providing links to speech synthesizers and other valuable information. For some of them, you can type in something you wish to hear synthesized. Then, assuming your computer has multimedia capabilities, you can experience state-of-the-art text-to-speech synthesis. Other useful links worth exploring are given below:
- http://www.haskins.yale.edu/featured/heads/syntheis.html
- http://www.ims.uni-stuttgart.de/~moehler/synthspeech/
- http://www.research.ibm.com/tts/

AT&T Labs Text-to-Speech Page: http://www.research.att.com/ ~ttsweb/tts/demo.php This demo illustrates the capabilities of the AT&T

Natural Voices™ speech synthesizer. Type in up to 300 characters and receive an audio file of what you've typed that is compatible with your computer and can be played using your multimedia capabilities. You can choose from among several voices.

 Acapela Text to Speech Demo: **http://www.acapela-group.com/text-to-speech-interactive-demo.html** Another site that allows you to type in what you want and hear it synthesized in several different male and female voices in Arabic, Danish, Dutch, English, and many other languages.

 SpeechLinks: **http://www.speech.cs.cmu.edu/comp.speech/ SpeechLinks.html** This speech technology hyperlinks page contains hundreds of links to projects around the world. Besides links to technical papers (most beyond the reach of beginning students), you'll find links to sites exploring speech recognition and speech synthesis.

 Ladefoged's Concatenative Speech Synthesis: **http://www.phonetics. ucla.edu/vowels/chapter8/chapter8.html** This site provides American, English, and Scottish synthesized text-to-speech renditions of "The North Wind and the Sun were disputing which was the stronger, when a traveler came along wrapped in a warm cloak. They agreed that the one who first succeeded in making the traveler take off his cloak should be considered stronger than the other."

Suggestions for Further Reading

- **Carlos Gussenhoven & Haike Jacobs**. 2005. *Understanding Phonology*, **2nd ed**. (London: Hodder Arnold). An excellent follow-up to this chapter; rich and largely accessible.
- **Bruce Hayes**. 2008. *An Introduction to Phonology* (Malden, MA: Blackwell). An excellent and richly illustrated follow-up to this chapter, relying more heavily on abstract features than we have used here.
- **April McMahon**. 2002. *An Introduction to English Phonology* (Edinburgh: Edinburgh University Press). A very basic, accessible treatment, including the phonology of words and phrases.
- **David Odden**. 2005. *Introducing Phonology* (Cambridge, UK: Cambridge University Press). A basic treatment, with separate chapters on phonetic transcription, allophonic relations, underlying representations, abstractness and psychological reality, and one devoted solely to analyses.

Advanced Reading

Clark et al. (2007) and Carr (1993) are basic textbooks that will be largely accessible to readers who have mastered some phonetics and the phonology of this chapter. The "problem book" by Halle and Clements (1983) covers a broad range of languages and has an excellent introductory chapter going beyond what we have covered; it has chapters on complementary distribution, natural classes, phonological rules, and systems of rules. Roca and Johnson (1999) is an excellent workbook, with scores of problems in a range of languages; it can be used independently or as an accompaniment to *A Course in Phonology* by the same authors. Kaye (1989) is a lively, provocative, and mostly accessible follow-up to this chapter. More specialized treatments are available in Bybee (2002) and Goldsmith (1996). The speech error data are taken from Fromkin (1971), which has a good many more examples and is accessible, at least to eager students.

References

Bybee, Joan. 2002. *Phonology and Language Use* (Cambridge, UK: Cambridge University Press).

Carr, Philip. 1993. *Phonology* (New York: St. Martin's).

Clark, John, Colin Yallop & Janet Fletcher. 2007. *An Introduction to Phonetics and Phonology*, 3rd ed. (Malden, MA: Blackwell).

Fromkin, Victoria A. 1971. "The Non-Anomalous Nature of Anomalous Utterances." *Language* 47, 1: 27-52.

Goldsmith, John A., ed. 1996. *The Handbook of Phonological Theory* (Malden, MA: Blackwell).

Hall, Rich. 1984. *Sniglets* (New York: Collier).

Halle, Morris & G. N. Clements. 1983. *Problem Book in Phonology* (Cambridge, MA: MIT Press).

Kaye, Jonathan. 1989. Phonology: *A Cognitive View* (Hillsdale, NJ: Erlbaum).

Roca, Iggy & Wyn Johnson. 1999. *A Course in Phonology* (Malden, MA: Blackwell).

———. 1999. *A Workbook in Phonology* (Oxford: Blackwell).

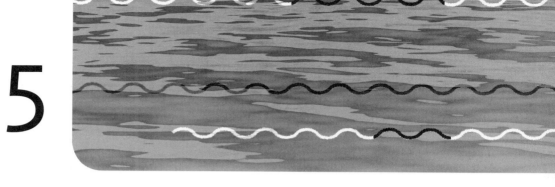

5

The Structure and Function of Phrases and Sentences: Syntax

What Do You Think?

- Your classmate Clarence says we readily produce routine expressions like "What time is it?" and "Fine, thanks" because we hear them so frequently. But he wonders how we produce and understand sentences we've never heard before. What do you think?
- Your sidekick Amber reports that reading Steven Pinker's *The Language Instinct* made her think about ambiguous language. She understands how a word like *bank* can mean 'savings bank' or 'bank of a river' but not how a string of unambiguous words like *new drug combinations* can mean both 'combinations of new drugs' and 'new combinations of (old) drugs.' What's your explanation?
- With the *Los Angeles Times* in hand, reader Ron asks whether it's legitimately grammatical to write, "Not a drop of rain had fallen on Roanoke Island, said John Wilson." He thinks the correct grammatical form is, "John Wilson said not a drop of rain had fallen on Roanoke Island." He wants to know about the correct order of subjects, verbs, and objects. What can you tell him?
- Nerdy Ned expresses annoyance that the grammar checker in his word processor objects to nearly every passive sentence he writes. Instead of *The winning team was hobbled together by a hodgepodge of friends*, the checker recommended *A hodgepodge of friends hobbled together the winning team*. Ned claims the checker assumes all passives are bad, and he disagrees. Is Ned right?

Introduction

In this chapter we explore how words are organized in phrases and sentences. We also explore the relationships between certain kinds of sentence pairs such as actives and passives and declaratives and interrogatives. We investigate how a finite grammar can generate an infinite number of sentences and how the "creative" aspects of producing and understanding novel sentences are normal parts of everyone's competence.

All languages have ways of referring to entities—people, places, things, ideas, events, and so on. The expressions used to refer to entities are noun phrases. The proper nouns *Pam* and *Pennsylvania*, the common nouns *cows* and *calories*, and the personal pronouns *he*, *she*, and *them* are noun phrases. So are more complex expressions such as *Pam's mother*, *that bag of tricks*, *the star of the show*, *a jaunty juggler from Jersey*, and *that feisty federal judge in Massachusetts who was nominated by Nixon in 1972*. All are referring expressions; all are noun phrases.

Languages also have ways of saying something about entities. They have ways of making affirmative and negative statements about entities. They enable speakers to ask questions, issue directives, and so on. Let's illustrate with affirmative statements. In the following sentences, reference is made to an entity and then a predication is made about it.

Referring Expression	Predication
Judge Jensen	married a butcher.
A poltergeist	appeared last night.
Julian	bought an iPad.

In the first example, reference is made to "Judge Jensen," and then something is predicated of her: she "married a butcher."

Try It Yourself In the second example above, reference is made to "a poltergeist" and then a predication is made of it. What's the predication? In "Nerdy Ned disagrees", identify the referent and the predication made of him.

Syntax is the part of grammar that governs the organization of words in phrases and sentences—the sentences speakers utter to make statements, ask questions, give directives, and so on. The study of syntax addresses the structure of sentences and their structural and functional relationships to one another. What are called referring expressions in functional terms are called noun phrases in syntactic terms. From a functional perspective, expressions such as *married a butcher* and *bought an iPad* are predicates or predications; from a syntactic point of view, they're verb phrases. Languages may differ from one another in many ways, but every language has noun phrases that act as referring expressions and verb phrases that act as predicates.

A simple sentence—often called a **clause**—contains a verb and, at a minimum, any other expressions required by the verb as part of its structural characteristics. In Chapter 2 we discussed *subcategories* of verbs and the fact that speakers understand the kinds of clause structure a verb permits. We noted that some verbs require a noun phrase complement, as in *Britney bought a new raincoat*. Others do not allow a noun phrase complement, as in *Danny tripped* or *He fell into the pool*. From a syntactic point of view, the verb is the pivotal element in a clause, and the verb's subcategorization determines the kinds of complements it may have. Verbs may consist of a single word, as with *bought, tripped,* and *fell,* or of several words such as those underlined in *She <u>had hidden</u> the gifts under a tree* and *The physician <u>should have alerted</u> the authorities*.

Constituency

It's essential in analyzing sentences to recognize that they consist not simply of words strung together like beads on a string, one after another, but of organized groups of words called **constituents**. We saw in earlier chapters that words and even syllables have linear and hierarchical organizations, so it shouldn't be surprising to learn that words in a sentence are organized not just in an obvious linear order but also hierarchically.

Consider the sentence *The elusive poltergeist frightened Alison's boyfriend during the night*. Plainly, it's made up of words in a particular order, and each word has sounds associated with it, so we could say that the sentence is made up of sounds (such as /d, u, r, ɪ, ŋ/) or of words (*poltergeist* and *night*). Though accurate to some degree, those analyses would miss a crucial point. Describing that sentence in terms of sounds or words would be akin to describing a shopping mall in terms of steel girders and copper wires—not wrong but beside the point. In any analysis the aim is to identify the *structural units* that are relevant to some purpose or level of organization. To characterize a shopping mall, we'd want to say that it comprises retail shops, restaurants, parking areas, movie theaters, and so on. We could go further and describe the composition of these units and their relationship to one another. In analyzing a sentence, the relevant structural units are its constituents. Thus, in our sentence, we'd want to say that *the elusive poltergeist* and *Alison's boyfriend* are unified in ways that *boyfriend during* and *during the* are not unified; *boyfriend during* and *during the* are not *constituents* of the sentence. For the moment we rely on native speaker intuitions in making those judgments. In the course of this chapter, we'll be more explicit about identifying constituents.

Tree Diagrams

A useful way to represent constituents and their relationships to one another is in a tree diagram. Figure 5.1 represents the fact that the sentence *Harry liked Peeves* consists of two parts: the referring expression *Harry* and the predicate *liked Peeves*. In the tree diagram, S stands for sentence, N for noun or pronoun, and V for verb. Notice that there are two branching **nodes** in the tree. The topmost branching node is labeled S, and the lower node to the right (not labeled for the moment) has two **branches**, one leading to V and the other to N. This same tree diagram could represent other sentences, such as *Harry saw it* in

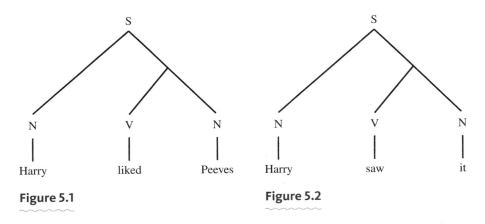

Figure 5.1   **Figure 5.2**

Figure 5.2. (As we'll see later, the trees in Figures 5.1 and 5.2 are simplified for ease of initial presentation.)

Linear Ordering of Constituents The words of every sentence occur in a particular—and obvious—order. To put it simply, sentences are expressed as an ordered sequence of words: *Harry liked Peeves*; *Hillary hated the harp*; *Xavier comes from Xanadu*; and *A plump plumber from Portland poked a poltergeist in the park*.

Hierarchical Ordering of Constituents As is apparent in the tree diagrams of Figures 5.1 and 5.2, there is more to the organization of a sentence than the linear order of its words. Figure 5.1 illustrates that *Harry liked Peeves* contains two constituents—one is *Harry* and the other is *liked Peeves*.

To explore the notion of internal structure a bit further, consider the expression *gullible boys and girls*. It has two possible readings: 'gullible boys and gullible girls' and 'girls and gullible boys.' This ambiguity reflects the fact that *gullible boys and girls* has two possible constituent structures, depending on whether *gullible* modifies *boys and girls* or only *boys*. Notice in the tree diagram of Figure 5.3 that from the highest node there are two branches, representing two constituents. By contrast, Figure 5.4 shows three branches—and thus three constituents—stemming from the highest node. Two observations are worth making. In Figure 5.3 the string *boys and girls* branches from a single node and thus forms a constituent, but the words *gullible* and *boys* do not branch from a single node and thus do not form a constituent. In Figure 5.4, however, the words *gullible* and *boys* do branch from a single node and thus form a constituent, whereas the string *boys and girls* does not branch from a single node and does not form a constituent. Figures 5.3 and 5.4 represent the two possible constituent structures for *gullible boys and girls* and capture the fact that the linear

Try It Yourself Draw tree diagrams that capture the different constituent structures of these ambiguous expressions: 1) *excessive light and heat*; 2) *current information technology*.

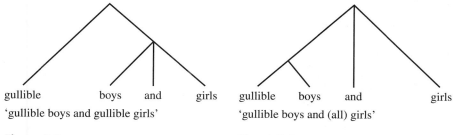

gullible   boys   and   girls   gullible   boys   and   girls

'gullible boys and gullible girls'   'gullible boys and (all) girls'

Figure 5.3   **Figure 5.4**

string has two possible internal organizations—and therefore two readings or interpretations.

Structural Ambiguity Just as structural ambiguity can occur in phrases like *gullible boys and girls*, it can occur in sentences. Examine sentence 1 below.

1. He sold the car to a cousin in Boston.

Although the individual words are not ambiguous, the sentence has more than one possible interpretation, and its ambiguity arises because the linear string of words has two possible constituent structures. We can use brackets to represent the possible constituent structures of sentence 1, as in 2 and 3 below.

2. He sold the car [to [a cousin in Boston]].
3. He sold the car [to a cousin] [in Boston].

Sentence 2 can be paraphrased as in 4 below, but not as in 5 or 6. By contrast, sentence 3 can be paraphrased as in 5 or 6, but not as in 4:

4. It was to a cousin in Boston that he sold the car.
5. It was in Boston that he sold the car to a cousin.
6. In Boston he sold the car to a cousin.

These examples illustrate that the words in a sentence have an internal organization that is not apparent from direct inspection. The linear order—which word is first, second, and so on—is obvious from inspection. But only a speaker of English can recognize constituent structure in an English sentence and the fact that a given string of English words may have more than one possible internal organization.

Major Constituents of Sentences: Noun Phrases and Verb Phrases

Besides their obvious linear order, then, the words in a sentence are organized into constituents that, while not apparent, are nevertheless understood by speakers. Consider the sentence in Figure 5.5, with its two constituents, and more elaborate sentences such as those in Figure 5.6.

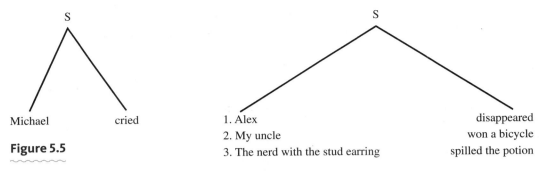

Figure 5.5

Figure 5.6

Noun Phrase and Verb Phrase

Sentences like those we've examined consist of two principal constituents: a noun phrase and a verb phrase, or NP and VP. (These structures correspond roughly to the functional features of referring expression and predicate discussed earlier.) In turn, each noun phrase contains a noun (*Alex, uncle, nerd*) and each verb phrase contains a verb (*disappeared, won, spilled*). As a matter of definition a noun phrase crucially contains a noun as its head, and a verb phrase crucially contains a verb as its head. The **head** of a phrase is its pivotal, central element. Noun phrases and verb phrases can be identified by the slots they fill in the architecture of a sentence and often by their functions. Thus in Figure 5.6, *Alex* in 1, *My uncle* in 2, and *The nerd with the stud earring* in 3 function as referring expressions about which a predication is made. Similarly, *disappeared, won a bicycle*, and *spilled the potion* make predications about a noun phrase.

Noun phrases can also be identified by substitution procedures such as those implied in the list of alternatives to the two-part structure shown in Figure 5.6. For *Alex* we could substitute *My uncle* or *The nerd with the stud earring*. All three are NPs and can occur in these slots: _____ won a bicycle; _____ spilled the potion; _____ disappeared.

In sentence 2 below, the verb phrase is *liked the song*. Unlike the VP of 1, which consists of the single word *vanished*, the VP of 2 contains the verb *liked* and the NP *the song*. Thus a VP may contain a noun phrase. Further, as 3 shows, a verb phrase may also contain a prepositional phrase (*on a bet*).

Noun Phrase	Verb Phrase
1. [Tina]	[vanished]
2. [Genaro]	[liked the song]
3. [The neighbor with the iPad]	[won a bike on a bet]

The noun phrases in the sentences above include *Tina, Genaro, the neighbor, the iPad, the song, a bike*, and *a bet*. A word string you can insert in the slots below would be an NP:

She enjoyed talking about _____.

Invariably, _____ upset her.

Inserted into either slot, the following expressions would produce well-formed English sentences and are therefore NPs; in each case, the *head noun* is italicized.

wild *wolverines*	that *loyalty* to his latest love
the *weather*	his *resolve* to reside in Riverdale
her yellow *yarn*	Wally's foolish *wager*
the *nitwit* who nicked her necklace	a cynical *cyclist* from Cincinnati

Notice, too, that a noun phrase can be a pronoun:

She enjoyed talking about *it/him/them/us.*

Invariably, *it/they/we* upset her.

Noun phrases and pronouns have the same distribution in sentences; where a noun phrase can occur, a pronoun can occur instead. Thus, pronouns are a kind of noun phrase (and a pronoun may be the head of a noun phrase). Later, we'll see how to exploit this fact in determining noun-phrase constituency.

Verb phrases can be identified using similar substitution procedures. Consider the sentence *Lou cried*, in which *cried* constitutes the verb phrase. Among many others, the following strings can substitute for *cried* in that sentence. They thus fit the frame and are verb phrases (the *head* in each verb phrase is italicized):

Lou
- *fell.*
- *lost* the race.
- *won* a prize for her success in the tournament.

To this point, we have seen two major constituents of a sentence: noun phrase and verb phrase.

Active and Passive Sentences

Regardless of how many words an NP contains, it may operate as a constituent in a sentence. Even elaborate NPs such as *the neighbor with the iPad* or *what she hoped to receive for her twenty-first birthday* are syntactic units, just like simple NPs such as *she, Genaro,* and *wolverines.* To see more clearly what is meant by a syntactic unit—a constituent—consider the sentences below. In each pair, the first sentence is characterized as "active," the second as "passive" (about which we'll explain more later):

1a. The coach blamed the referee. (*Active*)
   b. The referee was blamed by the coach. (*Passive*)

2a. Zimmershied discovered that dinosaur skeleton. (*Active*)
   b. That dinosaur skeleton was discovered by Zimmershied. (*Passive*)

3a. A jaunty judge from Jersey fined a plump plumber from Portland. (*Active*)
   b. A plump plumber from Portland was fined by a jaunty judge from Jersey. (*Passive*)

Try It Yourself Mimicking the pattern displayed in the sentence pairs above, provide the passive counterpart to *Dean Kamen invented the heart stent and the Segway* and the active counterpart to *The pantry must be stocked by husbands who stay at home and mind the kids.* Now try to specify as explicitly as you can the implicit knowledge of sentence constituents you relied on in order to form those counterpart sentences.

As speakers of English, we implicitly know how passive and active sentences are related to one another (even if we don't know the terms "active" and "passive"), but it is not possible to make that knowledge explicit without relying on the notion of constituency. For example, without knowledge of constituents, we might characterize the operation that relates sentences 1a and 1b above as follows: "To transform an active sentence to its passive counterpart, interchange the first two words (*the coach*) with the last two (*the referee*)." For present purposes, we ignore the additional steps needed, including introducing the verb *was* and the preposition *by*, but in a complete statement of the operation those steps would have to be specified as well. The operation of exchanging the first two and last two words produces the well-formed string 1b when applied to 1a. But if the same operation were applied to 2a, it would produce not 2b but the ill-formed string, "Dinosaur skeleton was that by Zimmershied discovered," and if applied to 3a would likewise produce an ill-formed string. Clearly, what speakers know about the relationship between active and passive counterparts involves something other than counting words. Implicitly, speakers know that active and passive sentences are related by a structure-dependent operation that interchanges noun phrase *constituents*, irrespective of the number of words contained in them.

Refer again to the constituents that get interchanged in the active/passive sentence pairs of 1, 2, and 3 above, and note that the word strings in each set below in 4 and 5 must share a structural property because the strings function similarly in those sentence pairs:

4. the coach; Zimmershied; a jaunty judge from Jersey

5. the referee; that dinosaur skeleton; a plump plumber from Portland

The NPs in 4 and 5 move *as units* in the operation that relates active and passive sentences: they are *constituents*.

Testing Constituency

For emphasis, we say it again: a sentence is not merely an ordered string of individual words but a structured string of words grouped into constituents that function as syntactic units. The tree diagrams earlier in this chapter relied on informal notions in determining constituency. Now we describe three kinds of tests that can be used for that purpose.

Movement In examining active and passive sentences, we relied on movement to identify noun phrase constituents. Any group of words that could be moved in transforming a sentence between active and passive we regarded as a constituent. We also relied on movement in paraphrasing the earlier sentences that presented structural ambiguity. In exploring the ambiguity of *He sold the car to a cousin in Boston*, we noted that one reading could be paraphrased as *In Boston he sold the car to a cousin*. Moving *in Boston* to the front of its sentence demonstrated that it functions as a syntactic unit—a constituent. Generally speaking, then, we say that a string of words that can be moved in a syntactic operation functions as a unit and is a constituent.

Substitution Substitution of pro-forms offers another method of identifying constituents. When a pro-form (for example, a pronoun or a "pro-verb") can substitute for a string of words in a sentence, that string is a constituent. In the sentences below, the substitution of a pro-form (underlined and **boldfaced**) for a preceding underlined string provides evidence that the preceding string is a constituent.

a. *Josh gained <u>a lead</u>, and Beth gained <u>**one**</u>, too.* (Thus, *a lead* is a constituent.)

b. *Josh gained <u>a huge lead</u>, and Beth gained <u>**one**</u>, too.* (Thus, *a huge lead* is a constituent.)

c. *Josh <u>gained a huge lead</u>, and Beth <u>**did**</u>, too.* (Thus, *gained a huge lead* is a constituent.)

Try It Yourself Because not every string of words in a sentence is a constituent, you'll discover strings for which pro-forms *cannot* be substituted. In sentence b above, attempt to identify a pro-form for these strings: *a huge*; *Josh gained*; and *gained a*. What do your results indicate about the status of those strings as constituents?

Coordination In identifying constituents a third test involves coordination. Because, generally, only constituents of the same kind can be conjoined by a coordinator such as *and* and *or*, coordination can offer evidence of constituency. Thus, in sentences like those below, the underlined conjoined strings are constituents (of the same kind).

a. For her birthday, Vanessa was given <u>a fancy new car</u> and <u>a thirty-foot sailboat</u>. (NPs)

b. Smokey <u>ran into the house</u> and <u>ate her dinner</u>. (VPs)

If you apply the tests described above, you'll uncover more constituents in a sentence than you might expect. Exploring levels of constituency has proven to be a productive enterprise for theories of syntax, as has comparing constituent structures across languages. Further exploration of levels of constituency lies beyond our scope, but we will occasionally introduce additional constituents, usually without explicitly justifying them.

Phrase-Structure Expansions

Expanding Noun Phrase

Relying on the analysis of categories (parts of speech) in Chapter 2, we can now characterize and exemplify certain NP types:

> Noun (N): *Karen, oracles, justice, swimming*
>
> Determiner (Det) + Noun: *that amulet, a potion, some gnomes, her coach*
>
> Determiner + Noun + Prepositional Phrase (PP): *the book on the table, that rise in prices, the marketplace of ideas, her plumber in Portland*
>
> Determiner + Adjective (A) + Noun: *an ancient oracle, these hellish precincts, my first Harley, a jaunty judge*

These various NP patterns can be represented by **phrase-structure expansion rules** such as the following:

> 1. NP → N (NP consists of N)
> 2. NP → Det N (NP consists of Det + N)
> 3. NP → Det N PP (NP consists of Det + N + PP)
> 4. NP → Det A N (NP consists of Det + A + N)

These four expansions can be merged into a single rule. N is the *only* constituent required in every NP expansion because every NP must contain a noun as its head. Other elements are placed in parentheses to represent their optionality. The merged rule looks like this:

> 5. NP → (Det) (A) **N** (PP)

Besides the four expansions (1–4) that we aimed to capture, rule 5 represents other expansions. Because Det, A, and PP are optional, we can expand NP not only as in 1, 2, 3, and 4 above, but also as in 6 and 7:

> 6. NP → A **N**
> 7. NP → Det A **N** PP

Rule 5 thus represents expansions we did not set out to capture. If English has well-formed NP structures consisting of A N (as in 6) and of Det A N PP (as in 7) and of any other expansions 5 would represent, then 5 is valid. Otherwise, it would need to be revised to exclude any impermissible structures.

As a matter of fact, some English NPs comprise an adjective and a noun—A N (*tall trees, ordinary superheroes, natural grace, youthful instructors*)—while others consist of Det A N PP (*his sorry life on the sidelines, the huge whale on the beach, those whimsical clouds in the sky*). An advantage of formalisms like rule 5 is that they often entail unanticipated claims that can be checked against other data and thus provide a test of their own validity.

Expanding Prepositional Phrase

PP stands for prepositional phrase, such as *in the car, from Xanadu, to a cousin, with the iPad*, and *by a jaunty judge*. PPs consist of a P (preposition) as head and typically an NP (noun phrase), so the phrase-structure expansion for PP is:

PP → **P** NP

If NP is treated as optional, as in *It fell off (the table)*, it would appear in parenthesis: PP → **P** (NP)

Expanding Sentence and Verb Phrase

That sentences and clauses have two basic constituents can be captured in this phrase-structure expansion:

S → NP VP

Every expansion rule can generate a tree diagram, and S → NP VP would generate this tree:

Having already explored expansions of NP, we turn now to the internal structure of VP. The following expansions of our frame for identifying VPs reveal that the structures on the right (those following *Lou*) are VPs, and constituents of the VP are labeled beneath them.

```
             _VP_
1. Lou       won
              V

           _____VP_____
2. Lou     won a bicycle
            V    NP

           _____VP_____
3. Lou     won the bike in May
            V    NP     PP
```

Sentences 1, 2, and 3 above indicate three VP expansions:

VP → **V**

VP → **V** NP

VP → **V** NP PP

V is the only constituent that occurs in all of these rules. It is the essential category in the VP constituent—its head. As is clear from sentence 1 above, NP and PP are optional constituents of VP. Using parentheses for optional elements, the three expansions above can be combined into a single phrase-structure rule:

VP → **V** (NP) (PP)

Just as we discovered unanticipated structural patterns when we merged four expansions of NP into a single rule, so the combined rule for VP generates an unanticipated V PP structure, which is not represented among sentences 1, 2, and 3, the basis for our VP expansion rule. We can check the validity of V PP as an expansion and see that it represents the internal structure of sentences like *(Finian) played in the yard, (Dana) raced through the exam,* and *(Pat) flew to Ballina,* the last of which is illustrated below.

```
            _____VP_____
Pat     flew to Ballina
          V       PP
```

Phrase-Structure Expansions and Tree Diagrams

We have formulated four phrase-structure expansion rules:

S   → NP VP
NP → (Det) (A) **N** (PP)
VP → **V** (NP) (PP)
PP → **P** (NP)

These represent the fact that S comprises NP and VP; NP contains N; VP contains V; and PP contains P. According to these phrase-structure expansion rules, all other possible constituents are optional.

The following tree diagram is one representation of our expansion rules:

It is the simplest structure generated by our rules and would represent sentences like *Lou disappeared* and *That stinks.* Now consider the more complex structure given in Figure 5.7, where *The runner from Butte won a prize at the fair* is an illustrative sentence for the structure. It is clear that our four expansion rules can represent structurally simple or structurally elaborate sentences.

Try It Yourself Limiting yourself to the four expansion rules used to produce the tree in Figure 5.7, draw a tree that would represent this sentence: *The runner from Butte won a car with a siren.* Before starting, ask yourself whether *a prize at the fair* is a constituent of the sentence in Figure 5.7, and take care to note the structural similarity of *the runner from Butte* and *a car with a siren.*

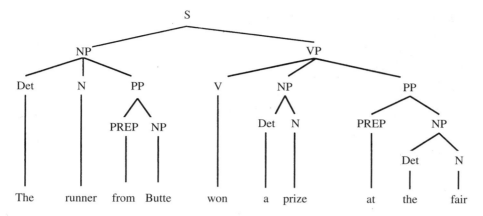

Figure 5.7

Grammatical Relations: Subject, Direct Object, and Others

Some traditional English grammar treatments offer notional definitions of subject (as doer of the action, for example) and object (receiver of the action). Others rely on structure and define a subject as the sentence constituent that a present-tense verb agrees with (for example, in *she sings* versus *they sing*). For various reasons, these and similar definitions leave a lot to be desired.

Using constituent structure, however, does enable analysts to define subject and direct object more precisely.

Try It Yourself Try identifying the doer and receiver of the action in these sentences. Then, relying on the agreement criterion mentioned here, identify the subject in each. 1) *New businesses and family-run businesses are often tiny.* 2) *It isn't known how many members the group has.* 3) *Landlords of buildings aim to burn fuel sparingly.* 4) *One consequence of the recession among 18- to 30-year olds living in New York is the availability of cheaper small apartments.* 5) *A sensitive camper taking this medicine may experience allergic reactions.* Do you regard these criteria as reliable?

Immediate Dominance

In Figure 5.8, the circled NP is directly under the S node, the boxed NP directly under the VP node, and the VP node directly under the S node. When a node is directly under another node—that is, when there are no intervening nodes—we say it is *immediately dominated* by that other node. Thus in Figure 5.8, V is immediately dominated by VP; the circled NP immediately dominated by S; the boxed NP immediately dominated by VP; and both VP and the circled NP immediately dominated by S.

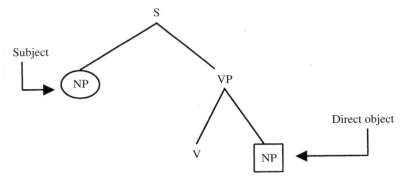

Figure 5.8

Subject and Direct Object

In English, **subject** is defined as the NP that is immediately dominated by S. In our diagram, the circled NP is immediately dominated by S and is thus the *subject*. **Direct object** is defined as an NP that is immediately dominated by VP. In Figure 5.8 it is the boxed NP. Because NP is an optional element in the expansion of VP, not every sentence will have a direct object.

Transitive and Intransitive Recall from Chapter 2 that a sentence lacking a direct object contains what is called an *intransitive* verb. Examples are *cry, laugh,* and *disappear,* all of which may occur without a direct object, as in *Hillary cried, Geoff laughed,* and *The jewels disappeared.* By contrast, verbs like *make, buy,* and *find* take a direct object and are called *transitive* verbs, as in *made a potion, buy a Harley,* and *found a penny.* While some verbs may be either transitive or intransitive, as exemplified in the first three sentence pairs below, others are only transitive (as in 4) or only intransitive (as in 5). (We use an asterisk to mark an ungrammatical structure, one that doesn't occur in the language.)

Try It Yourself Provide a sentence with a verb that can *only* be transitive and another with a verb that can *only* be intransitive. Then provide a pair of sentences in which the same verb is used once in a transitive and once in an intransitive structure.

	Intransitive	**Transitive**
1.	Josh won.	Josh won a prize.
2.	Taylor sings.	Taylor sings lullabies.
3.	Suze studied at Oxford.	Suze studied economics at Oxford.
4.	*Nicole frightened.	Nicole frightened the kittens.
5.	Miguel reappeared.	*Miguel reappeared the dishes.

Given the pivotal role of the verb in determining the structure of a clause, a verb's subcategorization as transitive or intransitive determines whether its clause may contain an object or not.

Grammatical Relations

Grammatical relation is the term used to capture the syntactic, or structural, relationship in a clause between an NP and the verb. In other words, grammatical relations indicate the syntactic role that an NP plays in its clause, and that role cannot be equated with anything else, including meaning. Besides the grammatical relations of subject and direct object, an NP in a clause can be an **indirect object**, an **oblique**, or a **possessor**. *Oblique* is the term for NPs that are not subject, object, or indirect object; in English an oblique is realized as the object of a preposition (*The vampire pointed to his teeth*). *Possessor* is the term for entities showing possession (*Josh's new Mini*). (Indirect objects are analyzed in exercises 5-5 and 5-6.)

Passive Sentences and Structure Dependence

Having defined subject and direct object in structural terms, we now return to a syntactic relationship examined earlier. Relying on the grammatical relations of subject and direct object, we can reformulate our description of the relationship between active and passive sentences as follows:

> To form a passive sentence from an active one, interchange the subject NP with the direct object NP. (As before, provision must be made for the preposition *by* and a form of the verb BE.)

Figure 5.9 provides an example:

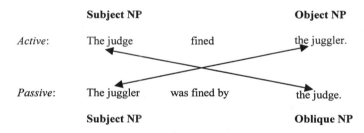

Figure 5.9

You can see that the direct object of the active sentence appears as the subject of the passive sentence, and the subject of the active sentence appears as an oblique (in a prepositional *by*-phrase) in the passive sentence.

Surface Structures and Underlying Structures

As we have seen in several ways, we understand considerably more about the architecture of sentences than is apparent in the linear order of their words. In fact, not only do we have implicit knowledge of constituent structure within the linear string of words in a sentence—what we call its **surface structure**—but we often perceive or understand constituents that are unexpressed in the linear string. For example, we readily understand the meaning of *didn't* in *Lisa won a* *prize, but Larry didn't,* as in option 5 below. But to understand that sentence requires implicit knowledge of syntactic operations:

Lisa won a prize, but Larry
1. didn't.
2. didn't care.
3. didn't tell Sarah.
4. didn't congratulate her.
5. didn't win a prize.

While the list of possible sentences following this pattern is endless, English speakers know that the only legitimate interpretation of 1 is 5 and that sentences 2 through 4 are not possible interpretations of 1.

To help explain this, recall that in Chapter 4 we postulated underlying forms of sounds and morphemes. Well, one way to account for implicit knowledge about sentence structure is to posit **underlying structures** for syntax. For instance, we could represent the meaning of sentence 1 by positing an underlying structure something like *Lisa won a prize, but Larry didn't win a prize.* If we assumed such an underlying structure and certain syntactic operations that deleted the repeated occurrence of the constituent *win a prize,* we would have a mechanism for understanding how English speakers know that only 5 above satisfies the meaning of 1.

Syntactic Operations: Question Formation and the Auxiliary

Among examples of syntactic operations in English, we have examined movement (as in passivization) and deletion (as in *Lisa won a prize, but Larry didn't*). Now we analyze other examples.

English has two principal kinds of questions. Yes/no questions are those that can be answered with a reply of yes or no, as in *Was it a candid discussion?* Information questions, on the other hand, include a WH-word like *who, what,* or *when* and require more than a simple yes or no reply.

Yes/No Questions Examine the statements below and their corresponding yes/no questions.

1. Suze <u>will</u> earn a fair wage.

   <u>Will</u> Suze earn a fair wage?

2. Last year's winner of the Tour de France <u>was</u> leading the pack on Tuesday.

   <u>Was</u> last year's winner of the Tour de France leading the pack on Tuesday?

If you compare the matched declarative and interrogative sentences, you'll see that the question requires moving the auxiliary verb of the statement to a position before the subject NP. Verbs such as *will* in 1 and *was* in 2 are called **auxiliary verbs**, or auxiliaries, and can be moved in front of a subject NP to form a question; auxiliary verbs are distinguished from main verbs such as *earn* in 1 and *lead* in 2 above and *study* in 3 and *hurt* in 4 below.

Notice that yes/no questions contain an auxiliary even when the corresponding declarative sentence does not, as 3 and 4 show:

3. Alvin *studied* journalism in college.

   Did Alvin *study* journalism in college?

4. Inflation always *hurts* the poor.

  Does inflation always *hurt* the poor?

In addition, an auxiliary usually must appear in the surface structure of negative sentences, as in the examples below.

5. Alvin *studied* journalism in college.

  Alvin *didn't study* journalism *in college.*

Auxiliaries can also be used to express contrast or emphasis (*She certainly does exercise every day!*) and other information such as future time (*She will win*) and aspect (*They were traveling then*). (Aspect and time reference are discussed in Chapter 6.)

Because an auxiliary often must appear in the surface structure of sentences (and also for other reasons not discussed here), a constituent representing the auxiliary is postulated in the underlying structure of *every* sentence. That means that, instead of the earlier expansion of S simply as NP VP, it must include AUX, as below:

  S → NP AUX VP

The operation that changes the constituent structure of the declarative sentences in 1, 2, 3, and 4 above to the constituent structure of their respective yes/no questions moves AUX to a site preceding the subject NP, as represented in Figure 5.10 below:

We thus represent the underlying structure of both *Suze will earn a fair wage* and *Will Suze earn a fair wage* as in the tree on the left in Figure 5.11. The tree on the right represents the constituent structure that results from application of the subject-auxiliary inversion operation.

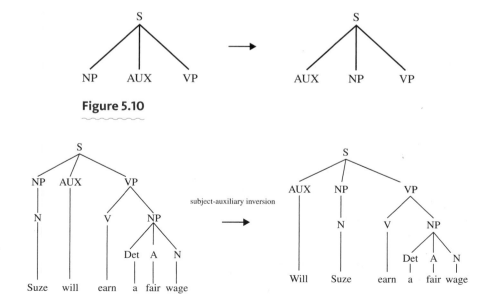

Figure 5.10

Figure 5.11

Information Questions In an information question, the information that is sought—the questioned constituent—is represented by a WH-word (*who* or *whom, why, when, where, which, what, how*), and such WH-questions occur in two forms. One echoes the form of the statement, as in these examples:

(He's boiling horsefeathers.)	He's boiling **what**?
(She was looking for Sigmund Freud.)	She was looking for **who**?

Intonation aside, the linear order of words in an echo question is identical to the linear order of words in the statement, except that a WH-word occurs in place of the questioned constituent—*what* for *horsefeathers, who* for *Sigmund Freud*. (For analysis of *who* and *whom*, see exercises 5-12 and 5-13.)

Much more common than echo questions are ordinary information questions. They take the form illustrated below, in which a syntactic operation called WH-movement fronts the WH-word to a position before the subject:

1. What is *he*   boiling—? (*He* is boiling what?)

2. Who was *she*   looking for—today? (*She* was looking for who today?)

If you compare these ordinary information questions with the parenthesized echo questions following them, you'll see that two movements have occurred:

- The WH-word (the questioned constituent *what* or *who*) appears at the front of its clause.

- The auxiliary (*is* or *was*) precedes the subject NP (which is *italicized* in the examples).

Notice, too, that ordinary information questions leave an understood "gap" in the structure at the site vacated by the fronted WH-word (indicated here by a dash—). By contrast, an echo question has no gap because the WH-word remains in its underlying site.

Embedded Clauses

We've been examining sentences consisting of a single clause, as in *Judge Jensen married a butcher* or *Lou cried*. Now we analyze sentences containing more than one clause—those consisting of a clause that is embedded as a constituent of another clause. In sentences 1 and 2 below, the *italicized clause* is embedded within another clause.

1. Suze said *Lou cried.*

2. *That Jen won the marathon* surprised Sheila.

In sentence 1, the clause *Lou cried* is embedded within the clausal structure *Suze said* ——. In 2, *(That) Jen won the marathon* is a clause embedded within the clausal structure —— *surprised Sheila* and corresponds structurally to the underlined NP in *It surprised Sheila*. These embedded clauses thus function like noun phrases within the embedding clause.

In sentences 1 and 2 above, an embedded clause functions as a constituent of an embedding clause, or what is often called a **matrix** clause. For example, in 3 below, the *italicized* embedded clause functions as a constituent of the matrix clause and has the same grammatical relation in the matrix clause as the underlined word in sentence 4 has within its clause:

3. *That Josh feared vampires* upset his wife.

4. <u>It</u> upset his wife.

In other words, *That Josh feared vampires* in 3 and *It* in 4 are both NPs with the grammatical relation of subject. Embedded clauses may have other functions within a matrix clause, including adverbial functions, as in *She failed most <u>when she tried least</u>*, but adverbial clauses lie beyond our scope.

Tree diagrams can be useful in illustrating the relationships among clauses in a sentence. In representing a sentence such as *Harry said he saw a ghost*, the embedded clause *he saw a ghost* fills the same sentence slot as the NP *it* in *Harry said it*, as shown in Figures 5.12 and 5.13. Figure 5.13 captures the fact that the embedded clause S_2 (*he saw a ghost*) functions structurally as part of the matrix clause S_1 (*Harry said —*). In the case of *Harry said it*, the NP immediately dominated by VP is *it*, which is an N. In the case of *Harry said he saw a ghost*, the NP immediately dominated by VP is *he saw a ghost*, which is an S. Figure 5.14 is a more detailed tree structure for the abbreviated one of Figure 5.13. Note that the phrase-structure rules given earlier would need to be refined in order to accommodate expansion of NP as S (as in Figures 5.13 and 5.14). As implied by these and other tree structures, we have begun to rely implicitly on certain elaborations of those expansion rules, and our expansions can be inferred from the tree diagrams.

Subordinators An embedded clause may be introduced by a word that would not occur if the clause stood as an independent sentence. Called a **subordinator** (or subordinating conjunction), such an introductory word serves to mark the

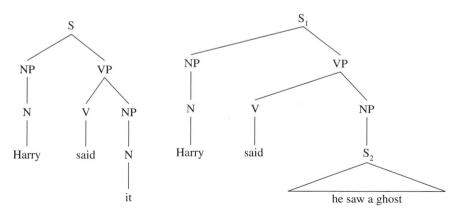

Figure 5.12   **Figure 5.13**

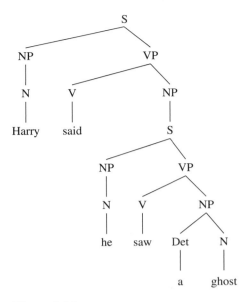

Figure 5.14

beginning of an embedded clause and helps identify its function in the sentence. Not all embedded clauses are introduced by a subordinator. Sentence 1 above may have a subordinator (*Suze said that Lou cried*), but it does not require one (*Suze said Lou cried*), whereas sentence 2 (*That Jen won the marathon surprised Sheila*) requires a subordinator.

Relative Clauses

Relative clause is the term used for a clause embedded within an NP to form structures such as those below (the relative clauses are *italicized*):

1. The dean criticized [the prof *who flunked me*].
2. [The jewels *that he stole*] were fakes.
3. Sarah saw a new film by [the French director *that Kim raves about*].
4. Sarah saw a new film by [the French director *Kim raves about*].

When NPs with the same referent occur in two clauses, a relative clause can be formed by embedding one clause into the other, as in the following example, where the identical indexes (subscript j) on *cousin* indicate identical referents:

I gave your address to my cousin$_j$ my cousin$_j$ lives in Dublin

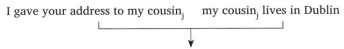

I gave your address to my cousin$_j$ who$_j$ lives in Dublin

English relative clauses are typically introduced by a relative pronoun such as *who* (or *whom* or *whose*), *which*, or *that*. As a comparison of 3 and 4 above illustrates, the relative pronoun may be omitted in specific circumstances.

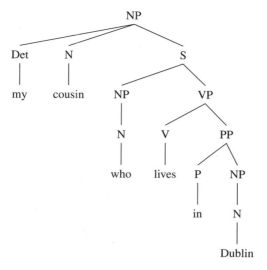

Figure 5.15

(Exercise 5-8 addresses these circumstances.) Relative clauses modify nouns, and the modified noun serves as the *head* of the entire noun phrase containng the relative clause. The head noun is repeated in the embedded clause, where it is *relativized* (taking the form of a relative pronoun). The structure of the resulting noun phrase can be represented as in Figure 5.15, in which the head noun *cousin* is labeled N. Notice in this instance that the relativized NP *who* functions as the subject of its clause (the NP immediately dominated by S).

In other clauses, the relativized NP may be the direct object, as here:

The jewels *that he stole* were fakes.

The relative clause *that he stole* derives from the underlying clause *he stole the jewels*, where *the jewels* is the direct object of the verb *stole* and has been relativized and moved to the front of its clause.

A relativized NP can also be an oblique as in 1 or a possessor as in 2:

1. This is the officer *whom I told you about.* (cf. *I told you about the officer*)
2. This is the officer *whose car was vandalized.* (cf. *the officer's car was vandalized*)

In English, then, a relativized NP can have any of these grammatical relations within its clause: subject, direct object, oblique, or possessor.

COMP Node

Now let's analyze the syntactic operations associated with relative clause formation in English. Examine the following sentences, noting the understood "gap" in the structure (indicated by a dash—):

1. There's the pothole that I warned you about —.

2. J. K. Rowling wrote the novel that I bought —.

3. The fans who — braved the weather paid a price.

We can represent the underlying constituent structure of these sentences in a tree diagram, as Figure 5.16 illustrates for sentence 2.

In order to form the relative clause structure of 2, the NP *the novel* (inside the lower clause *I bought the novel*) is relativized and moved to the front of its clause by the WH-movement operation we earlier introduced for information questions. Figure 5.16 shows a node labeled COMP (complementizer), which we have not previously identified. There is good reason to posit a COMP node in the underlying structure. Among other functions, COMP serves as a kind of placeholder and magnet for relative pronouns such as *that, which,* and *who,* as well as for the WH-constituents in information questions.

Since syntactic operations transform one constituent structure into another, we can represent the output of WH-movement as applied to Figure 5.16 by the tree given in Figure 5.17. Thus, WH-movement extracts a WH-constituent (*that*) from S and attaches it to the COMP node. The same syntactic operation could move any WH-constituent to COMP, including question words in the formation of information questions.

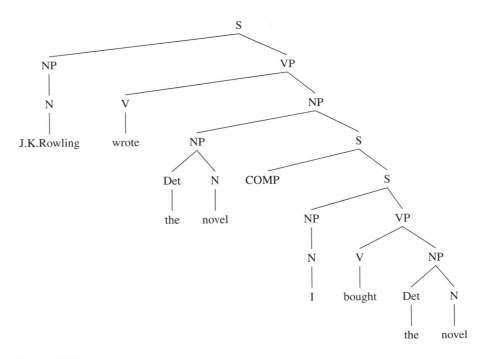

Figure 5.16

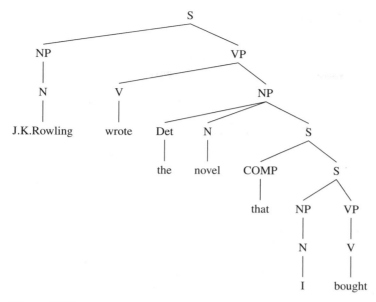

Figure 5.17

Types of Syntactic Operations

While it is not known how many types of syntactic operations exist in human languages, recent theories of syntax reflect evidence that syntactic operations are considerably more general than our relatively detailed specifications of examples from English or other languages might suggest. Movement operations are extremely common in the languages of the world, and some theoretical models of syntax limit all syntactic operations essentially to movement operations.

Functions of Syntactic Operations

We have examined several syntactic operations and stressed the point that all syntactic operations are structure dependent. We saw, for example, that irrespective of NP length or complexity, active and passive sentences are related in that the *object* NP of the active sentence (*A jaunty old judge fined Jody*) is the *subject* NP of the passive counterpart (*Jody was fined by a jaunty old judge*), and the *subject* of the active sentence (*a jaunty old judge*) is an *oblique* in the passive sentence (*by a jaunty old judge*).

You might wonder why languages have different ways of saying the same thing: what's the purpose of a syntactic operation like English passivization that essentially interchanges a subject and object but leaves the meaning of the sentence unchanged? To answer that question we exemplify with English examples, but comparable analyses in other languages could be used to illustrate the same point.

Yes/No Questions and Echo Questions

Yes/No Questions First, we analyze an example in which a syntactic operation does have a manifest effect on meaning. As we saw, yes/no questions are formed by moving the auxiliary in accordance with certain structural patterns. Thus, from the structure underlying *She will swear to it,* a syntactic operation produces the structure *Will she swear to it?* From a functional perspective the declarative structure makes a statement, the interrogative structure asks a question, and languages must provide speakers ways to make statements and ask questions. The point is that the form of the question is related to the form of the statement and is achieved by the syntactic operation called *subject-auxiliary inversion*. The meaning of the declarative and the meaning of the interrogative are not the same, of course.

Information Questions We saw that information questions have alternative forms—those in which the questioned constituent is fronted (*What* did they find? *Who* did she meet?) and those in which it isn't (*They found what? She met who?*). Both forms serve to ask questions and, broadly speaking, mean the same thing. But speakers use these forms for different purposes: they choose echo questions when they have failed to hear something completely or want to express surprise or incredulity at what they've heard. Thus, the alternative ways of asking questions serve different functions in a discourse.

Active and Passive Structures

Like the two forms of information questions, which have the same meaning but serve different discourse functions, active and passive pairs generally have the same meaning. After all, if Jody was fined by a jaunty old judge, it must also be the case that a jaunty old judge fined Jody. Why, then, should English have two ways of saying the same thing? To help answer that question, consider this passage about the baseball player Odalis Perez, taken from the Sports section of the *Los Angeles Times*:

Try It Yourself Explain why the writer of the passage below might have used the underlined passive structure in sentence 3 and why that sentence combines an active verb (*overran*) and a passive verb (*was thrown out*).

(1) *The Dodgers scored only one run despite twice loading the bases in the sixth inning, and Ward's base-running blunder in the ninth stirred more frustration for the team.* (2) *With one out and Cabrera on first base, Ward singled through the hole on the right side, sending Cabrera to third.* (3) *But Ward overran the bag and was thrown out, quickly dampening the Dodgers' mood.*

> **Perez** *gave up* an infield single to Barry Bonds before getting Andres Galarraga on another infield popup for the final out. **Perez** *re-engaged* Hernandez as he was walking off the field, triggering the ejection. **He** *was* also *ejected* June 13 against the Cleveland Indians at Jacobs Field.

Perez is the grammatical subject of the first two sentences, and *He* (also referring to Perez) is the subject of the third sentence. Of the three *italicized* verbs in the passage, the first two are active and both of them have Odalis Perez as the referent of their subject: Perez *gave up*; Perez *re-engaged*. The writer's focus was on Perez—and in order to keep the focus on Perez in the third sentence, he chose a passive structure, which allowed him to keep Perez in the spotlight: **He** <u>was</u> also <u>ejected</u> *June 13 against the Cleveland Indians at Jacobs Field*. Perez is the referent of the subject in *all* three sentences. An active structure (**An umpire** *ejected him June 13 against the Cleveland Indians at Jacobs Field*) would have introduced an extraneous person into the discourse and removed the focus from Perez.

As a further point, note that in a passive structure the subject of the corresponding active sentence may be omitted altogether. Instead of *He was ejected by an umpire June 13 against the Cleveland Indians at Jacobs Field*, the writer simply said *He was ejected June 13 against the Cleveland Indians at Jacobs Field*—without mentioning an umpire at all. By altogether omitting the subject of the active sentence, the focus remains on Perez.

Recursion and Novel Sentences

We have now seen that NPs and VPs can be expanded in various ways. We've also seen that VPs and PPs may contain NPs and that NPs may contain embedded sentences. That means we have seen the possibility of recursion—the ability of a sentence to incorporate another sentence that in turn could incorporate still another one, and so on. We've seen, in effect, that relying on a few expansion rules, English—or any other language—can be endlessly creative in forming novel sentences. Using those same few rules, speakers can also interpret novel sentences produced by others. Allowing for recursion, mastery of just a few rules enables speakers to produce and interpret sentences they haven't ever heard or read before. Thus is language endlessly novel, endlessly creative.

COMPUTERS AND THE STUDY OF SYNTAX

We saw in Chapter 2 that computer programs can do a good job of tagging words in a sentence with their correct part of speech, identifying lexical categories for nearly all the words. Beyond that, computer programs that can analyze a string of lexical categories for constituent structure are known as *parsers*, and some parsers achieve impressive success in assigning correct constituent structure to a string of lexical categories.

Tagging the words of a sentence for their lexical category is not the same thing as identifying constituent structure. Just as a string of words may have more than one constituent structure, so a string of lexical categories may represent more than one constituent structure. Just as the noun phrase *gullible boys and girls* has two possible constituent structures, so the string of categories for that phrase may have two bracketings:

[A [N Conj N]]   or   [A N] [Conj] [N]

Some computer programs can analyze tagged sentences and produce a labeled constituent structure or tree diagram. In the case of *gullible boys and girls*, a parser would produce two candidate constituent structures. Let's see how a parser would operate.

Given a sentence such as *That rancher saw the wolves*, a tagger would first assign parts of speech to the words as follows:

That$_{Det}$ rancher$_N$ saw$_V$ the$_{Det}$ wolves$_N$

In principle, *saw* could be a noun or a verb and *that* could have several possible tags, but even moderately sophisticated taggers would not have difficulty determining the correct tags here. Once part-of-speech tags have been assigned, a parser uses only a few phrase-structure expansion rules to produce a tree diagram or constituent-structure bracketing for the string. You can envision the process as something like working from the bottom of a tree structure to the top. For example, the phrase-structure expansion NP → Det N would bracket *that rancher* and *the wolves* as NPs, which yields the bracketing NP V NP. The expansion VP → V NP allows *saw the wolves* to be bracketed as VP, giving NP VP. That in turn is recognized as a representation of S. Taken together then, the tagged string can be parsed as in the figure at the bottom of this section. With more complicated strings, assigning correct constituent structure may be less straightforward.

Relying on their relatively simple parsers, grammar checkers in word processors sometimes suggest changes to your syntax in the interest of grammatical correctness or stylistic refinement. They often suggest revisions that indicate they have wrongly parsed a sentence. Often, too, they find natural sentences too long to parse, and the best they can do is suggest shortening the sentence.

$$[_S [_{NP} [\text{That }_{Det}] [\text{rancher }_N]_{NP}] [_{VP} [\text{saw }_V [_{NP} [\text{the }_{Det}] [\text{wolves }_N]_{NP}]_{VP}]_S]$$

This labeled bracketing is entirely equivalent to the tree diagram below:

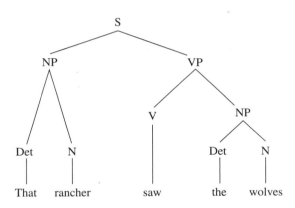

Summary

- The operations governing the formation of sentences constitute the syntax of a language. The study of sentence structure is also called syntax.
- All languages have referring expressions and predication expressions.
- In syntactic terms, a referring expression is an NP (noun phrase) and a predication expression a VP (verb phrase).
- A sentence (and a clause) consists of a verb with the appropriate set of NPs.
- Speakers of every language can generate an unlimited number of sentences from a finite number of operations for combining phrases.
- Phrase-structure expansion rules generate underlying constituent structures.
- Syntactic operations change one constituent structure into another one.

- Positing underlying constituent structures captures the striking regularity of certain relationships between sentences that are otherwise not apparent on the surface.
- Positing underlying structures helps explain some elements of meaning and certain syntactic and semantic relationships between sentences.
- In order to explain how speakers relate two structures to one another (such as *She doesn't believe in poltergeists* and *Doesn't she believe in poltergeists?*), linguists posit an operation that transforms the structure underlying the basic declarative sentence into the structure underlying the derived interrogative one.
- It appears that the most important and most general syntactic operations involve movement such as WH-movement.

What Do You Think? REVISITED

- *Clarence and productivity.* We hear some expressions so frequently that it's easy to imagine how we know them. Most of the things we say and read, though, we haven't said or heard or read before. But the structures that underlie what we say and hear are relatively few, and we have experience with them in everything we say and hear and read. By combining these few structures in different ways, we can generate and understand completely new sentences easily and accurately.
- *Amber and ambiguity.* Ambiguous words often don't call attention to themselves because context promotes a particular reading and efficiently eliminates alternatives. The utterance *I'm going to the bank to deposit a check* excludes the likelihood of a riverbank. Another kind of ambiguity arises when a string of words has more than one possible internal organization. *Gullible boys and girls* can mean 'girls and gullible boys' or 'gullible boys and gullible girls.' Likewise with *new drug combinations*, which may be organized as *[new drug] combinations* or *new [drug combinations]*.
- *Reader Ron.* The usual word order in an English sentence is subject-verb-object ("I hate turnips"), but there are grammatical alternatives ("Turnips I hate!"— which has an object-subject-verb order). Similarly, in "Not a drop of rain had fallen on Roanoke Island, said John Wilson," the main clause subject "John Wilson" appears after the main verb "said," which appears after the object clause "not a drop of rain had fallen on Roanoke Island." The ordinary subject-verb-object order (John Wilson—said—not a drop of rain had fallen on Roanoke Island) focuses a reader's attention on John Wilson. To focus it on the fact that not a drop of rain had fallen on Roanoke Island, the writer exploited the object-verb-subject order: Not a drop of rain had fallen on Roanoke Island—said—John Wilson.
- *Nerdy Ned.* Ned should consider offing a grammar checker that's so unsophisticated it recommends changing every passive sentence he writes. After all, sometimes a passive sentence is precisely what's needed to keep the focus

where a writer intends it to be. If Ned were writing about a winning team, he might choose to keep the focus there, and one way to do that would be by making *the winning team* the subject of the sentence, as in the one his checker balked at. ■

Exercises

Practice Exercises

A. In each sentence, identify the subject constituent and any direct object constituent.

  a. A political compromise will achieve that.

  b. That doesn't mean everybody will have a win-win situation.

  c. I would've noticed a progressive teacher's ideal pupil.

  d. What does the alternator do?

  e. A more radical position was held by the most prominent figure of the mission.

  f. Now the man who yearned for ten years to be a woman wants to remain a man.

B. Each sentence below has undergone one or more syntactic operations. Provide an appropriate underlying form for each, except those in parentheses, which are given simply for context.

  a. The scheme was initiated by displeased sophomores.

  b. The other girls were frustrated by our tactics.

  c. Erin could eat squid, but I couldn't.

  d. (I didn't expect that to happen.) Did you?

  e. (How are you?) Not bad.

  f. Do you know he failed his chemistry exam?

  g. Apples I love. Pears I hate.

Based on English

5-1. **a.** List as many examples of these constituents as you can identify in sentences 1 and 2 below: NP, PP, VP.

  b. List as many examples of these lexical categories as you can identify in sentences 1 and 2 below: N, PREP, V.

   1) A concert at an arena near St. Louis ended in disaster after fans staged a full-fledged riot.

   2) The trouble started when Axl Rose asked venue security to confiscate a camera he saw near the front of the stage.

c. For each of the expansions of VP given on page 161, provide an illustration. *Example:* **V NP**—*ate an apple.*

5-2. Match the following tree diagrams to one of these bracketed constituent structures: i) He sold the car [to a cousin] [in Boston]; or ii) He sold the car [to [a cousin in Boston]].

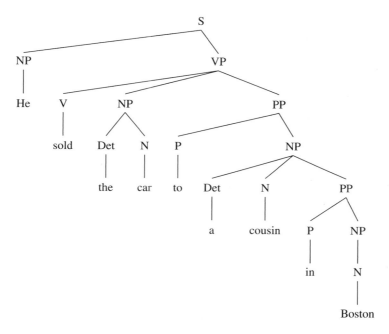

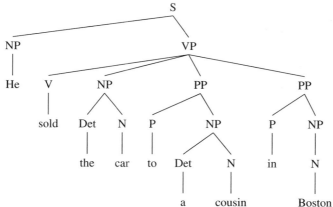

5-3. **a.** Draw a labeled tree diagram for each phrase below.

1) ancient inscriptions
2) in the dark night
3) concocted a potion

        4) borrowed the book that the teacher recommended

        5) the monstrous members of a terrible kingdom

    b. Provide a tree diagram for each sentence (for the moment, ignore the italics).

        1) Vampires *frighten him.*

        2) The skies deluged the earth *with water.*

        3) *A ghost has the spirit* of a dead person.

        4) *Do ghosts exist* in *the physical world?*

        5) *Does she* believe that ghosts exist?

        6) The teacher *that I described to you* won the race.

    c. For each *italicized* group of words in the sentences above, determine whether or not it is a constituent, and, if it is, provide its name.

5-4. What is the difference in the relationship between *Harry* and the verb *see* in 1 and 2 below? Draw tree diagrams of the underlying structure of the two sentences that reveal the difference in the structures.

    1) Josh advised Harry to see the doctor.

    2) Josh promised Harry to see the doctor.

5-5. English has a syntactic operation called dative movement that derives sentence 2 from the structure underlying sentence 1:

    1) I sent a letter to Hillary.

    2) I sent Hillary a letter.

The following also exemplify sentences with dative movement:

    He sold *his brother* a sailboat.

    Hal won't tell *me* Daniel's new phone number.

    I'm giving *my cousin* a new pair of pajamas.

    a. Give the three underlying sentences corresponding to the three derived sentences.

    b. Dative movement applies to prepositional phrases that begin with the preposition *to* but cannot apply to prepositional phrases that begin with most other prepositions:

        *I will finish you the homework. (from *I will finish the homework with you.*)

        *My neighbor heard the radio the news. (from *My neighbor heard the news on the radio.*)

But dative movement does not apply to all phrases that begin with the preposition *to*. The sentences in 3 below cannot undergo dative movement, as shown by the ungrammaticality of the corresponding sentences in 4.

    3) He's driving a truck to New Orleans.

        She's speaking nonsense to her boss.

    4) *He's driving New Orleans a truck.

        *She's speaking her boss nonsense.

    Describe dative movement in detail.

  c. Observe the ungrammatical sentences in 5 below, which are derived through dative movement from the sentences underlying the corresponding basic sentences in 6. How must you modify your description of dative movement so that it does not generate the ungrammatical sentences of 5?

    5) *I gave my new neighbor it.

        *I'm taking my little sister them.

        *They will probably send him me.

    6) I gave it to my new neighbor.

        I'm taking them to my little sister.

        They will probably send me to him.

5-6.   English has the grammatical relations of subject, direct object, oblique, and possessor. But it is debatable whether indirect object is a distinct grammatical relation and, if so, whether it occurs in sentences such as *The witch offered* **the child** *a potion* or *The witch offered a potion to* **the child**. The syntactic properties of *the child* differ in the two sentences. What syntactic evidence can you offer for arguing that *the child* does not have the same grammatical relation in each of these sentences? (*Hint*: At least one syntactic operation examined in this chapter does not produce grammatical strings for both the sentences.)

5-7.   English has two forms of relative clauses. Form 1 fronts the relativized noun phrase but leaves any preposition where it stood in the original clause.

This is the man [whom I talked *to* — last night]. (original clause: *I talked to the man last night*)

In Form 2, the preposition moves with the WH-word to the beginning of the clause.

This is the man [*to* whom I talked last night].

Describe the relative-clause operation for Form 2 relative clauses, focusing on how it differs from the operation for Form 1 relative clauses. Identify which relative pronouns can occur in which form of relative clause, and in which cases the two forms differ. Base your discussion on the following data:

This is the man [that left]. (Forms 1 and 2)

*This is the man [left]. (Forms 1 and 2)

This is the man [that I saw]. (Forms 1 and 2)

This is the man [who I saw]. (Forms 1 and 2)

This is the man [whom I saw]. (Forms 1 and 2)

This is the man [I saw]. (Forms 1 and 2)

This is the man [who I gave the book to]. (Form 1)

This is the man [whom I gave the book to]. (Form 1)

This is the man [that I gave the book to]. (Form 1)

This is the man [I gave the book to]. (Form 1)

*This is the man [to who I gave the book]. (Form 2)

This is the man [to whom I gave the book]. (Form 2)

*This is the man [to that I gave the book]. (Form 2)

*This is the man [to I gave the book]. (Form 2)

5-8.   In the earlier section on relative clauses, we noted that the relative pronoun may be omitted from certain structures. Thus, in the following sentence, Ø represents an omitted relative pronoun:

Sally saw a new film by the French director Ø Kim raved about.

a. For each of the following sentences, identify the grammatical relation of the relativized NP within its clause, using S for subject, DO for direct object, and Obl for oblique.

1) I lost the book [that you gave me].

2) He rented the video [that frightened you].

3) I bumped into the teacher [who taught me solid geometry].

4) I met the poet [who(m) we read about last week].

5) I found the video [that you lost].

6) I saw the oak tree [that you slept under].

7) The new teacher [that Lou liked] just quit.

8) The new teacher [who liked jazz] just quit.

9) I picked an apple from the tree [that you planted].

10) I like the new lyrics [that you complained about].

b. Which sentences would permit the relative pronoun to be omitted?

c. Which would not permit the relative pronoun to be omitted?

d. Which grammatical relations permit the relative pronoun to be omitted?

e. Which grammatical relations do not permit the relative pronoun to be omitted?

f. Rewrite sentences 4, 6, and 10, fronting the preposition with the relative pronoun.

g. Can the relative pronoun be omitted from the rewritten versions of 4, 6, and 10?

h. What generalization can you make about when a relative pronoun can be omitted from its clause?

5-9. Keeping in mind the movement operations for forming questions, analyze what has happened in the derivation of the sentences below to produce the ill-formed sentence. How would you formulate the auxiliary movement operation to avoid the ungrammatical example?

> The teacher who will give that lecture is Lily's aunt.
>
> *Will the teacher who give that lecture is Lily's aunt?
>
> Is the teacher who will give that lecture Lily's aunt?

5-10. Below are five examples of sentences that a word processor's grammar checker found objectionable, along with the comment that suggests a particular correction. In each case, the grammar checker has made an incorrect analysis, and the suggested correction would yield an ill-formed sentence. For each example, identify the word or constituent structure that the grammar checker has wrongly analyzed and explain the basis for its suggested correction.

Example: "In this sentence, each embedded clause functions as a grammatical unit in its matrix clause."

Comment: The word *each* does not agree with *functions*. Consider *function* instead of *functions*. Explanation: Likely that grammar checker incorrectly analyzed *functions* as a plural noun (rather than a third-person-singular verb) and took *embedded clause functions* to be a noun phrase. If the analysis were correct, "each embedded clause function" would be well formed.

1) "It is the word order in the sentence that signals who is doing what to whom."

Comment: Consider *are* instead of *is*.

2) "Do 'George Washington' and 'the first president of the United States' mean the same thing?"

Comment: Consider *presidents* instead of *president* or consider *means* instead of *mean*.

3) "When a student volunteers, 'Disneyland is fun,' . . ."

Comment: The word *a* does not agree with *volunteers*.

4) "Linguistic semantics is the study of the systematic ways in which languages structure meaning."

Comment: Consider *language's* or *languages'* instead of *languages*.

5) "Sentence 2 is true because we know the word *dogs* describes entities that are also described by the word *animals*."

Comment: Consider *describe* instead of *describes*.

Based on Languages Other Than English

5-11. Examine the tree diagram for this Fijian sentence:

ea-biuta	na	ŋone	vakaloloma	na	tamata	ðaa	e	na	basi
Past-abandon	the	child	poor	the	man	bad	on	the	bus

'The bad man abandoned the poor child on the bus.'

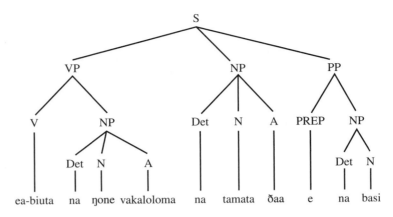

a. Provide the phrase-structure rules that will generate this constituent-structure tree.

b. Notice that the order of certain constituents in the Fijian sentence differs from that of English. With respect to constituent order, what are the major differences between Fijian and English?

c. On the basis of the tree structure, determine which of the following sequences of words are constituents and give the name of each constituent.

na basi	ea-biuta na ŋone vakaloloma
vakaloloma na tamata	e na
e na basi	na ŋone
na tamata ðaa	na ŋone vakaloloma na tamata ðaa
ðaa e na basi	ŋone vakaloloma
ea-biuta	e-biuta na ŋone

Especially for Educators and Future Teachers

5-12. Although we have downplayed the difference between *who* and *whom* in the examples in this chapter, writers and speakers who regularly make a distinction between them in relative clauses do so as follows:

1) It was Lynne *who* answered.

2) She's a keen golfer, *who* plays mostly in Morro Bay.

3) A nurse *who* walked his dog without a leash was fined $600.

4) Then came the meeting with the woman *whom* he intended to marry.

5) Her grandmother, *whom* she adored, was dangerously ill.

6) He married a woman from Devon, *whom* he'd met in Australia.

7) Ricardo, with *whom* we spent a week in Sitges, had learned to sail in Baja.

8) He said this to Eddie, *who* doesn't deny the lawyer's gut feeling.

9) This isn't solely for those *who* have decided to turn their lives around.

10) He was a friend of Truman, with *whom* he had an affair and *who* encouraged him to write.

After examining these sentences, formulate a statement that will capture the facts about when such writers and speakers use *who* and *whom* in relative clauses. (*Hint*: Bracket the relative clause and examine the grammatical relation of the relative pronoun within its clause.)

5-13. In this chapter, we discussed *who* and *whom* in different ways. On page 168, we took a *descriptive* approach, using the forms that speakers commonly use. But in Exercise 5.12, we considered a more traditional analysis associated with some teachers, editors, and parents, and sometimes referred to as prescriptive grammar, an approach that *prescribes* particular language forms as some people think they *should be*. What position do you think a teacher should take with respect to common usages that are criticized by prescriptive grammarians? What do you think students should understand about the role of language prescription in their lives? Do you think that role should be the same for them as writers and as conversationalists? Should teachers at different levels of education take different approaches to description and prescription? Explain your position and justify it.

Other Resources

Suggestions for Further Reading

- **Andrew Carnie. 2007. *Syntax: A Generative Introduction*, 2nd ed.** (Malden, MA: Wiley-Blackwell). A challenging introduction to generative syntax, with additional chapters on lexical-functional grammar and head-driven phrase-structure grammar.
- **Bernard Comrie. 1989. *Language Universals and Linguistic Typology: Syntax and Morphology*, 2nd ed.** (Chicago: University of Chicago Press). A clear discussion of syntactic universals across a wide range of languages; the chapters on Word Order, Subject, Case Marking, and Relative Clauses are particularly recommended.
- **Vivian J. Cook & Mark Newson. 2007. *Chomsky's Universal Grammar: An Introduction*, 3rd ed.** (Malden, MA: Wiley-Blackwell). A more advanced introduction to formal grammar, with chapters on principles and parameters, X-bar theory, and the minimalist program, going beyond the present chapter in accessible steps.
- **Jim Miller. 2009. *An Introduction to English Syntax*, 2nd ed.** (Edinburgh: Edinburgh University Press). A basic introduction to the syntax of English, combining structural and functional considerations; thorough and advanced.
- **Max Morenberg. 2009. *Doing Grammar*, 4th ed.** (New York: Oxford University Press). Focused on practical understanding of English grammar in traditional terms.
- **Maggie Tallerman. 2005. *Understanding Syntax*, 2nd ed.** (New York: Oxford University Press; London: Hodding-Arnold). A clear introduction to syntax as structure.

Advanced Reading

Comprehensive, if somewhat advanced, treatments of syntax, especially English syntax, can be found in Aarts (1997) and Radford (2009). The volumes edited by Shopen (2007) contain a wealth of useful material; probably accessible to interested readers who have mastered the present chapter are two excellent chapters of volume I: "Parts-of-Speech Systems" and "Passive in the World's Languages"; volume II contains valuable chapters discussing "Complementation," and "Relative Clauses." Thompson (2004) is a somewhat advanced treatment of functional grammar. Haegeman (2006) shows how to analyze sentence structure. Huddleston and Pullum (2002) is a rich grammar of English, with valuable theoretical discussion; at pages 1018–1022, interested readers will find arguments against treating clauses like *he saw a ghost* as an object noun phrase in sentences like *Harry said he saw a ghost,* but such arguments are beyond the scope of this chapter.

References

Aarts, Bas. 1997. *English Syntax and Argumentation* (New York: St. Martin's).

Haegeman, Liliane. 2006. *Thinking Syntactically: A Guide to Argumentation and Analysis* (Malden, MA: Blackwell).

Huddleston, Rodney & Geoffrey K. Pullum. 2002. *The Cambridge Grammar of the English Language* (Cambridge, UK: Cambridge University Press).

Radford, Andrew. 2009. *Analysing English Sentences: A Minimalist Introduction* (Cambridge, UK: Cambridge University Press).

Shopen, Timothy, ed. 2007. *Language Typology and Syntactic Description*, 2nd ed., 3 vols. (Cambridge, UK: Cambridge University Press).

Thompson, Geoff. 2004. *Introducing Functional Grammar*, 2nd ed. (London: Arnold; New York: St. Martin's).

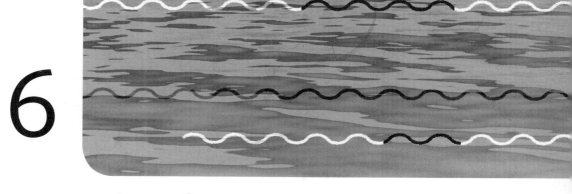

6

The Study of Meaning: Semantics

What Do You Think?

- Phyllis, a philosophy major, frequently poses language questions to her classmates. Recently she asked, "Do you think *George Washington* and *the first president of the United States* mean the same thing?" What do you tell her?
- Your friend Doug doubts that there are any true synonyms. You counter with *fast* and *quick* as synonyms that both mean 'speedy.' Doug one-ups you by pointing out that *a quick talker* isn't necessarily *a fast talker,* and he claims that since you can't always exchange *fast* and *quick,* they're not synonyms. Now what do you say?
- Your uncle Earnest knows you're studying linguistics and asks whether there's a term to capture the relationship between word pairs like *uncle* and *nephew, student* and *teacher, doctor* and *patient.* "They're not opposites like *hot* and *cold,*" he says. "But what are they?" What do you tell him?
- At a family picnic you listen to your cousin Kevin tease his four-year-old daughter about a coloring book he's taken from her. The girl says, "That's *mine.*" Kevin says, "That's right, it is mine." The girl repeats, "No, it's *mine.*" Kevin says, "That's what I said: it's *mine.*" "No, it's not," she insists. Then she grabs the book and walks away. What is it about the meaning of *yours* and *mine* that makes it possible to tease a four-year-old this way?

Introduction

Semantics has to do with meaning, and linguistic semantics is the study of the systematic ways in which languages structure meaning, especially in words and sentences. That will be the focus of this chapter. In Chapter 8 we'll discuss information structure, another aspect of meaning, and examine how it is encoded in language. In Chapter 9, we'll discuss still other aspects of meaning, especially certain kinds of inferential meaning.

In defining linguistic semantics (which we'll simply call "semantics"), we must invoke the word *meaning*. In everyday interaction, we use the words *meaning* and *to mean* in different contexts and for different purposes. For example:

The word *perplexity means* 'the state of being puzzled.'

Rash has two *meanings:* 'impetuous' and 'skin irritation.'

In Spanish, *espejo means* 'mirror.'

I did not *mean* that he is incompetent, just inefficient.

The *meaning* of the cross as a symbol is complex.

I *meant* to bring you my paper but left it at home.

What Is Meaning?

Linguists also attach different interpretations to the word *meaning*. Because the goal of linguistics is to explain precisely how languages are structured and used to represent situations in the world (among other things), it is helpful to distinguish among the different ways of interpreting the word *meaning*.

A few examples will illustrate why we need to develop a precise way of talking about meaning. Consider these sentences:

1. I went to the store this morning.

2. All dogs are animals.

The truth of sentence 1 depends on whether or not the speaker is in fact telling the truth about going to the store; nothing about the words of the sentence makes it inherently true. By contrast, sentence 2 is true because the word *dogs* describes entities that are also described by the word *animals*. The truth of 2 does not depend on whether or not the speaker is telling the truth; it depends solely on the meaning of the words *dogs* and *animals*.

Now compare the following pairs of sentences:

3. You are too young to drink.

   You are not old enough to drink.

4. Matthew spent several years in northern Tibet.

   Matthew was once in northern Tibet.

The sentences of 3 basically "say the same thing" in that the first describes exactly what the second describes and if the first is true, the second must also be true. We say they are *synonymous* sentences, or that they paraphrase each other.

In 4, the first sentence *implies* the second, but not vice versa. If Matthew spent several years in northern Tibet, he must have set foot there at some point in his life. On the other hand, if Matthew was once in northern Tibet, it is not necessarily the case that he spent several years there.

Next, consider the following sentences:

5. The unmarried woman is married to a bachelor.

6. My toothbrush is pregnant.

Sentences 5 and 6 are well formed syntactically, but there is something amiss with their semantics. The meanings of the words in 5 contradict each other: an unmarried woman cannot be married, and certainly not to a bachelor. Sentence 5 thus presents a *contradiction*. Sentence 6 is not contradictory but semantically *anomalous*: toothbrushes are not capable of being pregnant. To diagnose precisely what is wrong with these sentences, we need to distinguish between contradictory and anomalous sentences.

Finally, examine sentences 7 and 8:

7. I saw her duck.

8. She ate the pie.

Sentence 7 may be interpreted in two ways: *duck* may be a verb referring to the act of bending over quickly (while walking through a low doorway, for example), or it may be a noun referring to a type of waterfowl. These word meanings give the sentence two distinct meanings. Because there are two possible readings of 7, it is said to be **ambiguous**. On the other hand, 8 is not ambiguous but has an imprecise quality at least when considered out of context. While we know that the subject of 8 is female, we cannot know who it is that *she* refers to or which pie was eaten, although the phrase *the pie* indicates that the speaker has a particular one in mind. Taken out of context, 8 is thus *vague* in that certain details are left unspecified; but it is not ambiguous.

These observations illustrate that meaning is a multifaceted notion. A sentence may be meaningful and true because it states a fact about the world or because the speaker is telling the truth. Two sentences may be related to each other because they mean exactly the same thing or because one implies the other. Finally, when we feel that there is something wrong with the meaning of a sentence, it may be because the sentence is contradictory, anomalous, ambiguous, or merely vague. One purpose of semantics is to distinguish among these different ways in which language "means."

Linguistic, Social, and Affective Meaning

For our purposes we can initially distinguish three types of meaning. **Linguistic meaning** encompasses both sense and reference. **Social meaning** is what we rely on when we identify certain social characteristics of speakers and situations from the character of the language used. **Affective meaning** is the emotional connotation that is attached to words and utterances.

Linguistic Meaning

Meaning is a complicated matter and there is no single agreed-upon theory about how languages mean. Although analysis of meaning goes back at least to Plato and Aristotle, we remain quite far from a complete understanding of how languages encode meaning and how speakers interpret language.

Referential Meaning One way of defining meaning is to say that the meaning of a word or sentence is the actual person, object, abstract notion, event, or state to which the word or sentence makes reference, the entity the term picks out or identifies. (Some treatments refer to referential meaning as *extensional* meaning.) The **referential meaning** of *Alexis Rathburton*, for example, would be the person who goes by that name. The phrase *Scott's dog* refers to the particular domesticated canine belonging to Scott. That animal can be said to be the referential meaning of the linguistic expression *Scott's dog*, and the canine picked out or identified by the expression is its **referent**.

Words are not the only linguistic units to carry referential meaning. Sentences too refer to actions, states, and events in the world. *Rahul is sleeping on the sofa* refers to the fact that a person named Rahul is at the time of the utterance asleep on an elongated piece of furniture generally meant to be sat upon. The referent of the sentence is thus Rahul's state of being on the piece of furniture in question.

Sense Meaning Referential meaning is not sufficient to explain *how* some expressions mean what they mean. For one thing, not all expressions have referents. Neither *a unicorn* nor *the present king of France* has an actual referent in the real world, but both expressions have meaning. Even leaving social and affective meaning aside, if expressions had only referential meaning, then the sentences in 9 would mean exactly the same thing, as would those in 10, but they don't.

9. George Washington was the first president of the United States.

   George Washington was George Washington.

10. Michelle Robinson married Barack Obama in 1992.

    Michelle Robinson married the forty-fourth president of the United States in 1992.

Not only do the sentences of 10 mean different things, but the second one seems odd: after all, the United States did not have its forty-fourth president until 2009. If, *the forty-fourth president of the United States* had only a referential meaning, then the second sentence in 10 would seem perfectly ordinary.

Proper nouns such as *George Washington, Michelle Robinson*, and *Barack Obama* constitute a special category, and we might say that the meaning of proper nouns like those is the person named, the person to whom the proper noun refers. By contrast, the meaning of expressions such as *the president of the United States* and *the forty-fourth president of the United States* cannot be reduced to their referents. Consider the sentences of 11:

11. Al Gore nearly became the forty-third president of the United States.

    Al Gore nearly became George W. Bush.

Obviously, these sentences do not mean the same thing, despite the fact that *George W. Bush* and *the forty-third president of the United States* have the same referent. In general, we cannot equate the meaning of an expression with the referent of the expression. We say that expressions have "senses," as well as referents, and any theory of semantics must take sense meaning into account. In the first sentence in 11, the focus is on the sense of *the forty-third president of the United States*. (Just as extensional meaning is a term sometimes used for referential meaning, so *intensional* meaning is sometimes used for sense meaning.)

> **Try It Yourself** One of the sentences below focuses on the referential meaning of *the president of the United States* and the other focuses on its sense. Which is which?
>
> *The president of the United States* was born in Hawaii.
>
> By law, *the president of the United States* must be at least thirty-five years of age.

Social Meaning

Linguistic meaning is not the only type of meaning that speakers communicate to each other. Consider the following sentences:

1. So I says to him, "You can't do nothin' right."
2. Is it a doctor in here?
3. Y'all gonna visit over the holiday?
4. Great chow!

In addition to representing actions, states, and mental processes, these sentences convey information about the identity of the person who has uttered them or about the situation in which they've been uttered. In 1, use of the verb *says* with the first-person singular pronoun *I* indicates something about the speaker's social status. In 2, the form *it* where some other varieties use *there* indicates a speaker of an ethnically marked variety of English (African American English). In 3, the pronoun *y'all* identifies a particular regional dialect of American English (Southern). Finally, the choice of words in 4 indicates that the comment was made in an informal context. Social status, ethnicity, regional origin, and context are all social factors. In addition to linguistic meaning, therefore, every utterance also conveys social meaning, not only in the sentence as a whole but in word choice (*y'all* and *chow*) and pronunciation (*gonna* and *nothin'*).

Affective Meaning

There is a third kind of meaning besides linguistic and social meaning. Compare the following examples:

1. Tina, who always boasts about her two doctorates, lectured me all night on Warhol's art.
2. Tina, who's got two doctorates, gave me a fascinating overview of Warhol's art last night.

Because these two sentences can be used to represent exactly the same event, we say they have similar referential meaning. At another level, though, the information they convey is different. Sentence 1 gives the impression that the speaker considers Tina a pretentious bore. Sentence 2, in contrast, indicates that the speaker finds her interesting. The "stance" of the speaker in these utterances thus differs.

Word choice is not the only way to communicate feelings and attitudes toward utterances and contexts. A striking contrast is provided by sentences that differ only in terms of stress or intonation. This string of words can be interpreted in several ways depending on the intonation:

Erin is really smart.

The sentence can be uttered in a matter-of-fact way, without emphasizing any word in particular, in which case it will be interpreted literally as a remark acknowledging Erin's intelligence. But if the words *really* and *smart* are stressed in an exaggerated manner, the sentence may be interpreted as sarcastic and intended to convey exactly the opposite meaning. Intonation (often accompanied by appropriate facial expressions) can be used as a device to communicate attitudes and feelings, and it can override the literal meaning of a sentence.

Consider a final example. Suppose that Andy Grump, father of Sarah, addresses her as follows:

Sarah Grump, how many times have I asked you not to channel surf?

There would be reason to look beyond the words for the "meaning" of this unusual form of address. Mr. Grump may address his daughter as *Sarah Grump* to show his exasperation, as in this example. By addressing her as *Sarah Grump* instead of the usual *Sarah*, he conveys frustration and annoyance. His choice of name thus signals his exasperation. Contrast the tone of that sentence with a similar one in which he addresses her as *dear*.

The level of meaning that conveys a speaker's feelings, attitudes, and opinions about a particular piece of information or about the ongoing context is called *affective* meaning, and it is not an exclusive property of sentences. Words such as *Alas!* and *Hooray!* obviously have affective meaning, and so can words such as *funny*, *sweet*, and *obnoxious*. Even common words—such as *father*, *democracy*, and *old*—can evoke particular emotions and feelings in us. The difference between synonymous or near-synonymous pairs of words such as *vagrant* and *homeless* is essentially a difference at the affective level. In this particular pair, *vagrant* carries a negative affect, while *homeless* is neutral. Little is known yet about how affective meaning works, but it is of great importance in all verbal communication. From our discussion so far, you can see that meaning is not a simple notion but a complex combination of three aspects:

- **Linguistic meaning**: referential meaning (the real-world object or concept picked out or described by an expression) and sense meaning
- **Social meaning**: the information about the social nature of the speaker or of the context of utterance
- **Affective meaning**: what the speaker feels about the content or the ongoing context

The linguistic meaning of an expression is frequently called its *denotation*, in contrast to *connotation*, which includes both social and affective meaning.

This chapter focuses primarily on linguistic meaning, the traditional domain of semantics, but we occasionally refer to the three-way distinction. Social meaning is further explored in Chapters 10 and 11.

Word, Sentence, and Utterance Meaning

Meaning of Words and Sentences

We have talked about words and sentences as the two units of language that carry meaning. **Content words**—principally nouns, verbs, prepositions, adjectives, and adverbs—have meaning in that they refer to concrete objects and abstract concepts; are marked as characteristic of particular social, ethnic, and regional dialects and of particular contexts; and convey information about the feelings and attitudes of speakers. **Function words** such as conjunctions and determiners also carry meaning, though in somewhat different ways from content words, as you'll see later in this chapter. Like individual words, sentences also have social and affective connotations. The study of word meaning, however, differs from the study of sentence meaning because the units are different in kind.

In order for a sentence to convey meaning, we must rely on the meaning of the individual words it contains. How we accomplish the task of retrieving sentence meaning from word meaning is a complex question. One obvious hypothesis is that the meaning of a sentence is simply the sum of the meanings of its words. To see that this is *not* the case, consider the following sentences, in which the individual words (and therefore their *sum* meanings) are the same:

> The lion licked the trainer.
>
> The trainer licked the lion

Obviously, the sentences refer to different events and hence have distinct linguistic meanings. This is conveyed by the fact that the words of the sentences are ordered differently. We cannot say that all we need to do to retrieve the meaning of a sentence is add up the meanings of its parts. We must also consider the *semantic role* assigned to each word. By *semantic role* we mean such things as *who* did what *to whom, with whom,* and *for whom.* In other words, the semantic role of a word is the role that its referent plays in the action or state of being described by the sentence. Sentence semantics is concerned with semantic roles and with the relationship between words and constituents within a sentence.

Scope of Word Meaning

While it is important to distinguish between word meaning, on the one hand, and phrase and sentence meaning, on the other, the two interact on many levels. In Chapter 5 we examined the phrase *gullible boys and girls* and noted that it had two possible constituent structures and thus two possible meanings. Another way to think about the ambiguity of that phrase is to consider whether the adjective *gullible* has *boys and girls* within its scope (as in Figure 5.3) or only *boys* (as in Figure 5.4). In other words, does *gullible* modify *boys* alone or does it modify *boys and girls*? Scope is thus an important matter in determining meaning, and because the scope of modifiers has proven important in interpreting legal matters, including contracts and laws themselves, many a case has come before the courts—including the United States Supreme Court—contesting the scope of an adjective or adverb modifier.

In a sentence, the scope of individual words is also important in determining meaning. Consider this sentence:

He may leave tomorrow if he finishes his term paper.

The individual words *may, tomorrow,* and *if* have meanings: *may* denotes permission or possibility; *tomorrow* indicates a future time unit that begins at midnight on the day the sentence is spoken; and *if* indicates a condition. But the impact of these words reaches beyond the phrases in which they occur and affects the meaning of the entire sentence. Indeed, if we replace *may* with *will,* the sentence takes on an altogether different meaning:

He will leave tomorrow if he finishes his term paper.

With *may* the sentence denotes permission or possibility, but with *will* it simply describes a future event. Thus *may* affects the meaning of the *entire* sentence, and the *scope* of the meaning of the word *may* is the entire sentence. This is true also of *tomorrow* and *if*. Such examples illustrate that word meaning and sentence meaning are intimately related.

Try It Yourself Determine the scope of *only* in the sentences below. Using 1 as a model, provide a sentence that illustrates the scope of *only* for 2 and 3. Where the scope of *only* is ambiguous, give alternative "cf." sentences, each of which is *unambiguous*.

1. He wants *only* you to be happy. (cf.: He wants only you to be happy; he doesn't care about anyone else.)
2. *Only* she wants you to win.
3. She *only* wants to talk to her daughter.

Meaning of Utterances

In addition to words and sentences, there is a third factor that carries meaning, but we may not notice it as clearly because we take it for granted in day-to-day interactions. Consider this utterance:

I now pronounce you husband and wife.

This sentence may be uttered in very different sets of circumstances: (1) by an officiant at a ceremony, speaking to a couple getting married in the presence of their families and friends or (2) by an actor dressed as an officiant, speaking to two actors before a congregation of Hollywood extras assembled by a director filming a soap opera. In the first instance, *I now pronounce you husband and wife* creates a marriage for the couple intending to get married. But that same utterance has no effect on the marital status of any actor on the filming location. Thus the circumstances of utterance create different meanings even when the linguistic meaning of the sentence remains unchanged. It is therefore necessary to know the circumstances of an utterance in order to understand its effect or force. We say that the sentence uttered in the wedding context and the sentence uttered in the film context have the same linguistic meaning but are different **utterances**, each with its own *utterance meaning.*

The difference between sentence meaning and utterance meaning can be further illustrated by the question *Can you shut the window?* There are at least two ways in which an addressee might react to this question. One way would be to say *Yes* (meaning 'Yes, I am able to shut the window') and then do nothing about it. This is the "smart-aleck" interpretation, and it isn't the way such a question is usually intended. Alternatively, the addressee could simply shut the window. Obviously, these interpretations of the same question are different: the smart-aleck interpretation treats the question as a request for *information*; the alternative interpretation treats it as a request for *action*. To describe the difference between these interpretations, we say that they are distinct *utterances.*

Sentence semantics is not concerned with utterance meaning. (Utterances are the subject of investigation of another branch of linguistics called *pragmatics*, which we treat further in Chapters 8 and 9.) A premise of sentence semantics is that sentences must be divorced from the context in which they are uttered—in other words, that sentences and utterances must be distinguished. This premise may appear counterintuitive because meaning depends so heavily on context. The point is not to discard context as unimportant but to recognize that *sentences* may carry meaning independently of context, while utterance meaning depends crucially on the circumstances of the utterance. **Semantics** is the branch of linguistics that examines word and sentence meaning while generally ignoring context. By contrast, **pragmatics** pays less attention to the relationship of word meaning to sentence meaning and more attention to the relationship of an utterance to its context.

Lexical Semantics

The *lexicon* of a language can be viewed as a compendium of all its words. Words are sometimes called **lexical items,** or *lexemes* (the *-eme* ending as in *phoneme* and *morpheme*). The branch of semantics that deals with word meaning is called **lexical semantics**.

Lexical semantics examines relationships among word meanings. For example, it asks what the relationship is between the words *man* and *woman* on the one hand and *human being* on the other hand. How are the adjectives *large* and *small* in the same relationship to each other as the pair *dark* and *light*? What is the difference between the meaning of words such as *always* and *never* and the meaning of words such as *often* and *seldom*? What do speakers actually mean when they say that a dog is "a type of" mammal? Lexical semantics investigates such questions. It is the study of how the lexicon is organized and how the meanings of lexical items are interrelated, and its principal goal is to build a model for the structure of the lexicon by categorizing the types of relationships between words. Lexical semantics focuses on linguistic meaning.

Semantic Fields

Consider the following sets of words:

1. cup, mug, wineglass, tumbler, chalice, goblet
2. hammer, cloud, tractor, eyeglasses, leaf, justice

The words of set 1 all denote concepts that can be described as 'vessels from which one drinks,' while the words of set 2 denote concepts that have nothing in common. The words of set 1 constitute a **semantic field**—a set of words with an identifiable semantic affinity. The following set is also a semantic field, all of whose words refer to emotional states:

angry, sad, happy, exuberant, depressed, afraid

We see, then, that words can be classified into sets according to their meaning.

In a semantic field, not all lexical items necessarily have the same status. Consider the following sets, which together form the semantic field of color terms (of course, there are other terms in the same field):

1. blue, red, yellow, green, black, purple
2. indigo, saffron, royal blue, aquamarine, bisque

The colors referred to by the words of set 1 are more "usual" than those described in set 2. They are said to be less **marked** members of the semantic field than those of set 2. The less marked members of a semantic field are usually easier to learn and remember than more marked members. Children learn the term *blue* before they learn the terms *indigo, royal blue,* or *aquamarine.* Often, a less marked word consists of only one morpheme, in contrast to more marked words (contrast *blue* with *royal blue* or *aquamarine*). The less marked member of a semantic field cannot be described by using the name of another member of the same field, whereas more marked members can be thus described (*indigo* is a kind of blue, but *blue* is not a kind of indigo). Less marked terms also tend to be used more frequently than more marked terms; for example, *blue* occurs considerably more frequently in conversation and writing than *indigo* or *aquamarine.* (In the million-word Brown Corpus of written American English, there are 126 examples of *blue* but only one of *indigo* and none at all of *aquamarine.*) Less marked terms are also often broader in meaning

Try It Yourself Rust, silver, orchid, and champagne are members of the semantic field of colors, and you can readily identify the sources that gave rise to these color terms. Fruits, flowers, gems, and other natural objects are notable sources of terms in this semantic field. Can you identify five additional color terms directly borrowed from the name of a real-world object of that color?

than more marked terms; *blue* describes a broader range of colors than *indigo* or *aquamarine*. Finally, less marked words are not the result of the metaphorical usage of the name of another object or concept, whereas more marked words often are; for example, *saffron* is the color of a spice that lent its name to the color.

Using our understanding of semantic field and markedness, we now turn to identifying types of relationships between words. We'll see how the words of a semantic field can have different types of relationships to one another and to other words in the lexicon, and we'll classify these relationships.

Hyponymy

Consider again this set of unmarked color terms: *blue, red, yellow, green, black, purple*. What they have in common is that they refer to colors. We say that the terms *blue, red, yellow, green, black,* and *purple* are hyponyms of the term *color*. A **hyponym** is a subordinate, specific term whose referent is included in the referent of a superordinate term. Blue is a kind of color; red is a kind of color, and so on. They are specific colors, and *color* is the general term for them. We can illustrate the relationship by the following diagram, in which the lower terms are the hyponyms (*hypo*- means 'below'). The higher term—in this case, *color*—is called the superordinate term (technically, the *hypernym*).

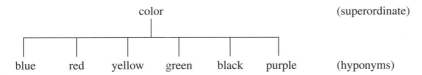

Another example is the term *mammal*, whose referent includes the referents of many other terms.

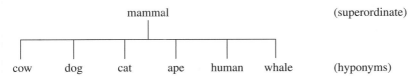

The relationship between each of the lower terms and the higher term is called *hyponymy*.

Hyponymy is not restricted to objects such as *mammal* or abstract concepts such as *color*—or even to nouns, for that matter. Hyponymy can be identified in many other areas of the lexicon. The verb *to cook*, for example, has many hyponyms.

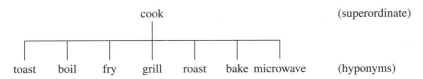

Not every set of hyponyms has a superordinate term. For example, *uncle* and *aunt* form a lexical field because we can identify a shared property in their meanings. Yet English does not have a term that refers specifically to both uncles and aunts (that is, to siblings of parents and their spouses).

?   (superordinate)

uncle   aunt   (hyponyms)

By contrast, some other languages have a superordinate term for the equivalent field. In Spanish, the plural term *tíos* can include both aunts and uncles, and the Spanish equivalents of the terms *uncle* and *aunt* are therefore hyponyms of *tíos*.

While hyponymy is found in all languages, the concepts that have words in hyponymic relationships vary from one language to the next. In Tuvaluan (a Polynesian language), the higher term *ika* (roughly, 'fish') has as hyponyms not only all terms that refer to the animals that English speakers would recognize as fish but also terms for whales and dolphins (which speakers of English recognize as mammals) and for sea turtles (which are reptiles). Of course, we are dealing with folk classifications here, not scientific classifications.

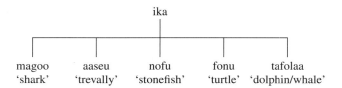

Thus there is variability across languages as to the exact nature of particular hyponymic relationships.

In a semantic field, hyponymy may exist at more than one level. A word may have both a hyponym and a superordinate term, as *blue* has in Figure 6.1. Because they refer to different "types" or "shades" of blue, the terms *turquoise*, *aquamarine*, and *royal blue* are hyponyms of *blue*. *Blue* in turn is a hyponym of *color*. We thus have a hierarchy of terms related through hyponymic relationships. Similar hierarchies can be established for many semantic fields, almost without limit. In the "cooking" field, *fry* has hyponyms in the terms *stir-fry*, *sauté*, and *deep-fry* and is itself a hyponym of *cook*. The lower we get in a hier-

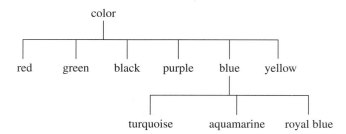

Figure 6.1

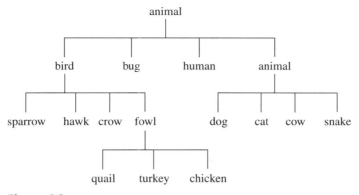

Figure 6.2

archy of hyponyms, the more marked the terms: *cook* is relatively unmarked; *stir-fry* is considerably more marked. The intermediate term *fry* is less marked than *stir-fry* but more marked than *cook*.

Examples of multiple layers of hyponymic relationships abound in the area of folk biological classification, as illustrated in Figure 6.2. Note that the term *animal* appears on two levels. English speakers use *animal* for at least two different referents: (1) animals as distinct from plants and rocks, and (2) animals (generally mammals other than humans) as distinct from humans, birds, and bugs. Cases in which a word has different senses at different levels of a hyponymic hierarchy are not uncommon.

Hyponymy is one of several relationship types with which speakers organize the lexicon. It is based on the notion of *inclusion*: if the referent of term *A* (for example, *color*) includes the referent of term *B* (for example, *red*), then term *B* (*red*) is a *hyponym* of term *A* (*color*). Hyponymy is important in everyday conversation—we use it whenever we say "B is a kind of A" (*red* is a kind of *color*)—and for such tasks as using a thesaurus, which is organized according to hyponymic relationships.

Meronymy: Part/Whole Relationships

A second important hierarchical relationship between words is the one found in pairs such as *hand* and *arm* or *room* and *house*. In each pair, the referent of the first term is part of the referent of the second term. A hand, however, is not "a kind of" arm, and thus the relationship between *hand* and *arm* is not hyponymic. Instead, we call it a *part/whole relationship* or a meronymic relationship. Part/whole relationships are not a property of pairs of words only: *hand, elbow, forearm, wrist,* and several other words are in a part/whole relationship with *arm*. Other examples of meronymy include words such as *second* and *minute, minute* and *hour, hour* and *day, day* and *week*, none of which could be described without reference to the fact that one is a subdivision of the other. Figure 6.3 illustrates the difference between a meronymic, or part/whole, relationship and a hyponymic relationship for the word *eye*.

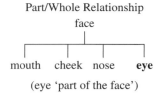
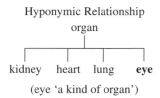

Figure 6.3

Synonymy

Two words are said to be **synonymous** if they mean the same thing. The terms *movie, film, flick,* and *motion picture* all have the same set of referents in the real world and are usually taken to be synonymous terms. To address the notion of synonymy more formally, we can say that term *A* is synonymous with term *B* if every referent of *A* is a referent of *B* and vice versa. For example, if every movie is a film and every film is a movie, the terms *movie* and *film* are synonymous. The "vice versa" is important: without it, we would be defining hyponymy.

You may wonder why speakers of a language bother to keep synonyms, given that they only add redundancy to the lexicon. English has many synonymous pairs such as *cloudy* and *nebulous*, *help* and *assist*, *skewed* and *oblique* (the result of English having borrowed the second term of each pair from French or Latin). When we assert that two terms are synonymous, we usually base that judgment on linguistic meaning only. Thus, even though *movie, film, flick,* and *motion picture* have the same linguistic meaning, they differ in social and affective meaning. *Film* may strike you as appropriate for movie classics or art movies; it is a more highbrow term. You recognize that *flick* is used chiefly in informal contexts, while *motion picture* is more traditional or industry related. Thus we can consider the terms to be synonymous if we specify that we are taking only linguistic meaning into account. At the social and affective levels, however, they are not synonymous.

In fact, there are very few true synonyms in the lexicon. More often than not, terms that appear to be synonymous have different social and affective connotations. Even if we restrict meaning to linguistic meaning, words that appear synonymous at first glance often refer to slightly different sets of concepts or are used in different situations. The adjectives *fast, quick,* and *rapid* may be used interchangeably in reference to someone's running speed, but a *fast talker* (a 'slippery or deceptive person') is different from a "quick talker"; some people live lives

Try It Yourself For each of these, provide a synonym or near synonym in the same word class. (An example is given for the first word in each set.)

Adjective: *keen (sharp), former, juvenile, speedy, speechless, strong, fertile, bare*

Noun: *bard (poet), juvenile, appointment, tool, agony, matrimony, rubbish, chief*

Verb: *enclose (fence), kidnap, stammer, seek, praise, clothe, agitate, pester, commit*

in the *fast lane*, not the "rapid lane"; and *quick* is the most appropriate term to describe a mind or a glance, while *rapid* is the usual term when reference is made to a person's *stride*, especially metaphorical strides, as in learning to type or do mathematics. Under the circumstances, is it accurate to say that these adjectives are synonymous?

The fact that there are few true synonyms in the lexicon of a language reflects the general tendency of speakers to make the most of what's available to them. If two terms have the same referent, the meaning of one is usually modified to express differences in linguistic, social, or affective meaning. Although true synonymy is rare, the notion is useful because it helps describe similarities between the meanings of different terms in the lexicon.

Antonymy

The word **antonymy** derives from the Greek root *anti-* ('opposite') and denotes opposition in meaning. In contrast to synonymy and hyponymy, antonymy is a *binary* relationship that can characterize a relationship between only two words at a time. Terms *A* and *B* are antonyms if when *A* describes a referent, *B* cannot describe the same referent, and vice versa.

The prototypical antonyms are pairs of adjectives that describe opposite notions: *large* and *small*, *wide* and *narrow*, *hot* and *cold*, *married* and *single*, *alive* and *dead*. Antonymy is not restricted to adjectives, however. The nouns *man* and *woman* are also antonyms because an individual cannot be described by both terms at once. *Always* and *never* form an antonymous pair of adverbs: they have mutually exclusive referents. The verbs *love* and *hate* can also be viewed as antonyms because they refer to mutually exclusive emotions. Antonymy is thus a binary relationship between terms with complementary meanings.

Intuitively, you can see a difference between the antonymous pair *large/small* and *single/married*. The first pair denotes notions that are relatively subjective. You would agree that blue whales are large mammals and mice are small mammals, but whether German shepherds are large or small dogs depends on your perspective. The owner of a Chihuahua will say German shepherds are large, but the owner of a Great Dane may judge them to be on the small side. Furthermore, adjectives such as *large* and *small* have superlative and comparative forms: blue whales are the *largest* of all mammals; German shepherds are *larger* than Chihuahuas but *smaller* than Great Danes. Antonymous pairs that have these characteristics are called *gradable* pairs.

In contrast to *large* and *small*, *single* and *married* are mutually exclusive and complementary. A person cannot be single and married at the same time. With respect to marital status, a person cannot be described with a term that does not have either *single* or *married* as a hyponym; thus *single* and *married* are complementary. Furthermore, *single* and *married* generally cannot be used in a comparative or superlative sense (someone's being legally "more single" than another single person is impossible). The pair constitutes an example of *nongradable* antonymy (also sometimes called *complementarity*).

There are thus two types of antonymy: gradable and nongradable. If terms *A* and *B* are *gradable* antonyms and if *A* can be used to describe a particular referent, then *B* cannot be used to describe the same referent, and vice versa. If *A* and *B* are *nongradable* antonyms, the same condition applies along with an additional condition: if *A* cannot describe a referent, then that referent must be describable by *B*, and vice versa. So *male* and *female*, *married* and *single*, *alive* and *dead* can be viewed as nongradable antonyms, while *hot* and *cold*, *love* and *hate*, *always* and *never* are gradable. Typically, for gradable antonyms, there will be words to describe intermediate stages: *sometimes, seldom, occasionally, often* are gradations between *always* and *never*.

As you recognize, the distinction between gradable and nongradable antonymy is sometimes blurred by speakers. In English, for example, it is reasonable to assume that whatever is alive is not dead and that whatever is dead is not alive, and thus that the adjectives *dead* and *alive* form a nongradable pair. However, we do have expressions such as *half dead, barely alive,* and *more dead than alive*. Such expressions suggest that, in some contexts, we see *alive* and *dead* as gradable antonyms.

Finally, antonymous words often do not have equal status with respect to markedness. For example, when you inquire about the weight of an object, you ask *How heavy is it?* and not *How light is it?*—unless you already know that the object is light. Notice also that the noun *weight*, which describes both relative heaviness and relative lightness, is associated with *heavy* rather than with *light* (as in the expressions *carry a lot of weight* and *throw one's weight around*). Of the antonymous pair *heavy* and *light, heavy* is more neutral than *light* and is thus less marked. In the same fashion, *tall* is less marked than *short, hot* less marked than *cold,* and *married* less marked than *single* (we say *marital status*, not "singleness status"). Although there is some variation across languages as to which word of a pair is considered less marked, there is a surprising agreement from language to language.

Try It Yourself For each of these, provide an antonym in the same word class:

Adjective: *palatable* (distasteful), *open, haughty, shallow, chilly, entire, rare*

Noun: *hindsight* (foresight), *insider, failure, benefit, chaos, certitude, fecundity*

Verb: *ignite* (extinguish), *reveal, remember, appear, expand, cleanse, bend*

Converseness

Another important relationship invokes the notion of oppositeness, although it does so in a way that differs from antonymy. Consider the relationship between *wife* and *husband*. If A is the husband of B, then B is the wife of A. Thus *wife* is the converse of *husband*, and vice versa. **Converseness** characterizes a reciprocal semantic relationship between pairs of words. Other examples of converse pairs include terms denoting many other kinship relations, such as *grandchild* and *grandparent* or *child* and *parent*; terms describing professional relationships, such as *employer* and *employee* or *doctor* and *patient*; and terms denoting relative positions in space or time, such as *above* and *below, north of* and *south of,* or *before* and *after*.

Converse pairs can combine with other types of opposition to form complex relationships. The antonymous pair *father: mother* is in a converse relationship with the antonymous pair *son: daughter*. Generally, converse pairs denote relationships between objects or between people. Some converse relationships are a little more complex. The verb *give*, for example, requires a subject and two objects (*She gave him the book*). The converse of *give* is *receive*, except that the relationship is neither a "reversal" of the subject and the direct object as it would be with *kiss* and *be kissed* (*Smith kissed Jones* versus *Jones was kissed by Smith*) nor a mutual subject/possessor relation such as *husband* and *wife*; rather, the relationship is between the subject and the indirect object.

> Siddharta gave Jessie a present.
>
> Jessie received a present from Siddharta.

Other pairs of words with a similar relationship include *lend* and *borrow* and *buy* and *sell*. Note that *rent* is its own converse in American English.

> Eve rents an apartment to Adam.
>
> Adam rents an apartment from Eve.

When there is a possibility of confusion, the preposition *out* can be attached to *rent* in the meaning of 'lending out for money.' In British English, this sense of *rent* is described by the verb *let* (*flat to let*). In some languages, a single word is used for 'buy' and 'sell.' In Samoan, for example, the word *faʔatau* carries both meanings, while the Mandarin Chinese words *măi* 'buy' and *mài* 'sell' are etymologically related. These facts suggest that converseness is an intuitively recognizable relationship.

Polysemy and Homonymy

Two other notions that are closely related to the basic relationship types are **polysemy** and **homonymy**. In contrast to the notions discussed above, polysemy and homonymy refer to similarities rather than differences between meanings. A word is *polysemous* (or polysemic) when it has two or more related meanings. The word *plain*, for example, can have several related meanings, including:

1. 'easy, clear' (*plain English*)
2. 'undecorated' (*plain white shirt*)
3. 'not good-looking' (*plain Jane*)

Homographs have the same spelling but different meanings (and pronunciations), such as *dove* 'a kind of bird' and *dove* 'past tense of *dive*' or *conduct* as a verb and *conduct* as a noun, where the verb has primary stress on the second syllable and the noun has it on the first syllable. *Homophones* have the same pronunciation but different senses: *sea* and *see*, *so* and *sew*, *two* and *too*, *plain* and *plane*, *flower* and *flour*, *boar* and *bore*, *bear* and *bare*, or *eye*, *I*, and *aye*. Words are *homonymic* when they have the same written *or* spoken form but different senses. A narrower definition of homonym limits the term to word sets that are both homographic and homophonous, as with *bank* of a river and savings *bank* or the adjective *still* 'quiet' (*still waters*) and the adverb *still* 'yet' (*still sick*). Languages exhibit polysemy and homonymy in their lexicons to varying degrees. A language such as Hawaiian, which has a restricted set of possible words because of its phonological structure, has a good deal more homonymy than English has (see "Sequence Constraints" in Chapter 4 and Figure 7.3).

A difficulty arises in distinguishing between homonymy and polysemy: How do we know if we have separate lexical items rather than a single word with different senses? Consider *plain*. How would we know whether or not the three adjectival senses ('easy,' 'undecorated,' 'not good-looking') constitute different words that happen to sound the same? Using spelling as a criterion is misleading: many sets of words are distinct but have the same spelling—as, for example, the noun *sound* 'noise' and the noun *sound* 'channel of water,' or *bank* 'financial institution' and *bank* 'shore of a river.' Yet the problem is important for anyone who wants to arrange or use the entries of a dictionary (in which different senses of the same word are grouped under a single entry but each homonymous form has its own distinct entry).

There is no simple solution. If there is a clear distinction between polysemy and homonymy, it must involve several criteria, no one of which would be sufficient by itself and some of which may yield different results. We have already excluded spelling as an unreliable criterion. One modestly reliable criterion is a word's historical origin, or *etymology*. We can consider that there are two words of the form *sound* corresponding to the two meanings given above because they derive from different historical roots. Likewise, the word *bank* meaning 'financial institution' is a borrowing from French, whereas *bank* meaning 'shore of a river' has a Scandinavian origin. The various antonyms and synonyms of a word provide a different kind of criterion for distinguishing between polysemy and homonymy. *Plain* in the sense of 'easy, clear' and *plain* in the sense of 'undecorated' share a synonym in *simple* and an antonym in *complex*. This fact suggests that they are indeed two meanings of the same polysemic word. No shared synonym or antonym can be identified for the two meanings of *sound*, as shown in Figure 6.4.

Finally, we can ask whether there is any commonality between different senses of what appears to be the same word. The two meanings of *plain* indicated above can be characterized as 'devoid of complexity,' which suggests that they are related, but no such superordinate description exists for *sound* 'stretch of water' and *sound* 'noise.' Thus *plain* in these two senses is polysemic, while the two senses of *sound* reflect homonymous lexical items. (Of course, other senses of *plain* may or may not belong to separate words.)

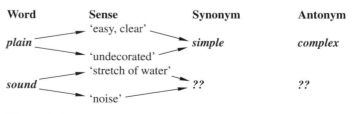

Word	Sense	Synonym	Antonym
plain	'easy, clear' 'undecorated'	*simple*	*complex*
sound	'stretch of water' 'noise'	??	??

Figure 6.4

While these criteria help distinguish between polysemy and homonymy, they are not foolproof. It is often difficult to decide whether a particular pair of lookalike and sound-alike word forms are separate homonymous words or simply the same polysemic word with different senses. Although homonymy and polysemy can be distinguished as different notions, the boundary between them may not be clear-cut in particular cases.

Metaphors

Difficulties in drawing a distinction between polysemy and homonymy arise partly from the fact that speakers often use words metaphorically. A traditional notion of **metaphor** sees it as an extension in the use of a word beyond its primary sense to describe referents that bear similarities to the word's primary referent. The word *eye*, for example, can be used to describe the hole at the dull end of a needle, the bud on a potato, or the center of a storm. The similarities between these referents and the primary referent of the word *eye* are their roundish shape and their more or less central role or position in a larger form. People frequently create new metaphors, and once a metaphor becomes accepted speakers tend to view the metaphorical meaning as separate from its primary sense, as in *booking* a flight, *tabling* a motion, *seeing* the *point*, *stealing* the *head*lines, *buying* time, studying a foreign *tongue*. It's thus tough to determine whether one word with two meanings exists or two words with different but metaphorically related meanings.

Metaphors occur constantly in day-to-day speaking and writing because they are a fundamental part of our thinking. The following examples were gleaned from newspaper headlines:

Tennis star Serena Williams <u>breezed</u> through the early matches

The dollar is <u>falling</u> *sharply*

His speech was the <u>catalyst</u> for a new popular *upheaval*

Oakland officials praise police for <u>curbing</u> protest violence

Oil *spill's* economic impact <u>muted</u>, so far

In the first example, the verb *breeze* is of course not meant literally; it is used to give the impression that Williams won the matches effortlessly, as a breeze might blow easily across a tennis court. Similarly, the underlined words in the other four sentences are meant to be interpreted as metaphors, whose effectiveness relies on our ability to see that in some contexts words are not to be interpreted literally. Besides the underlined words, other metaphors can be identified in the italicized words *sharply*, *upheaval*, and *spill*. (The mechanisms that we use in figuring out when a word must be interpreted metaphorically are discussed in Chapter 9.)

Metaphors aren't formed haphazardly. Observe, for example, the following metaphors that refer to the notion of time:

I look <u>forward</u> to seeing you again this weekend.

Experts do not <u>foresee</u> an increase in inflation in the near future.

He <u>drags up</u> old grudges from the past.

Once in a while, we need to <u>look back over our shoulders</u> at the lessons that history has taught us.

A pattern is apparent in these examples: In English, we construct time metaphors as if we physically move through time in the direction of the future. Thus the future is forward in the first two examples. Metaphors that refer to the past use words that refer to what is left behind, as in the latter two examples. Metaphors that violate this pattern would sound strange:

> *I look back to seeing you again this weekend.
>
> *He drags down old grudges from the past.

Another principle that governs the creation of metaphors is this: "Ideas are objects that can be sensed." Thus they can be smelled, felt, and heard.

> Your proposal smells fishy.
>
> I failed to grasp what they were trying to prove.
>
> I'd like your opinion as to whether my plan sounds reasonable.

Writers and critics often talk about the writing process as "cooking."

> I let my manuscript simmer for six months.
>
> Who knows what kind of a story he is brewing up!
>
> Their last book was little more than a half-baked concoction of earlier work.

"The heart is where emotions are experienced" is a common principle on which our metaphors for emotions are based.

> It is with a heavy heart that I tell you of her death.
>
> You shouldn't speak lightheartedly about this tragedy.
>
> The rescuers received the survivors' heartfelt thanks.

The construction of metaphors thus follows preset patterns.

Most of the metaphors discussed so far are relatively conventionalized—that is, they are common in speech and writing because they are preset. But language lends itself to creative activities, and speakers do not hesitate to create new metaphors. Even when we create our own metaphors, however, we must follow the principles that regulate conventionalized metaphors. In English, metaphors that refer to time obey the convention of "moving through time in the direction of the future."

Some metaphorical patterns are frequent across the world's languages, as with the word for 'eye' used metaphorically for roundish objects, as discussed above. But other principles of metaphor vary from language to language. For example, in many languages it is not the heart that is the seat of emotions. Polynesian languages such as Samoan and Tahitian treat the stomach as the metaphorical seat of emotions. It is likely that some of these principles reflect different cultures' views of the world. The exact workings of the link between culture and language are still not fully understood.

Metaphors play a significant role in the development of cognitive linguistics, which has demonstrated how big a role metaphorical thinking plays in our language, our thinking, and our lives more generally. Rather than as principally a poetic device, some researchers view our cognitive system as "fundamentally metaphorical in nature" and as having profound daily effects. Lakoff and John-son have written:

> How we think metaphorically matters. It can determine questions of war and peace, economic policy, and legal decisions, as well as the mundane choices of everyday life. Is a military attack a "rape," "a threat to our security," or "the defense of a population against terrorism"? The same attack can be conceptualized in any of these ways with very different military consequences.

Lexical Semantics: Discovering Relationships in the Lexicon

Hyponymy, part/whole relationships, synonymy, gradable and nongradable antonymy, converseness, polysemy, homonymy, and metaphor—lexical se-mantics is primarily concerned with discovering relationships in the lexicon of languages. The semantic relationships of a word are, in a sense, part of its meaning: the word *cold* can be defined as a gradable antonym of *hot*, as hav-ing the expression *sensation of heat* as a superordinate term, and as being more marked than *hot* but less marked than *chilly* and *freezing*. By knowing how the meaning of a word interacts with the meaning of other words, we can begin to understand its meaning.

Lexical semantics, of course, does not explain the difference in meaning be-tween words that are as unlike as *gorilla* and *doubtful*. For lexical semantics to be useful, it must be applied to particular areas of the lexicon in which word senses have shared characteristics. Thus the notion of semantic field becomes useful. If the word *gorilla* is placed in its appropriate semantic field, its relation-ship to *chimpanzee* and *great ape* can be investigated. Similarly, the word *doubt-ful* can be contrasted with *certain*, *probable*, *likely*, and other words that express likelihood or certainty.

The different types of relationships described above are the most basic tools of lexical semantics. They are basic because one type cannot be characterized in terms of another type. For example, an antonymous relationship between two words cannot be explained in terms of hyponymy, part/whole relationships, synonymy, converseness, or metaphor.

Function Words and Categories of Meaning

The lexicon is not made up exclusively of content words such as *father*, *pigeon*, *stir-fry*, and *democracy*, which refer to objects, actions, or abstract concepts. It also contains function words such as the conjunctions *if*, *however*, and *or*; the determiners *a*, *the*, and *these*; and the auxiliaries *may*, *should*, and *will*. The role of these categories is to signal grammatical relationships.

Tense and Modality

Many categories of meaning are associated with function words and function morphemes. Bound morphemes can denote several categories of meaning in

English, including number (*toys* v. *toy*) and tense (*walked* v. *walk*). In other languages, the same categories are expressed not by means of bound morphemes but by separate words. In Tongan, the function word *ʔoku* denotes present tense, while *naʔe* denotes past tense.

ʔoku	ʔalu	e	fineʔeiki	ki	kolo
Present	go	the	woman	to	town

'The woman is going to town.'

naʔe	ʔalu	e	fineʔeiki	ki	kolo
Past	go	the	woman	to	town

'The woman was going to town.'

Whether tense is expressed through bound morphemes or separate lexical items is not important for semantics. What is important is that there is the semantic category *tense* that affects the meaning of sentences in both Tongan and English.

Semantic categories such as tense are conveyed by function words and function morphemes, but their scope extends beyond the constituent in which they occur. The meaning of a tense morpheme affects the whole sentence because the **tense** of the verb determines the time reference of the entire clause. The category *tense* (and other semantic categories like it) thus refers to both word meaning and clause meaning.

Modality, or *mood*, is a category through which speakers can convey their attitude towards the truth or reliability of their assertions (called *epistemic modality*) or express obligation, permission, or suggestion (called *deontic modality*). The sentences in the following pairs differ as to their *epistemic* modality:

1. She has *probably* left town by now. (probability)

   She has left town by now. (assertion)

2. Harry *must've* been very tall when he was young. (conjecture)

   Harry was very tall when he was young. (assertion)

3. They *may* come to the party. (possibility)

   They are coming to the party. (assertion)

And those in the following pairs differ as to their *deontic* modality:

4. He *must* come tomorrow. (command)

   He is coming tomorrow. (statement)

5. They *may* take the dishes away. (permission)

   They are taking the dishes away. (statement)

The two types of modality are interrelated, as witnessed by the fact that the same words (*must* and *may*, for example) can denote either type, depending on the context. Modality can be expressed through auxiliary verbs such as *may*, *should*, or *must* (which are called *modal* auxiliaries); through *modal* verbs such as *order*, *assume*, and *allow*; through *modal* adverbs such as *possibly* or *certainly*; and in some languages through affixes attached to verbs or nouns. Such affixes are common in Native American languages, some of which can have extremely complex systems of modal affixes and particles.

Reference

A noun phrase in an utterance may or may not have a corresponding entity in the real world. **Reference** concerns the ability of linguistic expressions to refer to real-world entities. If someone says *I read a new biography of James Joyce last weekend*, the expressions *I* and *a new biography of James Joyce* refer to real-world entities. By contrast, if someone says *I'd like to find a short biography of James Joyce*, there is in the speaker's mind a real-world entity corresponding to *I* but not to *a short biography of James Joyce*. (A short biography of James Joyce may exist, but in this sentence the speaker does not have in mind a real-world entity to which the expression refers.)

In the examples below, note the difference in reference for different uses of a given phrase. In examples 1, 3, and 5, the underscored phrases do not have a referent; we say they are not referential or that they are nonreferential. In 2, 4, and 6, the very same expressions do have referents in the real world; they are referential.

1. Can you recommend <u>a good western</u> for kids? (nonreferential)
2. Last night I saw <u>a good western</u> on HBO. (referential)
3. She'd buy <u>a new Ford Explorer</u> if she found one on sale. (nonreferential)
4. She test-drove <u>a new Ford Explorer</u> that she liked. (referential)
5. I'm searching for <u>the best Chinese restaurant in the city</u>. (nonreferential)
6. On Tuesday I ate at <u>the best Chinese restaurant in the city</u>. (referential)

As these examples show, reference is a property, not of words or phrases as such, but of linguistic expressions as they occur in actual discourse. The same phrase can be referential in one utterance and nonreferential in another. Note, too, that reference cannot be equated with definiteness, a subject to which we return below. (Reference is investigated further in Chapter 8.)

Deixis

The word *deixis* is related to the Greek adjective *deiktikos*, meaning 'pointing, indicative.' **Deixis** is the marking of the orientation or position of entities and events with respect to certain *points of reference*. Consider the following sentence addressed to a waiter by a restaurant customer while pointing to items on a menu:

I want this dish, this dish, and this dish.

To interpret this utterance, the waiter must have information about who *I* refers to, about the time at which the utterance is produced, and about what the three noun phrases *this dish* refer to. We say that *I* is a *deictic expression*, and so are the present-tense form of the verb and the three noun phrases *this dish*. Our ability to interpret them enables us to interpret the sentence, and we can't interpret them out of context. The context is critical.

Deixis consists of three semantic notions, all related to the orientation or position of events or entities in the real world. *Personal deixis* is commonly conveyed through personal pronouns: *I* versus *you* versus *he* or *she*. *Spatial deixis* refers to orientation in space: *here* versus *there* and *this* versus *that*. *Temporal deixis* refers to orientation in time, as in present versus past, for example.

Personal Deixis Many of the utterances that we produce daily are comments or questions about ourselves or our interlocutors.

> *I* really should be going now.
>
> Did *you* return the video *I* asked *you* to?
>
> In this family, *we* never smoke and seldom drink.

The pronouns *I*, *you*, and *we*—along with *she*, *he*, *it*, and *they* (and alternative forms)—are markers of personal deixis. When we use these pronouns, we orient our utterances with respect to ourselves, our interlocutors, and third parties.

Personal pronouns are, of course, not the only tool used to mark personal deixis. The phrase *this person* in the sentence *You may enjoy scary roller-coaster rides, but this person doesn't care for them at all* may be used to refer to the speaker if the speaker wishes to express, say, annoyance or disdain. Likewise, in court, etiquette may require you to use the noun phrase *Your Honor* in addressing a judge: *Would Your Honor permit a brief recess?* Personal deixis is thus not associated exclusively with pronouns, although pronouns are the most common way to express personal deixis. In this discussion, we concentrate primarily on pronouns as markers of personal deixis.

The most basic opposition in personal-deixis systems is that between speaker (English *I*; German *ich*; Persian *man*; Thai *chăn*) and addressee (English *you*; German *du*; Persian *to*; Thai *thəə*). This opposition in *person* is so basic that it is reflected in the pronominal systems of all languages. Pronouns that refer to the speaker (or to a group including the speaker) are called *first-person* pronouns, and pronouns that refer to the addressee (or to a group including the addressee) are called *second-person* pronouns.

Besides the contrast between first person and second person, pronoun systems often have separate forms for the *third person*—that is, any entity other than the speaker and the person spoken to. In English, *he*, *she*, *it*, and *they* denote third-person entities. But third-person pronouns are not found in all languages. Some languages simply do not have special forms to refer to third-person entities. In these languages, third-person entities are referred to with a demonstrative such as *this* or *that*, or they remain unexpressed. In Tongan, a verb without an expressed subject is understood as having a third-person subject.

> na?e   a?u
> Past   arrive
> '(He/She/It) arrived.'

Tongan does have a third-person pronoun form but uses it only for emphasis.

> na?e   a?u   ia
> Past   arrive   he/she
> 'He/She is the one who arrived.'

That some languages lack separate third-person pronouns reflects the fact that the third person is less important than the first and second persons in personal deixis. In fact, the third person can be defined as an entity *other than* the first person and *other than* the second person. Because it can be described in terms of the other two persons, it is a less basic distinction in language in general. The singular pronoun system of English can thus be described as follows:

speaker only	I
hearer only	you
neither speaker nor hearer	he/she/it

Some languages make finer distinctions in their pronominal systems, while others make fewer distinctions (see the section on "Semantic Universals" in Chapter 7). In *all* languages, though, there are separate first-person and second-person pronouns.

Besides person, personal-deixis systems may mark distinctions in gender and number. In English, a gender distinction is made only in the third-person singular: *he* for masculine, *she* for feminine, and *it* for referents that are neither masculine nor feminine. In other languages, gender may be marked in other persons as well. In Hebrew, the second-person singular pronoun is *ata* for masculine referents but *at* for feminine referents. In some circumstances, Japanese distinguishes between masculine and feminine first-person singular pronouns. Number is marked on English pronouns in the first person (*I* versus *we*) and the third person (*he/she/it* versus *they*); the second-person pronoun *you* is used for reference to both singular and plural entities. In many languages, there are separate second-person singular and plural pronouns (French *tu* and *vous*; German *du* and *ihr*; Persian *to* and *shoma*). Singular and plural are not the only number categories that can be distinguished: some languages have distinct dual forms to refer to exactly two people, and a few languages even mark a distinction between "a few" and "many" referents (see the chart of Fijian pronouns in Chapter 7).

Finally, personal deixis frequently reflects the social status of referents. In French the choice of a pronoun in the second person depends on the nature of the speaker's relationship to the addressee. If speaker and addressee are of roughly equal social status, the pronoun *tu* is used; to mark or create social distance or social inequality, a speaker uses the plural pronoun *vous* instead of *tu*, even when addressing one person. Considerably more complex systems are found in languages such as Japanese, Thai, and Korean. Strictly speaking, the use of deictic devices to reflect facts about the social relationship of the participants is a distinct type of deixis, commonly referred to as *social deixis*.

Thus personal deixis can mark a number of overlapping distinctions: person, gender, number, and social relations. Languages express these distinctions in different combinations, marking some and not others. As noted, however, the basic distinction between first person and second person is found in all languages and appears to be a basic semantic category in all deictic systems.

Spatial Deixis Spatial deixis is the marking of the orientation or position in space of the referent of a linguistic expression. The categories of words most commonly used to express spatial deixis are demonstratives (*this, that*) and adverbs (*here, there*). Demonstratives and adverbs of place are by no means the only categories that have spatial deictic meaning; the directional verbs *go* and *come* also carry deictic information, as do *bring* and *take*.

Languages differ in terms of the number and meaning of demonstratives and adverbs of place. The demonstrative system of English distinguishes only between *this* (proximate—close to the speaker) and *that* (remote—relatively distant from the speaker). It is one of the simplest systems found. At the other extreme are languages such as Eskimo, which has 30 demonstrative forms. In all languages, however, the demonstrative system treats the speaker as a point of reference. Thus the speaker is a basic point of reference for spatial deixis.

Many spatial-deixis systems have three terms. Three-term systems fall into two categories. In one category, the meanings of the terms are 'near the speaker,' 'a little distant from the speaker,' and 'far from the speaker.' The Spanish demonstratives *este, ese, aquel* have these three respective meanings. In another type of three-term demonstrative system, the terms have the meanings 'near the speaker,' 'near the hearer,' and 'away from both speaker and hearer.' Fijian exemplifies such a system.

na   ŋone   o^{n}go
the   child   this (near me)
'this child (near me)'

na   ŋone   o^{n}gori
the   child   this (near you)
'that child (near you)'

na   ŋone   oya
the   child   that (away from you and me)
'that child (away from you and me)'

In both systems, however, the speaker is taken as either the sole point of reference or as one of two points of reference.

Spatial deixis thus represents the orientation of actions and states in space, and it is most commonly conveyed by demonstratives and by adverbs of place. Languages may have anywhere from 2 to 30 distinct demonstrative forms, but all demonstrative systems take the speaker as a basic point of reference.

Temporal Deixis A third type of deixis is temporal deixis—the orientation or position of the referent of actions and events in time. All languages have words and phrases that are inherently marked for temporal deixis, such as the English terms *before, last year, tomorrow, now,* and *this evening.* In many languages temporal deixis can be marked through tense, encoded on the verb with affixes, or expressed in an independent morpheme. In English, you must make an obligatory choice between the past-tense and the nonpast-tense form of verbs.

I walk to school every day. (nonpast tense)

I walked to school every day. (past tense)

To express a future *time*, English has no distinct verbal inflection (it lacks a future *tense*) but uses a multiword verb in the nonpast tense.

I will walk to school next week. (nonpast tense for future time)

Tuvaluan is like English: *e* denotes nonpast, while *ne* is a past-tense marker.

au	e	fano	ki	te	fakaala
I	Nonpast	go	to	the	feast

'I am going/will go to the feast.'

au	ne	fano	ki	te	fakaala
I	Past	go	to	the	feast

'I went to the feast.'

In some languages, the choice is between future and nonfuture (with undifferentiated present and past).

In a number of languages, temporal deixis can be marked only with optional adverbs. This Chinese sentence can be interpreted as past, present, or future, depending on the context:

xià	yŭ
down	rain

'It was/is/will be raining.'

When there is the possibility of ambiguity, an adverb of time ('last night,' 'right now,' 'next week') is added to the sentence.

In languages that do not mark tense on verbs, another semantic category called **aspect** is frequently obligatory. Aspect is not directly related to temporal deixis but refers to the ways in which actions and states are viewed: as continuous (*I was talking*), repetitive (*I talked [every day]*), instantaneous (*I talked*), and so on.

Tense is thus not the only marker of temporal deixis, although it is frequently exploited by languages as the primary means of marking temporal deixis.

The most basic point of reference for tense is the moment at which the sentence is uttered. Any event that occurs before that moment may be marked as past, and any event that occurs after that moment may be marked as future.

The train arrived. (any time before the utterance moment)

The train is arriving. (at the moment of utterance)

The train will arrive. (any time after the utterance moment)

When the point of reference is some point in time other than the moment of utterance, we say that tense is *relative*. Relative tense is used in many languages when speakers compare the time of occurrence of two events.

The dean finally invited me in after I had waited more than forty-five minutes.

Before I saw you yesterday, I had been sick for a week.

Some languages have complex rules of *tense concord* that dictate the form of verbs in relative contexts.

Deixis as a Semantic Notion The three types of deixis illustrate how semantic categories permeate language beyond the simple meaning of words. The deictic orientation of a sentence or part of a sentence can be conveyed through bound morphemes such as tense endings, through free morphemes and function words such as pronouns and demonstratives, or through content words such as *here* and *bring*. Deictic meaning is independent of the means used to convey it.

One purpose of semantics is to describe the important or essential parameters for characterizing deixis in language in general. We noted, for example, that distinguishing between speaker and addressee is an essential function of the personal deixis system of all languages. Similarly, every spatial deixis system has at least one point of reference, a location near the speaker. A spatial deixis system may also have a secondary point of reference near the hearer or addressee.

There is considerable overlap among the types of deixis. For example, personal, spatial, and temporal deixis share a basic point of reference: the speaker's identity and location in space and time. Some linguistic devices can be used to mark more than one kind of deixis. The English demonstrative *this* can be used for personal deixis (*this teacher*), spatial deixis (*this book*), and temporal deixis (*this morning*). Clearly, personal, spatial, and temporal deixis are closely related notions.

Textual Deixis   Another important type of deixis is *textual deixis*, which is the orientation of an utterance with respect to other utterances in a string of utterances. Consider, for example, the following pair of sentences:

He started to swear at me and curse. *That* made me even more angry.

The demonstrative *that* at the beginning of the second sentence refers not to a direction in space or time but rather to something previously mentioned. Often in this book, we use terms such as *above* or *below*, which refer to parts of the text with respect to other parts of the text. Such textual deixis enables speakers to package utterances together and indicate relationships across utterances. Because textual deixis is primarily concerned with utterances and their context, it goes beyond the scope of semantics as traditionally defined, although its importance is not to be underestimated.

Semantic Roles and Sentence Meaning

Although sentences, like words, must carry meaning in order for language speakers to understand each other at all, the meaning of sentences cannot be determined merely by adding up the meaning of each content word of the sentence. This fact was illustrated in the previous section, where we saw that bound morphemes and function words may carry meaning with semantic implications for the entire sentence. We also noted that sentences such as *The trainer licked the lion* and *The lion licked the trainer* convey different meanings despite the fact that they contain exactly the same words. Clearly, adding together the meaning of each word does not produce the full meaning of a sentence. More than the meaning of its individual content words must be taken into consideration when defining what contributes to the meaning of a sentence.

Consider the following active/passive counterparts, which, at the level of referential meaning, describe the same situation:

1. The lion licked the trainer.
2. The trainer was licked by the lion.

These sentences differ in that 1 is an active structure, 2 a passive structure. Since our concern here is with meaning, we ask how to account for the synonymy between 1 and 2.

Further, consider the following sentences:

3. David sliced the salami with a knife.

4. David used a knife to slice the salami.

Here is a situation not unlike the active/passive counterparts of 1 and 2, in that the sentences have the same referential meaning. Nevertheless, we need to characterize how sentences 3 and 4 mean "the same thing."

The situations just presented suggest that the crucial factor in the way sentence meaning is constructed is the *role* played by each noun phrase in relation to the verb, and to help with that we introduce the notion of **semantic role** of a noun phrase. (Some treatments of semantics use the term *thematic* role instead of *semantic* role.) *Semantic role* refers to the way in which the referent of a noun phrase contributes to the state, action, or situation described by the sentence. The semantic role of a noun phrase differs from its syntactic role (as subject, object, and so on), as illustrated by the contrast between sentences 1 and 2 above. In both sentences, the way in which the trainer is involved in the action is the same (and the way in which the lion is involved is the same). In other words, *the trainer* has the same semantic role in both sentences (and *the lion* has the same semantic role in both sentences). But despite its having the same *semantic* role in both 1 and 2, *the trainer* has different syntactic roles (direct object in 1 and subject in 2).

Semantic role is not an inherent property of a noun phrase: a given noun phrase can have different semantic roles in different sentences, as in the following:

5. Michael was injured by *a friend.*

6. Michael was injured with *a friend.*

Semantic role is a way of characterizing the meaning relationship between a noun phrase and the verb of a sentence, and above *a friend* is an agent in 5 but not in 6 (in 6, *a friend* could be characterized as having the semantic role of accompaniment).

Agents and Patients   The agent is the responsible initiator of an action; the patient is the entity that is affected by the verb and undergoes something of a change of state. In sentences 1 and 2 above, the agent is *the lion* and the patient is *the trainer.* That both sentences describe the same situation (and hence have the same referential meaning) can be explained by the fact that each noun phrase has the same semantic role in both sentences: *the lion* is the agent in both; *the trainer* is the patient in both.

Experiencers   In the following sentences the semantic role of the subject noun phrases is not agent: Courtney is not the responsible initiator of the actions denoted by the verbs but instead experiences a physical or mental sensation:

Courtney likes blueberry pancakes.

Courtney felt threatened by the lion.

In both sentences, the semantic role of Courtney is *experiencer*, which is defined as that which receives a sensory input. In English, experiencers can be either subjects or direct objects, depending on the verb. Compare the sentences about Courtney, in which the experiencer is the subject, with the following sentence, in which the experiencer is the direct object:

Dwayne sometimes astounds <u>me</u> with his wit.

Instruments and Causes   Now consider the semantic roles of the underscored noun phrases in the following sentences:

7. Michael was injured by <u>a stone</u>.
8. Michael was injured with <u>a stone</u>.

The difference between these sentences is that 8 implies that someone used a stone to attack Michael, while 7 does not require that implication. In 8, we say *a stone* is the *instrument*, or the intermediary, through which an unnamed agent performs the action; note that the definition of instrument requires that there be an agent, which is consistent with our interpretation of 8. In 7, *a stone* could be assigned the role of instrument only if an agent were doing the injuring. If the stone that injured Michael were part of a rockfall, *a stone* would be assigned the semantic role of *cause*, which is defined as any natural force that brings about a change of state. Instruments and causes can be expressed as prepositional phrases (as in examples 7 and 8) or as subjects, as in 9 and 10 below.

9. <u>The silver key</u> opened the door to the wine cellar. (INSTRUMENT)
10. <u>The heavy snow</u> caved in the roof. (CAUSE)

That the noun phrase *the silver key* is an instrument and not an agent is supported by the fact that it cannot be conjoined (linked by *and*) with an agent, as the following anomalous example shows:

*The silver key and John opened the door to the cellar.

However, an instrument *can* be conjoined with another instrument, and an agent can be conjoined with another agent.

<u>A push</u> and <u>a shove</u> opened the door to the cellar.

<u>John</u> and <u>Chelsey</u> opened the door to the cellar.

Recipients, Benefactives, Locatives, Temporals   A noun phrase can be a *recipient* (that which receives a physical object), a *benefactive* (that for which an action is performed), a *locative* (the location of an action or state), or a *temporal* (the time at which an action or state occurs).

I gave <u>Yolanda</u> a puppy. (RECIPIENT)

Stefan passed me a message for <u>Yolanda</u>. (BENEFACTIVE)

<u>The Midwest</u> is cold in winter. (LOCATIVE)

She left home <u>the day before yesterday</u>. (TEMPORAL)

The point of this enterprise is to characterize the possible semantic roles that noun phrases can fill in a sentence. Every noun phrase in a clause is assigned a semantic role, and, aside from coordinate noun phrases, the same semantic role cannot be assigned to two noun phrases in a single clause. Consequently, a sentence such as the following is semantically odd or anomalous because it contains two instrumental noun phrases, which are underlined:

*This ball broke the window with a hammer.

In addition, in most cases a noun phrase can be assigned only one semantic role. In rare instances, though, a noun phrase may be assigned two roles. For example, in the sentence *Geoff rolled down the hill*, if Geoff rolled down the hill deliberately, he is both agent and patient because he is at once the responsible initiator of the action and the entity that undergoes the change of state.

Semantic Roles and Grammatical Relations

Semantic roles and grammatical relations are not the same thing, as we have noted, and it is important to understand the relationship between them. For example, in English, the subject of a sentence can be an agent (as in the underlined noun phrase in sentence 1), a patient (as in 2), an instrument (3), a cause (4), an experiencer (5), a benefactive (or recipient) (6), a locative (7), or a temporal (8), depending on the verb.

1. The janitor opened the door. (AGENT)
2. The door opened easily. (PATIENT)
3. His first record greatly expanded his audience. (INSTRUMENT)
4. Bad weather ruined the grape harvest. (CAUSE)
5. Serge heard his father whispering. (EXPERIENCER)
6. The young artist won the prize. (BENEFACTIVE OR RECIPIENT)
7. Arizona attracts asthmatics. (LOCATIVE)
8. The next day found us on the road to Alice Springs. (TEMPORAL)

In certain English constructions, the subject may not have any semantic role, as with the "dummy *it*" construction, in which *it* fills the subject slot but is semantically empty.

It became clear that the government had jailed him.

So the notion of subject is independent of the notion of semantic role, and we could show the same thing of direct objects and other grammatical relations. Conversely, semantic roles do not appear to be constrained by grammatical relations. A locative, for example, may be expressed as a subject (as in 1 below), a direct object (2), an indirect object (3), or an oblique (4).

1. The garden will look great in the spring. (subject)
2. William planted the garden with cucumbers and tomatoes. (direct object)
3. The begonias give the garden a cheerful look. (indirect object)
4. The gate opens on the garden. (oblique)

Nevertheless, there is a relationship between grammatical relations and semantic roles. Consider the following sentences, all of which have *open* as a verb:

Michele opened the door with this key. (AGENT)

The door opened easily. (PATIENT)

This key will open the door. (INSTRUMENT)

The wind opened the door. (CAUSE)

The grammatical subjects of the sentences above are an agent (*Michele*), a patient (*the door*), an instrument (*this key*), and a cause (*the wind*). Such variety is not found with all verbs. The verb *soothe*, for example, can have an instrument or a cause as subject.

This ointment will soothe your sunburn. (INSTRUMENT)

The cold stream soothed my sore feet. (CAUSE)

To have an experiencer as the grammatical subject of the verb *soothe*, we use a passive construction.

I was soothed by the herbal tea. (EXPERIENCER)

Clearly, the verb controls the range of variation allowed in each case. Speakers know the semantic roles that each verb allows as subject, direct object, and so on. In the mental lexicon, there is what we might call a "tag" attached to the verb *soothe* indicating that only instruments and causes are allowed in subject position, whereas the tag attached to the verb *open* permits the subject to be agent, patient, instrument, or cause.

Semantic roles are universal features of the semantic structure of all languages, but how they interact with grammatical relations such as subject and direct object differs from language to language. Equivalent verbs in different languages do not carry similar tags. The tag attached to the English verb *like*, for example, permits only experiencers as subjects.

I like French fries. (EXPERIENCER)

But only patients can be the subjects of the equivalent Spanish verb *gustar*.

Las   papas fritas   me   gustan. (PATIENT)
the   French-fries   to-me   like
'I like French fries.' (Literally, 'French fries to me are pleasing.')

A similar situation is found for verbs of liking and pleasing in many other languages, including Russian. In some languages, the verb meaning to understand allows its subjects to be experiencers or patients, as in Samoan. The choice depends on emphasis and focus.

ʔua   maalamalama   aʔu   i   le   mataaʔupu.
Present-tense   understand   I   Object-marker   the   lesson
'I understand the lesson.'

ʔua	maalamalama	le	mataaʔupu		iate	aʔu.
Present-tense	understand	the	lesson		to	me

'I understand the lesson.' (Literally: 'The lesson understands to me.')

Some languages distinguish between agent and experiencer more carefully than English does. For example, the verb might take a subject when the action is intentional but a direct object when it is unintentional.

In addition to cross-linguistic variation with respect to specific verbs, languages vary in the degree to which different semantic roles fit into different grammatical slots in a sentence. In English, as we saw, the subject slot can be occupied by noun phrases of any semantic role—depending on the verb. Many English verbs allow different semantic roles for subject, direct object, and so on. But the situation is different in many other languages. Russian and German verbs do not allow nearly so much variation in semantic roles as English verbs do, and in those languages there is a much tighter bond between semantic roles and grammatical relations.

COMPUTERS, CORPORA, AND SEMANTICS

Computerized corpora are useful to dictionary makers and others in establishing patterns of language that are not apparent from mere introspection. For example, patterns of **collocation**—which words go together—are much more readily understood with the help of a computerized corpus of natural-language texts. Such patterns can be helpful in highlighting meanings, parts of speech, and words that co-occur with frequency.

Further, while it may appear that synonymous words can be used in place of one another, corpora can show that it is not common for words to be readily substitutable for one another. For example, *little* and *small*, *big* and *large*, and *fast* and *quick* are generally considered synonyms. But a cursory examination of key word in context (KWIC) concordances for these pairs shows that they are not straightforwardly substitutable. Table 6.1 shows a selection of KWIC entries for the word *little*, and Table 6.2 shows a selection of KWIC entries for *small*. (The samples come from the British National Corpus and have been concordanced using WordSmith. Either end of a KWIC line may show incomplete words.)

Note that quite a few sentences in Table 6.1 would not tolerate the substitution of *small* for *little*—including 2, 3, 5, 6, 9, 10, 11, 15, 16, 17, and 21. Taking 3 as an example, English does not permit "not a small irritated." Of those instances where substitution is possible, several would sound odd or convey a different connotation, such as 1, 4, and 8. In 1, "poor little rich boy" and "poor small rich boy" carry different senses. As the examples in Table 6.2 show, *little* is more readily substitutable for *small*; part of the reason is that in its use as an adjective *little* does in fact carry denotations and connotations much like those of most uses of *small*. But, looking again at Table 6.1, we see that the opposite is not true. This is because *little* is not only an adjective meaning 'small' but also part of an adverb, in the expressions *a little ruffled*, *a little dispirited*, and *a little open* (13, 20, 24) where it modifies an adjective, and *a little longer* (12) where it modifies an adverb. Yet dictionaries cite *little* and *small* as synonyms. In the "Other Resources" section at the end of this chapter, you'll find the link to a site that provides sample sentences containing any word or expression that you are interested in examining. From such a list you can learn a great deal about the semantics of any word or phrase. ■

Table 6.1 *Concordance for* little

1	ke council activities and so on. The poor	**little** rich boy was looked after by a second
2	a few hours of stall avoidance training and	**little,** if any, spinning. Vienna Dear Fräu
3	andt, I am deeply distressed, and also not a	**little** irritated, by the direction events hav
4	Even without the threat to his job, he had	**little** choice. There may be little or no
5	job, he had little choice. There may be	**little** or no hope of finding those particular
6	cted, some as yet unrecorded. But he had	**little** reason yet to ask for a search warrant
7	him if he so much as tried. But there is	**little** point, for instance, in turning on an
8	and those of his friends. You noticed my	**little** ploy. Current findings suggest a c
9	of success between classes have changed very	**little.** Objectively, he was little more a
10	changed very little. Objectively, he was	**little** more attractive to the Conservatives w
11	nd that it was necessary for him to retire a	**little** from the active life in which he had p
12	d energy upon his real work. We talked a	**little** longer, and then I bought some chocola
13	ess was still there, but the fur was maybe a	**little** ruffled. I wish all men enjoyed th
14	joyed their whole bodies, rather than just a	**little,** wobbly bit of it.' There is a nee
15	it.' There is a need, however, to look a	**little** more at the role of Parliament. ON
16	role of Parliament. ON A SLOW pitch with	**little** bounce, South Africa once again were u
17	and seven overs to spare. Addition of a	**little** silicone lubricant (vacuum grease, DOW
18	f air and quite softly-spoken and actually a	**little** shy-looking, and he'd made a point of
19	is ugly body quiet and still above them as a	**little** gravestone. Once the carriage was
20	motion, she closed her eyes, tired now and a	**little** dispirited. Then the front zip of
21	to his importuning hands and he eased away a	**little** so that his fingers could slide inside
22	original access to land, an issue upon which	**little** progress had been made—with the pos
23	survey, the privatization programme involved	**little** change in management or improvement in
24	rovement in efficiency. Might leave us a	**little** open sometimes, but with the pace we s
25	core a few goals!! we reckoned we knew a	**little** bit more about what makes children tic
26	unge and the dining room area was probably a	**little** bit smaller If you want to be happ
27	be happy and have a happy face and spread a	**little** joy around then there is just one way.

Table 6.2 *Concordance for* small

1	ad of papers with individual readerships too	**small** for us to analyse (the Scotsman, the G
2	into tears at the sight of the house and the	**small** familiar crowd waiting for her outside
3	McCloy, who lives here in town, runs a very	**small** unsuccessful sort of decorating busines
4	the Führer down to spring 1941 rested in no	**small** measure on the lack of serious interfer
5	ws volatile session His clothes were too	**small** now, pinching him at the neck, the wais
6	(although of course the numbers are far too	**small** for any quantitative analysis) can be s
7	illery and mortars, and themselves down to a	**small** amount of ammunition, the remnants of t
8	The Captain's white face had greyed, his	**small** mouth tightening into a cruel line.
9	esult, the individual may retain only a very	**small** percentage of the extra income earned a
10	unications products are helping both big and	**small** businesses in more than one hundred co
11	ex longed for a pond in the garden, but with	**small** children around the idea was shelved—
12	subsequent continuation of a large number of	**small** unions and, as a secondary consequence,

Table 6.2 *Concordance for* small (continued)

13	le, often near remote skerries, headlands or **small**	uninhabited islands, and this necessita
14	ime of the Russian conquest, although only a **small**	remnant of this nationality survives to
15	d bought their house and provided her with a **small**	income. perfect like a small velvet
16	ences for arbitrage risk were also generally **small,**	and 88% of the cases fell within the r
17	ntract). In doing so, she knocked down a **small**	boy and immediately went down again to
18	essible to teachers, along with a monitor (a **small**	black and white one would do), then it
19	In the end they hauled the Gnomes into a **small**	ante-room across the galleried landing
20	e famous Shaker pegged wall-rail for hanging **small**	cupboards, shelves, mirrors and even ch
21	ne.' The most marked contrast between the **small**	towns and their larger counterparts is
22	ment. Thirty years later what had been a **small**	village was a big town and would have b
23	ves that churchyards provide a focus and are **small**	enough for a group of local enthusiasts
24	s pursuing a policy of devaluing the yuan in **small,**	frequent steps, in an effort to boost
25	any factors specific for countries, even for **small**	regions within a country and for groups
26	5°F/Gas Mark 3), allowing 40 minutes for the **small**	basins and 50 minutes for the large bow
27	and the back of the Admiralty proper runs a **small**	unnamed side-street which I must have p
28	might reply 'Yes, but these cost savings are **small**	compared to the fuel savings you get wi

Summary

- Semantics is the study of meaning in language.
- Semantics traditionally focuses on linguistic meaning, but languages also convey social meaning and affective meaning.
- Words, sentences, and utterances can all carry meaning, and sentence meaning and utterance meaning must be distinguished.
- The study of sentence meaning falls primarily within the domain of semantics.
- Within a sentence, words may have *scope* over other constituents, as *only* has scope over the bracketed constituent in *He only knew [what he had read in the letter]*.
- Pragmatics is the branch of linguistics that concerns itself with utterance meaning.
- Lexical semantics is the study of meaning relationships in vocabulary. The *types* of relationships that hold among sets of words are universal, though the particular word sets to which they apply vary from language to language.
- Semantic fields are sets of words whose referents belong together on the basis of fundamental semantic characteristics.
- The words in a semantic field can be arranged in terms of these relationships: hyponymy (a kind of), meronymy or part/whole (subdivision), synonymy (similar meaning), gradable and nongradable antonymy (opposite meaning), converseness (reciprocal meaning), polysemy (multiple meanings), homonymy (same written or spoken form), and metaphor (derived meaning).

- Semantic notions such as deixis can be expressed by bound morphemes (*-ed* in *walked*) and function words (*that* in *that one*) as well as by content words (*tomorrow*).
- There are several types of deixis: personal (*you, me*), spatial (*here, there*), and temporal (*now, then*). All require that a point of reference be identified.
- In relation to the speaker and the moment of utterance, the here and now is highly privileged as a point of reference in all three types of deixis.
- The meaning of a sentence is not simply the sum meaning of its words.
- Sentence semantics aims to uncover the basic relationships between the noun phrases and the verb of a sentence.
- Semantic roles (e.g., agent or instrument) are not inherent properties of noun phrases but are relational notions. They are independent of the grammatical relations (e.g., subject or object) of the noun phrase. The verb determines which semantic role may be used in particular grammatical slots of a sentence.
- This chapter has described nine semantic roles:

  agent: the responsible initiator of an action
  patient: the entity that undergoes a certain change of state
  experiencer: the entity that receives a sensory input
  instrument: the intermediary through which an agent performs an action
  cause: the natural cause that brings about a change of state
  benefactive: the entity for which an action is performed
  recipient: the entity that receives a physical object
  locative: the location of an action or state
  temporal: the time at which the action or state occurs

- Semantic roles are universal, but languages differ as to how particular roles are encoded in syntax.

What Do You Think? REVISITED

- *Phyllis's questions. George Washington* and *the first president of the United States* usually refer to the same person, namely that man who lived from 1732 to 1799 and became president of the United States in 1789. *George Washington* is his name, but *George Washington* does not mean 'the first president of the United States.' The two expressions have the same *referent* but different *senses*. The fact that two expressions refer to the same entity does not necessarily entail that they *mean* the same thing. Consider this example: "Some Maryland residents like to claim that John Hanson was the first president of the United States." Even though that statement is true, it would not be true to say, "Some Maryland residents like to claim that John Hanson was George Washington." The fact that one is true but not the other demonstrates that they do not mean the same thing.

- *Doug's doubt.* Although synonyms might not have the same co-occurrence patterns with other words, they may still mean the same thing in some contexts. Doug has identified a frame into which you could slot *fast* or *quick* but not with the same meaning, and that fact seems to be an argument that the two words are not used exactly the same way, but they are synonymous. And of course "fast talker" is an idiom that may have its origin in someone's talking quickly, but the idiom identifies someone who persuades by smooth or deceptive talk.
- *Uncle Earnest.* The term that characterizes the semantic relationship between *uncle* and *nephew* is "converse," by no means the same as opposite. Among other meanings, *hot* means 'not cold,' but *nephew* is not the same as 'not uncle.' In addition, opposites usually represent the extremes of words that can be arrayed along a continuum, for example from *hot* to *warm* to *lukewarm* to *cold*, where *hot* and *cold* are opposites. Converse terms, by contrast, usually involve a reciprocal relationship—as with the verbs *buy* and *sell*, *give* and *receive*, or *teach* and *learn* and the nouns *doctor* and *patient* or *employer* and *employee*.
- *Cousin Kevin.* Words like *mine* and *yours* are "deictic" expressions, and their meaning depends, in this case, on who is saying them. *Mine* means something like 'belonging to the speaker' (or the reported speaker), so when cousin Kevin says "It's mine," he's claiming ownership, and when his daughter uses the very same words she's claiming ownership. Deictic words must be interpreted in context. ■

Exercises

Practice Exercise

A. Provide a word whose referent has the specified semantic relationship to the words below.

1. *mother* and *father* are the hyponyms.
2. *knee* is the part.
3. *jewel* is the superordinate term.
4. *bicycle* is the whole.
5. *tall* is the antonym.
6. *grandmother* is the converse.
7. *niece* is the converse.
8. *obese* is the synonym.

B. From Table 6.1, provide the numbers of the KWIC concordance lines in which the word *little* could be glossed in each of these senses:

1. 'small'
2. 'not much'
3. 'small amount of'

Based on English

6-1.   The following sentences are ambiguous. Based on the discussion in this chapter and Chapter 5, describe the ambiguity.

  1) They found the peasants revolting.

  2) The car I'm getting ready to drive is a Lamborghini.

  3) There is nothing more alarming than developing nuclear power plants.

  4) Erika does not like her husband, and neither does Natalie.

  5) They said that they told her to come to them.

  6) He met his challenger at his house.

6-2.   Identify the differences in linguistic, social, and affective meaning among the words and phrases in each of the following sets:

  1) hoax, trickery, swindle, rip-off, ruse, stratagem

  2) delightful, pleasant, great, far-out, nice, pleasurable, bad, cool

  3) man, guy, dude, jock, imp, lad, gentleman, hunk, boy

  4) eat, wolf down, nourish, devour, peck, ingest, graze, fill one's tummy

  5) tired, fatigued, pooped, weary, languorous, zonked out, exhausted, spent

  6) stupid person, idiot, nerd, ass, jerk, turkey, wimp, punk, airhead, bastard

6-3.   Some of the sets of terms below form semantic fields. For each set:

  a. Identify the words that do *not* belong to the same semantic field as the others in the set.

  b. Identify the superordinate term of the remaining semantic field, if there is one (it may be a word in the set).

  c. Determine whether some terms are less marked than others, and justify your claim.

  1) acquire, buy, collect, hoard, win, inherit, steal

  2) whisper, talk, narrate, report, tell, harangue, scribble, instruct, brief

  3) road, path, barn, way, street, freeway, avenue, thoroughfare, interstate, method

  4) stench, smell, reek, aroma, bouquet, odoriferous, perfume, fragrance, scent, olfactory

6-4.   For each semantic relationship specified below, provide one or more examples of words whose referents have that relationship to the specified word and identify the name of the semantic category that is used to cover your answer.

  Example: *fish* is the superordinate term (hypernym).

Answer: *salmon, trout, ling cod, flounder, swordfish, tuna* are its hyponyms.

1) *Irish setter, dalmatian, cocker spaniel* are the hyponyms.

2) *tabby, tom, Persian, alley* are the hyponyms.

3) *dog, cat, goldfish, parakeet, hamster* are the hyponyms.

4) *knife, fork, spoon* are the hyponyms.

5) *true* is the antonym.

6) *inaccurate* is the antonym.

7) *sister* is the converse.

8) *teacher* is the converse.

9) *partner* is the converse.

10) *toe* is the part.

11) *menu* is the whole.

12) *friend* is the synonym.

13) *teacher* is the synonym.

6-5. In the following sets of sentences one or more words are used metaphorically. Provide a general statement describing the principle that underlies each set of metaphors; then add to the set one metaphor that follows the principle.

Example:

I let my manuscript *simmer* for six months.

She *concocted* a retort that readers will appreciate.

There is no easy *recipe* for writing effective business letters.

General statement: "The writing process is viewed as cooking." Additional example: "He is the kind of writer who *whips up* another trashy novel every six months." ~assault / attack~

1) Members of the audience besieged him with counterarguments.

His opponents tore his arguments to pieces.

My reasoning left them with no ammunition.

The others will never be able to destroy this argument.

His question betrayed a defensive stance.

2) This heat is crushing.

The sun is beating down on these poor laborers.

The clouds seem to be lifting.

The northern part of the state is under a heavy snowstorm.

The fresh breeze cleared up the oppressive heat.

6-6. Determine whether the words in each of the following sets are polysemic, homonymous, or metaphorically related. In each case, state the criteria used to arrive at your conclusion. You may use a dictionary.

1) to run down (the stairs); to run down (an enemy); to run down (a list of names)

2) the seat (of one's pants); the seat (of government); the (driver's) seat (of a car)

3) an ear (for music); an ear (of corn); an ear (as auditory organ)

4) to pitch (a baseball); pitch (black); the pitch (of one's voice)

5) to spell (a word); (under) a spell; a (dry) spell

6) vision (the ability to see); (a man of) vision; vision (as a hallucination)

7) the butt (of a rifle); the butt (of a joke); to butt (as a ram)

6-7. Identify the semantic role of each underscored noun phrase in these sentences:

1) In October, I gazed from the wooden bridge into the small river behind our college.

2) I have forgotten everything that I learned in grade school.

3) The snow completely buried my car during the last storm.

4) Fifty kilos of cocaine were seized by the DEA.

5) Natalie was awarded one thousand dollars' worth of travel.

6) The hurricane destroyed the island.

7) Their ingenuity never ceases to amaze me.

6-8. **a.** Examine Table 6.1 to determine which words frequently co-occur with *little*, either preceding or following it.

b. List all the immediate constituents of which *little* is an element in the examples of Table 6.1; on that basis say what kind of a phrase *little* functions in—for example, an adjective phrase or adverb phrase.

Example 12: *a little longer*—adverb phrase; 20: *a little dispirited*—adjective phrase

Based on English and Other Languages

6-9. A "tag" is attached to every verb in the lexicon, indicating which semantic role can be assigned to each noun argument. For example, the verb *bake* can have an agent as its subject (as in sentence 1), a patient (as in sentence 2), a cause (3), or an instrument (4). But in subject position it does not allow locatives (5) or temporals (6).

1) Matthew baked scones.

2) The cake is baking.

3) The sun baked my lilies to a crisp.

4) This oven bakes wonderful cakes.

5) *The kitchen bakes nicely.

6) *Tomorrow will bake nicely.

a. Determine which semantic roles these verbs allow as subject on the basis of the sentences provided: *feel, provide, absorb, thaw, taste.*

1) His hands felt limp and moist.

I could feel the presence of an intruder in the apartment.

This room feels damp.

They all felt under the blanket to see what was there.

This semester feels very different from last semester.

2) Gas lamps provided light for the outdoor picnic.

These fields provide enough wheat to feed a city.

Who provided these scones?

The accident provided me plenty to worry about.

Your textbooks provide many illustrations of this phenomenon.

The bylaws provide for dissolution of the board in these cases.

3) The students have absorbed so much material that they can't make sense of it anymore.

This kind of sponge does not absorb water well.

The United States absorbed the Texas Republic in 1845.

My work hours are absorbing all my free time.

The soil is absorbing the rain.

4) If Antarctica suddenly thawed, the sea level would rise dramatically.

Chicken does not thaw well in just two hours.

The crowd thawed after Kent arrived.

Kent's arrival thawed the party.

The heat of the sun will thaw the ice in the ice chest.

Ice thaws at 0 degrees Celsius.

The peace treaty will thaw relations between the United States and China.

5) This wine tastes like vinegar.

He's tasted every single hors d'oeuvre at the party.

I can taste the capers in the sauce.

b. Languages may differ with respect to the semantic roles that particular verbs may take. The following are semantically well-formed French sentences with the verb *goûter* 'taste':

Il n'a   jamais goûté au caviar.

he not-have ever   tasted the caviar

'He's never tasted caviar.'

Je goûte un goût amer dans ce   café.

I   taste a   taste bitter in   this coffee

'I taste a bitter taste in this coffee.'

By contrast, the following sentence is not well constructed:

*Les cuisses de grenouille goûtent bon.

the thighs of frog   taste   good

'Frogs' legs taste good.'

What is the difference between English *taste* and French *goûter* in terms of the range of semantic roles that they permit as subject?

Especially for Educators and Future Teachers

6-10. Your high school ESL class asks you whether *bank* in *bank of a river* and in *savings bank* are the same word. You note that the terms are both nouns and are spelled alike and pronounced alike. By trying to identify synonyms and antonyms (as in Figure 6.4), you construct an argument designed to persuade your students that they are different words and not the same word with different senses. To show the contrast, identify another pair of word forms that represent different senses of the same word, again constructing the argument by identifying synonyms and antonyms.

6-11. In your first year of teaching, you tell your middle school English class that the subject of a sentence is the "doer" of the action, and give as an example, *Devon scored the most points*. When you ask for other examples, a student volunteers *Disneyland is fun*, and you immediately see a problem: *Disneyland* is the subject of the sentence but not the doer of any action. Relying on your knowledge of semantic roles, what do you say to correct your explanation about the roles that subjects play in sentences?

6-12. Draw up characterizations of one or two sentences each to help your students remember the difference between a grammatical relation (e.g., subject or object) and a semantic role (e.g., agent or instrument).

6-13. Cite three pairs of expressions in each of which the referent for the two expressions is the same but the sense is different. Ex.: *Mt. McKinley* and *the highest peak in the United States*.

6-14. Writing handbooks sometimes urge writers to be cautious about where in a sentence to position the word *only*. They may recommend placing *only* immediately in front of the constituent within its scope (handbooks may phrase it as placing *only* in front of the words it *modifies*). In the sentences below, bracket the constituent within the scope of *only* and insert a caret where *only* could be placed to have it directly preceding the structure in its scope. (*Note*: These sentences are adapted from the British National Corpus.)

Example: That *only* leaves [one logical explanation]. (= That leaves *only* one logical explanation.)

a. She *only* needed to rest.

b. I *only* saw one tiny bit of it.

c. The opportunities have *only* been adopted halfheartedly.

d. Ads in newspapers usually *only* offer one product or a small range of products.

e. Cassie *only* knew of one stone like that.

Other Resources

Internet

LISU website: http://www.CengageBrain.com For users of this textbook. Provides updated Internet links as well as supplemental material for students and instructors. Here you will find interactive learning tools.

British National Corpus: http://www.natcorp.ox.ac.uk/ Here you can obtain up to 50 authentic sentences containing any word or expression you specify, chosen at random from the 100-million-word resources of the British National Corpus.

 Internet Thesaurus: http://thesaurus.com At this website you'll find access to an online thesaurus. With it you can explore the relationships among words, especially those in synonymous and antonymous relationships.

 WordNet: http://wordnet.princeton.edu/ In the words of its website, WordNet is a lexical database of English, developed under the direction of George A. Miller, with support from the National Science Foundation and other agencies. Nouns, verbs, adjectives and adverbs are grouped into sets of cognitive synonyms called "synsets," each expressing a distinct concept. The synsets are interlinked by means of conceptual-semantic and lexical relations. You can explore the network of related words and concepts with the browser at the website. The site also provides some information about ongoing research supported by NSF and Google into ways of enhancing and improving WordNet. There is so much to be learned at this website that you owe it to yourself to pay a visit and enjoy the experience!

 Thinkmap's Visual Thesaurus: http//www.visualthesaurus. com/ Type in a word at this site and venture into a visual thesaurus. Besides an impressive network of lexical and semantic relations usefully displayed, the site provides access to a visual thesaurus and pronunciations for modest fees. Clicking on any word in a displayed net rearranges the configuration to reveal a new set of relationships. Well worth at least a trial visit.

Suggestions for Further Reading

- **Stephen R. Anderson & Edward L. Keenan. 1985. "Deixis," in Timothy Shopen, ed.,** *Language Typology and Syntactic Description*, vol. 3 (Cambridge, UK: Cambridge University Press), pp. 259–308. A relatively brief and comprehensive treatment of deixis.
- **Alan Timberlake. 2007. "Aspect, Tense, and Mood," in Timothy Shopen, ed.,** *Language Typology and Syntactic Description*, vol. 3: *Grammatical Categories and the Lexicon*, **2nd ed.** (Cambridge, UK: Cambridge University Press), pp. 280–333. Provides a concise discussion of the semantic notions named in the title.
- **George Lakoff & Mark Johnson. 2003.** *Metaphors We Live By* (Chicago: University of Chicago Press). An update of the 1980 classic work on metaphors, reissued with an "Afterword, 2003," from which comes our quote in the section on "Metaphors."
- **George A. Miller. 1996.** *The Science of Words* (Indianapolis: W. H. Freeman). An accessible and award-winning treatment of the psychology of lexical meaning.
- **Sebastian Lobner. 2002.** *Understanding Semantics* (London: Arnold; New York: Oxford University Press). Appearing in the "Understanding Language Series," this is a thorough and wide-ranging introduction to semantics in general. It goes beyond the current chapter by treating sentence meaning more fully and by treating cognition, translation, and formal semantics.
- **Simon Winchester. 1998.** *The Professor and the Madman: A Tale of Murder, Insanity, and the Making of the* **Oxford** English Dictionary (New York: HarperCollins). Whether you're interested in a tale of murder and insanity or the making of the OED, this page-turner proves that lexicographers aren't harmless drudges.

Advanced Reading

Accessible treatments of semantics can be found in Lyons (1995) and Saeed (2009). Lexical semantics is discussed in Lehrer (1974), which focuses on semantic universals (discussed in Chapter 7 of this textbook). Cruse (1986) is a good overview of lexical semantics. Several of the papers in Holland and Quinn (1987) investigate connotation and the cultural elements in the organization of semantic fields. Other valuable works in related veins are Lakoff and Johnson (1989) and Fauconnier and Turner (2002). Cognitive linguistics and cognitive grammar, which we only mention in this chapter but which are increasingly important in semantic understanding, are discussed in Croft and Cruse (2004) and Langacker (2008). Deixis is discussed in Chapter 2 of Levinson (1983). General and practical treatments of lexicography can be found in Landau (2001) and the somewhat more advanced Atkins and Rundell (2008), the latter complemented by Fontenelle (2008), a collection of previously published influential articles, accessible to keen students.

References

Atkins, B. T. Sue & Michael Rundell. 2008. *The Oxford Guide to Practical Lexicography* (Oxford: Oxford University Press).

Croft, William & D. Alan Cruse. 2004. *Cognitive Linguistics* (Cambridge, UK: Cambridge University Press).

Cruse, D. A. 1986. *Lexical Semantics* (Cambridge, UK: Cambridge University Press).

Fauconnier, Gilles & Mark Turner. 2002. *The Way We Think: Conceptual Blending and the Mind's Hidden Complexities* (New York: Basic Books).

Fontenelle, Thierry, ed. 2008. *Practical Lexicography: A Reader* (Oxford: Oxford University Press).

Holland, Dorothy & Naomi Quinn, eds. 1987. *Cultural Models in Language and Thought* (Cambridge, UK: Cambridge University Press).

Lakoff, George & Mark Johnson. 1989. *More than Cool Reason: A Field Guide to Poetic Metaphor* (Chicago: University of Chicago Press).

Landau, Sidney I. 2001. *Dictionaries: The Art and Craft of Lexicography,* 2nd ed. (Cambridge, UK: Cambridge University Press).

Langacker, Ronald W. 2008. *Cognitive Grammar: A Basic Introduction* (New York: Oxford University Press).

Lehrer, Adrienne. 1974. *Semantic Fields and Lexical Structure* (Amsterdam: North-Holland).

Levinson, Stephen C. 1983. *Pragmatics* (Cambridge, UK: Cambridge University Press).

Lyons, John. 1995. *Linguistic Semantics: An Introduction* (Cambridge, UK: Cambridge University Press).

Saeed, John I. 2009. *Semantics,* 3rd ed. (Chichester: Wiley-Blackwell).

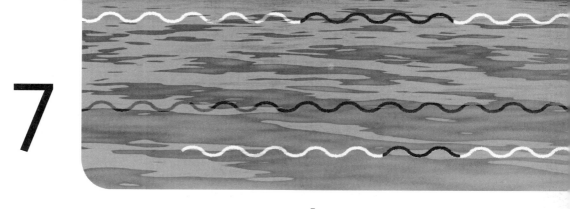

7

Language Universals and Language Typology

What Do You Think?

- Your niece announces one day that her teacher said English has 13 vowels, and she asks whether all languages have 13 vowels. What do you tell her?
- When cousins visit you in Chicago for your twenty-first birthday, you notice that in addressing more than one person Terry from Texas says "y'all" and Jerry from Jersey says "youse." You know those pronouns aren't "standard," but you wonder whether English ought to have a separate second-person plural pronoun. You also wonder whether languages typically have equivalents of *y'all* and *youse*. What's your conclusion?
- Your classmate Clarence is studying Japanese and comments that its word order is illogical: verbs appear at the *end* of the sentence and prepositions *after* the noun. He claims the logical order is Subject-Verb-Object, as in English, and says *pre-position* obviously means *before* the noun. What arguments might persuade Clarence that Japanese and English word orders are equally logical (or illogical)?
- Bruce wonders why his coworker Francesca, originally from the Philippines, mixes up English pronouns, referring even to her daughter as "he" and her son as "she." "Whenever she talks about someone, she uses the wrong pronoun," Bruce says. What would you suppose about pronouns in Tagalog that could cause such confusion?

Similarity and Diversity Across Languages

The languages of the world exhibit many different patterns of phonology, morphology, syntax, and semantics. Some have large inventories of phonemes; others only a few. In some languages, including French, Italian, and English, the basic structure of the clause is SVO: the subject comes before the verb, and the direct object follows the verb, as in these examples:

	Subject (S)	Verb (V)	Object (O)
French	Haussmann	fait aménager	la place.
English	Haussmann	redesigned	the square.
Italian	Keplero	modificò	la teoria di Copernico.
English	Kepler	modified	Copernicus's theory.

In languages such as Japanese and Persian, the subject and the direct object both occur before the verb, in an SOV pattern:

	Subject (S)	Object (O)	Verb (V)	
Japanese	Sono hebi ga	inu o	korosita.	
	That snake	the dog	killed.	'That snake killed the dog.'
Persian	Ali	ketabhara	mibæræd.	
	Ali	the books	is carrying.	'Ali is carrying the books.'

Given such variation, you might wonder whether the world's languages share any characteristics. As it happens, there are basic principles that govern the structure of *all* languages. These **language universals** determine what is possible and what is impossible in language structure. For example, while some languages have voiced and voiceless stops (b and p; d and t) and others have only voiceless stops (p and t), no language has yet been encountered that has voiced stops but no voiceless stops. This observation can be translated into a generalization expressing what is possible in the structure of a language (that is, a language can have both voiced and voiceless stops or only voiceless stops in its phonemic inventory) and excluding a combination of phonemes that is not known to occur in any of the world's languages (that is, voiced stops without voiceless stops).

Why Uncover Universals?

Language universals are statements of what is possible and impossible in languages. Viewed from a purely practical perspective, such principles are useful in that, if we can assume them to apply to all languages, they need not be repeated in the description of each language. Thus the study of language universals underscores the unity underlying the enormous variety of languages found in the world.

Much more important, language universals are important to our understanding of the brain and of the principles that govern interpersonal communication in all cultures. In the course of evolution, the human species alone has developed the ability to speak, thus distinguishing itself from all other animals, including other higher mammals. Humans have developed not one single language that is spoken and understood by everybody, but nearly 7,000 different ones, all complex and all sophisticated. If basic principles govern *all* languages, they are likely to be the result of whatever cognitive and social skills enabled human beings to develop the ability to speak in the first place. By studying language universals, we begin to understand what in the human brain and the social organization of everyday life enables people to communicate through language. The study of language universals offers a glimpse of the cognitive and social foundations of human language, about which so much remains to be discovered and about which so much research has been actively pursued in recent decades.

When postulating language universals, researchers must exercise caution because only relatively few of the world's languages have been adequately described. Further, much more is known about European languages and the major non-Western languages (such as Chinese, Japanese, Hindi, and Arabic) than about the far more numerous other languages of Africa, Asia, the Americas, and Oceania. In Papua New Guinea alone (an area about the size of the states of Washington and Oregon combined), over 700 languages are spoken, although grammatical descriptions of only a few dozen are available; very little or nothing at all is known about the others. Linguists proposing language universals must ensure that the proposed principles are applicable to more than the familiar European languages. Universals must be generally valid, whether for languages spoken by only a few dozen people in a highlands village of Papua New Guinea or by millions of people in Europe, Africa, or Asia. Since little or nothing is known about the structure of hundreds of languages, universal principles can be proposed only as tentative hypotheses based on the languages for which descriptions are available.

Caution must also be exercised in drawing inferences from language universals. These universal principles help explain why language is species specific, but there is a big step between uncovering a universal and explaining it in terms of human cognitive or social abilities. More often than not, explanations for language universals as symptoms of cognitive or social factors rely on logical arguments rather than on solid scientific proof. Of course, the fact that explanations can be only tentative does not mean they should not be proposed, but it does mean that linguists must be cautious and keep in mind that languages fulfill many roles at once.

Language Types

A prerequisite to the study of universals is a thorough understanding of the variety found among the world's languages. **Language typology** focuses on classifying languages according to their structural characteristics. (*Typology* means the study of types or the classification of objects into types.) Examples of typological classifications are "languages that have both voiced and voiceless stops in their phonemic inventories" (like English, French, and Japanese) and "languages that have only voiceless stops" (like Mandarin Chinese, Korean, and Tahitian). Since no language has voiced stops without voiceless stops, that type does not exist. Naturally, the languages in each category will differ, based on the criteria of classification. Of course, linguists can establish categories only according to specific criteria; the world's languages are so diverse in so many different ways that no overall typological classification of languages exists, even within a single level of linguistic structure such as phonology.

Typological categories have no necessary correspondence with groups of languages that have descended from the same parent language; in fact, typological categories cut across language families. Language types are independent of language families in principle, but members of the same family often do share certain typological characteristics as a result of their common heritage. Consequently, linguists include as many unrelated languages as possible in their proposed language types to ensure that the similarities among languages of any category are not the result of familial relationships.

This chapter explores both the variety found among the world's languages and the unity that underlies this variety. Uncovering language universals and classifying languages into types are complementary tasks. In order to uncover universal principles, we first need to know the extent to which languages differ from one another in terms of their structure. We would not want to posit a language universal on the basis of a limited sample of languages, only to discover that the proposed universal did not work for a type of language that we had failed to consider. A universal must work for all language types and all languages.

Similarly, the way in which we go about classifying languages and describing the different types of structures is determined in large part by the search for universals. It would be possible, for example, to set up a typological category grouping all languages that have the sound /o/ in their phonemic inventory. But such a typology tells us nothing about any universal principle underlying the structure of these languages, and their structures might have little in common other than the fact that /o/ appears in their phonemic inventory. In contrast, a typology of languages based on the presence or absence of nasal vowels reveals interesting patterns. It turns out that no language in the world has only nasal vowels. All languages must have oral vowels, whether or not they also have nasal vowels. This suggests that oral vowels are in some sense more "basic" or more indispensable than nasal vowels, which could be of great interest to our understanding of language structure. Therefore, this typology is useful, in that it has helped uncover a language universal. Whether a particular typological classification is interesting or useful depends on whether it helps uncover universal principles in the structure of languages.

The next few sections present examples of language universals and language types from semantics, phonology, syntax, and morphology. For each example, observe the interaction of typologies with universals, and note how different kinds of language universals are stated. Some examples will be taken up again toward the end of the chapter, where we examine cognitive and social explanations that have been proposed to account for language universals and language types.

Semantic Universals

Semantic universals govern the composition of the vocabulary of all languages. That semantic universals should exist at all may seem surprising at first. Anyone who has studied a foreign language knows how greatly the vocabularies of two languages can differ. Some ideas that are conveniently expressed with a single word in one language may require an entire sentence in another language. The English word *privacy*, for example, does not have a simple equivalent in French. (That doesn't mean that the French lack the notion of privacy!)

Similarly, English lacks an equivalent for the Hawaiian word *aloha,* which can be roughly translated as 'love,' 'compassion,' 'pity,' 'hospitality,' or 'friendliness' and is also used as a general greeting and farewell. Despite these cross-linguistic differences, however, there are some fundamental areas of the vocabulary of every language that are subject to universal rules. These areas include color terms, body part terms, animal names, and verbs of sensory perception.

Semantic universals typically deal with the less marked members of semantic fields (see Chapter 6), which are called *basic terms* in this context. As an example, consider the following terms, which all refer to shades of blue: *turquoise, royal blue,* and *blue. Blue* is a more basic term than the others: *turquoise* derives from the name of a precious stone of the same color, while *royal blue* refers to a shade of blue. The word *blue* is thus more basic than each of the other words, although for different reasons: unlike *turquoise, blue* refers primarily to a color, not an object; unlike *royal blue, blue* is a simple, unmodified term. The combination of these characteristics makes *blue* a less marked—more basic—color term than the others. *Basic terms* have three characteristics:

1. They are morphologically simple.
2. They are less specialized in meaning than other terms.
3. They are not recently borrowed from another language.

Semantic universals deal with terms like *blue* and not with terms like *turquoise* and *royal blue.*

Pronouns

Although pronoun systems can differ greatly from language to language, the pronoun system of every language follows the same set of universal principles.

All known languages have pronouns for at least the speaker and the addressee: the first person (*I, me*) and the second person (*you*). But there is great variability among the world's languages in the number of distinctions that are made by pronouns. The following chart presents the English pronominal system (we limit ourselves to subject pronouns).

English Pronouns

	SINGULAR	PLURAL
FIRST PERSON	I	we
SECOND PERSON	you	you
THIRD PERSON	he, she, it	they

In this chart, columns represent number: "singular" and "plural." The rows list person: first-person pronouns, second-person pronouns, and third-person pronouns. Standard American English uses the same form for both the singular and plural second-person pronoun (*you*).

The pronoun systems of other languages display other patterns. Spoken Castilian Spanish has separate forms for the singular and plural in each person;

in the example below, the two plural forms are the masculine and feminine pronouns. (Spanish also has "polite" pronoun forms, but we ignore them here.)

Castilian Spanish Pronouns

	SINGULAR	PLURAL	
		M	F
FIRST PERSON	yo	nosotros	nosotras
SECOND PERSON	tú	vosotros	vosotras
THIRD PERSON	él, ella	ellos	ellas

Some languages make finer distinctions in number. Ancient Sanskrit made a distinction between two people and more than two people. The form for two people is called the *dual*, and the form for more than two is called the *plural*. (In the chart below, the three words for the third person are the masculine, feminine, and neuter forms.)

Sanskrit Pronouns

	SINGULAR	DUAL	PLURAL
FIRST PERSON	aham	āvām	vayam
SECOND PERSON	tvam	ūvām	yāyam
THIRD PERSON	sas, tat, sā	tau, te, te	te, tāni, tās

Other languages have a single pronoun to refer simultaneously to the speaker and the addressee (and sometimes other people) and a separate pronoun to refer to the speaker along with other people but excluding the addressee. The first of these is called a first-person *inclusive* pronoun, the second a first-person *exclusive* pronoun. In English, both notions are encoded in *we*.

In contrast, Tok Pisin has separate inclusive and exclusive pronouns.

Tok Pisin Pronouns

	SINGULAR	PLURAL
FIRST-PERSON EXCLUSIVE	mi	mipela
FIRST-PERSON INCLUSIVE		yumi
SECOND PERSON	yu	yupela
THIRD PERSON	em	ol

Tok Pisin is an English-based creole (see Chapter 12), with most of its vocabulary coming from English. The English pronouns and other words that were taken by Tok Pisin speakers to form their pronoun system are easily recognizable: *mi* from *me*, *yu* from *you*, *em* probably from *him*, *yumi* from *you-me*, *ol* from *all*, and the plural suffix *-pela* probably from *fellow*.

Fijian has one of the largest pronoun systems of any language. It has a singular form for each pronoun, a dual form for two people, a separate "trial" form that refers to about three people, and a plural form that refers to more than three people (in actual usage, trial pronouns refer to a few people and the plural refers to a multitude). In addition, in the first-person dual, trial, and plural, Fijian, like Tok Pisin, has separate inclusive and exclusive forms.

Fijian Pronouns

	SINGULAR	DUAL	TRIAL	PLURAL
FIRST-PERSON EXCLUSIVE	au	keirau	keitou	keimami
FIRST-PERSON INCLUSIVE		kedaru	kedatou	keda
SECOND PERSON	iko	kemudrau	kemudou	kemunii
THIRD PERSON	koya	rau	iratou	ira

Between the extremes represented by English and Fijian are many variations. Some languages have separate dual pronouns; others do not. Some systems make a distinction between inclusive and exclusive pronouns; others do not.

All the world's languages have distinct first- and second-person pronouns, and most languages have third-person pronouns, inclusive first-person pronouns, and exclusive first-person pronouns. A four-person system (inclusive first-person and exclusive first-person, second-person, and third-person pronouns) is by far the most common. The four-person pronoun system is thus somehow more basic than a two-person or three-person type. In this respect, English is atypical.

Variations in pronoun systems are governed by a set of universal rules. To discover these universals, we need to establish a typology of pronoun systems.

Some Types of Pronoun Systems in the World's Languages
Systems with singular and plural forms—e.g., English, Spanish
Systems with singular, dual, and plural forms—e.g., Sanskrit
Systems with singular, dual, trial, and plural forms—e.g., Fijian
Systems lacking inclusive/exclusive distinction in first-person plural—
    e.g., English, Spanish
Systems with inclusive/exclusive distinction in first-person plural—e.g., Tok
    Pisin, Fijian

Some Types of Pronoun Systems That Do *Not* Occur
Systems lacking first-person and second-person pronouns
Systems with singular and dual forms but no plural forms
Systems with singular, dual, and trial forms but no plural forms
Systems that make an inclusive/exclusive distinction, but not in the first person
    (a logical impossibility)

Based on what we do and don't find in our typology, we postulate some universal rules.

Some Universal Rules

1. All languages have at least first-person and second-person pronouns.
2. If a language has singular and dual forms, then it will also have plural forms.
3. If a language has singular, dual, and trial forms, then it will also have plural forms.
4. If a language makes an inclusive/exclusive distinction in its pronoun system, it will make it in the first person.

Note that the converse of these rules is not true. The converse of universal rule 2, for instance, would state that if a language had separate plural forms, it would have separate dual forms. But even English proves this generalization wrong: it has separate plural forms but no dual. The implications thus go in only one direction.

It is important to note that semantic typologies and universals do not represent a measure of complexity in language or culture. The most we can infer from these differences is that some categories are more salient in some cultures than in others. Comparing the two examples of semantic universals discussed in this section, we also see that the pronoun system of English is one of the most restricted in the world, despite the fact that English has very rich scientific and color lexicons, to mention only two arenas. Thus, different arenas of the lexicon exhibit different degrees of elaboration in different languages. This does not mean that some languages are "richer" or "better" or "more developed" than others.

Phonological Universals

Vowel Systems

Another level of linguistic structure in which we can identify universal rules and classify languages into useful typological categories is phonology. In Chapter 3 we discussed the fact that languages can have very different inventories of sounds. Figure 7.1 represents the vowel system of standard American English, classified according to place of articulation. Compare this with Figure 7.2, which represents the vowel system of standard Parisian French (a conservative dialect retaining certain oppositions that have been lost in many other French dialects). The symbol /ü/ represents a high front rounded vowel as in the word

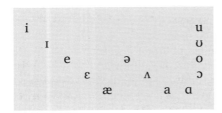

Figure 7.1 Vowels of American English

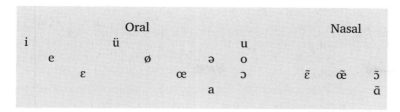

Figure 7.2 Oral and Nasal Vowels of Parisian French

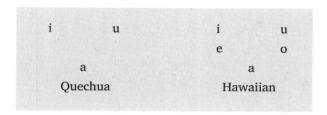

Figure 7.3 Vowels of Quechua and Hawaiian

/ʁü/ *rue* 'street'; /ø/ is an upper mid rounded vowel as in /fø/ *feu* 'fire'; /œ/ is a lower mid rounded vowel as in /bœʁ/ *beurre* 'butter'; and /ɛ̃/, /œ̃/, /ɔ̃/, and /ɑ̃/ are nasal vowels. Finally, Figure 7.3 compares the vowel systems of Quechua (spoken in Peru and Ecuador) and Hawaiian.

The first thing these four examples demonstrate is that different languages may have very different sets of vowels: English has several vowels in its inventory that French does not have, and vice versa. Second, the number of vowels in a language can vary considerably. Quechua has only 3 distinct vowels; along with the vowel systems of Greenlandic Eskimo and Moroccan Arabic, the Quechua vowel system is one of the smallest in the world. Hawaiian has 5 vowels, a very common number among the world's languages. At the other end of the spectrum, English has 13 vowels and French has 15, including the four nasal vowels.

Underlying such diversity, however, we find universal patterns. If we charted the vowel inventories of all known languages, we would confirm that languages usually have vowel systems that fall between the two extremes represented by Quechua and French. Thus every language has at least 3 vowel phonemes. Some have 4 vowels, like Malagasy, the language of Madagascar (whose vowels are /i ɛ ə ʊ/), and the Native American language Kwakiutl (which has /i a ə ʊ/). Some have 5 vowels, such as Hawaiian, Mandarin Chinese, and, as shown in Tables 3.3 and 3.5, Spanish and Japanese. Others, such as Persian and Malay, have 6 vowels; and so on up to 15.

Comparing the charts, we find that all languages include in their vowel inventory a high front unrounded vowel (/i/ or /ɪ/), a low vowel (/a/), and a high back rounded (/u/ or /ʊ/) or unrounded (/ɯ/) vowel. These vowels have allophones in some languages, particularly in languages with few vowels. In Greenlandic Eskimo, for example, /i/ has the allophones [i], [e], [ɛ], and [ə], depending on the consonants that surround it; but there are no minimal pairs that depend on these variants. Small variations also exist, but these variations do not really contradict the universal rule, which can be stated as follows: **All languages have a high front unrounded vowel, a low vowel, and a high back rounded or unrounded vowel in their phoneme inventory.** Note that this first universal rule describes what constitutes the minimal type and what is included in all other types.

The second universal rule is stated: **Of the languages that have four or more vowels, all have vowels similar to /i a u/** (as indicated by the first universal rule) **plus either a high central vowel /ɨ/** (as in Russian *vɨ* 'you') **or a mid front unrounded vowel /e/ or /ɛ/.** The third universal rule we can uncover from our vowel charts is this: **Languages with a five-vowel system include a mid front unrounded vowel.** In the five-vowel system of Hawaiian, for example, /e/ has allophones [ɛ] and [e]. Other languages with five-vowel inventories include Japanese (whose inventory is /i ɛ a ɔ ɯ/) and Zulu (/i ɛ a ɔ u/). Most languages with five vowels have a mid back rounded vowel (either /ɔ/ or /o/) in their inventory, like Japanese, Hawaiian, and Zulu. A few languages with a five-vowel system lack a mid back rounded vowel, although a similar sound is often included, as with Mandarin Chinese, whose inventory (/i ü a ë u/) includes the lower-mid back unrounded vowel /ë/.

We can thus state that languages with five-vowel inventories *generally* (but not always) have a mid back rounded vowel. This observation is applicable to languages with more than five vowels as well. The fourth universal rule thus reads: **Languages with five or more vowels in their inventories generally have a mid back rounded vowel phoneme.** This rule is stated in a different way from the first three rules in that it is not absolute. But it is a useful observation because it describes a significant tendency across languages.

Languages with six-vowel inventories like Malayalam (spoken in southwestern India) include /ɔ/ in their inventory and either /ɨ/ or /e/. Malayalam has in its inventory the three "obligatory" vowels /i a u/; the vowels /e/ and /ɔ/, as predicted by the second and third universal rules; and /ɨ/. These universal rules can be summarized as in Figure 7.4.

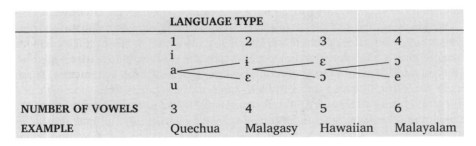

	LANGUAGE TYPE			
	1	2	3	4
NUMBER OF VOWELS	3	4	5	6
EXAMPLE	Quechua	Malagasy	Hawaiian	Malayalam

Figure 7.4 Summary of Universal Vowel Rules

Nasal and Oral Vowels

Other universal rules that regulate the vowel inventories of the world's languages can be uncovered, but we will mention only two more. The first states: **When a language has nasal vowels, the number of nasal vowels never**

exceeds the number of oral vowels. We can find examples of languages with fewer nasal vowels than oral vowels: Standard French, for example, has four nasal vowels and eleven oral vowels. We can also find examples of languages with an equal number of oral and nasal vowels: Punjabi (a language of northern India) has ten of each. But there are no known languages with a greater number of nasal vowels than oral vowels.

The second universal rule of interest is not a rule in the usual sense but a description of the most common vowel system: a five-vowel system consisting of a high front unrounded vowel (/i/ or /i/), a mid front unrounded vowel (/e/ or /ɛ/), a low vowel (/a/), a mid back rounded vowel (/o/ or /ɔ/), and a high back rounded vowel (/u/ or /ʊ/). Hawaiian is an example of such a system, as you can see by looking at the symmetry in the chart for Hawaiian vowels. Each vowel is maximally distant from the others, which minimizes the possibility of two vowels being confused. Such a five-vowel system thus has an ideal quality, a matter to which we return later in this chapter.

Consonants

Vowel systems are not the only area of phonology in which universal rules operate. The consonant inventories of the languages of the world also exhibit many universal properties. A few examples are presented here, although not in great detail, since they do not differ in nature from universals of vowel systems.

Recall (from Chapter 3) that the sounds /p t k/ are voiceless stops. Every language has at least one of these voiceless stops as a phoneme. While some languages lack affricates or trills, voiceless stops are found in all languages. In fact, most languages have all three of these sounds, even languages with small consonant inventories. Niuean (a Polynesian language), for example, has only three stops, three nasals, three fricatives, and an approximant, totaling ten consonants (in contrast to the twenty-four of American English). Yet the three stops are /p t k/. Put in the form of a universal, this generalization reads: **Most languages have the three stops /p t k/ in their consonant inventory**. This universal suggests that these three consonants are in some sense more basic than others.

It is clear, given our discussion, that this universal is not an absolute rule. Hawaiian (a language related to Niuean) has only /p/ and /k/. (That is why English words with the sound /t/ are borrowed into Hawaiian with a /k/, like *kikiki* 'ticket'). This universal is thus a *tendency*, rather than a statement of what is and isn't found among the world's languages.

Another important universal referring to stops has already been mentioned. Recall that the difference between the two sets of stops /p t k/ and /b d g/ is that the first set is voiceless, the second voiced. All six sounds have phonemic status in English, as is true in French, Spanish, Quechua, and many other languages. In some languages, however, we find only voiceless stops, such as in Hawaiian (and all other Polynesian languages), Korean, and Mandarin Chinese. Thus far, we have identified two types of languages: languages with both voiced and voiceless stops, and languages with only voiceless stops. As noted, every language has at least one voiceless stop in its inventory; consequently, there are no languages that have voiced stops but no voiceless stops, and no languages that have neither voiced nor voiceless stops. This typology allows us to derive the following universal rule: **No language has voiced stops without voiceless stops**.

Note that of the universals of stop inventories explored thus far, only one rule (and it is only a tendency) says anything about *which* stops are included in the inventories of languages. But there are other universals that deal with this question. We give only one example here: **If a language lacks a stop, there is a strong tendency for that language to include in its inventory a fricative sound with the same place of articulation as the missing stop.** For instance, Standard Fijian, Amharic (the principal language of Ethiopia), and Standard Arabic all lack the phoneme /p/, which is a labial stop. As predicted by the universal rule, all these languages have a fricative /f/ or /v/, whose place of articulation is similar to that of /p/. The fricative thus "fills in" for the missing stop. This rule, too, is only a tendency, as there are languages that violate it. Hawaiian, which lacks a /t/, has none of the corresponding fricatives /ð/, /θ/, /z/, or /s/. But most languages do follow the rule.

Syntactic and Morphological Universals

Word Order

Speakers of English and other European languages commonly assume that the normal way of constructing a sentence is to place the subject first, then the verb, and then the direct object (if there is one). Indeed, in English, the sentence *Mary saw John*, which follows this order, is well formed, while variations like *John Mary saw* and *saw Mary John* are not.

However, normal word order in a sentence differs considerably from language to language. Consider the following Japanese sentence, in which the subject is *Akiko*, the verb is *butta* 'hit (past tense),' and the direct object is *Taro*.

> akiko ga   taroo o   butta
> Akiko Subject Taro Object hit
> 'Akiko hit Taro.'

In Japanese, the normal word order is thus subject, direct object, and verb (SOV). If we changed this order, the result would be ungrammatical.

Now consider Tongan, in which the verb must come first, the subject second, and the direct object last (VSO). In the following sentence, the verb is *taaʔi* 'to hit,' the subject is a person named *Hina*, and the direct object is a person called *Vaka*.

> naʔe taaʔi ʔe   hina ʔa   vaka
> Past hit   Subject Hina Object Vaka
> 'Hina hit Vaka.'

Of course, not all English sentences follow the order subject-verb-direct object, or SVO. To emphasize particular noun phrases, English speakers sometimes place direct objects in clause-initial position as with *sewing* in *Sewing I hate, but I'll do it for you*. In questions like *Who(m) did you see?* the direct object *who(m)* is in first position. Similar word order variants are found in most languages. Sentences like the *sewing* and *whom* examples derive from more basic sentences, however, and are also less common than sentences that follow SVO order. Thus, even though some English constructions do not follow this order, we say that SVO order is basic in English, and that English is an SVO language. Examples of SVO languages include Romance languages (such as French, Spanish, and Italian), Thai, Vietnamese, and Indonesian. Japanese is an SOV language, as are Turkish, Persian, Burmese, Hindi, and the Native American languages Navajo, Hopi, and Luiseño. Tongan is a VSO language, as are most other Polynesian languages, Welsh, a number of Native American languages such as Salish, Squamish, Chinook, Jacaltec, and Zapotec, and some dialects of Arabic.

There are three other logical possibilities for combining verbs, subjects, and direct objects besides VSO, SVO, and SOV. Remarkably, however, very few languages have VOS, OVS, or OSV as basic word orders. Only a handful of languages are VOS, the best known being Malagasy and Fijian. Following is a basic sentence in Fijian showing that the direct object precedes the subject.

> ea   taya na   ŋone na yalewa
> Past hit   the child the girl
> 'The girl hit the child.'

OVS and OSV are the basic word order of only a handful of languages of the Amazon Basin, including Hixkaryana (OVS) and Nadëb (OSV). By far the most common word orders found among the world's languages are SVO, SOV, and, to a lesser extent, VSO.

Try It Yourself What characterizes the ordering of S and O in SVO, SOV, and VSO languages (the most common ones) and differentiates them from VOS, OVS, and OSV languages (the uncommon ones)?

In each of the three common configurations, S *precedes* O; in the uncommon configurations, S *follows* O. We can thus make a generalized statement: **In the basic word orders of the languages of the world there is an overwhelming tendency for the subject of a sentence to precede the direct object**.

There is a great deal more to universals of syntax. Two extreme cases are languages in which the verb comes first in the clause (called verb-initial languages and illustrated by Tongan) and languages in which the verb comes last (called verb-final languages and illustrated by Japanese). For the sake of simplicity, we exclude VOS and OSV languages from our discussion, though they follow basically the same rules as VSO and SOV languages respectively.

Possessor and Possessed Noun Phrases

If we look at the order of other syntactic constituents in verb-initial and verb-final languages, we find strikingly regular and interesting patterns. First of all, in most verb-final languages such as Japanese, possessor noun phrases precede possessed noun phrases.

> taroo no imooto
> Taro of sister
> 'Taro's sister'

In verb-initial languages the opposite order is most commonly found; in the following example from Tongan, the possessed entity is expressed first, the possessor last.

> ko e tuonga?ane ?o vaka
> the sister of Vaka
> 'Vaka's sister'

We have thus established the following rule: **There is a strong tendency for possessor noun phrases to precede possessed noun phrases in verb-final languages and to follow possessed noun phrases in verb-initial languages.**

Prepositions and Postpositions

To express position or direction, many languages use prepositions. As the word indicates, *prepositions* come *before* modified noun phrases (NP). In Tongan, for example, the prepositions *ki*, which indicates direction, and *?i*, which denotes location, both precede the NP they modify.

> ki tonga   ?i tonga
> to Tonga   in Tonga

Other languages have postpositions instead of prepositions. *Postpositions* fulfill the same functions as prepositions, but they follow the NP, as in this Japanese example.

> tookyoo ni
> Tokyo to
> 'to Tokyo'

Overwhelmingly, verb-initial languages have prepositions and verb-final languages have postpositions. The third rule can be stated as follows: **There is a strong tendency for verb-initial languages to have prepositions and for verb-final languages to have postpositions.**

Relative Clauses

Depending on the language, relative clauses either precede or follow head nouns. In English relative clause constructions (*the book that Judith wrote*), the relative clause (*that Judith wrote*) follows its head (*the book*). The same is true in Tongan.

ko e tohi [naʔe faʔu ʔe   hina]
the book Past write Subject Hina
'the book that Hina wrote'

In Japanese, by contrast, the relative clause precedes its head.

[hiroo ga   kaita] hon
Hiro   Subject wrote book
'the book that Hiro wrote'

The great majority of verb-initial languages place relative clauses after the head noun, and the great majority of verb-final languages place relative clauses before the head noun. We can therefore note the following universal: **There is a strong tendency for verb-initial languages to place relative clauses after the head noun and for verb-final languages to place relative clauses before the head noun.**

Overall Patterns of Ordering

We have established that verb-initial languages (VSO) place possessors after possessed nouns, place relative clauses after head nouns, and have prepositions. Verb-final languages (SOV), on the other hand, place possessors before possessed nouns, place relative clauses before head nouns, and have postpositions.

In all these correlations a pattern emerges. Notice that possessors and relative clauses modify nouns; the noun is a more essential element to a noun phrase than any of the modifiers. In a similar sense, noun phrases modify prepositions or postpositions; likewise, though it is not intuitively obvious, the most important element of a prepositional phrase is the preposition itself, not the noun phrase—it is the preposition that makes it a prepositional phrase. Finally, in a verb phrase, the direct object modifies the verb. In light of these observations, we can draw a generalization about the order of constituents in different language types: **In verb-initial languages the modifying element follows the modified element**, while in verb-final languages the modifying element precedes the modified element. This pattern is illustrated in Table 7.1.

This generalization is of course based on tendencies rather than absolute rules. At each level of the table some languages violate the correlations. Persian,

Table 7.1 *Summary of Constituent Orders*

VERB-INITIAL LANGUAGES (EXAMPLE: TONGAN)	VERB-FINAL LANGUAGES (EXAMPLE: JAPANESE)
Modified—Modifier	*Modifier—Modified*
verb—direct object	direct object—verb
possessed—possessor	possessor—possessed
preposition—noun phrase	noun phrase—postposition
head noun—relative clause	relative clause—head noun

for example, is an SOV language like Japanese and thus should have the properties listed in the right-hand column of the table. But in Persian possessors follow possessed nouns, prepositions are used, and relative clauses follow head nouns—all of which are properties of verb-initial languages. Such counterexamples to the correlations are rare, however.

Notice that our discussion has mentioned nothing about verb-medial (SVO) languages like English. These languages appear to follow no consistent pattern. English, for example, places relative clauses after head nouns and has prepositions (both properties of verb-initial languages). With respect to the order of possessors and possessed nouns, English has both patterns (*the man's arm* and *the arm of the man*). In contrast, Mandarin Chinese, another verb-medial language, has characteristics of verb-final languages.

Word order universals are an excellent illustration of the level that linguists attempt to reach in their description of the universal properties of language. Table 7.1 implies that in the structure of virtually all verb-initial and verb-final languages, the same ordering principle is at play at the levels of the noun phrase, the prepositional phrase, and the whole sentence. This is remarkable in that it applies to a great many languages whose speakers have never come in contact with each other. It is thus likely that some cognitive process shared by all human beings may underlie this ordering principle.

Relativization Hierarchy

Another area of syntactic structure in which striking universal principles are found is the structure of relative clauses. English can relativize the subject of a relative clause, the direct object, the indirect object, obliques, and possessor noun phrases (see Chapter 5). The following set of English examples illustrates these different possibilities.

the teacher [*who* talked at the meeting] (subject)

the teacher [*whom* I mentioned —to you] (direct object)

the teacher [*that* I told the story to —] (indirect object)

the teacher [*that* I heard the story from —] (oblique)

the teacher [*whose* book I read] (possessor)

Other languages do not allow all these possibilities. Some languages allow relativization on only some of these categories but not others. For example, a relative clause in Malagasy is grammatical only if the relativized noun phrase is the subject of the relative clause.

ny mpianatra [izay nahita ny vehivavy]
the student   who saw   the woman
'the student who saw the woman'

In Malagasy there is no way of directly translating a relative clause whose direct object has been relativized ('the student that the woman saw'), or the indirect object ('the student that the woman gave a book to'), or an oblique ('the student that the woman heard the news from'), or a possessor ('the student whose book the woman read'). If speakers of Malagasy need to convey what is represented by these English relative constructions, they must make the relative clause passive, so that the noun phrase to be relativized becomes the grammatical subject of the relative clause ('the student *who* was seen by the woman'). Alternatively, they can express their idea in two clauses—that is, instead of 'the woman saw the student who failed his exam,' they might say that 'the woman saw the student, and that same student failed his exam.'

Some languages have relative clauses in which subjects or direct objects can be relativized, but indirect objects, obliques, or possessors cannot. An example of such a language is Kinyarwanda, spoken in East Africa. Other languages, like Basque, spoken in northwestern Spain and southwestern France, have relative clauses in which the subject, the direct object, and the indirect object can be relativized, but not an oblique or a possessor. Yet another type of language adds obliques to the list of categories that can be relativized; such is the case in Catalan, spoken in northeastern Spain. Finally, languages like English allow all possibilities.

Table 7.2 recapitulates the types of relative clause systems found among the world's languages; the plus sign indicates a grammatical category that can be relativized, while a minus sign indicates one that cannot be relativized. Notice that a plus sign does not imply anything about the signs to the right of it—they may be plus or minus. A plus sign implies that all categories to the left can be relativized.

It is a remarkable fact that there are no languages in which, for example, an oblique can be relativized ('the man [that I heard the story from]') but not subjects, direct objects, and indirect objects as well. Indeed, relative clause formation in all languages is sensitive to a *hierarchy* of grammatical relations:

Relative Clause Hierarchy
Subject < Direct object < Indirect object < Oblique < Possessor

The hierarchy predicts that if a language allows a particular category on the hierarchy to be relativized, then the grammar of that language will also allow all positions to the left to be relativized. For example, possessors in English can be relativized ('the woman [*whose* book I read]'). The hierarchy predicts that English would allow all positions to the left of possessor (namely, oblique, indirect object, direct object, and subject) to be relativized. The hierarchy also predicts

Table 7.2 *Relativization Hierarchy: Types of Relative Clause Systems*

LANGUAGE TYPE	SUBJECT	DIRECT OBJECT	INDIRECT OBJECT	OBLIQUE	POSSESSOR	EXAMPLE
1	+	−	−	−	−	Malagasy
2	+	+	−	−	−	Kinyarwanda
3	+	+	+	−	−	Basque
4	+	+	+	+	−	Catalan
5	+	+	+	+	+	English

that Basque, which permits indirect objects to be relativized, will allow direct objects and subjects to be relativized; Basque does *not* allow categories to the right of indirect object on the hierarchy (obliques or possessors) to be relativized. The hierarchy is thus a succinct description of the types of relative clause formation patterns found in the languages of the world.

Types of Language Universals

In this section we draw on the universals treated in the previous sections in order to classify the different types of universals. It should be clear by now that language universals are not all alike. Some do not have any exceptions. Others hold for most languages but not all. It is important to distinguish between these two types of universals because the first type appears to be the result of an absolute constraint on language in general, while the other is the result of a tendency.

Absolute Universals and Universal Tendencies

The first two types of universals are distinguished by whether they can be stated as absolute rules. The typology of vowel systems established earlier indicates that the minimum number of vowels in a language is three: /i a u/. The two universal rules that are suggested by the typology read as follows:

1. All languages have at least three vowels.
2. If a language has only three vowels, these vowels will be /i a u/.

From the descriptions of all languages studied to date, it appears that these two rules have no exceptions. The two rules are thus examples of **absolute universals**—universal rules that have no exceptions. Other examples of absolute universals include: If a language has a set of dual pronouns, it must have a set of plural pronouns; if a language has voiced stops, it must have voiceless stops.

In contrast to absolute universals, a number of universal rules have some exceptions. A good example is the rule stating that if a language has a gap in its inventory of stops, it is likely to have a fricative with the same place of articulation as the missing stop. This rule holds for most languages that have gaps in their inventory, but not all. Such rules are called **universal tendencies**. (A possible explanation for universal tendencies is that they represent the coming together of partly competing universal rules.)

Naturally, researchers must be careful when deciding that a particular rule is absolute. Until relatively recently, it would have been easy to assume that no language existed with OVS or OSV as basic word order (since none had been described) and that there was an absolute universal stating that "no language has OVS or OSV for basic word order." But we now know of a few OVS and OSV languages, all spoken in the Amazon Basin. Thus the rule that had been stated as an absolute universal seemed absolute only because no one had come across a language that violated it.

Implicational and Nonimplicational Universals

Independently of the contrast between absolute universals and tendencies, we can draw another important distinction—between implicational and nonimplicational universals. Some universal rules are in the form of a conditional implication, as in the following examples:

◆ If a language has five vowels, it generally has the vowel /o/ or /ɔ/.

◆ If a language is verb-final, then in that language possessors are likely to precede possessed noun phrases.

All rules of the form "if condition P is satisfied, then conclusion Q holds" are called **implicational universals**. Other universals can be stated without conditions: All languages have at least three vowels. Such universals are called *nonimplicational universals*.

There are thus four types of universals.

Types of Universals
Absolute implicational universal
> If a language has property X, it must have property Y.

Implicational tendency
> If a language has property X, it will probably have property Y.

Absolute nonimplicational universal
> All languages have property X.

Nonimplicational tendency
> Most languages have property X.

Explanations for Language Universals

Given the extreme structural diversity that they otherwise exhibit, it is remarkable that all languages of the world fall into clearly defined types and are subject to universal rules. It is thus reasonable to ask why universal rules exist at all. The question is extremely complex, and no one has come up with a definitive explanation for any universal. But for many universals we can make hypotheses or at least educated guesses about the reasons for their existence.

Original Language Hypothesis

The first explanation for language universals that may come to mind is that all languages derive historically from the same original language. This hypothesis is difficult to support, however. First of all, archaeological evidence strongly suggests that the ability to speak developed in our ancestors in several parts of the globe at about the same time, and it is difficult to imagine that different groups of speakers not in contact with one another would have developed exactly the same language. Second, even if we ignore the archaeological evidence, the existence of an original language is impossible to prove or disprove because we have no evidence for or against it. Thus the original language hypothesis is not a very good explanation; it is so hypothetical that it does not adequately fulfill the function of an explanation.

Universals and Perception

A more likely hypothesis explaining language universals is that they are symptoms of how all humans perceive the world and conduct verbal interactions. In the following sections, several such explanations will be applied to the universals established earlier in this chapter. In the discussion of vowel systems, you may have noticed that the three vowels found in all languages—/i a u/—are mutually very distant in a vowel chart. The two vowels /i/ and /u/ differ in terms of frontness and usually rounding, and /a/ differs from the other two in terms of frontness and height. From these observations, it is not difficult to hypothesize why these three vowels are the most fundamental vowels across languages: There is no other set of three vowels that differ from each other more dramatically.

Acquisition and Processing Explanations

Some language universals have psychological explanations with no physiological basis. The explanations that have been proposed for word order universals, for example, are based on the notion that the more regular the structure of a language, the easier it is for children to acquire. Thus the fact that verb-initial languages have prepositions and place adjectives after nouns, possessors after possessed nouns, and relative clauses after head nouns can be summarized by the following rule: **In verb-initial languages, the modifier follows the modified element**. Languages that strictly follow this rule exhibit a great deal of regularity from one construction to another; a single ordering principle regulates the order of verbs and direct objects, adpositions and noun phrases, nouns and adjectives, possessors and possessed nouns, and relative clauses and head nouns. It seems that such a language would be easier to acquire than a language with two or more ordering principles underlying different areas of the syntax. The fact that so many languages in the world follow one overall ordering pattern (modified-modifier) or the other (modifier-modified) with such regularity thus reflects the suggested general tendency for the structure of language to be as regular as possible so as to be as easy as possible to acquire.

Psychological explanations have also been proposed to explain the relative clause formation hierarchy. Relative clauses in which the head functions as the subject of the relative clause ('the woman [who left]') are easier to learn and understand than relative clauses in which the head functions as the direct object of the relative clause ('the man [that I saw]'). Children generally acquire the first type before they begin using the second type. Furthermore, people take less time to understand the meaning of relative clauses on subjects than on direct objects. Relative clauses on direct objects, in turn, are easier to understand than those on indirect objects, and so on down the hierarchy: Subject < Direct object < Indirect object < Oblique < Possessor. There is thus a psychological explanation for the cross-linguistic patterns in the typology of relative clause formation: A language allows a "difficult" relative clause type only if all the "easier" types are also allowed.

Social Explanations

Finally, recall that language is both a cognitive and a social phenomenon. Some language universals have a basis in cognition; others reflect the fact that language is a social tool.

Universals of pronoun systems can be explained in terms of the uses of language. Why, for example, do all languages have first-person and second-person singular pronouns? Consider that the most basic type of verbal interaction is face-to-face conversation. Other contexts in which language is used to communicate (in writing, over the telephone, on the radio, texting, and so on) are relatively recent inventions compared to the ability to carry on a conversation; they occur less frequently and perhaps less naturally than face-to-face interactions. In a face-to-face interaction, it is essential to be able to refer efficiently and concisely to the speaker and the addressee, the two most important entities involved in the interaction. An argument between two individuals who were unable to use *I* and *you* or had to refer to themselves and each other by name would be notably less efficient. Obviously, first-person and second-person singular pronouns are essential for ordinary efficiency of social interaction. It is thus not surprising that every language has first-person and second-person singular pronoun forms, even though its pronoun system may have a gap elsewhere. The universal that all languages have first-person and second-person pronoun forms thus has a social motivation.

Furthermore, as noted earlier, the most frequent pronoun system has separate first-person, second-person, and third-person forms, and separate first-person inclusive ('you and me and perhaps other people') and exclusive ('other people and me, but not you') forms. Why would this system be so frequent and in some way more basic than other systems? Pronoun systems can be viewed as a matrix, with each slot of the matrix characterized by whether the speaker and the addressee are included in the reference of the pronoun, as in Table 7.3.

In light of the fact that speaker and addressee are the more important elements of face-to-face interactions, it should come as no surprise that speaker and addressee inclusion or exclusion should be the crucial factor in defining each slot of the matrix. The most basic (and most common) type of pronoun system is thus the most balanced matrix, one in which each slot is filled with a separate form.

Table 7.3 *Matrix of Pronoun Systems*

	SPEAKER INCLUDED	SPEAKER EXCLUDED
ADDRESSEE INCLUDED	——	second-person singular
		second-person plural
	first-person inclusive plural	
ADDRESSEE EXCLUDED	first-person singular	third-person singular
	first-person exclusive plural	third-person plural

Language universals may thus stem from the way in which humans perceive the world around them, learn and process language, and organize their social interactions. Underlying the search for universals is the desire to learn more about these areas of cognition and social life.

Language Universals, Universal Grammar, and Language Acquisition

Throughout this chapter we've examined various linguistic generalizations. Some have been typological, having to do with the various aspects of the world's languages. We've also examined language universals—characteristic of every language, of language in general—and we noted absolute and implicational universals. We've seen examples in phonology, morphology, and syntax and semantics. We noted that the ultimate goal in the study of universals is to explain them (not merely describe them), and we pointed in the direction of physiological, psychological, and social reasons.

In recent decades, the question of the nature of language universals has taken on increased prominence. What do language universals tell us about the human mind, the brain? What questions do they raise about how human language is acquired and how it functions in the brain and interfaces with perceptions of the world, on the one hand, and with phonological or manual realization, on the other? Is there a separate faculty in the brain that is devoted specifically to language? Or does a combination of other, more general, mental processes support the acquisition and functioning of language?

In our discussions of syntax in Chapter 5, we pointed out relationships between active and passive sentences, declarative and interrogative sentences, sentences with and without embedded clauses, and so on. We took a structural/ generative approach, modern but mindful of more traditional grammar. In our analyses we addressed the question, "How does English (or Spanish or Japanese or . . .) work? How are its sentences shaped and related to one another?" We described operations like those for passivization and subject-auxiliary inversion that change one constituent structure into another. Toward the end of that chapter, we indicated that some theories of syntax do not rely on particular operations for relating sentences to one another, but instead rely on a very general movement rule operating on much more abstract structures than we portrayed. In the traditions in which our analyses are rooted, syntax in particular has become increasingly abstract, far more so than we indicated in our treatment, and the reason for its increasing abstractness is related to an understanding of language universals as described in the present chapter.

Among the wealth of research in linguistics in recent decades, two strands are particularly noteworthy here. The generative enterprise, spearheaded by Noam Chomsky, focused especially in its early years on descriptions of various languages and the operations that were thought to underlie relationships between one sentence and another (e.g., active and passive). Part of the aim was to characterize a universal grammar that children brought to the task of learning their language. The other enterprise, inspired by the work of Joseph H. Greenberg, looked at scores of languages in search of universal properties, some of which we've described in this chapter. Greenberg's work highlighted the facts about universals and went a long way toward characterizing them.

In the past two decades, those research strands have begun in some ways to converge. In the generative enterprise it was essential to understand what a child brought to the acquisition task innately because it was clear that to master the astonishingly complex system that constitutes a human language, and to do so in a very short time, presumed an initial state of mind somehow rich in language (or in aptitude for language). Generative linguists took as a principal objective to characterize that initial state. While, generally speaking, it is language *diversity* that is most apparent in viewing languages, generativists sought to show that "the apparent richness and diversity of linguistic phenomena is illusory and epiphenomenal, the result of interaction of fixed principles under slightly varying conditions" (as Chomsky himself put it). In other words, from an underlying universal grammar and some language-specific determinants, all the world's linguistic diversity can arise. Meanwhile, inheritors of the Greenberg tradition have also actively engaged in efforts to understand the universality of linguistic patterns around the globe.

As a result, linguists and other language scientists are undertaking active collaboration with biologists, computational linguists and computer scientists, cognitive neuroscientists, and others in pursuit of whatever it is in the human brain that allows children to acquire language so well and efficiently and gives rise to the universals that underlie the more apparent diversity of nearly 7,000 human languages around the world.

COMPUTERS AND THE STUDY OF LANGUAGE UNIVERSALS

For more than half a century researchers have been trying to craft devices that can translate between languages. Except in limited ways, however, that goal has eluded even the best attempts thus far. Word-for-word translation does not do the trick because, for one thing, languages differ in their word orders and, for another, the metaphors of one language may not translate into the relevant metaphor of another language. Countless other reasons also contribute to the failure of word-for-word translation.

Consider two models of translation. In a *transfer translation model*, one set of rules or procedures is established for translating from language A into language B and a second set for translating in reverse—that is, from B into A. The rules would have to be completely explicit, and a set of procedures in *each* direction would be needed, because translation is not symmetrical. If a machine translation

(MT) device were established for even six languages, then 6 × 5 (i.e., 30) sets of procedures would be needed to translate each language into all of the other five.

Now consider an alternative system—an *interlingual translation model*—in which the basic semantic elements of each language can be represented abstractly and then encoded into other languages. A procedure would be needed for each language to decode it into abstract semantic elements (forming an abstract semantic representation), along with a second procedure for encoding abstract semantic representations into the lexicon, syntax, and (for spoken texts) phonology of each target language.

The interlingual translation model would require twelve procedures—one *decoding* procedure and one *encoding* procedure for each of the six languages.

Transfer Translation

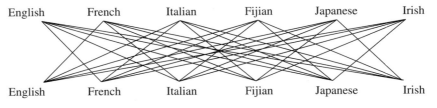

Interlingual Translation

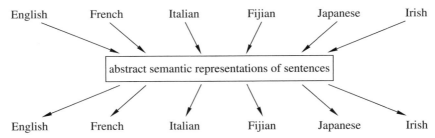

Such a model is simpler than the transfer translation model that requires 30 procedures. Unfortunately, we don't know the extent to which sentences can be decomposed into the kinds of abstract semantic representations needed for an interlingual model, especially in making a language-neutral intermediate representation.

Difficulties related to translation in either model concern what one language encodes that another may not encode. Fijian, for example, as shown in the chart of that language's pronouns, has four second-person pronouns, while English has only one. That would make it very easy to translate any second-person pronoun from Fijian into English, provided the abstract semantic representation of the Fijian pronouns contains the element 'second person.' All such representations would be mapped onto English *you*. But would translating the other way around be equally straightforward? Given an English sentence containing the pronoun *you*, no machine could determine from the word itself its underlying semantic representation, other than second person. Because English does not code a distinction among singular, dual, trial, and plural number in the second person, an MT device could not decide which Fijian pronoun to choose. We can represent the first part of the problem in the following schema, where translating from Fijian to English would be easy.

But translating English *you* into Fijian would be a challenge. While the text or context might make clear the number of addressees represented by the pronoun *you*, that information would prove difficult or impossible for an MT device to decipher except in rare cases (e.g., *you two*, *the three of you*).

To confound things, the situation is reversed for third-person singular pronouns. Fijian does not distinguish between masculine, feminine, and neuter singular pronouns, but English does; as indicated in the accompanying chart, Fijian has only the pronoun *koya* corresponding to the English pronouns *he*, *she*, and *it*.

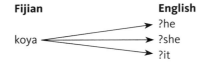

From *koya* alone, no device could decide which English pronoun would be the correct translation. Again, context might make it clear, but interpreting context creates an even more difficult challenge for an MT device.

The problems we've discussed can be minimized by limiting the translation machinery to two languages and to very specialized domains of discourse. For example, if you were translating only medical texts or only technical documents from English into another language, you would deal with a limited subset of vocabulary and structures. Analysis of particular kinds of text may reveal that certain lexical or grammatical options rarely (or never) occur in them. When creating a list of words that appear in medical journals, for example, most informal vocabulary could be eliminated from consideration.

Similarly, to return to the pronoun problem discussed above, English-language medical journals would almost certainly not use the full range of potential semantic distinctions represented in Fijian, so for projects translating medical documents, some possible Fijian pronouns might be eliminated for practical purposes.

The need for translation has grown urgently in recent decades with the formation of the European Union, and considerable financial resources have been made available for exploring automatic translation. In pursuit of better methods of machine translation, corpora containing more than one language have been created, and analysis of them will yield findings helpful for designing automatic translation devices.

Some multilingual corpora contain the same *kinds* of texts but not identical texts. For example, the texts in the Aarhus Corpus of Danish, French, and English law are not translations of one another, but they represent a reservoir of information about the legislative language in these languages. Other corpora contain texts that are translations of one another, as with the Canadian Hansard Corpus, which contains parliamentary proceedings in French-to-English and English-to-French translations.

When a corpus contains translations it is possible to create a "parallel aligned corpus." This is a corpus containing texts in different languages that have been aligned, sometimes automatically, so that sections correspond to one another—paragraph to paragraph or sentence to sentence. Researchers can use these corpora to explore the mathematical properties of vocabulary and syntax in languages and pairs of languages. By relying on knowledge of such properties, automatic translation may be able to avoid some of the difficulties of either of the transfer translation or interlingual translation models depicted above. Instead, certain mathematical properties of languages would help determine likely translations, independently of how the human mind processes languages and makes translations. ∎

Summary

- Underlying the great diversity of the world's languages, universal principles are at play at all levels of language structure—phonology, morphology, syntax, and semantics.
- The study of typology aims to catalog languages according to types, while the study of universals aims to formulate the universal principles themselves.
- In lexical semantics, the composition of pronoun systems, in which cross-linguistic variation is found, is dictated by several universal rules that regulate distinctions in number and person.
- Vowel systems and inventories of stops are two examples of universals at play in phonology.
- In syntax and morphology, universals are found that regulate the basic order of constituents in sentences and phrases.
- In syntax, the relativization hierarchy is a striking example of a universal principle.
- The salient characteristic of all universals is that the most common patterns are the most regular and harmonious.

- Four types of universals can be distinguished, depending on whether they have exceptions (absolute versus tendency) and according to their logical form (implicational versus nonimplicational):

  Absolute implicational universals: Languages with property X must have property Y.

  Implicational tendencies: Languages with property X will probably have property Y.

  Absolute nonimplicational universals: All languages have property X.

  Nonimplicational tendencies: Most languages have property X.

- The ultimate goal of the study of language universals is to provide explanations for such universal principles.
- Language universals may have physiological, psychological, or social explanations.

  Physiological: Universals are often indicative of how we perceive the world around us. Thus, languages tend to highlight categories that are physiologically and perceptually salient, as with vowels.

  Psychological: Structural simplicity and consistency make languages easier to acquire and process. Thus many universals predict that the simplest and most consistent systems will be preferred.

  Social: Distinctions drawn on the expression side of language reflect important social distinctions on the content side.

What Do You Think? REVISITED

- *Your niece.* Many people tend to think about a language in terms of its written form rather than its spoken form. That's why so many people report that English has 5 vowels (*a, e, i, o,* and *u*). But Figure 7.1 shows your niece to be correct. Besides its 13 vowels, English has 3 diphthongs, as in the words *buy, toy,* and *cow.* Languages vary in the number of vowels they have. Quechua, Greenlandic Eskimo, and Moroccan Arabic have 3 vowels; Hawaiian has 5; English 13; Parisian French 15.
- *Cousins in Chicago.* Many speakers of English say *you* whether they're addressing one person or several, but other speakers use a distinct form for more than one addressee: *y'all, youse,* or *y'uns* (*y'uns* in Western Pennsylvania and parts of the Ohio Valley). Probably quite a few of your friends say *you guys* when addressing more than one person. As shown in the pronoun charts in this chapter, it is not unusual for languages to have distinct singular and plural forms for second-person pronouns—or even to distinguish two addressees from more than two. Fijian, for example, has four distinct forms: for addressing one person (singular), two persons (dual), three (trial), and more than three (plural). In English some dialects distinguish between second-person singular and second-person plural pronouns, and *you guys* is gaining

in popularity among speakers who don't otherwise have a distinct plural form like *y'all* or *youse.*

- *Clarence on Japanese.* It seems inevitable to think one's own language natural and logical and to suspect that other languages are odd or illogical if they differ. Perhaps nowhere is this more true than with word order. Like other aspects of language, though, word order isn't a matter of logic. Some languages have a basic SVO order, but others favor SOV or VSO or some other order. German uses SVO in main clauses and SOV in subordinate clauses, whereas English uses SVO for main clauses (*I bought it*) and subordinate clauses (*because I wanted it*). Despite its having a basic SVO word order, other word orders are possible in English: *Carrots I like, peas I hate!* And while English has "prepositions," there's nothing that says words that function *like* prepositions but *follow* the noun phrase can't be called by another name, such as postpositions. Certain word order patterns often go together in a language, and such patterns invite speculation and hypotheses as to why they do so.
- English has separate masculine and feminine third-person pronouns (*he* and *she*), but Tagalog and many other languages use the same pronoun for masculine and feminine referents (see the discussion of Fijian pronouns in this chapter). When speaking a second language, it's easier to ignore a distinction made in one's native tongue than to make a distinction your own language doesn't make. Francesca wouldn't use the wrong pronoun *every* time she speaks about someone, but she could do it often enough to create that impression. ■

Exercises

Practice Exercise

The statements in sets A and B contain universal statements, some true and some false. Identify which set contains absolute universals and which set contains implicational universals, and for each universal say whether it is true or false. Also, then, for set C, say whether each statement is true or false.

A. i. Every language has vowels and consonants.

 ii. Every language has Subject-Verb-Object as its basic word order.

 iii. Every language has the same number of personal pronouns.

 iv. Every language in its pronouns differentiates between singular and plural 'you.'

 v. Every language in its pronouns differentiates between inclusive and exclusive 'we.'

B. i. If a language has only three vowels, they may all be front vowels.

 ii. If a language has only three vowels, they may all be back vowels.

 iii. If a language has only three vowels, they may all be high vowels.

 iv. If a language has stop consonants, they may all be voiced.

C. i. Language universals probably exist because all languages derive historically from one original language.

ii. There is no limit to the ways in which human languages may differ from one another.

iii. Some language universals have a basis in human cognition.

iv. Some language universals have a basis in human social interaction.

Based on English and Other Languages

7-1. Make a judgment about how usual or unusual the following features of standard English are in comparison with other languages discussed in this chapter. Explain your judgment in each case.

1) a 13-vowel system

2) no (phonemically distinct) nasal vowels

3) Subject-Verb-Object word order

4) adjectives preceding head nouns

5) relative clauses following head nouns

6) no dual pronoun forms

7) no trial pronoun forms

8) no distinct second-person plural pronouns

9) no distinction between inclusive and exclusive pronouns

7-2. Determine whether each of the following is an absolute implicational universal, an absolute nonimplicational universal, an implicational universal tendency, or a nonimplicational universal tendency.

1) The consonant inventories of all languages include at least two different stops that differ in terms of place of articulation.

2) Languages always have fewer nasal consonants than oral stops.

3) In all languages, the number of front vowels of different height is greater than or equal to the number of back vowels of different height.

4) Most VSO languages have prepositions, not postpositions.

5) Diminutive particles and affixes tend to exhibit high vowels.

6) If a language has separate terms for 'foot' and 'leg,' then it must also have different terms for 'hand' and 'arm.'

7) The future tense is used to express hypothetical events in many languages, and the past tense is often used to express nonhypothetical events.

8) Languages that have a relatively free word order tend to have inflections for case.

9) Many verb-initial languages place relative clauses after the head of the relative clause.

7-3. In English, conditions can be expressed in two ways: by placing the conditioning clause first and the conditioned clause second, as in (1) below, or by placing the conditioning clause second and the conditioned clause first, as in (2). In numerous languages, however, only the first pattern is grammatical. In Mandarin Chinese, the conditioning clause must come first, as in (3); if it is placed second, as in (4), the resulting string is ungrammatical. No language allows only pattern (2)—conditioning clause second, conditioned clause first.

    1) If you cry, I'll turn off the TV.

    2) I'll turn off the TV if you cry.

    3) rúguǒ wǒ dìdi   hē   jiǔ   wǒ jiù hěn shēngqì

        If   my younger-brother drink wine I   then very angry

        'If my younger brother drinks wine, I'll be very angry.'

    4) *wǒ hěn shēngqì rúguǒ wǒ dìdi   hē   jiǔ

        I   very angry   if   my younger-brother drink wine

    a. From this information, formulate descriptions of an absolute implicational universal, an absolute nonimplicational universal, and a universal tendency, all of which refer to conditional clauses.

    b. Propose an explanation for the universal ordering patterns that you formulated in (a). (*Hint*: Think of the order in which the actions denoted by the conditioning and the conditioned clauses must take place.)

7-4. The composition of vowel inventories of the world's languages is predicted by the hierarchy given in Figure 7.4. The hierarchy predicts the composition of a vowel inventory consisting of six phonemes. Complete the next step in the hierarchy by determining the composition of seven-vowel inventories. Use the following information on the composition of the seven-vowel inventories of three languages, which you should assume are representative of possible seven-vowel inventories.

Burmese	i e ɛ a ɔ o u
Sundanese	i ɨ ɛ a ɔ u ə
Washkuk	i ɨ e ɛ a ɔ u

7-5. Consider the following typology of pronoun systems found among the world's languages. The first column of each set represents singular pronouns; the second column, dual pronouns; and the third column, plural pronouns. An example of a language also is given for each type (incl. = inclusive, excl. = exclusive).

8-pronoun Systems

    1) I   we-2   we   Greenlandic Eskimo

        thou   you-2   you

        s/he   they

    2) I   we   Arabic

        thou   you-2   you

        s/he   they-2   they

3)	I	we-2-incl.	we-incl.	Southern Paiute (North America)
	thou		you	
	s/he		they	

9-pronoun Systems

1)	I	we-2	we	Lapp (Arctic Scandinavia)
	thou	you-2	you	
	s/he	they-2	they	

2)	I	we-2-incl.	we-incl.	Maya (Central America)
		we-2-excl.	we-excl.	
	thou		you	
	s/he		they	

3)	I	we-2-incl.	we	Lower Kanauri (India)
		we-2-excl.		
	thou	you-2	you	
	s/he		they	

10-pronoun Systems

1)	I	we-2-incl.	we	Coos (North America)
		we-2-excl.		
	thou	you-2	you	
	s/he	they-2	they	

2)	I	we-2-incl.	we-incl.	Kanauri (India)
		we-2-excl.	we-excl.	
	thou	you-2	you	
	s/he	they-2	they	

11-pronoun Systems

1)	I	we-2-incl.	we-incl.	Hawaiian
		we-2-excl.	we-excl.	
	thou	you-2	you	
	s/he	they-2	they	

2)	I	we-2-incl.	we-incl.	Ewe (West Africa)
		we-2 excl.	we-excl.	
	thou	you-2	you	
	s/he	they-2	they	
			he and they	

a. On the basis of these data, which you may assume to be representative, formulate a set of absolute universal principles that describe the composition of 8-, 9-, 10-, and 11-pronoun systems. State your principles as generally as possible.

b. Of these systems, the most common is the 11-pronoun system of type 1, exemplified by Hawaiian, followed by the 9-pronoun system of type 1, exemplified by Lapp. Formulate a set of universal tendencies that describe the preponderance of examples of these two systems.

7-6. From a logical standpoint, the possible basic ordering combinations of subject, verb, and direct object are SOV, SVO, VSO, VOS, OVS, and OSV. We have seen that there is great variation in the percentage of languages exhibiting each combination as a basic word order. Linguists have recognized this fact for several decades, but there has been little agreement on the exact distribution of these basic word order variations across the world's languages. Here are results from five researchers who conducted cross-linguistic analyses of the distribution of basic word order possibilities. (The figures are cited from Tomlin 1986.)

RESEARCHER	LANGUAGES SAMPLED	PERCENTAGE						UNCLASSIFIED
		SOV	SVO	VSO	VOS	OVS	OSV	
Greenberg	30	37	43	20	0	0	0	0
Ultan	75	44	34.6	18.6	2.6	0	0	0
Ruhlen	427	51.5	35.6	10.5	2.1	0	0.2	0
Mallinson/Blake	100	41	35	9	2	1	1	11
Tomlin	402	44.8	41.8	9.2	3.0	1.2	0	0

a. In what ways do these researchers' data agree, and where do they disagree? Describe in detail.

b. What are the possible causes of the discrepancies in the results?

c. What lesson can typologists learn from this comparison?

7-7. Relative clauses can be formed in a variety of ways. In English, we "replace" the relativized element by a relative pronoun that links the relative clause to its head (type 3). Other languages do not have distinct relative pronouns but replace the relativized element by a personal pronoun (type 2). For example, in Gilbertese (spoken in the central Pacific), the position of the relativized element in the relative clause is marked with a personal pronoun.

Type 2	**Type 2**
te ben [e bwaka iaon te auti]	te anene [i nori-a]
the coconut it fall on the house	the coconut I saw-it
'the coconut [that fell on the house]'	'the coconut [that I saw]'

In other languages, such as Finnish, relative clauses are formed by simply deleting the relativized element from the relative clause; no relative pronoun or personal pronoun is added to the relative construction (type 1).

Type 1	**Type 1**
[tanssinut] poika	[näkemäni] poika
had-danced boy	I-had-seen boy
'the boy [that had danced]'	'the boy [that I had seen]'

Some languages have several types of relative clauses. Mandarin Chinese has types 1 and 2. (In Mandarin the relative clause is ordered before its head and is separated from the head by the particle *de*.)

Type 1

[mǎi píngguǒ de]   rén

buy apples   Particle man
'the man [who bought apples]'

Type 2

[tā jiějie zài měiguó de]   rén

he sister is-in America Particle man
'the man [whose sister is in America]'

In Mandarin Chinese, type 1 is used only when relativizing a subject or direct object, while type 2 can be used when relativizing a direct object, an indirect object, an oblique, or a possessor, as indicated in the accompanying table. Whenever two types of relative clauses are found in a language, the pattern is the same: as we go down the relativization hierarchy (from subject to direct object to indirect object to oblique to possessor), one type can end but the other type takes over. Here are the patterns for some languages:

Grammatical Relation Relativized

	SUBJECT	DIRECT OBJECT	INDIRECT OBJECT	OBLIQUE	POSSESSOR
Aoban (South Pacific)					
Type 1	+	−	−	−	−
Type 2	−	+	+	+	+
Dutch					
Type 1	+	+	−	−	−
Type 2	−	−	+	+	+
Japanese					
Type 1	+	+	+	+	+
Type 2	−	−	−	−	+
Kera (Central Africa)					
Type 1	+	−	−	−	−
Type 2	−	+	+	+	+
Mandarin Chinese					
Type 1	+	+	−	−	−
Type 2	−	+	+	+	+
Roviana (South Pacific)					
Type 1	+	+	+	−	−
Type 2	−	−	−	+	+
Tagalog (Philippines)					
Type 1	+	−	−	−	−
Type 2	+	−	−	−	−
Catalan (Spain)					
Type 1	+	+	+	−	−
Type 2	−	−	−	+	−

What cross-linguistic generalizations can you draw from these data on the distribution of relative clause types in each language? How can we expand the universal rules associated with the hierarchy to describe these patterns?

7-8. Below is a sentence from the program notes to *Officium*, produced by ECM Records. After that, in sections, the sentence is repeated with translations from the program notes in German and French. Comparable sections are marked typographically. After examining the English sentence and the three translations, answer the questions that follow.

> The oldest pieces on this record (if one can use words like "new" and "old" in this context) are the chants, the origins of which are not known to us.

The **oldest** pieces				*on this record*		
Die **ältesten** Stücke				*dieser Aufnahme*		
Les morceaux **les**	**plus**	**anciens**	figurant	*sur*	*ce*	*disque*
THE PIECES	THE	MOST	OLD	FIGURING	ON THIS	RECORD

(if one *can use words* like "new" and "old" in this context)

—so man in diesem Zusammenhang überhaupt von „neu" und „alt" *sprechen kann*—
IF ONE IN THIS SITUATION AT ALL OF NEW AND OLD SPEAK CAN

(si tant est que les termes «nouveau» et «ancien» *conviennent* à ce contexte)
IF SUCH IT IS THAT THE TERMS NEW AND OLD SUIT TO THIS CONTEXT

are	the chants,	the	origins of which	<u>are not known</u> **to**	**us.**
sind	Gesänge,	deren	Ursprung	**uns** <u>nicht</u>	<u>bekannt</u> ist.
ARE	CHANTS	WHOSE	ORIGIN	TO-US NOT	KNOWN IS.
sont	les chants,	dont	l'origine	**nous** <u>est</u>	<u>inconnue.</u>
ARE	THE CHANTS	WHOSE	ORIGIN	TO-US IS	UNKNOWN

a. Which of the languages have prepositions, and which of them have postpositions?

b. Each of the translations contains three clauses, the equivalents of

  i. the oldest pieces on this record are the chants

  ii. if one can use words like *new* and *old* in this context

  iii. the origins of which are not known to us

Do any of the languages use a word order other than SVO in the main clause? In the subordinate clauses? If any other word orders are represented, identify them.

c. Which languages have adjectives preceding head nouns? Which have adjectives following head nouns?

d. Neither German nor French uses a prepositional phrase to express what English expresses as *to us*. What do they do instead, and how is the meaning conveyed without a preposition?

Especially for Educators and Future Teachers

7-9. This chapter describes "language universals." Do you think everything said here about language universals applies to all varieties of every language—including all dialects of a language as well? What about nonstandard dialects? Explain your position.

7-10. At an appropriate level for the students you teach or are preparing to teach, explain what a language universal is and how there can be so much diversity in the world's languages when such universals exist.

Other Resources

Suggestions for Further Reading

- **Bernard Comrie. 1989.** *Language Universals and Linguistic Typology: Syntax and Morphology*, **2nd ed.** (Chicago: University of Chicago Press). Accessible and basic; highly recommended.
- **William Croft. 2003.** *Typology and Universals,* **2nd ed.** (Cambridge, UK: Cambridge University Press). More advanced and wide-ranging than Comrie (1989); particularly good on explanations for various kinds of universals.
- **Jae Jung Song. 2001.** *Linguistic Typology* (Harlow, Essex: Pearson). Also accessible, focuses on morphological and syntactic typologies.
- **Lindsay J. Whaley. 1997.** *Introduction to Typology: The Unity and Diversity of Language* (Thousand Oaks, CA: Sage). This book is the most basic of the four listed.

Advanced Reading

Mallinson and Blake (1981) is a good introduction to typology. Shopen (2007) is a collection of excellent essays by distinguished researchers on selected areas of syntactic typology and is also useful on the range of morphological and syntactic variation found among the world's languages. Some of the most influential work on language universals was conducted by Greenberg, who edited a four-volume compendium of detailed studies of universals on specific areas of linguistic structure (1978); these volumes provided data for some of the exercises in this chapter. Brown (1984) is an interesting investigation of universals of words for plants and animals. Lehrer (1974) is a good summary of research on semantic universals. Tomlin (1986) surveys the basic word orders of the world's languages. The relativization hierarchy was uncovered by Edward L. Keenan and Bernard Comrie, and Chapter 7 of Comrie (1989) offers a clear discussion of the topic. Butterworth, Comrie, and Dahl (1984) is a collection of papers on theoretical explanations for language universals. Christiansen et al. (2009) points to the converging strands of universals research, with chapters by specialists in linguistics, biology, psychology and cognitive neuroscience, computer science and computational linguistics, and philosophy; while not all chapters will be accessible to LISU's readers, students and instructors will find some of them highly instructive (the LISU website provides links to some chapters available in published journals or elsewhere on the Internet). Chomsky (2004) is an accessible overview of highly abstract approaches to universals and their explanation, in essence encapsulating what appears in much greater detail in Chomsky (1995), from which our quote in this chapter comes.

References

Brown, Cecil H. 1984. *Language and Living Things: Uniformities in Folk Classification and Naming* (New Brunswick, NJ: Rutgers University Press).

Butterworth, Brian, Bernard Comrie & Östen Dahl, eds. 1984. *Explanations for Language Universals* (Berlin: Mouton).

Chomsky, Noam. 1995. *The Minimalist Program* (Cambridge, MA: MIT Press).

———. 2004. "Language and Mind: Current Thoughts on Ancient Problems." In Lyle Jenkins, ed., *Variation and Universals in Biolinguistics* (Amsterdam: Elsevier). [Also available at http://fccl.ksu.ru/papers/chomsky1.htm]

Christiansen, Morten H., Chris Collins & Shimon Edelman, eds. 2009. *Language Universals* (New York: Oxford University Press).

Greenberg, Joseph H., ed. 1978. *Universals of Human Language,* 4 vols. (Stanford: Stanford University Press).

Lehrer, Adrienne. 1974. *Semantic Fields and Lexical Structure* (Amsterdam: North-Holland).

Mallinson, George & Barry J. Blake. 1981. *Language Typology* (Amsterdam: North-Holland).

Shopen, Timothy, ed. 2007. *Language Typology and Syntactic Description,* 2nd ed., 3 vols. (Cambridge, UK: Cambridge University Press).

Tomlin, Russell S. 1986. *Basic Word Order: Functional Principles* (London: Croom Helm).

Part Two

Language Use

In Part One you examined the structure of words, phrases, and sentences. In Part Two you'll examine how you use those structures in ordinary social interactions. You'll see that languages provide alternative ways of saying the same thing and what those alternative ways accomplish socially and communicatively. Languages exist only to be used, and our use of language distinguishes us from all other animals. It is language use that makes us uniquely human. By putting language to use, we do things, we accomplish things, and we can achieve social and intellectual satisfaction. In this section, you'll explore how putting sentences together into texts—spoken and written discourse—affects choices among alternative sentence structures and how what is actually said and what is relied upon in context interact to achieve successful communication between one person and another.

Besides communicating what you intend to communicate, the forms of language that you use reflect your social identity and mirror the character of the situation in which you are communicating. Part Two explores the patterns of linguistic variation across diverse social groups—whose language varieties are called *dialects*—and the patterns of linguistic variation across communicative situations—where characteristic varieties are called *registers*.

8

Information Structure and Pragmatics

What Do You Think?

- Annie, an international student you are tutoring, asks about the function of definite and indefinite articles in English. You explain that the definite article refers to particular persons, places, or things—*the Golden Gate Bridge, the mayor*—whereas the indefinite article refers to *any* entity—*a chef, a park, an apple*. Annie says she's been paying attention to what people say, and your explanation doesn't match what she's heard. She points out that you yourself had recommended "a movie" you'd seen, and you meant *Avatar*, a particular movie. You immediately recognize that she's right. What better explanation can you offer her for the use of definite and indefinite articles?
- During an ESL class discussion about active and passive sentences, Thom from Taiwan asks why English has two ways of saying exactly the same thing, and as an example he cites this active/passive pair of sentences:

Spain won the 2010 World Cup. (active)

The 2010 World Cup was won by Spain. (passive)

You're saved by the bell and think about your answer overnight. At the next class meeting, what do you tell Thom?
- Your classmate Clint, who's majoring in business, wants to know when objects can precede subjects in English. He noticed a TV commentator say about the mayor of New York City, *Him I like!* Clint wants to know what you think.

Introduction: Encoding Information Structure

Syntax and semantics are not the only regulators of sentence structure. A sentence may be grammatically and semantically well formed but still exhibit problems when used in a particular context. Examine the following versions of a local news report. (The sentences of Version 1 are numbered because we refer to them later.)

Version 1

(1) At 3 A.M. last Sunday, the Santa Clara Fire Department evacuated two apartment buildings at the corner of Country Club Drive and Fifth Avenue. (2) Oil had been discovered leaking from a furnace in the basement of one of the buildings. (3) Firefighters sprayed chemical foam over the oil for several hours. (4) By 8 A.M., the situation was under control. (5) Any danger of explosion or fire had been averted, and the leaky furnace was sealed. (6) Residents of the two apartment buildings were given temporary shelter in the Country Club High School gymnasium. (7) They regained possession of their apartments at 5 P.M.

Version 2

As for the Santa Clara Fire Department, it evacuated two apartment buildings at the corner of Country Club Drive and Fifth Avenue at 3 A.M. last Sunday. In the basement of one of the buildings, someone had discovered a furnace from which oil was leaking. What was sprayed by firefighters over the oil for several hours was chemical foam. It was by 8 A.M. that the situation was under control. What someone had averted was any danger of explosion or fire, and as for the leaky furnace, it was sealed. What the residents of the two apartment buildings were given in the Country Club High School gymnasium was temporary shelter. Possession of their apartments was regained by them at 5 P.M.

Virtually the same words are used in the two versions, and every sentence in both versions is grammatically and semantically well formed. Still, something is strikingly odd about Version 2. It runs counter to our expectations of how information should be presented in a text. Somehow, it emphasizes the wrong elements or emphasizes the right elements at the wrong time. Though grammatical, the sentence structures of Version 2 seem inappropriate to this news report.

The problem with Version 2 is the way in which different pieces of information are marked for relative significance. In any sequence of sentences, it is essential to mark elements as more or less important or necessary. Speakers and writers are responsible for foregrounding certain elements and backgrounding others, just as a painter uses contrasts of color, shape, and value to highlight some details and deemphasize others.

In language texts, such highlighting and deemphasizing is called **information structure**. Unlike syntax and semantics, which are sentence-based aspects of language, information structure requires consideration of discourse—coherent sequences of sentences rather than isolated ones. Out of context, there is nothing wrong with the first sentence of Version 2:

As for the Santa Clara Fire Department, it evacuated two apartment buildings at the corner of Country Club Drive and Fifth Avenue at 3 A.M. last Sunday.

But as the *opening* to a news report it strikes us as odd and inappropriate. It feels as though something has been said before this or that we have missed out on a reference to something or other. When we talk about information structure we need to account for *discourse context*—the environment in which a sentence is produced and especially what precedes that sentence. We can describe a **discourse** as a sequence of utterances that "go together" in a particular situation. A conversation at dinner, a newspaper column, a personal letter, a radio interview, and a subpoena to appear in court are examples of discourse. We could even say that an utterance like *Oh, look!* (intended to draw attention to a beautiful sunset, for example), although not a sequence of utterances, is nevertheless discourse because it is produced within a situational context that helps determine an appropriate information structure.

In order to mark information structure in an utterance, speakers rely on the fact that syntactic operations permit alternative ways of shaping sentences. For example, the following sentences are alternative ways of saying the same thing.

1. The firefighter discovered a leak in the basement.
2. In the basement, the firefighter discovered a leak.
3. A leak in the basement was discovered by the firefighter.
4. It was the firefighter who discovered a leak in the basement.
5. What the firefighter discovered in the basement was a leak.
6. It was a leak that the firefighter discovered in the basement.
7. What was discovered by the firefighter was a leak in the basement.
8. The firefighter, he discovered a leak in the basement.

Exploiting such a choice of alternatives enables us to mark information structure. You might ask yourself what question each of the sentences above is an appropriate answer to. This chapter will describe how that can be discovered.

Pragmatics is the branch of linguistics that studies information structure. In Chapter 9, we'll discuss other aspects of language use that fall under the umbrella of *pragmatics*.

Try It Yourself To the eight sentences above, add two more that say the same thing, stated differently but containing the same information as sentence 1 (and all the others), no more, no less.

Categories of Information Structure

In order to describe the differences between alternative ways of saying the same thing, we identify the basic categories of information structure. These categories must be applicable to all languages (although how each category is used may differ). With these categories, we want to explain how discourse is constructed in any language. These explanations ultimately may suggest hypotheses about how different components of the human mind (such as memory, attention, and logic) work and interact. Thus, categories of information structure, like other aspects of linguistics, should be as independent of particular languages as possible.

There is an important difference between the types of syntactic constructions found in particular languages and the categories of information structure. The range of available syntactic constructions differs considerably from language to language. As an example, some languages have a passive construction (*She was tricked by a con artist*), while others do not. Since the categories of information structure are not language-dependent, they cannot be defined in terms of particular structures. Nevertheless, there is a close kinship between pragmatics and syntax, and one principal function of syntax in all languages is to encode pragmatic information. What differs from language to language is how pragmatic structure maps onto syntax.

Given Information and New Information

One category of information structure is the distinction between given and new information. **Given information** is information currently in the forefront of an addressee's mind; **new information** is information just being introduced into the discourse. Consider the following two-turn interaction:

Alice: Who ate the pizza?

Dana: Erin ate the pizza.

In Dana's answer, the noun phrase *Erin* represents new information because it is being introduced into the discourse there; by contrast, *the pizza* in the reply is given information because it can be presumed to be in the mind of Alice, who has just introduced it in the previous turn. We'll see shortly that given information often finds expression in condensed form, for example as *Erin ate it* or *Erin did*.

In the following sequence of sentences, uttered by a single speaker, the underlined element represents given information because it has just been introduced in the previous sentence and can thus be assumed to be in the addressee's mind.

A man called while you were on your break. He said he'd call back later.

As another example, look at Version 1 of the Santa Clara Fire Department newspaper piece in the introduction to this chapter. Notice in (1) that the noun phrase *two apartment buildings* is new information and in (2) that *oil* and *a furnace* are new information; they have not been mentioned earlier and cannot be presumed to exist in a reader's mind. Note, also, that in (2) *the buildings* is given information, following mention of *two apartment buildings* in (1). In (3), *the oil* is given information by virtue of *oil* having been previously mentioned in (2). Likewise, in (5) reference is made to *the leaky furnace*, which is given information because in (2) *a furnace* was mentioned, along with the fact that it was leaking. Below, we'll see that the difference between new information and given information is reflected in the use of indefinite and definite articles, as in the phrases *a furnace* and *the furnace*.

A piece of information need not be explicitly mentioned in order for it to be *given* information. Information is sometimes taken as given because of its close association with something that has been introduced into the discourse. For example, when a noun phrase is introduced into a discourse, all the subparts of the referent can be treated as given information.

> When Kent returned <u>my car</u> last night, <u>the gas tank</u> was nearly empty and <u>the glove compartment</u> was stuffed with candy wrappers.

> Ellen went on <u>a Caribbean cruise</u> last year and loved <u>the food</u> and <u>the sights</u>.

In the first sentence, *my car* is new information, but because a car typically has a gas tank and a glove compartment, mention of *my car* suffices to make its *gas tank* and *glove compartment* given information. Similarly, *the food* and *the sights* represent given information in the second example because mention of *a Caribbean cruise* suffices to enable an addressee to have in mind those things customarily associated with a cruise, including meals and sightseeing.

Try It Yourself Examine Version 1 of the Santa Clara Fire Department newspaper report in the introduction to the chapter. In sentence (2), note the constituent *a furnace in the basement of one of the buildings*. Sentence (1) mentions two apartment buildings, but prior to (2) there has been no mention of a furnace or a basement. Assess whether *a furnace* and *the basement* in (2) represent given or new information, and explain your assessments.

Because face-to-face conversation and most other kinds of discourse have at least implicit speakers and addressees, participants always take the speaker and first-person pronouns such as *I* and the addressee and second-person pronoun *you* to be given information. They do not need to be introduced into the discourse as new information.

Expressing New Information Noun phrases representing new information usually receive more stress in speech than those representing given information and are commonly expressed in a more elaborated fashion—for example, with a full noun phrase (rather than a pronoun) and sometimes with a prepositional phrase, relative clause, or other modifier that helps identify the referent. The following are typical of how new information is introduced into a discourse.

> When I entered her office, I saw <u>a tall man wearing an old-fashioned hat</u>.

> Before she went to dinner, she found <u>a tidy note he'd written</u>.

Expressing Given Information Given information is commonly expressed in more reduced or abbreviated ways. Typical reducing devices for encoding given information include *pronouns* and *unstressed noun phrases*. Sometimes given information is left out of a sentence altogether. In the following interaction, the information given by Adam's question (namely, *is at the door*) is entirely omitted from Bella's answer, which expresses only new information.

Adam: Who's at the door?

Bella: The mail carrier.

The contrast between given and new information is important in characterizing the function of several constructions in English and other languages, as you'll see in the next section.

Topics

The **topic** of a sentence is its *center of attention*—what it's about, its point of departure. The notion of topic is contrasted with the notion of *comment*, which is the element of a sentence that says something about the topic. Often, given information is the sentence element about which we say something and is thus the topic. New information represents what we say about the topic and is thus the comment. For example,

Try It Yourself   Look for abbreviating devices used for given information in Version 1 of the Santa Clara Fire Department newspaper report discussed earlier in the chapter. For example, in (4) instead of saying *By 8 A.M. last Sunday*, the report omits *last Sunday* because, having already been expressed in (1), it is given information, whereas *by 8 A.M.* is new information. Identify two additional instances of given information omitted from the sentences of Version 1; identify a pronoun used to encode given information; and specify which full noun phrase the pronoun represents.

if *Erin ate the pizza* is offered in answer to the question *What did Erin do?*, the topic would be *Erin* (the given information) and the comment would be *ate the pizza* (the new information). The topic of a sentence can sometimes be phrased as in these examples:

Speaking of Erin, she ate the pizza.

As for Erin, she ate the pizza.

The topic is not always given information. In the second sentence of the sequence below, the noun phrase *her little sister* is new, not given, information, but it is the topic.

Erin ate the pizza. As for her little sister, she preferred the ice cream.

Note that in the phrase *her little sister*, the word *her* anchors the new information to the given information represented by *Erin*.

In conversation, we often first establish a topic with a preliminary remark or question and only then make a comment about it.

Sheila: Remember that guy I said was pestering me?

Ammon: Yeah.

Sheila: Well, he fell off his skateboard in front of the whole class today.

In Sheila's second turn, *he* is the topic and *fell off his skateboard in front of the whole class today* is the comment.

Given information can sometimes serve as comment, as in the underlined element in the following sequence:

Hal didn't believe anything the charlatan said. As for Sara, she believed it all.

So the given/new contrast differs from the topic/comment contrast.

It is difficult to define precisely what a topic is. While the topic is the element of a sentence that functions as the center of attention, a sentence like *Oh, look!*, uttered to draw attention to a stunning sunset, has an unexpressed topic (the setting sun or the sky). Thus, topic is not necessarily a property of the sentence; it may be a property of the discourse context.

Topics are less central to the grammar of English than to the grammar of certain other languages. In fact, the only construction that unequivocally marks topics in English is the relatively uncommon *as for* construction in sentences such as the following:

> As for Colin, he'd seen enough and went to bed.

> As for British politicians, John Major was no match for Clinton's youthful vigor.

In English, marking the topic of a sentence is far less important than marking the subject.

Although topics aren't usually marked in English, writers take advantage of the fact that topics usually occur toward the beginning of a sentence to maintain topic continuity in a paragraph. One way of doing that (but not the only one) is by having the same referent as the topic for a series of sentences.

Marking topics is considerably more important in certain other languages than it is in English. Korean and Japanese, for example, have function words whose sole purpose is to mark a noun phrase as topic. In Chinese and some other languages, no special function words attach to topic noun phrases, but topics are marked by word order. In Korean, Japanese, and Chinese, noun phrases marked as topic occur very frequently. Thus, despite difficulty in defining it, topic is an important notion and needs to be distinguished from other categories of information structure.

Try It Yourself In the excerpt below, identify the noun phrase that is the topic in each sentence. What is noteworthy about the referents of those topics?

(1) Jennifer Weiner, the best-selling author of eight books, had been battling traffic for close to an hour before landing at the Four Seasons Hotel in Beverly Hills. (2) With her kids ensconced in an upstairs room, she collapses into a perfect leather chair and sweetly, if sweatily, orders off the bar menu. (3) The unpretentious 40-year-old is different from many other novelists. (4) She's online, engaged, and quick to speak up for women's fiction. (5) And she's one of the few authors a publisher will book into a hotel in Beverly Hills.

[Adapted from "Calendar," *Los Angeles Times*, July 30, 2010]

Contrast

A noun phrase is said to be **contrastive** when it occurs in opposition to another noun phrase in the discourse. Here, for example, *Sara* in Beth's answer is contrasted with *Matt* in Alan's question.

> **Alan**:   Did Matt see the accident?
>
> **Beth**:   No, <u>Sara</u> did.

Contrast Beth's answer with another possible one in which the noun phrase would not be contrastive: *Yes, he did.*

Contrast is also marked in sentences that express the narrowing down of a choice from several candidates to one. In such sentences, the noun phrase that refers to the candidate thus chosen is marked contrastively.

Of everyone present, only <u>Chloe</u> knew what was going on.

Compare that sentence with the following one, in which *Chloe* is not contrastive.

Gerard knew what was going on, and Chloe did, too.

A simple test exists for contrast: if a noun phrase can be followed by *rather than*, it is contrastive.

Speaker A: Did Matt see the accident?

Speaker B: No, <u>Sara</u>, rather than Matt, saw the accident.

A single sentence can have several contrastive noun phrases. In the following exchange, *Dina* contrasts with *Milo*, and *an entire cast of spirits* contrasts with *a ghost*.

Aaron: Did Milo see a ghost?

Bella: Yes, Milo saw a ghost, but <u>Dina</u> saw <u>an entire cast of spirits</u>.

The entity with which a noun phrase is contrasted may be understood from the discourse or from the situational context. In the following example, *Rachel* could be marked contrastively if the sentence were part of a conversation about how the interlocutors dislike going to Maine during the winter.

<u>Rachel</u> likes going to Maine during the winter.

Below, in an exchange between an employee and one of several managers, the noun phrase *I* in the manager's reply can be made to contrast with *other managers*, which is not expressed but is understood from the situational context.

Employee: Can I leave early today?

Manager: <u>I</u> don't mind.

With strong stress on *I*, the implication of the manager's answer is, 'It's fine with me, but I don't know about the other managers.' The employee can readily understand the implication from shared knowledge of the situational context.

In English, contrastive noun phrases can be marked in a variety of ways, most commonly by pronouncing the contrastive noun phrase with strong stress.

You may be smarter, but <u>he</u>'s more popular.

Other ways of marking contrastiveness will be investigated in the next section.

Definite and Indefinite Expressions

Among other possible reasons, speakers mark a noun phrase as **definite** when they assume that the addressee can identify its referent. Otherwise, the noun phrase is marked as **indefinite**. In the example below, the definite noun phrase *the neighbor* in Bundy's answer presupposes that Andrea can determine which neighbor Bundy is talking about.

Andrea: Who's at the door?

Bundy: It's <u>the neighbor</u>.

Bundy's answer is appropriate if she and Andrea have only one neighbor or have reason to expect a particular neighbor at the door. If they have several neighbors and Bundy cannot assume that Andrea will be able to identify which neighbor is at the door, the answer to Andrea's question would be indefinite: *It's a neighbor*.

Proper nouns and pronouns are generally definite. Pronouns such as *you* and *we* usually refer to individuals who are identifiable in the discourse context. And a speaker who refers by name to someone (say, *Hillary Clinton* or *Michelle*) or something (*Hamilton High School* or *Iowa*) assumes that the addressee will be able to determine the referents of those proper nouns. Still, there are exceptions, as when clerks in a government office say to each other:

> I have a Susie Schmidt here who hasn't paid her taxes since 2006.

Use of the indefinite article *a* marks *Susie Schmidt* as indefinite. It marks the fact that neither the speaker nor the addressee knows the particular individual who goes by the name of Susie Schmidt and that Susie Schmidt is new information in the discourse.

> **Try It Yourself** To determine how English expresses indefiniteness with plural noun phrases, examine the first words of sentences (3) and (6) in Version 1 of the Santa Clara Fire Department newspaper report in the chapter introduction. Also in Version 1, compare the phrase *two apartment buildings* in (1) with *the two apartment buildings* in (6) and identify which is definite and which is indefinite.

Definiteness in English and many other languages is marked by the choice of articles (definite *the* versus indefinite *a*) or by demonstratives (*this* and *that*, both definite). Indefinite noun phrases in English are marked by *a* or *an* (*a furnace, an apartment building*) or by the absence of any article (*oil, fire, apartment buildings*). While the definite article can be used with singular and plural nouns (*the building, the firefighters*), the indefinite article can be used only with singular nouns (*a building, *a firefighters*). Even lacking an indefinite article, plural nouns can still be indefinite.

Article choice is not always a way to mark definiteness. Some languages have only one article. Fijian has only a single article—*na*—and it is definite. To mark indefiniteness, speakers of Fijian use the expression *e dua*, which means 'there is one.'

1. na   tuuraŋa   (definite)
   Article gentleman
   'the gentleman'

2. e dua   na   tuuraŋa   (indefinite)
   there is one Article gentleman
   'a gentleman'

Hindi, in contrast, has only an indefinite article *ek*, and a noun phrase with no article is interpreted as definite.

1. maĩ kitaab ḍʰūũṛʰ rahii tʰii   (definite)
   I   book   search -ing Past-tense
   'I was looking for the book.'

2. maĩ ek kitaab ḍʰūũṛʰ rahii tʰii   (indefinite)
   I   a book   search -ing Past-tense
   'I was looking for a book.'

Many languages do not have articles and rely on other means to mark definiteness, if it is marked at all. Mandarin Chinese relies on word order. A subject that comes before the verb, as in 1 below, is definite; if it follows the verb, as in 2, it is indefinite.

1. huǒchē lái   le   (definite)
   train   arrive New-situation
   'The train has arrived.'

2. lái   huǒchē le   (indefinite)
   arrive train   New-situation
   'A train has arrived.'

Other systems also exist. In Rotuman, spoken in the South Pacific, most nouns have two forms, one definite and one indefinite.

Definite		Indefinite	
futi	'the banana'	füt	'a banana'
vaka	'the canoe'	vak	'a canoe'
rito	'the young shoot'	rjot	'a young shoot'

The indefinite form derives from the definite form through a set of phonological rules.

Definite versus Given Definiteness and givenness are not the same thing. A noun phrase can be definite and given, definite and new, indefinite and given, or indefinite and new, with the first and last combinations being the most common. Below, *a lecture* is indefinite and new, and *the lecturer* is definite and given.

> Last night, we went to Hayden Planetarium for <u>a lecture</u>, and <u>the lecturer</u> fainted.

A noun phrase referring to new information can also be definite. The following sequence, in which *the plumber* is definite, is acceptable whether or not the speaker has introduced a particular identifiable plumber into the previous discourse.

> The kitchen faucet is leaking; we'd better call <u>the plumber</u>.

In certain circumstances, a noun phrase can be both *indefinite* and *given*, as with the underlined noun phrase in this example:

> I ate a hamburger for lunch—<u>a hamburger</u> that was the worst I've ever eaten.

Clearly, definiteness and givenness are distinct categories of information structure.

Try It Yourself In Version 1 of the newspaper report in the chapter introduction, identify at least one noun phrase in each of the following categories: (a) indefinite and new; (b) definite and new; (c) indefinite and given; (d) definite and given.

Referential Expressions

A noun phrase is **referential** when it refers to a particular entity (or more than one). In the first example below, the expression *a Greek with blue eyes* does not refer to anyone in particular and is thus nonreferential. By contrast, in the second example the same phrase does have a referent and is referential.

> Jen wants to marry <u>a Greek with blue eyes</u> but hasn't met one yet.
>
> (nonreferential)
>
> Jen wants to marry <u>a Greek with blue eyes</u>; his name is Yanni.   (referential)

Out of context, *Jen wants to marry a Greek with blue eyes* is ambiguous because nothing in the sentence indicates whether or not a particular Greek is intended. In everyday discourse, sentences of this type are rarely ambiguous, given the power of context to clarify.

Because referentiality and definiteness are not the same thing, a noun phrase can be

> *referential and definite*—Where are <u>the keys</u> to <u>the office</u>?
>
> *referential and indefinite*—She leased <u>a new Ford Raptor</u>.
>
> *nonreferential and definite*—What's <u>the smartest thing</u> to do now?
>
> *nonreferential and indefinite*—You've got to buy <u>a new car</u>.

While pronouns and proper nouns are usually referential, certain pronouns such as *you, it, they,* and *one* are often nonreferential.

> In this county, if <u>you</u> own a house <u>you</u> have to pay taxes.
>
> <u>It</u> is widely suspected that the commissioner had links to the insurance industry.
>
> <u>They</u>'re forecasting thunderstorms for tonight.
>
> <u>One</u> just doesn't know what to do for the best.

Because none of these pronouns refers to a particular entity, they are nonreferential.

Generic and Specific Expressions

A noun phrase may be *generic* or *specific* depending on whether it refers to a category or to particular members of a category. In the first example below, *the bombardier beetle* is generic because it refers to the set of all bombardier beetles; but in the second, which could have been uttered during a visit to a zoo, *The giraffe* refers to a particular animal and is thus specific.

> It describes the bombardier beetle, which squirts a lethal mixture into the face of its enemy.
>
> The giraffe bent slowly forward and gingerly took a carrot from my palm.

In the first sentence, *the bombardier beetle* is generic and definite, while *a lethal mixture* is generic and indefinite. In the second sentence, *The giraffe* is specific and definite, and *a carrot* is specific and indefinite. Thus, the generic/specific contrast differs from the definite/indefinite contrast.

Try It Yourself The sentence below appears in a U.S. Supreme Court decision about trucks on interstate highways in Iowa. Identify one underscored noun phrase that is specific and another that is generic. Is the remaining noun phrase specific or generic? Which of the noun phrases are definite and which indefinite? Which referential and which nonreferential?

> Indeed, <u>the State</u> points to only <u>three ways</u> in which <u>the 55-foot single</u> is even arguably superior.

Categories of Information Structure

Information structure is not marked solely on noun phrases. Other parts of speech, verbs in particular, can represent given or new information and can also be contrastive. In the following exchange, the underlined verb represents contrastively marked new information.

> Jerry visits occasionally, but Sara <u>encamps</u> every holiday.

Similarly, prepositions can sometimes be marked for information structure, as in this example of contrastive marking.

> I said *on* the table, not *under* it!

In this chapter, we concentrate almost exclusively on the marking of information structure on noun phrases, in part because the role of other constituents in the structure of discourse is still not well understood.

Information Structure: Intonation, Morphology, Syntax

Languages differ in how much pragmatic information they encode and in how they encode it. In many languages intonation is used to mark contrast. While intonation is an important tool for marking information structure in English, it is less important in that role in languages such as French and Chinese. Other languages, such as Japanese, have function words whose sole purpose is to indicate pragmatic categories. Still others, including English, depend on syntactic structures such as the passive to convey pragmatic information. Thus, different languages use different strategies to encode pragmatic information. What follows is a sampling of these strategies.

New-Information Stress

In English and some other languages, intonation is an important device for marking information. Generally, noun phrases representing new information receive stronger stress than those representing given information, and they are uttered on a slightly higher pitch than the rest of the sentence. This is called *new-information stress*.

> **Aaron:** Whose footprints are these on the sofa?
>
> **Bianca:** They're *Lou's footprints*.

English speakers also exploit stress to mark contrast.

1. **Aaron:** Are these your footprints on the sofa?

   Bianca: They're not mine, they're *Lou's*.

2. She told Hal he needed two more years to graduate, but she gave *Zoe full clearance*.

Phonetically, new-information stress and contrastive stress are similar, but functionally they differ. English uses stress in complex ways, much more so than such languages as French and Chinese.

Information Structure Morphemes

Some languages have grammatical morphemes whose sole function is to mark categories of information structure. In Japanese, the function word *wa*, which is placed after noun phrases, marks either givenness or contrastiveness. When a noun phrase is neither given nor contrastive, it is marked with a different function word (usually *ga* for subjects and *o* for direct objects). That *wa* is a marker of given information is illustrated by the following exchange:

> **Kenn:** basu ga   kimasuka
> bus Subject come-Question
> 'Is the bus coming?'
>
> **Yumiko:** basu wa   kimasu
> bus Given coming-is
> 'The bus is coming.'

In Kenn's question, *basu* could not be marked with *wa* unless he and Yumiko had been talking about the bus in the previous discourse. But in Yumiko's answer, *basu* is given information and must be marked with *wa*.

Japanese *wa* also marks contrastive information, as in the following sentence:

> basu wa   kimasu   demo takushi wa   kimasen
> bus Contrast coming-is but   taxi   Contrast coming-isn't
> 'The bus is coming. But the taxi isn't (coming).'

Here, *basu wa* need not represent given information, for *wa* can simply mark the fact that the noun phrase to which it is attached is in contrast with another noun phrase also marked with *wa* (*takushi* 'taxi').

The most transparent way of marking information structure is with function words, and this is the preferred way in many languages. Such grammatical morphemes as Japanese *wa* do not affect the overall shape of a sentence. Rather, they straightforwardly point out which sentence element is given, which is contrastive, and so on.

Fronting

Among several syntactic operations that serve to mark information structure is *fronting*. Fronting operates in many languages, although its exact function varies from language to language. In English, it creates sentence 1 from the structure underlying sentence 2, which has the same meaning.

1. A boy he may be, but just a boy he's certainly not.
2. He may be a boy, but he's certainly not just a boy.

In English, one function of fronting is to mark givenness, and a fronted noun phrase must represent given information.

Avi: I heard that you really like mushrooms.

Bert: <u>Mushrooms</u> I'd kill for.

A noun phrase can be fronted if its referent is part of a set that has been mentioned previously in the discourse, even though the referent itself may not have been mentioned. In the following example, *Barnyard* is a hyponym of *family movies*, which is mentioned in the question asked of Courteney Cox-Arquette that immediately precedes the fronted noun phrase; the result is pragmatically acceptable.

Q: Did you deliberately make two family movies back to back?

CCA: No, *Barnyard* I did when I was breast-feeding.

Fronted noun phrases are often contrastive in English.

Ali: Do you like <u>Lady Gaga</u>?

Basho: I like her early songs, but <u>Lady Gaga herself</u> I'm not crazy about.

Fronted noun phrases do not always have the same function in other languages as they do in English. In Mandarin Chinese, fronted noun phrases commonly represent the topic of the sentence.

1. zhèi běn   shū pízi hěn hǎo kàn
   this Classifier book cover very good-looking
   'This book, the cover is nice looking.'

2. zhèi ge   zhǎnlǎnhuì wǒ kàndào hěn duō yóuhuàr
   this Classifier exhibition I   see   very many painting
   '(At) this exhibition, I saw many paintings.'

What is interesting about Chinese fronted noun phrases is that they do not necessarily have a semantic role in the rest of the sentence. In the following sentence, for example, *mógū* 'mushrooms' cannot be a patient because the sentence already has a patient: *zhèi ge dōngxi* 'that sort of thing.' Yet the sentence is both grammatical and pragmatically acceptable.

mógū   wō hěn xǐhuan chī zhèi ge   dōngxi
mushroom I   very like   eat this Classifier thing
'Mushrooms, I like to eat that sort of thing.'

Furthermore, fronted noun phrases do not need to be contrastive in Chinese, though they frequently are in English. The comparison of English and Chinese fronting illustrates an important point: a grammatical process such as a movement operation may have comparable syntactic properties in two languages, but its pragmatic functions may differ considerably.

Left-Dislocation

Left-dislocation is an operation that derives sentences such as 1 from the structure underlying basic sentences such as 2.

1. Holly, I can't stand her.
2. I can't stand Holly.

Left-dislocation is syntactically similar to fronting, but there are notable differences between the two. In particular, a fronted noun phrase does not leave a pronoun in its stead, whereas a left-dislocated noun phrase does.

Holly I can't stand. (fronting)

Holly, I can't stand *her*. (left-dislocation)

Unlike a fronted noun phrase, a left-dislocated noun phrase is set off from the rest of the sentence by a very short pause, represented in writing by a comma. Left-dislocation is similar in nature and function to *right-dislocation*, which moves a noun phrase to the right of a sentence.

I can't stand her, Holly.

In our discussion, we concentrate on left-dislocation.

Left-dislocation is used primarily to reintroduce given information that has not been mentioned for a while. In the following example, the speaker names and comments on a number of people. Hal, mentioned early in the discourse, is reintroduced in the last sentence. There, because nothing has been said about him in the previous two sentences, the speaker reintroduces *Hal* as a left-dislocated noun phrase.

I've kept in touch with lots of classmates. Occasionally, I still see Hal, who was my best friend in high school. And then there's Jim, my college roommate. And Stan and Sara. I met them as sophomores at Ohio State. I really like Jim and Stan and Sara. But *Hal*, I can't stand him now.

In addition to reintroducing given information, left-dislocation may be contrastive. In the example above, *Hal* clearly contrasts with *Jim*, *Stan*, and *Sara*. As a result of its double function, left-dislocation is typically used when speakers go through lists and make comments about each element in the list. Some languages exploit left-dislocation more frequently than English does. In colloquial French, left-dislocated noun phrases are more frequent than the equivalent basic sentences.

<u>Mon</u> <u>frère</u>,   il s'en va en Mongolie.
my   brother he is-going to Mongolia
'My brother, he is leaving for Mongolia.'

Right-dislocation, illustrated by the following sentence, is also common.

> J'sais   pas, <u>moi</u>, c'qu'il   veut.
> I know not me   what-he wants
> 'Me, I don't know what he wants.'

Left-dislocation in colloquial French differs in function from the equivalent operation in English. In French, a left-dislocated noun phrase represents a topic. Left-dislocated noun phrases are particularly frequent when a new topic is introduced into the discourse (as in the first of the following examples) or when the speaker wishes to shift the topic of the discourse (as in the second example).

1. [Asking directions of a stranger in the street]
   Pardon,   <u>la gare</u>, où   est-elle?
   excuse-me the station where is it
   'Excuse me, where is the station?'
2. **Pierre**: <u>Moi</u>, j'aime bien les croissants.
             me   I like a lot the croissants
             'Me, I like croissants a lot.'

   Marie: Oui, mais <u>le pain frais</u>, c'est bon aussi.
             yes but   the bread fresh it-is good too
             'Yes, but fresh bread is also good.'

The pragmatic function of left-dislocation is thus broader in French than in English.

It Clefts and WH Clefts

Clefting operations are used in many languages to mark information structure. In the English examples below, 1 is an *it*-cleft sentence, 2 is a WH-cleft sentence, and 3 is the basic sentence that corresponds to 1 and 2.

1. It was a very strange sight that Stan saw at the party.   (*it*-cleft)
2. What Stan saw at the party was a very strange sight.   (WH-cleft)
3. Stan saw a very strange sight at the party.

It-cleft sentences are of the form *It is/was . . . that*, in which what comes between the first part and the second part of the construction is the clefted noun phrase, prepositional phrase (*It was in March that she last visited*), or adverb (*It's only recently that she's learned to sing*). WH-cleft constructions can be of the form WH-*word . . . is/was/will be*, in which the WH-word is usually *what*. In WH-cleft constructions, the clefted noun phrase, clefted prepositional phrase, or clefted adverb is placed after the verb *be*, and the rest of the clause is placed between the two parts of the construction. Other variants of WH-cleft sentences also exist, as in these examples:

> <u>The one who</u> saw Nick at the party <u>was</u> Stan.

> Nick <u>is who</u> Stan saw at the party.

Besides *is* and *was*, some other forms of *be* may also occur in clefts.

Both *it*-cleft and WH-cleft constructions are used to mark givenness. In an *it*-cleft construction, the clefted phrase presents new information, while the rest of the sentence is given information. Thus, the information question in 1 below can be answered with 2, in which the answer to the question (that is, the new information) is clefted, but it can't be answered with 3 because the clefted element is not the requested new information.

1. Who did Stan see at the party?
2. It was Nick that Stan saw at the party.
3. *It was Stan who saw Nick at the party.

That the part of the sentence following *that/who* in a cleft sentence presents given information is illustrated by the fact that it can refer to something just mentioned in the previous sentence. In the following example, the second sentence contains a cleft construction in which the elements following *that* are simply repeated from the previous sentence in the discourse.

> Alice told me that Stan saw someone at the party that he knew from his high school days. It turns out it was Nick <u>that Stan saw at the party</u>.

Clearly, the element following *that* in a cleft sentence represents given information. WH-cleft constructions are similar to *it*-cleft constructions. In WH-cleft sentences, the new information comes after the verb *be*, and the rest of the clause is placed between the WH-word and the *be* verb.

1. What did Stan see at the party?
2. What Stan saw was Nick salsa dancing.

Question 1 could not be answered with either of the following clefted sentences because in neither 3 nor 4 is the clefted noun phrase the new information.

3. *The one who saw Nick salsa dancing was Stan.
4. *Where Stan saw Nick was at the party.

The rest of a WH-clefted sentence marks given information, as in an *it*-clefted sentence. The following sentence pair, in which given information is underlined, illustrates this fact.

> I liked her latest novel very much. In particular, what <u>I liked about it</u> was the character development.

Both *it*-clefting and WH-clefting highlight which element is new information and which is given information.

In addition, both constructions can mark contrast. Consider the following sequences. In 1 (whose second sentence is an *it*-cleft construction) and 2 (whose second sentence is a WH-cleft), the new information can readily be understood as contrastive. Possible implied information is provided in square brackets after each example.

1. Alice said Stan saw someone at the party that he knew from his high school days. It turns out it was Nick that Stan saw at the party [. . . not Larry, as you might have thought].

2. I liked her latest novel very much. In particular, what I liked about it was the way the characters' personalities are developed. [I liked the character development more than the style of writing.]

You might wonder why English should have two constructions with the same function. Languages usually exploit different structures for different purposes—and, indeed, there is a subtle difference in the uses for these two constructions. An *it*-cleft construction can be used to mark given information that the listener or reader is not necessarily thinking about. In a WH-cleft construction, though, the listener or reader must be thinking about the given information. Thus, it is possible to begin a narrative with an *it*-cleft construction but not with a WH-cleft construction. The first sentence below, an *it*-cleft construction, would be an acceptable opening for a historical narrative, but the second sentence is a WH-cleft construction and would not normally make a good beginning.

> It was to gain their independence from Britain that the colonists started the Revolution.

> *What the colonists started the Revolution to gain was their independence from Britain.

The first sentence is an acceptable opening because it does not necessarily assume that the reader has in mind the given information (*the colonists started the Revolution*) when the narrative begins. The second sentence does assume that the given information (*[what] the colonists started the Revolution to gain*) is in the reader's mind and thus does not make a good opening sentence.

The difference between *it*-cleft and WH-cleft constructions shows that given information is not an absolute notion. There may be different types of givenness: information that the addressee knows but is not necessarily thinking about at the moment and information that the addressee both knows and is thinking about.

Passives

As with other languages that have a passive construction, the choice between an active structure and its passive equivalent can be exploited in English to mark information structure. Compare the following sentences:

1. Bureaucrats could easily store and retrieve data about the citizenry. (active)

2. Data about the citizenry could easily be stored and retrieved by bureaucrats. (passive)

3. Data about the citizenry could easily be stored and retrieved. (passive)

Of these three sentences, all of which may represent the same situation, sentence 1 is an active sentence, whereas the other two are passives. In 2, the agent is expressed (*bureaucrats*) in what is called an *agent passive* or *by-passive* construction. Because no agent is expressed in sentence 3, it is called an *agentless passive* or short passive.

Agentless passives and agent passives serve specific purposes. An agentless passive serves well if the agent is particularly unimportant in the action or state represented by the sentence—for example, when the agent is a generic entity whose identity is irrelevant to the point of the sentence.

A new shopping mall is being built near the airport.

Those laws, however noxious, are rarely enforced.

In the first sentence, the agent is likely a real-estate developer; in the second one, police authorities. In each case, the exact identity of the particular agent is either known or irrelevant to the situation represented by the sentence. In spoken language, instead of agentless passives, active sentences with the indefinite and nonreferential pronoun *they* often occur, as in these examples:

They're building a new shopping mall near the airport.

They issue new Christmas stamps every year.

They rarely enforce those noxious laws.

An agent passive construction is used when a noun phrase other than the agent is the given information. Imagine a news report that begins as follows:

The World Health Organization held its annual meeting last week in Geneva.

This sentence establishes the annual meeting as given information for the rest of the report. If the sentence that follows it uses the noun phrase *the meeting*, that phrase will likely occur in subject position because it represents given information. In that following sentence, if *the meeting* does not have the semantic role of agent, the sentence is likely to be expressed as a passive construction in order to allow *the meeting* to be the grammatical subject.

The meeting was organized by health administrators from 50 countries.

This generalization is not absolute, and there is nothing fundamentally wrong with a sequence in which the second sentence is active rather than the passive predicted by the generalization, as shown below:

The World Health Organization held its annual meeting last week in Geneva. Health administrators from 50 countries organized the meeting.

But the equivalent sequence with a passive second sentence flows better and may be easier to understand:

The World Health Organization held its annual meeting last week in Geneva. The meeting was organized by health administrators from 50 countries.

In English, the choice of a passive sentence over its active counterpart is regulated by information structure. Specifically, agentless passives are used when the agent is known or not particularly significant (as in this very sentence). Agent passives (with *by*) are used when a noun phrase other than the agent of the sentence is more prominent as given information than the agent itself.

Try It Yourself In the following sentences, identify the two agentless passives and say what the agent is likely to be. For the agent passive, specify the agent.

1) Two state governors were mentioned by the president. 2) Most people would feel fear if their capital were attacked. 3) The Japanese auto maker has been hurt as stock markets fell.

Not all languages have a passive construction. Chinese and Samoan, for example, do not. But such languages have other ways of saying what English expresses with the passive. In Samoan, when the agent of a sentence is not important, it is simply not expressed; the sentence remains an active structure.

?ua   ?oteŋia le   teiŋe
Present-tense scold   the young-woman
'The young woman is being scolded.' (Literally: 'Is scolding the young woman.')

Word Order

Many languages use the sequential order of noun phrases to mark differences in information structure. English cannot use the full resources of word order for this purpose because it uses word order to mark subjects and direct objects (see Chapter 5). In the sentence *The cat is chasing the dog*, it is word order that indicates who is doing the chasing and who is being chased. If we invert the two noun phrases, the semantics of the sentence (who is agent and who is patient) changes: *The dog is chasing the cat.*

In a language like Russian, however, the noun phrases can be scrambled without changing the semantics. All the following sentences mean the same thing. (Note that š is pronounced [ʃ], like *sh* in English *ship*.)

1. koška presleduet sobaku
   cat   is chasing dog
2. sobaku presleduet koška
3. presleduet koška sobaku   'The cat is chasing the dog.'
4. presleduet sobaku koška
5. koška sobaku presleduet
6. sobaku koška presleduet

In each of these sentences we know *who* is doing *what* to *whom* because the inflections on the noun differ from one another. The *-u* ending of *sobaku* 'dog' marks it as the direct object (if it were the subject, it would be *sobaka*), and the *-a* ending of *koška* 'cat' marks it as the subject (as direct object, it would be *košku*).

The differences among these versions of the same sentence reside in their information structure. More precisely, in Russian, word order marks givenness. The information question *Što koška presleduet?* 'What is the cat chasing?' can only be answered as follows:

koška presleduet sobaku
cat   is-chasing dog
'The cat is chasing the dog.'

On the other hand, the question *Što presleduet sobaku?* 'What is chasing the dog?' must be answered as follows:

sobaku presleduet koška
dog   is-chasing cat
'The cat is chasing the dog.'

Thus, what comes first in the Russian sentence is not the subject but the given information, and what comes last is the new information. In answer to the question *What is the cat chasing?*, *the dog* is new information and comes at the end of the Russian sentence. By contrast, in answer to the question *What is chasing the dog?*, *the cat* is new information and comes last in the sentence. Word order in Russian, as in many other languages, is thus used to mark givenness. Similar explanations could be offered for the other variants of the Russian sentence we have cited, but we will not develop them here. (See Exercise 8-9.)

Typically, in languages that exploit word order to encode pragmatic information, syntactic constructions such as passives, *it*-clefts, and WH-clefts do not exist (or are rare). Russian has a grammatical construction that resembles the English passive, but it is rarely used. The reason is simple: given the rich inflectional system for marking grammatical relations, word order is left free to mark information structure, and there is no need to use complex structures like the passive to mark givenness. Passives are useful in languages that exploit word order for other purposes and thus cannot manipulate it to indicate pragmatic information.

The Relationship of Sentences to Discourse: Pragmatics

We have outlined some of the basic notions needed to describe how information is structured in discourse and analyzed a number of constructions in terms of information structure. From the discussion in this and previous chapters, it should be clear that the syntactic structure of any language is driven by two factors. On the one hand, syntax must encode semantic structure: the syntactic structure of a sentence must enable language users to identify who does what to whom—the agent, patient, and so on for other semantic roles. On the other hand, syntax must encode information structure: which constituents represent given information, which represent new information, which can be easily identified by the addressee, which cannot, and so on. Schematically, the relationship can be viewed as follows:

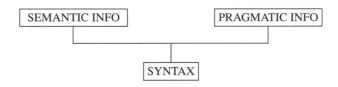

Syntax is thus used to convey both semantic information and pragmatic information.

COMPUTERS AND PRAGMATICS

A thorough understanding of pragmatics will eventually prove important for speech recognition and, to a lesser extent, for speech synthesis. To date, however, features of pragmatics have been less well explored in computational linguistics than morphological, lexical, phonological, grammatical, and semantic features of texts.

One reason for the relative neglect of pragmatics is that modeling the world knowledge and discourse knowledge that speakers rely on when producing and understanding texts is even more challenging than creating models of structural aspects of language. Another is that the kinds of linguistic features by which some pragmatic categories are realized are not always expressed in ways that computers can readily track.

As we have seen, speakers base some aspects of expression on their beliefs about what addressees know and are thought to have in the forefront of their minds. This is true in marking noun phrases as definite or indefinite, in choosing between active and passive structures, and in indicating contrast by intonation, for example. While these three features have some representation in a text, others such as given and new information have little or no textual realization and would be extremely challenging or even impossible for a computer to identify.

If you've ever used a grammar checker, you know that even rudimentary ones readily spot passive verbs. What checkers cannot do is distinguish between those passives that effectively serve a pragmatic function such as topicalization and those that do not. If a writer rewrote all passives as actives, the individual rewritten sentences would remain grammatical, but the changes would likely do serious damage to the pragmatic structure of the text. (Exercise 8-7 asks you to consider revising the passives in a short text.)

Computer programs can identify pragmatic categories only if they are somehow marked in the text. For example, the Japanese function word *wa* can be automatically identified as easily as an English passive, and most English noun phrases can be automatically identified as definite or indefinite. But other categories—for example, topic, givenness, and referentiality—cannot be identified automatically. If researchers wanted to make use of such categories, their texts would have to be manually tagged to reflect those categories. To do this, an interactive analysis program would tag each *potential* item—say, all referring expressions—as "given" and then present a human editor with a menu of alternatives for the tentative tag, much as a spell checker offers alternative spellings. Once such categories were tagged in the texts of a corpus, researchers could explore related matters, relying on the computer's capacity for speed and accuracy.

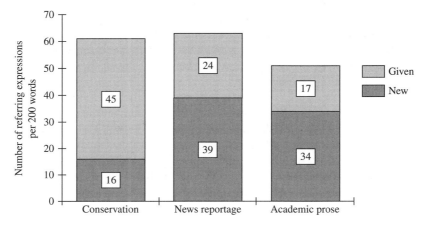

Figure 8.1 Average Number of Given and New Referring Expressions in Three Kinds of Text

Source: D. Biber, S. Conrad, R. Reppen, 1998.

Suppose a corpus contained referring expressions that had been manually tagged as given or new. It would be a simple matter to calculate the number of given and new references for any group of texts in the corpus—for conversations, say, or for news reportage in newspapers. It turns out that different kinds of texts differ significantly in the average number of given and new references they contain, and that similar facts have implications for artificial intelligence, for speech recognition, and for teaching, especially teaching foreign languages for specific purposes such as law or science.

Figure 8.1 shows two sets of relations: those between given and new information in each column for three kinds of text and the relationships among the three kinds of text. For example, conversation has about three times as many given noun phrases as new ones. Academic prose, by contrast, has half as many given noun phrases as new ones. Likewise, while conversation and news reportage have approximately the same number of noun phrases per 200 words of text, the proportion of given and new noun phrases is reversed between them. Conversational-

ists use noun phrases that are mostly given. News reportage introduces new referents about twice as often as it mentions given referents. A good many noun phrases in conversation are first-person and second-person pronouns, which always represent given information. (By contrast, the use of first-person and second-person pronouns in news reportage is virtually limited to quoted speech and do not constitute the bulk of news reportage.)

As Figure 8.1 shows, a second kind of information can be drawn from counts of given and new referring expressions in different kinds of text. For example, the number of new noun phrases is relatively low in conversation as compared with academic prose or news reportage. Not surprisingly, news reportage contains more than twice the number of new references as conversation, and so does academic prose.

With suitably tagged corpora, a good deal can be learned about the character of different kinds of texts. Such information will prove critical in speech recognition, machine translation, foreign language teaching, and other real-world applications of linguistics where computers and natural language meet. ■

Summary

- Pragmatics is concerned with the encoding of information structure—the relative significance of different elements in a clause, principally noun phrases. It treats the relationship of sentences to their discourse environment.
- Relational categories include *givenness* (whether a piece of information is new or already exists in the discourse context), *topic* (the center of attention), and *contrast* (whether a piece of information is contrasted with another piece).
- Nonrelational notions include *definiteness* (whether the referent of a noun phrase is identifiable) and *referentiality* (whether a noun phrase has a referent).
- Some syntactic operations serve to mark certain elements of sentences for pragmatic categories. In English, fronting, left-dislocation, *it*-cleft, WH-cleft, and passivization single out particular noun phrases as sentence topics or as given information or new information.
- Contrast is marked through sentence stress and is a secondary function of certain syntactic operations such as fronting.
- Many languages exploit word order or grammatical morphemes to mark information structure.

- The functions of a particular syntactic operation or information-structure device may differ from language to language because each language favors particular strategies over others.
- Syntax encodes two types of information: semantic information (the semantic role of a noun phrase) and pragmatic information (the relative significance of noun phrases in a discourse).

What Do You Think? REVISITED

- *Annie, the international student.* Sources sometimes suggest that definite articles are used to refer to particular persons, places, and things, as in *the Eiffel Tower* and *the president.* But it is inaccurate to say indefinite articles are used exclusively to refer to *any* person, place, or thing (i.e., not a particular one). That is one function of an indefinite article (*I'm looking for a present in the $50 range for Toni; got a suggestion?*). Commonly, though, an indefinite article signals that the speaker believes the addressee does not have the (particular) referent already in mind (*I bought Toni a present after I got a suggestion from Barry*). In other words, an indefinite noun phrase can signal to a hearer (or reader) that an entity is new to the discourse. Once the entity is in the addressee's mind, speakers use definite noun phrases (*the present, the suggestion, it*) to signal that the referent is given information and the speaker believes the addressee can identify it. In a conversation (or newspaper article or other discourse, for that matter), it is routine for an initial mention of something to be indefinite and subsequent mentions to be definite.
- *Thom from Taiwan and the ESL class discussion.* The active and passive versions of the sentence about the World Cup mean the same thing. For example, if one version is true, the other must be true; if one is false, the other must be false. Also, they describe the same situation. Still, the sentences would not be used in the same circumstances because they're *about* different things. The active version (*Spain won the 2010 World Cup*) says something about the Spanish team. The sentence is *about* Spain's team. The passive version (*The 2010 World Cup was won by Spain*) is *about* the 2010 World Cup. Thus, the sentences have the same referential meaning, but they present different perspectives. Ask Thom to consider the two requests below and decide whether the active and passive versions above could be used equally well as answers:

   Tell me something good about Spain's team.

   Tell me something about the 2010 World Cup.

   Speakers (and writers) tend to be efficient, and while two sentences might *mean* the same thing, that doesn't mean they could be used interchangeably in all discourse contexts. Different versions serve different purposes and situations.
- *Your classmate Clint.* English generally places subjects before verbs and verbs before objects (*I like popcorn!*), but to express contrast an object can sometimes be moved into first position before the subject (*Popcorn I like!*). ■

Exercises

Based on English

8-1. In an article called "Ellen's 'Heart Issue': A Friend's Report," actress Kathy Najimy writes as follows about her first meeting with Ellen DeGeneres. After examining the passage (sentence numbers have been added), answer the questions that follow:

[handwritten: voice of peggy hill, Hocus Pocus witch]

[handwritten:).]

> (1) I met Ellen three or four years ago when I was a guest on her show. (2) She was funny, smart and charming, and I was moved by her vulnerability and what she was going through in regards to her sexuality. (3) We would sit in the trailer and talk about what was happening to her personally and politically. (4) It was interesting to me because I know lots of gay people, and I know lots of famous people, but I had never known anyone who was famous and gay and struggling with what to do about it. [*Los Angeles Times*, "Calendar," December 21, 1997, p. 79]

a. In 1, is the first-person pronoun *I* given or new information? Explain the basis for your answer.

b. In 2, is *She* given or new information? Explain the basis for your answer.

c. In 3, is *We* given or new information? Explain the basis for your answer.

d. In 4, is *It* given or new information, and what constituent does *It* refer to?

e. Identify the noun phrase that is the topic in sentences 2, 3, and 4. *[handwritten: Pronouns]*

f. From your answers to b through e above, what inference can you draw about topics in this paragraph?

g. From the examples you have just examined and the other pronouns in the passage, would you say that personal pronouns generally represent given information or new information?

h. In 1, is *Ellen* given or new information? Definite or indefinite? Explain.

i. In 1, whose show does *her show* refer to? Is *her show* definite or indefinite? *[handwritten: not marked with the.]*

j. List *all* indefinite noun phrases in the passage. (Remember that pronouns are noun phrases.)

k. Prior to its mention in 3, *the trailer* has not been mentioned, so how do you explain that it is definite?

8-2. Examine the passage below and answer the questions that follow:

> (1) They were metal mirrored sun glasses, the kind you buy at a drugstore on the way to the beach, standard Angeleno equipment, as noteworthy as sunscreen or sandals. (2) But when Lane Kiffin stared down from behind them on the Rose Bowl's outdoor stage at Pac-10 media

day—while the conference's other nine coaches removed their shades—
they were reflections of a reputation. (3) What is he hiding? (4) Who
is he hiding? [Adapted from the *Los Angeles Times* "Sports," July 30,
2010, C1]

a. From the following list, identify all the *non-referential noun phrases*:
sun glasses, a drugstore, the beach, the Rose Bowl's outdoor stage,
a reputation.

b. From the following list, identify all the *generic noun phrases*: sun glasses,
a drugstore, the beach, sunscreen, sandals, their shades, a reputation.

c. Identify any contrastive noun phrases in the passage.

d. In 2, *they* represents given information and is definite. What noun phrase
in 1 has the same referent as *they* but is indefinite? Explain why the first
of these noun phrases is indefinite and the second definite even though
they have identical referents.

e. From the passage, identify a noun phrase in each of the following
categories:

(i). referential and definite
(ii). referential and indefinite
(iii). nonreferential and definite   *the*
(iv). nonreferential and indefinite
(v). generic and definite   *a*
(vi). generic and indefinite

8-3. Consider the following text as a complete story in a newspaper. Analyze each
sentence in its context and state what is odd about it in terms of information
structure.

(1) As for the Santa Clara Fire Department, it evacuated two apartment
buildings at the corner of Country Club Drive and Fifth Avenue at 3
A.M. last Sunday. (2) Nancy Jenkins had discovered a furnace in the
basement of a building at the corner of Country Club Drive and Fifth
Avenue, and the furnace was leaking oil. (3) What the firefighters did
was to spray chemical foam over the oil for several hours. (4) It was
by 8 A.M. last Sunday that the situation was under control. (5) What
someone had averted was any danger of the explosion or the fire, and
as for a leaky furnace, it was sealed. (6) What the residents of the
two apartment buildings at the corner of Country Club Drive and Fifth
Avenue were given in the Country Club High School gymnasium was
temporary shelter. (7) Possession of their apartments was regained by
the residents of the two apartment buildings at the corner of Country
Club Drive and Fifth Avenue at 5 P.M. last Sunday.

8-4. Choose a short article (approximately one newspaper column) or an excerpt
of an article from a newspaper's front page. Identify all the sentences that
have undergone a syntactic operation of some kind (such as passivization or
clefting). In each case, explain the most likely reason for using a transformed
sentence instead of the equivalent basic sentence.

8-5. In certain dialects of English, a syntactic operation moves a noun phrase to the beginning of its clause. It derives sentence (1) from the same underlying structure as the basic sentence (2):

1) A bottle of champagne and caviar he wants.

2) He wants a bottle of champagne and caviar.

The operation is called "Yiddish movement" because it is characteristic of the English dialect spoken by native speakers of Yiddish. Yiddish movement is syntactically similar to fronting but differs in its pragmatic function. Here are three pragmatic contexts in which Yiddish movement is appropriate. On the basis of these data, describe succinctly the pragmatic function of Yiddish movement.

1) Speaker A: What does he want?
   Speaker B: A bottle of champagne and caviar he wants!

2) Speaker A: How's your daughter?
   Speaker B: So many worries she causes me to have!

3) Speaker A: Are you willing to help me?
   Speaker B: Not a finger would I lift for you!

Compare in particular the following interactions. In the first, the answer can undergo Yiddish movement; in the second, it cannot.

4) Speaker A: Who is Deborah going to marry?
   Speaker B: A scoundrel Deborah is going to marry!

5) Speaker A: Who is going to marry Deborah?
   Speaker B: *Deborah a scoundrel is going to marry!

8-6. Below is an excerpt, taken and slightly adapted from a U.S. Supreme Court case (*Kassel v. Consolidated Freightways Corp.*); some noun phrases have been underscored and the sentences numbered. Read it attentively and answer the questions that follow.

(1) None of these findings is seriously disputed by Iowa. (2) Indeed, the State points to only three ways in which the 55-foot single is even arguably superior: singles take less time to be passed and to clear intersections; they may back up for longer distances; and they are somewhat less likely to jackknife. (3) The first two of these characteristics are of limited relevance on modern interstate highways. (4) As the District Court found, the negligible difference in the time required to pass, and to cross intersections, is insignificant on 4-lane divided highways because passing does not require crossing into oncoming traffic lanes, and interstates have few, if any, intersections. (5) The concern over backing capability also is insignificant because it seldom is necessary to back up on an interstate. (6) In any event, no evidence suggested any difference in backing capability between the 60-foot doubles that Iowa permits and the 65-foot doubles that it bans. (7) Similarly, although doubles tend to jackknife somewhat more

than singles, 65-foot doubles actually are less likely to jackknife than 60-foot doubles.

a. Using notions of given and new information and definite and indefinite noun phrases, explain how you know in sentence 2 that *the State* refers to Iowa.

b. Identify one underscored noun phrase in each of these categories: (i) generic and definite; (ii) specific; (iii) definite; (iv) generic and indefinite; (v) definite and referential; (vi) indefinite and referential; (vii) given and definite; (viii) given and indefinite; (ix) indefinite and new.

c. In light of the discussion of the relationship between indefinite and new, on the one hand, and definite and given, on the other, explain why these indefinite noun phrases in sentence 7 represent given information: *doubles, singles, 65-foot doubles, 60-foot singles*.

d. Identify the noun phrase that is the topic of sentences 1, 3, 4, and 5.

e. Sentence 1 uses a passive structure. The active equivalent would be, *Iowa does not seriously dispute any of these findings*. Which noun phrase is topicalized in the passive version? Given the topic that you have just identified, what is the paragraph preceding this excerpt likely to be about?

8-7. Examine the passage that follows and note the underscored passive verbs. Then offer a pragmatic reason that may have motivated the authors to use each of the underscored passives. Next, for any clause or sentence whose passive verb you cannot justify, rewrite it using an active verb. Finally, consider your revised passage, and judge whether the text is more pragmatically effective than the original. Explain your judgment.

> This work examines linguistic and structural features present in written criminal statements for predictive value in determining the likelihood of veracity or deception. Statements written by suspects and victims <u>were identified</u> through the investigation of criminal incidents and serve as data. Support <u>was found</u> for a positive relationship between deception and the attributes of equivocation, negation, and relative length of the prologue. A positive relationship <u>was</u> also <u>found</u> between veracity and unique sensory details. Weak support <u>was found</u> for a relationship between veracity and emotions in the epilogue. More than 80 per cent of the statements <u>were</u> correctly <u>classified</u> as containing veracity or deception. [Adapted from Susan H. Adams and John P. Jarvis. 2006. "Indicators of Veracity and Deception: An Analysis of Written Statements Made to Police." *International Journal of Speech, Language and the Law*, 13.1: p. 1.]

Based on Languages Other Than English

8-8. As in Russian, word order in Spanish is used to encode information structure. The constituents of a sentence may be ordered in a variety of ways, as shown by the following examples from Castilian Spanish, all of which can describe the same event. (S = subject; V = verb; O = direct object)

Consuelo envió el paquete. (SVO)
Consuelo sent the package

Envió Consuelo el paquete. (VSO)
sent Consuelo the package

Envió el paquete Consuelo. (VOS)
sent the package Consuelo

El paquete lo envió Consuelo. (OVS)
the package it sent Consuelo

'Consuelo sent the package.'

Consider the following conversational exchanges, focusing on the order of constituents in the answers.

1) Q: ¿Qué hizo Consuelo?
   what did Consuelo
   'What did Consuelo do?'

   A: Consuelo preparó la sangria.
   Consuelo prepared the sangria
   'Consuelo made the sangria.'

2) Q: ¿Quién comió mi bocadillo?
   who ate my sandwich
   'Who ate my sandwich?'

   A: Tu bocadillo lo comió Consuelo.
   your sandwich it ate Consuelo
   'Consuelo ate your sandwich.'

3) Q: ¿A quién dió Consuelo este regalo?
   to whom gave Consuelo this present
   'Who did Consuelo give this present to?'

   A: Este regalo lo dió Consuelo a su madre.
   this present it gave Consuelo to her mother
   'Consuelo gave this present to her mother.'

4) Q: ¿Que pasó?
   what occurred
   'What happened?'

   A: Se murió Consuelo.
   died Consuelo
   'Consuelo died.'

5) Q: ¿Recibió Consuelo el premio?
   received Consuelo the prize
   'Did Consuelo get the prize?'

   A: No, el premio lo recibió Paquita.
   no the prize it received Paquita
   'No, *Paquita* got the prize.'

6) Q: ¿Recibió Consuelo esta carta?
received Consuelo this letter
'Did Consuelo get this letter?'

A: No, Consuelo recibió   este paquete.
no Consuelo received this package
'No, Consuelo got this *package*.'

7) Q: ¿Recibió Consuelo el   premio?
received Consuelo the prize
'Did Consuelo get the prize?'

A: Si, el   premio lo recibió   Consuelo.
yes the prize   it received Consuelo
'Yes, Consuelo got the prize.'

a. On the basis of these data, describe how word order is used to mark information structure in Spanish statements (but not in questions). In particular, state which categories of information structure are marked through which word order possibility. Make your statement of the rules as general as possible.

b. Notice that in certain sentences the pronoun *lo* 'it' appears before the verb. What is the syntactic rule that dictates when it should and should not appear? Which rule of English does the presence of the pronoun in these sentences remind you of?

8-9. In light of the function of Russian word order, provide an information question (in English) to which sentences 5 and 6 in the "Word Order" section of this chapter would be pragmatically acceptable Russian answers.

8-10. Examine the Japanese utterances below, made while two friends were waiting at a bus stop. Explain why Yumiko used *basu ga* to refer to the bus, while Kimiko used *basu wa*.

Yumiko: basu ga   kimasu
bus   Subject coming-is   'The bus is coming.'

Kimiko: basu wa   konde-imas
bus   Given crowded-is   'The bus is crowded.'

8-11. Tongan has an operation that incorporates the direct object (Object) into the verb, forming a verb-noun compound. It generates a sentence like (a) from the underlying structure of the basic sentence (b):

a) naʔa   ku inu   pia   (Object incorporated)
Past-tense I   drink beer
'I drank beer.' (literally: 'I beer-drank.')

b) naʔa   ku inu   ʔa   e   pia   (Object not incorporated)
Past-tense I   drink Object the beer
'I drank the/a beer.'

Below are three more examples of object-incorporated constructions (translated loosely to highlight the meaning of the Tongan sentence):

| ʔoku | | nau | fie kai | ika | (Object incorporated) |
| Present-tense | | they | hungry-for | fish | |

'They are fish-hungry.'

| naʔa | | ma | sio | faiva | (Object incorporated) |
| Past-tense | | we | see | movie | |

'We (went) movie-watching.'

| ʔoku | | ne | faʔu | hiva-kakala | (Object incorporated) |
| Present-tense | | she | compose | love-song | |

'She is love-song composing.'

An incorporated direct object cannot be followed by a restrictive relative clause, but a direct object that has not been incorporated can be. Compare:

*naʔa	ku	inu	pia	[naʔa	nau omai]	
						(Object incorporated)
Past-tense	I	drink	beer	Past-tense	they give-me	

'I drank beer [that they gave me].'

naʔa	ku	inu	ʔa	e	pia	[naʔa	nau omai]
							(Object not incorporated)
Past-tense	I	drink	Object	the	beer	Past-tense	they give-me

'I drank the/a beer [that they gave me].'

Assuming that restrictive relative clauses have the same function in Tongan and English, describe the pragmatic function of Tongan object incorporation.

Especially for Educators and Future Teachers

8-12. To jog your students' memories about what constitutes given and new information and how information status affects the marking of a noun phrase as definite or indefinite, you offer this short report: *Last weekend I went to a wedding. The bride and groom were friends of mine.* Then you give your students these opening lines (below) from a newspaper article about Annika Sorenstam (adapted from the *Los Angeles Times*, March 20, 2003). You instruct them to fill in the blanks with *a/an* or *the*, as appropriate. Using a level of explanation you deem appropriate for your students, tell a classmate how you would teach your students about their ability to restore definite or indefinite articles to the piece.

The best female golfer in the world is standing at __ grill, on __ black rubber mat, __ squadron of pots and pans flying in formation on hooks above her head. Annika Sorenstam feels very much at home as she conducts __ tour of __ kitchen at the Lake Nona resort, where her thoughts are far removed from her world of professional golf. In __ kitchen, it's not Pak or Webb or Inkster on her mind. It's crab cakes, stuffed mushrooms and tiramisu. That's why chef Gary Hoffman handed her 60 fillets to sear for

__ recent evening meal in __ club's dining room. Sorenstam also knows how to carve __ flower out of __ wedge of melon, the easiest way to peel potatoes, and how to whip up rice pilaf.

Here's __ story she enjoys telling. One evening at dinner, __ club member enjoyed his meal. "He said, 'Bring out the chef,'" Sorenstam said. "So Gary came out and __ member said, 'No, not that chef, the other one.' So I came out."

8-13. In a dictionary appropriate to your current or prospective students (or a desk dictionary you use yourself), examine the entries for *a* and *the* to identify which definition among the several listed for each word best matches your understanding as discussed in this chapter. Then assess whether those definitions adequately represent the facts about indefinite and definite articles as you understand them. If they don't, write an amended definition at a level appropriate for your students.

Other Resources

Internet

 LISU website: http://www.CengageBrain.com For users of this textbook. Provides updated Internet links as well as supplemental material for students and instructors. Here you will find interactive learning tools.

 AT&T text-to-speech demonstration: http://www.research.att. com/~ttsweb/tts/demo.php In an earlier chapter, you may have visited this website for a demonstration of speech synthesis and been impressed with the synthesizer's ability to produce the consonantal and vocalic sounds of the sentence you submitted. It's worth returning to the site to submit sentences that illustrate some information structure devices such as left-dislocation or contrast. Judge for yourself to what extent this speech synthesis engine captures the intonation that conveys such pragmatic information.

Suggestions for Further Reading

- **Geoffrey N. Leech. 1983.** *Principles of Pragmatics* (London: Longman). An accessible introduction.
- **Kenneth R. Rose & Gabriele Kasper, eds. 2001.** *Pragmatics in Language Teaching* (Cambridge, UK: Cambridge University Press). Especially for language teachers and those learning a second language, these essays emphasize matters often overlooked in language learning and language teaching.
- **George Yule. 1996.** *Pragmatics* (Oxford: Oxford University Press). A brief and accessible introduction, appearing in a series designed to introduce students to various linguistic subfields. Besides material covered in the current chapter, it treats material covered in Chapters 6 and 9.

Advanced Reading

Overviews of the issues addressed in this chapter can be found in Lambrecht (1994), Foley (2007), Givón (1979a), Chafe (1976), McCarthy (1991), and Georgakopolou and Goutsos (2004). A thoughtful discussion of topics discussed in this chapter can be found in Chafe (1994). The papers in Givón (1979b) and Li (1976) investigate the interaction of syntax and pragmatics in various languages, while Chafe (1970) examines this interaction in English.

Givenness and related topics are discussed in Prince (1979), definiteness in Lyons (1999). The discussion of *it*-cleft and WH-cleft constructions in this chapter relies on Prince (1978), and the discussion of fronting and Yiddish movement on Prince (1981). Lambrecht (1981) analyzes left-dislocation and right-dislocation in spoken French. English passive constructions are investigated in Thompson (1987). A concise discussion of the function of Russian word order can be found in Comrie (1987). For an overview of research on intonation and sentence stress and their pragmatic functions, see Bolinger (1986). Other means of marking pragmatic structure in English are discussed in Halliday and Hasan's classic (1976). Schiffrin et al. (2001), a broad treatment of discourse, is a useful resource for instructors. Our Figure 8.1, modeled on Figure 5-2 from Biber et al. (1998), infers approximate numerical counts from the purely visual representation in the original; Biber et al.'s chapter treating "The Study of Discourse Characteristics" accessibly discusses interactive methods for tracking discourse features.

References

Biber, Douglas, Susan Conrad & Randi Reppen. 1998. *Corpus Linguistics: Investigating Language Structure and Use* (Cambridge, UK: Cambridge University Press).

Bolinger, Dwight L. 1986. *Intonation and Its Parts: Melody in Spoken English* (Stanford: Stanford University Press).

Chafe, Wallace L. 1970. *Meaning and the Structure of Language* (Chicago: University of Chicago Press).

Chafe, Wallace L. 1976. "Givenness, Contrastiveness, Definiteness, Subjects, Topics, and Point of View," in Li (1976), pp. 25–55.

Chafe, Wallace L. 1994. *Discourse, Consciousness, and Time: The Flow and Displacement of Conscious Experience in Speaking and Writing* (Chicago: University of Chicago Press).

Comrie, Bernard. 1987. "Russian," in Timothy Shopen, ed., *Languages and Their Status* (Philadelphia: University of Pennsylvania Press), pp. 91–151.

Foley, William A. 2007. "A Typology of Information Packaging in the Clause," in Timothy Shopen, ed., *Language Typology and Syntactic Description*, 2nd ed. (Cambridge, UK: Cambridge University Press), 1, pp. 362–446.

Georgakopolou, Alexandra & Dionysis Goutsos. 2004. *Discourse Analysis: An Introduction*, 2nd ed. (Edinburgh: Edinburgh University Press).

Givón, Talmy. 1979a. *On Understanding Grammar* (New York: Academic).

Givón, Talmy, ed. 1979b. *Syntax and Semantics 12: Discourse and Syntax* (New York: Academic).

Halliday, M. A. K. & Ruqaiya Hasan. 1976. *Cohesion in English* (London: Longman).

Lambrecht, Knud. 1981. *Topic, Antitopic, and Verb Agreement in Non-standard French* (Amsterdam: Benjamins).

Lambrecht, Knud. 1994. *Information Structure and Sentence Form: Topic, Focus, and the Mental Representation of Discourse Referents* (Cambridge, UK: Cambridge University Press).

Li, Charles N., ed. 1976. *Subject and Topic* (New York: Academic).

Lyons, Christopher. 1999. *Definiteness* (Cambridge, UK: Cambridge University Press).

McCarthy, Michael. 1991. *Discourse Analysis for Teachers* (Cambridge, UK: Cambridge University Press).

Prince, Ellen F. 1978. "A Comparison of WH-clefts and *It*-clefts in Discourse," *Language* 54:883–906.

Prince, Ellen F. 1979. "On the Given/New Distinction," *Papers from the Fifteenth Regional Meeting of the Chicago Linguistics Society* (Chicago: Chicago Linguistics Society), pp. 267–78.

Prince, Ellen F. 1981. "Topicalization, Focus Movement, and Yiddish Movement: A Pragmatic Differentiation," *Proceedings of the Seventh Annual Meeting of the Berkeley Linguistics Society* (Berkeley: Berkeley Linguistics Society), pp. 249–64.

Schiffrin, Deborah, Deborah Tannen & Heidi E. Hamilton. 2001. *The Handbook of Discourse Analysis* (Malden, MA: Blackwell).

Thompson, Sandra A. 1987. "The Passive in English: A Discourse Perspective," in Robert Channon & Linda Shockey, eds., *In Honor of Ilse Lehiste* (Dordrecht: Foris), pp. 497–511.

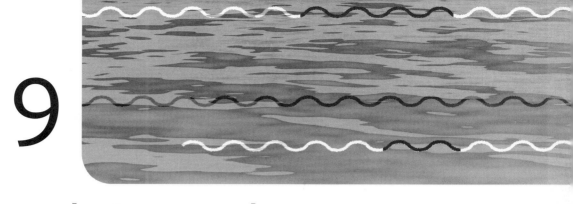

9

Speech Acts and Conversation

What Do You Think?

- Your friend Isabella wonders aloud why the words "I now pronounce you husband and wife" will create a legal marriage between two people at a wedding but not when uttered on stage in a play. At first you dismiss the question as silly. "No, really," she says. "What makes the difference?" You think the answer's obvious, but you try. What's the best explanation you can give?

- Kimberly complains that just last week her boyfriend Tyler promised to take her along the next time he went skiing. Then this weekend he went skiing and didn't invite her. Asked what Tyler said when he made his promise, Kimberly reports that he said, "I will. I will. Honestly, I will." You ask whether Tyler said, "I promise," and Kimberly says "No." You tell her you think Tyler's a lout, but you're not sure he made a promise because he didn't use that word. "C'mon," she says, "a promise is a promise." How do you explain your interpretation of a promise to her?

- Your younger brother Brandon complains that when Daniel, a French friend from college, phones to speak with you, he takes forever to get to the point and apologizes endlessly for nothing! Brandon wonders why Daniel can't get to the point. You're aware that people from different cultures behave differently on the telephone. What explanation do you offer Brandon for Daniel's telephone behavior?

Language in Use

People use language principally as a tool to *do* things: request a favor, make a promise, report a piece of news, give directions, offer a greeting, seek information, extend an invitation, request help, and do hundreds of other ordinary things. Sometimes what we do with language has serious consequences: propose marriage, swear to tell the truth, fire an employee, declare a mistrial, and so on. Such *speech acts* are part of *speech events*—conversations, lectures, student-teacher conferences, news broadcasts, marriage ceremonies, and courtroom trials. In addition to births, deaths, fires, robberies, hurricanes, automobile accidents, and the like, which are not speech acts, much of what is reported in newspapers, blogs, and radio and television news broadcasts are speech acts: arrests, predictions, denials, promises, accusations, announcements, warnings, threats, exhortations, and so forth. Earlier chapters in this book examined the structure of words and sentences. Now we examine what we do with linguistic structures and how our utterances accomplish their work.

Knowing a language is not simply a matter of knowing how to encode a message and transmit it to a second party, who then decodes it in order to understand what we intended to say. If language use were a matter simply of encoding and decoding messages—in other words, of *grammatical competence*—every sentence would have a fixed interpretation irrespective of its context of use. But that's not the case, as the scenarios below illustrate.

1. You're stopped by a police officer, who surprises you by informing you that you've just driven through a stop sign. "I didn't see the stop sign," you say.

2. A friend has given you directions to her apartment, including instructions to turn left at the first stop sign after the intersection of Oak and Broad. You arrive about 30 minutes late and say, "I didn't see the stop sign."

3. You're driving with an aunt who's in a hurry to get to church. You slow down and glide through a stop sign, knowing that on Sunday mornings there is seldom traffic at that intersection. As you enter the intersection, you see a car approaching and jam on the brakes, startling your aunt. "I didn't see the stop sign," you say.

To the police officer, your utterance ("I didn't see the stop sign") is an *explanation* for failing to stop and a subtle *plea* not to be cited for the violation. To the friend, your utterance is an *excuse* for your tardiness and a *claim* that it was neither intended nor entirely your fault. To your aunt, the same sentence (an untruthful one in this case) is uttered as an *apology* for having frightened her. She recognizes your intention to apologize and says, "It's all right. But *please* be careful." The linguistic meaning of the sentence *I didn't see the stop sign* is the same in all three cases, but uttering it in these different contexts serves different purposes, conveys distinct messages, and <u>does</u> different things.

Sentence Structure and the Function of Utterances

Traditional grammar books say that declarative sentences make statements (*It's raining*), imperative sentences issue directives (*Close the door*), and interrogative sentences ask questions (*What time is it?*). That analysis is oversimplified, even misleading. Consider the sentence, *Can you shut the window?* Taken literally, its interrogative structure asks a question about the addressee's *ability* to shut a particular window. If asked this question by a roommate trying to study while a college marching band practiced nearby, you would probably interpret it not as a question about your abilities (and thus requiring a verbal response) but as a request to close the window. (A request in question form is usually marked in speech by the absence of voice raising and sometimes in writing by the absence of a question mark: *Would you please respond promptly.*) Conversely, the imperative structure *Tell me your name again* would normally be taken not as a directive to do something but as a request for information.

Take another case: Suppose a knock is heard at the door, and Megan says to Alex *I wonder who's at the door*. If Megan believed Alex knew the answer, this declarative sentence might be uttered as a request for information. Often, though, it would be a polite request for Alex to open the door.

Finally, interrogative sentences can sometimes be used to make statements, as in Suze's reply to Eric's question.

Eric: Is Amy pretty easy to get along with?

Suze: Do hens have teeth?

Suze's *question* communicates an emphatically negative *answer* to Eric's inquiry. Two things are clear, then: (1) People often employ declarative, interrogative, and imperative sentences for purposes other than making statements, asking questions, and issuing commands, respectively; and (2) a pivotal element in the interpretation of an utterance is the context in which it is uttered. Recall the three faces of language use depicted in Chapter 1, showing *context* as the base of a triangle linking *meaning* and *expression*.

You recognize that a sentence is a structured string of words carrying a certain meaning. By contrast, an *utterance* is a sentence that is said, written, or signed *in a particular context* by someone *with a particular intention*, by means of which the speaker intends *to create an effect* on the addressee. Thus, as an interrogative sentence, *Can you close the window?* may be said to carry the meaning of a request for *information* ('Are you able to close the window?'), but as a contextualized *utterance* it would typically be a request for *action* ('Please shut the window'). Drawing the appropriate inferences from conversation is an essential ingredient for interpreting utterances. To understand utterances, you must be skilled at "reading between the lines," and the skills you employ in using and interpreting the sentences shaped by *grammatical competence* are part of your *communicative competence*.

Speech Acts

Besides what we accomplish through physical acts such as cooking, eating, bicycling, gardening, or getting on a bus, we accomplish a great deal each day by verbal acts. In face-to-face conversation, telephone calls, job application cover letters, notes scribbled to a roommate, and a multitude of other speech events, we perform verbal actions of different types. In fact, language is the principal means we have to greet, compliment, and insult one another, to plead and flirt, to seek and supply information, and to accomplish hundreds of other tasks in a typical day. Actions that are carried out through language are called **speech acts**, and, as noted in Chapter 8, a surprisingly large number of reports in newspapers are reports of speech acts.

Try It Yourself Which headlines report speech acts and which report physical acts:

Fight Brews at FCC	CSC Awarded Contract
Judge Limits Skid Row Sweeps	Winds Wreak Havoc
Smuggling Suspects Acquitted	POW Rescued from Captors
Tut's Chariot Arrives in Times Square	F.B.I. Challenges Use of Seal
Two Convicted in Kennedy Airport Plot	Woods Denies Taking Drugs

Types of Speech Act

Among the various kinds of speech act, six have received particular attention:

1. *Representatives* represent a state of affairs: assertions, statements, claims, hypotheses, descriptions, suggestions. Representatives can generally be characterized as true or false.

2. *Commissives* commit a speaker to a course of action: promises, pledges, threats, vows.

3. *Directives* are intended to get the addressee to carry out an action: commands, requests, challenges, invitations, entreaties, dares.

4. *Declarations* bring about the state of affairs they name: blessings, hirings, firings, baptisms, arrests, marryings, declaring mistrials.

5. *Expressives* indicate the speaker's psychological state or attitude: greetings, apologies, congratulations, condolences, thanksgivings.

6. *Verdictives* make assessments or judgments: ranking, assessing, appraising, condoning. Because some verdictives (such as calling a baseball player "out") combine the characteristics of declarations and representatives, these are sometimes called *representational declarations*.

Locutions and Illocutions

Every speech act has several principal components, two of which directly concern us here: the *utterance itself* and the *intention of the speaker* in making it. First, every utterance is represented by a sentence with a grammatical structure and a linguistic meaning; this is the **locution**. Second, speakers have some intention in uttering the locution, and what they intend to accomplish is called the **illocution**. (A third component of a speech act—one we do not discuss at length—is the effect of the act on the hearer; this is the *perlocution,* or the "uptake.")

Consider the utterance, *Can you shut the window?* Like all utterances, it can be viewed as comprising a locution and an illocution. The locution is a *yes/no* question about the addressee's ability to close a particular window; as such, convention would require an answer of *yes* or *no.* Let's assume that the speaker's intention (the illocution) is to request the addressee to shut the window; as such, convention would enable the addressee to recognize the structural question as a request for action and to comply or not. In discussions of speech acts, it is common for the illocutionary act itself to be called the speech act; thus promises, assertions, threats, invitations, and so on are all speech acts.

Distinguishing Among Speech Acts

How do people distinguish among different types of speech acts? How do we know whether a locution such as *Do you have the time?* is a *yes/no* question (*Do you have the time* [to help me]*?*) or a request for information about the time of day? To put the matter in more technical terms, given that a locution can serve many functions, how do addressees understand the illocutionary force of a speaker's utterance? The answer of course is "context." But how do people interpret context accurately?

We begin our analysis by distinguishing between two broad types of speech act. Compare the following two utterances:

1. I now pronounce you husband and wife.
2. It is going to be a very windy day.

In the appropriate context, the first utterance creates a new relationship between two individuals; it is a declaration that effectuates a marriage. The second utterance is a simple statement or representation of a state of affairs. As any weather forecaster will attest, it will have no effect on the weather. As you saw earlier, utterances such as sentence 2 make assertions or state opinions and are *representatives.* Utterances such as sentence 1 change the state of things and are *declarations;* they provide a striking illustration of how language in use is a form of action. Children exposed to fantastical declarations such as *Abracadabra, I change you into a frog!* eventually learn that real-life objects are more recalcitrant than fairy-tale objects, but all speakers come to recognize a verbal power over certain aspects of life, especially with respect to social relationships.

With the utterance *I now pronounce you husband and wife,* the nature of the social relationship between two people can be profoundly altered. Similarly, the utterance *You're under arrest!* can have consequences for one's social freedom, as can *Case dismissed.* An umpire can change the outcome of a baseball game with a simple declaration like *Safe!* or *Strike three!* Typically, to be effective, declarations of this type must be uttered by a specially designated person. If called by a nondesignated individual—a fan in the stands, for example—*Out!* would be a verdictive, not a declaration. Indeed, a declaration by a single designated umpire will override the opposite call by an entire stadium of fans.

Appropriateness Conditions and Successful Declarations

The efficacy of any declaration depends on well-established conventions. *I now pronounce you husband and wife* can bind two individuals in marriage, but only if several conditions are satisfied: the setting must be a wedding ceremony and the utterance made at the appropriate moment; the speaker must be a designated officiator approved to marry others (minister, rabbi, justice of the peace) and must intend to officiate at a marriage; the two individuals must be legally eligible to marry each other; and they must intend to become spouses. Finally, of course, the words themselves must be uttered. If any condition is not satisfied, the utterance of the words will be ineffectual as a *performative* speech act— one whose words effectuate the act. Made on a Hollywood movie set by an actor in the role of a pastor and addressed to two actors playing characters about to marry, the utterance may help secure an Academy Award, but it will not effectuate a marriage.

The conventions that regulate the conditions under which an utterance serves as a particular speech act—as a marriage, promise, arrest, invitation—have been called **appropriateness conditions** by philosopher John Searle, and they can be classified into four categories.

1. *Propositional content condition* requires merely that the words of the sentence be conventionally associated with the intended speech act and convey the content of the act. The locution must exhibit conventionally acceptable words for effecting the particular speech act: *Is it raining out?*, *I now pronounce you husband and wife, You're under arrest, I promise to . . . , I swear . . . .*

2. *Preparatory condition* requires a conventionally recognized context in which the speech act is embedded. In a marriage, the situation must be a genuine wedding ceremony (however informal) at which two people intend to exchange vows in the presence of a witness.

3. *Sincerity condition* requires the speaker to be sincere in uttering the declaration. At a wedding, the speaker must intend that the marriage words effectuate a marriage; otherwise, the *sincerity condition* will be violated and the speech act will not be successful.

4. *Essential condition* requires that the involved parties all intend the result; for example, in a wedding ceremony, the participants must intend by the utterance of the words *I now pronounce you husband and wife* to create a marriage bond.

Successful Promises Now consider the commissive, *I promise to help you with your math tonight.* In order for such an utterance to be successful, it must be recognizable as a promise; in addition, the preparatory, sincerity, and essential conditions must be met. In the propositional content condition, the speaker must use the conventional term *promise* to state the intention of helping the addressee. The preparatory condition requires that speaker and hearer are sane and responsible, that the speaker believes he or she is able to help with the math, and that the addressee wishes to have help. The preparatory condition would be violated if, for example, the speaker is knowingly not available or unable to do the math himself or herself, or if the participants were reading the script of a movie in which the utterance appears. If the speaker knew that the hearer did not *want* help, the promise would not succeed. For the sincerity condition to hold, the speaker must sincerely intend to help the addressee. This condition would be violated (and the promise formula abused) if the speaker had no such intention. Finally, the essential condition of a promise is that the speaker intends by the utterance to place himself or herself under an obligation to provide some help to the hearer. These four appropriateness conditions define a successful promise.

Successful Requests and Other Speech Acts Appropriateness conditions are useful in describing not only declarations and commissives but all other types of speech acts. In a typical request (*Please pass me the salt*), the content of the utterance must identify the act requested of the hearer (passing the salt), and its form must be a conventionally recognized one for making requests. The preparatory condition includes the speaker's beliefs that the addressee is capable of passing the salt and that, had the speaker not asked the addressee to pass it, he or she would not have ventured to do so. The sincerity condition requires that the speaker genuinely desires the hearer to pass the salt. Finally the essential condition is that the speaker intends by the utterance to get the hearer to pass the salt.

The Cooperative Principle

The principles that govern the interpretation of utterances are diverse and complex, and they differ somewhat from culture to culture. Even within a single culture, they are so complex that we may wonder how languages succeed at communication as well as they do. The principles that we examine in this section, however commonsensical they may seem to Western readers, are by no means universal; as you'll see later, what seems commonsense to one group may not be commonsense to all groups.

Despite occasional misinterpretations, people in most situations manage to understand utterances essentially as they were intended. The reason is that, without cause to expect otherwise, interlocutors normally trust that they and their conversational partners are honoring the same interpretive conventions. *Hearers* assume simply that speakers have honored the conventions of interpretation in constructing their utterances. *Speakers*, on the other hand, must make a twofold assumption: not only that hearers will themselves be guided by the conventions, but also that hearers will trust speakers to have honored those conventions in constructing their utterances. There is an unspoken pact that people will *cooperate* in communicating with each other, and speakers rely on this cooperation to make conversation efficient.

The **cooperative principle**, as enunciated by philosopher H. Paul Grice, is as follows:

> Make your conversational contribution such as is required, at the stage at which it occurs, by the accepted purpose or direction of the talk exchange in which you are engaged.

This pact of cooperation touches on four areas of communication, each of which can be described as a *maxim*, or general principle.

Maxim of Quantity

First, speakers are expected to give as much information as is necessary for their interlocutors to understand their utterances but to give no more than is necessary. If you ask an acquaintance whether he has any pets and he answers, *I have two cats*, it is the *maxim of quantity* that permits you to assume he has no other pets. The conversational implication of such a reply is 'I have two (and only two) cats (and no other pets).' Notice that *I have two cats* would be true even if the speaker had six cats or six cats, two dogs, and a llama. But if he had such other pets, you would have reason to feel deceived. While his reply was not false as far as it went, your culturally defined expectation that relevant information will not be concealed would have been violated. In most Western cultures (but not in all cultures), listeners expect speakers to abide by this maxim, and—equally important—speakers know that hearers believe them to be abiding by it. It is this unspoken cooperation that creates conversational implicatures.

To take another example, suppose you asked a couple painting their house what color they had chosen for the living room, and one of them replied:

> The walls will be an eggshell white to contrast with the black sofa and the Regency armchair I inherited from my grandmother. Bless her soul, she passed away last year after a lengthy marriage to my grandfather, who never appreciated grandmother's love of the performing arts—or the visual arts, for that matter. Then the trim will be peach except near the door, which our consultant said should be salmon so it doesn't clash with the black and red Picasso print we brought back from Spain when we vacationed there in, uh, let's see, I think it was 2008. Or was it 2009? I forget, actually. Gosh! time flies, doesn't it? And the stairway leading to the bedrooms will be a pale yellow, which is my favorite color.

In providing too much information, far more than was sought or expected, the speaker is as uncooperative as the man who withheld information about his pets. The maxim of quantity provides that, in normal circumstances, speakers say just enough, that they supply no less information—and no more—than is necessary for the purpose of the communication: *Be appropriately informative.*

Society stigmatizes individuals who habitually violate the maxim of quantity; those who give too much information are described as "never shutting up" or "always telling everyone their life story," while those who habitually fail to provide enough information are branded sullen, secretive, or uncommunicative.

Maxim of Relevance

The second maxim directs speakers to organize their utterances in such a way that they are relevant to the ongoing context: *Be relevant at the time of the utterance*. The following interaction illustrates a violation of this maxim.

Zach: How are you and Zora getting along?

Zane: There's a great movie on HBO Thursday night.

On its face, Zane's reply seems unrelated to what Zach has asked; if so, it would violate the *maxim of relevance*. Owing to the maxim of relevance, when someone produces an apparently irrelevant utterance, hearers typically strive to understand how it might be relevant (as a joke, perhaps, or an indication of displeasure with the direction of the conversation and a desire to change it). Chronic violations of this maxim are characteristic of schizophrenics, whose sense of "context" differs radically from that of other people.

Maxim of Manner

Third, people follow a set of miscellaneous rules that are grouped under the *maxim of manner*. Summarized by the directive *Be orderly and clear*, this maxim dictates that speakers and writers avoid ambiguity and obscurity and be orderly in their utterances. In the following example, the maxim of manner is violated with respect to orderliness.

A birthday cake should have icing; use unbleached flour and sugar in the cake; bake it for one hour; preheat the oven to 325 degrees; and beat in three fresh eggs.

This recipe is odd for the simple reason that English speakers normally follow a chronological order of events in describing a process such as baking.

Orderliness is dictated not solely by the order of events: in any language there are rules that dictate a "natural" order of details in a description. Because in American English more general details usually precede more specific ones, when a speaker violates this rule the result appears odd, as in the example below, where sentences have been numbered.

(1) My hometown has five shopping malls. (2) It is the county seat. (3) My father and my mother were both born there. (4) My hometown is a midwestern town of 105,000 inhabitants, situated in the middle of the Corn Belt. (5) I was brought up there until I was 13 years old.

As a third example, consider the utterance *Ted died and was hit by lightning*. If it was the lightning that killed Ted, the maxim of manner has been violated here. Although in logic *and* joins clauses whose time reference is not relevant (thus, *She studied chemistry and she studied biology* is logically equivalent to *She studied biology and she studied chemistry*), the maxim of manner dictates that an utterance such as *They had a baby and got married* has different

Try It Yourself In accordance with the maxim of manner (and placing more general details before more specific ones), what would be a better order for sentences (1)–(5) just above?

conversational implications from those in the utterance *They got married and had a baby*. The maxim of manner in this instance suggests that the sequence of expressions reflects the sequence of events or is irrelevant to an appropriate interpretation. Of course, English and other languages provide ways around misinterpretation: *They had a baby before they got married; First they had a baby and then they got married; They got married after they had a baby;* and so on.

Maxim of Quality

The fourth general principle governing norms of language interpretation is the maxim of quality: *Be truthful*. Speakers and writers are expected to say only what they believe to be true and to have evidence for what they say. Again, the other side of the coin is that speakers are aware of this expectation; they know that hearers expect them to honor the *maxim of quality*. Without the maxim of quality, the other maxims are of little value or interest. Whether brief or lengthy, relevant or irrelevant, orderly or disorderly, all lies are false. Still, it should be noted that the maxim of quality applies principally to assertions and certain other representative speech acts. Expressives and directives can hardly be judged true or false in the same sense.

It is useful to reflect further on the maxim of quality. On the one hand, it is this maxim that constrains interlocutors to tell the truth and to have evidence for their statements. Ironically, on the other hand, it is this maxim that makes lying possible. Without the maxim of quality, speakers would have no reason to expect hearers to take their utterances as true, and without the assumption that one's interlocutors assume one to be telling the truth, it would be impossible to tell a lie. Lying requires that speakers are expected to be telling the truth.

Violations of the Cooperative Principle

It is no secret that people sometimes violate the maxims of the cooperative principle. Certainly not all speakers are completely truthful; others have not observed that efficiency is the desired Western norm in conversational interaction. More interestingly, speakers are sometimes forced by cultural norms or other external factors to violate a maxim. For example, irrespective of your aesthetic judgment, you may feel constrained to say *What a lovely painting!* to a host who is manifestly proud of a newly purchased artwork. The need to adhere to social conventions of politeness sometimes invites people to violate maxims of the cooperative principle.

Indirect Speech Acts

As mentioned earlier, interrogative structures can be used to make polite requests for action, imperative structures can be used to ask for information, and so on. Such uses of a structure with a supposed meaning to accomplish a different task frequently play a role in ordinary interaction, as in this exchange between colleagues who have stayed at the office after dark.

Kayla: Is the boss in?

Ryan: The light's on in her office.

Kayla: Oh, thanks.

Ryan's answer makes no apparent reference to the information Kayla is seeking and would thus appear to violate the maxim of relevance. Yet Kayla is satisfied with the answer. Recognizing that the *literal* interpretation of Ryan's reply violates the maxim of relevance but assuming that as a cooperative interlocutor Ryan is being relevant, Kayla seeks an *indirect* interpretation. To help her, she knows certain facts about the boss's habits: she works in her own office, doesn't work in the dark, and isn't in the habit of leaving the light on when gone for the day. Relying on this information, Kayla infers an interpretation from Ryan's utterance: Ryan believes the boss is in.

Ryan's reply is an example of an **indirect speech act**—one that involves an apparent violation of the cooperative principle but is in fact indirectly cooperative. For example, an indirect speech act can be based on an apparent violation of the maxim of quality. When we describe a friend as *someone who never parts with a dime*, we don't mean it literally; we are exaggerating. By exaggerating the information, we may seem to flout the maxim of quality. But listeners usually appreciate that the statement should not be interpreted literally and make an appropriate adjustment in their interpretation. Similarly, we may exclaim in front of the Willis Tower in Chicago, *That's an awfully small building!* This utterance appears to violate the maxim of quality in that we are expressing an evaluation that is manifestly false. But speakers readily spot the irony of such utterances and take them to be indirect speech acts intended to convey an opposite meaning.

Characteristics of Indirect Speech Acts   From these examples, we can identify four characteristics of indirect speech acts:

1. Indirect speech acts violate at least one maxim of the cooperative principle.
2. The literal meaning of the locution of an indirect speech act differs from its intended meaning.
3. Hearers and readers identify indirect speech acts by noticing that an utterance has characteristic 1 (it violates a maxim) and by assuming that the interlocutor is following the cooperative principle.
4. As soon as hearers and readers have identified an indirect speech act, they identify its intended meaning with the help of knowledge of the context and of the world.

Thus, to interpret indirect speech acts, hearers use the maxims to sort out the discrepancy between the literal meaning of the utterance and an appropriate interpretation for the context in which it is uttered.

Indirect Speech Acts and Shared Knowledge   One prerequisite for a successful indirect speech act is that interactors share sufficient background about the context of the interaction, about each other and their society, and about the

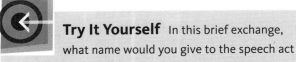

Try It Yourself In this brief exchange, what name would you give to the speech act in A? In B? Does D represent a direct speech act or an indirect one? What about A? Direct or indirect?

A. Anna: Who ate the bread I made yesterday?
B. Juan: With the raisins?
C. Anna: Yeah.
D. Juan: Did you ask Raul?

world in general. If Jacob asks Emma *Have you finished your sociology paper?* and she replies as in either B or B¹ below, Jacob will certainly recognize her answer as an indirect speech act. But whether or not he can interpret it will depend on his knowledge of the world.

A. **Jacob:** Have you finished your sociology paper?
B. **Emma:** Is Rome in Spain?
B¹. **Emma:** Is the Pope Catholic?

Using and understanding indirect speech acts requires familiarity with both language and society. To cite an example from another culture, when speakers of the Polynesian language Tuvaluan want to comment on the fact that a particular person is in the habit of talking about himself, they may say *koo tagi te tuli ki tena igoa* 'The plover bird is singing its own name.' The expression derives from the fact that the plover bird's cry sounds like a very sharp "tuuuuuliiiii," from which speakers of Tuvaluan have created the word *tuli* to refer to the bird itself. Thus the expression has become an indirect way of criticizing the trait of singing one's own praises. In order to interpret the utterance as an indirect speech act, one must be familiar not only with the plover bird's cry and the fact that it resembles the bird's name but also with the fact that Tuvaluans view people who talk about themselves as being similar to a bird "singing its own name." Clearly, considerable background information about language, culture, and environment is needed to interpret indirect speech acts.

Politeness

Indirect speech acts appear to be a complicated way of communicating. Not only must you spot them, but you must then go through a complex reasoning process to interpret them. One might think it would be more efficient to communicate directly. The fact is, though, that indirect speech acts have uses besides asking and answering questions, criticizing others, and so on. They sometimes add humor and sometimes show politeness. Emma's indirect reply (*Is Rome in Spain?*) to Jacob's question suggests 'Don't be ridiculous; of course I'm not done.' By contrast, the alternative reply (*Is the Pope Catholic?*) would suggest 'You know I always get my papers done on time!' Questions such as *Can you shut the window?* are perceived as more polite and less intrusive and abrasive than a command such as *Shut the window!* One message that indirect speech acts convey is, 'I am being polite toward you.' Indirect speech acts are thus an efficient tool of communication: they can convey two or more messages simultaneously.

Respecting Independence and Showing Involvement

There are two basic aspects to being polite. The first rests on the fact that human beings respect one another's privacy, independence, and physical space. We *avoid* intruding on other people's lives; we try *not* to be overly inquisitive about their activities; and we take care *not* to impose our presence on them. We respect their independence and don't intrude (sometimes called *negative politeness*). On the other hand, when we let people know we enjoy their company, feel comfortable with them, like something about their personality, or are interested in their well-being, we show involvement (sometimes called *positive politeness*). While everyone expects both independence and involvement, the first requires us to leave people alone, while the second requires us to do the opposite. Fortunately, these competing needs usually arise in different contexts. When we shut ourselves in a room or take a solitary walk on the beach, we affirm our right to independence. When we attend a party, invite someone to dinner, or call friends on the telephone to check up on them, we show involvement. Both are forms of politeness.

In conversation, interlocutors give one another messages about their needs for independence and their wishes for involvement and also acknowledge one another's needs for both types of politeness. The expectation that others won't ask embarrassing questions about our personal lives stems from the need for independence. By contrast, when you tell a friend about a personal problem and expect sympathy, you are seeking involvement. Excusing yourself before asking a stranger for the time acknowledges the stranger's right to freedom from intrusion. When we express the hope of meeting an interlocutor at a later date (*Let's get together soon!*), we acknowledge the interlocutor's need for involvement and sociability.

Speech Events

News broadcasts, public speeches, classroom lectures, religious sermons, and conversations are **speech events** in which members of a community interact on one or more topics, for a particular purpose, and with awareness of the social relations among the interlocutors. "Speech" events need not involve *speaking*: personal letters, shopping lists, office memos, birthday cards, and newspaper editorials also count as speech events.

Conversation provides the matrix in which native languages are acquired, and it stands out as the most frequent, most natural, and most representative of verbal interactions. A person can spend a lifetime without writing a letter, composing a poem, or debating public policy, but only in rare circumstances does someone not have frequent conversation with friends and companions. Conversation is an everyday speech event. We engage in it for entertainment (gossiping, passing the time, affirming social bonds) and for accomplishing work (getting help with studies, renting an apartment, ordering a meal at a restaurant). Whatever its purpose, conversation is our most basic verbal interaction.

Although lovers in movies can conduct heart-to-heart conversations with their backs to each other, conversation usually involves individuals facing each other and taking turns at speaking. They neither talk simultaneously nor let the conversation lag. In some societies, even with several conversationalists in a single conversation, there are only tenths of a second between turns and extremely little overlap in speaking. At the beginning of a conversation, people go through certain rituals, greeting one another or commenting about the weather. Likewise, at the end of a conversation, people don't simply turn their backs and walk away; they take care that all participants have finished what they wanted to say and only then utter something like "I have to run" or "Take care." Throughout the entire interaction, conversationalists maintain a certain level of orderliness—taking turns, not interrupting one another too often, and following certain other highly structured but implicit guidelines for conversation.

These guidelines can be considered norms of conduct that govern how conversationalists comport themselves. Though it is tempting to think of relaxed conversation as essentially free of rules or constraints, the fact is that many rules are operating, and the unconscious recognition of these rules helps identify particular interactions as conversations.

The Organization of Conversation

If it seems surprising that casual conversation should be organized by rules, the reason is that, as in most speech events, more attention is paid to content than to organization; we take the organization of conversations for granted. A conversation can be viewed as a series of speech acts—greetings, inquiries, congratulations, comments, invitations, requests, refusals, accusations, denials, promises, farewells. To accomplish the work of these speech acts, some organization is essential: we take turns at speaking, answer questions, mark the beginning and end of a conversation, and make corrections when they are needed. To accomplish such work expeditiously, interlocutors could give one another traffic directions.

> Okay, now it's your turn to speak.
>
> I just asked you a question; now you should answer it, and you should do so right away.
>
> If you have anything else to add before we close this conversation, do it now because I am leaving in a minute.

Such instructions would be inefficient, however, and would deflect attention from the content. In unusual circumstances, conversationalists do invoke the rules (*Would you please stop interrupting?* or *Well, say something!*), but invoking the rules underscores the fact that they have been violated and can itself seem impolite. Conversations are usually organized covertly, and the organizational principles provide a discreet interactional framework.

The covert architecture of conversation must achieve the following: organize turns so that more than one person has a chance to speak and the turn taking is orderly; allow interlocutors to anticipate what will happen next and, where there is a choice, how the selection is to be decided; provide a way to repair glitches and errors when they occur.

Turn Taking and Pausing

Participants must tacitly agree on who should speak when. Normally we take turns at holding the floor and do so without overt negotiation. A useful way to uncover the conventions of turn taking is to observe what happens when they break down. When a participant fails to take the floor despite indications that it is her turn, other speakers usually pause, and then someone else begins speaking. In this example, Emily repeats her question, assuming that Sarah either didn't hear it or didn't understand it the first time.

Emily: But he didn't like it?

  [pause]

Emily: [louder] So he didn't like it?

Sarah: Oh, no. But then later, he said he did.

Turn-taking conventions are also violated when two people attempt to speak simultaneously. In the next example, the beginning and end of the overlap are marked with brackets.

Speaker 1: After John's party we went to Ed's house.

Speaker 2: So you—   so you—you—

  [   ]

Speaker 3: What— what—time did you get there?

When such competition arises in casual conversation, a speaker may either quickly relinquish the floor or turn up the volume and continue speaking. Both silence and simultaneous speaking are serious problems in conversation, and the turn-taking norms are designed to minimize them.

Different cultures have different degrees of tolerance for silence between turns, overlaps in speaking, and competition among speakers. In the Inuit and some other Native American cultures, for example, people sit comfortably together in silence. At the other extreme, in French and Argentine cultures several conversationalists often talk simultaneously and interrupt each other more frequently than Americans typically feel comfortable doing.

However much tolerance they may have for silences and overlaps, people from all cultures appear to regulate turn taking in conversation in essentially similar ways: Speakers signal when they wish to end their turn, either selecting the next speaker or leaving the choice open; the next speaker takes the floor by beginning to talk. These simple principles, which seem second nature to us, regulate conversational turn taking very efficiently.

Turn-Taking Signals Speakers signal that their turn is about to end with verbal and nonverbal cues. As turns commonly end in a complete sentence, the completion of a sentence may signal the end of a turn. A sentence ending in a tag question (*isn't it?, are you?*) explicitly invites an interlocutor to take the floor.

Speaker A: Pretty windy today, isn't it?

Speaker B: Sure is!

The end of a turn may also be signaled by sharply raising or lowering the pitch of your voice, or by drawling the last syllable of the final word of the turn. In very informal conversations, one common cue is the phrase *or something*.

Speaker 1: So he was behaving as if he'd been hit by a truck, or something.

Speaker 2: Really?

Other expressions that can signal the completion of a turn are *y'know, kinda, I don't know* (or *I dunno*), and a trailing *uhm*. As with *y'know*, some of these can also function within a turn to help the speaker keep the floor while thinking about what to say next. Another way to signal the completion of a turn is to pause and make no attempt to speak again.

Daniel: I really don't think he should've said that at the meeting, particularly in front of the whole group. It really was pretty insensitive.

[pause]

David: Yeah, I agree.

Of course, speakers often have to pause in the middle of a turn to think about what to say next, to emphasize a point, or to catch a breath. To signal that a speaker has finished a turn, the pause must be long enough, but "long enough" differs from culture to culture.

Nonverbal as well as verbal signals can indicate the end of a turn. Although in speaking the principal role of gestures is to support and stress what we say, continuing our hand gestures lets our interlocutors know we have more to say. Once we put our hands to rest, our fellow conversationalists may infer that we are yielding the floor.

In a more subtle vein, eye gaze can help control floor holding and turn taking. In mainstream American society, speakers do not ordinarily stare at their interlocutors; instead, their gaze goes back and forth between their listener and another point in space, alternating quickly and almost imperceptibly. But because listeners, on the other hand, usually fix their gaze on the speaker, a speaker reaching the end of a turn can simply return her gaze to an interlocutor and thereby signal her own turn to listen and the interlocutor's to speak. In cultures in which listeners look away while speakers stare, a speaker who wishes to stop talking simply looks away. While eye gaze plays a supportive role in allocating turns, the success of telephone conversations makes it clear that eye gaze is not essential in the allocation of turns.

Getting the Floor In multiparty conversations, the speaker holding the floor can select who will speak next, or the next speaker can select himself or herself. In the first instance, the floor holder may signal the choice by addressing the next speaker by name (*What've you been up to, Helen?*) or by turning toward the selected next speaker. If the floor holder does not select the next speaker, anyone may take the floor, often by beginning the turn at an accelerated pace so as to block other potential claims for the floor.

When the floor holder does not select the next speaker, competition can arise, as in the following example, in which overlaps are indicated with square brackets.

Speaker 1:	Who's gonna be at Jake's party on Saturday?
	[pause]
Speaker 2:	Todd to—
	[ ]
Speaker 3:	I don't kn—
	[pause]
Speaker 2:	Todd told me—
	[ ]
Speaker 3:	I don't know who's—
	[short pause]
Speaker 2:	[to speaker 3] Go ahead!
Speaker 3:	I don't know who's gonna be there, but I know it'll be pretty crowded.
Speaker 2:	Yeah, that's what I was gonna say. Todd told me a lotta people would be there.

Friendly participants strive to resolve such competition quickly and smoothly.

Social inequality between conversationalists (boss and employee, parent and child, doctor and patient) is often reflected in how often and when participants claim the floor. In American work settings, superiors commonly initiate conversations by asking a question and letting subordinates report. Thus subordinates hold the floor for longer periods of time than superiors; subordinates perform while superiors act as spectators. In some cultures, superiors talk while subordinates listen.

Adjacency Pairs

One useful mechanism in the covert organization of conversation is that certain turns have specific follow-up turns associated with them. Questions that request information take answers. The reply to a greeting is usually also a greeting, to an invitation an acceptance or refusal, and so on. Certain sequences of turns go together, as in these *adjacency pairs*.

Request for Information and Providing Information
Adam: Where's the milk I bought this morning?
Betty: On the counter.

Invitation and Acceptance
Alex: I'm having friends to dinner Saturday, and I'd really like you to come.
Bert: Sure!

Assessment and Disagreement
Angel: I don't think Nick would play such a dirty trick on you.
Brit: Well, you obviously don't know Nick very well.

Explanation and Concurrence

Mary: You can get them at Thrifty for about ten bucks.

Sylvia: Right.

Such **adjacency pairs** comprise two turns, one of which directly follows the other. In a question/answer adjacency pair, the question is the first part, the answer the second part. Here are other examples of adjacency pairs.

Request for a Favor and Granting

Guest: Can I use your phone?

Host: Sure.

Apology and Acceptance

Eli: Sorry to bother you this late at night.

Dave: No, that's all right. What's up?

Summons and Acknowledgment

Mark: Bill!

Bill: Yeah?

Structural Characteristics of Adjacency Pairs Three characteristics of adjacency pairs can be noted.

1. **They are contiguous.** The two parts of an adjacency pair are contiguous and are uttered by different speakers. A speaker who makes a statement before responding to a question that has been asked sounds strange (and can provoke frustration) because adjacency pairs are structured to be consecutive:

   Adam: Where's the milk I bought this morning?

   Betty: They said on the radio the weather would clear up by noon. It's on the counter.

2. **They are ordered.** The two parts of an adjacency pair are ordered. Except on TV game shows like *Jeopardy*, the answer to a question cannot precede the question. Ordinarily, you cannot accept an invitation before it has been offered, and an apology cannot be accepted before it is uttered (except sarcastically).

3. **They are matched.** The first and second parts of an adjacency pair are appropriately matched. Appropriate matching avoids odd exchanges such as the following:

   Kimi: Do you want more coffee?

   Sasa: That's all right. You're not bothering me in the least!

Insertion Sequences Sometimes the requirement that the two parts of an adjacency pair be contiguous is violated in a socially recognized way.

Adam: Where's the milk I bought this morning?

Betty: The skim milk?

Adam: Yeah.

Betty: On the counter.

In that exchange, in order to provide an accurate answer to Adam's question, Betty must first know the answer to another question, and to find out she initiates an *insertion sequence*—an adjacency pair that interrupts the original one and puts it "on hold." The interaction thus consists of an adjacency pair embedded within another one. Here's another example from a telephone call.

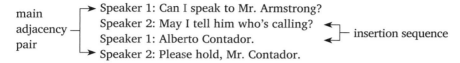

main adjacency pair

Speaker 1: Can I speak to Mr. Armstrong?
Speaker 2: May I tell him who's calling?
Speaker 1: Alberto Contador.
Speaker 2: Please hold, Mr. Contador.

insertion sequence

Preferred and Dispreferred Responses   Certain kinds of adjacency pairs are marked by a preference for a particular type of second part. For example, requests, assessments, and invitations have preferred and dispreferred answers. Compare the following interactions, in which the first exchange displays a preferred second part and the second exchange a dispreferred one.

Fran: I really enjoyed the movie last night. Did you?
Frank: Yeah, it was pretty good.

Fran: I really enjoyed the movie last night. Did you?
Frank: Well, I thought it was a bit sappy, but I can see how you might've liked parts of it.

The preferred second part is agreement to an assessment as well.

Fiona: I think Ralph's a pretty good writer.
Kieran: I think so, too.

Fiona: I think Ralph's a pretty good writer.
Kieran: Well, his imagery's colorful, but apart from that I'm not sure he writes well at all.

Dispreferred second parts tend to be preceded by a pause or begin with a hesitation particle such as *well* or *uh*. Preferred second parts tend to follow the first part without a pause and to consist of structurally simple utterances.

Michelle: Wanna meet for lunch tomorrow?
Michael: Sure!

Michelle: Wanna meet for lunch tomorrow?
Michael: Well, uh . . . tomorrow's Tuesday, right? I told Lori I'd have lunch with her. And it's her birthday, so I can't cancel. How about Wednesday?

In addition, even dispreferred second parts often begin with a token agreement or acceptance, or with an expression of appreciation or apology, and characteristically include an explanation.

Wade: Can I use your phone?

Frank: Oh, I'm sorry; I'm expecting a business call. Could you wait a bit?

Try It Yourself To an apology, a preferred second part is an acceptance, while a dispreferred second part is a refusal to accept it. For each of these speech acts, name one preferred and one dispreferred second part: request for information; invitation to a party; greeting; accusation; offer of congratulations; assessment.

Opening Sequences

Conversations are opened in socially recognized ways. Before beginning their first conversation of the day, conversationalists normally greet each other, as when two office workers meet in the morning.

Jeff: Mornin', Stan!

Stan: Hi. How's it goin'?

Jeff: Oh, can't complain, I guess. Ready for the meeting this afternoon?

Stan: Well, I don't have much choice!

Greetings exemplify opening sequences, utterances that ease people into a conversation. They convey the message "I want to talk to you."

Greetings are usually reserved for acquaintances who have not seen each other for a while, or as opening sequences for longer conversations between strangers. Some situations do not require a greeting, as with a stranger approaching in the street to ask for the time: *Excuse me, sir, do you know what time it is?* The expression *Excuse me, sir* serves as an opening sequence appropriate to the context. Thus, greetings are not the only type of opening sequences.

Very few conversations do not begin with some type of opening sequence, even as commonplace as the following:

Eric: Guess what.

Jo: What?

Eric: I broke a tooth.

Conversationalists also use opening sequences to announce that they are about to invade the personal space of their interlocutors. Here, two friends are talking on a park bench next to a stranger; at a pause in their conversation, the stranger interjects:

Stranger: Excuse me, I didn't mean to eavesdrop, but I couldn't help overhearing you mention Dayton. I'm from Dayton.

[Conversation then goes on among the three people.]

It's not surprising that opening sequences take the form of an apology in such situations.

Finally, opening sequences may serve as a display of your voice to enable the interlocutor to recognize who is speaking, especially at the beginning of telephone conversations. Here, the phone has just rung in Alfred's apartment.

Alfred:	Hello?
Helen:	Hello!
Alfred:	Oh, hi, Helen! How you doin'?

In the second turn, Helen displays her voice to enable Alfred to recognize her. In the third turn, Alfred indicates his recognition and simultaneously provides the second part of the greeting adjacency pair initiated in the previous turn.

Opening Sequences in Other Cultures In many cultures, the opening sequence appropriate to a situation in which two people meet after not having met for a while is an inquiry about the person's health, as in the American greeting *How are you?* Such inquiries are essentially formulaic and not meant literally. Indeed, most speakers respond with a conventional upbeat formula (*I'm fine* or *Fine, thanks*) even when feeling terrible. In other cultures, the conventional greeting may take a different form. Traditionally, Mandarin Chinese conversationalists ask *Nǐ chī guo fàn le ma?* 'Have you eaten rice yet?' When two people meet on a road in Tonga, they ask *Ko hoʔo ʔalu ki fe?* 'Where is your going directed to?' These greetings are as formulaic as *How are you?*

In formal contexts, or when differences of social status exist between participants, many cultures require a lengthy and formulaic opening sequence. In Fiji, when an individual visits a village, a highly ceremonial introduction is conducted before any other interaction takes place. This event involves speeches that are regulated by a complex set of rules governing what must be said, and when, and by whom. This ceremony serves the same purpose as opening sequences in other cultures.

Functions of Opening Sequences A final aspect of opening sequences in which cultural differences are found is the relative importance of their various functions. In telephone conversations in the United States, opening sequences serve primarily to identify speakers and solicit the interlocutor's attention. In France, opening sequences for telephone conversations normally include an apology for invading someone's privacy.

Person called:	Allô?
Person calling:	Allô? Je suis désolé de vous déranger. Est-ce que j'peux parler à Marie-France?
	('Hello? I'm terribly sorry for disturbing you. Can I speak to Marie-France?')

In a U.S. telephone conversation, such an opening sequence is not customary. Thus, in two relatively similar cultures, the role played by the opening sequence in a telephone call is different. As a result, the French can find Americans intrusive and impolite on the telephone, while Americans may be puzzled by French apologetic formulas, which they find pointless and exceedingly ceremonious.

Closing Sequences

Conversations must also be closed appropriately. A conversation can be closed only when the participants have said everything they wanted to say. Furthermore, a conversation must be closed before participants begin to feel uncomfortable about having nothing more to say. As a result, conversationalists carefully negotiate the timing of closings, seeking to give the impression of wanting neither to rush away nor to linger on. These objectives are reflected in the characteristics of the closing sequence. First of all, a closing sequence includes a conclusion to the last topic covered in the conversation. In conclusions, conversationalists often make arrangements to meet at a later time or express the hope of so meeting. These arrangements may be genuine, as in the first example here, or formulaic, as in the second.

Carl:	Okay, it's nice to see you again. I guess you'll be at Kathy's party tonight.
Dana:	Yeah, I'll see you there.

Elizabeth:	See you later!
Farouk:	See ya!

The first step of a closing sequence helps ensure that no one has anything further to say. This is accomplished by a simple exchange of short turns such as *okay* or *well*. Typically, such preclosing sequences are accompanied by a series of pauses between and within turns that decelerate the exchange and prepare for closing down the interaction. In the following example, Dana takes the opportunity to bring up one last topic, after which Carl initiates another closing sequence.

Carl:	Okay, it's nice to see you again. I guess you'll be at Kathy's party tonight.
Dana:	Yeah, I'll see you there.
Carl:	Okay.
Dana:	I hear there's gonna be lots of people there.
Carl:	Apparently she invited half the town.
Dana:	Should be fun.
Carl:	Yeah.
Dana:	Okay.
Carl:	Okay. See you there.
Dana:	Later!

Sometimes, after a preclosing exchange, speakers refer to the original motivation for the conversation. In a courtesy call to inquire about someone's health, the caller sometimes refers to this fact after the preclosing exchange.

Person calling:	Well, I just wanted to see how you were doing after your surgery.
Person called:	Well, that was really nice of you.

If the purpose of a conversation was to seek a favor, this short exchange might take place:

Alex:	Well, listen, I really appreciate your doing this for me.
Beth:	Forget it. I'm glad to be of help.

Finally, conversations close with a parting expression: *bye*; *goodbye*; *see ya*; *catch you later*; *later, dude*.

A striking thing about closings is their deceptive simplicity. In fact, they are complex. Participants exercise care not to give the impression that they are rushing away or that they want to linger, and they try to ensure that everything on the unwritten agenda of any participant has been touched on. However informal and abbreviated they may be, closing sequences are characterized by a good deal of negotiated activity.

Conversational Routines

Both openings and closings are more routinized than the core parts of conversations. Core parts are relatively less predictable; while people are trained from childhood not to ask certain kinds of questions, they are also drilled on the proper way to open and close conversations. Because of the routinized nature of openings and closings, conversations can be begun and, equally important, ended expeditiously.

Repairs

A **repair** takes place in conversation when a participant feels the need to correct herself or another speaker, to edit a previous utterance, or simply to restate something, as in the following examples.

1. **Speaker:** I was going to Mary's—uh, Sue's house.

2. **Speaker:** And I went to the doctor's to get a new—uh—a new whatchamacallit, a new prescription, because my old one ran out.

3. **Alex:** Aren't those roses pretty?
   Kate: They're pretty, but they're tulips.

4. **Winston:** Todd came to visit us over the spring break.
   David: What?
   Winston: I said Todd was here over the spring break.

In 2, the *trouble source* is the fact that the speaker cannot find a word. In 4, David initiates a repair because he has not heard or has not understood Winston's utterance. Conversationalists thus make repairs for a variety of reasons.

To initiate a repair is to signal that you have not understood or have misheard an utterance, that a piece of information is incorrect, or that you are having trouble finding a word. To resolve a repair, someone must repeat the misunderstood or misheard utterance, correct the inaccurate information, or supply the word. To initiate a repair, interlocutors may ask a question, as in 4 above; repeat part of the utterance to be repaired, as in 5 below; abruptly stop speaking, as in 6; or, as in 1 above, use particles and expressions like *uh*, *I mean*, or *that is*.

5. **Speaker:** I am sure— I am *absolutely* sure it was him I saw last night prowling around.

6. **Nelson:** And here you have what's called the—
   [pause]
   Juan: The carburetor?
   Nelson: Yeah, that's right, the carburetor.

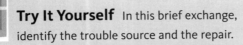

Try It Yourself In this brief exchange, identify the trouble source and the repair. Then note which of the four possibilities the repair represents: self-initiated, self-repaired; other-initiated, self-repaired; self-initiated, other-repaired; other-initiated, other-repaired.

> **Eric:** She shows her this garden furniture, and she says we got—
>
> **Sylvia:** PATIO furniture!
>
> **Eric:** Patio furniture.

Repairs can be initiated and resolved by the person who uttered the words that need to be repaired or by another conversationalist. There are thus four possibilities: repairs that are self-initiated and self-repaired; repairs that are other-initiated and self-repaired; repairs that are self-initiated and other-repaired; and repairs that are other-initiated and other-repaired. Of these possibilities, conversationalists show a strong preference for self-initiated self-repairs (as in 1 and 2 above), which are least disruptive to the conversation and to the social relationship between the conversationalists. In general, conversationalists wait for clear signals of communicative distress before repairing an utterance made by someone else. The least preferred pattern is for repairs that are other-initiated and other-repaired (as in 3 above). Individuals in the habit of both initiating and repairing utterances for others get branded as poor conversationalists or know-it-alls (although such repairs seem not uncommon among couples long familiar with one another).

Found in many cultures, these preference patterns reflect a widespread but unspoken rule that all participants in a conversation among equals be given a chance to say what they want to say by themselves. Conversationalists provide assistance to others in initiating and resolving repairs only if no other option is available.

Politeness: An Organizational Force in Conversation

Violating the turn-taking principles by interrupting or by failing to take turns is considered impolite. Turning your back on interlocutors at the end of a conversation without going through a closing sequence is also stigmatized in the conventions of politeness. Other aspects of politeness are more subtle but nevertheless play an important role in structuring conversation.

There are covert ways in which we communicate respect for independence and involvement. When we expect interlocutors to allow us to both initiate and resolve a repair ourselves, we are expecting them to respect our right to make a contribution to the conversation without intrusion from others; that is, we are asking them to respect our independence. Similarly, we recognize another person's need for independence when, instead of ending a conversation abruptly, we initiate a preclosing exchange, affording our interlocutors a chance to say something further before closing. In contrast, when we initiate a conversation with a greeting, we convey concern about our addressee's health and well-being, thereby acknowledging the other's need for involvement. Many of the principles of conversational architecture can be explained in terms of politeness and the recognition of the politeness needs of others.

Cross-Cultural Communication

When people of different cultures have different norms about what type of politeness is required in a particular context, trouble can easily arise. We've described how callers in France begin telephone conversations with an apology; such apologies seldom form part of the opening sequence of an American telephone conversation. Obviously, members of the two cultures view telephone conversations differently: Americans generally see the act of calling as a sign of involvement, while the French tend to view it as a potential intrusion.

As a consequence of such variability, people from different cultures often misinterpret each other's signals. In the conversations of Athabaskan Indians, a pause of up to about one and a half seconds does not necessarily indicate the end of a turn, and Athabaskans often pause that long within a turn. In contrast, most European Americans consider a pause of more than one second sufficient to signal the end of a turn (although there may be social variation). When Athabaskan Indians and Euro-Americans interact with each other, the latter often misinterpret the Athabaskans' midturn pauses as end-of-turn signals and feel free to claim the floor. From the Athabaskans' perspective, the Euro-Americans' claim of the floor at this point constitutes an interruption. With the same situation occurring time and again in interactions between the two groups, negative stereotypes arise. Athabaskans find Euro-Americans rude, pushy, and uncontrollably talkative, while Euro-Americans find Athabaskans conversationally uncooperative, sullen, and incapable of carrying on a coherent conversation. Unwittingly carrying those stereotypes into a classroom, Euro-American teachers may judge Athabaskan students unresponsive or unintelligent because the teachers' unspoken cultural expectations are for students to speak up, interact, and be quick in their responses. While these tend to be the actions of children in mainstream Euro-American culture, Athabaskan children, honoring the norms of their own culture, tend not to behave in that manner. Though most people are unaware of such subtle cross-cultural differences, they can have profound social consequences.

COMPUTERS, SPEECH ACTS, AND CONVERSATION

As we saw in the previous chapter in this section, pragmatics has not yet been thoroughly explored in computational linguistics and corpus studies. It remains necessary to create models of politeness, turn taking, and the other phenomena discussed in this chapter before many of the applications of computer technology to speech will be mastered.

The building of corpora of written language has proceeded more quickly than the compilation of spoken corpora, and the reasons are obvious. Especially in recent years, machine-readable texts initially published as books, magazines, and newspapers have been widely available, as is the Web. In addition,

scanners can effectively transform many older printed materials into machine-readable text. Creating electronic representations of transcribed spoken language is quite a different matter. First of all, it must be captured, on audio or video. Then it must be transcribed—a challenging and expensive task, and one partly dependent on the quality of the recording and the degree of ambient noise in the original environment.

Still, a substantial part of the British National Corpus is based on speech. About one hundred volunteers throughout Britain carried recorders in the course of several days' ordinary activities, observing in a note-book the conditions surrounding the conversations and other exchanges recorded, such as the participants and their relationships to one another, the physical setting of the recorded speech, and so on. The recordings were then transcribed in ordinary English spelling. We have reported findings from the British National Corpus in earlier "Computer" sections of this book (for example, see the "conversation" category in Figure 8.1) and will report other findings in later chapters. For American speech, other corpora have been compiled, including the American National Corpus and the Corpus of Contemporary American English (see the "Other Resources" section in this chapter and the next chapter). ■

Summary

- Utterances accomplish things such as asserting, promising, pleading, and greeting. Actions accomplished through language are called speech acts.
- That language is commonly used to perform actions is most clearly illustrated by declarations such as *You're fired!* or *Case dismissed!* Whether declarations or not, all speech acts can be described with four appropriateness conditions that identify aspects of or prerequisites for a successful speech act: the content, the preparatory condition, the sincerity condition, and the essential condition.
- In most normal circumstances, language users are bound by an unspoken pact that they adhere to and expect others to adhere to. This "cooperative principle" consists of four maxims—quantity, quality, relevance, and manner.
- On occasion, a speaker may flout a maxim to signal that the literal interpretation of the utterance is not the intended one.
- To encode and decode the intended meaning of indirect speech acts, people use patterns of conversational implicature based on knowledge of their language, their society, and the world around them.
- Indirect speech acts convey more than one message and are commonly used for politeness or humor.
- Respecting other people's needs for privacy demonstrates independence politeness, while showing interest and displaying sympathy expresses involvement politeness.
- A speech event is a social activity in which language plays an important role.
- Speech events are structured, and appropriate verbal and nonverbal behavior characteristics of particular speech events can be described systematically.
- Conversations are organized according to certain regulatory principles.
- Turn taking is regulated by one set of norms.
- Adjacency pairs are structured by a local set of organizational principles, and many have preferred and dispreferred second parts.
- Organizational principles shape conversational openings and closings.
- The organization of repairs can be described with a set of rules that rank different repair patterns in terms of preference. Repairs that are self-initiated and self-made are favored.
- At the root of many organizational principles in conversation is the need to display independence politeness and involvement politeness to other people.

- Culture-specific norms determine when and where independence politeness and involvement politeness behaviors are appropriate.
- Because the organization of polite conversational behavior differs from culture to culture, miscommunication of intent across cultures is common.

 ## What Do You Think? REVISITED

- *Isabella's question.* Every speech act has appropriateness conditions surrounding it. Among those associated with the act of pronouncing two people married by saying certain words is the intention of the two people to get married to one another at that time. In the case of a play, the actors intend merely to depict a wedding ceremony but not to marry. As a consequence, an essential condition of a marriage pronouncement is lacking, and the utterance is ineffectual as a marriage pronouncement.
- *Kimberly's complaint.* Making a promise requires using the word *promise*, as in, *I promise to do the dishes if you'll cook dinner.* Without the word, there's no promise. (Of course, if someone asks, *Do you promise?* and the reply is *Yes*, the reply would constitute a promise.) Pledges and expressed intentions don't require the word *promise*, so Tyler may have had good intentions, but he didn't make a promise.
- *Brandon's complaint.* Brandon's observation probably has less to do with Daniel as an individual than with his French social practices. The French regard telephoning people as intruding on them and may apologize for phoning and take longer to get to the point than Americans expect. By contrast, Americans regard calling a friend as showing involvement, being generally positive, and not requiring apology. ∎

Exercises

Based on English

9-1. Make a list of the headlines on the front page or home page of a daily newspaper. Indicate which of the headlines report physical actions and which report speech acts.

9-2. Observe a typical lecture meeting of one of your courses and identify the characteristics that define it as a lecture (as distinct from an informal conversation, workshop, seminar, or lab meeting). Identify characterizing features of the areas listed below. To what extent is there room for variability in how a lecture is conducted (depending, for example, on the personality of the participants)? When does a lecture stop being a lecture?

    a. Setting (physical setting, clothing, social identity of the participants, and so on)

    b. Nonverbal behavior of the participants (body movement, stance and position with respect to each other, and so on)

    c. Verbal behavior of the participants (turn taking, openings, closings, assignment of pair parts among participants, and so on)

    d. Topic (what is appropriate to talk about? to what extent can this be deviated from? and so on)

9-3. Make a tape recording of the first minute of a radio interview. Transcribe what is said during that first minute in as much detail as possible (indicating, for example, who talks, when pauses occur, and what hesitations occur). Label each turn as to its illocutionary force (greeting, inquiry, compliment, and so on). Then describe in detail the strategies used in opening the radio interview. Illustrate your description with specific examples taken from your transcript.

9-4. Make a tape recording of the first minute of a broadcast of the evening news on radio or television. Transcribe what is said during that minute in as much detail as possible. Then answer the following questions, citing specific illustrations from your transcript.

    a. What effect do radio or television newscasters try to achieve initially?

    b. How is this accomplished? Describe at least two strategies, using specific illustrations.

    c. Suppose you played your tape recording to friends without identifying what was taped. Exactly what features would help them recognize it as a recording of the evening news? Cite three specific telltale characteristics other than content.

    d. Which of the news items are reports of physical actions and which are reports of speech acts?

9-5. Observe the following interaction between two people who are working at nearby desks.

    Amy: Zach?

    Zach: Yeah?

    Amy: Do you have a ruler?

Amy's first turn is an opening sequence. What does it signal, and what does Zach's response indicate? Why did Amy not open merely with *Do you have a ruler?*

9-6. The next time you talk on the telephone to a friend, observe the distinctive characteristics of talk over the telephone, and take notes immediately after you hang up. Identify several ways in which a telephone conversation differs from a face-to-face conversation. Try to re-create specific linguistic examples from your telephone conversation to illustrate your points.

9-7. Consider the following excerpts, each of which contains a repair. For each excerpt, determine whether the repair is (a) self-initiated and self-repaired,

(b) self-initiated and other-repaired, (c) other-initiated and self-repaired, or
(d) other-initiated and other-repaired.

a. **Jan:**   What's the sales tax in this state?

   James: Seven cents on the dollar.

   Patricia: Seven cents on the dollar? You mean eight and a half cents.

   James: Oh, yeah, eight and a half cents.

b. **Anne:**   There's a party at Rod's tonight. Wanna go?

   Sam: Rod's? Rod's outta town!

   Anne: I mean Rick's.

c. **Peter:**   And then he comes along an' tells me he's droppin' his ac-
                  counting cl— uh, his economics class.

   Frank: Yeah, he told me the same thing the next mornin'.

d. **Rick:**   His dog's been sick since last month an' he won't be able to go
                  to the wedding 'cause he's gotta take care of it.

   Alice: Well, his dog's been sick for at least two months. So it's nothin'
                  new.

e. **Sam:**   Do you remember the names of all their kids? The oldest one
                  is Daniel, the girl's Priscilla, then there's another girl—What's
                  her name again?

   Regie: Susie, I think.

   Sam: Yeah, Susie, that's it.

f. **Ellie:**   What do they charge you for car insurance?

   Ted: Two thousand bucks a year, but then there's a three-hundred-
                  dollar deductible. Three hundred or one hundred—I can't
                  remember.

   Ellie: Probably one hundred, right?

   Ted: Yeah, I think you're right. One hundred sounds right.

g. **Sarah:**   He's been cookin' all day for her birthday party.

   Anne: Actually he's been cooking for three days now.

h. **Will:**   There wasn't much I could do for her. She needed five thou-
                  sand bucks for tuition and I jus' didn't have it.

   David: I thought it was four thousand.

   Will: Yeah, four thousand, but I didn't have that much.

9-8. Consider the following excerpts, all of which are prestructures initiating
conversation. Describe in detail the structure and the function of each pre-
structure using the terms *turn* (or *turn taking*), *signal*, *adjacency pair*, *first part*,
second part, and *claiming the floor*.

a. **Larry:**   Guess what.

   Lauren: What?

   Larry: Pat's coming tomorrow.

    b. Tom: [reading the newspaper] I can't believe this!

        Fred: What?

        Tom: Congress passed another new immigration law.

    c. Ruth: [chuckles while reading a book]

        Anne: What're you chuckling about?

        Ruth: This story—it's so off the wall!

9-9. Consider the following excerpt from a conversation among three friends.

    1) Cindy: Heard from Jill recently? She hasn't written or called in ages.

    2) Larry: Yeah, she sent me a postcard from England.

    3) Barb: From England?

    4) Larry: Uh, maybe it was from France, I can't remember.

    5) Cindy: What's she doin—

    6) Barb: No, I know it must've been from France 'cause she was gonna stay there all year.

    7) Cindy: What's she doin' in France?

    8) Larry: Why are you asking about her?

    9) Cindy: I don't know, I've just been thinkin' about her.

    10) Larry: She's on some sort of exchange program. Studying French or something.

    11) Cindy: Sounds pretty nice to me.

    12) Larry: Yeah. Well, I don't know. She said she was tired of Europe and wants to come home.

    a. In the conversation above, how many turns does each interlocutor have?

    b. Identify an example of each of the following in the conversation above: *turn-taking signal*, *claiming the floor*, *preferred response*, *dispreferred response*, *repair*, *trouble source*, *initiation*, and *resolution*.

    c. Identify an *adjacency pair* in the conversation, giving the name of the *first part* and *second part*.

9-10. Conversations in fiction and drama and those re-created in movies or on stage often differ from ordinary everyday conversations. The following is an excerpt from a conversation in Isak Dinesen's autobiographical novel *Out of Africa* (New York: Random House, 1937).

    "Do you know anything of book-keeping?" I asked him.

    "No. Nothing at all," he said, "I have always found it very difficult to add two figures together."

    "Do you know about cattle at all?" I went on. "Cows?" he asked. "No, no. I am afraid of cows."

"Can you drive a tractor, then?" I asked. Here a faint ray of hope appeared on his face. "No," he said, "but I think I could learn that."

"Not on my tractor though," I said, "but then tell me, Emmanuelson, what have you even been doing? What are you in life?"

Emmanuelson drew himself up straight. "What am I?" he exclaimed. "Why, I am an actor."

I thought: Thank God, it is altogether outside my capacity to assist this lost man in any practical way; the time has come for a general human conversation. "You are an actor?" I said, "that is a fine thing to be. And which were your favourite parts when you were on the stage?"

"Oh I am a tragic actor," said Emmanuelson, "my favourite parts were that of Armand in 'La Dame aux Camelias' and of Oswald in 'Ghosts.'"

On the basis of this example, analyze the differences between the organization of conversations represented in writing and the organization of actual conversations. Why do these differences exist?

9-11. The transcribed conversational excerpt below includes two adjacency pairs. Provide the letter or letters of the turn(s) for each of these categories: (1) insertion sequence, (2) first part of first adjacency pair, (3) second part of first adjacency pair, (4) first part of second adjacency pair, (5) second part of second adjacency pair. Next, match each of these speech acts to a turn that exemplifies it: (6) clarification, (7) rejection, (8) proposal, (9) request for clarification.

    A. Eric: Wanna watch *Civil War* tonight?

    B. Nan: The Ken Burns series?

    C. Eric: He made it with his brother.

    D. Nan: Sorry. I've got an econ quiz tomorrow.

Especially for Educators and Future Teachers

9-12. Below are two sets of turns from conversations among college students, most spoken within a few months after graduating from high school. In utterances (1) to (4), the highlighted word **like** is used in at least two distinct ways. Analyze (1)–(4) and characterize the two ways. In utterances (5) to (7), the word **all** is highlighted. Characterize its function in these turns. Then imagine a discussion with your students in which you and they are analyzing a transcription. One student reports that another teacher pokes fun at the use of *like*, and another student chimes in that her father ridicules it, too. What points would you make to indicate that these relatively new uses for *like* and *all* function in conversation in ways that are similar to other, more traditional expressions? With what words can *like* and *all* be compared? Discuss why these newer usages are sometimes ridiculed.

    1) Adam: I don't want to break up with her **like** . . . this time.

      Brent: Yeah don't break up this time.

      Break up **like** Thanksgiving or something.

2) **Ben:** So she called and was **like,**

I can't believe you did this,

I can't believe you did this.

I'm **like**—,

3) **Ali:** I was like,

I was **like** why,

why,

you know . . .

4) **Rod:** I was **like** all happy and stuff.

5) **Jose:** Wait. Why is she **all** bitchin' at you first of all?

6) **Jaime:** I am **all** sitting here trying to read.

7) **Danny:** I was like **all** happy and stuff.

9-13. Your students are probably familiar with a version of the old adage that claims, "Sticks and stones may break my bones, but words will never hurt me." At a level appropriate for your students, draw up a lesson plan that analyzes this saying in terms of the power of speech acts. You might consider beginning the lesson by inquiring whether any students have ever been hurt by what others have said to them or about them.

9-14. Call upon students of various cultural backgrounds to discuss their experience calling and being called on the phone by members of other cultural groups. Also discuss their attitudes toward telemarketing calls and how their attitudes might reflect cultural values.

Other Resources

Internet

 LISU Website: http://www.CengageBrain.com On the site for this textbook (LISU), you'll find an audio recording and transcription of a conversation among four university students about an outing to buy a birthday present. In the conversation, from which a couple of modified examples appear within this chapter, Eric and Sylvia (boyfriend and girlfriend) tell the Chia Pets story to their friends Mary and Maria. The interaction illustrates several features of conversation discussed in this chapter.

 Corpus of Contemporary American English: http://www. americancorpus.org Compiled by Mark Davies at Brigham Young University, "COCA" contains significant quantities of American English speech and writing, the latter in the categories of fiction, magazine, newspaper, and academic. It groups its materials into five-year periods beginning in 1990, with the most recent materials coming from the summer of 2010. The site allows a variety of search types (including KWIC concordances—discussed toward the end of Chapter 6) and provides guidance for several kinds of research inquiries, with access free of cost.

Video

- **John J. Gumperz, T. C. Jupp, and C. Roberts. 1979.** *Crosstalk: A Study of Cross-Cultural Communication* (London: National Centre for Industrial Language Training and BBC) A one-hour video illustrating and discussing miscommunication between East Indian immigrants and bank clerks, librarians, and other institutional figures in London; a moving demonstration of the painful difficulties that can arise from differing conversational norms across cultural boundaries.

Suggestions for Further Reading

- **Diane Blakemore. 1992.** *Understanding Utterances: An Introduction to Pragmatics* (Oxford: Blackwell). A basic introduction; a natural follow-up to the contents of this chapter.
- **Peter Grundy. 2008.** *Doing Pragmatics,* **3rd ed.** (London: Hodder Education). A basic and clear introduction, with an effective conversational and interactive style, containing a chapter on doing project work in pragmatics and others on politeness, speech acts, and deixis (the last of which we treated in Chapter 6); examples mostly British.
- **Barbara Johnstone. 2008.** *Discourse Analysis,* **2nd ed.** (Malden, MA: Blackwell). Covering material treated in the present chapter and Chapter 8. Well written, highly stimulating, and including a wide range of critical analyses.
- **Jacob L. Mey. 2001.** *Pragmatics: An Introduction,* **2nd ed.** (Oxford: Blackwell). A thorough and more advanced treatment than Grundy, containing chapters on speech acts, pragmatics across cultures, and conversation analysis, as well as literary pragmatics.
- **Deborah Tannen. 1990.** *You Just Don't Understand: Women and Men in Conversation* (New York: Ballantine). Accessible and highly popular best-seller discusses misunderstanding between the sexes; also treats Gricean maxims very simply.
- **Deborah Tannen. 1994.** *Gender and Discourse* (New York: Oxford University Press). An accessible treatment of the background to Tannen's *You Just Don't Understand.*
- **Ronald Wardhaugh. 1985.** *How Conversation Works* (New York: Blackwell). A well-focused, basic, and accessible textbook.

Advanced Reading

The analysis of speech acts has been an enterprise chiefly of philosophers. Austin (2005) is a set of 12 readable lectures laying out the nature of locutionary and illocutionary acts (as well as perlocutionary acts). Grice (1975, 1989) formulates the cooperative principle and enumerates the conversational maxims we've discussed. Searle (1976) discusses the classification of speech acts and their syntax, while Searle (1975) lays out the structure of indirect speech acts. Besides these primary sources, Levinson (1983) remains invaluable.

Profoundly differing from the philosophical traditions in their methodological approach, the inductive studies of the conversation analysts are challenging to read: turn taking was first analyzed systematically by Sacks et al. (1974), closings by Schegloff and Sacks (1973), and repairs by Schegloff et al. (1977). More accessible for student readers are these treatments of conversation analysis and language use in informal contexts: Levinson (1983) and Chapters 11 and 12 of Wardhaugh (2010).

The theoretical background to the study of speech events is presented in Goffman (1986; original edition 1974) and Hymes (1974). Goffman (1981) presents interesting and entertaining analyses of various speech events, including lectures and radio talk. Goodwin (1981) describes how talk and gestures are integrated in conversation. The organization of conversation in the workplace is investigated in Boden (1988). The characterization of communication between subordinates and superordinates as spectator/performer or performer/spectator was proposed by Bateson (2000), a new edition of a classic text, laying out the philosophical foundation for the study of human communication. Cross-social and cross-cultural differences in the organization of conversation are analyzed in Gumperz (1982a, 1982b), Blum-Kulka et al. (1989), Trosborg (1995), and Scollon and Scollon (1981, 1995), from the last of which a few examples appear in this chapter. Godard (1977) is an interesting study of Franco-American differences in behavior on the telephone, and this and other aspects of French interaction are discussed in Chapter 10 of Ager (1990). Brown and Levinson (1987) and chapters of Levinson (1983) and Wardhaugh (2010) discuss politeness. Drew and Heritage (1993) is a collection of essays discussing interaction in institutional settings.

References

Ager, Dennis E. 1990. *Sociolinguistics and Contemporary French* (Cambridge, UK: Cambridge University Press).

Austin, John. 2005. *How to Do Things with Words*, 2nd ed. (Cambridge, MA: Harvard University Press).

Bateson, Gregory. 2000. *Steps to an Ecology of Mind: Collected Essays in Anthropology, Psychiatry, Evolution, and Epistemology* (Chicago: University of Chicago Press).

Blum-Kulka, Shoshana, Juliane House & Gabriele Kasper, eds. 1989. *Cross-cultural Pragmatics: Requests and Apologies* (Norwood, NJ: Ablex).

Boden, Deirdre. 1988. *The Business of Talk: Organizations in Action* (Cambridge, UK: Polity).

Brown, Penelope & Stephen C. Levinson. 1987. *Politeness: Some Universals in Language Usage* (Cambridge, UK: Cambridge University Press).

Drew, Paul & John Heritage, eds. 1993. *Talk at Work* (Cambridge, UK: Cambridge University Press).

Godard, Daniele. 1977. "Same Setting, Different Norms: Phone Call Beginnings in France and the United States," *Language in Society* 6:209–19.

Goffman, Erving. 1986. *Frame Analysis: An Essay on the Organization of Experience* [Repr. ed., with a foreword by Bennett Berger] (Boston: Northeastern University Press).

Goffman, Erving. 1981. *Forms of Talk* (Philadelphia: University of Pennsylvania Press).

Goodwin, Charles. 1981. *Conversational Organization: Interaction between Speakers and Hearers* (New York: Academic).

Grice, H. Paul. 1975. "Logic and Conversation," in Peter Cole & Jerry L. Morgan, eds., *Syntax and Semantics 3: Speech Acts* (New York: Academic), pp. 41–58.

Gumperz, John J. 1982a. *Discourse Strategies* (Cambridge, UK: Cambridge University Press).

Gumperz, John J., ed. 1982b. *Language and Social Identity* (Cambridge, UK: Cambridge University Press).

Hymes, Dell. 1974. *Foundations in Sociolinguistics* (Philadelphia: University of Pennsylvania Press).

Levinson, Stephen C. 1983. *Pragmatics* (Cambridge, UK: Cambridge University Press).

Sacks, Harvey, Emanuel A. Schegloff & Gail Jefferson. 1974. "A Simplest Systematics for the Organization of Turn-Taking in Conversation," *Language* 50:696–735.

Schegloff, Emanuel A., Gail Jefferson & Harvey Sacks. 1977. "The Preference for Self-Correction in the Organization of Repair in Conversation," *Language* 53:361–82.

Schegloff, Emanuel A. & Harvey Sacks. 1973. "Opening Up Closings," *Semiotica* 7:289–327.

Scollon, Ron & Suzanne B. K. Scollon. 1981. *Narrative, Literacy and Face in Interethnic Communication* (Norwood, NJ: Ablex).

Scollon, Ron & Suzanne Wong Scollon. 1995. *Intercultural Communication* (Oxford: Blackwell).

Searle, John R. 1975. "Indirect Speech Acts," in Peter Cole & Jerry L. Morgan, eds. *Syntax and Semantics 3: Speech Acts* (New York: Academic), pp. 59–82.

Searle, John R. 1976. "A Classification of Illocutionary Acts," *Language in Society* 5:1–23.

Trosborg, Anna. 1995. *Interlanguage Pragmatics: Requests, Complaints and Apologies* (Berlin: Mouton de Gruyter).

Wardhaugh, Ronald. 2010. *An Introduction to Sociolinguistics*, 6th ed. (Malden, MA: Blackwell).

10

Language Variation Across Situations of Use: Registers and Styles

What Do You Think?

- English major Michael comments that the dialogue in a P. D. James novel he's reading is "awesome, totally natural." You scoff because you've recently corrected a transcribed deposition you'd given in connection with an insurance claim for an automobile accident, and your answers to the attorney's questions were peppered with false starts and *uhms* and *uhs*. Your answers didn't resemble the tidy fictional dialogue of novels at all. And neither did the attorney's questions! What can you tell Michael about what's totally natural in fictional dialogue?
- Nina, a ninth grader, asks why her teachers dislike slang and colloquialisms, and she wonders what's the difference between them. What do you tell her?
- Your classmate Clarence says he's shocked to see contractions like *it's* and *don't* used in this textbook and claims they're supposed to be avoided in college textbooks and in college writing classes. You think they create an informal, relaxed tone and are appropriate in the textbook. What justification can you offer for your preference?
- Poring over a cookbook, your uncle Colin laments: "What strange English this is! 'Toast pine nuts in medium skillet. Remove and add 1 tbsp. oil and garlic. Cook 4 minutes and drain remaining liquid. Sprinkle salt and pepper inside trout cavity and stuff with spinach mixture. Brush trout with remaining oil.' What ever happened to words like *of* and *for* and *them* and *the* and the other Anglo-Saxon glue of the language?" What do you say?

Introduction

Language varieties characteristic of particular social situations—for example, *face-to-face conversation*, *telephone conversation*, *interviews*, and *biography*—are called **registers** (or styles). Across different circumstances, everyone varies language forms. For example, you may call one person *Michelle* or *Ted*; another person *Dr. Lavandera* or *Mr. Olson*; and still others *Your Honor* or *Mr. President*; to some you say *Sir* or *Madam* or *Miss*. If you use the address term *dude*, you don't use it indiscriminately for anyone at all. Speakers of French address some individuals with the second-personal singular pronoun *tu* but others with the plural pronoun *vous*. In some communities, different social situations call for alternative forms of a single language; in other communities, different social situations call for different languages altogether.

Language Varies Within a Speech Community

Language Choice in Multilingual Societies

You might assume that in multilingual countries such as Switzerland, Belgium, and India different languages are spoken by different groups of people, and that's true of course. Typically, though, one language or another is also systematically allocated to specific social situations. In communities employing several languages, the choice of one language or another is not arbitrary. Instead, a particular setting such as a classroom or government office may favor or even require one language, while other languages will be appropriate to other speech situations. Although there may be roughly equivalent expressions in two languages, the social meaning that attaches to use of one particular language generally differs from that attached to use of another. As a result, speakers must attend to the social import of language choice, however unconsciously they make their choice.

Linguistic Repertoires in Brussels, Tehran, and Los Angeles

The use of selected varieties from two languages among government workers in the capital of Belgium illustrates the nature of language choice in one European community.

Government functionaries in Brussels who are of Flemish origin do not always speak Dutch to *each other*, even when they all know Dutch *very* well and *equally* well. Not only are there occasions when they speak French to *each other* instead of Dutch, but there are some occasions when they speak standard Dutch and others when they use one or another regional variety of Dutch with each other. Indeed, some of them also use different varieties of French with each other as well, one variety being particularly loaded with governmental officialese, another corresponding to the nontechnical conversational French of highly educated and refined circles in Belgium, and still another being not only a "more colloquial French" but the colloquial French of those who are Flemings. All in all, these several varieties of Dutch and of French constitute the *linguistic repertoire* of certain social networks in Brussels (Fishman [1972], pp. 47–48).

The language variety that Brussels residents use is prompted by the setting in which the talk takes place, by the topic, by the social relations among the participants, and by certain other features of the situation. In general, the use of Dutch is associated with informal and intimate interaction, whereas French has more official or "highbrow" connotations. Given these associations, the choice to speak French or Dutch carries a social meaning in addition to the referential meaning of the words and utterances.

We use the term **linguistic repertoire** for the set of language varieties exhibited in the speaking and writing patterns of a speech community. As in Brussels, the linguistic repertoire of any speech community may consist of several languages and include several varieties of each language.

In the mid-1970s, there was considerable multilingualism in Tehran, the capital of Iran. Christian families spoke Armenian or Syriac at home and in church, Persian at school, all three in different situations while playing or shopping, and Azerbaijani Turkish at shops in the bazaar. Muslim men from northwest Iran, who were working as laborers in the then-booming capital city, spoke a variety of Persian with their supervisors at construction sites but switched to a variety of Turkish with their fellow workers and to a local Iranian dialect when they visited their home villages on holidays; in addition, they listened daily to radio broadcasts in standard Persian and heard passages from the Koran recited in Arabic. It was not uncommon for individuals to command as many as four or five languages and deploy them in different situations. Much the same situation exists today.

In Los Angeles, the Korean-speaking community supports bilingual institutions of various sorts: banks, churches, stores, and a wide range of services from pool halls and video rental shops to hotels, construction companies, and law firms. At some banks in the neighborhood known as Koreatown all the tellers are bilingual, and in the course of a day's work many often switch between Korean and English. As the tellers alternate between customers, they naturally switch between Korean and English as appropriate.

Try It Yourself Identify a situation on your campus or in your community where people can be heard switching between languages in the course of a conversation, depending on who it is they're speaking with or the topic or who else is present or some other aspect of the social situation.

Switching Varieties Within a Language

If we examine the situation in Europe, besides switching between languages we see examples of language-internal switching. Brussels residents switch not only between French and Dutch but among varieties of French and varieties of Dutch. In Hemnes, a village in northern Norway, residents speak two distinct varieties of Norwegian. Ranamål, the local dialect, serves to identify speakers of that region. Bokmål, one of two forms of standard Norwegian (the other being Nynorsk), is in use for education, religion, government transactions, and the mass media. All members of the Hemnes community control both Ranamål and Bokmål and regard themselves at any given time as speaking one or the other. Between Ranamål and Bokmål there are differences of pronunciation, morphology, vocabulary, and syntax, and speakers do not perceive themselves as mixing the two varieties in their speech. Here's an illustration with a simple sentence, meaning 'Where are you from?'

ke du e ifrå	(Ranamål)
vor ær du fra	(Bokmål)

Bokmål is the expected variety in certain well-defined situations, and residents of Hemnes do not accept its use among themselves outside those situations. In situations in which speakers customarily use Ranamål, speaking Bokmål would signal social distance and disregard for community spirit. To use Bokmål in Hemnes with fellow locals is to *snakkfint* or *snakk jalat* 'put on airs.' As the researchers who reported these findings note, "Although locals show an overt preference for the dialect, they tolerate and use the standard in situations where it conveys meanings of officialdom, expertise, and politeness toward strangers who are clearly segregated from their personal life" (Blom and Gumperz [1972], pp. 433–34). Regard for the social situation is thus highly important in choosing varieties of the same language, just as it is in switching between languages.

Speech Situations

As we have seen in Hemnes, Los Angeles, Brussels, and Tehran, language switching can be triggered by a change in any one of several situational factors, including the setting and purpose of the communication, the person addressed, the social relations between the interlocutors, and the topic.

Elements of a Speech Situation

If we define a **speech situation** as the coming together of significant situational factors such as purpose, topic, and social relations, then each speech situation in a bilingual or multilingual community generally allows only one of the community's languages to be used. Table 10.1 illustrates this concept for an English/Spanish bilingual community in Los Angeles.

As you see, in situation A, a variety of Spanish is appropriate, but in situation C a variety of English. Only in the relatively uncommon case of situation E

Table 10.1 *Linguistic Repertoire*

Situation	Relation of Speakers	Place	Topic Type	Spanish	English
A	intimate	school	not academic	X	
B	intimate	home	not academic	X	
C	not intimate	school	not academic		X
D	not intimate	home	academic		X
E	intimate	school	academic	X	X

Table 10.2 *Elements of a Speech Situation*

Purpose	Setting	Participants
Activity	Topic	Speaker
Goal	Location	Addressee
	Mode	Social roles of speaker and addressee
		Character of audience

might an individual have a genuine choice between Spanish and English without calling attention to the language chosen. In situation E, the competing values of intimacy (which usually requires Spanish, as in situations A and B) and an academic topic (for which English is usually preferred) may sometimes yield Spanish and sometimes English.

Table 10.2 charts certain aspects of a speech situation that may prompt or require a change in language variety.

In terms of *purpose*, the kind of activity is crucial and so is the goal. Are you making a purchase, giving a sermon, telling a story? Entertaining, reporting information, greeting a friend, or affirming a social relationship? The activity may have an influence on your language selection.

As to *setting*, you may switch from one language to another as the *topic* switches from one of local interest, say, to one of national concern, or from a personal matter to one about your college. *Location*, too, can influence language choice in that you might well use one language in an academic setting but a different one in a religious setting or at home for otherwise roughly comparable situations. The *mode*—that is, whether you are speaking or writing (or using ten fingers or two thumbs)—can also influence the forms of language you select, as is clear, for example, in contrasting instant messaging, telephone conversations, and texting.

As to *participants*, the identity of the speaker will influence language choice, as will the identity of the person being addressed. Speakers typically adapt utterances to the age of an addressee. In some societies, the older a person, the higher his or her social standing; younger people must address older people more respectfully than they address their peers. As noted, in French the second-person singular pronoun 'you' has two forms: *tu* for a social equal or to express intimacy, *vous* for a person of higher social status or to mark social distance (and for addressing more than one person, irrespective of social relations). A younger person addressing an older person may be expected to use *vous*, not *tu*, unless the older person is a close relative. Given that *tu* is the grammatically singular form and *vous* the plural form, and given that verbs exhibit agreement with their subject, French illustrates one way in which even verb morphology may vary according to the age or social status of the addressee. Persian shows similar patterns with singular *to* [to] and plural *shoma* [ʃomɑ] and with appropriate verbal agreement with the grammatical number of the subject, as do several other European tongues.

It is not just the social identity of speaker and addressee that is relevant, but also their *roles* in the particular speech situation. A judge, for example, typically speaks one variety at home—where she may be mother, wife, neighbor—and another as judge in the courtroom. A parent who works as a teacher and has his child for a student may speak different varieties at home and at school, even when topic and addressee are the same.

The various aspects of the speech situation come together in a particular choice of language variety. In each situation—a general one such as home or church or a specific one such as discussing politics in a cafe with a close friend—one variety is usually more appropriate than others. In fact, people get so accustomed to speaking a particular language in a given setting that they can experience difficulty using another language in that setting, no matter how familiar that language may be in other settings. (Of course, professional translators, bilingual educators, and certain businesspersons who regularly engage in negotiations with members of their own and another culture will be among the exceptions to this generalization.) As a result, switching between language varieties is common throughout the world and is known as **code switching**. It is far, far more common than many monolingual speakers might guess.

Registers in Monolingual Societies

The recognition that in multilingual societies there are settings and speech situations in which one language is appropriate but not another has a parallel in monolingual speech communities, where varieties of a single language constitute the entire linguistic repertoire. Consider the difference between the full forms of careful speech and the abbreviations and reductions characteristic of fast speech that occur in relaxed face-to-face communication: not only workaday contractions like *he's* and *I'll* but reduced sentences like *Jeetyet?* [ʤitjɛt] for 'Did you eat yet?' and *Wajjasay?* [wɑʤəse] for 'What did you say?'

To take another example, you know that you don't typically use the same terms for certain body parts when speaking to friends and when speaking to a physician. You might use *collarbone* at home and *clavicle* with a physician, while either term might be used with friends, depending on other aspects of the speech situation. Lexical choices made for more intimate body parts would be yet more strikingly different.

The distribution of alternative terms for the same referent may seem arbitrary and without communicative benefit. With body parts, for example, all the terms may be known and used by all the parties in equivalent situations. A physician may use *clavicle* speaking with her own physician, but *collarbone* with family and friends. Since all the terms could communicate referential meaning and be equally well understood, the choice of a socially appropriate variant is *cognitively* unhelpful. But such variation as has lasted for centuries in a society can be assumed to serve an important function, and you may wonder why linguistic expression differs from one speech situation to another. The answer is that different expressions for the same content can indicate different affective relationships to salient aspects of the situation (setting, topic, social relations between speaker and addressee, and so on) and even help define a situation.

From a young age, everyone learns to control several language varieties for use in different speech situations. No one is limited to a single variety in a single language. These language varieties may belong to one language or several. Just which speech situations—which purposes, settings, participants—prompt which variety depends on social norms. In one society, the presence of in-laws may call for a different variety (as in Dyirbal and several other aboriginal Australian societies). In other societies, the presence of children or members of the opposite sex may be crucial. In Western societies, adults have a slew of words they avoid saying in the presence of children (and children struggle to avoid saying in the presence of adults). There are also differences associated with mode—for example, written versus spoken. You are familiar with the term *colloquial*: it is merely a label for informal speech.

Markers of Register

Languages differ from one another in vocabulary, phonology, grammar, and semantics, and registers of a single language may also differ at every level. Different speech situations may call for different interactional patterns as well—for example, the allocation of turns in conversation differs starkly from how turns are allocated in courtrooms and classrooms. In addition, social rules govern nonlinguistic behaviors such as physical proximity, face-to-face positioning, standing and sitting, which accompany register variation. Interactional patterns and body language are beyond the scope of this book, but they are part and parcel of social and cultural communication.

Generally speaking, when you find characteristic features of a register at one level of the grammar, you can expect corresponding features at other levels as well. For example, to describe legalese or face-to-face conversation requires attention to characteristic vocabulary, sentence structure, semantics, and phonology. There are some provisos that need to be made in this regard. It is customary to talk about slang and jargon when discussing registers, but their characteristic linguistic features are limited to vocabulary, and the concomitant linguistic forms (for example, in pronunciation and grammar) are those of the situation in which that vocabulary is being used.

Lexical Markers of Register

Registers vary along certain social dimensions. For example, people speak (and write) in markedly different fashions in formal and informal situations. Formality and informality can be seen as polar opposites of a situational continuum along which forms of expression may be arranged.

The words *pickled, high, drunk,* and *intoxicated* may all refer to the same state of inebriation, but you can rank them on a scale of formality, and you would likely agree on a ranking from least formal to most formal in the order given. In one context, to suggest inebriation may require the word *intoxicated*, while another may require *drunk* or *under the influence. Bombed, buzzed,* and *pissed* are terms favored by younger people in situations of considerable informality.

One thesaurus lists more than 125 expressions for 'intoxicated.' Needless to say, they are not situationally equivalent and cannot be substituted for one another irrespective of the social situation.

Not every word that can be glossed as 'inebriated' is suitable for use on all occasions when reference to intoxication is intended. The chosen words can indicate quite different attitudes toward the addressees, the person being described, the state of intoxication itself, and so on. It can also index the speech situation in which the term is being used as intimate or distant, formal or informal, serious or jocular. Consider this fictitious dialogue between judge and defendant at an arraignment in a courtroom:

Judge: I see the cops say you were wasted last night and drove an old junker down the middle of the road. That right?

Defendant: Your honor, if I might be permitted to address this baseless allegation, I should like to report that I was neither inebriated nor under the influence of an alcoholic beverage of any kind; for the record, I imbibed no booze last evening.

In the first place, the judge's language seems out of place: words like *cops*, *wasted*, and *junker* seem inappropriate for a judge presiding at an arraignment. The abbreviated form *That right?* may be appropriate in relaxed conversation, but it suggests a level of informality unsuitable in a courtroom interaction between a judge and someone charged with an offense. As for the defendant's response, it too seems out of place, even more so following the extremely informal language used by the judge. Even if the judge had used courtroom-appropriate language, the defendant's language seems overly formal. And, of course, it seems odd for the informal word *booze* to appear in an utterance characterized by the formal words *imbibed*, *inebriated*, *beverage*, and *allegation*.

Compare the judge's language above with the following, which seems more appropriate to an arraignment.

Judge: You are charged with driving a 2004 blue Ford while under the influence of alcohol. How do you plead?

Even within a single language, then, registers or styles match specific situations of use.

Try It Yourself Name a speech situation of your choosing (e.g., a conference with a professor, dinner with your grandparents, a job interview) and list five words for things you would likely talk about in that situation but for which the expression you'd likely use would differ from the one you'd use for the same referent when speaking with a close friend. Provide both words.

Terms of Address Along with other lexical, grammatical, and phonological features, appropriate forms of address for a given person may differ from situation to situation. The Queen of England is addressed by her subjects and others as *Your Majesty* (or *Ma'am*), though Prince Philip, her husband, presumably uses a more intimate address term when speaking to her in private. In court, judges are addressed as *Your Honor* or *Judge*, though their friends and neighbors may call them *Judy* or

Vaughn. Each of us is addressed in multiple ways, depending on the situation: by first name (*Pat*); family name (*Smith*); family name preceded by a title (*Doctor Smith, Ms. Jones*); the second-person pronoun (*you*); terms showing respect (*Sir, Madam*); and various informal generic terms (*guy, dude*). At the opposite end of the scale are terms of disrespect such as *buster* or *you bastard*.

Phonological Markers of Register Registers are marked not only by lexical choices but also by features of syntax, morphology, semantics, pragmatics, and for spoken registers, phonology. In a study of New York City speechways that we will discuss further in the following chapter, considerable phonological variation was uncovered among all groups of speakers in different situations of use.

Figure 10.1 presents frequencies for the pronunciation of -*ing* as /ɪŋ/ (that is, "with the g") in three speech situations. We use -*ing* to represent the pronunciation of the suffix in words like *talking, running, eating,* and *watching.* The speech situations in this case consist of three kinds of interaction during a sociolinguistic interview in the homes of four groups of respondents (labeled LC, WC, LMC, and UMC). The style of the interview, with its interlaced questions and answers, can be regarded as "careful" speech. Respondents also read a set passage aloud, and "reading" style was taken to represent more careful speech than interview style. In order to prompt more relaxed speech, at the end of the interview the interviewer asked respondents whether they'd ever had a close call with death, and this gambit usually elicited a relaxed, unguarded variety, here called "casual" speech.

In their casual speech, LC respondents (LC is an abbreviation for lower class, a socioeconomic ranking based on a combination of income, education, and employment type) pronounced the -*ing* suffix as /ɪŋ/ 20 percent of the time (the other 80 percent as /ɪn/). In their careful speech, the occurrence of /ɪŋ/ increased to 47 percent (while /ɪn/ decreased to 53 percent). When reading a passage aloud, the LC respondents pronounced /ɪŋ/ 78 percent of the time (and /ɪn/ only 22 percent). This represents a dramatic increase of /ɪŋ/ pronunciations in increasingly formal speech situations. The same overall pattern holds

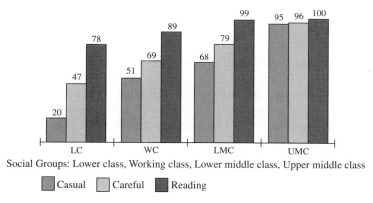

Social Groups: Lower class, Working class, Lower middle class, Upper middle class

■ Casual ▢ Careful ■ Reading

Figure 10.1 Percentage of -*ing* Pronounced as /ɪŋ/ in Three Speech Situations among Four Social Groups in New York City

Source of data: Labov 2006.

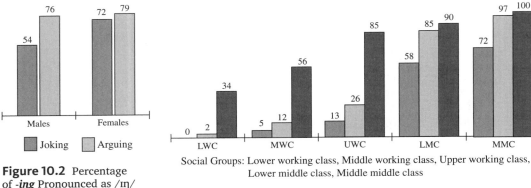

Figure 10.2 Percentage of *-ing* Pronounced as /ɪŋ/ in Two Speech Situations by Males and Females in Los Angeles

Source of data: B. Wald and T. Shopen, "A Researcher's Guide to the Sociolinguistic Variable (ING)" in Shopen and Williams (1981), p. 247.

Social Groups: Lower working class, Middle working class, Upper working class, Lower middle class, Middle middle class

Figure 10.3 Percentage of Pronunciation of *-ing* Pronounced as /ɪŋ/ in Three Speech Situations among Five Social Groups in Norwich, England

Source of data: Trudgill 2000.

for the other social groups. Each group used more /ɪŋ/ pronunciations in careful speech than in casual speech and more in reading style than in careful speech. In this New York City speech community, then, /ɪŋ/ indexes formality, with more frequent /ɪŋ/ pronunciations signaling increased formality.

In another study, college students in Los Angeles gathered data showing that both males and females used more /ɪŋ/ pronunciations in arguments than in joking. Again, we can view arguing as a more careful register than joking. The frequencies are given in Figure 10.2. Although men and women don't have the same percentages for the distribution of *-ing* (a topic we return to in Chapter 11), they exploit this phonological feature in the same way as an index to situations of use.

A study in Norwich, England, uncovered similar patterns. Among five social groups, the highest-ranking group in the study (the middle middle class) *always* used /ɪŋ/ in the formal register of reading style, while the lowest group in the study (lower working class) *never* used it in their most casual speech. Thus, while all five social groups used both pronunciations, the range of difference was 100 percentage points at the extremes of socioeconomic status and situational formality.

As the frequencies in Figure 10.3 show, the Norwich and New York City patterns are the same: each social group uses most /ɪŋ/ in reading style and least in its casual speech, with an intermediate percentage for careful speech. It is clear that widely separated English-speaking communities use /ɪŋ/ to index the formality of a situation. Note that it is not the absolute percentage that indexes situations but the *relative* percentages across situations. This linguistic marker is a continuous variable, able to indicate fine distinctions in degrees of formality across a range of speech situations.

As another example of phonological variation (or its equivalent spelling variation), the distribution of ordinary contractions like *can't, won't,* and *I'll* shows that speakers exhibit differential use of such forms across speech situations.

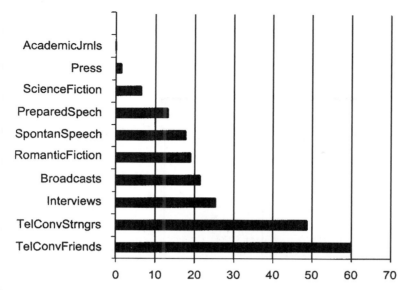

Figure 10.4 Number of Contractions per 1,000 Words in Different Registers
Source of data: Biber 1988.

Based on a corpus of written and spoken British English, the frequency counts in Figure 10.4 represent the average number of contractions per 1,000 words. Notice that in going from telephone conversations with friends to telephone conversations with strangers to interviews to broadcasts and so on up the list, there is a graded increase in formality, which is accompanied by fewer and fewer contractions.

Grammatical Markers of Register

Situations of use are also marked by syntactic variables. As an example, consider the occurrence of prepositions at the end of a clause or sentence. You may recall from your school days that some teachers frown on sentence-final prepositions. Instead of *That's the teacher I was telling you about*, they recommend *That's the teacher about whom I was telling you*. Well, it's no secret that, despite the admonition to avoid them, sentence-final prepositions abound in English. What's less well known is that they don't occur with equal frequency in all speech situations. Using the same corpus of texts as was used for contractions, Figure 10.5 presents the number of sentence-final prepositions per 1,000 prepositions for nearly a dozen spoken and written registers. This figure does not show the same continuous incline from least formal to most formal that we saw with contractions. Instead, it shows a major distinction between speech and nonfiction writing, with fiction writing (which includes fictional dialogue) having intermediate values. In the spoken registers, average counts of between 33 and 56 prepositions per 1,000 appear in sentence-final position. In the registers of nonfiction writing, though, final prepositions are fewer than in any of the spoken registers.

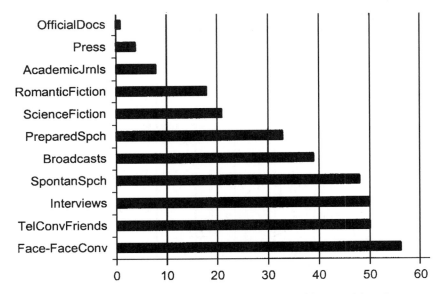

Figure 10.5 Number of Sentence-Final Prepositions per 1,000 Prepositions in Different Registers

Source of data: Biber 1988.

Thus, there is a notable difference between speech and writing with respect to sentence-final prepositions.

As a second, more striking, example of grammatical variation across registers, examine this brief passage of *legalese*.

> Upon request of Borrower, Lender, at Lender's option prior to full reconveyance of the Property by Trustee to Borrower, may make Future Advances to Borrower. Such Future Advances, with interest thereon, shall be secured by this Deed of Trust when evidenced by promissory notes stating that said notes are secured hereby.

This passage illustrates several syntactic features characteristic of legalese:

1. Frequent use of passive structures: *shall be secured, are secured*
2. Preference for repetition of nouns instead of pronouns: *Lender/at Lender's option, promissory notes/said notes, Future Advances/Such Future Advances*
3. Variable omission of indefinite and definite articles: *Upon request, of Borrower, to Borrower, Lender, at Lender's, by Trustee*

Semantic Markers of Register

A given word form often carries different meanings in different registers. Consider the word *notes*. As used in the legalese passage above, it means promissory note, or IOU. In its everyday meaning, *note* refers to a brief, informal written message (and it may have other senses, such as a musical note); the point is simply that *note* carries a sense specific to legalese. Among words carrying one sense in everyday use but a different sense in legal register are these.

Expressions Carrying a Distinctive Sense in Legalese

to continue	hearing	sentence
to alienate	action	rider
to serve	executed	motion
save	suit	reasonable man
party	note	consideration

Not only lawyers but also some of their clients may give specialized meanings to words. Criminal jargon contains many words and expressions that are in common use but carry a different meaning when used in the context of criminal behavior. The following lists are illustrative.

General Criminal Jargon

mob	sing	bug
hot	rat	bird cage
fence	racket	slammer
sting	a mark	joint ('prison')

Drug World Jargon

crack	pot	downer
coke	grass	speed
snow	toot	pusher
rock	high	dealer
dime	down	joint ('marijuana cigarette')

Each of these expressions bears one sense in ordinary situations but a different sense in the underworld. While the words carry specialized meanings when used in such specific speech situations, they do not constitute separate registers with their own phonological, morphological, grammatical, and pragmatic markers. But they do index a social situation by drawing on characteristics of wider social situations such as informality and conversation, while at the same time relying on specialized words or words with situation-specific meanings.

Slang The vocabulary sometimes used in situations of extreme informality is called **slang**. Like jargon, slang functions as the lexical part of a highly informal register, such as conversation, instant messaging, or texting. It is sometimes said that slang signals rebellious undertones or an intentional distancing of its users from certain mainstream values, and it is certainly popular among teenagers and college students. But its use isn't limited to those groups, and by no means does it always signal rebellion or rejection of mainstream values. Slang has some of its wellsprings in specialized groups of all sorts, from physicians and computer "hackers" to police officers and stockbrokers. But, fundamentally, it is the characteristic vocabulary of highly informal usage.

While slang may change as quickly as some clothing fashions, the fact that there are slang dictionaries suggests that some slang expressions lead longer

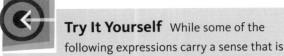

Try It Yourself While some of the following expressions carry a sense that is not slang, each also carries a slang sense in extremely informal situations. Provide a slang sense for each term: the nouns *skinny*, *cougar*, *hunk*, *buzz*, *nerd*, *wuss*, and *tube*; the verbs *veg out*, *wig out*, *party*, and *nuke*; the adjectives *awesome*, *cool*, and *clueless*; the directives *get a life*, *get a clue*, and *get real*; and the exclamation *Not!*

lives. These examples from the dust jacket of a slang dictionary are illustrative of relatively recent slang: *awesome, bells and whistles, cover your ass, designer drug, dork, kick ass, netiquette, pocket pool, puzzle palace, spam, tits and zits,* and *whatever!* The effectiveness of slang depends crucially on the circumstances of its use. In an appropriate situation, anyone of any age and any social standing can legitimately use slang.

Just as informal clothing can extend its welcome from informal circumstances into somewhat more formal circumstances, so slang expressions often climb up the social ladder, becoming acceptable in more formal circumstances. The words *mob* and *pants* are among many that were slang at an earlier period of their history but can now be used in relatively formal circumstances. As words become established in more formal circumstances, they lose their status

College Slang: The Top 20

In *Slang and Sociability*, Connie Eble reports the top slang expressions used by students at the University of North Carolina between 1972 and 1993. Which of them are still in use on your campus? Have any gone completely out of use, so far as you know, or have any changed their meaning? Can you suggest current alternatives in use on your campus?

sweet	'excellent, superb'	*chill/chill out*	'relax'
slide	'easy course'	*blow off*	'neglect, not attend'
bag	'neglect, not attend'	*killer*	'excellent, exciting'
jam	'play music, dance, party'	*scope*	'look for partner for sex or romance'
wasted	'drunk'	*clueless*	'unaware'
diss	'belittle, criticize'	*pig out*	'eat voraciously'
bad	'good, excellent'	*crash*	'go to sleep'
cheesy	'unattractive, out of fashion'	*hook (up)*	'locate a partner for sex or romance'
buzz/catch a buzz	'experience slight intoxication'	*tool*	'socially inept person'
trip (out)	'have a bizarre experience'	*cool*	'completely acceptable'

as slang, and newer slang terms may replace them. Among the slang terms illustrated on the dust jacket of the dictionary mentioned above is *emoticon*. Since 1995, when the dictionary was published, *emoticon* has become the standard term for facial glyphs used to indicate emotions in emails and certain other contexts. Such a rise up the social ladder is far from uncommon, but some slang expressions endure *only* in informal circumstances. *Bones* meaning 'dice' was used by Chaucer in the fourteenth century and remains marked in dictionaries today as informal or slang.

Jargon Specialist terms used by groups with shared specialized interests when engaged in activities surrounding those interests, including talk about them, are called jargon. **Jargon** is the specialized vocabulary associated with professions such as medicine, finance, and engineering and with activities such as sports, music, and computing. Unlike slang, jargon isn't limited to situations of extreme informality but may be used wherever professionals interact with one another (and sometimes with others). **Argot** is another term associated with "professional" language or activities, but *argot* tends to suggest the language of underground or criminal activities.

Because jargon consists of terms that are used elsewhere in a different sense or perhaps not used elsewhere at all, discourse that deals with specialized topics and displays jargon may perplex the uninitiated. Here's a sentence from a *Los Angeles Times* story about a baseball game. If you're familiar with the sport, the meaning of the sentence will be transparent, but otherwise you're not likely to understand it despite its straightforward and ordinary grammatical structure:

Try It Yourself Besides the baseball jargon noted in the nearby discussion, identify six additional terms (including nouns and verbs) with senses particular to baseball in the short illustrative sentence. On the basis of your familiarity with baseball or because you are unfamiliar with the sport, you should be able to identify the jargon.

> The momentum carried them to load the bases in the bottom of the sixth on two walks and an error, but Suppan struck out Jose Valentin and had Chavez fly to center to end the inning.

The newspaper story contains plenty of baseball jargon, including the nouns *plate, pitch, curveball, fastball, changeup, swing, hit, run, out, home run, left fielder, baseman, starter, closer, stand-in, runner, reliever, warning track,* and *pocket,* as well as the verbs *tied, doubled, pitched, singled,* and *homered.* For baseball fans, such jargon is easy to understand; for others, it can be utterly opaque.

Similarities and Differences Between Spoken and Written Registers

Although it is sometimes said that writing is simply speech written down—visual as distinct from audible language—writing and speaking ordinarily serve different purposes and have highly distinctive linguistic characteristics. Conversation is not a written register, of course, but it can be represented in novels and screenplays. Nor are legal contracts ordinarily spoken. Imagine how the words and syntax of a handwritten last testament would differ from one made by a person who leaves a will or last testament by speaking on a camcorder. Or consider the linguistic differences between a note stuck on a refrigerator door and the same basic message spoken to someone face-to-face. You'll quickly recognize that speaking and writing are not mirror images of each other.

1. **Oral communication can exploit intonation and voice pitch to convey information**. Face-to-face communication can also utilize gestures, posture, and physical proximity between participants. In writing, the only channels available are words and syntax, supplemented by typography and punctuation. In speaking, communication is possible on multiple channels simultaneously. We can criticize someone's personality in a seemingly objective manner while expressing with intonation or body language how much we greatly admire the person, or vice versa. In writing, much more must be communicated lexically and syntactically, although there are ways of achieving ironic and sarcastic tones that enable addressees to read "between the lines."

2. **Speech and writing differ in the amount of planning that is possible**. Most written registers allow time for composing and revising. But pausing to find just the right word in a highly interactive conversation can test your interlocutor's patience and cost you the floor. The difference in the available time for planning and editing in written registers produces characteristic syntactic patterns that are difficult to achieve under the real-time or "online" processing constraints imposed in spontaneous speech. Written registers typically show a more specific and varied vocabulary, in part because writers have time to choose their words carefully (or even consult a thesaurus). Of course, not every written register is more planned than every spoken register. Academic lectures and job interviews may reflect some characteristics of planned discourse more common with writing. On the other hand, some types of writing are produced with relatively little planning, and the language of an email note typed in a hurry is likely to be quite speechlike.

3. **Speakers and addressees often stand face-to-face, whereas writers and readers ordinarily do not**. In face-to-face interactions, the immediacy of the interlocutors and the contexts of interaction allow them to refer to themselves (*I think*, *you see*) and their own opinions and to be more personal in their interaction. By contrast, the contexts of writing limit the degree to which written expression can be personal. But we wouldn't want to overgeneralize. Consider, for example, a personal letter and a face-to-face friendly conversation. People may feel they have a right to be equally personal in both

contexts. An impersonal stance is thus a feature of only some written registers, as a personal stance is a feature of only some spoken registers.

4. **Written registers tend to rely less on the context of interaction than spoken registers do.** Writing is more independent of context. In spoken registers, expressions of spatial deixis (such as demonstrative pronouns like *this* and *that*) and temporal deixis (like *today* and *next Tuesday*) can be understood with reference to the here and now of the utterance. By contrast, in writing, the lack of a shared environment may make such expressions opaque or confusing. To which day would *today* refer in an undated written text? And to what would *this* refer when found in a printed document? Like other distinctions among registers, reliance on deictic expressions does not constitute an absolute difference between speech and writing. In telephone conversations, for example, you cannot say *this thing* (referring to something in the speaker's environment) without risking confusion. In contrast, you can leave a written note on the kitchen table that reads *Please don't eat this!*—provided the referent of *this* is obvious from what lies near the note; an author of a textbook can reliably refer to *this page* or *this sentence*.

There are many ways in which spoken and written registers differ. But when we examine the differences, we don't find an absolute dichotomy between them. For example, not many words could occur only in speech or only in writing, even though certain words may occur more frequently in one mode or the other. Most written registers tend to be more formal, more informational, and less personal. Along a personal/impersonal continuum, the type of writing found in biographies falls toward the impersonal end, while informal conversation tends toward the personal end. But personal letters may be close to conversation in their linguistic character, whereas instant text messages, though written, exhibit some characteristics of speech. Writing and speaking thus do not form a simple dichotomy, and to describe their differences we must observe *which* written register and *which* spoken register is being considered. With all language choices, the situation of use is the *most* influential factor in determining linguistic form.

Two Registers Compared

To illustrate the linguistic character of different registers, let's examine excerpts from two kinds of text, both biographical. The first comes from a Pulitzer Prize–winning biography of Harry S. Truman and the second from an interview with Truman. The first is thus a written text, the second a transcribed spoken text.

In 1945 Truman had been vice-president for only a few months when President Franklin D. Roosevelt died in office. In the first passage, biographer David McCullough, reporting events surrounding Truman's preparing to address the American people about a nationwide steel workers strike, takes the occasion to introduce a staffer who worked on Truman's address.

Written Biography of Harry S. Truman	Line	Sentence
But the main work, and at Truman's request,	1	1
was done by a rising new star at the White House,	2	
Navy Captain Clark Clifford, who had been posted temporarily	3	
the summer before as assistant to Jake Vardaman,	4	
and then, when Vardaman was removed,	5	
had stepped in as naval aide.	6	
Clifford was thirty-nine years old, over six feet tall,	7	2
broad in the shoulders, slim-waisted, and handsome as a screen actor,	8	
with wavy blond hair and a silky baritone voice.	9	
In his Navy uniform he looked almost too glamorous	10	3a
to be true, or to be taken seriously;	11	
but he was calm, clearheaded, polished as a career diplomat,	12	3b
and, as Truman had quickly perceived, exceedingly capable.	13	
Indeed, Clifford's almost chance presence on the staff	14	4
would prove to be one of the luckiest breaks of Truman's presidency.	15	

The second passage is from a face-to-face interview conducted with Truman by Merle Miller.

Oral Interview with Harry S. Truman	Line	Sentence
Q. What do you consider the biggest mistake you made as President?	1	1
A. That damn fool from Texas that I first made Attorney General	2	2
and then put on the Supreme Court.	3	
I don't know what got into me.	4	3
He was no damn good as Attorney General, and on the Supreme	5	4
Court . . . it doesn't seem possible, but he's been even worse.	6	
He hasn't made one right decision that I can think of.	7	5
And so when you ask me what was my biggest mistake, that's it.	8	6a
Putting Tom Clark on the Supreme Court of the United States.	9	6b
I thought maybe when he got on the Court he'd improve,	10	7
but of course, that isn't what happened.	11	
I told you when we were discussing that other fellow.	12	8a
After a certain age it's hopeless to think people are going to	13	8b
change much.	14	

It's apparent at a glance how strikingly different these passages are. They contain about the same number of words (the biography excerpt 132, the interview exchange 135), but a close examination reveals many differences. For one, their average sentence lengths differ. The biography comprises only four sentences (or, if we count 3a and 3b separately, five), while the interview contains eight sentences. (Although the interviewer represented Truman's spoken words in nine sentences, we twice combined pairs of the transcribed sentences

into single sentences so as to avoid exaggerating the already small number of
sentences.) That means the spoken sentences are strikingly shorter than the
written ones.

Lexicon and Grammar

Another difference between the spoken
and written registers can be seen in the
lexicon of the excerpts. Truman's direct
(and sometimes earthy) vocabulary is
characteristic of conversations, including such relatively informal interviews
as the one quoted, and his language
would likely strike readers of a narra-

Try It Yourself Before you consider
the analysis that follows, examine the two
passages above with some care yourself. Compare
the complexity of the syntax—for example, how
much coordination occurs and whether it coordinates
clauses or phrases. Consider which lexical categories
are favored in each passage (more nouns or pronouns,
adjectives or adverbs?) and whether both passages
use active and passive voice equally. What other
observations can you make?

tive biographical passage as inappropriate except in quoted speech. By the same
token, the biography contains words and phrases that would seem perhaps stiff
or even snooty in an interview. Striking differences in the preferred lexical categories and in syntax are also apparent, as we'll see. Such features—not in isolation but taken together—mark passages as particular kinds of text, particular
registers, reflective of particular speech situations, including the circumstances
of their production.

Vocabulary Truman's spoken language during the interview relies on short
everyday words, ones that are easy to retrieve and produce in the course of real-
time talking: *damn fool, what got into me, no damn good, maybe, when you ask
me, that isn't what happened*. By contrast, a biographer composing text and with
opportunities to reflect on word choice has time to retrieve more semantically
specific words, such as *request, posted, temporarily, perceived, exceedingly*, and
polished—and, if need be, to revise them afterward, an option not available to
speakers reaching for words as they speak.

Lexical Bundles and Repetition Because conversations and interviews rely on
real-time speech production, they take advantage of expressions already spoken and of lexical bundles. Local repetitions are expressions that get echoed
exactly or nearly exactly within a very short space of time. Truman's near
repetition of *and then <u>put on the Supreme Court</u>* (line 3) and *<u>putting</u> Tom Clark
<u>on the Supreme Court</u>* (line 9) exemplifies the pattern; another example is his
saying *my <u>biggest mistake</u>* (line 8), echoing the interviewer's *the <u>biggest mistake</u>
you made* (line 1).

The term *lexical bundle* refers to a group of words that occur frequently together in particular registers and serve common needs of that register. In conversation and informal interviews such as Truman's, several lexical bundles serve
to introduce other thoughts; they offer a ready frame for saying things. Among
lexical bundles occurring frequently in conversations are several that appear in
the interview: *I don't know what* . . . ; *that isn't what* . . . ; *I thought* . . . ; and *I told
you* . . . . Such lexical bundles, which need not be particular kinds of phrases,
stand ready for use as "launchers" of something to follow; they are ready-made

frames for producing fluent speech in real time. Another kind of lexical bundle, not a launcher but a relative clause, can be seen in *that I can think of* (line 7), illustrating how relative clauses can help define or delimit a referent (here, *one right decision*).

Nouns and Pronouns In comparable amounts of text, the written biography contains about thirty nouns, the spoken interview only about half that number. By contrast, the interview exhibits a dozen first-person and second-person pronouns, whereas the biographical excerpt has none and shows fewer third-person pronouns than the spoken interview.

There are other differences in pronominal use as well. In his speaking, Truman uses the demonstrative pronoun *that* as a "sentential" pronoun, referring to an entire clause (not merely a noun phrase, the most common referent of a pronoun): *that isn't what happened* (line 11). Elsewhere, in *that's it* (line 8), *that* is used somewhat vaguely, referring back to *my biggest mistake* or ahead to *Putting Tom Clark on the Supreme Court of the United States* or to both. The biography contains no such examples and, if a vague pronoun were to find its way into a draft version, the author or an editor would likely clarify it at revision.

Prepositions and Prepositional Phrases The biography and the interview have about the same number of prepositional phrases, but the interview contains a sentence-final preposition (*He hasn't made one right decision that I can think of*), a feature that occurs rarely in formal writing of any kind but is relatively frequent in interviews and conversation, as shown in Figure 10.5.

Verbs The excerpt from the interview contains twenty-four verb groups (main verbs with any auxiliaries: *told, would prove, were discussing, are going to change*), twice as many as appear in the biography. Since each verb group represents a clause, the spoken interview contains twice as many clauses as the biographical excerpt. Frequent verbs—thus frequent and shorter clauses for an equivalent number of words—are far more characteristic of spontaneous speech than of planned and edited writing. As to particular verbs, Truman uses several "private" verbs such as *think* and *know*, and his interviewer uses *consider*—verbs that represent a person's internal mental state. Such private verbs are characteristic of conversation and interviews but not of the narrative portions of a biography.

Because speakers in an interview (as in a conversation) face real-time pressure to retrieve words as they speak, speech produced in real time tends to show relatively frequent use of verbs with broad semantic scope (which are apparently easier to retrieve from the internal lexicon). By contrast, registers such as written biographies, whose composition allows time for retrieving semantically more precise verbs, show relatively higher frequencies of verbs with narrower scope. Quite a few of Truman's verbs—*made, put, get, happen*—have broad semantic scope. Even in this short passage, he uses *made* and *got* twice each (*that I first made*; *he hasn't made*;

Try It Yourself In the biographical passage, identify four instances of the auxiliary verb *be* used as part of a passive verb structure, and note whether each is a *by*-passive or an agentless passive. Then try to explain the function of including or omitting the *by* phrase in each of the passive structures.

what got into me; he got on the Court) and *put* (*then put on the Supreme Court*) instead of, say, *nominated* or *appointed*.

One feature of the written biography is its use of passive voice verbs (*was done, had been posted, was removed, to be taken*), which number a third of all the verbs in the passage. By contrast, the spoken interview contains no passive voice verbs. This difference in our excerpts mirrors a more general contrast between active and passive verbs in written and spoken registers.

The interview concerns the years of Truman's presidency, as the preponderance of past-tense verbs reflects. Among its two dozen verb groups, more than half are in the past-tense (including *made, put, got, was, thought, happened, told*), while most of the present-tense verbs refer to the ongoing interaction between Truman and his interviewer or to Truman's own thought processes in the course of the interview: *when you ask, I don't know, I can think*. The biographical passage, entirely narrative, contains past-tense verbs almost exclusively. There are also striking differences in verb *aspect* (see Chapter 6), but we do not address aspect here.

Try It Yourself In the biographical passage, identify an example of four conjoined adjective phrases other than those in the series of five noted in our discussion. Can you identify any conjoined adjective phrases in the interview? What do you make of that difference?

Adverbs Truman uses adverbs for reference to time sequencing (*first, then*) and as hedges to indicate his stance toward what he is saying, as with *of course* and *maybe*. He uses the emphatic adverbs *damn* and *even* (*damn good, even worse*). In the biographical passage, adverbs refer to time sequencing (*before, then*), as in the interview, and also serve as emphatics (*too, exceedingly*) and hedges (*almost* in lines 10 and 14). Only the biographical passage exhibits manner adverbials (*temporarily, seriously, quickly*).

Coordination and Subordination The interview shows several examples of conjoining, using the conjunctions *and* and *but*, chiefly to link clauses, as in lines 5, 6, and 8. The biographical passage shows a preference for conjoining phrases rather than clauses, including noun phrases (*wavy blond <u>hair</u> and a silky baritone <u>voice</u>*), adjective phrases (*thirty-nine years <u>old</u>, over six feet <u>tall</u>, <u>broad</u> in the shoulders, <u>slim-waisted</u>, and <u>handsome</u> as a screen actor*), and verb phrases (*had been posted . . . and . . . had stepped aside* and *to <u>be</u> true, or to <u>be taken</u> seriously*).

By contrast, the biographical passage contains several subordinate clauses: a relative clause starting in line 3 (*who had been posted . . .*); adverbial clauses in lines 5 (*when Vardaman was removed*) and 13 (*as Truman had quickly perceived*); and the conjoined complement clauses after *glamorous* in line 10 (*to be true, or to be taken seriously*). The interview also contains several subordinate clauses, including those in lines 4, 8, 10, 12, and 13. Among other subordinate clauses are those that complement the verb *think* in lines 10 and 13. In both cases, the subordinator *that* has been omitted, rendering *I thought [that] maybe . . . he'd improve* and *it's hopeless to think [that] people are going to change much*. Omission of the complementizer *that*—especially after the verb *think* and a few others—is very frequent in conversation and informal interviews and relatively uncommon at all in academic prose and the kind of writing represented in our biographical excerpt. The excerpt happens not to have any possible examples of complementizer *that*-omission. (We are not addressing relative clauses in the interview, where *that* is sometimes omitted, as in line 1, but not invariably, as in line 7).

Syntactic Shortening and Syntactic Incompleteness Syntactic shortening is a well-known linguistic feature, and it is particularly common in conversation and certain other kinds of interaction, including interviews. In answer to the interviewer's question in line 1, Truman does not offer a complete sentence but only a noun phrase, albeit a noun phrase containing a relative clause. Similarly, Truman's utterance in line 9 (*Putting Tom Clark on the Supreme Court of the United States*) is not a complete sentence (although our considering that phrase as a possible part of the preceding utterance could lead to a different syntactic analysis).

Questions Almost too obvious to mention, the interview contains a question (as interviews must), a syntactic structure that would be uncommon in a biography except in quotations. Strikingly, though, in his reply Truman uses the syntax of a direct question (*When you ask me <u>what was my biggest mistake</u>*), rather than an indirect question (*When you ask me <u>what my biggest mistake was</u>*). His repetition of the form of the question in his answer is not uncommon in conversation and contributes to an impression of informality.

Phonology

We can't make straightforward comparisons of pronunciation because only the interview is speech-based. Nor do we have a phonetic transcription of Truman's words, but the interviewer's transcribed text suggests that Truman, like most speakers, exhibited frequent phonological contraction during the interview. Instead of full forms like *do not* and *has not*, the excerpt exhibits eight contracted forms: *don't, doesn't, isn't, hasn't, he's, he'd, that's,* and *it's.* The biographical excerpt maintains (line 3) the full form *who had* rather than *who'd*, the only possible contraction in the excerpt. (Figure 10.4 shows the relative frequency of contractions in various registers, confirming the patterns in our excerpts.)

Comparing Registers

No single feature identifies the registers our excerpts exemplify. Instead, features occurring in combination characterize the first passage as a planned and revised written biography or narrative and the second as a spoken face-to-face interview produced in real time. Truman's style is so casual that it suggests conversation more than a formal interview, perhaps the result of the interviewer's having spent several months with him, morning and afternoon. With the passing days and an increased familiarity between Truman and the interviewer, the interview came to resemble conversation between acquaintances or friends.

We have now seen some of the ways in which linguistic features differ from one speech situation to another and thus help characterize the respective registers. We've seen that often there is more of one feature in a given register than in another, and occasionally a feature occurs in (or is absent from) one register exclusively or almost exclusively, as with contractions. Sometimes the same linguistic form occurs in more than one register but with different meanings or uses, as we saw for example with coordination.

COMPUTERS AND THE STUDY OF REGISTER VARIATION

In the field of artificial intelligence, in expert systems, and in a number of critically important high-tech fields today, the role of registers is crucial. The reasons are complex. Consider the different patterns of syntax and vocabulary across registers that any system would need to master, such as information given in the form of headlines or medicalese or legalese or conversation. Think of it this way: if your corpus contained nothing but writings from newspapers but failed to distinguish among the distinctly different kinds of newspaper texts (reportage, personal ads, editorials and editorial letters, advertising, cartoons, sports commentary, business analysis, stock market and weather reports, and so on), it would have to be immeasurably more complicated than would a set of individual systems designed to handle various registers one by one.

It would be difficult to overestimate the importance of computers to the study of register and register variation. Compilers of corpora have always been mindful of the importance of sorting texts into registers. (In effect, this means designating each text as belonging to a particular register.) Since so much study of registers has been quantitative, large-scale corpora help ensure reliability and validity, although the design of a corpus is critically important in establishing validity. Earlier we saw that the Brown and LOB corpora of English ran to about 1 million words each. By today's standards, those are not big corpora. Although even the British National Corpus is not the biggest corpus in the world, it has more than one hundred million words. According to information provided at the BNC website,

> The Corpus occupies about 1.5 gigabytes of disk space—the equivalent of more than a thousand high capacity floppy diskettes.

To put these numbers into perspective, the average paperback book has about 250 pages per centimeter of thickness; assuming 400 words a page, we calculate that the whole corpus printed in small type on thin paper would take up about ten metres of shelf space. Reading the whole corpus aloud at a fairly rapid 150 words a minute, eight hours a day, 365 days a year, would take just over four years.

Some of the research findings reported in this chapter, with its emphasis on quantitative assessments of corpora, have relied on computers. Leaving aside the tasks of their physical creation on paper, the data in several tables and figures were generated without computers, such as Figure 10.2, which reports the frequency of *-ing* pronounced as /ɪŋ/ among males and females in Los Angeles. But for other data, computers were needed, at least in a practical sense. Identifying some features would be utterly straightforward, given a tagged corpus. In the straightforward category we can include nouns, prepositions, demonstrative pronouns, private verbs, and so on. Depending on the extent of the tagging, other categories could be identified, such as past-tense verbs, but if the corpus weren't tagged for tense, an algorithm would have to be specified to instruct the computer what to look for. Algorithms would also be necessary to identify such structures as sentence pronouns and sentence-final prepositions. Some algorithms would prove particularly tricky to design. Think about the nature of an algorithm that would instruct a computer how to identify *that* omissions, as in *She said he tried* rather than *She said that he tried*. After all, it's one thing to write an algorithm that identifies a feature that is present, but identifying a feature that is not present is more challenging. ∎

Summary

- Three principal elements determine each *speech situation*: setting, purpose, and participants.
- Topic and location are part of *setting*.
- Activity type and goals are part of *purpose*.

- With respect to *participants*, it is not only the people themselves who influence language form but also the roles they are playing in that speech situation.
- As we wear different clothing for different occasions and different activities, so we generally do not speak the same way in court, at dinner, and on the soccer field.
- In multilingual communities, different speech situations call sometimes for different languages and sometimes for different varieties of the same language.
- *Registers* are language varieties characteristic of particular speech situations. Registers are sometimes also called *styles*.
- The set of varieties used in a speech community in various speech situations is called its *linguistic repertoire* or its *verbal repertoire*.
- The linguistic repertoire of a monolingual community contains many registers, which differ from one another in their linguistic features either in an absolute sense or, usually, in a relative sense.
- Each register is characterized by a set of linguistic features, not by a single feature.
- The sum total of such features (lexical, phonological, grammatical, and semantic), together with the characteristic patterns for the use of language in a particular situation, determines a register.
- Because register or style varieties within a language draw on the same grammatical system, the differential exploitation of that system to mark different registers occurs not in absolute but in relative terms.
- Writing differs from speaking in a number of fundamental ways, but the linguistic differences between the two *modes* are not absolute.
- Spontaneous spoken language relies heavily on lexical bundles and local repetition of expressions to achieve fluency.

What Do You Think? REVISITED

- *Michael and fictional dialogue.* Not many people have had occasion to read a transcript of actual speech, and fewer still have transcribed an ordinary recorded conversation. Given the spontaneous character of conversation, speakers often need to search for words and sort out their syntax to convey what they intend. They sometimes wander down syntactic dead ends and have to backtrack. For Michael, "natural" may simply mean dialogue that seems genuinely colloquial and doesn't appear stiff. If he had to read a transcription of an actual conversation (with its hesitations and restarts and *uhms* and *uhs*), he would doubtless grow impatient. To prevent such impatience, novelists scrupulously avoid making their dialogue entirely natural.
- *Nina and slang.* Probably not all Nina's teachers dislike slang and colloquialisms, and it's a safe bet that not all of them dislike them in all situations. But teachers understand that slang is characteristic of extreme informality and probably regard most classroom interactions as relatively formal situations and written essays as an especially formal register. By definition, colloquial expressions characterize spoken

language, and given that language-related school tasks focus chiefly on reading and writing, teachers may discourage "colloquial" expressions in student essays. Language appropriate to an informal conversation may not be appropriate in a written essay.

- *Clarence and contractions.* Contractions are a shortcut and in writing usually represent words as they are commonly spoken in informal situations. Written contractions thus mimic the relaxed tone of conversation. When they're used, say, in friendly letters, they mimic the informality of conversation. By extension, textbooks may aim for a more conversational and engaging tone by using contractions to help create something of an informal, perhaps conversational, tone. In this textbook, an interactive tone is established partly by asking readers to figure things out ("Try it yourself") and answer questions ("What do you think?") and partly by using contractions that help create an informal tone.

- *Uncle Colin's recipe.* Sometimes passed on from cook to cook and written hurriedly on index cards or scraps of paper, family cooks may be inclined to omit unnecessary words, using a kind of telegraphic language for speed and efficiency. It shouldn't be surprising, then, that any omitted words in a recipe would be ones carrying little information and easily restored from context: 'Toast **the** pine nuts in **a** medium skillet. Remove **them** and add 1 tbsp. [tablespoon] **of** oil and garlic. Cook **them for** 4 minutes and drain **the** remaining liquid. Sprinkle **some** salt and pepper inside **the** trout cavity and stuff **it** with **the** spinach mixture. Brush **the** trout with **the** remaining oil.' It's a common, if somewhat old-fashioned, recipe style.   ■

Exercises

Based on English

10-1. Consider the following expressions.

> *Kindly extinguish the illumination upon exiting.*

> *Please turn off the lights on your way out.*

The content of the directive is basically the same in both expressions, but the social meanings differ notably. Identify features that highlight the differences between the two directives; then discuss the impression that each is likely to make and under which circumstances each might be appropriate.

10-2. **a.** List five pairs of terms for body parts or bodily functions, such as *clavicle/ collarbone* or *urinate/pee*, that could mark a distinction between a discussion you were having with a physician, say, and a friend on the same topic.

  b. Rank the words in each set below in order of formality:

  1) prof, teacher, instructor, mentor, educator

  2) guru, mullah, maestro, trainer, coach, don

  c. Are any of the words in (1) or (2) above so informal as to be slang? Explain.

10-3. Collections of campus slang are popular, and gathering and discussing examples can be helpful in understanding aspects of language structure and language use. At the University of Southern California, students of Professor Carmen Silva-Corvalán identified the words below as examples of slang. For each term, indicate whether you hear it used in situations of extreme informality on your campus, identify its lexical category (e.g., noun, adjective), and give a concise definition for any you are familiar with. Note, too, which processes of word formation were employed to create these slang terms (e.g., semantic shift, conversion, blending—see Chapter 2). If you regard any term as geographically limited, explain yourself. As an extension to the exercise, the next time you hear someone use any of these terms over the next week, jot down the full utterance as though you were collecting citation examples for a dictionary of slang, and note whether the speech situation was informal or not.

Ex: *bounce*. Yes, verb 'leave, usually in a quick or abrupt manner'; semantic shift.

cheese
chill
chillax
clutch
dank
hella
ride it
sick
sketch
tight
weaksauce
wingman

10-4. Record about 30 seconds of a radio news report and a television news report (if possible, use the same news item). After transcribing the passages, compare them to see what effect the medium and, in particular, the presence of visuals has on the choice of linguistic forms.

10-5. Here's the continuation to the Truman interview quoted in this chapter; the sentences have been numbered for reference.

Q. (1) How do you explain the fact that he's been such a bad Justice?

A. (2) The main thing is . . . well, it isn't so much that he's a *bad* man. (3) It's just that he's such a dumb son of a bitch. (4) He's about the dumbest man I think I've ever run across. (5) And lots of times that's the case. (6) Being dumb's just about the worst thing there is when it comes to holding high office, and that's especially true when it's on the Supreme Court of the United States. (7) As I say, I never will know what got into me when I made that appointment, and I'm as sorry as I can be for doing it. [*Plain Speaking*, p. 242].

a. Is it clear what *that* refers to in *that's the case* (sentence 5) and *that's especially true* (sentence 6)? If so, what type of constituent does *that* refer to in these instances?

b. What is the name of the linguistic feature you examined in question a above?

c. Identify all instances of *be* as a main verb. How many are there?

d. What is the function of *well* in sentence 2?

e. Wherever possible, supply a noun phrase that would have the same referent as the pronoun *it* in sentences 2, 3, 6 (two instances), and 7. Explain those cases where a noun phrase could not be identified as having the same referent as *it*.

10-6. **a.** Look up the definition of *slang* in a good desk dictionary and, using the definition as a guideline, list as many slang words and expressions as you know for two notions each in (1) and (2) below.

    1) drunk; sexually carefree person; ungenerous with money; sloppy in appearance

    2) sober; chaste person; generous with money; neat and tidy

b. What is it about the notions represented in (1) that makes them more susceptible to slang words and expressions than those in (2)?

c. To the extent you could cite slang terms for the items in (2), do they carry negative or positive connotations?

d. Does the dictionary definition of slang help explain the differential distribution of slang terms in (1) and (2) and the connotations associated with the slang terms in (2)? If so, explain how. If not, revise the dictionary definition to accommodate what you have discovered about the connotations of slang terms.

10-7. Some of the most common words of English (*the, of, and, a, to, it, is, that*) appear in both the biography and the interview, as well as in nearly all other registers of English. But one register in which these words are relatively infrequent is headlines.

a. Identify two other registers in which you can observe a relatively infrequent use of these words.

b. Choose a sample from one of the two registers you've identified or from newspaper headlines, and identify the lexical categories that strike you as occurring with higher frequency than in conversation. Note which lexical categories, if any, occur relatively infrequently.

c. Offer a hypothesis as to why the distribution is as you found it.

d. Examine *of course* in line 11 of the Truman interview. On one level it could be analyzed as a prepositional phrase consisting of the preposition *of* and the noun *course*. If instead you think of it as a compound, what lexical category would it belong to? (*Hint:* Substitute single words for the compound and decide which category the substitutes belong to.)

e. In terms of its distribution with respect to other word classes, determine which lexical category *too* belongs to in line 10 of the biography. Using the same criterion, what is the lexical category of *almost* in the same line? What about *so* in line 8 and *much* in line 14 of the interview?

f. Make a list of the determiners in the biographical passage and a list of those in the interview. Specify the particular word class for each determiner in your list (for example, article, demonstrative).

g. The biography has no examples of *that*, whereas the interview has six: lines 2 (twice), 7, 8, 11, and 12. Identify the word class for each instance of *that*.

h. Give an argument for not categorizing *in* (biography, line 6) as a preposition.

i. The passages contain several compounds (for example, the compound noun *Navy Captain* in the biography, line 3). Identify all the compounds in both passages, and note their lexical categories and the lexical categories of their parts (for example, *Navy Captain* is a noun, comprising a noun and a noun). What similarities exist in the categories of compounds in the biography and the interview? What differences?

j. Examine occurrences of *to* in the biography (lines 4, 11, 15) and the interview (twice in line 13). Which, if any, is a preposition? What are the others?

k. Assuming that the passages are typical of their registers, what generalizations can you make about the registers in terms of their exploitation of particular word classes?

10-8. Examine the letters below. The first is a recommendation for a student seeking admission to a master's degree program in linguistics, the second a letter to a magazine, and the third a personal note from a young woman to a female friend in another state. Identify two particular linguistic characteristics of each type of letter.

Letter of Recommendation (182 words)

I have known Mr. John Smith as a student in three of my courses at State, and on the basis of that acquaintance with him, it is my recommendation that he should certainly be admitted to graduate school.

John was a student of mine in Linguistics 100, where he did exceptionally well, writing a very good paper indeed. On the basis of that paper, I encouraged him to major in linguistics and subsequently had the good fortune to have him in two more classes. In one of these (historical linguistics) he led the class, manifestly working more insightfully than the other seventeen students enrolled. In the other course (introduction to phonology), he did less well, perhaps because he was under some financial pressure and was forced to work twenty hours a week while carrying a full academic load. In all three courses, John worked very hard, doing much more than was required.

I recommend John Smith to you without reservation of any kind. He knows what he wants to achieve and is clearly motivated to succeed in graduate school.

Editorial Letter (91 words)

Your story on Afghanistan was in error when it stated that the Russian-backed coup of 1973 was bloodless. As a Peace Corps volunteer in

Afghanistan at the time, I saw the bodies and blood and ducked the bullets. It was estimated that between 1,000 and 1,500 died, but it is hard to get an accurate count when a tank pulls up to the house of the shah's supporters and fires repeatedly into it from 30 feet away, or when whole households of people disappear in the middle of the night.

Personal Letter (142 words)

So, what's up? Not too much going on here. I'm at work now, and it's been so slow this week. We haven't done anything. I hate it when it's so slow. The week seems like it's never going to end.

Well how have you all been? Did you get the pictures and letter I sent you? We haven't heard from you in a while. Mother has your B'day present ready to send and Dan's too, but no tellin' when she'll get around to sending it. How are the kids? Does Dan like kindergarten? Well, Al has gone off to school. I miss him so much. He left Monday to go to LLTI. It's a trade school upstate. You only have to go for two years, and he's taking air conditioning and refrigeration and then he's going to take heating.

10-9. Below are personal ads (slightly adapted) from a weekly newspaper published in Los Angeles. Examine their linguistic characteristics and answer the questions that follow.

1) Aquarius SWM, 33, strong build, blue eyes. You: marriage-minded, bilingual Latin Female 23–30, children ok.

2) Busty, brilliant, stunning entrepreneur, 40s (looks 30). Seeks possibly younger, tall, handsome, caring SWM, who respects individuality. Someone who lives the impossible dream, financially secure, good conversation, for relationship, n/s.

3) SWM, 28, attractive college student, works for major US airlines, enjoys traveling. Seeks Female, 23–32, humorous and intelligent for world-class romance and possibly marriage.

4) English vegetarian. SWM, 31. Sincere, sensitive, original, thinking, untypical, amusing, shy, playful, affectionate professional. Seeking warm, witty, open-minded WF, under 29, to share my life with.

5) Slim, young, GWM, straight appearance, masculine, athletic, healthy, clean-shaven, discreet. Seeks similar good-looking WM, under 25, for monogamous relationship.

6) Very romantic SBM, 24, college educated. Seeks wealthy, healthy and beautiful Lady for friendship and maybe romance. Phonies and pranksters need not apply.

7) Hispanic DF, petite but full of life, likes sports, dancing, traveling, looking for someone with same interests, 30+, race unimportant.

8) Evolved, positive thinking, spiritual, affectionate, honest, handsome, healthy, secure, 36, 6', 160#, blue-eyed, unpretentious, unencumbered, professional. Seeking counterpart, soul mate, marriage, family.

    a. Compared to conversation, which lexical categories are very frequent in the ads? Which ones are particularly rare?

    b. Identify eight characteristic linguistic features of personal ads. They may be features of syntax, morphology, vocabulary, abbreviation conventions, and so on.

    c. List the verbs in all the ads, and identify their grammatical person (first, second, third) and number (singular, plural) where possible. (*Hint*: Supply the pronoun that would serve as subject of each verb in order to determine person and number.)

    d. Choose one of the ads and attempt to write it out fully in conversational English solely by supplying additional words; keep the word order and word forms of the original ad.

    e. On the basis of your attempt, what indication is there that the ads represent a reduced or abbreviated form of conversational English? If you judge the ads not to be reductions of the sentences of conversational English, what explanation can you offer for the form of their sentences?

    f. Which linguistic features of personal ads strike you as conventionalized to the point of requiring previous knowledge of the register in order to understand it?

10-10. Examine a current issue of your campus newspaper and identify as many different registers as you can find in it (for example, editorials and movie reviews). Choose a passage from one register and list eight linguistic features that contribute by their high frequency to the characterization of that register; provide an example of each feature from your passage.

10-11. Headline styles vary somewhat across newspapers and other sources. Consider the linguistic characteristics of the headlines below, selected from *The New York Times* (online edition) in the summer of 2010. Identify all the prepositions and adjectives. Identify any adverbs. (Review Chapter 2 if necessary so as to distinguish between adjectives and nouns used attributively—that is, preceding other nouns.) What is noteworthy about the use of determiners? What accounts for the difference between the relative lack of determiners and the relatively high frequency of prepositions? Can you offer an explanation for which lexical categories predominate in these headlines? What tense do these verbs exhibit: *rules, is, cites,* and *faces*? In which headlines are other tenses used? Do any of the headlines lack verbs altogether? What do you find noteworthy about the use of auxiliary verbs in 5, 8, 10, 24? Rewrite the following examples as though they were complete sentences within the article captioned by the headline: 2, 3, 15, 17, 21, 22, and 25.

    1) U.S. Judge Rules Against Obama's Stem Cell Policy

    2) Graft Dispute in Afghanistan Is Test for U.S.

    3) New Orleans Levees Nearly Ready, but Mistrusted

    4) U.S. General Cites Goals to Train Afghan Forces

    5) Plotting Doubted in WikiLeaks Case

6) Scant Progress in Effort on Racial Killings

7) Egg Industry Faces New Scrutiny After Outbreak

8) Drive to Overhaul Low-Performing Schools Delayed

9) McCain Looks to Complete a Comeback

10) Bush Ties Disputed as Crucial in Ohio Senate Race

11) U.S. Judges Sound Off on Bank Statements

12) Hacker's Arrest Offers Glimpse Into Crime in Russia

13) Nordstrom Links Online Inventory to Real World

14) Yankees Rookie Gives as Good as He Gets

15) Venezuela, More Deadly Than Iraq, Wonders Why

16) In S.E.C. Fraud Suit, Texas Brothers Stand Firm

17) Floods Force Thousands From Homes in Pakistan

18) Students, Welcome to College; Parents, Go Home

19) Florida Candidate Veers From Tea Party's Script

20) In Alaska, Names Not on Ballot Play Roles

21) Scrutiny for Chinese Telecom Bid

22) Crowded Field for Bringing Web Video to TVs

23) As Semenya Returns, So Do Questions

24) Canceled Brooklyn Concert Reinstated

25) Proposed Muslim Center Draws Opposing Protests

Based on English and Other Languages

10-12. Identify several instances of linguistic features that vary across registers in a foreign language you have studied. (Some features may be mentioned in your foreign language textbook, others by your instructor.) Identify at least one phonological feature, one grammatical feature, and several vocabulary items that vary across situations of use. For each feature, specify the situation in which it is appropriate and another in which it would not be. (*Hint:* Consider such differences of situation as writing versus speaking, formal versus informal, fast speech versus careful speech, interaction between you and, say, a teacher versus you and a close friend.)

Especially for Educators and Future Teachers

10-13. Examine a foreign language textbook, and identify any evidence the author has provided that the particular language varies from situation to situation. That evidence may focus on formality versus informality, differences between speech and writing, forms of address for addressees of different social status, slang terms or jargon, or any other linguistic variation that depends on situation of use. What's your assessment about how clear the book is about the importance of such differences in sounding like a native speaker or writing like one?

10-14. Examine the front matter of your dictionary (or the one you recommend to students) and locate the discussion of how it treats slang. (You may have to look under "usage" or "labels" for the discussion.) Compare what the dictionary says about slang in the front matter with the definition it gives in the main body of the dictionary's list of entries. Finally, look up six common slang words your students (or classmates) use and see whether the dictionary notes the slang sense you have in mind and whether that sense is labeled as slang. On the basis of this exercise, would you judge that particular dictionary to be a useful source of information about slang for you? For your students? Who would ordinarily use a dictionary to determine slang meanings? Would students ordinarily use a dictionary to gather information about slang? To what extent should a dictionary attempt to include slang terms and slang senses?

10-15. From one of the registers listed or from another that you deem interesting, choose one that is be appropriate for your students and craft an exercise that would help guide them to collect a small set of examples and analyze them appropriately: texting, instant messages, classified ads, course descriptions in college catalogs, recipes, rental agreements. Exercises 10-9 and 10-10 may serve as examples.

10-16. What implications for teaching ESL/EFL (or any foreign or second language) do you see in the fact that even in a brief passage like the Truman interview so much of the language is already structured either by repetition or by lexical bundling? How important a role should lexical bundles play in creating model conversations for second language learners?

Other Resources

Internet

LISU Website: http://www.CengageBrain.com For users of this textbook. Provides updated Internet links as well as supplemental material for students and instructors. Here you will find interactive learning tools.

British National Corpus: http://www.natcorp.ox.ac.uk/ The home page for the British National Corpus permits you to submit queries and receive sample sentences containing the expression you queried.

American National Corpus: http://www.americannationalcorpus.org/ A project of the Language Data Consortium, ANC aims eventually to match the contents of the British National Corpus. ANC remains under development and welcomes documents of any kind (including student essays and email) created by native speakers of English (visit the website for details). Meanwhile, OANC (O for "open") provides material for research on American English, including transcripts of about 3.2 million words of face-to-face and telephone interactions and about 11.4 million words of written English.

Suggestions for Further Reading

- **Allan Bell. 1991.** *The Language of News Media* (Cambridge, MA: Blackwell). The most accessible in-depth analysis of a single register.

- **Vijay K. Bhatia. 1993.** *Analysing Genre: Language Use in Professional Settings* (London: Longman). A qualitative approach to registers, a next step beyond this textbook.
- **Robert L. Chapman, ed. 1995.** *Dictionary of American Slang*, **3rd ed.** (New York: HarperCollins). A handsome dictionary of slang; also discusses the nature and sources of slang. We have taken examples of slang for illustration in this chapter from dust jackets of this volume.
- **David Crystal & Derek Davy. 1969.** *Investigating English Style* (London: Longman). Contains accessible chapters on the language of conversation, religion, newspaper reporting, and legal documents.
- **Connie Eble. 1996.** *Slang and Sociability: In-group Language among College Students* (Chapel Hill: University of North Carolina Press). Highly informative with a glossary of over 1,000 slang terms.
- **J. E. Lighter, ed. 1997— .** *Random House Historical Dictionary of American Slang* (New York: Random House). A major work of interest to historians of American English and American slang and anyone interested in the history of particular slang terms. Two volumes (through the letter O) have been published.
- **Timothy Shopen & Joseph M. Williams, eds. 1981.** *Style and Variables in English* (Cambridge, MA: Winthrop). Essays treating discourse, literary style, and other styles.

Advanced Reading

Brown and Fraser (1979) surveys the elements of speech situations that can influence language. Joos (1962) is a popular treatment of the notion of linguistic style. The description of switching in Brussels comes from Fishman (1972), while Blom and Gumperz (1972) describes switching between Bokmål and Ranamål. Biber (1988) is a quantitative study of variation in a corpus of spoken and written English, while Biber (1995) discusses textual variation in Korean, Somali, and other languages. O'Donnell and Todd (1991) treats English in the media, advertising, literature, and the classroom. Discussions of other written registers can be found in Ghadessy (1988). Crystal (2006) discusses how email, instant messaging, and chat may be influencing English, while Crystal (2009) tackles the same subject with respect to texting and argues against the widespread view that it is harming the language or young people's mastery of it. Chapters in Biber and Finegan (1994) describe sports-coaching registers, personal ads, and dinner-table conversations, as well as register variation in Somali and Korean. Andersen (1990) describes register use among children. Finegan (1992) discusses the evolution of fiction, essays, and letters over the course of several centuries, along with attitudes toward standardization during that formative period. Lambert and Tucker (1976) reports several social-psychological studies of address forms, principally in Canadian French, Puerto Rican Spanish, and Colombian Spanish. Useful and insightful discussions of French registers can be found in Sanders (1993) and George (1993), while French slang and colloquial usage is abundantly illustrated in Burke (1988). Barbour and Stevenson (1990) contains two chapters that discuss aspects of situational variation in German, and Clyne (1999) touches on situational variation as well. More advanced discussions of register can be found in Duranti and Goodwin (1992), which provides descriptive and theoretical perspectives on the importance of context. Eckert and Rickford (2001) reflects anthropological approaches to style, the traditional sociolinguistic notion of style as attention paid to speech, the important matter of audience design, and functionally motivated situational variation. Accessible chapters on American slang (by Connie Eble), rap and hip hop (by H. Samy Alim), the language of cyberspace (by Denise E. Murray), and talk between doctors and patients (by Cynthia Hagstrom) appear in Finegan and Rickford (2004). The biographical passage about Truman comes from McCullough (1992:502) and the interview passage from Miller (1974:242). Many of the generalizations about spoken and written registers discussed in this chapter are based on information reported in Biber et al. (1999), an exceptionally rich source of information about grammar and the occurrence of linguistic forms across four registers.

References

Andersen, Elaine S. 1990. *Speaking with Style* (London: Routledge).

Barbour, Steven & Patrick Stevenson. 1990. *Variation in German: A Critical Approach to German Sociolinguistics* (Cambridge, UK: Cambridge University Press).

Biber, Douglas. 1988. *Variation across Speech and Writing* (Cambridge, UK: Cambridge University Press).

———. 1995. *Dimensions of Register Variation: A Cross-Linguistic Comparison* (Cambridge, UK: Cambridge University Press).

Biber, Douglas & Edward Finegan, eds. 1994. *Sociolinguistic Perspectives on Register* (New York: Oxford University Press).

Biber, Douglas, Stig Johansson, Geoffrey Leech, Susan Conrad & Edward Finegan. 1999. *Longman Grammar of Spoken and Written English* (Harlow, UK: Longman).

Blom, Jan-Petter & John J. Gumperz. 1972. "Social Meaning in Linguistic Structure," in John J. Gumperz & Dell Hymes, eds., *Directions in Sociolinguistics* (New York: Holt), pp. 407–34.

Brown, Penelope & Colin Fraser. 1979. "Speech as a Marker of Situation," in Klaus Scherer & Howard Giles, eds., *Social Markers in Speech* (Cambridge, UK: Cambridge University Press), pp. 33–62.

Burke, David. 1988. *Street French: How to Speak and Understand French Slang* (New York: John Wiley).

Crystal, David. 2006. *Language and the Internet*, 2nd ed. (Cambridge, UK: Cambridge University Press).

———. 2009. *Txtng: The Gr8 Db8* (Cambridge, UK: Cambridge University Press).

Clyne, Michael G. 1999. *The German Language in a Changing Europe* (Cambridge, UK: Cambridge University Press).

Coupland, Nikolas. 2007. *Style: Language Variation and Identity* (Cambridge, UK: Cambridge University Press).

Duranti, Alessandro & Charles Goodwin, eds. 1992. *Rethinking Context: Language as an Interactive Phenomenon* (Cambridge, UK: Cambridge University Press).

Eckert, Penelope & John R. Rickford, eds. 2001. *Style and Sociolinguistic Variation* (Cambridge, UK: Cambridge University Press).

Finegan, Edward. 1992. "Style and Standardization in England: 1700–1900," in Tim William Machan & Charles T. Scott, eds., *English in Its Social Contexts: Essays in Historical Sociolinguistics* (New York: Oxford University Press), pp. 102–30.

Finegan, Edward & John R. Rickford, eds. 2004. *Language in the USA: Themes for the Twenty-first Century* (Cambridge, UK: Cambridge University Press).

George, Ken. 1993. "Alternative French," in Carol Sanders, ed., *French Today: Language in Its Social Context* (Cambridge, UK: Cambridge University Press), pp. 155–70.

Ghadessy, Mohsen, ed. 1988. *Registers of Written English: Situational Factors and Linguistic Features* (London: Pinter).

Joos, Martin. 1962. *The Five Clocks* (New York: Harcourt).

Labov, William. 2006. *The Social Stratification of English in New York City*, 2nd ed. (Cambridge, UK: Cambridge University Press).

Lambert, Wallace E. & G. Richard Tucker. 1976. *Tu, Vous, Usted: A Social-Psychological Study of Address Patterns* (Rowley, MA: Newbury House).

McCullough, David. 1992. *Truman* (New York: Touchstone).

Miller, Merle. 1974. *Plain Speaking: An Oral Biography of Harry S. Truman* (New York: Berkley Books).

O'Donnell, W. R. & Loreto Todd. 1991. *Variety in Contemporary English*, 2nd ed. (London: HarperCollins).

Sanders, Carol. 1993. "Sociosituational Variation," in Carol Sanders, ed., *French Today: Language in Its Social Context* (Cambridge, UK: Cambridge University Press), pp. 27–54.

Trudgill, Peter. 2000. *Sociolinguistics: An Introduction to Language and Society*, 4th ed. (New York: Penguin).

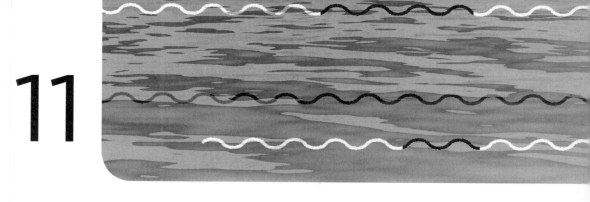

11

Language Variation Among Social Groups: Dialects

What Do You Think?

- Returning from summer camp, your 9-year-old niece Nina reports that one of the counselors "talked funny": he called the TV a *telly*; trucks, *lorries*; dish towels, *tea towels*; and cookies, *biscuits*. What do you tell Nina about who "talks funny" and who doesn't?

- Your friend Daniel, a teacher in Chicago, tells you that after a substitute teacher who grew up in Alabama replaced him one day, the students reported that the sub spoke with a distinct Southern accent. But, they said, the sub claimed he had no accent at all. They wondered how the sub could possibly imagine he didn't have an accent. What explanation would you offer them?

- In a discussion about whether teachers in the United States should know something about the structure and pronunciation patterns of Ebonics, your classmate Evan claims Ebonics is "just broken English" and teachers shouldn't have to study it. What arguments can you make that if Ebonics is "broken," then every variety of English is "broken" when viewed from the perspective of every other variety?

- In the cafeteria, you and some classmates are discussing to what degree male and female college students talk differently. Sammy says they speak the same. What do you tell her?

Language or Dialect: Which Do You Speak?

It is an obvious fact that people of different nations tend to use different languages: Spanish in Spain, Portuguese in Portugal, Japanese in Japan, Somali in Somalia, and so on. Along with other cultural characteristics, language is part of what distinguishes one nation from another. Of course, it isn't only across national boundaries that people speak different languages. In the Canadian province of Quebec, ethnic French-Canadians maintain a strong allegiance to the French language, while ethnic Anglos maintain a loyalty to English. In India, scores of languages are spoken, some confined to small areas, others spoken regionally or nationally.

Among speakers of any widely spoken language there is considerable international variation, as with Australian, American, British, Indian, and Irish English, among others. Striking differences can be noted between the varieties of French spoken in Montreal and Paris and among the varieties of Spanish in Spain, Mexico, and various Central and South American countries. In addition, even casual observers know that residents of different parts of a country speak regional varieties of the same language. When Americans speak of a "Boston accent," a "Southern drawl," or "Brooklynese," they reveal their perception of American English as varying from place to place. These linguistic markers of region identify people as belonging to a particular social group, even when that group is as loosely bound together as are most American regional groups. In countries where regional affiliation may have social correlates of ethnicity, religion, or clan, regional varieties may be important markers of social affiliation. Like the existence of different languages, the existence of regional varieties of a language suggests that people who speak *with* one another tend to speak *like* one another. It's also reasonable to think that people who view themselves as distinct from other groups may tend to mark that distinction in their speech.

A language can be thought of as a collection of dialects that are historically related and similar in vocabulary and structure. Dialects of a single language characterize social groups whose members choose to say they are speakers of the same language.

Social Boundaries and Dialects

Language varies from region to region and also across ethnic, socioeconomic, and gender boundaries. Speakers of American English know that many white Americans and black Americans tend to speak differently, even when they live in the same city. Similarly, middle-class speakers can often be distinguished from working-class speakers. Women and men also differ from one another in their language use. Throughout the world, in addition to regional dialects, there are ethnic varieties, social class varieties, and gender varieties. These constitute what some call **social dialects**, although the word *dialect* is commonly limited to a regional variety.

Distinguishing Among Dialect, Register, and Accent

Dialect and Register The term **dialect** refers to the language variety characteristic of a particular regional or social group. Partly through his or her dialect we recognize a person's regional, ethnic, social, and gender affiliation. Thus the term *dialect* has to do with language *users*, with groups of speakers. In addition, as we saw in the preceding chapter, all dialects vary according to the situation in which they are used, creating what in the previous chapter we called *registers*: language varieties characteristic of *situations of use*. In this chapter we deal with *dialects*—language varieties characteristic of particular social groups. Languages, dialects, and registers are all language **varieties**. What this means is that there is no linguistic distinction between a language and a dialect. Every dialect is a language, and every language is realized in its dialects. From a linguistic point of view, what is called a language and what is called a dialect are indistinguishable.

Dialect and Accent *Dialect* refers to a language variety in its totality—including vocabulary, grammar, pronunciation, pragmatics, and any other aspect of the linguistic system. The terms *language* and *variety* also refer to an entire linguistic system. By contrast, the word **accent** refers to pronunciation only. When we discuss a "Southern accent" or a "Boston accent," we mean the *pronunciation* characteristic of the Southern dialect or the Boston dialect.

How Do Languages Diverge and Merge?

How is it that over time certain language varieties, once similar to one another, come to differ while other varieties remain very much alike? There is no simple answer to that question, but the more people interact, the more alike their language remains or becomes. The less the contact between social groups, the more likely it is that their language varieties will develop distinctive characteristics.

Geographical separation and social distance promote differences in speechways. From the Proto-Indo-European language spoken about 6,000 years ago have come most of today's European languages and many languages of Central Asia and the Indian subcontinent. Not only the Romance languages but the Germanic, Celtic, Greek, Baltic, Slavic, and Indo-Iranian languages have developed from Proto-Indo-European. When you consider that only about 200 generations have lived and died during that 6,000-year period, you can appreciate how quickly a multitude of languages can develop from a single parent language.

Just as physical distance can promote dialect distinctions, social distance can help create and maintain distinct dialects. In part, middle-class dialects differ from working-class dialects because of a relative lack of sustained interactional contacts across class boundaries in American society. African-American English remains distinct from other varieties of American English partly because of the social distance between whites and many African Americans in the United States. A dialect links its users through recognition of shared linguistic characteristics, and speakers' abilities to use and understand a dialect mark them as "insiders" and allow them to identify (and exclude) "outsiders." But as we will see, it is not necessarily the case that varieties differ from one another in a tidy fashion. It may be that two varieties share vocabulary but differ in pronunciation, or share a good deal of their phonology but differ in some other respects. All language varieties change and develop continuously.

Language Merger in an Indian Village

Just as physical and social distance enable speakers of one variety to distinguish themselves from speakers of other varieties, so close contact and frequent communication foster linguistic *similarity*. As varieties of the same language spoken by people in close social contact tend to become alike, different languages spoken in a community may also tend to merge.

Kupwar is a village in India on the border between two major language families: the Indo-European family (which includes the languages of North India) and the unrelated Dravidian family (the languages of South India). Kupwar's 3,000 inhabitants fall into three groups and regularly use three languages in their daily activities. The Jains speak Kannada (a Dravidian language), the Muslims speak Urdu (an Indo-European language closely related to Hindi), and the Untouchables speak Marathi (the regional Indo-European language surrounding Kupwar and the principal literary language of the area). These groups have lived in the village for centuries, and most men are bilingual or multilingual. Over the course of time, with individuals switching back and forth among at least two of these languages, the varieties used in Kupwar have come to be more and more alike. In fact, the grammatical structures of the village varieties are now so similar that a word-for-word translation is possible among the languages because word order and other structural characteristics of the three languages are now virtually identical. This merging is remarkable because the varieties of these languages that are used elsewhere are very different from one another.

Even in Kupwar, though, where the three grammars have been merging, the vocabulary of each language has remained largely distinct. On the one hand, the need for communication among the different groups has encouraged grammatical convergence. On the other hand, the social separation needed to maintain religious and caste differences has supported the continuation of separate vocabularies. As things now stand, communication is relatively easy across groups, while affiliation and group identity remain clear. This is the linguistic equivalent of having your cake and eating it, too.

In the following example sentence, the word order and morphology are relatively uniform across the three Kupwar varieties, but the vocabulary identifies which language is being spoken.

Language Merger in Kupwar

URDU	pala	jəra	kaat	ke	le	ke	a		ya
MARATHI	pala	jəra	kap	un	gʰe	un	a	l	o
KANNADA	tapla	jəra	kʰod	i	təgond	i	bə		yn
	greens	a little	cut	having	taken	having	come	past	I

'I cut some greens and brought them.'

To a remarkable extent the three grammars have merged by combining grammatical elements from each language, while social distinctions have been preserved (and are partly maintained) by differences in vocabulary.

Language/Dialect Continua

In contrast to the situation in Kupwar, the Romance languages, which include Spanish, French, Italian, and Portuguese, have evolved distinct national varieties from the colloquial Latin spoken in their regions in Roman times. Whereas the varieties of language spoken in Kupwar have converged, the language varieties arising from Latin have diverged over the centuries. The reasons in both cases are the same. First, people use language to mark their social identity. Second, people who talk with one another tend to talk *like* one another. A corollary of the second principle is that people not talking with one another tend to become linguistically differentiated.

Today the languages of Europe look separate and tidily compartmentalized on a map. In reality they are not so neatly distinguishable. Instead, there is a continuum of variation, and languages "blend" into one another. The national border between France and Italy also serves as a dividing line between French-speaking and Italian-speaking areas. But the French spoken just inside the French border shares features with the Italian spoken just outside it. From Paris to the Italian border lies a continuum along which local French varieties become more and more "Italianlike." Likewise, from Rome to the French border, Italian varieties become more "Frenchlike."

Swedes of the far south can communicate better with Danish speakers in nearby Denmark using their local dialects than with their fellow Swedes in distant northern Sweden. A similar situation exists with residents along the border between Germany and the Netherlands. Using their own local varieties, speakers of German can communicate better with speakers of Dutch living near them than with speakers of southern German dialects. Examples of geographical dialect continua are found throughout Europe. In fact, while the standard varieties of Italian, French, Spanish, Catalan, and Portuguese are not mutually intelligible, the local varieties form a continuum from Portugal through Spain, halfway through Belgium, then through France down to the southern tip of Italy. There are also a Scandinavian dialect continuum, a West Germanic dialect continuum, and South Slavonic and North Slavonic dialect continua.

In the case of Kupwar, if there were no outside reference varieties against which to compare the varieties spoken in the village, we might be inclined to say that the varieties spoken there were dialects of one language. The residents of Kupwar, however, have found it socially valuable to continue speaking "different" languages, despite increasing grammatical similarity. What counts most in deciding on designations for language varieties and on whether such names represent dialects of a single language or separate languages are the views of their speakers.

National Varieties of English

In this section we briefly examine some national varieties of English, with emphasis on American English and British English.

American and British National Varieties

The principal varieties of English throughout the world are customarily divided into British and American types. British English is the basis for the varieties spoken in England, Ireland, Wales, Scotland, Australia, New Zealand, India, Pakistan, Malaysia, Singapore, and South Africa. American (or North American) includes chiefly the English of Canada and the United States.

Despite the groupings just suggested, certain characteristics of Canadian English are closer to British English, while certain characteristics of Irish English are closer to North American English. And there are many differences between, say, standard British English and standard Indian English. But we can still make a number of generalizations about British-based varieties and American-based varieties, provided we recognize that neither group is completely homogeneous.

Spelling Of the well-known spelling differences between British and American English, some are systematic, others are limited to a particular word. American red, white, and blue are *colours* in Britain, and many other words ending in *-or* in American English end in *-our* in British English. Among idiosyncratic spellings are British *tyres* and *kerb* versus American *tires* and *curb*. Interestingly, Canadians use some British and some American spellings, a reflection of their close historical association with the two countries. For the most part, these spelling differences don't reflect spoken differences. Below are listed some common American ~ British spelling correspondences.

American	British	American	British
labor, favor	labour, favour	tire	tyre
license, defense	licence, defence	curb	kerb
spelled, burned, spilled	spelt, burnt, spilt	program	programme
analyze, organize	analyse, organise	pajamas	pyjamas
center, theater	centre, theatre	check	cheque
judgment, abridgment	judgement, abridgement	ton	tonne
dialed, canceled	dialled, cancelled	catalog	catalogue
installment, skillful	instalment, skilful	czar	tsar

Pronunciation Differences in vowel and consonant pronunciation, as well as in word stress and intonation, combine to create American and British accents. Speakers of both varieties pronounce the vowel of words in the *cat, fat, mat* class with /æ/. For similar words ending in a fricative such as *fast, path,* and *half,* American English has /æ/, while some British varieties have /ɑ:/, the stressed vowel of *father*. Americans pronounce the vowel in the *new, tune* and *duty* class with /u/, as though they were spelled "noo," "toon," and "dooty." Varieties of British English often pronounce them with /ju/, as though spelled "nyew," "tyune," and "dyuty," a pronunciation also heard among some older Americans.

As to consonants, perhaps the most noticeable difference has to do with intervocalic /t/. When /t/ occurs between a stressed and an unstressed vowel, Americans and Canadians usually pronounce it as a flap [ɾ]. As a result, the word *sitter* is pronounced [sɪɾər], and *latter* and *ladder* are pronounced alike. By contrast, speakers of some British varieties pronounce intervocalic /t/ as [t]. As another example, most American varieties have a retroflex /r/ in word-final position in words such as *car* and *near* and also preceding a consonant as in *cart*

and *beard*, whereas some British varieties, including standard British English,
do not. With respect to post-vocalic /r/,
speakers of Irish and Scottish English
follow the American pattern, while
speakers of dialects in New York City,
Boston, and parts of the coastal South
follow the British pattern.

Among differences of word stress,
British English tends to stress the
first syllable of *garage, fillet,* and *ballet*, while American English places stress
on the second syllable. The same is true for *patois, massage, debris, beret,* and
other borrowings from French. In certain polysyllabic words such as *laboratory,*
secretary, and *lavatory* the stress patterns differ, with American English
preserving a secondary stress on the next-to-last syllable.

Try It Yourself Use the IPA symbols
given on the inside front and back covers
of this text to transcribe the word *laboratory* to
represent both British and American pronunciations
with four syllables.

Syntax and Grammar Some noun phrases that denote locations in time or space
take an article in American English but not in British English.

American	British
in the hospital	in hospital
to the university	to university
the next day	next day

Some collective nouns (those that refer to groups of people or to institutions)
are treated as plural in British English but usually as singular in American
varieties. An American watching a soccer game might say *Cornell is ahead by two*,
whereas a British observer might say *Manchester are ahead by two*. Americans rely
more on form than on sense. Thus, speaking of the Los Angeles Angels of Anaheim
baseball team, a writer or sportscaster might say *Los Angeles has won again* or *The
Angels have won again*. In both British and American English, a noun such as *police*
takes a plural verb, as in *The police are attempting to assist the neighbors.*

A further illustration of the grammatical differences between the two varieties is the use of the verb *do* with auxiliaries. If asked *Have you finished the assignment?*, American English permits *Yes, I have*, while British English allows that
and *Yes, I have done*. Asked whether flying time to Los Angeles varies, a British
Airways flight attendant might reply, *It can do.*

Vocabulary There are also vocabulary differences between American and British
English, such as those below.

American	British	American	British
elevator	lift	second floor	first floor
TV	telly	flashlight	torch
hood (of a car)	bonnet	trunk (of a car)	boot
cookies	biscuits	dessert	pudding
gas/gasoline	petrol	truck	lorry
can	tin	intermission	interval
line	queue	exit	way out
washcloth/facecloth	flannel	traffic circle/rotary	roundabout

Try It Yourself In some cases, a word used in Britain is hardly known in the United States. In other cases, the most common British term happens not to be the most common American term. For each of the following, give the ordinary American English equivalent: *fortnight*, *holiday*, *motorway*, *diversion*, *roadworks*, *joining points*, *tailback*, *hire car*, *car park*, *windscreen*, *spanner*.

Regional Varieties of American English

Starting in the 1940s, investigation of vocabulary patterns in the eastern United States suggested Northern, Midland, and Southern dialects. Midland was divided into North Midland and South Midland varieties. Boston and metropolitan New York were seen as distinct varieties of the Northern dialect. Midwestern states such as Illinois, Indiana, and Ohio, which had formerly been thought of as representing "General American," were seen as situated principally in the North Midland dialect, with a narrow strip of Northern dialect across their northernmost counties and a small strip belonging to the South Midland variety across their southern counties. More recent investigations suggest refinements of that scheme, such as those represented in the geographical patterns of Figure 11.1, and the term "General American" has fallen out of favor because it came to mean very little.

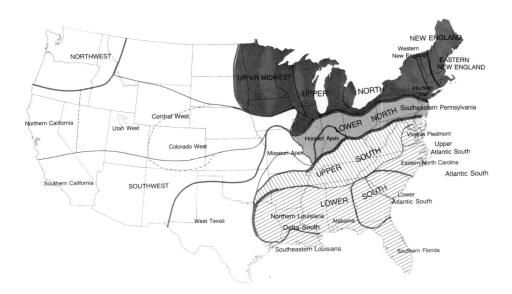

Figure 11.1 Major Dialectic Regions of the USA, Based on Vocabulary

Source: Carver 1987.

Mapping Dialects

To propose a map such as the one in Figure 11.1, dialectologists investigate vocabulary, pronunciation, or grammar. Typically, a researcher with a questionnaire visits a town and inquires of residents what they call certain things or how they express certain meanings. Based solely on regional vocabulary, Figure 11.1 divides the United States into two main dialects (North and South), each divided into Upper and Lower sections, with the West viewed as an extension of the North dialect. The map in Figure 11.1 relies on fieldwork undertaken in the 1960s and 1970s for the *Dictionary of American Regional English*, or *DARE*.

Prior to *DARE*, several linguistic atlas projects were undertaken, part of a project called the Linguistic Atlas of the United States and Canada. Data collection in several regions was completed and the results published, but parts of the project remain incomplete. Still, the data collected provide a useful view of regional variation. To take an example, when atlas investigators asked respondents for the commonly used term for the large insect with transparent wings often seen hovering over water, local terms came to light. Figure 11.2 shows *darning needle* as the most common term in New England, upstate New York, metropolitan New York (including northern and eastern New Jersey and Long Island), and northern Pennsylvania. Elsewhere, other terms predominated: *mosquito hawk* in coastal North Carolina and Virginia, *snake doctor* in inland Virginia, and *snake feeder* along the northern Ohio River in West Virginia, Ohio, western Pennsylvania, and the upper Ohio Valley toward Pittsburgh.

Figure 11.2 shows that not all the terms for 'dragonfly' were neatly distributed. In some areas only a single form occurred, in others more than one. The larger Os on the map in New England indicate that *darning needle* was the only regional term found there. Figures 11.3 and 11.4 show that *mosquito hawk* was virtually the only regional response given in parts of southeast Texas and portions of central Texas, as well as all of Louisiana and Florida, and much of southern Alabama, Mississippi, and Georgia. But *snake doctor* was the favored form in west, north, and northwest Texas, the western half of Tennessee, the northern parts of Alabama and Mississippi, and part of northwestern Georgia. *Snake feeder* occurred occasionally in Oklahoma along the Canadian and Arkansas rivers (which aren't labeled in our figure but can be identified within Oklahoma near the solid triangles of Figure 11.3). Both *mosquito hawk* and *snake doctor* were used in the southern half of Arkansas (in Figures 11.3 and 11.4). *Darning needle*, so popular in New York and New England, occurred too infrequently even to be recorded on these maps of the South. Some respondents were unacquainted with local terms and reported using only *dragonfly*. (If you live in or come from an area represented on the maps but find the terms indicated there unfamiliar, bear in mind that the data were often gathered in rural areas and represent "folk" speech as well as "cultivated" speech. Moreover, some of the interviews took place decades ago, and word usage may have changed in the meanwhile.)

Determining Isoglosses Once a map has been marked with symbols for various features, lines called **isoglosses** can often be drawn at the boundary for the different forms. For example, in Figure 11.5 the four isoglosses traversing the North-Central states of Ohio, Indiana, and Illinois represent the northernmost

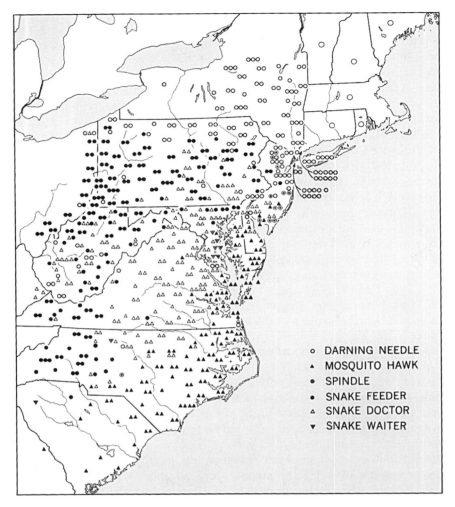

Figure 11.2 Words for 'Dragonfly' in the Eastern States
Source: Kurath 1949.

limits of *greasy* pronounced with a /z/ [grizi], of *snake feeder* as the term for 'dragonfly,' and of two other features.

Figure 11.6 represents seven isoglosses in the Upper Midwest. Three of them mark the southernmost boundaries of Northern features: *humor* pronounced [hjumər] (/hj/ is represented in the map's legend as /hy/); *boulevard* referring to the grass strip between the curb and sidewalk; and *come in (fresh)*, meaning 'to give birth' and (in rural areas) usually said of a cow. The four other isoglosses mark the northernmost boundaries of Midland features: the word *on* pronounced with a rounded vowel (/ɔ/ or /ɒ/, where /ɒ/ is like /ɑ/ but pronounced with lip rounding) instead of an unrounded /ɑ/; the term *caterwampus*, meaning 'askew' or 'awry'; the term *roasting ears* for 'corn on the cob'; and *lightbread* for 'white bread.'

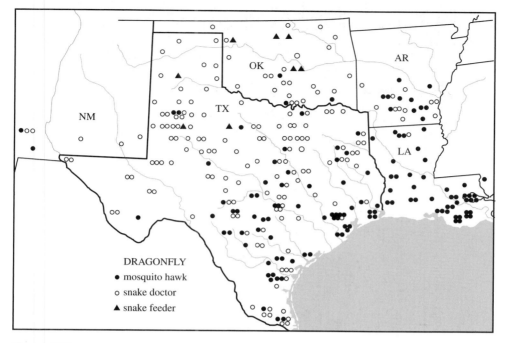

Figure 11.3 Words for 'Dragonfly' in Texas, Arkansas, Louisiana, Oklahoma
Source: Atwood 1962.

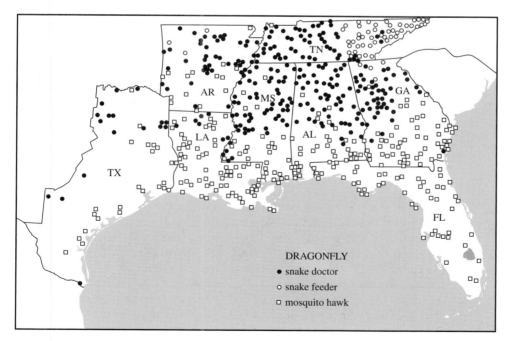

Figure 11.4 Words for 'Dragonfly' in the Gulf States
Source: Pederson 1986.

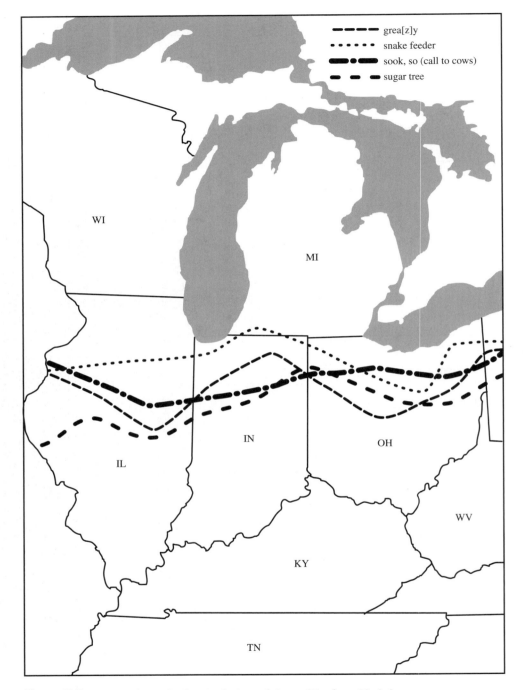

Figure 11.5 Four Isoglosses in the North-Central States (Northern Limits)
Source: Marckwardt 1957.

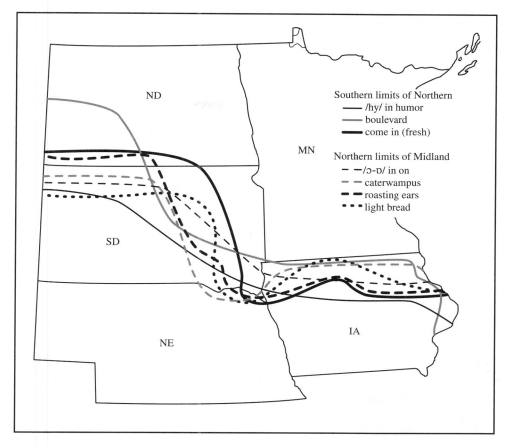

Figure 11.6 Seven Isoglosses in the Upper Midwest
Source: Allen 1973.

Dialect Boundaries

Imagine the isogloss maps stacked on top of one another on a transparency. The result would be a map similar to the one in Figure 11.6 and would show the extent to which the isoglosses from different maps "bundle" together. The geographical limit for the use of a particular word (say, *caterwampus*) often corresponds roughly to the limit for other terms or pronunciations. Where isoglosses bundle, dialectologists draw dialect boundaries. Thus, a *dialect boundary* is simply the location of a bundle of isoglosses. The map in Figure 11.1 is a distillation of dozens of maps similar to those in Figures 11.5 and 11.6.

Speech patterns are influenced partly by the geographical and physical boundaries that facilitate or inhibit communication and partly by the migration routes followed in settling a place. Among the isoglosses of Figure 11.5, the one for /grisi/ versus /grizi/ essentially follows a line (now approximated by Interstate 70)

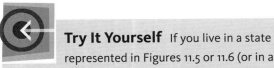

Try It Yourself If you live in a state represented in Figures 11.5 or 11.6 (or in a neighboring state), identify the location of your town or city with respect to one of the isoglosses and determine whether your usual pronunciation of the initial sound in *humor* or the intervocalic consonant in *greasy* is accurately reflected in the figure.

that was the principal road for the westward migration of pioneers during the postcolonial settlement period.

In the western United States, the dialect situation is more complex than in the longer established areas of the East, South, and Midwest. The West drew settlers speaking dialects from various parts of the country. California continues to welcome immigrants from other parts of the country and the world.

Dictionary of American Regional English

The *Dictionary of American Regional English* makes available more information about regional words and expressions throughout the United States than has ever been known before.

Based on answers to more than 1,800 questions asked by field workers who traveled to 1,002 communities across the country, the maps used for exhibiting *DARE*'s findings do not represent geographical space, as most maps do, but population density. Thus the largest states on a *DARE* map are those with the largest populations. As a result, *DARE* maps depict states in somewhat unfamiliar shapes. (To view a *DARE* map with labeled state names, follow the lead given in the "Other Resources" section at the end of this chapter.)

Figure 11.7 shows the distribution of the terms *mosquito hawk* and *skeeter hawk* on a *DARE* map and a conventional map. Along with an occasional occurrence in California and New Mexico, you can see the distribution of these terms through the Gulf states and up the eastern seaboard and appearing occasionally in Minnesota, Wisconsin, Michigan, and a few other states. The name *cruller*, for 'a twisted doughnut,' has a different distribution, as shown in Figure 11.8. *Cruller* is used in the northeast, in New England, New York, New Jersey, Pennsylvania, and so on, as well as in some Great Lakes states and California, but does not occur in Alaska, Washington, Oregon, Nevada, New Mexico, Montana, Wyoming, North Dakota, and Hawaii.

As the result of various regional dialect projects, especially *DARE*, a complex picture of American English dialects emerges, as Figure 11.1 shows. In the figure, the darker the shading of a dialect area, the greater the number of vocabulary items that distinguish it from other dialect areas. As you can see, the farther west you go, the fewer the special vocabulary characteristics that appear. To judge by vocabulary, boundaries for American dialects are better established in the eastern states than in the more recently settled western ones.

Based on the vocabulary findings of *DARE*, the United States appears to have basically North and South dialects, each divided into upper and lower regions as shown in Figure 11.1. The Upper North contains the dialects of New England, the Upper Midwest, and the Northwest, with some lesser-marked dialect boundaries in the Central West and Northern California. The Southwest is also a dialect area, with Southern California having some distinct characteristics. The South is divided into Upper South and Lower South, and each of those has subsidiaries.

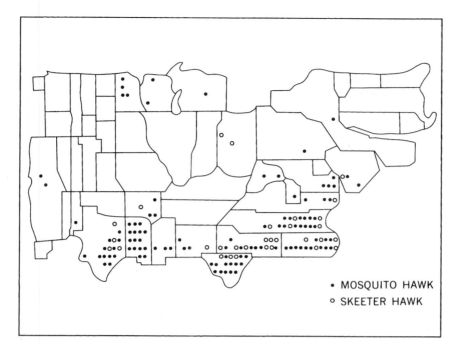

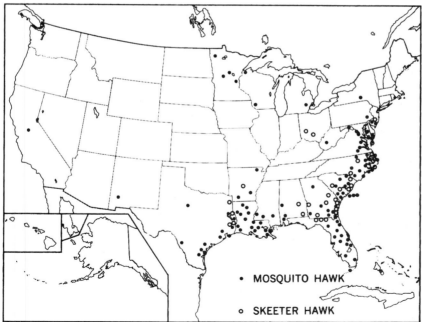

Figure 11.7 Distribution of *Mosquito Hawk* and *Skeeter Hawk* on *DARE* Map
and Conventional Map

Source: *Dictionary of American Regional English*, I, 1985.

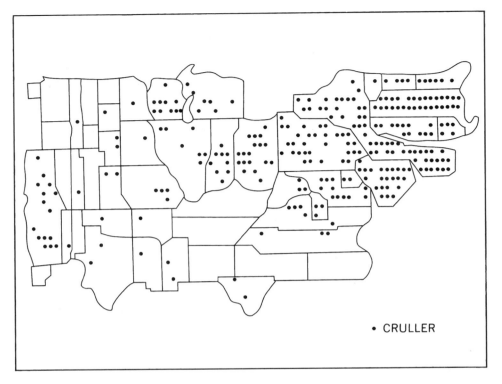

Figure 11.8 Distribution of *Cruller* on a *DARE* Map

Source: *Dictionary of American Regional English*, I, 1985.

The Atlas of North American English

A major investigation of pronunciation in U.S. and Canadian urban areas took place in the 1990s. The Atlas of North American English, or ANAE, is independent of the Linguistic Atlas of North America and Canada and of *DARE* in its aims, methods, and findings. ANAE was created with data from a telephone survey of North American urban centers in a project called Telsur.

On the basis of telephone discussions with respondents who identified themselves as born or raised in the speech community in which they were reached, Telsur combined impressionistic judgments of pronunciation with rigorous acoustic analysis of recorded conversations. Telsur and ANAE focused on vowel sounds, in particular several vowel pronunciations known to be in flux.

Vowel Mergers

Among notable changes taking place in North American pronunciation are mergers of vowels that were formerly separate: /ɑ/ and /ɔ/ in words like *cot* and *caught* and /ɪ/ and /ɛ/ in words like *pin* and *pen*. To distinguish these last two items, many speakers who pronounce them the same call the first a *straight pin* or *safety pin* and the second an *ink pen*.

Cot ~ Caught Merger The traditional pronunciations of *cot* and *caught* have been distinct, the first with the nucleus /ɑ/ and the second with /ɔ/. Because /ɑ/ is a low back vowel and /ɔ/ is a lower-mid back vowel, the merger is often called the **low back merger**. It involves word pairs like *Don* and *Dawn, wok* and *walk,* and *hock* and *hawk.* For the many speakers of American English who don't merge these vowels, /ɑ/ and /ɔ/ are distinct phonemes, and those word pairs are *minimal pairs* (which we discussed in Chapter 4). With the merger of these two phonemes, the number of vowels in the English inventory is reduced, and a good many homophonous pairs may result.

Pin ~ Pen Merger Another merger involves the vowels in word pairs like *pin ~ pen, him ~ hem, lint ~ lent,* and *cinder ~ sender.* For many speakers, these vowels are kept distinct as [ɪ] and [ɛ], but for others they are homophonous and cannot be distinguished in speech. This merger is sometimes called the IN ~ EN merger.

Conditioned and Unconditioned Mergers The merger of /ɑ/ and /ɔ/ isn't limited to specific phonological environments within a word but occurs everywhere. Such an *unconditioned* merger affects all words that contain the sounds, with the result that a vowel contrast is lost. By contrast, the vowels /ɪ/ and /ɛ/ merge only when they precede the nasals /n/ or /m/ but not elsewhere. Speakers who pronounce *pin* and *pen* identically don't merge *pit* and *pet, lit* and *let, whipped* and *wept,* and so on, because these words don't match the phonological environment required for the merger.

We can summarize the discussion of mergers in the chart below.

Name	Vowels	Condition	Examples
cot ~ caught merger	/ɑ/ ~ /ɔ/	unconditioned	*cot ~ caught, hock ~ hawk*
pin ~ pen merger	/ɪ/ ~ /ɛ/	preceding /n/ or /m/	*pin ~ pen, cinder ~ sender*

Vowel Shifts

Other major changes in North American English involve shifting the pronunciation of vowels from one location in the mouth to another. The effect is that a word pronounced with a given vowel is heard by outsiders as having a different vowel. As an example, the word spelled *cod* may be heard as *cad.* You know that vowels can be represented in a chart such as the one on the inside front cover and in Figure 3.4. In addition to the simple vowels in the figure, English has three diphthongs: /aj/ (*my, line*), /ɔj/ (*toy, coin*), and /aw/ (*cow, town*). (In this book, we generally represent other English vowels as simple vowels, or *monophthongs.* Thus, we represent the underlying vowel of *made* as /e/, of *flowed* as /o/, and of *food* as /u/. These vowels are often pronounced as diphthongs and represented as diphthongs in some books, which give their underlying forms as, for example, /ey/, /ow/, and /uw/.)

Northern Cities Shift Across the major cities of the North—including Syracuse, Rochester, and Buffalo in New York, Cleveland and Akron in Ohio, Detroit in Michigan, Chicago and Rockford in Illinois, and Milwaukee and Madison in Wisconsin—a set of vowel shifts is occurring that is remarkable in its

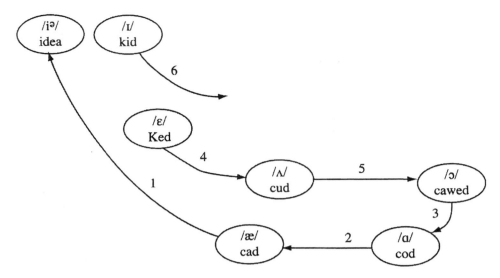

Figure 11.9 Northern Cities Shift
Source: Adapted from Labov 1996.

scope. They constitute the Northern Cities Shift and can be represented as in Figure 11.9. This shift includes Canadian as well as U.S. cities. The shift's characteristics include those given below. (The numbers in parentheses refer to the numbered shifts in Figure 11.9; for simplicity, we don't include shift number 6 in our list.)

1. /æ/ is raised and fronted to [iᵊ]—*man* and *bad* can even sound like the under-scored vowel in *id<u>ea</u>*: [miᵊn], [biᵊd] (1 in figure)
2. /ɑ/ is fronted to [æ]—*cod* sounds like *cad* (2 in figure)
3. /ɔ/ is lowered and fronted to [ɑ]—*cawed* sounds like *cod* (3 in figure)
4. /ɛ/ is lowered and centered to [ʌ]—*Ked* sounds like *cud* (4 in figure)
5. /ʌ/ is backed to [ɔ]—*cud* sounds like *cawed* (5 in figure)

Southern Shift In the South, a different set of vowel shifts is occurring, as represented as in Figure 11.10. This Southern Shift's qualities include the five listed below in which italicized words serve as examples. (The parentheses refer to the numbered shifts in Figure 11.10; for simplicity, we don't include shifts 7 or 8 in our list.)

1. /aj/ is monophthongized to [a]—*hide* sounds like [had] or [haːd] (1 in figure)
2. /e/ is lowered, centralized, and diphthongized to [aj]—*slade* sounds like *slide* (2 in figure)
3. /i/ is lowered, centralized to [ɪ]—*keyed* [ki-əd] sounds like *kid* [kɪ-əd] (3 in figure)
4. /o/ is fronted—*code* and *boat* sound like [kɛᵒd] and [bɛᵒt] (6 in figure)

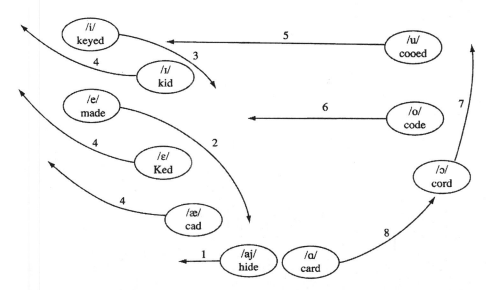

Figure 11.10 Southern Shift
Source: Adapted from Labov 1996.

5. /ɪ/, /ɛ/, /æ/ are raised, fronted, and diphthongized—*kid* sounds like *keyed* ([ki-əd]), *Ted* like *tid* ([tɪ-əd]), *pat* like *pet* ([pɛ-ət]) (4 in figure)

6. /u/ is fronted—*cooed* sounds like "kewl" ([kʲu-əl]) (5 in figure)

It is worth noting the widespread diphthongization of vowels in the South, making some of the illustrative words above possibly misleading for speakers of other varieties. It may be helpful to bear in mind how a Southern linguist characterized this process when he reported the voice of a local restaurant server asking whether he wants "swuheet tuhee with a leeuhd"—sweet tea with a lid.

ANAE Findings

Relying on 439 telephone respondents for whom acoustic analyses have been completed, the Atlas of North American English provides a map of the United States and Canada in which new dialect boundaries are proposed. You can get a clear picture of these results at the ANAE website. Meanwhile, the map in Figure 11.11 (on the following page) suggests the major North American dialect regions, as based on Telsur pronunciation data. The map indicates four main U.S. pronunciation regions: West, North, Midland, and South. Within the North are Inland North and Western New England dialects and within the South are Texas South and Inland South dialects. You'll also note designations for dialects named Mid-Atlantic, New York City (NYC), Eastern New England (ENE), Western Pennsylvania, and others. There are also two pronunciation regions in Canada—one labeled simply Canada and the other Atlantic Provinces.

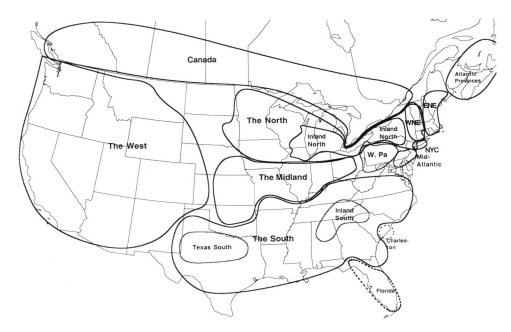

Figure 11.11 Urban Dialect Areas of the United States, Based on Pronunciation

Source: Adapted from Labov 1996.

Below is a table adapted from the ANAE website that indicates some salient characteristics of the pronunciation of some dialects. In keeping with the representation of Figure 11.11, we indicate characteristics of each region as a whole and sometimes of dialects within the region.

NORTH	Less fronting of /o/ than in other areas
Inland North	Northern Cities Shift
Western New England	Less advanced Northern Cities Shift
SOUTH	Monophthongization of /aj/
Inland South	Southern Shift
Texas South	Southern Shift
MIDLAND	Transitional low back merger
	Fronting of /o/
WEST	Low back (*cot* ~ *caught*) merger
	Stronger fronting of /u/ than of /o/
CANADA	Low back (*cot* ~ *caught*) merger
Atlantic Provinces	No low back merger

Additional data on the map are not sufficiently accessible in this black-and-white image to discuss further. Among the information you can glean from the color maps at the website are the fact that the St. Louis Corridor (which isn't marked on Figure 11.11) falls within the Midland region but nevertheless displays the Northern Cities Shift. You can also note that nearly all of Florida lies outside the South region. This is because Florida does not participate in the Southern Shift, although it does display the fronting of /u/ (step 5 in Fig. 11.10) but not of /o/ (step 6 in Fig. 11.10). In Canada, the Atlantic Provinces are conservative in pronunciation and don't (at least yet) participate in the changes characteristic of other parts of Canada such as the low back (*cot* ~ *caught*) merger.

Ethnic Varieties of American English

Just as oceans and mountains separate people and may eventually lead to distinct speech patterns, so social boundaries also promote distinct speechways. Perhaps the most notable social varieties of American English are *ethnic varieties*. Ethnicity is sometimes racial and sometimes not. For example, differences in the speech of Jewish and Italian New Yorkers have been noted, and the variety of English influenced by Yiddish speakers who settled in America is sometimes called "Yinglish." But the social separation that leads to ethnic varieties of language is particularly noticeable in the characteristic speech patterns of many urban African Americans. In Philadelphia and other cities, the speech of African-American residents is becoming increasingly distinct from the speech of white residents.

Such a distinction between social groups is also noticeable in the characteristic speech patterns of other ethnic groups. Spanish-speaking immigrants in Los Angeles, New York, Chicago, Miami, and elsewhere have learned English as a second language, and their English is marked by a foreign accent. The children and grandchildren of these immigrants acquire English as a native language (and many are bilingual), but the native variety of English that many Hispanic Americans speak identifies them as being of Hispanic ancestry or growing up in neighborhoods with children of Hispanic ancestry.

The discussion that follows identifies certain characteristics of African-American English and Chicano English. Both are bona fide varieties of American English like any other regional or social variety. Both have complete grammatical systems overlapping to a great degree with other varieties of English. And, like standard American English, both have a spectrum of registers. While both varieties share many characteristics with other varieties of American English, they also exhibit certain distinctive features and a set of shared features that taken together distinguish each of them from all others.

Like all other social varieties, these two have rules that determine what is well formed and what is ill formed. Rules govern the structures and use of all dialects, and no dialect exists without phonological, morphological, and syntactic rules. All the language universals described in Chapter 7 apply to African-American English and Chicano English as well.

African-American English

Not all African Americans are fluent speakers of African-American English, and not all speakers of African-American English are African Americans. After all, people grow up speaking the language variety around them. In an ethnically diverse metropolitan area like Los Angeles, you can meet teenaged and young adult speakers of African-American English whose foreign-born parents speak Chinese or Vietnamese. The variety of English spoken by these Asian-Americans reflects the characteristic speechways of their friends and of the neighborhoods in which they acquired English. To underscore an obvious but often overlooked fact, the acquisition of a particular language or dialect is as independent of skin color as it is of height or weight.

The history of African-American English is not completely understood, and there are competing theories about its origins and subsequent development. But there is no disagreement concerning its structure and functioning. Like all varieties, it has characteristic phonological, morphological, and syntactic features, as well as some vocabulary of its own. Like all other social groups, speakers of African-American English also share characteristic ways of interacting. In this section we examine some phonological and syntactic features of African-American English, but not lexical or interactional characteristics. It is important to recognize that while it is customary to talk about regional and ethnic varieties of a language in terms of particular features, no variety is simply a set of features. Every social variety represents a rich syntax, phonology, lexicon, and pragmatics, most of which is shared with other varieties of the same language.

Phonological Features We examine four characteristic pronunciation features of African-American English (AAE).

1. **Consonant cluster simplification** Consonant clusters are frequently simplified. Typical examples occur in the words *desk*, pronounced as "des" [dɛs], *passed* pronounced as "pass" [pæs], and *wild* pronounced as "wile" [wajl]. Consonant cluster simplification also occurs in all other varieties of American English. Among speakers of standard English, the consonant clusters <sk> in *ask* and <ld> in *wild* are also commonly simplified, as in "asthem" [æsðəm] for *ask them* and "tole" [tol] for *told*. But consonant cluster simplification occurs more frequently and to a greater extent in African-American English than in other varieties.

2. **Deletion of final stop consonants** Final stop consonants, such as /d/, may be deleted in words like *side* and *borrowed*. Speakers of AAE frequently delete some word-final stops, pronouncing *side* like *sigh* and *borrowed* like *borrow*. This deletion rule is systematically influenced by the phonological and grammatical environment:

   a. Whether a word-final stop consonant represents a separate morpheme (as in the past tense marking of *followed* and *tried*) or doesn't represent a separate morpheme but is part of the word stem (as in *side* and *rapid*). Final [d] is preserved much more frequently when it is a separate morpheme.

   b. Whether word-final stops occur in a strongly stressed syllable (*tried*) or a weakly stressed syllable (*rapid*)—note that the second syllable of *rapid* is not as strongly stressed as the first syllable. Strongly stressed syllables tend to preserve final stops more than weakly stressed syllables do.

c. Whether a vowel follows the stop (as in *side angle* and *tried it*) or a consonant follows it (as in *tried hard* and *side street*). A following vowel helps preserve the stop; in fact, it appears to be the most significant factor in determining whether a final stop is deleted.

3. **Interdental ~ labiodental substitution** Other phonological features are less widespread. For some speakers of AAE, the *th* of words like *both*, *with*, and *Bethlehem* may be realized not as the voiceless interdental fricative /θ/ but the voiceless labiodental fricative /f/, yielding [bof] or [wɪf], for example. Likewise the voiced interdental fricative /ð/ in words like *smooth* or *bathe* and *brother* or *mother* may be realized with the voiced labiodental fricative /v/, yielding [smuv], [bev], [brʌvə], and [mʌvə]. Note too in *brother* and *mother* the absence of word-final /r/, a feature that AAE shares with the English of New York City, eastern New England, and parts of the coastal South.

4. ***Aunt* and *ask*** Two other pronunciations are often noted. The first is that the initial vowel of *aunt* and *auntie* is pronounced as /ɑ/, a pronunciation also characteristic of eastern New England, but not of most other U.S. dialects, which have /æ/. The second is the pronunciation of *ask* as [æks] instead of [æsk]. By no means is this pronunciation unique to AAE, but it is a feature that has been stereotyped and stigmatized.

In investigations of ongoing changes in the pronunciation of American English, researchers have been surprised to discover that African Americans living in those cities affected by the Northern Cities Shift don't seem to participate in it. This is one indication that leads some observers to conclude that AAE and standard American English are diverging rather than becoming more alike.

Grammatical Features We examine four grammatical features of African-American English.

1. **Copula deletion** Compare the uses of the copula—the verb BE—in African-American English and standard American English below. Sentences 1 and 2 illustrate that AAE permits deletion of *be* in the present tense precisely where standard English permits a contracted form of the copula.

AFRICAN-AMERICAN	STANDARD AMERICAN
1. That my bike.	That's my bike.
2. The coffee cold.	The coffee's cold.
3. The coffee be cold there.	The coffee's (always) cold there.

2. **Habitual *be*** As example 3 above indicates, speakers of AAE express recurring or habitual action by using the form *be*. It may seem to speakers of other varieties that AAE *be* is equivalent to standard American English *is*. In fact, though, in sentences such as 3 *be* is equivalent to a verb expressing a habitual or continuous state of affairs. As African-American linguist Geneva Smitherman wrote about sentences such as 2 and 3, "If you the cook and *the coffee cold*, you might only just get talked about that day, but if *The coffee bees cold*, pretty soon you ain't gon have no job!" Thus, the verb *be* (or its inflected variant *bees*) is used to indicate continuous, repeated, or habitual action. The following examples further illustrate this function.

AFRICAN-AMERICAN	STANDARD AMERICAN
Do they be playing all day?	Do they play all day?
Yeah, the boys do be messin' around a lot.	Yeah, the boys do mess around a lot.
I see her when I bees on my way to school.	I see her when I'm on my way to school.

3. **Existential *it*** Another feature of African-American English is the use of the expression *it is* where standard American English uses *there is*, as when after hurricane Katrina a resident of New Orleans reported, *It's nothing left*. Below are two more examples of existential *it*:

AFRICAN-AMERICAN	STANDARD AMERICAN
Is it a Miss Jones in this office?	Is there a Miss Jones in this office?
She's been a wonderful wife and it's nothin' too good for her.	She's been a wonderful wife and there's nothing too good for her.

4. **Negative concord** The African-American English sentences below contain more than one word marked for negation—a syntactic phenomenon technically called **negative concord** but better known as double negation or multiple negation. In AAE, multiple-negative constructions are well formed, as they are in some other varieties of American English and as they were more generally in earlier periods of English.

AFRICAN-AMERICAN	STANDARD AMERICAN
Don't nobody never help me do my work.	Nobody ever helps me do my work.
He *don't never* go *nowhere*.	He *never* goes anywhere.

The fact that these constructions are not regarded as standard English *today* has no bearing on their grammaticality or appropriateness in other varieties.

Chicano English

Another important set of ethnic dialects of American English are those called Latino English or Hispanic English. The best known variety is Chicano English, spoken by many people of Mexican descent in major U.S. urban centers and in rural areas of the Southwest.

As with African-American English and all other varieties of English, many features of Chicano English are shared with other varieties, including other varieties of Hispanic English, such as those spoken in the Cuban community of Miami and the Puerto Rican community of New York City. Chicano English comprises many registers for use in different situations. Some characteristic features doubtless result from the persistence of Spanish as one of the language varieties of the Hispanic-American community, but Chicano English has become a distinct variety of American English and cannot be regarded as English spoken with a foreign accent. It is acquired as a first language by many children and is the native language of hundreds of thousands of adults. It is thus a stable variety of American English, with characteristic patterns of grammar and pronunciation.

Phonological Features Phonological features of Chicano English include consonant cluster simplification, as in [ɪs] for *it's*, "kine" for *kind*, "ole" for *old*, "bes" for *best*, and "un-erstan" [ʌnərstæn] for *understand*. Much of this can be represented in the phrase, *It's kind of hard*, which is pronounced [ɪs kanə har]. Another notable characteristic is the devoicing of /z/, especially in word-final position. Because of the widespread occurrence of /z/ in the inflectional morphology of English (in plural nouns, possessive nouns, and third-person-singular present-tense verbs such as *goes*), this characteristic is stereotyped. Chicano English pronunciation is also characterized by the substitution of stops for the standard fricatives represented in spelling by *th*: [t] for [θ] and [d] for [ð], as in "tick" for *thick* and "den" for *then*. Also characteristic is pronunciation of verbal *-ing* as "een" [in] rather than /ɪn/ ([ən]) or /ɪŋ/, as in *waiting* or *building*. Other *-ng* words such as *sing* and *long* end with a combined velar nasal /ŋ/ and velar stop /g/, as in [sɪŋg], not [sɪŋ], and *long* [lɔŋg], not [lɔŋ]. A well-known and stereotyped feature is substitution of "ch" [tʃ] for "sh" [ʃ], as in pronouncing *she* as [tʃi] instead of [ʃi], *shoes* as [tʃuz] (homophonous with *choose*) instead of [ʃuz], and *especially* as [ɛspɛtʃəli]. There is also substitution of "sh" for "ch," as in "preash" [priʃ] for *preach* and "shek" [ʃɛk] for *check* [tʃɛk], though this feature seems not to be stereotyped. Chicano English also exhibits certain intonation patterns that may strike speakers of other dialects of American English as uncertain or hesitant.

As with speakers of AAE, speakers of Hispanic varieties of English who live in cities affected by the Northern Cities Shift don't appear to be participating in these shifts, at least to the same extent as other groups.

Grammatical Features Chicano English also has characteristic syntactic patterns. It often omits the past-tense marker on verbs that end with the alveolars /t/, /d/, or /n/, yielding "wan" for *wanted* and "wait" for *waited*. At least in Los Angeles, *either . . . or either* is sometimes heard instead of *either . . . or*, as in *Either I will go buy one, or either Terry will*. Another feature is the use of dialect-specific prepositions such as *out from* for *away from*, as in *They party to get out from their problems*. As with many other varieties, Chicano English permits multiple negation, as in *You don't owe me nothing* and *Us little people don't get nothin'*.

Ethnic Varieties and Social Identification

It's important to reemphasize that some customary features of Chicano English and African-American English are characteristic of other varieties of American English. In some cases, as with consonant cluster simplification, these features are widespread in mainstream varieties, including standard English. In other cases, as with negative concord, they are not characteristic of standard American English but are shared with other nonstandard varieties. What makes any variety distinct is *not* a single feature but a cluster of features, some of which may also occur in other varieties to a greater or lesser degree.

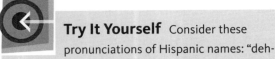

Try It Yourself Consider these pronunciations of Hispanic names: "deh-lah-CROOS" for *de la Cruz*; "FWEHN-tehs" for *Fuentes*; "GAHR-sah" for *Garza*, and "ehr-NAHN-dehs" for *Hernandez*. Say these names aloud as you think they would be said without an ethnic pronunciation. Compare those pronunciations with the ones in quotation marks, and identify two features in the Hispanic pronunciations that are characteristic of Chicano English. Identify two other features we did not discuss but that you think may reflect characteristics of Hispanic English.

Ethnic dialects are an important ingredient in social identity, and features that are recognized as characteristic of specific social groups can be used to promote or reinforce affiliation with that identity. When speaking, an African-American man or woman who wants to stress his or her social identity as an African American may choose to emphasize or exaggerate features of African-American English. The same is true for speakers of Hispanic English varieties who wish to emphasize their Hispanic identity. News correspondents on English-language radio and television broadcasts generally speak without marked social group accents. To emphasize their ethnic identity, however, some correspondents use a marked ethnic pronunciation of their own names at the conclusion of a report. A broadcast journalist named Maria Hinojosa identifies herself as mah-REE-ah ee-noh-HOH-sah, with a trill /r̃/ in REE. Another, Geraldo Rivera, pronounces his first name heh-RAHL-doh. Such ethnically marked pronunciations highlight pride in one's ethnic identity.

Socioeconomic Status Varieties: English, French, and Spanish

Less striking than regional and ethnic varieties, but equally significant, are the remarkable patterns of speech that characterize different socioeconomic status groups. Here we describe some speech patterns of the English spoken in New York City and in Norwich, England, as well as of the French of Montreal and the Spanish of Argentina.

New York City

New Yorkers sometimes pronounce /r/ and sometimes drop it in words like *car* and *beer*, *cart* and *fourth* (where /r/ follows a vowel in the same syllable and appears either word finally or preceding another consonant). The presence or absence of this /r/ does not change a word's referential meaning. A "cah pahked" in a red zone is ticketed as surely as a similarly *parked car*. And whether you live in New York or "New Yoahk," you have the same mayor (or "maya").

Still, the occurrence of /r/ in these words is anything but random and anything but meaningless. Linguist William Labov hypothesized that /r/ pronunciations in New York correlated with social-class affiliation and that any two socially ranked groups of New Yorkers would differ in their pronunciation of /r/. On the basis of preliminary observations, he predicted that members of higher socioeconomic status groups would pronounce /r/ more frequently than would speakers in lower socioeconomic class groups.

To test his hypothesis, Labov investigated the speech of employees in three Manhattan department stores of different social rank: Saks Fifth Avenue, an expensive, upper-middle-class store; Macy's, a medium-priced, middle-class store; and S. Klein, a discount store patronized principally by working-class New Yorkers. He asked supervisors, sales clerks, and stock boys the where-abouts of merchandise he knew to be displayed on the fourth floor of their store. In answer to a question such as "Where can I find the lamps?" he elic-ited a response of *fourth floor*. Then, pretending not to have caught the answer, he said, "Excuse me?" and elicited a repeated—and more careful—utterance of *fourth floor*. Each employee thus had an opportunity to pronounce postvocalic /r/ four times (twice each in *fourth* and *floor*) in a natural and realistic setting in which language itself was *not* the focus of attention.

Employees at Saks, the highest-ranked store, pronounced /r/ more often than those at S. Klein, the lowest-ranked store. At Macy's, the middle-ranked store, employees pronounced an intermediate number. Figure 11.12 presents the re-sults of Labov's survey. The darker sections represent the percentage of employ-ees who pronounced /r/ four times; the lighter sections above the darker areas represent the percentage who pronounced it once, twice, or three times (but not four). Employees who did not pronounce /r/ at all are not directly represented in the bar graph. As can be seen, 30 percent of the Saks employees pronounced all /r/, and an additional 32 percent pronounced some /r/. At Macy's, 20 percent pronounced /r/ four times, and an additional 31 percent pronounced some /r/. At S. Klein, only 4 percent of the employees pronounced all /r/, with an addi-tional 17 percent pronouncing one, two, or three /r/s. Labov's hypothesis about the social stratification of postvocalic /r/ seemed strikingly confirmed.

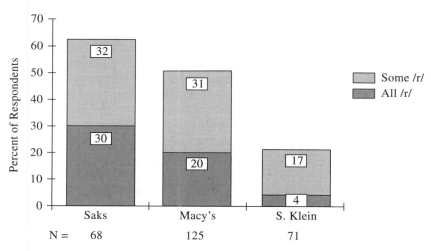

Figure 11.12 Overall Stratification of /r/ by Store in New York City
Source: Labov 2006.

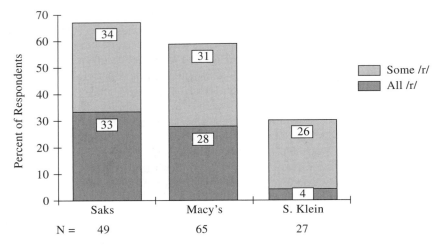

Figure 11.13 Stratification of /r/ by Store in New York City: White Female Sales Clerks
Source: Labov 2006.

You may be able to suggest other possible explanations for these findings because factors other than socioeconomic status might have influenced the results, as Labov recognized. For example, if he spoke to more men than women in one store or more stock boys than sales clerks, or more African Americans than whites, the difference in pronunciation of /r/ could have been produced by gender, job, or ethnic differences. As it happened, there were more white female sales clerks than any other single group, and looking at their pronunciations separately from those of everyone else would eliminate the possibility of findings skewed by gender, job, or ethnicity. Figure 11.13 reveals an overall pattern of distribution similar to that for the whole sample of respondents. The white female sales clerks at Saks pronounced more /r/ than those at Macy's, who in turn pronounced more than those at S. Klein. Thus Labov could rule out the possibility that his findings reflected ethnic, gender, or in-store job differences.

Following the department store study, Labov undertook a different and complementary kind of investigation. Equipped with detailed sociological descriptions of individual residents of Manhattan's Lower East Side, he spent several hours with each of about a hundred respondents there and recorded the conversations. His interviewing techniques prompted the respondents to use speech samples characteristic of different speech situations, or registers, as we discussed in Chapter 10. Here are six variables he examined:

◆ postvocalic /r/ (as in the department store survey)

◆ *th* in words such as *thirty*, *through*, and *with* (New Yorkers say *thirty* sometimes with /θ/ and sometimes with /t/)

◆ *th* in words such as *this*, *them*, and *breathe* (the infamous "dis, dat, dem, and dose" words, with variants /ð/ and /d/)

- alternate pronunciation of -ing words like *running* and *talking*, with /ɪŋ/ and /ɪn/ variants (Often referred to as "dropping the g," you know from Chapter 3 that the alternation is between the velar nasal /ŋ/ and the alveolar nasal /n/; only the spelling has a "g" to drop.)
- pronunciation of the vowel in the word class *soft, caught, coffee*
- pronunciation of the vowel in the word class *bad, care, sag*

In the interviews, Labov spoke with women and men, parents and children, African Americans and whites, Jews and Italians—a representative sample of Lower East Side residents. On the basis of extensive information about their background, he assigned each respondent to a socioeconomic status group based on a combination of three factors:

- the *education* of the respondent
- the *income* of the respondent's household
- the *occupation* of the principal breadwinner in the household

Using these criteria, he placed individuals into one of four socioeconomic status categories, which he called lower class, working class, lower middle class, and upper middle class. As expected, and as Figure 11.14 shows, upper-middle-class (UMC) respondents exhibited more /ɪŋ/ than lower-middle-class (LMC) respondents, who in turn exhibited more than working-class (WC) respondents, who used more than lower-class (LC) respondents. Each group also pronounced more /ɪŋ/ as attention paid to speech was increased in various styles. Through several graded speech registers—casual style, interview style,

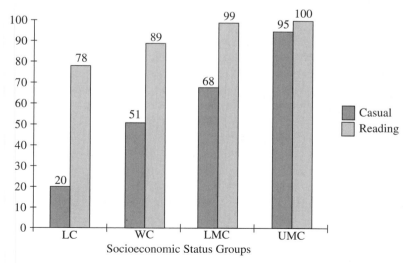

Figure 11.14 Percent of -ing pronounced as /ɪŋ/ by Four Socioeconomic Groups in New York City

Source of data: Labov 2006.

and reading style—respondents in all socioeconomic groups increased the percentage of /ɪŋ/ pronounced. Interview style is not shown here.

Labov found that all six variables were socially stratified. Each socioeconomic status group had characteristic patterns of pronunciation, and the percentage of pronunciation of the variants was ranked in the same way as the groups themselves. The upper middle class pronounced most /θ/ for *th* (as in *thing*), most /ð/ for *th* (as in *then*), most /ɪŋ/ (as in *running*), and most /r/ (as in *car*). The lower-class respondents pronounced fewest of these variants, while the lower middle class and working class fell in between, with the lower middle class pronouncing more than the working class. Such regular patterns of variation suggest that even subtle differences in social stratification may be reflected in language use.

The vowels were stratified in a similar way. New Yorkers have several pronunciations of the first vowel in *coffee*, ranging from high back tense [u] through mid back [ɔ] down to low back [ɑ]. The vowel of words in the *bad* class also varies—from low front lax [æ] to high front tense [iᵊ] with an **offglide**, as we saw in our discussion of the Northern Cities Shift. In New York City, higher socioeconomic status groups favored lower vowels in both cases.

Norwich, England

British linguist Peter Trudgill investigated the speech patterns of residents of Norwich, England, and found strikingly similar results in syntactic as well as phonological variation. Respondents were divided into five groups: middle middle class (MMC), lower middle class (LMC), upper working class (UWC), middle working class (MWC), and lower working class (LWC). Figure 11.15 illustrates the distribution of final /ɪŋ/ in the suffix *-ing* among these groups in casual and reading styles.

Comparing data from New York City (Figure 11.14) and Norwich (Figure 11.15) shows that the patterns of distribution for socioeconomic status are similar in the two cities. Each successively higher socioeconomic status group pronounces more /ɪŋ/ than the group immediately below it.

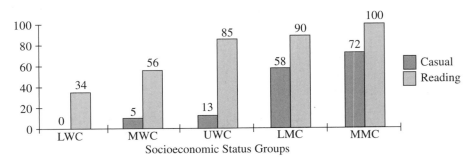

Figure 11.15 Percent of *-ing* Pronounced as /ɪŋ/ by Five Socioeconomic Groups in Norwich

Source of data: Trudgill 2000.

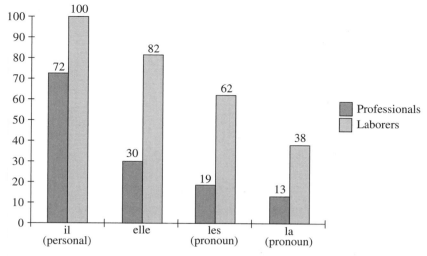

Figure 11.16 Percent of /l/-Deletion in Montreal French for Two Occupational Groups
Source of data: Sankoff and Cedergren 1971.

Montreal, Canada

In Montreal, French speakers vary the pronunciation of pronouns and definite articles. Except in the word *le*, /l/ is sometimes pronounced and sometimes omitted in personal pronouns such as *il* 'he' and *elle* 'she' and articles (and pronouns) such as *les* 'the (plural)' and *la* 'the (feminine).' (See Table 2.11.) In the usage of two occupational groups, professionals and laborers, the laborers consistently omitted /l/ more frequently than the professionals did, as shown for four such words in Figure 11.16.

Argentina

Spanish speakers show similar patterns of phonological variation. To cite one example in Argentina, speakers sometimes delete /s/ before pauses (as in English, /s/ is a common word-final sound in Spanish, occurring on plural nouns and on several verb forms). In a study of six Argentinian occupational groups, the percentage of /s/-deletion was greatest in the lowest-status occupations and least in the higher-status occupations, as shown in Figure 11.17.

General Comments

On the basis of evidence from these and other studies, parallel patterns of distribution may be expected for phonological variables wherever comparable social structures are found. Morphological and syntactic variation also exists, though evidence about variation at these levels of the grammar is scanty. What holds true of variation in English, French, and Spanish presumably holds true of similarly structured communities speaking other languages, although here, too, evidence is scanty.

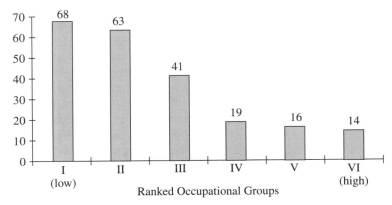

Figure 11.17 Percent of Prepausal /s/-Deletion in Argentine Spanish for Six Occupational Groups

Source of data: Terrell 1981.

The Language Varieties of Women and Men

You know that in many speech communities women and men don't speak identically. In the United States, certain words are associated more with women than men and may "sound" feminine as a result. Adjectives such as *lovely*, *darling*, and *cute* may carry feminine associations, as do words that describe precise shades of color, such as *mauve* and *chartreuse*.

In some languages, the differences between women's and men's speech are more dramatic than in English. In informal situations among speakers of Japanese, even the first-person pronoun 'I' differs for women (*atasi*) and men (*boku*). In French, *je* is the first-person pronoun for men and women, but because adjectives are marked for gender agreement, *Je suis heureux* 'I am happy' identifies a male speaker, while *Je suis heureuse* identifies a female speaker.

Reports of striking differences between gender varieties have been reported for Chukchee (spoken in Siberia) and for Thai. In polite Thai conversation between men and women of equal rank, women say *dičʰàn* while men say *pʰŏm* for the first-person singular pronoun 'I.' Thai also has a set of particles used differently by men and women, especially in formulaic questions and responses such as 'thank you' and 'excuse me.' The polite particle used by men is *kʰráp*, while women use *kʰá* or *kʰâ*. Because these politeness particles occur frequently in daily interaction, speech differences between men and women can seem highly marked in Thai, despite the fact that few words are so differentiated.

There are also more subtle differences between men's and women's speech, the kinds of quantitative differences we saw between other social groups. For example, in Montreal, where professionals delete /l/ from articles and pronouns less frequently than laborers do, men and women also differ in pronouncing these same words. Figure 11.18 shows that men delete /l/ more frequently than women for *il* (personal, as in *il chante* 'he sings'), for *elle*, and for the pronouns *les* and *la*.

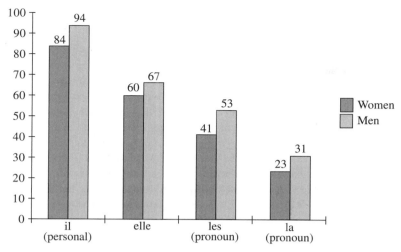

Figure 11.18 Percent of /l/-Deletion in Montreal French for Women and Men
Source of data: Sankoff and Cedergren 1971.

Patterns in which women delete sounds less frequently than men also appear in New York City and Norwich. In these cities, when higher socioeconomic classes behave linguistically in one way to a greater extent than lower ones, women tend to behave like the higher socioeconomic groups to a greater extent than men do.

In English, besides vocabulary differences, more subtle linguistic differences between the sexes can go largely unnoticed. One study examined the pronunciation of the *-ing* suffix in words like *running* and *talking*. In a semirural New England village, the speech patterns of a dozen boys and a dozen girls between the ages of 3 and 10 showed that, even in such young children, all but three used both alveolar [n] and velar [ŋ] pronunciations for verbal *-ing*. Interestingly, twice as many girls as boys showed a preference for the /ɪŋ/ forms, as shown below.

Pronunciation of *-ing* by 12 Boys and 12 Girls in a New England Village

	PREFERENCE FOR /ɪŋ/	NO PREFERENCE FOR /ɪŋ/
GIRLS	10	2
BOYS	5	7

The finding that girls and boys differ in this way may seem surprising, given that in this New England village (as generally in Western societies) girls and boys are in frequent face-to-face contact with each other, although they also play separately. A significant separation in the communication channels, suggested earlier as a motivating factor in the differentiation of dialect speech patterns, does not appear to explain this case. What, then, is the explanation? One hypothesis is the "toughness" characteristic associated with working-class

Masculinity and the Toughness Factor

There's evidence for the greater prestige of *running* and *talking* pronunciations with [ŋ] over those that "drop the *g*" (that is, pronounce *–ing* with [n]). Here are two facts. (1) English speakers who use both variants (that's virtually all of us) tend to pronounce *–ing* with [ŋ] more often when speaking in situations of greater formality. (2) Social groups with higher socioeconomic status pronounce *–ing* with [ŋ] more often than lower status groups. Interestingly, girls and women pronounce *–ing* with [ŋ] more frequently than boys and men do. One explanation may be that women are more status conscious than men—sociologists have found that to be the case in other arenas, so why not in language, too? But linguists suggest an additional reason. Think of it as the "toughness factor." Boys and men may associate pronunciations like *runnin'* and *talkin'* with working-class "toughness"—and that connection apparently outweighs any link to prestige because the less prestigious pronunciation marks "masculinity" and masculinity outranks prestige. Now you might object that using the term "masculinity" to explain the linguistic behavior of boys and men seems to beg the question. After all, what's gained by calling a pronunciation "masculine" just because men use it more than women? Well, masculinity and femininity are not the same thing as male and female. Sex differences (male and female) are biological, and language differences don't reflect biology. Instead, what they do reflect is the phenomenon of *gender*—what it *means* to be male or female in a particular sociocultural environment. You're aware of gender differences marked by clothing, hair length, body decoration, and jewelry use. ("Wear some earrings, for God's sake," the mother of Emma Thompson's character in the movie "The Winter Guest" tells her after she's cut her hair short. "Let folks know you're a woman!") So you shouldn't be surprised that language also reflects the important social identity of gender roles.

lifestyles combined with the "masculinity" characteristic associated with the *-in'* forms. In other words, an association between masculinity and "dropping the *g*" may outweigh the associations with prestige and higher socioeconomic status that otherwise accompany the *-ing* variant with the *g* (that is, [ŋ]). This analysis suggests that linguistic differences between males and females are related not to biological sex but to socially constructed gender roles.

Why Do Stigmatized Varieties Persist?

You may wonder why speakers don't give up their stigmatized varieties for more prestigious ones. The explanation lies partly in the fact that a person's identity—as a woman or man, as an American or Australian, as a member of a particular ethnic or socioeconomic group—is entwined with the speech patterns of the group he or she belongs to. To change the way you speak is to signal changes in who you are or how you want to be perceived. For a New Yorker transplanted to California, speaking like a Californian is to relinquish some identity as a New Yorker. To give up speaking African-American English is to relinquish some identity as an African American. To give up working-class speech patterns acquired in childhood is to take on a new identity. In short, to take on new speech patterns is to reform oneself and present oneself anew.

Language is a major symbol of our social identity, and we have seen how remarkably fine-tuned to that identity it can be. If you wish to identify with "non-native" regional, socioeconomic, or ethnic groups and have sufficient contact with them, your speech will naturally and gradually come to resemble theirs.

We can illustrate with a telling story of linguistic and social identity on Martha's Vineyard, an island off the coast of Massachusetts. There the vowels /aj/ and /aw/ have two principal variants, with the first element of each diphthong sometimes pronounced [a] and sometimes with a more centralized [ə]. Words like *night* and *why* may be pronounced [aj] or [əj]; words like *shout* and *how* may be pronounced with [aw] or the more centralized [əw]. These variants are not typical dialect features: they don't reflect gender, ethnicity, or socioeconomic status. Instead, vowel centralization represents identity with traditional values of the island and its life. In an investigation carried out by sociolinguist William Labov, the up-island residents showed more vowel centralization than the residents in sections catering to summer visitors. Young men intending to leave the island and lead their lives on the mainland showed the least vowel centralization, while the greatest vowel centralization was shown by a young man who had moved to the mainland but returned to Martha's Vineyard. Thus the centralized diphthongs may be viewed as representing rejection of mainland values and a positive view of the values of island life.

The symbolic value of a person's language variety cannot be overestimated. In Britain speakers of regional varieties who were asked to evaluate oral arguments rated the *quality* of an argument higher when it was presented in a standard accent but found the same argument more *persuasive* when it was made using a regional accent.

It's easy for speakers higher on the socioeconomic ladder to ask about speakers lower on the ladder, "Why don't they start talking like us?" The answer may not be so difficult to recognize: their social identity is different, and they don't necessarily share the values of other groups, including higher socioeconomic groups. Think about gender dialects: it is perfectly acceptable for women to speak like women and men to speak like men. Imagine men asking women to speak like them in order to get ahead in "a man's world." Or imagine a female CEO or manager asking her company's male truck drivers to speak more like women to get ahead in "a woman's world." These are patently unacceptable scenarios.

Language is a central factor in a person's identity. Asking people to change their customary language patterns is not like asking them to wear different styles or colors of sweaters. It is asking them to assume a new identity and to espouse the values associated with that identity, that is the identity of speakers of a different dialect. One reason nonstandard varieties successfully resist the urgings of education is that vernacular language varieties are deeply entwined with the social identities and values of their speakers.

COMPUTERS AND THE STUDY OF DIALECT

Given the mass of both quantitative and qualitative data represented in our discussion of dialects, it should be no surprise that computers are being used by dialectologists to accomplish their goals. Researchers are digitizing the kinds of data that in the past have been manually represented, as on some maps in this chapter. For example, researchers for the Linguistic Atlas of the Middle and South Atlantic States (LAMSAS) have used a program called Map-Info to plot longitude and latitude coordinates for the residences of all 1,162 LAMSAS informants, which will enable maps of various sizes and degrees of detail to represent features that were elicited from the informants. In Figures 11.7 and 11.8 you saw the use of computers in generating nontraditional maps for dialectology. In a different vein, the work represented in the Telsur project and the Atlas of North American English depends crucially on using computers to perform acoustic analyses of vowel sounds.

In addition to a wide variety of tasks that have used computers for map-related activities, the kinds of resources that corpora make available to researchers interested in language variation are beginning to revolutionize the study of dialects. A project called the International Corpus of English aims to provide texts totaling about one million words of written and spoken English of the 1990s from each of 20 centers around the world, representing the English spoken in the Caribbean, Fiji, Ghana, Hong Kong, India, Kenya, Nigeria, the Philippines, Singapore, and other regions. The texts of these corpora will be tagged and annotated, making their use in dialect comparisons extremely valuable.

In our discussions of variation across dialects, we have seen that vocabulary and pronunciation vary. In the real world, an understanding of vowel variation has proven useful in keeping an innocent person out of jail. Computers have been used to help analyze the vowel characteristics in tape recordings that contained illegal speech acts—in this case, acts of threatening. Someone had telephoned a major airline with a serious threat of violence, and workers who heard the call thought they recognized the voice as belonging to a disgruntled former employee. A computer analysis of the vowel quality of the caller showed that his dialect was not the same as that of the former employee. ∎

Summary

- When separated physically or socially, people with shared speechways come to speak differently. Given sufficient time and separation, distinct languages can arise.
- Conversely, the speech of people talking as members of the same community can develop in unison, even tending to merge in some situations.
- There is no linguistic basis upon which to distinguish between a dialect and a language. Every language is made up of dialects, and in terms of linguistic principles and linguistic universals every dialect is a language.
- Linguistic differences exist among social groups within every speech community.
- Linguistic forms can vary greatly from one social group to the next, and social groups may be defined in a number of ways besides regionally.
- Both ethnicity and socioeconomic status are bases for social group affiliation.
- Women and men may also be thought of as belonging to different social groups, called gender groups.
- Combining these different group distinctions yields a complex picture of the composition of society. Within a particular ethnic group, we find socioeconomic

classes whose members are male or female. Differences in speechways support such social identities.

- Whatever the social group, its language variety will typically exhibit characteristics that distinguish it from the language varieties of other social groups.
- The linguistic features that characterize social varieties may also serve as markers (or symbols) of social identity.
- One way to stress membership in an ethnic group is to emphasize or even exaggerate the characteristic features of that ethnic language variety.
- If a woman wants to appear particularly feminine, she may choose to exhibit features associated with women's speech and avoid "masculine-sounding" expressions.
- Individuals can use socially marked language characteristics for their own purposes.
- Everyone speaks with a pronunciation that is characteristic of social identity. No one can speak without an accent, though we tend to be acutely aware of the accents of others and to think members of our own social groups do not carry accents.

What Do You Think? REVISITED

- *Nina talks "funny," too.* Nina's camp counselor appears to be a speaker of British English. As funny as the counselor's dialect may have struck Nina, this camper's dialect might have sounded just as unusual to the counselor. Every group's language variety differs—more or less—from those of other groups. Of course, there is nothing "funny" about anyone's speech, except possibly that it's different, and patterns that differ from our own may seem odd simply because they differ from what we're accustomed to.
- *Daniel's Alabama sub.* There is no speaker of any language who doesn't carry an accent; everyone speaks a language variety whose pronunciation reflects something about his or her social identity. Speakers of English recognize British, American, Canadian, and Australian accents, among others. Even if you could shed your native accent, you'd have to replace it with another one because you can't speak a language without an accent. (See Ex. 11–11a.)
- *Evan and Ebonics.* In 1997, at the height of the Ebonics controversy, much of the comment in newspapers and other media indicated a widespread perception that a dialect of a language can legitimately be judged good or bad by how closely it resembles the "standard" variety of the language. All language varieties differ from one another to greater or lesser degrees. French is ungrammatical if judged by the rules of Spanish or Japanese and American English if judged by the rules of British English. Ebonics is ungrammatical if judged by the rules of standard English. And standard English is ungrammatical if judged by the rules of Ebonics or standard French. The very notion of a "standard" English is problematic, given the great differences among spoken varieties even of U.S. presidents.
- *Women talk, men talk.* The degree to which the talk of men and women differs isn't the same from one cultural group to the next. This is also true for variation

across social groups within a given culture. Research has found some differences, such as different words for the same item or some forms used more frequently by men or women. If Sammy recalls the many ways in which boys and girls are brought up differently, she shouldn't be surprised that men and women also *speak* somewhat differently. ■

Exercises

Based on English

11-1. Distinguish between an accent and a dialect. Distinguish between a dialect and a language. What is meant by a "language variety"? Does it make any sense to say of a language variety that "it isn't a language, it's *only* a dialect"?

11-2. Examine a copy of a newspaper or magazine published in Britain (for example, *The Times, The Economist, Punch, The Spectator, The Listener*) and list as many examples of differences between American and British English as you can notice on any two pages. Include examples of vocabulary, syntax, spelling, and punctuation.

11-3. Which of the following words are you familiar with? Make two lists, one consisting of those you normally use and the other consisting of those you don't use but have heard others use. With what regional or national group do you associate the words you have heard others use but don't use yourself? Compare your judgments with those of your classmates.

dragonfly	darning needle, mosquito hawk, spindle, snake feeder, snake doctor
pancake	fritter, hotcake, flannel cake, batter cake
cottage cheese	curds, curd cheese, clabber cheese, dutch cheese, pot cheese
string beans	green beans, snap beans
earthworm	night crawler, fishing worm, angle worm, rain worm, red worm, mud worm
lightning bug	firefly, fire bug
baby carriage	baby buggy, baby coach, baby cab, pram

11-4. The following questions (some slightly adapted) are from the questionnaire used to gather data for *DARE*. Answer each question yourself, and then compare your answers with those of your classmates. Do you and your classmates agree on the regions in which the particular variants are used? (*DARE* provides maps for answers to these questions.)

a. How do you speak of roads that have numbers or letters? For example, if someone asks directions to get to (Supply local city name), you might say, "Take __."

b. What names are used around here for:

1) the part of the house below the ground floor?

2) the kind of sandwich in a large, long bun, that's a meal in itself?

    3) a small stream of water not big enough to be a river?

    4) a round cake of dough, cooked in deep fat, with a hole in the center?

    5) a piece of cloth that a woman folds over her head and ties under her chin?

    6) the common worm used as bait?

    7) vehicles for a baby or small child, the kind it can lie down in?

    8) a mark on the skin where somebody has sucked it hard and brought the blood to the surface?

    9) a bone from the breast of a chicken, shaped like a horseshoe?

    10) the place in the elbow that gives you a strange feeling if you hit it against something?

    11) very young frogs, when they still have tails but no legs?

11-5. What was Labov's hypothesis about the distribution of /r/ in New York City department stores? If in your city or town there are three socially ranked stores that could be similarly investigated, can you name two phonological features you would expect to be socially differentiated? Design a question for each feature that would uncover the data needed to test your hypothesis. (Make the question a natural one for the kind of store you have in mind.) Would you ask your respondents to repeat their answers as Labov did? Explain why or why not.

11-6. "William Labov . . . once said about the use of black English, 'It is the goal of most black Americans to acquire full control of the standard language without giving up their own culture.' . . . I wonder if the good doctor might also consider the goals of those black Americans who have full control of standard English but who are every now and then troubled by that colorful, grammar-to-the-winds patois that is black English. Case in point—me."

So wrote a twenty-one-year-old African-American college student in *Newsweek* (Dec. 27, 1982, p. 7). She cites several features of African-American English such as those described in this chapter.

    a. Look up the meaning of *patois* in your desk dictionary and note its connotations in referring to particular language varieties. Are those connotations positive or negative? What does her use of the phrase "grammar-to-the-winds" suggest about the student's attitude toward the grammaticality of African-American English?

    b. What features of African-American English do you think the student means in calling it a "grammar-to-the-winds patois"?

    c. What would be the implications for communication if any speech variety were indeed "grammarless"? Give two reasons why African-American English cannot accurately be called a "grammar-to-the-winds" dialect.

    d. What would you assume to be the reason for the student's attitudes toward African-American English? What might you explain to her about patterns of language in every variety and about the status of particular varieties *in terms of their linguistic features*?

11-7. Describe two ways in which you have noticed that the speech of women and men differs in greetings, threats, swearing, and promises. What do you think accounts for these differences? Do you think such differences are increasing or decreasing? Explain the bases for your answers.

11-8. Among many functions of the word *like* in English, it is used by certain speakers to mark the beginning of a direct quotation. Here are two examples of this quotative *like*:

"And then she's like, 'I don't want to go.'"

"So he's like, 'But you promised!'"

To complete this exercise, you will need natural data from the speech of your acquaintances. Collect 20 naturally occurring examples of quotative *like* from the speech of at least five people (including some people younger and others older than you). Write down the examples exactly as they were spoken, taking care not to call attention to the speech of your acquaintances or the fact that you are observing their language. Relying on five-year ranges (15–19, 20–24, and so on), note the approximate age of every speaker you set out to observe (whether or not he or she actually uses quotative *like*).

a. Some researchers call this feature "quotative *be like*" because their data indicate that this use of *like* generally occurs with the verb *be*, as in the examples above. Explain whether or not your data lend support to using the alternative name.

b. Identify the tense (past or nonpast) of the verbs that precede quotative *like* in your data. Identify the time (present, past, or future) that the verbs refer to. Keep in mind that tense and time are not the same phenomena.

c. In both the examples above, the verb form has been contracted to '*s*. What percentage of your examples show a similar contraction?

d. In both of the examples above, the subject of *be* in the quotative *like* clauses is a pronoun (*he, she*). What lexical categories are the subjects in your examples?

e. Identify which age groups use this feature and which don't. On the basis of your admittedly limited evidence, propose a hypothesis about whether use of this feature is age related.

f. Compare your findings about use and age with the findings of some classmates, and reconsider your hypothesis in light of the pooled data.

g. Do you think that younger users will continue using quotative *like* as they get older (which would make it an example of language change in progress) or that they will not continue using it beyond a certain age (which would make it an age-graded feature)? Explain your view.

h. In your data, do you note any examples that represent uses of *like* other than the quotative, leaving aside its use as a preposition (*He looks like his dad*), subordinating conjunction (*Winstons taste good like a cigarette should*),

or verb (*She likes asparagus*)? If so, analyze those uses and try characterizing them; what name(s) might suit them?

   i. What other expressions have you heard that function like quotative *like*?

Especially for Educators and Future Teachers

11-9. **a.** Below are the opening words of a presentation by a college teacher to a
group of Southern teachers at a professional meeting. (Imagine it spoken
with a distinctive Southern accent: the college teacher was born in the
South and clearly wished to play upon those affiliations.)

"Years ago, during my first week in Wisconsin, I was asked by a fellow
teacher, 'Do you mean they let *you* teach English?' The speaker was a
Canadian with what I thought a very peculiar accent. Soon after that, a
woman working on a degree in speech asked me with all the kindness
and gentleness of which she was capable whether I would let her teach
me how to talk right. If I had had her zeal and patience and kindness,
I might very well have made the offer first, for I thought her speech
highly unsatisfactory."

Provide answers to these questions, most of which the teacher posed to her
audience:

   1) Who should teach whom how to speak "right"?

   2) Is there a standard pronunciation in American English and, if so, what
is it?

   3) Should education aim to make everyone sound like everyone else?

   4) Is it possible that training could make everyone sound like everyone
else?

   5) If the training succeeded, how would everyone sound?

   6) Assuming uniformity could be achieved, how long could it last?

   b. The same college teacher reported these comments from a Southern
teacher and a Southern physician ([ʍ] represents [hw]):

Teacher: [a: hæv dɪlɪbərɪtlɪ wəkt tu gɛt rɪd av ɪnɪ tresɪz av æksɪnt æz a:
θɪŋk owl ɛʤəketɪd pipəl ʃʊd du a: prad masɛf ðæt a: hæv nat wən ʍɪt av ɪnɪ
tresəbəl æksɪnt ɪn ma: spitʃ]

Physician: [mɪnɪ av ma pəjʃəns θɪŋk a: æm fram ðə nɔəθ bɪkɔwz æz ən
ɛʤəketɪd pəsən a: don av kɔəs hæv ə səðən æksɪnt]

   1) After reading the comments aloud, write them out in standard
orthography.

   2) Give the standard orthography for these words as pronounced in the
same dialect:

      i) [mɔwnɪn] ii) [kaəd] iii) [kent] iv) [hɛp] v) [spikɪn] vi) [həjd] vii)
[mɪnɪ] viii) [bɪnɪfɪt]

   c. Compare Figure 11.10 and the description of the Southern Shift
with the transcriptions of comments by the Southern teacher and

physician. For each of these features of the Southern Shift, cite two words from the comments or the list of words in (2) that exemplify it: (i) monophthongization of /aj/; (ii) /ɛ/ pronounced higher and more fronted; (iii) /æ/ pronounced higher and more fronted. (For all examples, provide the words in standard orthography and the transcribed version.)

d. Cite a pair of words in the transcriptions that indicate whether the *pin* ~ *pen* merger is characteristic of this dialect. Cite a pair of words with /r/-omission after vowels. Cite a pair with /l/-omission after vowels.

(Adapted from Jane Appleby, "Is Southern English Good English?" In David L. Shores and Carol P. Hines, eds., *Papers in Language Variation* [Tuscaloosa: University of Alabama Press, 1977], p. 225.)

11-10. Looking at the content of what the physician and teacher reported in Ex. 11-9, answer these questions:

a. Does the physician believe that Northerners have accents?

b. Does he or she believe that education removes or should remove a regional accent?

c. Do you think the physician is pleased that the patients believe their physician is from the North?

d. The teacher twice uses the word *traces* in reference to accent. Does the choice of this term suggest whether the teacher regards regional accents positively or negatively? Had this teacher grown up speaking a Northern accent, do you think he or she would have reported trying to get rid of any *traces* of accent? What do you think of this teacher's view of the relationship between education and accent?

e. Do you like it when people recognize where you're from? Do you have an accent that outsiders admire? Has anyone ever said anything unfavorable about your accent to you? Have you ever tried to get rid of any "traces" of accent in your speech? All things considered, what do you think about your own accent?

f. Putting yourself into the frame of mind of the Southern teacher, why might he or she believe that educated people should rid themselves of any traces of accent in their speech?

g. To judge from the transcribed comments of the teacher and the physician, how easy is it for a person to get rid of all traces of accent?

11-11. a. What would it mean to speak without an accent? (Think globally as well as regionally: what would it mean to speak English without an American, British, Canadian, Australian, or other national accent? What would it mean to speak French without a North American, European, or other accent?) Why do you imagine some people appear to think it's better to be from nowhere than somewhere?

b. Provide a list of four regional features of *your own* pronunciation that others have called to your attention or you are otherwise aware of.

c. Make a list of features you admire in the speech of others. What's admirable about those features?

d. Make a list of features you dislike in the speech of others. Can you specify what it is about those features that you dislike?

e. What explanation can you offer for the fact that many people believe they speak *without* an accent?

11-12. Cockney is a British dialect spoken by working-class Londoners, and the number of Cockney speakers doubtless exceeds the estimated 1.5 million speakers of the variety of English known as RP (Received Pronunciation) or BBC (British Broadcasting Corporation) English that is taught in England's private schools. Among the features of Cockney is /h/-dropping, especially in unstressed words, such as the pronouns *he*, *him*, and *her*, the verbs *has*, *have*, and *had*, as well as in all other word classes: nouns like *hospital*, *heaven*, and *hell*, adjectives like *hot* and *heavy*, verbs like *help* and *hiss*. Cockney speakers pronounce a glottal stop for the medial /t/ in words like *bitter* and *later* and accompanying medial /p/ as in *paper*. Also characteristic is an /f/ pronunciation for the initial consonant of words like *thin* and the final consonant of words like *with* and *mouth*, as well as the medial consonant in words like *pithy* and *Cathy*. Instead of [θɪn] for *thin*, Cockney speakers say "fin," and "wif" for *with*, and "Caffee" [kæfi] for *Cathy*. They merge /ð/ and /v/ in specific phonological environments: word finally, as in "breave" and "bave" for *breathe* and *bathe*, and in medial position, yielding "bruvver" for *brother* and "muvver" for *mother*. Comment on the phonological similarity and differences between Cockney and African-American English. What do the pronunciation similarities between (largely white) Cockney speakers and black speakers of African-American English indicate about the relationship between race and pronunciation? What do the similarities suggest about the systematic nature of phonological variants within dialects?

Other Resources

Internet

LISU Website: http://www.CengageBrain.com For users of this textbook. Provides updated Internet links as well as supplemental material for students and instructors. Here you will find interactive learning tools.

Dictionary of American Regional English: http://dare.wisc.edu/ ?q = node/17 Contains information about *DARE*, including base map with state codes compared to a U.S. geographical map.

American Dialect Society: http://www.americandialect.org Offers information about the American Dialect Society (ADS), including a special page for student members. Also provides links to pages for *DARE* and various Linguistic Atlas projects.

Linguistic Atlas Projects: http://www.lap.uga.edu/ An ambitious website providing information about the nine Linguistic Atlas projects. Best represented is LAMSAS—Linguistic Atlas of the Middle and South Atlantic States (ranging from New York to northern Florida and including West Virginia and

Pennsylvania)—but you can find useful information about all the atlas projects.

 Linguist List's Topic Page on Ebonics: http://linguistlist.org/topics/ ebonics/ Linguist List is the major discussion list among linguists for issues of general interest. Ebonics was such a popular topic in 1996 and 1997 that the list managers collected all the information Linguist List has on it at one site.

 Atlas of North American English: http://www.ling.upenn.edu/phono_ atlas/home.html ANAE is based on a systematic telephone survey of the major urban areas of the United States and Canada in a project called Tel-sur, based at the University of Pennsylvania. The website presents the latest research, with color maps showing vowel pronunciation. When you visit the site, keep in mind that in this textbook we represent only three English vowels as diphthongs, but the ANAE site uses a different set of representations, which are provided here for convenience:

LISU	**ANAE**	**WORDS**
/aw/	/aw/	pout, plowed
/aj/	/ay/	my, mine
/ɔj/	/oy/	boy, soy
/e/	/ey/	made, frayed
/o/	/ow/	flowed, code
/u/	/uw/	food, cooed
/ɔ/	/oh/	talk, dawn, caught
/ɛ/	/e/	pet, Seth, wedge
/ʊ/	/u/	wood, could

 Ebonics Information Page: http://www.cal.org/topics/dialects/aae. html Maintained by the Center for Applied Linguistics, a rich page, full of valuable discussion and analysis of African-American English and issues related to Ebonics.

 Survey of English Usage: http://www.ucl.ac.uk/english-usage/ Information about the International Corpus of English, especially the million-word British contribution.

 LSA: Videos on the Web: http://www.uga.edu/lsava/Wolfram/Wolfram. html Clips from "Indian by Birth: The Lumbee Dialect," reflecting Walt Wolfram's work among the Lumbee Indians of Robeson County, North Carolina, and from "The Ocracoke Brogue" (about the dialect of English spoken on Ocracoke Island).

 The Language Samples Project: http://www.ic.arizona.edu/~lsp/ main.html Under development at the University of Arizona, this project provides information about varieties of English, including African-American English, Southern (American) English, and British English.

Video and Audio

Some of the videos and DVDs listed below are available in libraries and video rental outlets. Some can be purchased through educational video suppliers, such as Insight Media (**http://www.insight-media.com**) or PBS.

- **American Tongues** This award-winning video treats regional accents from Boston to Texas, with a focus on the speech of some very engaging teenagers.
- **Black on White** From the BBC's 1986 *Story of English* series narrated by Robert MacNeil, this video explores the origins and spread of African-American English.
- **Communities of Speech** In this video Walt Wolfram and Deborah Tannen debate issues as they examine the concept of standard American English and other American dialects.
- **Do You Speak American?** Robert MacNeil travels the United States in 2003, exploring traditional dialect characteristics and new developments.

Suggestions for Further Reading

- **Craig M. Carver. 1987.** *American Regional Dialects*: *A Word Geography* (Ann Arbor: University of Michigan Press). An overview of American English dialects based upon vocabulary findings in the *Dictionary of American Regional English*.
- **Frederick Cassidy, Joan Houston Hall, eds. 1985–.** *Dictionary of American Regional English* (Cambridge, MA: Belknap Press). The most comprehensive treatment of American regional vocabulary, with four volumes published so far, up to the word *sky writer*.
- **Edward Finegan & John R. Rickford, eds. 2004.** *Language in the USA* (Cambridge, UK: Cambridge University Press). Treats a wide range of topics related to dialects, including American regional dialects and social varieties, Ebonics, hip hop, slang, and adolescent language (the "Advanced Reading" section below cites several chapters in this collection).
- **Carmen Fought. 2006.** *Language and Ethnicity*: *Key Topics in Sociolinguistics* (Cambridge, UK: Cambridge University Press). Ethnicity is an increasingly important topic of investigation, and this accessible treatment asks not only what ethnicity is but whether there are "white" ways of speaking and what it means to construct an ethnic identity and to borrow features of another's ethnic identity.
- **Arthur Hughes, Peter Trudgill & Dominic Watt. 2005.** *English Accents and Dialects*: *An Introduction to Social and Regional Varieties of English in the British Isles*, 4th ed. (London: Arnold). Particularly good on pronunciation. Includes discussion not only of London, but of Belfast, Dublin, South Wales, Edinburgh, and speakers from 11 other regions, with a CD containing edited interviews with the speakers.
- **William Labov, Sharon Ash & Charles Boberg. 2006.** *The Atlas of North American English*: *Phonetics, Phonology, and Sound Change* (Berlin: Mouton de Gruyter). A richly illustrated multimedia analysis of recent vowel pronunciation in North America, with colorful maps illustrating patterns of distribution and their relationship to older dialect patterns, this extraordinary work won the 2008 Leonard Bloomfield Book Award from the Linguistic Society of America.
- **Rosina Lippi-Green. 1997.** *English with an Accent*: *Language, Ideology, and Discrimination in the United States* (London: Routledge). A provocative introduction to facts and myths surrounding discussion of accent and other aspects of dialect in the United States.
- **Salikoko S. Mufwene, John R. Rickford, Guy Bailey & John Baugh, eds. 1998.** *African-American English*: *Structure, History and Use* (London: Routledge). Distinguished researchers analyze the structure and use of African-American English. Besides treatment of phonology, lexicon, grammar, discourse, and the history of African-American English, you can learn what linguists and anthropologists think of Ebonics, the Oakland school district resolution, obscenity, hip-hop, and Ice-T.
- **Peter Trudgill. 2000.** *The Dialects of England* (Oxford: Blackwell). A reliable treatment of traditional and modern dialects in England, with maps.
- **Peter Trudgill. 2000.** *Sociolinguistics*: *An Introduction to Language and Society*, 4th ed. (New York: Penguin). A basic, brief, and accessible treatment.
- **Peter Trudgill & J. K. Chambers, eds. 1991.** *Dialects of English*: *Studies in Grammatical Variation* (New York: Longman). Contains 22 descriptions of grammar in various dialects of the United States, Australia, Canada, Scotland, and especially England.

Advanced Reading

Chambers and Trudgill (1998), Hudson (1996), and Wardhaugh (2010) discuss dialects generally. The discussion of convergence in Kupwar in this chapter is based on Gumperz and Wilson (1971). Green (2002) is a thorough and accessible treatment of African-American English. More popular treatments can be found in Rickford and Rickford (2000) and Smitherman (1986), the latter providing some of the examples in this chapter. Baugh (2004) addresses the Ebonics controversy of 1996–1997. Ornstein-Galicia (1988) and Fought (2003) are useful on Chicano English. On the sociolinguistics of French, see Sanders (1993) and Ball (1997); on German, see Stevenson (1997); on Spanish, see Mar-Molinero (1997).

Ferguson and Heath (1981) is a collection of essays describing language use among Native Americans, Filipinos, Puerto Ricans, Jews, Italian Americans, French Americans, German Americans, and others. The principal findings for the Linguistic Atlas of the United States for the East Coast can be found in Kurath (1949), Atwood (1953), and Kurath and McDavid (1961). See Allen (1973–76) for the Upper Midwest, Pederson (1986–91) for the Gulf states, Bright (1971) for California and Nevada, Atwood (1962) for Texas. Discussion of the Southern Shift can be found in Nunnally (2008), which inspired several of the diphthongizations given in connection with Figure 11.10 (and my appreciation to Nunnally himself for the "sweet tea with a lid" report and translation in my discussion of the Southern Shift above). From a highly knowledgeable outsider's point of view, Tottie (2002) offers a fresh perspective on American English.

The relationship between language and gender is treated in Eckert and McConnell-Ginet (2003). A chapter-length overview, including discussion of the contributions of lesbians and women of color to an understanding of multicultural feminism can be found in Bucholtz (2004). The data in the present chapter on gender differences in Thai come from Haas (1940), who also discusses Chukchee. Fischer (1958) reports the New England -*ing* data cited here. Johnson and Meinhof (1997) is a collection of essays on masculine sociolinguistics, addressing power, conversation, gossip, expletives, and other topics. Holmes (1995) asks whether women are more polite than men. Ochs (1992) relates language and gender through social activities, social stances, and social acts. Labov and Harris (1994) report the story of the threatening phone call to an airline and the dialect identification task they undertook. Language and social identity—and the linguistic construction of social identity—are treated in Alim (2004a,b), Bucholtz (1999), Eckert (1989, 2000), and Fought (2006; cited in "Suggestions for Further Reading").

References

Alim, H. Samy. 2004a. *You Know My Steez*: *An Ethnographic and Sociolinguistic Study of Styleshifting in a Black American Speech Community*. Publication of the American Dialect Society, No. 89.

———. 2004b. "Hip Hop Nation Language." In Finegan & Rickford, pp. 387–409.

Allen, Harold B. 1973–1976. *The Linguistic Atlas of the Upper Midwest*, 3 vols. (Minneapolis: University of Minnesota Press).

Atwood, E. Bagby. 1953. *A Survey of Verb Forms in the Eastern United States* (Ann Arbor: University of Michigan Press).

———. 1962. *The Regional Vocabulary of Texas* (Austin: University of Texas Press).

Ball, Rodney. 1997. *The French-Speaking World*: *A Practical Introduction to Sociolinguistic Issues* (London: Routledge).

Baugh, John. 2004. "Ebonics and Its Controversy." In Finegan & Rickford, pp. 305–18.

Bright, Elizabeth S. 1971. *A Word Geography of California and Nevada* (Berkeley: University of California Press).

Bucholtz, Mary. 1999. "You da Man: Narrating the Racial Other in the Production of White Masculinity." *Journal of Sociolinguistics* 3: 443–60.

———. 2004. "Language, Gender, and Sexuality." In Finegan & Rickford, pp. 410–29.

Chambers, J. K. & Peter Trudgill. 1998. *Dialectology*, 2nd ed. (Cambridge, UK: Cambridge University Press).

Eckert, Penelope. 1989. Jocks and Burnouts: Social Categories and Identity in the High School (New York: Teachers College Press).

———. 2000. *Linguistic Variation as Social Practice*: The Linguistic Construction of Identity in Belten High (Malden, MA: Blackwell).

Eckert, Penelope & Sally McConnell-Ginet. 2003. *Language and Gender* (Cambridge, UK: Cambridge University Press).

Ferguson, Charles A. & Shirley Brice Heath, eds. 1981. *Language in the USA* (Cambridge, UK: Cambridge University Press).

Fischer, John L. 1958. "Social Influences on the Choice of a Linguistic Variable," *Word* 14:47–56; repr. in Hymes 1964, pp. 483–88.

Fought, Carmen. 2003. *Chicano English in Context* (New York: Palgrave Macmillan).

Green, Lisa J. 2002. *African American English*: Character and Contexts (Cambridge, UK: Cambridge University Press).

Gumperz, John J. & Robert Wilson. 1971. "Convergence and Creolization: A Case from the Indo-Aryan/Dravidian Border in India," in Dell Hymes, ed., *Pidginization and Creolization of Languages* (Cambridge, UK: Cambridge University Press), pp. 151–67.

Haas, Mary R. 1940. "Men's and Women's Speech in Koasati," *Language* 20:142–49; repr. in Hymes 1964, pp. 228–33.

Holmes, Janet. 1995. *Women, Men and Politeness* (London: Longman).

Hudson, R. A. 1996. *Sociolinguistics*, 2nd ed. (Cambridge, UK: Cambridge University Press).

Hymes, Dell, ed. 1964. *Language in Culture and Society* (New York: Harper & Row).

Johnson, Sally & Ulrike Hanna Meinhof, eds. 1997. *Language and Masculinity* (Oxford: Blackwell).

Kurath, Hans. 1949. *A Word Geography of the Eastern United States* (Ann Arbor: University of Michigan Press).

Kurath, Hans & Raven I. McDavid, Jr. 1961. *The Pronunciation of English in the Atlantic States* (Ann Arbor: University of Michigan Press).

Labov, William. 2006. *The Social Stratification of English in New York City*, 2nd ed. (Cambridge, UK: Cambridge University Press).

———. 1972. *Sociolinguistic Patterns* (Philadelphia: University of Pennsylvania Press).

———. 1996. "The Organization of Dialect Diversity in America." Available at http://www.ling.upenn.edu/phono_atlas/ICSLP4.html

——— & Wendell Harris. 1994. "Addressing Social Issues through Linguistic Evidence." In John Gibbons, *Language and the Law* (London: Longman), pp. 265–305.

Marckwardt, Albert H. 1957. *Principal and Subsidiary Dialect Areas in the North-Central States*. Publication of the American Dialect Society, No. 27.

Mar-Molinero, Clare. 1997. *The Spanish-Speaking World*: A Practical Introduction to Sociolinguistic Issues (London: Routledge).

Nunnally, Thomas, ed. 2008. *Tributaries*. Journal of the Alabama Folklife Society, No. 10.

Ochs, Elinor. 1992. "Indexing Gender," in Alessandro Duranti & Charles Goodwin, eds., *Rethinking Context* (Cambridge, UK: Cambridge University Press), pp. 335–58.

Ornstein-Galicia, Jacob, ed. 1988. *Form and Function in Chicano English* (Malabar, FL: Robert E. Krieger).

Pederson, Lee. 1986–1991. *Linguistic Atlas of the Gulf States*, 7 vols. (Athens: University of Georgia Press).

Rickford, John R. & Russell J. Rickford. 2000. *Spoken Soul* (New York: John Wiley & Sons).

Sanders, Carol, ed. 1993. *French Today*: Language in its Social Context (Cambridge, UK: Cambridge University Press).

Sankoff, Gillian & Henrietta Cedergren. 1971. "Some Results of a Sociolinguistic Study of Montreal French," in R. Darnell, ed., *Linguistic Diversity in Canadian Society* (Edmonton: Linguistic Research), pp. 61–87.

Smitherman, Geneva. 1986. *Talkin and Testifyin*: The Language of Black America (Detroit, MI: Wayne State University Press).

Stevenson, Patrick. 1997. *The German-Speaking World: A Practical Introduction to Sociolinguistic Issues* (London: Routledge).

Terrell, Tracy D. 1981. "Diachronic Reconstruction by Dialect Comparison of Variable Constraints," in David Sankoff & Henrietta Cedergren, eds., *Variation Omnibus* (Edmonton: Linguistic Research), pp. 115–24.

Tottie, Gunnel. 2002. *An Introduction to American English* (Oxford: Blackwell).

Wardhaugh, Ronald. 2010. *An Introduction to Sociolinguistics*, 6th ed. (New York: Wiley-Blackwell).

Part Three

Language Change, Language Development, and Language Acquisition

Part Three combines Part One's focus on language structure with Part Two's emphasis on language use. Here we investigate three topics that are perennial favorites:

- how languages change over time and are related to one another
- how English developed from *Beowulf* to the twenty-first century
- how children and adults learn languages.

You know that French and Spanish are related languages in that they derive from the same historical source. You also know that the English of Shakespeare differs from today's English. In Part Three you'll learn how languages change and develop, which languages are related to one another, and which ones have no known relatives.

You'll also investigate language acquisition by children and adults. For children acquiring a first language and for anyone interacting with them during that process, a child's first words and early utterances prompt wonder and tickle the imagination. In contrast to the frolicsome time children have acquiring their first tongue, adolescents and adults often must exert strenuous efforts to learn a second language. For children, success with a native language is guaranteed. For adults, learning a second language can be a challenge and is not always successful. You'll see why.

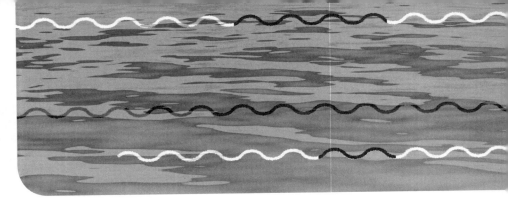

12

Language Change Over Time: Historical Linguistics

What Do You Think?

- Pre-med Melissa conjectures that English must derive from Latin because it contains so many Latin words. What can you tell her about the historical relationship between Latin and English and about why English contains so many Latin words?
- On a field trip to Chinatown in San Francisco with your sixth-grade class, a colleague from Taiwan accompanies you. When she tries to buy pieces of jade from a Chinese street vendor, they cannot understand one another and enlist help from a translator. Afterward your colleague explains that she speaks Mandarin dialect, and the vendor spoke only Cantonese dialect. Your students claim that if speakers of Mandarin and Cantonese cannot understand one another, they must be speaking different *languages*. They're not both speaking Chinese! Are they right?
- Examining a map of the Middle East, classmates notice that many places in Iraq have names beginning with *al, an,* or *as* (*Al Fallūjah, Al Basrah, An Najaf, As Sulaymānīyah*), but those in neighboring Iran don't. Someone claims Persian and Arabic must be related because the writing systems look the same. What can you tell them about the relationship between Persian and Arabic? Between speech and writing?
- Students in a geography class note two kinds of place names in Oklahoma—transparent ones like *Sweetwater, Sand Springs, Granite, Grove, Beaver,* and *Mountain View* and others like *Okmulgee, Oktaha, Chickasha, Comanche, Chattanooga, Manitou, Cherokee, Arapaho,* and *Wynona*, which don't have independent meanings in English. What can you tell them about languages in contact with one another and how place-names come to be?

Do Living Languages Always Change?

It's no secret that languages change over the years. Usually the most noticeable differences between generations are in vocabulary. What one generation called *hi-fi, car phone,* and *studious young man or woman,* a younger generation calls *iPod, cell phone* or *mobile phone,* and (in some instances) *nerd.* Your parents' grandparents may not have used the terms *tank tops, six-packs, sitcoms,* or *cyberspace* in their youth, nor referred to certain verbal actions as *bad-mouthing, dissin,* or *dumping on* someone. Until relatively recently none of us had heard of a *Segway,* an *SUV,* or *smartphones*; we weren't yet *googling* for information or *friending* and *defriending* on Facebook and MySpace.

Pronunciation also changes—in individual words and whole classes of words containing a particular sound. For example, a few decades ago the word *nuclear* was commonly pronounced [nukliər], but today you often hear "nukular" [nukjələr]. In the same vein, *realtor,* formerly pronounced "re-al-tor" [riəltər], is increasingly pronounced "real-a-tor" [rilətər]. Sound changes that affect individual words like *nuclear* and *realtor* are called **sporadic sound changes**.

Regional accents and dialects change as well. As we saw in Chapter 11, in much of Canada and the western United States, the vowel sounds in the words *cot* and *caught* are pronounced identically, so that these words—and similar pairs like *Don* and *Dawn* and *wok* and *walk*—are no longer distinguished, although in other regions of the United States they remain distinct. Sound changes that affect all the words in which a particular sound occurs in a particular sound environment are called **regular sound changes**, and they may be conditioned or unconditioned, as we'll see.

Sometimes a change affects a sound only when it occurs in a particular linguistic environment. For example, in some dialects of the American South, the vowels /ɪ/ and /ɛ/ are merging, but only when they occur before the nasal consonants /n/ or /m/. In those dialects, *him* and *hem* sound the same, but *pit* and *pet* remain distinct in pronunciation. This kind of regular sound change is called **conditioned sound change**. We also saw extensive shifting of North American vowels in the Northern Cities Shift and the Southern Shift. These shifts are **unconditioned sound changes**: they affect every word in which the particular sound appears.

The meaning of terms can also change. About 1,000 years ago, the English verb *starve* (Old English *steorfan*) meant simply 'die' (by any cause). Today, it refers principally to deprivation and death by hunger (or, by metaphorical extension, to 'deprive of affection'). Until recently, the adjective *natural,* which has been used in English for over 700 years, did not have the meaning 'without chemical preservatives,' which it commonly has today, as in *all-natural ice cream.* The meanings of *joint, bust, fix, high, hit,* and many other words have been extended, in these cases by their use in the world of drugs. To take a final example, if you check the meaning of the expression *to beg the question,* you'll find that the *Oxford English Dictionary* defines it as 'take for granted the matter in dispute,' but among your friends and on radio and television you'll notice that it often means simply 'lead to another question.' When enough people in enough contexts use it this way, the new definition will be added to the existing one in the *OED* and other dictionaries.

There can also be grammatical differences in the speech of different generations. *Goes the king hence today?* Shakespeare's Lennox asks Macbeth. Today, the same inquiry (were there occasion to use it) would more likely be *Is the king going away today?* The simple fact is that certain grammatical features of seventeenth-century English are no longer in use. To cite a more recent development, in many parts of the American South, double modals have come into use, and it's not uncommon to hear people using them in sentences such as *I might could do it.* Whether these "double modal" constructions will spread remains to be seen, but they have a certain appeal.

Try It Yourself Decide whether you say "nu-kyu-ler" or "nu-cle-er" and which of the two you think your parents say and your friends say. Then listen attentively over the next few days to see whether your impressions match the facts. Afterward, check one or two dictionaries to see whether the pronunciation you've actually heard people using is recorded in the dictionary or not. Should it be?

Generalizing from one's own linguistic experience may be risky, but it is safe to say that the common experience of noticing linguistic differences between one generation and another reflects the simple fact that languages do not stand still. Languages are always in the process of changing—and they change at all levels of the grammar: phonology, morphology, syntax, and semantics.

Language Families and the Indo-European Family

One result of ongoing language changes is that a single language can develop into several languages. The early stages of such development are apparent in differences among Australian, American, Canadian, Indian, and Irish dialects of English, all of which have sprung from English spoken in Britain. In order for different dialects to develop into separate languages, groups of speakers must remain relatively isolated from one another, separated by physical barriers such as mountain ranges and great bodies of water or by social and political barriers such as those drawn along tribal, religious, ethnic, or national boundaries.

You've probably heard it said that French, Spanish, and Italian come from Latin. The "Vulgar Latin" spoken in parts of the Roman empire lives on in to-day's French, Italian, Spanish, Portuguese, Rumanian, Catalan, Galician, and Provençal, all of which are its direct descendants. On the other hand, the classical Latin of Cicero, Virgil, Caesar, and other Roman writers is "dead," and the written varieties of French, Spanish, and Italian are based on the modern spoken languages, not the classical written language.

You may also have heard it claimed that English comes from Latin. English and Latin are indeed related, but Latin is not an ancestor of English. Both languages come from a common ancestor, but they traveled along different paths. During the Renaissance, English borrowed hundreds and hundreds of words from Latin—for example, *conspicuous, dexterous, eradicate, halo, insane,* and *jocular.* But borrowed words don't affect genealogy. English is descended from Proto-Germanic, a language spoken about the time of classical Latin and a few centuries earlier, a language that ultimately gave rise not only to English but to German, Dutch, Norwegian, Danish, and Swedish (among others). Thus, as

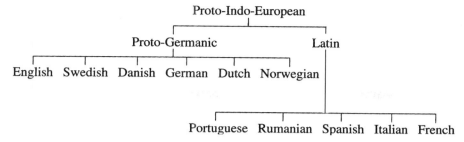

Figure 12.1 Germanic and Romance Branches of the Indo-European Family

Latin is the parent language of French and Spanish, so Proto-Germanic is the parent language of English and its Germanic relatives.

Except for a few carved runic inscriptions from the third century A.D., Proto-Germanic (unlike Latin) has left no written records. Modern knowledge of Proto-Germanic has been inferred from the character of its daughter languages through comparative reconstruction, a technique explained in this chapter. Proto-Germanic and Latin are themselves daughters of Proto-Indo-European, another unattested (unrecorded) language. In a simplified manner, we can represent the situation by the family tree in Figure 12.1, which has two branches.

While the fact that languages change and give rise to new languages is familiar to modern readers, it is a notion that was postulated clearly only two centuries ago. In 1786, while he was serving as a judge in Calcutta, Sir William Jones addressed the Royal Asiatic Society of Bengal about his linguistic experience.

> The Sanskrit language, whatever be its antiquity, is of a wonderful structure; more perfect than the Greek, more copious than the Latin, and more exquisitely refined than either, yet bearing to both of them a stronger affinity, both in the roots of verbs and in the forms of grammar, than could possibly have been produced by accident; so strong indeed, that no philologer could examine them all three, without believing them to have sprung from some common source, which, perhaps, no longer exists: there is a similar reason, though not quite so forcible, for supposing that both the Gothic and the Celtic, though blended with a very different idiom, had the same origin with the Sanskrit; and the old Persian might be added to the same family . . . .

Today linguists would avoid such judgmental statements as Sanskrit having a "more perfect" structure than Greek and being "more exquisitely refined" than Latin, but Jones recognized that languages give rise to other languages. Indeed, Sanskrit, Latin, Greek, Celtic, Gothic, and Persian *did* spring from a "common source" that "no longer exists." Jones had achieved an important insight. The common source of Latin, Greek, Sanskrit, Celtic, Gothic, Persian, and many other languages (including English and its Germanic relatives, and French and Spanish and their Romance relatives) is Proto-Indo-European. A parent language and the daughter languages that have developed from it are collectively referred to as a **language family**, and the family that Jones recognized is called the **Indo-European** family. While there are no written records of Proto-Indo-European itself, a rich vein of inferences about its words and structures can be mined from the inherited linguistic characteristics of its daughter languages.

The working assumption of historical linguists is this: a feature that occurs widely in daughter languages and cannot be explained by reference to language typology, language universals, or borrowing from another tongue is likely to have been inherited from the parent language.

How to Reconstruct the Linguistic Past

There is evidence of massive migrations from Central Asia to Europe about 4000 B.C. by a people who probably spoke Proto-Indo-European. There are no written records to document these earlier migrations, but archaeologists have found buried remains from the daily life of people who inhabited particular parts of the globe. Combined with what we can reconstruct of ancestral languages, archaeological records enable researchers to make educated guesses about where our ancestors came from and where they migrated to, as well as how they lived and died.

When scholars reconstruct an ancestral language, they also implicitly reconstruct an ancestral culture. Every culture lives on the lips of its speakers, so words ascribed to a prehistoric group represent artifacts in their culture and facets of their daily social and physical activities. In this chapter, we concentrate not on Indo-European culture and the Indo-European homeland but on the Polynesians, whose linguistic development presents another interesting case of reconstruction of a protolanguage and the culture of its speakers. (At the end of this chapter you'll find references for similar reconstructions of the Indo-European and Algonquian families.)

Polynesian and Pacific Background

On land, the only physical obstacles to sustained contacts between people are insurmountable mountains and wide rivers, which are in fact not very common. Boundaries between languages and cultures therefore are often blurred. In contrast, once people settle on an isolated island, contact with inhabitants of other islands is difficult and limited, and languages and cultures develop in relative isolation. Islands thus offer an opportunity to study what happens when a protolanguage evolves into distinct daughter languages. Because the South Pacific region consists of small islands and isolated island groups, it provides an almost ideal "laboratory" for researchers interested in the past.

The South Pacific is home to three cultural areas—Polynesia ('many islands'), Melanesia ('black islands'), and Micronesia ('small islands')—whose approximate boundaries are shown in Figure 12.2. Among other things, each area is distinguished by the physical appearance of its inhabitants: Polynesians are generally large, with olive complexions and straight or wavy hair; Melanesians typically are dark-skinned, with smaller frames and curlier hair; and Micronesians tend to be slight of frame, with light brown complexions and straight hair. We will concentrate on Polynesians and ask what can be learned about their origins and their early life in Polynesia from the languages they speak today.

The islands of Polynesia vary greatly in size and structure. The main island of Hawaii and the islands of Samoa and Tahiti are comparatively large land masses formed through volcanic eruptions. Other islands are tiny atolls, little more than

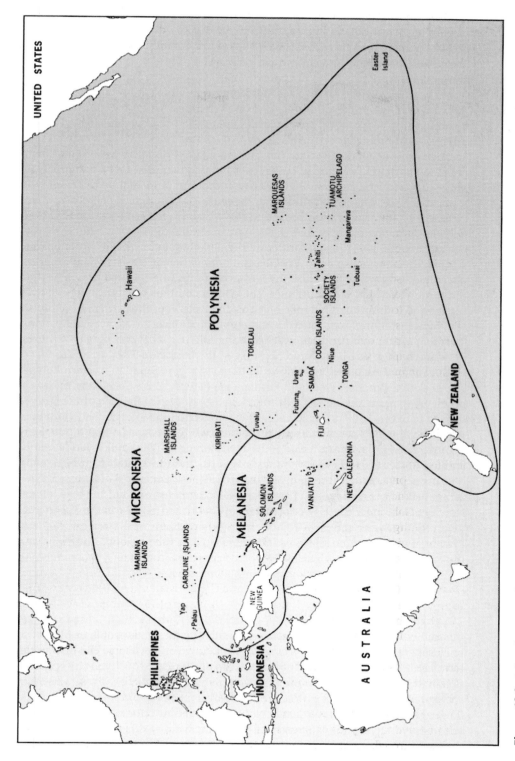

Figure 12.2 Cultural Areas in the Pacific

sand banks and coral reefs that barely reach the surface of the ocean; typically, one can walk or wade around an atoll in a few hours. Atolls are found in Tuvalu, the Tuamotu Archipelago, and the northern Cook Islands. Some coral islands in Tonga and elsewhere have been raised by underground volcanic activities and are medium-sized and hilly, in contrast to atolls, which are utterly flat.

No written records exist to aid in tracing the Polynesians' cultural and linguistic development because they had no system of writing before literacy was introduced by Westerners. But modern languages and the archaeological record provide useful tools for reconstruction.

There is every indication that all the islands of Polynesia were settled by a people who shared a common language, a common culture, and a common way of dealing with the environment. We know that they traveled by sea from west to east, settling islands on their way, because the languages of Polynesia are clearly related to languages spoken to the west in Melanesia but have no connection with languages spoken to the east in South America. In addition, Polynesian cultures have many affinities with Melanesian cultures but virtually none with those of South America. Finally, the human bones, artifacts, and other archaeological remains found on the western islands of Polynesia are older than those found on the eastern islands. The conclusion that western Polynesia was settled prior to eastern Polynesia contradicts the hypothesis that the Polynesians originated in South America, a theory popularized by Norwegian explorer Thor Heyerdahl, who in 1947 reached Polynesia in a raft after setting sail from Peru and who subsequently told his story in the book *Kon-Tiki*.

The oldest archaeological records in Polynesia were found in western Polynesia: in Tonga, Samoa, Uvea, and Futuna (see Figure 12.2). Consisting mostly of pottery fragments similar to those found farther west in Melanesia, these records date to between 1500 and 1200 B.C. This implies that people moved from somewhere outside Polynesia and settled on these western islands about 3,500 years ago. No pottery has been found in eastern Polynesia (the Cook Islands, Tahiti and the Society Islands, the Marquesas Islands, and the Tuamotu Archipelago), but other archaeological remains indicate that these eastern islands were settled around the first century A.D. The most recent remains are found in Hawaii and New Zealand. That these two island groups were settled last is not surprising, given that they are the most remote from other islands of the region. The earliest artifacts found on these islands suggest that the ancient Hawaiians and the ancestors of the New Zealand Maoris first arrived on their respective island homes between the seventh and eleventh centuries A.D.

Polynesian Languages and Their History

We said earlier that all of Polynesia was settled by the same people or by groups of closely related people from a single region. Linguistic evidence can help us determine the original homeland of the Polynesians. In Table 12.1 you can see some striking similarities among words in five Polynesian languages. These and other widespread similarities of expression for equivalent content demonstrate that the languages of Polynesia are related. Not finding similar close correspondences in vocabulary between the languages of Polynesia and any other language, we can safely say that Polynesian languages form a language family. In other words, all the Polynesian languages are daughter languages of a single parent language, the

Table 12.1 *Common Words in Five Polynesian Languages*

Tongan	Samoan	Tahitian	Maori	Hawaiian	
manu	manu	manu	manu	manu	'bird'
ika	iʔa	iʔa	ika	iʔa	'fish'
kai	ʔai	ʔai	kai	ʔai	'to eat'
tapu	tapu	tapu	tapu	kapu	'forbidden'
vaka	vaʔa	vaʔa	waka	waʔa	'canoe'
fohe	foe	hoe	hoe	hoe	'oar'
mata	mata	mata	mata	maka	'eye'
ʔuta	uta	uta	uta	uka	'bush'
toto	toto	toto	toto	koko	'blood'

ancestor of the 30 or so Polynesian languages and of no other existing language. Known as Proto-Polynesian, the parent language was spoken by the people who first settled western Polynesia between 1500 and 1200 B.C.

In Table 12.1, the word *manu* 'bird' is exactly the same—in form and sense— in all five languages. The other words have the same vowel correspondences (where one has /a/, all have /a/) and differ slightly from one another in some of the consonants. The Polynesian words in each line of the table are **cognates**— words that have developed from a single, historically earlier word. In examining other words, you'll find the consonant correspondences between the different languages to be strikingly regular. On the basis of many word sets in addition to the nine in Table 12.1, you can see that in words where the phonemes /m/ and /n/ (as in *manu*) occur in one Polynesian language, they tend to occur in all. On the other hand, Tongan, Samoan, Tahitian, and Maori /t/ corresponds to /k/ in Hawaiian, as in the words for 'forbidden' and 'eye.' We can represent these *sound correspondences* as in Table 12.3 on page 429.

If we examine still other words, these sound correspondences are maintained, and additional **correspondence sets** can be established. As the words in Table 12.2 reveal, Tongan and Maori /k/ corresponds to a glottal stop /ʔ/ in Samoan, Tahitian, and Hawaiian, while Tongan, Samoan, and Maori /ŋ/ corresponds to Tahitian /ʔ/ and Hawaiian /n/. We can thus establish regular sound correspondences among modern-day Polynesian languages.

Table 12.2 *Cognates in Five Polynesian Languages I*

Tongan	Samoan	Tahitian	Maori	Hawaiian	
toki	toʔi	toʔi	toki	koʔi	'axe'
taʔi	taŋi	taʔi	taʔi	kani	'to cry'
taŋata	taŋata	taʔata	taŋata	kanaka	'man'
kafa	ʔafa	ʔaha	kaha	ʔaha	'rope'
kutu	ʔutu	ʔutu	kutu	ʔuku	'louse'
kata	ʔata	ʔata	kata	ʔaka	'to laugh'
moko	moʔo	moʔo	moko	moʔo	'lizard'

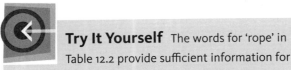

Try It Yourself The words for 'rope' in Table 12.2 provide sufficient information for two correspondence sets of consonant sounds. The final line in Table 12.3 gives k-ʔ-ʔ-k-ʔ as one of those correspondence sets. What's the other one that can be proposed from the words for 'rope'?

In comparative reconstruction, it is important to exclude all *borrowed* words because the only words that can profitably provide sounds for use in a correspondence set are those that have descended directly from the ancestor language. For example, because Proto-Polynesian *s became /h/ in Tongan (but remained /s/ in some daughter languages), Tongan has very few words with /s/—among them *sikaleti*, meaning 'cigarette.' While *sikaleti* was obviously borrowed from a language outside the Polynesian family, words borrowed from other languages within the same family may not be so easy to spot.

Comparative Reconstruction

The method just illustrated is known as **comparative reconstruction**. It aims to reconstruct an ancestor language from the evidence that remains in daughter languages. Its premise is that, borrowing aside, similar forms with similar meanings across related languages are *reflexes* of a single form with a related meaning in the parent language. This commonsense approach is at the foundation of the comparative method and, indeed, of historical linguistics.

When we examine correspondence sets such as m-m-m-m-m and t-t-t-t-k in Table 12.3, it seems reasonable to assume that *m and *t existed in the parent language and that /m/ was retained in each of the daughter languages, while /t/ was retained except in Hawaiian, where it became /k/. Such assumptions are the everyday fare of historical linguistics. When we assume the existence of a sound (or other structure) in a language for which we have no evidence except what can be inferred from daughter languages, that sound (or structure) is said to be reconstructed. Reconstructed forms are "starred" to indicate that they are unattested. We can represent the reconstructions from correspondence sets this way:

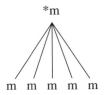

In describing the development of Hawaiian from Proto-Polynesian, we would postulate a historical rule of the form: *t > k. (A shaftless arrow indicates that one form developed into another form over time.) A sound change in which one sound (*t) develops into two or more sounds (t and k) is called a **split**.

Instead of *t, we could have reconstructed a *k in Proto-Polynesian. We would then say that *k was retained in Hawaiian and became /t/ in *all* the other languages. But we posit *t because experience with many languages has led historical linguists to prefer reconstructions that assume the *least* change consistent with the facts, unless there is good reason to do otherwise. In this instance, reconstructing *t assumes fewer subsequent changes than would a reconstruction of *k. You can think of this as the majority rule.

Table 12.3 *Sound Correspondences in Five Polynesian Languages*

Tongan	Samoan	Tahitian	Maori	Hawaiian
m	m	m	m	m
n	n	n	n	n
ŋ	ŋ	ʔ	ŋ	n
p	p	p	p	p
t	t	t	t	k
k	ʔ	ʔ	k	ʔ

Now let's inspect the reconstruction of *m more closely. To postulate that /m/ existed in the protolanguage and was retained in all the daughter languages is the simplest hypothesis but not the only logical one. You could hypothesize some other sound in the protolanguage that independently became /m/ in each daughter language.

Because /m/ is a bilabial nasal, both the bilabial /b/ and the nasal /n/ would be other likely candidates for this reconstruction because they share phonetic features with the /m/ found in all the daughter languages. On the other hand, Polynesian languages generally lack the phoneme /b/, so it seems more reasonable to assume that the parent language also lacked /b/. Alternatively, you could reconstruct an /n/ that changed to /m/ in all the daughter languages independently of one another. But there are two reasons to reject this hypothesis. First, it is not a minimal assumption, and, second, the daughter languages have an /n/ that also requires a source in the parent language. We thus postulate Proto-Polynesian *m and *n, which were retained unchanged in all the daughter languages.

Let's examine one other correspondence set: ŋ-ŋ-ʔ-ŋ-n. We have just postulated Proto-Polynesian *n as the reconstructed earlier form (technically, the **etymon**) of the correspondence set n-n-n-n-n. It's interesting to compare this reconstruction with one for the correspondence set ŋ-ŋ-ʔ-ŋ-n, for which the most likely reconstruction is *ŋ.

> **Try It Yourself** Given that /m/, the sound in all the daughter languages of Table 12.3, is a bilabial nasal, which other two sounds would make good candidates as the sound from which /m/ might have developed in the five daughter languages represented in the table?

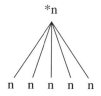

*n

n n n n n

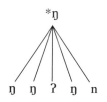

*ŋ

ŋ ŋ ʔ ŋ n

Given these reconstructions, *ŋ was retained in Tongan, Samoan, and Maori but became /ʔ/ in Tahitian and /n/ in Hawaiian. As a result, the distinction between *n and *ŋ that existed in Proto-Polynesian and is maintained in Tongan, Samoan, and Maori does not exist in Hawaiian, where *n and *ŋ have merged in /n/. Hawaiian /n/ therefore has two historical sources. When two sounds merge into one, that sound change is called a **merger**. We can represent this historical merger either in rules (*n > n; *ŋ > n) or schematically.

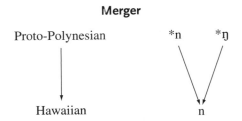

Merger

Subgroups On the basis of lexical and structural characteristics, it is apparent that some Polynesian languages are more closely linked than others. As shown in Table 12.4, Tongan differs from other Polynesian languages in at least two respects: it has initial /h/ where other languages do not have anything; and it has nothing where other languages have either /l/ or /r/. Niuean, another Polynesian language, shares these and certain other characteristics with Tongan. On the basis of such evidence, Tongan and Niuean can be seen to form a **subgroup**, or *branch*, of Polynesian. This implies that Tongan and Niuean were at one time a single language distinct from Proto-Polynesian and that Proto-Tongic, as that language is called, developed certain features before splitting into Tongan and Niuean. The retention in both languages of these features (those that developed after Proto-Tongic split from Proto-Polynesian but before Tongan and Niuean split into separate languages) constitutes the characteristic shared features of the Proto-Tongic branch of the Polynesian family.

In the meantime, the other branch of Proto-Polynesian also evolved independently after its speakers lost contact with speakers of Proto-Tongic. As this second branch, called Proto-Nuclear-Polynesian, developed its distinctive characteristics, it emerged as a separate language that gave rise to still other languages. Except for Tongan and Niuean, all modern Polynesian languages share certain features inherited from Proto-Nuclear-Polynesian. In turn, Proto-Nuclear-Polynesian has two main subgroups: Samoic-Outlier and Eastern Polynesian. The evolution of Polynesian languages can be represented in the family tree shown in Figure 12.3. Such family trees usefully represent the general genealogical relationships in a family of languages, although they inevitably oversimplify the complex facts of history, especially by excluding borrowings and other influences that languages in contact can exert on one another.

Table 12.4 *Cognates in Five Polynesian Languages II*

Tongan	Samoan	Tahitian	Maori	Hawaiian	
hama	ama	ama	ama	ama	'outrigger'
hiŋoa	iŋoa	iʔoa	iŋoa	inoa	'name'
mohe	moe	moe	moe	moe	'to sleep'
hake	aʔe	aʔe	ake	aʔe	'up'
ua	lua	rua	rua	lua	'two'
ama	lama	rama	rama	lama	'torch'
tui	tuli	turi	turi	kuli	'knee'

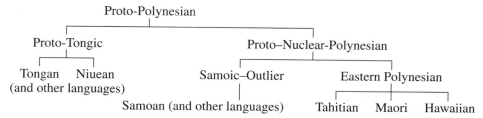

Figure 12.3 Polynesian Languages

Reconstructing the Proto-Polynesian Vocabulary

On the basis of the evidence provided by modern-day Polynesian languages, we can reconstruct the sound system and vocabulary of Proto-Polynesian (and make educated guesses about its grammatical structure). In turn, reconstructed linguistic information can tell us a good deal about the people who first settled Polynesia more than 3,000 years ago.

A word can be reconstructed in Proto-Polynesian if we find **reflexes** of it—that is, cognates—in at least one language of each major subgroup (Tongic, Samoic-Outlier, and Eastern Polynesian; see Figure 12.3) and are confident that the cognates are not borrowed words. If we reconstructed a lexical item for Proto-Polynesian based simply on evidence from Tongan and, say, Samoan, we would run the risk of having found a word that existed originally only in Tongan—after Tongan became a separate language—and that was borrowed by the early Samoans. You can see from the map in Figure 12.2 that Tonga and Samoa are geographically close enough to have had contacts in prehistoric times.

For example, since cognate words for 'bird,' 'fish,' and 'man' are found in all major subgroups of the Polynesian family (as shown in Tables 12.1 and 12.2), we can reconstruct a Proto-Polynesian form for each word. According to regular sound correspondences and the most plausible reconstructed sounds, these words are *manu, *taŋata, and *ika. In contrast, the word for a 'night of full moon,' which in Maori and Tahitian is *hotu* and in Hawaiian *hoku*, cannot be reconstructed for Proto-Polynesian because there is no cognate in any Tongic or Samoic-Outlier language. Similarly, an etymon for the Tongan and Niuean word *kookoo* 'windpipe' cannot be reconstructed for Proto-Polynesian because there is no reflex in any Samoic-Outlier or Eastern Polynesian language.

Using the comparative method of historical reconstruction just outlined, the lexical items in Table 12.5, all referring to the physical environment, can be reconstructed for Proto-Polynesian. From Table 12.5, you can see that the Proto-Polynesian people had words for ocean-related notions (the left-hand column) and for topographic features typically found on large volcanic islands (the right-hand column). As it happens, there are no waterfalls, precipices, mountains, or lakes on coral atolls, and only rarely are they found on raised coral islands.

In interpreting such results, linguists make the assumption that the presence of a word for a particular object in a language usually indicates the presence of that object in the speakers' environment. (There are exceptions to this rule, as we will see, but they are few and far between.) In particular, complete land-lubbers will not normally have an elaborate native vocabulary for the sea and

Table 12.5 *Reconstructed Terms in Proto-Polynesian I*

*awa	'channel'	*hafu	'waterfall'
*hakau	'coral reef'	*lanu	'fresh water'
*kilikili	'gravel'	*lolo	'flood'
*peau	'wave'	*mato	'precipice'
*sou	'rough ocean'	*maʔuŋa	'mountain'
*tahi	'sea'	*rano	'lake'
*ʔone	'sand'	*waitafe	'stream'

for seafaring activities, barring the possibility of a recent move inland from a coastal area. We thus surmise that the early Polynesians inhabited a high island or a chain of high islands but lived close enough to the ocean to be familiar with the landscape and phenomena of the sea.

In Table 12.6, we reconstruct other Proto-Polynesian names for animals and make the assumption that the ancient Polynesians were familiar with them. Names of many other reef and deepwater fish and other sea creatures can be reconstructed besides those listed in the left-hand column. In contrast, we can reconstruct only a handful of names for land animals: a few domesticated animals (dog, pig, chicken) and a few birds and reptiles. We surmise that the Polynesians' original habitat was rich in sea life but probably relatively poor in land fauna—that the Polynesians originally inhabited coastal regions and not island interiors. The character of the land fauna offers pointed information about the Proto-Polynesian homeland. Since the Proto-Polynesian terms *peka* 'bat' and *lulu* 'owl' can be reconstructed, we can exclude as possible homelands Tahiti, Easter Island, and the Marquesas, where bats and owls are not found.

Furthermore, snakes are found only east of Samoa. Though we find reflexes of Proto-Polynesian *ŋata* 'snake' in many languages, we find no snakes west of Samoa. Had the Proto-Polynesians inhabited an island west of Samoa, they

Table 12.6 *Reconstructed Terms in Proto-Polynesian II*

*maŋoo	'shark'	*kulii	'dog'
*kanahe	'mullet'	*puaka	'pig'
*sakulaa	'swordfish'	*moko	'lizard'
*ʔatu	'bonito'	*kumaa	'rat'
*ʔono	'barracuda'	*ŋata	'snake'
*ʔume	'leatherjacket'	*fonu	'turtle'
*manini	'sturgeon'	*peka	'bat'
*nofu	'stonefish'	*namu	'mosquito'
*fai	'stingray'	*lulu	'owl'
*kaloama	'goatfish'	*matuku	'reef heron'
*palani	'surgeonfish'	*akiaki	'tern'
*toke	'eel'	*moa	'chicken'

would very likely have lost the term *ŋata over the centuries. Similarly, we know that pigs (for which the word *puaka can be reconstructed) are not native to Polynesia, but Europeans first arriving between the sixteenth and nineteenth centuries found them everywhere except on Niue, Easter Island, and New Zealand. These three regions are thus unlikely homelands.

Words for some animals have undergone interesting changes in certain Polynesian languages. For example, New Zealand is much colder than the rest of Polynesia, and its native animals are very different from those found on the tropical islands to the north. Upon arrival in New Zealand, the ancient Maoris encountered many new species to which they gave the names of animals they had left behind in tropical Polynesia; thus, the following correspondences exist.

Proto-Polynesian		Maori	
*pule	'cowrie shell'	pure	'bivalve mollusk'
*ŋata	'snake'	ŋata	'snail'
*ali	'flounder'	ari	'small shark'

Names for other animals were either dropped from the Maori vocabulary or applied to things commonly associated with the animal.

Proto-Polynesian		Maori	
*ane	'termite'	ane	'rotten'
*lupe	'pigeon'	rupe	'mythical'

Other changes are more complex. The word *lulu* (or *ruru*) refers to owls in languages such as Tongan, Samoan, and Maori, which are spoken in areas where owls are found. On some islands, such as the Marquesas and Tahiti, owls do not exist, and the reflex of Proto-Polynesian *lulu* 'owl' has either disappeared from the language, as in Marquesan, or been applied to another species, as in Tahitian. Owls inhabit Hawaii, but the Proto-Polynesian term *lulu* has been replaced by the word *pueo* there.

Why would the early Hawaiians replace one word with the other? In the Marquesas, as we noted, there are no owls, and the language spoken there has no reflex of *lulu*. Apparently the ancient Polynesians settled the Marquesas and stayed for several centuries, during which they lost the word *lulu* for lack of anything to apply it to. When they subsequently traveled north and settled Hawaii, they encountered owls, but by that time the word *lulu* had been forgotten, and a new word had to be found.

The linguistic evidence argues that the ancestors of the Polynesians were fishermen and cultivators. Here are a few of the many terms that refer to fishing and horticulture.

*mataʔu	'fishhook'	*too	'to plant'
*rama	'to torch fish'	*faki	'to pick'
*paa	'fish lure'	*lohu	'picking pole'
*kupeŋa	'fish net'	*hua	'spade'
*afo	'fishing line'	*maʔala	'garden'
*faaŋota	'to fish'	*palpula	'seedling'

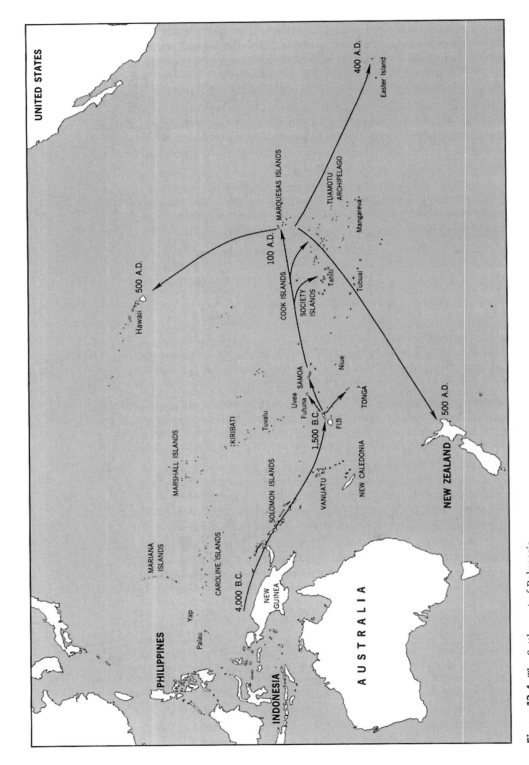

Figure 12.4 The Settlement of Polynesia

By contrast, hunting terms are limited, with three words apparently exhausting all possible reconstructions for verbs related to hunting: *fana* 'to shoot with a bow,' *welo* 'to spear,' and *seu* 'to snare with a net.' It is probably safe to infer that the major source of food for the ancient Polynesians was not the bush but the sea and garden.

One field with a notable array of vocabulary is canoe navigation, with the following reconstructions: *folau* 'to travel by sea,' *ʔuli* 'to steer,' *fohe* 'paddle,' *fana* 'mast,' *laa* 'sail,' *kiato* 'outrigger boom,' *hama* 'outrigger.' That the speakers of Proto-Polynesian were expert seafarers comes as no surprise, given that they traveled enormous distances between islands (2,000 miles stretch between Hawaii and the closest inhabited island).

Historical Linguistics and Prehistory

Linguistic evidence combined with archaeological evidence leads to the following hypotheses, which are summarized (and can be tracked) in Figure 12.4.

1. The speakers of Proto-Polynesian inhabited the coastal region of a high island or group of high islands.

2. This homeland is likely to have been in the region between Samoa and Fiji, including the islands of Tonga, Uvea, and Futuna.

3. The ancient Polynesians were fishermen, cultivators, and seafarers.

4. Around the first century A.D., the ancient Polynesians traveled eastward from their homeland, settling eastern Polynesia: Tahiti, the Cook Islands, the Marquesas, the Tuamotu, and the neighboring island groups.

5. Then, between the fourth and sixth centuries, Easter Island, Hawaii, and New Zealand were settled from eastern Polynesia.

Our discussion has focused on Polynesian origins and migrations. By judiciously combining linguistic evidence with evidence from other disciplines, we have constructed a probable picture of an ancient people, the environment they lived in, and the skills they developed for survival. These same methods have been used for other peoples and to reconstruct other migration patterns, including the Indo-Europeans and the Algonquian Indians.

What Are the Language Families of the World?

The comparative method that is used to trace the historical development of languages can also be applied to determine which languages are related within families. In this section we survey the major language families of the world.

Counting Speakers and Languages

It is not easy to determine with certainty how many people speak languages such as English, Chinese, and Arabic. Nevertheless, these and a few others stand out for the sheer number of people that claim them as a native language. Of the world's

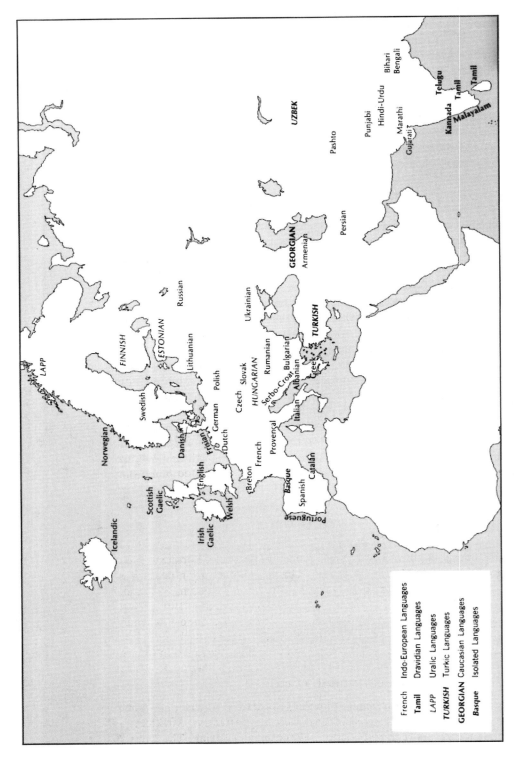

Figure 12.5 Location of the Major Indo-European, Dravidian, Caucasian, Uralic, and Turkic Languages

several thousand languages, ten are spoken natively by 100 million individuals or more. (For purposes of counting speakers, we have coupled Hindi and Urdu.)

Chinese	1.2 billion
English	325 million
Spanish	325 million
Hindi-Urdu	245 million
Arabic	220 million
Bengali	180 million
Portuguese	180 million
Malay	150 million
Russian	145 million
Japanese	120 million

Of these, Chinese, English, Spanish, Arabic, and Russian are, alongside French, the working languages of the United Nations.

Equally difficult to estimate is the number of languages currently spoken in the world. It is difficult to determine, in many cases, whether particular communities speak different dialects of one language or different languages. Furthermore, little is known about many of the world's languages. In Papua New Guinea, a nation of only 5.4 million people, more than 800 languages are spoken, although we have descriptions of a mere handful. Many Papuan languages are spoken in remote communities by only a few hundred speakers, or even a few dozen.

The following discussion is arranged by language family, beginning with Indo-European, Sino-Tibetan, Austronesian, and Afroasiatic, which are the four most important families in terms of numbers of speakers and numbers of languages. The three major language families of sub-Saharan Africa are then discussed, followed by other language families of Europe and Asia, including important isolated languages such as Japanese. Finally, we discuss the native languages of the Americas, Australia, and central Papua New Guinea. Pidgins and creoles are discussed after a brief discussion of the proposed Nostratic macrofamily.

The Indo-European Family

To the Indo-European language family belong most languages of Europe (which are now spoken natively in the Americas and Oceania and play prominent roles in Africa and Asia), as well as most languages of Iran, Afghanistan, Pakistan, Bangladesh, and most of India. Of the ten languages with more than 100 million native speakers, six belong to the Indo-European family. Yet Indo-European languages number only several hundred, about 6 percent of the world's languages. The extensive spread of Indo-European languages is shown in Figure 12.5. The Indo-European family is divided into several groups. Figure 12.6 is a family tree showing a few languages for each group.

Germanic Group Modern-day Germanic languages include English, German, Yiddish, Swedish, Norwegian, Danish, Dutch (and its derivative Afrikaans), and a few other languages such as Icelandic, Faroese, and Frisian. The closest

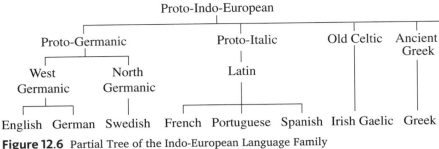

Figure 12.6 Partial Tree of the Indo-European Language Family

Table 12.7 *Common Words in Seven Germanic Languages*

English	German	Dutch	Swedish	Danish	Norwegian	Icelandic
mother	Mutter	moeder	moder	moder	moder	móðir
father	Vater	vader	fader	fader	fader	faðir
eye	Auge	oog	öga	øje	øye	auga
foot	Fuss	voet	fot	fod	fot	fótur
one	ein	een	en	en	en	einn
three	drei	drie	tre	tre	tre	þrír
month	Monat	maand	månad	måned	måned	mánaður

relative to English is Frisian, spoken in the northern Netherlands. As Table 12.7 illustrates, Germanic languages bear striking similarities to one another in vocabulary, and similarities in phonology and syntax are also numerous. Some Germanic languages are mutually intelligible, and all bear the imprint of a common ancestor. English has diverged significantly in the course of its history, as discussed in Chapter 13.

Swedish, Danish, Norwegian, Icelandic, and Faroese—the North Germanic group—are more closely related to each other than to the other languages of the Germanic group. They descended from Proto-North-Germanic, which evolved as a single language for a longer period of time than the West Germanic subgroup that includes English, German, Frisian, and Dutch. We also have written records of Gothic, which was spoken in central Europe but disappeared around the eighth century. Gothic alone forms the East Germanic subgroup. Figure 12.7 is the family tree for the Germanic group (with Gothic in parentheses because it is extinct).

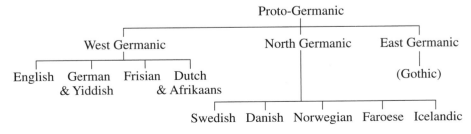

Figure 12.7 Germanic Languages

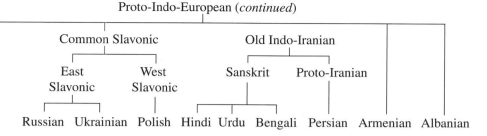

With about 325 million speakers, English is spoken in the British Isles, the United States, most of Canada, the Caribbean, Australia, New Zealand, and South Africa. In addition, there are numerous bilingual speakers of English and another language on the Indian subcontinent, in eastern and southern Africa, and in Oceania. To these we must add the countless speakers of English as a second language scattered around the globe. English is the second most populous spoken language in the world after Chinese, but it is unrivaled in terms of its geographical spread and popularity as a second language. German, which has not spread as much as English, is still one of the world's most widely spoken languages. It claims 95 million native speakers, mostly in central Europe.

Italic Group and Romance Subgroup   The Romance languages include French, Spanish, Italian, Portuguese, and Rumanian, as well as Provençal (in the south of France), Catalan (in northern Spain), Galician (in the Autonomous Region of Galicia in northwest Spain), and Romansch (in Switzerland). The Romance languages are closely related to each other, as witnessed by the sample of vocabulary correspondences in Table 12.8. The Rumanian words for 'mother,' 'father,' 'foot,' and 'month,' which are not derived from the same roots as those in the other Romance languages, illustrate the type of historical change that can hinder communication between speakers of closely related languages. Such examples are particularly common in Rumanian, which is geographically isolated from other Romance languages.

The languages of the Romance family are descendants of Vulgar Latin. Because the Romance languages have remained in close contact over the centuries, subgroups are more difficult to identify than for Germanic languages. Latin is one descendant of Proto-Italic. Oscan and Umbrian, the other principal descendants, were once spoken in central and southern Italy but are now extinct and little is

Table 12.8 *Common Words in Six Romance Languages*

French	Italian	Spanish	Rumanian	Catalan	Portuguese	
mère	madre	madre	mamă	mare	mãe	'mother'
père	padre	padre	tată	pare	pai	'father'
œil	occhio	ojo	ochiu	ull	ôlho	'eye'
pied	piede	pie	picior	peu	pé	'foot'
un	uno	uno	un	un	um	'one'
trois	tre	tres	trei	tres	três	'three'
mois	mese	mes	luna	mes	mês	'month'

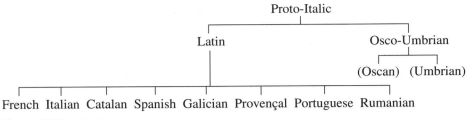

Figure 12.8 Italic Languages

Figure 12.9 Slavonic Languages

known about them. Spanish, with approximately 325 million native speakers in Spain and the Americas, is the second or third most populous language. Portuguese is spoken by nearly 180 million people, principally in Portugal and Brazil. French has about 65 million native speakers in France, Canada, and the United States, as well as many second-language speakers, particularly in North Africa and West Africa. The tree for Italic and Romance languages is shown in Figure 12.8.

Slavonic Group Slavonic languages are spoken in eastern Europe and the former Soviet Union. The Slavonic group can be divided into three subgroups: East Slavonic, which includes Russian (spoken in Russia), Ukrainian (spoken in Ukraine), and Belarusan (spoken in Belarus); South Slavonic, which includes Bulgarian, Serbian, and Croatian; and West Slavonic, which groups together Polish, Czech, Slovak, and a few minor languages. All are derived from Common Slavonic (see Figure 12.9). Even more so than the Germanic and Romance languages, Slavonic languages are remarkably similar, especially in their vocabulary (see Table 12.9).

Table 12.9 *Common Words in Six Slavonic Languages*

Russian	Ukrainian	Polish	Czech	Serbian/ Croatian	Bulgarian	
mat'	mati	matka	matka	mati	mayka	'mother'
otec	otec'	ojciec	otec	otac	baʃʧa	'father'
oko	oko	oko	oko	oko	oko	'eye'
noga	noga	noga	noha	noga	krak	'foot'
odin	odin	jeden	jeden	jedan	edin	'one'
tri	tri	trzy	tři	tri	tri	'three'
mesjac	misjac'	miesiac	meʃíc	mjesec	mesec	'month'

Note: Russian *oko* 'eye' is archaic; the modern word is *glaz*.

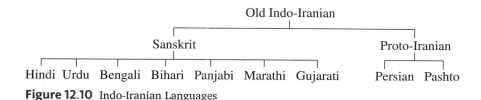

Figure 12.10 Indo-Iranian Languages

By far the most widely spoken Slavonic language is Russian, with 145 million speakers. Ukrainian has 39 million speakers, Polish 43 million, Serbian 11 million, Croatian 6 million, Czech 11 million, and Belarusan 9 million.

Indo-Iranian Group At the other geographical extreme of the Indo-European family is the Indo-Iranian group, subdivided into Iranian and Indic (see Figure 12.10). Persian (or Farsi) has 32 million speakers principally in Iran and Afghanistan, and Pashto has 20 million speakers principally in Pakistan. Indic languages include Hindi-Urdu, spoken in India (where it is called Hindi and is written in Devanāgarī script) and Pakistan (where it is called Urdu and uses Arabic script). Other Indic languages include:

Bengali	170 million	Bangladesh, India, and Nepal
Marathi	68 million	Central India
Gujarati	46 million	Western India, Tanzania, Uganda, Kenya
Panjabi	61 million	Pakistan and Northern India
Bihari	37 million	Northeastern India, Nepal (also called Bhojpuri)

Many of these languages are also spoken by ethnic Indian populations in Southeast Asia, Africa, the Americas, Great Britain, and Oceania. The parent language of the modern Indic languages is Sanskrit, the ancient language of India immortalized in the Vedas and other classical texts.

Table 12.10 presents sample vocabulary correspondences among a few Indo-Iranian languages. Not all the words with one meaning are cognates because some have sources other than a common parent language.

Hellenic Group The sole member of the Hellenic group is Greek. Certain languages, while belonging to a major language family, were isolated early enough

Table 12.10 *Common Words in Six Indic Languages*

Hindi	Bengali	Marathi	Gujarati	Persian	Pashto	
mã:	ma	ma:	ma:	mɑdær	mo:r	'mother'
ba:p	ba:p	baba:	ba:p	pedær	pla:r	'father'
ã:kʰ	cókʰ	dola	a:nkʰ	tʃæʃm	starga	'eye'
pã:w	pa:	pa:	pa:g	pɑ	pʂa	'foot'
ek	ak	ek	e:k	jek	jaw	'one'
ti:n	ti:n	ti:n	tra:n	se	dre:	'three'
mahi:na:	mas	mahi:na:	mahi:no	mɑh	mia:ʃt	'month'

Note: c represents a voiceless unaspirated palatal obstruent; ʂ represents a voiceless retroflex fricative.

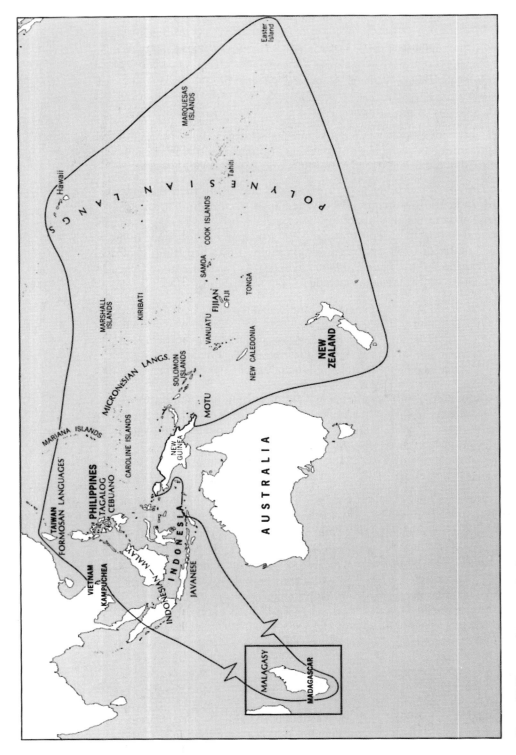

Figure 12.11 Map of Austronesian Languages

that they do not bear any particularly close affiliations to other languages of the family. Such is the case with Greek, which evolved through the centuries in relative isolation. Greek stands out from other isolated Indo-European languages because of its relatively large number of speakers (12 million) and its historical importance in Indo-European linguistics, owing to the survival of early written records of Ancient Greek.

Other Indo-European Language Groups Of the other Indo-European groups, Celtic includes Irish Gaelic, Scots Gaelic, Breton, and Welsh, which together are spoken by fewer than 1 million people today. Baltic includes Lithuanian and Latvian. Tocharian and Anatolian (including Hittite) are now extinct. Armenian and Albanian form two additional groups.

The Sino-Tibetan Family

Included in the Sino-Tibetan family are about 400 East Asian languages, many of which remain relatively unexplored. This family is divided into a Sinitic, or Chinese, group and a Tibeto-Burman group.

The Sinitic group includes more than a dozen named varieties (including Hakka, Jinyu, Mandarin, Min Nan, Wu, Xiang or Hunan, Yue or Cantonese). Most are structurally similar and are regarded by their speakers as dialects of a single language. With more than one billion speakers, this is the world's most populous language; it is, of course, Chinese. Five dialect groups can be identified. Mandarin includes the Běijīng dialect, which serves as the official language of the People's Republic of China; Yue includes the dialect of Guǎngzhōu (Canton), which is spoken by the greatest number of overseas Chinese.

By contrast, the Tibeto-Burman group includes nearly all of the Sino-Tibetan languages, but each has relatively few speakers. Among the languages of this group with more than a million speakers are Burmese (spoken in Myanmar), Meitei or Manipuri (spoken in India), Kam or Khams Tibetan, and Tibetan.

The Austronesian Family

The Austronesian family has over 1,200 languages scattered over one-third of the Southern Hemisphere. It includes Malay, spoken by about 150 million people in Indonesia and Malaysia; Javanese, with 75 million speakers on the island of Java in Indonesia; Tagalog or Pilipino, the official language of the Philippines; Cebuano, another language of the Philippines; and Malagasy, the principal language of Madagascar. Most other Austronesian languages have fewer than a million speakers each, and many of them are spoken by only a few hundred people.

The Austronesian family contains several groups. The most ancient division is between three groups of minor Formosan languages spoken in the hills of Taiwan and all other Austronesian languages; the latter group is called Malayo-Polynesian. The most important split divides Western Malayo-Polynesian (languages spoken in Indonesia, Malaysia, Madagascar, the Philippines, and Guam) from Oceanic or Eastern Malayo-Polynesian (extending from the coastal areas of Papua New Guinea into the islands of the Pacific). Fijian and the Polynesian languages are Oceanic languages. Table 12.11 gives a sample of vocabulary correspondences between representative Austronesian languages. Figure 12.12 is a simplified family tree, and the distribution of Austronesian languages is illustrated in Figure 12.11.

Table 12.11 *Common Words in Six Austronesian Languages*

Malay	Malagasy	Tagalog	Motu	Fijian	Samoan	
ibu	ineny	inâ	sina	tina	tinaa	'mother'
bapa	ikaky	amá	tama	tama	tamaa	'father'
mata	maso	mata	mata	mata	mata	'eye'
satu	isa	isa	ta	dua	tasi	'one'
tiga	telo	tatló	toi	tolu	tolu	'three'
batu	vato	bato	nadi	vatu	fatu	'stone'
kutu	hao	kuto	utu	kutu	ʔutu	'louse'

Note: Samoan *fatu* actually means 'fruit pit,' a meaning closely related to 'stone.'

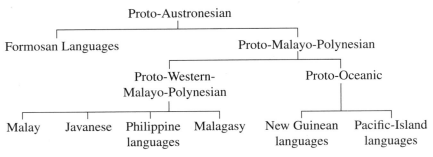

Figure 12.12 Tree of Austronesian Languages

The Afroasiatic Family

The Afroasiatic family comprises about 375 languages scattered across the northern part of Africa and western Asia. It includes Arabic, dialects of which are spoken across the entire northern part of Africa and the Middle East; Hebrew, the traditional language of the Jewish nation and revived in the twentieth century as the national language of Israel; Egyptian, the now extinct language of the ancient Egyptian civilization; and Hausa, one of Africa's major languages, spoken natively in Nigeria, Niger, and neighboring nations (see Figure 12.13).

Hebrew and Arabic form the Semitic group, to which also belong Amharic, the official language of Ethiopia, and Akkadian, a language of ancient Mesopotamia (modern Iraq). Akkadian appears to have been the first language ever written, but it was replaced largely by Aramaic, which is also Semitic. Aramaic dialects include Palestinian Aramaic (the language Jesus spoke) and Modern Syriac, spoken by Christians in Iran, Iraq, and Georgia (in the former Soviet Union).

Somali, the principal language of Somalia, is one of almost 50 members of the Cushitic group. Kabyle and other languages that belong to the Berber group are scattered across North Africa. Hausa and close to 200 other languages form the Chadic group, all of which have developed tone systems. Ancient Egyptian forms a separate Afroasiatic group; Coptic is used as a liturgical language of the Coptic Church but has no native speakers. Table 12.12 is a comparative vocabulary for representative members of the Afroasiatic family.

Table 12.12 *Common Words in Six Afroasiatic Languages*

Arabic	Hebrew	Amharic	Kabyle	Hausa	Somali	
um	ɛm	annat	jemma	inna	hoojjo	'mother'
ab	av	abbat	baba	baba	aabe	'father'
ʕain	ajin	ajn	allen	ido	il	'eye'
ʔeʒer	rɛgɛl	agar	aḍaṛ	k'afa	ʕag	'foot'
waḥad	ɛxad	and	waḥed	'daya	hal	'one'
ṭalaṭa	ʃloʃa	sost	tlata	uku	saddeħ	'three'
ʃaher	xodɛʃ	wár	eccher	wata	bil	'month'

Note: ħ is the symbol for a voiceless pharyngeal fricative and ʕ for its voiced counterpart; ṭ represents an "emphatic" or pharyngealized t, represented by a superscripted ʕ [tˤ] in the International Phonetic Alphabet.

The Three Major Language Families of Sub-Saharan Africa

Besides the Afroasiatic family spoken north of the Sahara Desert, Africa is home to three other language families: the Niger-Congo (or Niger-Kordofanian) family, with perhaps 1,500 languages spoken by about 150 million people in a region that stretches from Senegal to Kenya to South Africa; the Nilo-Saharan family, with 200 languages spoken in and around Chad and the Sudan; and the Khoisan family in southern Africa, with 25 languages. The Khoisan family, traditionally associated with the Bushmen of the Kalahari Desert, is the only language family in the world that has click sounds (discussed in Chapter 3). The boundaries between these language families are shown in Figure 12.13.

Most of the better-known languages of sub-Saharan Africa belong to the Niger-Congo family. These include Akan, spoken in Ghana; Congo, spoken in Angola and the Democratic Republic of Congo; Fula (also called Fulani and Fulfulde), spoken in Guinea and Senegal; Wolof, spoken principally in Senegal, Gambia, and Guinea; Yoruba, spoken in Nigeria; Éwé, spoken in Ghana and Togo; Igbo, spoken in Nigeria; Swahili, with relatively few first-language speakers and perhaps 30 million second-language speakers, chiefly in East Africa; and other Bantu languages of southern Africa such as Zulu and Sotho.

Other Language Families of Asia and Europe

Scattered throughout Asia and Europe are a few smaller language families and a few languages that are not genealogically related to any other language family, so far as linguists can determine, and are therefore called *isolates*.

The Dravidian Family Languages of the Dravidian family are spoken principally in southern India (see Figure 12.5).

Try It Yourself Compare the words for 'month' in the four Dravidian languages given in Table 12.13 (page 447) with the words for 'month' in the six Indic languages of Table 12.10 (page 441). Which Dravidian language appears to have borrowed the word for 'month' from an Indic language? Which Indic language has the word for 'month' most like the one borrowed by the Dravidian language?

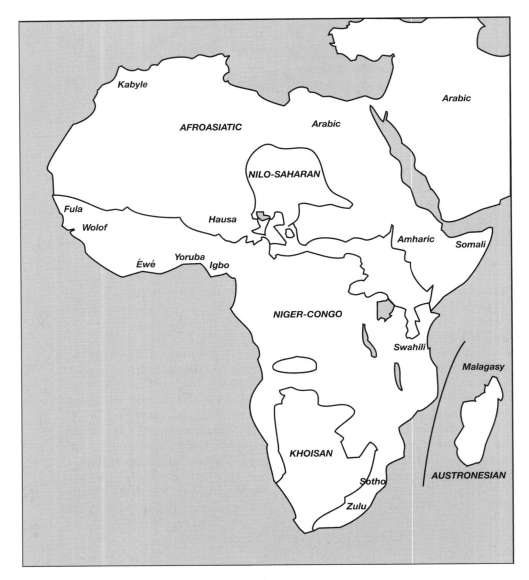

Figure 12.13 The Language Families of Africa

Source: Adapted from Gregersen, Edgar A. 1977. *Language in Africa: An Introductory Survey* (New York: Gordon & Breach).

The four major Dravidian languages are Tamil, Malayāḷam, Kannaḍa, and Telugu, all of which have been written for centuries. All Dravidian languages have been somewhat influenced by the Indic languages spoken to their north.

The Mon-Khmer Family The Mon-Khmer family includes almost 150 languages spoken in Southeast Asia (Vietnam, Laos, Cambodia, Thailand, and Myanmar), China, and India. The most important of these are Vietnamese, spoken mostly in Vietnam, and Cambodian or Khmer, the official language of Cambodia. Coupled with the Munda languages (such as Santali, Mundari, and Ho) spoken chiefly in

Table 12.13 *Common Words in Four Dravidian Languages*

Tamil	Malayāḷam	Kannaḍa	Telugu	
amma:	amma	awwa	amma	'mother'
appa:	a:cchan	tande	na:nna	'father'
kaṇṇu	kaṇṇu	kannṇu	kannu	'eye'
ka:lu	ka:l	ka:lu	ka:lu	'foot'
onru	oru	ondu	okaṭi	'one'
mu:nru	mu:nnu	mu:ru	mu:ḍu	'three'
ma:sam	nela	tingaḷu	tingḷu	'month'

Note: Subscript dots represent retroflection.

India, the Mon-Khmer languages constitute what some scholars call the Austro-Asiatic family.

The Tai Family The best-known languages of the Tai family are Thai and Lao, the official languages of Thailand and Laos respectively. There are about 50 other members of the Tai family scattered throughout Thailand, Laos, Vietnam, Myanmar, eastern India, and southern China, where they intertwine with Sino-Tibetan and Mon-Khmer languages. Tai languages have been related to a number of languages spoken in Vietnam, with which they form a Kam-Tai family, and to still others in Vietnam and China, forming a Tai-Kadai family.

The Caucasian Family With about 35 languages, the Caucasian family is confined to the mountainous region between the Black Sea and the Caspian Sea in Turkey, Iran, and what was part of the former Soviet Union. Caucasian languages typically have complex phonological and morphological systems. The best-known Caucasian language is Georgian, spoken in Georgia (see Figure 12.5).

The Turkic Family This family comprises about 60 languages, all of which are quite similar. The better-known members are Turkish and Uzbek. Most Turkic languages are spoken in Turkey and central Asia (see Figure 12.5). Some scholars include Turkic in a larger Altaic family.

The Uralic Family With about 40 members, the Uralic family is thought by some to be related to the Turkic family, though this link is tenuous. The better-known Uralic languages are Finnish and Hungarian; also included are Estonian and Lapp (see Figure 12.5).

Japanese The Japanese language does not have any universally agreed-upon relatives, although many scholars regard Japanese and Korean as belonging to an Altaic family, along with Turkic. Ryukyuan, spoken in Okinawa, is a dialect of Japanese, and Ainu, a nearly extinct language spoken in the north of Japan, may also be related but is generally considered an isolate. Japanese has absorbed considerable influence from Chinese, to which it is *not* related.

Korean Many scholars regard Korean and Japanese as related members of the Altaic family, but this hypothesis remains unproven. Like Japanese, Korean has been greatly influenced by Chinese over the centuries.

Other Isolated Languages of Asia and Europe Of the remaining isolated languages of Eurasia, Basque is the best known. It is spoken in an area that straddles the Spanish-French border on the Atlantic coast (see Figure 12.5).

Native American Languages

Compared to the Old World, the linguistic situation in the New World is bewildering, with numerous Native American language families in North and South America. While proposals for the genealogical integration of these languages have been made, solid evidence for a pan-American link is lacking. Below are listed a few of those families and some of their members.

Eskimo-Aleut In North America, we distinguish the Eskimo-Aleut family (whose speakers are *not* genetically related to Amerindians) from other language families. Inuktitut has about 14,000 speakers across northern Canada and Alaska, and Yupik has about 17,000 speakers in Alaska and a few score in Siberia.

Algonquian Also called Algic, the Algonquian languages include Cree (with 90,000 speakers in Canada and Montana) and Ojibwa (with 64,000 speakers in Ontario, Manitoba, Michigan, Minnesota, and North Dakota). Represented by fewer speakers are Arapaho (Wyoming), Blackfoot (Canada and Montana), Cheyenne (Montana and Oklahoma), Kickapoo (Kansas, Oklahoma, and Coahuila, Mexico), Malecite-Passamaquoddy (Maine and New Brunswick), Micmac (Maritime Canada and Boston and Maine), Potawatomi (a mere 50 speakers spread across Wisconsin, Michigan, Kansas, and Ontario), and Shawnee (Oklahoma).

Muskogean Related to the Algonquian languages are the Muskogean languages. The largest language is Choctaw, with speakers in Oklahoma, Mississippi, and Louisiana. Also Muskogean are Chickasaw (Oklahoma), Koasati (Louisiana and Texas), and Alabama (Texas).

Athabaskan In the Athabaskan family, some varieties of Apache are becoming extinct, but Western Apache has speakers in Arizona, and Mescalero-Chiricahua Apache has speakers, chiefly in New Mexico. Navaho has nearly 150,000 speakers in Arizona, Utah, and New Mexico. Chipewyan has a few thousand speakers in Alberta, Saskatchewan, Manitoba, and the Northwest Territories. Often included with the Athabaskan languages in a group called Na-Dene are Tlingit and Haida, both spoken in Alaska and British Columbia.

Iroquoian Excepting principally Cherokee (with speakers in Oklahoma and North Carolina), the Iroquoian languages Cayuga, Mohawk, Oneida, and Seneca are spoken mainly in Ontario, Quebec, and upstate New York.

Siouan Located mainly in the upper Midwest of the United States and in Canada, the Siouan family includes Dakota (20,000 in Minnesota, Montana, Nebraska, and the Dakotas, as well as Manitoba and Saskatchewan). Crow has speakers in Montana, and Lakota has speakers in Nebraska, Minnesota, Montana, and the Dakotas, as well as Manitoba and Saskatchewan. Winnebago (or Ho-Chunk) has speakers in Nebraska and Wisconsin, while Omaha has speakers in Nebraska and Oklahoma.

Penutian The Penutian family includes Tsimshian (spoken mostly in British Columbia), Yakima (Washington), and Walla Walla (Oregon).

Salishan Among the languages of the Salishan family are Shuswap (British Columbia), Spokane (Washington), and Thompson (British Columbia).

Uto-Aztecan The Uto-Aztecan language family remains robust. Varieties of Nahuatl are spoken by about 1 million people in central and southern Mexico. On a much smaller scale, Huichol has speakers in Nayarit and Jalisco, and Papago-Pima (also called Tohono O'odham) in Arizona and Mexico. Hopi is spoken in Arizona, and Yaqui near Phoenix and Tucson and in Mexico. Shoshoni has a couple thousand speakers in California, Nevada, Idaho, Wyoming, and Utah, while Ute-Southern Paiute is spoken by about the same number in Colorado, Utah, Arizona, and Nevada. Comanche has a couple hundred speakers in Oklahoma. Also Uto-Aztecan are Cahuilla and Luiseño, spoken by no more than a score or two in Southern California.

Hokan Hokan includes Kumiái, or Diegueño (Baja California and Southern California), Havasupai-Walapai-Yavapai (Arizona), Karok (northwestern California), Maricopa (near Phoenix), Mohave (spoken on the California-Arizona border), and Washo (on the California-Nevada border).

Mayan The largest Mayan language is Yucatec, whose 940,000 speakers live mostly in the Yucatán Peninsula. Mam has about 400,000 speakers, most in Guatemala. The Mayan family also embraces Kekchi (with perhaps 365,000 speakers), Quiché (with perhaps 600,000), Cakchiquel (with perhaps 400,000), and about two dozen other languages.

Quechua Quechua was the language of the ancient Incan Empire. Today it has perhaps 6 million speakers in the Andes and is the most popular indigenous South American language; its genealogical affiliation is unclear.

Tupi The Tupi family includes Guaraní, with nearly 5 million speakers in Paraguay (where it is an official language), Bolivia, and southwestern Brazil.

Oto-Manguean Members of the Oto-Manguean family include Zapotec (with almost half a million speakers), Mixtec (about a quarter of a million), and Otomi (100,000), all spoken in central and southern Mexico.

Totonacan Totonacan includes eleven languages, including nine varieties of Totonac, spoken by about 250,000 speakers in Mexico.

Extinct and Dying Amerindian Languages Scores of indigenous languages of the Americas have fallen silent over the past few decades. The last speaker of Tillamook, a Salishan language, died in 1970, eight years after the last speaker of Wiyot, related to the Algonquian languages. Algonquian has also lost Miami, spoken in Indiana and Oklahoma, and Massachusett (also called Natick and Wampanoag). Also extinct are Huron (or Wyandot) of the Iroquoian family, and the Hokan languages Chumash, from Santa Barbara, California, but extinct since 1965, and Salinan, from California's central coast, as well as the Uto-Aztecan language Cupeño, formerly spoken in Southern California, and Penobscot in Maine, and Shasta in California. Other extinct Amerindian languages include Chinook, of

Washington and Oregon; Natchez and Tonkawa, both of Oklahoma; and Mohegan-Montauk-Narragansett, spoken earlier in Wisconsin and from Long Island to Connecticut and Rhode Island; and Iowa-Oto of Oklahoma, Iowa, and Kansas.

Amerindian languages are disappearing in the face of mounting pressure for younger speakers to adopt English, Spanish, or Portuguese, and many native languages are known only to a few older speakers. Besides several varieties of Apache, here are a few other languages with fewer than 50 speakers each (in fact, fewer than a handful in most cases); the family name is given in italics.

Abnaki (Quebec)—*Algic/Algonquian*

Coeur d'Alene (Idaho), Squamish (near Vancouver)—*Salishan*

Menominee (Wisconsin), Delaware—*Algic/Algonquian*

Osage (Oklahoma)—*Siouan*

Wichita (Oklahoma)—*Caddoan*

Miwok, Yokuts (both California), Coos (Oregon)—*Penutian*

Pomo (California)—*Hokan*

Tuscarora (formerly North Carolina, now near Niagara Falls, New York, and in Ontario, Canada)—*Iroquoian*

Languages of Aboriginal Australia

Before settlement by Europeans in the eighteenth century, Australia had been inhabited by Aborigines for up to 50 millennia. It is estimated that at the time of first contact with Europeans about 200 to 300 Aboriginal languages were spoken. Today many have disappeared, along with their speakers, decimated by imported diseases and sometimes (as on the island of Tasmania) by genocide. Today, only about 100 Aboriginal languages survive, most spoken by tiny populations of older survivors.

Try It Yourself In many places in the world, including the United States, Canada, Australia, Latin America, and South America, indigenous languages are still spoken, sometimes by very few speakers, most of whom may be elderly. Use the web—for example, the on-line *Ethnologue*—to discover which endangered language is geographically closest to you and how many speakers remain. See, too, whether there are efforts being made to record or preserve it.

Virtually all Australian languages fall into a single family with two groups: the large Pama-Nyungan group, which covers most of the continent and includes most Aboriginal languages, and the Non–Pama-Nyungan group, which includes about 50 languages spoken in northern Australia.

Papuan Languages

Papuan languages are spoken on the large island of New Guinea, which is divided politically between the nation of Papua New Guinea and the Indonesian-controlled section called Irian Jaya. While the inhabitants of coastal areas of the island speak Austronesian languages, about 800 of the languages are not Austronesian languages. Referred to as Papuan languages, most are not in any danger of extinction, though many are spoken by small populations. They fall into more than 60 different families, with no established genealogical link among them. Little is known about most of these languages.

Nostratic Macrofamily

Recent years have seen renewed focus on linking certain language families within larger "macrofamilies." The proposed Nostratic macrofamily has received attention even in the popular press. Some scholars have proposed that several language families that are generally regarded as distinct should be viewed as having a common source further back in time. The languages hypothesized to belong to Nostratic differ slightly from scholar to scholar, but most scholars espousing this theory include Indo-European, Afroasiatic, Uralic, Altaic, Dravidian, and Eskimo-Aleut. Assuming that detailed comparative reconstruction confirmed this hypothesis, the Nostratic macrofamily would then make distant cousins of English (Indo-European); Hebrew, Arabic, Somali, and Hausa (Afroasiatic); Finnish and Hungarian (Uralic); perhaps Korean and Turkish (Altaic); Tamil (Dravidian); and Inuktitut (Eskimo-Aleut).

Although the links among these far-flung languages are not widely accepted among scholars, the hypothesis is provocative in an important way. As demonstrated in this chapter, the principal method for establishing genealogical relations among languages is by comparative reconstruction, whereby the forms of a parent language are hypothesized and the forms of the various daughter languages are derived by regular rules. Before any comparative reconstruction can be attempted, there must be hypotheses about which languages are and are not related. With the Nostratic hypothesis in mind, you may find it thought provoking to reexamine the tables of common words for those Nostratic languages illustrated in this chapter: Tables 12.7 through 12.10 for four Indo-European groups, Table 12.12 for Afroasiatic, and Table 12.13 for Dravidian. Bear in mind that the sound correspondences among these languages would not be directly between sounds of the daughter languages but between sounds of the reconstructed parent languages, so any immediate correspondences you might spy could be deceptive.

Languages in Contact

At no other time in history have there been such intensive contacts between language communities as in recent centuries. As a result of the exploratory and colonizing enterprises of the English, French, Dutch, Spanish, and Portuguese, European languages have come into contact with languages of Africa, Native America, Asia, and the Pacific. These colonizing efforts put members of different speech communities in contact with each other. For example, the importing of slaves from Africa to the Americas forced speakers of different African languages to live side by side. Several language contact phenomena can arise when speakers of different languages interact.

Multilingualism

Bilingualism The first of these phenomena is **bilingualism** or multilingualism, in which members of a community natively acquire more than one language. In a multilingual community, children grow up speaking several languages. Use of each language is often compartmentalized, as when one is used at home and another at school or work. Multilingualism is such a natural solution to the challenge of language contact that it is extremely widespread throughout the world. In this respect, industrialized societies such as the United States and Japan, in which bilingualism is not widespread, are exceptional. In the United States, bilingualism is mostly relegated to immigrant communities, whose members are expected to learn English upon arrival. This adaptation is one-sided in contrast to what is found in most areas of the globe, where neighboring communities learn each other's languages with little ado. In central Africa, India, and Papua New Guinea, it is commonplace for small children to grow up speaking four or five languages. In Papua New Guinea, multilingualism is a highly valued attribute that enhances a person's status in the community.

Nativization A possible side effect of multilingualism is **nativization**, which takes place when a community adopts a new language (in addition to its native language) and modifies the structure of the new language, thus developing a characteristic dialect of the community. That is precisely what happened with English in India, where Indian English is recognized as a separate dialect of English with some of its own structural characteristics. Indeed, it has become one of India's two national languages (along with Hindi) and is used in education, government, and communications within India and with the rest of the world.

Pidgins Another process that may take place in language contact situations is pidginization. Although it is probably derived from the word *business*, the origin of the word **pidgin** is unclear, but the term refers to a contact language that develops where groups are in a dominant/subordinate situation, often in the context of colonization. Pidgins arise when members of a politically or economically dominant group do not learn the native language of the political or economic subordinates they interact with. To communicate, members of the subordinate community create a simplified variety of the language of the dominant group as their own second language. These simplified varieties then become the language of interaction between the colonizer and the colonized. Pidgins are thus defined in terms of sociological and linguistic characteristics. They are structurally simpler versions of the language of the dominant group. They lack native speakers and are typically used for a restricted range of purposes.

Pidgins have arisen in many areas of the world, including West Africa, the Caribbean, the Far East, and the Pacific. Many pidgins have been based on English and French, the languages of the two most active colonial powers in the eighteenth and nineteenth centuries. Portuguese, Spanish, Dutch, Swedish, German, Arabic, and Russian, among others, have also served as a base for the development of pidgins. Today, most pidgins have given way to creole languages.

From Pidgin to Creole At some point, a pidgin may begin to fulfill a greater number of roles in social life. Instead of using the pidgin only in the workplace to communicate with traders or colonizers, speakers may begin to use it at home or among themselves. Such situations frequently arise when the colonized population is linguistically diversified, and members of such a diversified community may find it convenient to adopt the new language as a **lingua franca**—a means to communicate across language boundaries. As a result, children begin to grow up speaking the new language, and as greater communicative demands are put onto that language its structure becomes more complex in a process called creolization. A **creole** language is thus a former pidgin that has "acquired" native speakers. Creoles are structurally complex, eventually as complex as any other language, and they differ from pidgins in that they exhibit less variability from speaker to speaker than pidgins do.

The boundary between pidgin and creole is often difficult to establish. Creolization is a gradual process, and in many places pidgins are undergoing creolization. In such situations, there will be much variability from speaker to speaker and from situation to situation. For some speakers and in some contexts, the language will clearly be at the pidgin stage; for speakers whose language is more advanced in the creolization process, or in contexts that call for a more elaborated variety, the language will be structurally more complex. Furthermore, as a creole gains wider usage and becomes structurally more complex, it often comes to resemble the language on which it is based. For example, in the Caribbean and in Hawaii, English-based creoles are very similar to standard English for many speakers. Typically in such situations we find a continuum from speaker to speaker and from situation to situation—from a nonstandard dialect of the parent language to a very basic pidgin.

Figure 12.14 shows the location of the more important creoles in the world. Note that in common parlance many creoles are called pidgins, as with Hawaiian Pidgin and Papua New Guinea Tok Pisin (from 'talk Pidgin'), both of which are actually creoles.

Some creoles have low status where they are spoken. Hawaiian creole, or Da Kine Talk, is often referred to as a "bastardized" version of English or "broken English." The fact is that Hawaiian creole has its own structure, different from that of English, and you could not pretend to speak Da Kine Talk by speaking "broken" English.

In contrast, in many areas of the world creoles have become national languages used in government proceedings, education, and the media. In Papua New Guinea, Tok Pisin is one of the three national languages (along with English and Kiri Motu, also a creole) and has become a symbol of national identity. Some creoles have become the language of important bodies of literature, particularly in West Africa. Elsewhere, creoles are used in newspapers and on the radio for various purposes, including cartoons and commercials. Figure 12.15 is a publicity cartoon in Papua New Guinea Tok Pisin; the English translation of the captions is given underneath. Tok Pisin is even used to write about linguistics, as illustrated by the following discussion of relative clause formation in Tok Pisin; it begins with three example sentences.

1. Ol ikilim pik bipo.
2. Na pik bai ikamap olosem draipela ston.
3. Na pik *ia* [ol ikilim bipo *ia*] bai ikamap olosem draipela ston.

Sapos yumi tingting gut long dispela tripela tok, yumi ken klia long tupela samting. Nambawan samting, sapos pik istap long (1) em inarapela pik, na pik istap long (2) em inarapela, orait, yumi no ken wokim (3). Tasol sapos wanpela pik tasol istap long (1) na (2), em orait long wokim (3). Na tu, tingting istap long (1) ia, mi

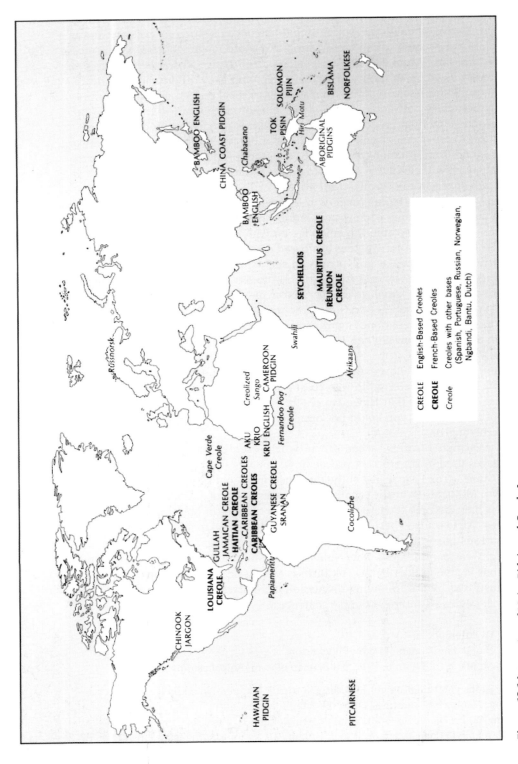

Figure 12.14 Location of Major Pidgin and Creole Languages

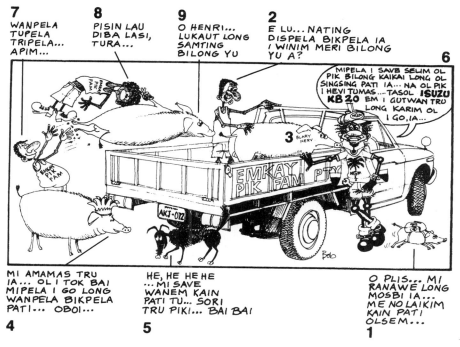

7
WANPELA
TUPELA
TRIPELA...
APIM...

8
PISIN LAU
DIBA LASI,
TURA...

9
O HENRI...
LUKAUT LONG
SAMTING
BILONG YU

2
E LU... NATING
DISPELA BIKPELA IA
I WINIM MERI BILONG
YU A?

6
MIPELA I SAVE SELIM OL
PIK BILONG KAIKAI LONG OL
SINGSING PATI IA... NA OL PIK
I HEVI TUMAS....TASOL **ISUZU
KB20** EM I GUTWAN TRU
LONG KARIM OL
I GO, IA...

3 BLARY
NERY

EMKAY PIK FAM PTY

AKJ-072

MI AMAMAS TRU
IA... OL I TOK BAI
MIPELA I GO LONG
WANPELA BIKPELA
PATI... OBOI...

4

HE, HE HE HE
...MI SAVE
WANEM KAIN
PATI TU... SORI
TRU PIKI... BAI BAI

5

O PLIS... MI
RANAWE LONG
MOSBI IA...
ME NO LAIKIM
KAIN PATI
OLSEM...

1

1. Oh, please. I'm running away to Port Moresby. I don't like this kind of party.
2. Hey, Lu! It's not for nothing that this big fat one beats your wife (in size).
3. The bloody nerve!
4. I am so happy. They all say that we are going to a big party. Oh, boy.
5. Hee, hee, hee, hee. I know what kind of party too. Very sorry, Piggy. Bye bye.
6. We frequently sell pigs for eating at dance parties. But pigs are very heavy so Isuzu KB20s are excellent to carry them all away.
7. One, two, three, up . . .
8. (speaking in Hiri Motu) Friend, I don't speak Tok Pisin.
9. Hey, Henry! Watch out for your things.

Figure 12.15 Publicity Cartoon in Tok Pisin

bin banisim insait long tupela banis long (3), long wonem, em bilong kliaim yumi long wonem pik Elena itok en.

[Translation]

1. They killed the pig.
2. The pig looks like a big rock.
3. The pig [that they killed] looks like a big rock.

If we think carefully about these three sentences, we can obtain two interpretations. First, if the pig of sentence (1) is one pig, and the pig of sentence (2) is another pig, then we cannot construct (3). However, if the pig in (1) and (2) is the same, then we can construct (3). Thus, I have bracketed in (3) the meaning corresponding to (1) with two brackets, because it has the purpose of identifying for us which pig Elena [the speaker who produced these sentences] is talking about. [Gillian Sankoff, "Sampela Nupela lo Ikamap Long Tok Pisin," 1975.]

In short, creoles can fulfill all the demands that are commonly imposed on a language. The structural similarities among creoles worldwide are striking. For example, many creoles lack indefinite articles and a distinction between the future and other tenses, and many have preposition stranding (as in the English expression *the house I live in*). Such similarities have led some researchers to propose that the development of pidgins and creoles follows a "program" that is genetically innate in humans. There are, however, many differences among the world's creoles, in which the imprint of various native languages is clear. In many South Pacific creoles, for example, a distinction is made in the pronoun system between dual and plural and between inclusive first-person dual and plural and exclusive first-person dual and plural (see Chapter 7, where the Tok Pisin pronoun system is given). These distinctions are not found in West African creoles, and their presence in South Pacific creoles reflects the fact that many languages spoken in the South Pacific make these distinctions. In Nigerian creole, on the other hand, we find honorific terms of address (*Mom* and *Dad*) that are used when addressing high-status individuals. These honorifics are not found in any other creole; again, they are transferred from local languages. Thus there is both homogeneity and heterogeneity among the creoles of the world.

COMPUTERS AND THE HISTORY OF LANGUAGES

In the study of historical linguistics and language change, computers have been particularly helpful in their ability to manipulate large quantities of data accurately and efficiently. Several major historical corpora have been compiled over the past couple of decades, and their ability to aid researchers in tracing lexical, morphological, semantic, and syntactic change in language has proven impressive and interesting.

Among the influential historical corpora is the Helsinki Corpus of English Texts: Diachronic and Dialectal (called the Helsinki Corpus for short). Here we concentrate on the historical (diachronic) part. Compiled by researchers at the University of Helsinki, this corpus contains texts of English from the Old English period (starting at about A.D. 800) and continuing through the early eighteenth century in the period known as Early Modern English. Unlike the LOB and Brown corpora, which contain 2,000-word extracts of texts, the Helsinki Corpus contains texts varying in length from 2,500 to almost 20,000 words. Altogether, there are 242 text files totaling about 1.5 million words of running text. For each text, information is included about the author's name, sex, education, origin, and social status, as well as about the date of composition and the genre of the text (akin to what we have called register). Using the Helsinki Corpus, researchers have been able to investigate patterns of development with certain genres across time, across genres within a given period of time, between male and female writers, and between British and American English, to mention just some of the dimensions along which it is possible to explore.

ARCHER (A Representative Corpus of Historical English Registers) includes eight registers over the centuries from 1650 to 1990, broken into half-century periods. For the periods 1750 to 1799, 1850 to 1899, and 1950 to 1999, it contains parallel British and American texts; for the other periods, only British texts. The eight registers include written (such as fiction, medicine) and speech-based registers (fictional conversation, drama, sermons). All told, ARCHER contains over 1,000 texts and about 1.7 million words. ∎

Summary

- Languages are always changing.
- All levels of the grammar change: phonology, morphology, lexicon, syntax, and semantics.
- From one language many others can develop in the course of time if groups of speakers remain physically or socially separated from one another.
- Comparative reconstruction enables linguists to make educated guesses about the structure and vocabulary of prehistoric peoples and to infer a good deal about their cultures from the nature of the reconstructed lexicon.
- The thousands of languages in the world can be grouped for the most part into language families whose branches represent languages that are genealogically closer to one another than to other languages of the family.
- When speakers of different languages come into contact, bilingualism may develop, with speakers commanding two or more languages.
- In some circumstances—usually when a dominant and a subordinate group are in contact—a pidgin may spring up for limited use, usually in trade. Over time, if the pidgin comes to be used for other purposes and children learn it at home as a first language, the process of creolization starts.
- Creolization is a process of linguistic expansion in both uses and structures.

 ## What Do You Think? REVISITED

- *Pre-med Melissa.* Both English and Latin are descended from Indo-European, but English has come down through the Germanic branch and Latin through the Romance branch. English borrowed thousands of words from Latin during the Renaissance when scientific writing moved from Latin to the local languages, and those borrowings from Latin may create a mistaken impression that English derives from Latin, but it does not.
- *Chinatown jade.* Mandarin and Cantonese derive from the same historical sources and are regarded by their speakers as dialects of one language. In addition, using a set of Chinese characters, speakers of both dialects can comprehend a given written text, though if they read it aloud it would not be understood by speakers of the other dialect. There is no precise point in the historical development of languages at which linguists can say two varieties that have descended from a common parent language have become different *languages* as opposed to different *dialects* of the same language.
- *Iraqi place names.* The *al, an,* and *as* in Iraqi place names such as *Al Basrah, An Najaf,* and *As Sulaymānīyah* are forms of the Arabic definite article. (The article also appears in words like *algebra* and *alcohol* that English has borrowed from Arabic.) The language of Iran is Persian, an Indo-European language distantly related to English but not to Arabic. For writing, though, both Persian and Arabic use forms of Arabic script, in part as a consequence of their being Muslim countries with Muslim culture and history. Of course, any spoken

language can be written in a variety of scripts so it is a mistake to assume that two languages using the same script are necessarily derived from a single ancestor tongue.

- *Oklahoma.* Oklahoma place names such as *Okmulgee, Comanche, Chattanooga, Manitou, Cherokee, Arapaho,* and *Wynona* are now "naturalized" English names, borrowed from Native Americans and now pronounced by speakers of English as English words. Languages in contact often borrow from one another, and newcomers may ask local inhabitants for the name of a place and incorporate that name into their own language. The more transparent names—Grove and Granite and the like—appear to be descriptive terms, presumably given to places by English speakers or in a few cases perhaps translations of Native American names. ■

Exercises

Based on Languages Other Than English

The Amara data used here are taken from an unpublished Amara lexicon by Bil Thurston; the Hiw, Sowa, Mota, and Raɣa data from Darrell Tryon, *New Hebrides Languages* (Pacific Linguistics, C, 50, 1976); the Waskia data from Malcolm Ross and John Natu Paol, *A Waskia Grammar Sketch and Vocabulary* (Pacific Linguistics, B, 56, 1978); the Lusi and Bariai data from Rick Goulden, "A Comparative Study of Lusi and Bariai" (M.A. thesis, McMaster University, 1982).

12-1. The following is a comparative word list from seven languages spoken in the South Pacific. (β represents a voiced bilabial fricative and ɣ a voiced velar fricative.)

Hiw	Waskia	Motu	Amara	Sowa	Mota	Raɣa	
yoŋ	utuwura	lai	akauliŋ	laiŋ	laŋ	laŋi	'wind'
en	laŋ	miri	olov	on	one	one	'sand'
βət	maŋa	nadi	epeiouŋo	βət	βət	fatu	'stone'
yə	didu	matabudi	opon	tariβanaβi	uwə	afua	'turtle'
eyə	wal	gwarume	ouŋa	ek	iɣa	iɣa	'fish'
noya	kasim	namo	ovinkin	tapken	nam	namu	'mosquito'
yo	nup	lada	serio	se	sasa	iha	'name'
moɣoɣe	kulak	natu	emim	dozo	natu	nitu	'child'
suɣe	buruk	boroma	esnei	bo	kpwoe	poe	'pig'
tø	kemak	tohu	elgo	ze	tou	toi	'sugarcane'

a. Identify which languages are likely to be related and which are not, and justify your claims.

b. Of the languages that appear to be part of the same family, which are more closely related? Justify your answer.

12-2. The following is a comparative word list from Lusi and Bariai, closely related languages spoken on the island of New Britain in Papua New Guinea.

Lusi	Bariai		Lusi	Bariai	
βaza	bada	'to fetch'	βua	bua	'Areca nut'
kalo	kalo	'frog'	niu	niu	'coconut'
ɣali	gal	'to spear'	uβu	ubu	'hip'
ahe	ae	'foot'	rai	rai	'trade wind'
zaŋa	daŋa	'thing'	oaɣa	oaga	'canoe'
tazi	tad	'sea'	mata	mata	'eye'
tupi	tup	'to peek'	zoɣi	dog	a type of plant
tori	tol	'to dance'	hani	an	'food'
ŋiŋi	ŋiŋ	'to laugh'	aŋari	aŋal	a type of bird

a. List the consonant correspondences between Lusi and Bariai.

b. Identify which vowel is lost in Bariai and give a rule that states the environment in which it is lost.

12-3. Table 12.3 provides some correspondence sets among five Polynesian languages. We noted that Tongan had lost a phoneme /r/ from its inventory, which was kept as /r/ or became /l/ in the other four languages. Furthermore, Tongan has kept a phoneme /h/ in certain words, which has been lost in all other Polynesian languages. The following cognates illustrate these two changes.

Tongan	Samoan	Tahitian	Maori	Hawaiian	
hama	ama	ama	ama	ama	'outrigger'
ama	lama	rama	rama	lama	'torch'

a. On the basis of this information and the following words, complete the table of consonant correspondences for Tongan, Samoan, Tahitian, Maori, and Hawaiian.

Tongan	Samoan	Tahitian	Maori	Hawaiian	
leʔo	leo	reo	reo	leo	'voice'
ʔuha	ua	ua	ua	ua	**'rain'**
lili	lili	riri	riri	lili	'angry'
hae	sae	hae	hae	hae	'to tear'
hihi	isi	ihi	ihi	ihi	**'strip'**
huu	ulu	uru	uru	ulu	**'to enter'**
fue	fue	hue	hue	hue	type of vine
afo	afo	aho	aho	aho	'fishing line'
vela	vela	vera	wera	wela	'hot'
hiva	iva	iva	iwa	iwa	**'nine'**

b. Using your table of consonant correspondences and assuming that vowels have not undergone any change in any Polynesian language, complete the following comparative table by filling in the missing words.

Tongan	Samoan	Tahitian	Maori	Hawaiian	
kaukau	_____	_____	_____	_____	'to bathe'
_____	mata	_____	_____	_____	'eye'
_____	tafe	_____	_____	kahe	'to flow'
laʔe	_____	_____	_____	_____	'forehead'
laŋo	_____	_____	_____	_____	'fly'

    c. Reconstruct the Proto-Polynesian consonant system on the basis of the information you now have; take into account the genealogical classification of Polynesian languages discussed in this chapter. (*Hint*: The protosystem has to be full enough to account for all the possible correspondences found in the daughter languages. No daughter language has innovated new phonemes, but all have lost one or more from the protosystem.)

    d. Reconstruct the Proto-Polynesian words for 'outrigger,' 'rain,' 'to enter,' 'strip,' and 'nine.'

12-4. Below is a list of Modern French words in phonetic transcription with the Vulgar Latin words from which they derive. (Notice that word-initial /k/ in Latin becomes /k/, /ʃ/, or /s/ in Modern French, depending on its environment.)

Modern French	Vulgar Latin	
kɔʁd	korda	'rope'
ʃã	kampus	'field'
sɛdʁ	kɛdrus	'cedar'
kʁaʃe	krakkaːre	'to spit'
ʃamo	kameːlus	'camel'
sɛʁkl	kirkulus	'circle'
kuʁiʁ	kurrere	'to run'
ʃaʁ	karrus	'carriage'
kle	klavis	'key'
sitɛʁn	kistɛrna	'tank'
kɔlõb	kolomba	'dove'
ʃa	kattus	'cat'
ku	kollum	'neck'

    a. Provide a rule that predicts which of the three French phonemes will appear where Latin had /k/. (Address only the initial consonant of words.)

    b. Consider the additional data below.

Modern French	Vulgar Latin	
ʃov	kalvus	'bald'
ʃɛn	katena	'chain'
ʃo	kalidum	'hot'
ʃɛʁ	karo	'flesh'

At first glance, these forms are problematic for the rule you stated in (a). Note, however, that in Modern French these four words are spelled *chauve*, *chaine*, *chaud*, and *chair*, respectively. Given the fact that French orthography often reflects an earlier pronunciation of the language, explain in detail what has likely happened to the four words in the history of the language.

12-5. Consider the following Proto-Indo-European reconstructions. Conspicuously, no word for 'sea' can be reconstructed for Proto-Indo-European.

*rtko	'bear'	*peisk	'fish'
*laks	'salmon'	*sper	'sparrow'
*or	'eagle'	*trozdo	'thrush'
*g^{w}ou	'cow/bull'	*su:	'pig'
*kwon	'dog'	*agw^{h}no	'lamb'
*mori	'lake'	*sneig^{wh}	'snow'
*b^{h}erəg	'birch'	*gr̥ano	'grain'
*yewo	'wheat'	*med^{h}u	'honey'
*weik	'village'	*sel	'fortification'
*se:	'to sow'	*kerp	'to collect (food)'
*yeug	'to yoke'	*web^h	'to weave'
*sne:	'to spin'	*arə	'to plow'
*ayes	'metal'	*agro	'field'

a. Describe in detail what these reconstructions (or lack of reconstructions) tell us about the activities and environment of the Proto-Indo-Europeans.

b. Based on these reconstructions and on what you know about the current distribution of Indo-European languages, which area or areas of the world would be the best candidates as the homeland of the Proto-Indo-Europeans? Defend your claim.

12-6. Here is a list of Proto-Indo-European reconstructions with Modern English glosses. Cite a Modern English word (perhaps itself borrowed from another language) that contains a reflex for each of the reconstructions.

*ak^{w}a	'water'	*agro	'field'
*k^{w}etwer	'four'	*b^{h}ugo	'ram, goat'
*b^{h}reu	'to boil'	*pel	'skin'
*reg	'to rule'	*gel	'to freeze'
*wen	'to strive for'	*g^{h}ans	'goose'
*med	'to measure'	*yeug	'to join together'
*ped	'foot'	*genə	'to give birth'

Especially for Educators and Future Teachers

12-7. Think about conversations you've had with your grandparents and their peers and identify several of their words or expressions that you regard as old-fashioned and no longer in use by you or your peers. Are there any characteristic pronunciations that identify speakers you know as belonging to an older generation? Are there any characteristics of your speech or that of your fellow teachers that your students would regard as old-fashioned? Do you teach any particular views of language use that your students regard as old-fashioned? Are there usages you insist your students not use that may now be judged acceptable by respected usage guides?

12-8. Given that languages change within a lifetime, teachers need to be attentive to such changes and consider whether usages they may have been taught as correct in the past remain the only correct form. Identify two prescriptive rules you were taught that you believe may reflect outdated usage. Check a good usage handbook or dictionary to see what they report about current usage for those linguistic features.

Other Resources

Internet

 LISU Website: http://www.CengageBrain.com For users of this textbook. Provides updated Internet links as well as supplemental material for students and instructors. Here you will find interactive learning tools.

 Ethnologue: Languages of the World: http://www.ethnologue.com/ The *Ethnologue* is a catalog of the world's languages, an extraordinary source of information about all languages—where they are spoken, by how many people, and to what family they belong. It is the source of much of the data presented in this chapter. The Ethnologue website provides an electronic version and includes a language name index and a language family index. A typical entry is given below:

> UTE-SOUTHERN PAIUTE [UTE] POPULATION: 1,980 (2000 census). 20 monolinguals (1990 census). 3 Chemehuevi on Chemehuevi Reservation, 10 on Colorado River Reservation (1994 L. Hinton). Ethnic population: 5,000 (1977 SIL).
>
> REGION: Ute in southwest Colorado, southeast and northeast; Southern Paiute in southwest Utah, north Arizona, and south Nevada; Chemehuevi on lower Colorado River, California.
>
> LANGUAGE USE: Mostly adults.
>
> LANGUAGE DEVELOPMENT: Literacy rate in L1: Below 1%. Literacy rate in L2: 75%–100%. Bible portions: 2006.
>
> WRITING SYSTEM: Latin script.

 Ethnologue Maps of Native American and all other Languages: http://www.ethnologue.com/country_index.asp At this site you can access maps representing the distribution of languages by country, including maps of Native American languages.

 Lydia Green's Project: http://www.lydiajewlgreen.com/yupik/ Focusing on Central Yupik in Alaska, a language spoken by fewer than 17,000, Lydia Green demonstrates how a college student can carry out a firsthand investigation of a Native American language.

 Joseph Henderer's Project: http://www.archive.org/details/SouthernCaliforniaIndigenousLanguagesPilotFilm In this short film, college student Joseph Henderer hits the road to find the last fluent speakers of Southern California's indigenous languages.

Video

• **In Search of the First Language**
Part of the NOVA video series, this fascinating exploration was first broadcast in 1997. It includes discussion by prominent linguists on a wide range of topics related to language change and language families, including the controversial Nostratic hypothesis. (No longer available

for purchase. A transcript of the broadcast is available at http://www.pbs.org/wgbh/nova/transcripts/2120glang.html.)

Suggestions for Further Reading

- **Jean Aitchison. 2001.** *Language Change: Progress or Decay?* **3rd ed.** (Cambridge, UK: Cambridge University Press). Combines traditional historical analysis with sociolinguistic insights.
- **Lyle Campbell. 1997.** *American Indian Languages: The Historical Linguistics of Native America* (New York: Oxford University Press). Called a landmark in the analysis of Native American languages, this comparative and historical analysis won the Linguistic Society of America's Leonard Bloomfield Award in 2000.
- **Bernd Heine & Derek Nurse. 2000.** *The Languages of Africa* (Cambridge, UK: Cambridge University Press). An excellent introduction to the languages of Africa, written specifically for undergraduate students. Contains chapters on each of the families and on the phonology, morphology, and syntax of African languages, along with chapters on comparative linguistics, language in society, and language and history.
- **Calvert Watkins. 2000. "Indo-European and the Indo-Europeans."** *The American Heritage Dictionary of the English Language*, 4th ed. (Boston: Houghton Mifflin). Conveniently appended to the dictionary and included on its CD-ROM version, this article describes Indo-European and the cultural inferences that can be drawn from the reconstructed lexicon, providing an introduction to a dictionary of Indo-European roots, with cognates in several languages.

Advanced Reading

Many good textbooks treat historical linguistics, among them Crowley and Bowern (2010) and Campbell (2004). Lehmann (1967) contains many of the original documents of historical work from the nineteenth century, including the speech of Sir William Jones quoted earlier. Bellwood (1979; 1987) and Jennings (1979) survey research on Polynesian and Austronesian migrations, including extensive discussion of language history. Pawley and Green (1971) discusses the linguistic evidence for the location of the Proto-Polynesian homeland. Bomhard (1992) and Kaiser and Shevoroshkin (1988) discuss the Nostratic macrofamily.

A convenient reference work treating about a dozen language families and 40 of the world's major languages is Comrie (2009), with a list of references for each family and language. The Cambridge Language Survey Series includes volumes on lesser-known areas and language families by Comrie (1981), Foley (1986), and Suárez (1983), and on major languages, such as Shibatani (1990). The languages of China are succinctly surveyed in Ramsey (1987), Native North American languages in Mithun (1999), Amazonian languages in Derbyshire and Pullum (1986–1998), and South American languages in Manelis Klein and Stark (1985). An accessible chapter-length treatment of Native American languages is Yamamoto and Zepeda (2004), while Hinton (1994) offers informative chapters on Native American languages in California. Romaine (1991) includes chapters on the indigenous and non-indigenous languages of Australia with an emphasis on their sociolinguistic contexts. Using a method like the one that determined the Proto-Polynesian homeland, Siebert (1967) discusses the original home of the Proto-Algonquian people.

Nativization is discussed in Kachru (1982). Good surveys of the structure and use of pidgins and creoles include Romaine (1988) and Holm (2000). A provocative look at the origins and evolution of language can be found in Bickerton (2009). The death of Texas German is described in detail in Boas (2009), an award-winning work offered as a model for the study of other endangered dialects and languages. Nettle and Romaine (2000) discusses the extinction of languages around the world.

References

Bellwood, Peter. 1979. *Man's Conquest of the Pacific: The Prehistory of Southeast Asia and Oceania* (New York: Oxford University Press).

————. 1987. *The Polynesians: Prehistory of an Island People*, rev. ed. (London: Thames and Hudson).

Bickerton, Derek. 2009. *Adam's Tongue: How Humans Made Language, How Language Made Humans* (New York: Hill and Wang).

Boas, Hans C. 2009. *The Life and Death of Texas German*, Publications of the American Dialect Society 93 (Durham, NC: Duke University Press).

Bomhard, Allan R. 1992. "The Nostratic Macrofamily (with Special Reference to Indo-European)," *Word* 43:61–83.

Campbell, Lyle. 2004. *Historical Linguistics: An Introduction*, 2nd ed. (Cambridge, MA: MIT Press).

Comrie, Bernard. 1981. *The Languages of the Soviet Union* (Cambridge, UK: Cambridge University Press).

Comrie, Bernard, ed. 2009. *The World's Major Languages*, 2nd ed. (London: Routledge).

Crowley, Terry & Claire Bowern. 2010. *An Introduction to Historical Linguistics*, 4th ed. (New York: Oxford University Press).

Derbyshire, Desmond C. & Geoffrey K. Pullum, eds. 1986-1998. *Handbook of Amazonian Languages*, 4 vols. (Berlin: Mouton de Gruyter).

Foley, William A. 1986. *The Papuan Languages of New Guinea* (Cambridge, UK: Cambridge University Press).

Hinton, Leanne. 1994. *Flutes of Fire*, rev. ed. (Berkeley, CA: Heyday).

Holm, John. 2000. *An Introduction to Pidgins and Creoles* (Cambridge, UK: Cambridge University Press).

Jennings, Jesse D., ed. 1979. *The Prehistory of Polynesia* (Cambridge, MA: Harvard University Press).

Kachru, Braj, ed. 1982. *The Other Tongue: English across Cultures* (Urbana: University of Illinois Press).

Kaiser, M. & V. Shevoroshkin. 1988. "Nostratic," *Annual Review of Anthropology* 17:309–29.

Lehmann, Winfred, ed. 1967. *A Reader in Nineteenth-Century Historical Linguistics* (Bloomington: Indiana University Press).

Manelis Klein, Harriet E. & Louisa R. Stark, eds. 1985. *South American Indian Languages: Retrospect and Prospect* (Austin: University of Texas Press).

Mithun, Marianne. 1999. *The Languages of Native North America* (Cambridge, UK: Cambridge University Press).

Nettle, Daniel & Suzanne Romaine. 2000. *Vanishing Voices: The Extinction of the World's Languages* (New York: Oxford University Press).

Pawley, Andrew & Kaye Green. 1971. "Lexical Evidence for the Proto-Polynesian Homeland," *Te Reo* 14:1–35.

Ramsey, S. Robert. 1987. *The Languages of China* (Princeton: Princeton University Press).

Romaine, Suzanne. 1988. *Pidgin and Creole Languages* (London: Longman).

———. 1991. *Language in Australia* (Cambridge, UK: Cambridge University Press).

Sankoff, Gillian. 1975. "Sampela Nupela lo Ikamap Long Tok Pisin." In K. A. McElhanon, ed., *Tok Pisin i Go We*? (Ukarumpa: Linguistic Society of New Guinea).

Shibatani, Masayoshi. 1990. *The Languages of Japan* (Cambridge, UK: Cambridge University Press).

Siebert, Frank T. 1967. "The Original Home of the Proto-Algonquian People," *Bulletin No. 214* (Ottawa: National Museum of Canada), pp. 13–47.

Suárez, Jorge A. 1983. *The Mesoamerican Indian Languages* (Cambridge, UK: Cambridge University Press).

Yamamoto, Akira Y. & Ofelia Zepeda. 2004. "Native American Languages." In Edward Finegan & John R. Rickford, eds., *Language in the USA* (Cambridge, UK: Cambridge University Press), pp. 153–81.

13

Historical Development in English

What Do You Think?

- You visit Ye Olde Coffee Shoppe with your friend Scott, who reads on the back of the menu that the word "Ye" in the shop name should *not* be pronounced "yee." The menu says *Y* is a variant of an older letter pronounced like *th* and the name of the shop is actually *The Old Coffee Shop*. Scott scoffs. What do you say to skeptical Scott?
- Your niece Agnes, who's recently moved west from Cleveland, notices on a map in her geography textbook that many cities in California and the Southwest have names like San Diego and Santa Monica that include the words "San" or "Santa," and she asks why such names don't occur elsewhere in the United States. What do you tell her?
- Jeremy, a secondary school teacher of modern languages, wonders why English has so few inflections on its nouns when its close relative German has so many. Do you know?
- Isabelle, an international student, asks why some English nouns such as "sheep" and "deer" do not have ordinary plural forms like most English nouns. They're irregular, you say, but she wants to know why. What explanation can you offer?
- Stodgy Stan is stewing over a correction made by his English composition instructor to his essay on fraud. Stan wrote, "In every case the fraud victim had signed a document without understanding what they agreed to," and his instructor corrected "they" to "he or she." Stan says everyone uses "they" because "he or she" sounds clumsy. "What's the point?" he asks. What can you suggest?

A Thousand Years of Change

Nearly every secondary school student in the English-speaking world has studied the writings of Shakespeare and Chaucer. You may recall that when you read Shakespeare's plays, some lines were opaque, as with these opening lines of *Henry IV*:

So shaken as we are, so wan with care

Find we a time for frighted peace to pant

And breathe short-winded accents of new broils

To be commenced in stronds afar remote.

The English spoken in and around London four centuries ago is sometimes subtly and sometimes strikingly different from the English spoken there and throughout the English-speaking world today. Still, much of it is accessible and very little of it is so foreign that it eludes us completely. Many of the words in the brief passage just cited are familiar enough, although some are used in ways that strike a modern reader as peculiar. While the words of the opening line are familiar and can be sorted out syntactically as poetic English, the second line is a bit tougher, even though all the words except *frighted* exist in Modern English in exactly the same forms. (The line means 'Let us find a time for frightened peace to catch its breath.')

As the many worldwide Shakespearean productions testify to, reciting Shakespeare's plays with their sixteenth-century vocabulary and syntax but with a modern pronunciation enables audiences today to follow the plays with little difficulty. With costumed actors interacting, there is not much in *Romeo and Juliet*, *Henry IV*, or *King Lear* that modern audiences fail to grasp.

Far more difficult to understand is Middle English, the language of Chaucer, who lived in London two centuries earlier. His *Canterbury Tales*, whose opening lines follow, was the first major book to be printed in England. William Caxton published it in 1476, almost a century after it was written and well after Chaucer's death in 1400.

Whan that April with his shoures soote

The droghte of March hath perced to the roote,

And bathed every veyne in swich licour,

Of which vertu engendred is the flour . . .

Thanne longen folk to goon on pilgrimages.

> **Try It Yourself** Examine the opening lines of the *Canterbury Tales* above and identify 10 words besides *that* and *with* that appear exactly the same as Modern English words. Then identify five others that appear almost, but not exactly, the same as Modern English words.

Although Chaucer's pronunciation of these words differed dramatically from ours, quite a few of them still have the same written form as they did then.

Several other words in the passage may be recognizable, although their Modern English counterparts differ a bit: *droghte* is 'drought,' *perced* 'pierced,' *veyne* 'vein,' *vertu* 'virtue, strength,' and *flour* 'flower.' Others are more opaque, such as *soote*, which is 'sweet'; *swich*, which is 'such'; *thanne*, which is 'then'; and the verbs *longen* 'to long' and *goon* 'to go.' As a whole, the Chaucer passage is harder to grasp than the one written by Shakespeare. In the two centuries between Chaucer's death in 1400 and Shakespeare's in 1616, English changed—as languages always do. Chaucer understood language change and the arbitrariness of linguistic form for accomplishing the goals of language, as he indicates in these lines from *Troilus and Criseyde* (II, 22–26), with a modern version on the right.

Ye knowe ek, that in forme of speche is chaunge	You know also that in speech's form (there) is change
Withinne a thousand yeer, and wordes tho	Within a thousand years, and words then
That hadden pris, now wonder nyce and straunge	That had value, now wondrously foolish and strange
Us thinketh hem, and yet thei spake hem so,	To us seem them, and yet they spoke them so,
And spedde as wel in love as men now do.	And fared as well in love as men now do.

The English spoken in Chaucer's time is far enough removed from today's English that students often study the *Canterbury Tales* in "translation"—from fourteenth- into twenty-first-century English. We're not yet so estranged from Shakespeare's language that we require a translation, but published editions of his plays have abundant glosses and footnotes to help explain his language to speakers of Modern English.

If we now examine the language of the epic poem *Beowulf*, written down almost four centuries before Chaucer lived, we are struck by its utterly foreign appearance. Indeed, speakers of Modern English cannot recognize *Beowulf* as English, and it seems as far removed from Modern English as today's Dutch and German are. We don't know the identity of the *Beowulf* poet, but he composed his grim epic about 600 years before Chaucer, who would have found its language about as unintelligible as modern readers do. Here are the first three lines from a *Beowulf* manuscript transcribed around the year A.D. 1000, with a rough word-for-word translation on the right:

Hwæt wē Gār–Dena in geārdagum	What! We of Spear-Danes in yore-days
þēodcyninga þrym gefrūnon,	People's-kings glory have heard,
hū ðā æþelingas ellen fremedon.	How the nobles heroic-deeds did.

A more colloquial rendering might be: *Yes, we have heard of the might of the kings of the Spear-Danes in days of yore, how the chieftains carried out heroic deeds.*

Old English seems "foreign." Scarcely a word in the passage is familiar (although when you have finished reading this chapter, a few may seem not quite so strange). Even certain letters are different: Modern English no longer uses <æ>, <þ>, or <ð>. Still, an imaginative inspection may reveal that some function words remain in present-day English (*wē* = *we*, *in* = *in*, and *hū* = *how*). Perhaps you also suspected that *hwæt* is *what*, but it is not easy to recognize *geārdagum* as *yore* plus *days* or *cyninga* as *kings*. Even knowing these words, you would find the passage far from transparent. You would need to know the meaning of the nouns *þēod*, *þrym*, and *æþelingas* (none of which survives in Modern English), the verbs *gefrūnon* and *fremedon*, and the adjective *ellen* (here used as a noun). And given all that lexical information, the syntax of Old English would still be elusive.

Where Does English Come From?

Before the beginning of the modern era, Britain was inhabited by Celtic-speaking peoples, ancestors of today's Irish, Scots, and Welsh. In 55 B.C., Britain was invaded by Julius Caesar, but his attempt to colonize it failed, and the Romans conquered Britain only in A.D. 43 and remained there for nearly four centuries. When the Roman legions withdrew in 410, the Celts, who had long been accustomed to Roman protection, were at the mercy of Picts and Scots from the north of Britain. In a profoundly important development for the English language, Vortigern, king of the Romanized Celts in Britain, sought help from three Germanic tribes. Around the year 449 these tribes set sail from what is today northern Germany and southern Denmark, but when they landed in Britain they liked it and decided to settle, leaving the Celts only the remote corners—Scotland, Wales, and Cornwall.

The invaders spoke closely related varieties of West Germanic, the dialects that were to become English. The word *England* derives from the name of one of the tribes, the Angles: thus England, originally *Englaland*, is the 'land of the Angles.' The Old English language used by the Germanic inhabitants of England and their offspring up to about A.D. 1100 is often called Anglo-Saxon, after two of the tribes (members of the third tribe were called Jutes). The oldest surviving English-language written materials come from the end of the seventh century, with an increasing quantity after that, giving rise to an impressive literature, including *Beowulf*.

Once the Anglo-Saxon peoples had settled in Britain, there were additional onslaughts from other Germanic groups starting in 787. In the year 850, a fleet of 350 Danish ships arrived. In 867, Vikings captured York. Danes and Norwegians settled in much of eastern and northern England and from there launched attacks into the kingdom of Wessex in the southwest. In 878, after losing a major battle to King Alfred the Great of Wessex, the Danes agreed by the Treaty of Wedmore to become Christian and to remain outside Wessex in a large section of eastern and northern England that became known as the Danelaw because it was subject to Danish law. After the treaty, Danes and Norwegians were assimilated to Anglo-Saxon life, so much so that 1,400 English place-names are Scandinavian, including those ending in *-by* 'farm, town' (*Derby*, *Rugby*), *-thorp* 'village' (*Althorp*), *-thwaite* 'isolated piece of land' (*Applethwaite*), and *-toft* 'piece of ground' (*Brimtoft*, *Eastoft*).

Attacks from the Scandinavians continued throughout the Viking Age (roughly 750–1050) until finally King Svein of Denmark was crowned king of England and was succeeded almost immediately by his son Cnut in 1016. England was then ruled by Danish kings until 1042, when Edward the Confessor regained the throne lost to the Danes by his father Æthelred. The intermingling between the

Anglo-Saxon invaders and the subsequent Scandinavian settlers created a mix of Germanic dialects in England that molded the character of the English language and distinguishes it from its cousins.

English Is a Germanic Language

We noted in Chapter 12 that West Germanic is distinguished from two other branches of the Germanic group of Indo-European languages: North Germanic (which includes Swedish, Danish, and Norwegian) and East Germanic (including only Gothic, which has since died out).

During the first millennium B.C., before Germanic had split into three branches but after it had split from the other branches of Indo-European, Common (or Proto-) Germanic developed certain characteristic features that continue in its daughter languages, setting them apart as a group from all other Indo-European varieties. Among these characteristics are features belonging to every level of grammar, including phonology, lexicon, morphology, and syntax.

Consonant Shifts The most striking phonological characteristic of the Germanic languages, including English, is a set of consonant correspondences found in none of the other Indo-European languages. In 1822, Jacob Grimm, one of the Brothers Grimm of fairy-tale fame, formulated these correspondences in what is now called Grimm's law. Grimm described the sound shifts that had occurred within three natural classes of sounds in developing from Indo-European into Germanic.

Grimm's Law

1. Voiceless stops became voiceless fricatives:

    p > f   t > θ   k > h

2. Voiced stops became voiceless stops:

    b > p   d > t   g > k

3. Voiced aspirated stops became voiced unaspirated stops:

    bʰ > b   dʰ > d   gʰ > g

The impact of these changes can be seen in Figure 13.1 by examining the shift of voiceless stops in Indo-European to voiceless fricatives in Germanic. We illustrate this shift by citing English words that have inherited the sounds /f θ h/ from Germanic as in part 1 of Grimm's law and by contrasting them with corresponding words in Romance languages, which (like all the other branches of Indo-European) did not undergo these sound shifts.

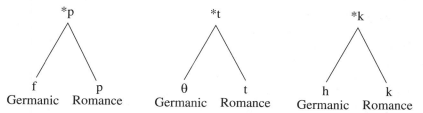

Figure 13.1 Reflexes of Indo-European Voiceless Stops in Germanic and Romance

Germanic	Romance		
English	*Latin*	*French*	*Spanish*
fish	piscis	poisson	pez
three	tres	trois	tres
heart	cor	cœur	corazón

Stress Shifts Another important phonological development of Common Germanic was a shift in stress patterns. Indo-European had variable stress on its words, so that a morpheme could be stressed on a particular syllable in one word but elsewhere in a different word. But in Common Germanic, stress shifted systematically to a word's first or root syllable, where it remained, irrespective of the word in which the morpheme occurred. Contrast Modern English *fáther, fátherly, unfátherly,* and *fátherless,* all with stress on the root syllable in the Germanic fashion, to the Greek borrowings *phótograph, photógrapher, and photográphic,* with variable stress in the Indo-European fashion.

Vocabulary The pattern of consonant shifting described by Grimm's law set apart the pronunciation of the Germanic vocabulary from that of other Indo-European languages (as seen in the Romance examples above). In addition, the Germanic languages have a set of words found nowhere else in Indo-European. Once the Germanic tribes separated from the rest of the Indo-European peoples, any words borrowed from speakers of a non-Indo-European tongue or innovated would be distinctively Germanic within Indo-European. Among the English words found in other Germanic languages but not in any other Indo-European languages are the nouns *arm, blood, earth, finger, hand, sea,* and *wife;* the verbs *bring, drink, drive, leap,* and *run;* and the adjectives *evil, little,* and *sick.* Here are the strictly Germanic nouns from English and German (to illustrate the similarity among Germanic tongues) and from French (to illustrate the striking contrast between Germanic and Romance languages).

English	**German**	**French**
arm	Arm	bras
blood	Blut	sang
earth	Erd	terre
finger	Finger	doigt
hand	Hand	main
sea	See	mer
wife	Weib	femme

These Germanic words could have existed in Indo-European and been lost in all the daughter languages except Germanic, but that isn't likely, so we can assume they were not inherited from Indo-European but innovated during the Common Germanic period or borrowed from a now-lost source at that time.

Morphology and Syntax in Indo-European

Indo-European—at least at some stages—was a highly inflected language. In fact, Sanskrit, one of the oldest attested Indo-European languages, had eight case inflections on nouns, so it is possible that Indo-European itself had eight cases (although, alternatively, case distinctions absent from Proto-Indo-European could have arisen in the Indic branch to which Sanskrit belongs). If we assume that the rich inflectional morphology of Sanskrit reflects the complexity of Indo-European, then Indo-European nouns would have had eight *cases*, three *numbers* (singular, dual, plural), and three *genders* (masculine, feminine, neuter). Verbs were also highly inflected, probably for two *voices* (active and a kind of passive), four *moods* (indicative, imperative, subjunctive, optative), and three *tenses* (present, past, future). In addition, verbs carried markers for *person* and *number*.

The Indo-European system of indicating verb tenses was principally word internal (as in English *sing/sang/sung*). While this internal sound *gradation* (sometimes called *ablaut*) is typical of Indo-European languages, the typical English inflection for the past tense, pronounced [-t] (*kissed*) or [-d] (*judged*), is characteristically Germanic. Thus the two-tense system, with past tense marked by a dental or alveolar suffix, sets the Germanic group apart from all its Indo-European cousins.

Periods in the History of English

Because languages change continuously, any division into historical stages or periods must be somewhat arbitrary. Scholars have nevertheless divided the history of English into three main periods representing different stages of the language. We refer to the language spoken in England from the end of the seventh century to the end of the eleventh century (700–1100) as Old English or Anglo-Saxon. The English spoken since 1450 or 1500 is called Modern English and that spoken in between—roughly from 1100 to 1450 or 1500—is Middle English. Thus *Beowulf* is written in Old English, Chaucer's *Canterbury Tales* in Middle English, and Shakespeare's *Henry IV* in (early) Modern English.

Old English: 700–1100

The Angles, Saxons, and Jutes who first invaded England settled in different parts of the island, and four principal Old English dialects sprang up: Northumbrian in the north (north of the Humber River); Mercian in the Midlands; Kentish in the southeast; and West Saxon in the southwest (see Figure 13.2). Because Wessex was the seat of the powerful King Alfred, its dialect, West Saxon, achieved a certain status, and it forms the basis of most surviving Old English literature and of the study of Old English today.

Like the classical Latin of Roman times and today's German and Russian, Old English was a highly inflected language. It had an elaborate system of inflectional suffixes on nouns, pronouns, verbs, adjectives, and even determiners. Only traces of these inflectional forms survive in Modern English.

Old English Script

Only a few Old English graphs, or letters, differ from those of Modern English, but they occurred in some of the most frequently used words, giving Old English an exaggerated air of strangeness. Among the graphs no longer used in

Figure 13.2 The Old English Dialects

English are <þ> (called thorn), <ð> (eth), <p> (wynn), and <æ> (ash). Editors usually let the graphs thorn, eth, and ash remain in modern texts but substitute <w> for wynn.

Thorn <þ> and eth <ð> (and their respective capitals <Þ> and <Ð>) were alternative spellings for the sounds [θ] or [ð], which were allophones of a single phoneme in Old English. Scribes did not assign one graph to the sound [θ] and the other to [ð] because, being allophones of a single phoneme, these sounds were not perceived as different. Old English speakers were no more aware of the difference between [θ] and [ð] than Modern English speakers are aware of the different *p* sounds in *pot* and *spot*.

The graph <æ>, rarely used in Modern English, represented a pronunciation in Old English much like the vowel of *hat*. The Old English vowel combinations <ēo> and <ēa> represented the diphthongs [eːɔ] and [ɛːə] respectively. The letter sequence <sc> is equivalent to Modern English <sh> [ʃ], so that Old English *scip* was pronounced just like Modern English *ship*. The letter <c> represented one of two sounds: [k] as in *cȳpmenn* or [tʃ] as in *æðellīce*. The letter <g> represented three sounds: it was pronounced as [j] word-initially when it preceded a front vowel (as in *gelamp* and *gȳt*) and word-finally when it followed one (as in *Rōmānabyrig*); elsewhere it was pronounced as [g] or [ɣ]. The letter <y> was always the high front rounded vowel [ü]. The letters <j> and <q> were not used in Old English, and <k> was rare (hence *folc* 'folk'), although the sounds they represent today did exist as in *cwēn* 'queen' and *cēpan* 'keep.' The letter <x> was an alternative spelling of <cs>, pronounced [ks], as in *axode* [aksɔdɛ] 'asked.' Finally, we might mention that <⁊> 'and' was the customary representation in original manuscripts of the Old English equivalent of an ampersand sign <&>.

Old English Sounds

Much could be said about the Old English sound system. We make only a few comments about some patterns that have implications for the development of Modern English.

Vowels Old English had long and short vowels and diphthongs, although in late Old English the diphthongs tended to become monophthongs. (A similar simplification occurs today in American dialects of the South, in which words such as *time* /tajm/ tend to be pronounced [tʰaːm]; throughout the United States the pronunciation of *I* is simplified from [aj] to [a] or [aː] in a phrase such as *I'm gonna* [amgʊnə].) Over the centuries the short vowels have remained relatively constant so that many words are pronounced today much as they were pronounced in Old English: *fisc* 'fish,' *æt* 'at,' *þorn* 'thorn,' *benc* 'bench,' and *him* 'him.' By contrast, the long vowels have undergone significant changes. Suffice it to say that Old English long vowels had their "continental" values, as in the words *stān* [staːn] 'stone,' *sēon* [seːɔn] 'see,' *sōðlīce* [soːðliːʧɛ] 'truly,' *būton* [buːtɔn] 'without, except,' and *swīðe* [swiːðɛ] 'very.'

Consonants Old English permitted certain word-initial consonant clusters that Modern English does not allow; hence /hl/ in *hlud* 'loud,' /hr/ in *hring* 'ring,' and /kn/ in *cniht* 'knight.' Three pairs of sounds whose members are distinct phonemes in Modern English were allophones of single phonemes in Old English: [f] and [v]; [θ] and [ð]; and [s] and [z]. The voiceless allophones [f θ s] occurred at the beginning and

Try It Yourself Using the description given in the paragraph above, determine the allophone of /f/ or /θ/ that occurs in each of these words: *fōt* 'foot,' *līf* 'life,' *heofon* 'heaven,' *stæð* 'shore,' *stæðe* 'shore (dative singular form),' *ōþer* 'other,' *oð* 'until,' *oft* 'often,' *hwæðer* 'whether,' *hæðen* 'heathen.'

end of words and when adjacent to voiceless sounds within words; between voiced sounds, however, the voiced allophones occurred. Thus in the nominative case of the word *wīf* [wiːf], <f> represented the allophone [f], but in the genitive case it represented the allophone [v]: *wīfes* [wiːvɛs] (note the final [s], too). The phonemes /s/ and /θ/ figure prominently in the history of English because they occur in so many inflections and function words.

Old English Vocabulary and Morphology

Compounds Old English writers were fond of compounding. The three lines of *Beowulf* cited earlier contain three compounds: *Gār-Dena* meaning 'spear Danes,' *geār* + *dagum* meaning 'yore days,' and *þēod* + *cyninga* meaning 'nation kings.' Others from *Beowulf* include *seglrād* 'sail road' and *hrōnrād* 'whale road' for *sea* and *bānhūs* 'bone house' for *body*.

Noun Inflections Old English had several inflections for noun phrases, depending on their grammatical and semantic role in a sentence. Four principal cases could be distinguished: *nominative* (usually for subjects), *genitive* (for possessives and certain other functions), *dative* (for indirect objects and certain other functions), and *accusative* (for direct objects and objects of certain prepositions). Each noun carried a grammatical gender, which occasionally reflected natural gender; *guma* 'man' and *brōðor* 'brother' were masculine, while *brȳd* 'bride' and *sweostor* 'sister' were feminine. But usually gender had little to do with the natural sex of a noun's referent. For example, the nouns *mīl* 'mile,' *wist* 'feast,' and *lēaf* 'permission' were feminine; *hund* 'dog,' *hungor* 'hunger,' *wīfmann* 'woman,' and *wingeard* 'vineyard' were masculine; and *wīf* 'woman, wife,' *manncynn* 'mankind,' and *scip* 'ship' were neuter. Grammatical gender is simply a category that determined the way a noun was inflected and the inflections on adjectives and other constituents of the noun phrase, as well as pronominal agreement.

Table 13.1 shows the paradigms for the nouns *fox* 'fox,' *lār* 'learning, lore,' *dēor* 'animal,' and *fōt* 'foot.' From the Old English *fox* declension (*declension* is the name for a noun paradigm) come the only productive Modern English noun inflections: the genitive singular in *-s* and all plurals in *-s*. The *dēor* declension survives in uninflected modern plurals such as *deer* (whose meaning has been narrowed from 'animal') and *sheep*, but new words never follow this pattern. The *fōt* declension has yielded a few nouns (such as *goose*, *tooth*, *louse*, *mouse*, and *man*) whose plurals are signaled by an internal vowel change rather than by the common *-s* suffix. Modern English phrases such as *a ten-foot pole* are relics of the Old English genitive plural ('a pole of ten feet'), whose form *fōta* has yielded *foot*. Over the centuries, most nouns that had been inflected according to other declensions have come to conform to the *fox* paradigm, and new nouns (with the exception of a few loanwords such as *alumni* and *phenomena*) are also inflected like it. Irregular forms of words tend to be relics that have been inherited from earlier regularities.

Articles The Modern English definite article *the* has a single orthographic shape with two standard pronunciations, [ði] before vowels and [ðə] elsewhere. In sharp contrast, the Old English demonstratives—forerunners of today's definite article—were inflected for five cases and three genders in the singular and for

Table 13.1 *Four Old English Noun Declensions*

	Masculine 'Fox'	Feminine 'Learning'	Neuter 'Animal'	Masculine 'Foot'
Singular				
Nominative	fox	lār	dēor	fōt
Accusative	fox	lār-e	dēor	fōt
Genitive	fox-es	lār-e	dēor-es	fōt-es
Dative	fox-e	lār-e	dēor-e	fēt
Plural				
Nom./Acc.	fox-as	lār-a	dēor	fēt
Genitive	fox-a	lār-a	dēor-a	fōt-a
Dative	fox-um	lār-um	dēor-um	fōt-um

Table 13.2 *Old English Declension of Demonstrative 'That'*

	Singular			Plural
	Masculine	**Feminine**	**Neuter**	**All Genders**
Nominative	sē	sēo	þæt	þā
Accusative	þone	þā	þæt	þā
Genitive	þǣs	þǣre	þæs	þāra
Dative	þǣm	þǣre	þǣm	þǣm
Instrumental	þȳ	þǣre	þȳ	þǣm

three cases without gender distinction in the plural (see Table 13.2). The fifth case, the instrumental, was used with or without a preposition to indicate such semantic roles as accompaniment or instrument ('with the chieftains,' 'by an arrow'). It's instructive to compare the Old English demonstrative in Table 13.2 with the Modern German definite article in Table 2.10. The similarities are striking.

As with Modern English indefinite plural noun phrases (*She writes novels*), Old English indefinite noun phrases frequently lacked an explicit marker of indefiniteness. But sometimes *sum* 'a certain' and *ān* 'one' occurred in the singular for emphasis and were inflected like adjectives.

Adjective Inflections Old English adjectives owe their complexity to innovations that arose in Common Germanic and consequently do not appear in other Indo-European languages.

Old English adjectives were inflected for gender, number, and case to agree with their head noun. There were two adjective declensions. When a noun phrase had as one of its constituents a highly inflected possessive pronoun or demonstrative, adjectives were declined with the so-called weak, or *definite*, declension. In other instances, such as predicative usage (*It's tall*), when indicators of grammatical relations were few or nonexistent, the more varied forms of the strong, or *indefinite*, declension were required. Table 13.3 gives the indefinite and definite adjective paradigms for *gōd* 'good.' Notice that Old English has ten forms, as compared to the single form *good* in Modern English.

Nothing remains of the Old English inflectional system for adjectives. Today all adjectives occur in a single shape such as *tall*, *old*, and *beautiful* (with comparative and superlative inflections, as in *taller* and *tallest*). For any gender, number, or case of the modified noun, and for both attributive functions (*the tall ships*) and predicative functions (*the ship is tall*), the form of a Modern English adjective remains invariant.

Personal Pronouns Modern English personal pronouns preserve more of their earlier complexity than any other word class. The Old English paradigms are given in Table 13.4, alongside their modern counterparts. As you can see, besides singular and plural pronouns, Old English had a dual number in the first and second persons to refer to exactly two people ('we two' and 'you two'). The dual was already weakening in late Old English and eventually disappeared. So did the distinct number and case forms for the second-person pronoun (*þū* 'thou'/*þē* 'thee' and *gē* 'ye'/*ēow* 'you' are all now *you*) and the distinct dative case form for the third-person-singular neuter pronoun.

Table 13.3 *Old English Declensions of the Adjective 'Good'*

	SINGULAR			PLURAL		
	Masc.	Fem.	Neut.	Masc.	Fem.	Neut.
Indefinite						
Nom.	gōd	gōd	gōd	gōd-e	gōd	gōd
Acc.	gōd-ne	gōd-e	gōd	gōd-e	gōd	gōd
Gen.	gōd-es	gōd-re	gōd-es	gōd-ra	gōd-ra	gōd-ra
Dat.	gōd-um	gōd-re	gōd-um	gōd-um	gōd-um	gōd-um
Ins.	gōd-e	gōd-re	gōd-e	gōd-um	gōd-um	gōd-um
Definite				*All genders*		
Nom.	gōd-a	gōd-e	gōd-e	gōd-an		
Acc.	gōd-an	gōd-an	gōd-e	gōd-an		
Gen.	gōd-an	gōd-an	gōd-an	gōd-ra (gōd-ena)		
Dat.	gōd-an	gōd-an	gōd-an	gōd-um		

Table 13.4 *Old English and Modern English Pronouns*

	OLD ENGLISH					MODERN ENGLISH				
	First	Second	Third Person			First	Second	Third Person		
			Masc	Fem	Neut			Masc	Fem	Neut
Singular										
Nom.	ic	þū	hē	hēo	hit	I	you	he	she	it
Acc.	mē	þē	hine	hie	hit	me	you	him	her	it
Gen.	mīn	þīn	his	hiere	his	mine	yours	his	hers	its
Dat.	mē	þē	him	hiere	him	me	you	him	her	it
Dual										
Nom.	wit	git								
Acc.	unc	inc								
Gen.	uncer	incer								
Dat.	unc	inc								
		All Genders						All Genders		
Plural										
Nom.	wē	gē	hīe			we	you	they		
Acc.	ūs	ēow	hīe			us	you	them		
Gen.	ūre	ēower	hiera			ours	yours	theirs		
Dat.	ūs	ēow	him			us	you	them		

Relative Pronouns In Old English, an invariant particle *þe* or *ðe* marked the introduction of a relative clause, though *þe* was often compounded with the demonstrative *sē, sēo, þæt*, as in *sē þe* (for masculine reference) and *sēo þe* (for feminine reference) 'who, that.' Forms of the demonstrative *sē, sēo, þæt* could also occur alone as relatives:

ānne	æðeling	sē	wæs	Cyneheard	hāten
a	prince	Rel	was	Cyneheard	called

'a prince who was called Cyneheard'

Old English relative clauses were also sometimes introduced by *þe* and a form of the personal pronoun; as in this example with *þe* and *him*.

Nis	nū	cwicra	nān	þe	ic	him	mōdsefan	mīnne	durre	āsecgan.
(there) isn't	now	alive	no one	Rel	I	him	mind	my	dare	speak

'There is no one alive now to whom I dare speak my mind.'

As this example shows, Old English relativized indirect objects (*him*). According to the relative clause hierarchy that we examined in discussing universals in Chapter 7, Old English should also have relativized direct objects and subjects—and in fact it did.

Verbs and Verb Inflections Like other Germanic languages, Old English had two types of verbs. The characteristically Germanic ones have a [d] or [t] suffix in the past tense (and are called "weak"). The traditional Indo-European ones are called "strong" and show a vowel alternation (as in *sing/sang/sung*). Old English had seven patterns for strong verbs. Table 13.5 lists the principal parts (the forms from which all other inflected forms can be derived) of these seven classes. All the illustrative strong verbs in Table 13.5 survive as irregular verbs in Modern English, but many others have developed into regular verbs in the course of time. For example, *shove, melt, wash,* and *step* followed strong patterns in Old English but are regular in Modern English.

Two tenses (present and past) and two moods (indicative and subjunctive) could be formed from a verb's principal parts. Table 13.6 gives a typical Old English regular verb conjugation for *dēman* 'judge, deem' (*conjugation*

Table 13.5 *Seven Classes of Old English Strong Verbs*

Infinitive	Past Singular	Past Plural	Past Participle	
1. rīdan	rād	ridon	geriden	'ride'
2. frēosan	frēas	fruron	gefroren	'freeze'
3. drincan	dranc	druncon	gedruncen	'drink'
4. beran	bær	bǣron	geboren	'bear'
5. licgan	læg	lǣgon	gelegen	'lie'
6. standan	stōd	stōdon	gestanden	'stand'
7. feallan	fēoll	fēollon	gefeallen	'fall'

Table 13.6 *Conjugation of 'Judge, Deem' in Old English*

	Indicative Mood	Subjunctive Mood
Present Tense		
Singular		
first person	dēm-e	
second person	dēm-st (or dēm-est)	dēm-e
third person	dēm-þ (or dēm-eþ)	
Plural		
first, second, and third	dēm-aþ	dēm-en
Past Tense		
Singular		
first person	dēm-d-e	
second person	dēm-d-est	dēm-d-e
third person	dēm-d-e	
Plural		
first, second, and third	dēm-d-on	dēm-d-en
Gerund	tō dēm-enne (or dēm-anne)	
Present Participle		dēm-ende
Past Participle	dēm-ed	

is the name for a verb paradigm). Note that the present-tense indicative had three singular forms and one plural, but the present-tense subjunctive had only one singular and one plural form. In contrast to the twelve distinct forms of an Old English weak verb paradigm, the Modern English regular paradigm has only four distinct forms (*judge, judges, judged,* and *judging*) and does not include any distinct subjunctive forms.

Compared to its elaborate Indo-European ancestors and some of its even more elaborate cousins, Old English had a simple verbal system. Old English verbs were inflected for person, number, and tense in the indicative mood and for number and tense in the subjunctive mood; the subjunctive was used more frequently in Old English than in Modern English.

Inflections and Word Order in Old English

Having a rich inflectional system, Old English could rely on its morphological distinctions to indicate the grammatical relations (subject, object) of nouns (and, to a lesser extent, their semantic roles). Noun phrases had agreement in gender, number, and case among the demonstrative/definite article, the adjective, and the head noun. Adjectives were declined, either definite or indefinite, as already described. Using some of the declensions provided in Tables 13.1, 13.2, and 13.3 and two other adjectives, we can form the following Old English noun phrases. Note that in each instance the adjective and demonstrative article *agree* with the noun (that is, they have inflections that match the noun in gender, case, and number).

sē gōda fox	'the good fox' (masculine nominative singular)
gōd dēor	'good animals' (neuter nominative/accusative plural)
þā gōdan fēt	'the good feet' (masculine nominative/accusative plural)
langra fōta	'of long feet' (masculine genitive plural)
þǣre micelan lāre	'of/for the great learning' (feminine genitive/dative singular)

The rich inflectional system operating within Old English noun phrases could indicate grammatical relations and certain semantic roles without having to rely on word order the way Modern English does. Word order was therefore more flexible in Old English than in Modern English. Still, by late Old English, word order patterns were already similar in many respects to those of Modern English. In main clauses, both Old English and Modern English show a preference for SVO order (subject preceding verb preceding object). Modern English prefers SVO in subordinate clauses as well. Old English (like Modern German) preferred verb-final word order (SOV) in subordinate clauses.

As in Modern English, the order of elements in Old English noun phrases was usually determiner-adjective-noun: *sē gōda mann* 'the good man.' Far more frequently than in Modern English, genitives preceded nouns, as in the following:

folces weard	'people's protector'	
mǣres līfes mann	'splendid life's man'	('a man of splendid life')
fotes trym	'foot's space'	('the space of a foot')

Old English generally had prepositions, although when used with pronouns they often occurred in postposition (that is, after the pronoun), as in this example:

sē	hālga Andreas	him	tō	cwæþ ...
the	holy Andrew	him	to	said ...
'St. Andrew said to him ...'				

Like Modern English adjectives, Old English adjectives almost uniformly preceded their head nouns (*sē foresprecena here* 'the aforesaid army'), although they could sometimes follow them:

wadu weallendu
waters surging
'surging waters'

As they do in Modern English, relative clauses generally followed their head nouns.

ðā	cyningas	ðe	ðone	onwald	hæfdon
the	kings	who	the	power	had
'the kings who had the power'					

Companions of Angels: A Narrative in Old English

The Old English passage in Figure 13.3 originates in Bede's *Ecclesiastical History of the English People*, which was completed in A.D. 731 and subsequently translated from Latin into English, perhaps by Alfred the Great during his reign as king of Wessex (871–899). The passage here is a slightly edited version of a later translation by the English abbot Ælfric (c. 955–1020). The story tells how Gregory the Great, who reigned as pope between 590 and 604, first learned of the English people as he walked through a marketplace in Rome and saw boys being sold as slaves. The passage seems as foreign as any language written in

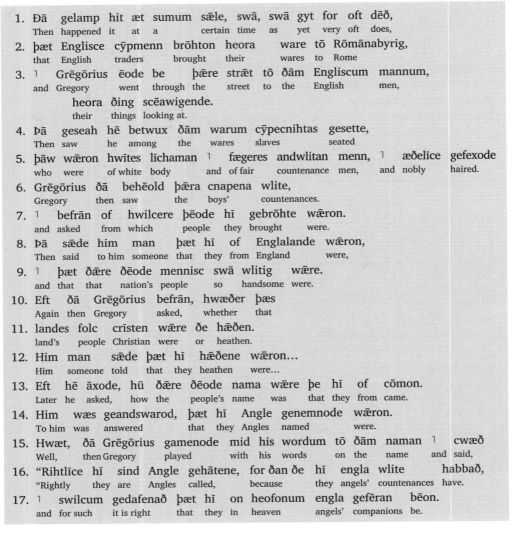

1. Ðā gelamp hit æt sumum sǣle, swā, swā gyt for oft dēð,
   Then happened it at a certain time as yet very oft does,
2. þæt Englisce cȳpmenn brōhton heora ware tō Rōmānabyrig,
   that English traders brought their wares to Rome
3. ⁊ Grēgōrius ēode be þǣre strǣt tō ðām Engliscum mannum,
   and Gregory went through the street to the English men,
   heora ðing scēawigende.
   their things looking at.
4. Þā geseah hē betwux ðām warum cȳpecnihtas gesette,
   Then saw he among the wares slaves seated
5. þāw wǣron hwītes līchaman ⁊ fægeres andwlitan menn, ⁊ æðelīce gefexode
   who were of white body and of fair countenance men, and nobly haired.
6. Grēgōrius ðā behēold þǣra cnapena wlite,
   Gregory then saw the boys' countenances.
7. ⁊ befrān of hwilcere þēode hī gebrōhte wǣron.
   and asked from which people they brought were.
8. Þā sǣde him man þæt hī of Englalande wǣron,
   Then said to him someone that they from England were,
9. ⁊ þæt ðǣre ðēode mennisc swā wlitig wǣre.
   and that that nation's people so handsome were.
10. Eft ðā Grēgōrius befrān, hwæðer þæs
    Again then Gregory asked, whether that
11. landes folc crīsten wǣre ðe hǣðen.
    land's people Christian were or heathen.
12. Him man sǣde þæt hī hǣðene wǣron...
    Him someone told that they heathen were...
13. Eft hē āxode, hū ðǣre ðēode nama wǣre þe hī of cōmon.
    Later he asked, how the people's name was that they from came.
14. Him wæs geandswarod, þæt hī Angle genemnode wǣron.
    To him was answered that they Angles named were.
15. Hwæt, ðā Grēgōrius gamenode mid his wordum tō ðām naman ⁊ cwæð
    Well, then Gregory played with his words on the name and said,
16. "Rihtlīce hī sind Angle gehātene, for ðan ðe hī engla wlite habbað,
    "Rightly they are Angles called, because they angels' countenances have.
17. ⁊ swilcum gedafenað þæt hī on heofonum engla gefēran bēon.
    and for such it is right that they in heaven angels' companions be.

Figure 13.3 Old English Narrative Written Around the Year 1000

the Roman alphabet and more so than some, given its unfamiliar letters. (Don't be shy about reading it aloud, at least in private.)

Vocabulary in the Narrative

There is greater difference between Old English and Modern English in nouns, verbs, and adjectives than in function words.

Function Words Focusing on prepositions, demonstratives, and pronouns, you'll see notable similarities between the Old English passage and Modern English: in the prepositions *æt* 'at,' *tō* 'to,' *betwux* 'between, among,' *of* 'of, from'; in the conjunction < ⅂ > 'and,' which occurs more than half a dozen times in the passage; in the conjunction *þā* 'then,' used frequently to introduce sentences. The subordinator *þæt* (lines 8 and 17) was used as it is in Modern English. Some of the personal pronouns functioned exactly as they do in Modern English: *hit* 'it,' *he* 'he,' *hi* 'they,' *him* 'him.' (Note that some of the demonstratives in the passage differ slightly in spelling from those in Table 13.2, as with the dative plural *þām* in lines 3 and 4 as compared to *þǣm*.)

Content Words Some of the unfamiliarity of nouns, verbs, and adjectives is due to inflections (*mannum*, the dative plural of 'man') and much of it to spelling differences or pronunciation rather than to loss or gain of words themselves. Thus you can see earlier forms of the nouns *English*, *street*, *thing*, *men*, and *name* in *Englisce*, *strǣt*, *ðing*, *menn*, and *nama*. In *brōhton*, *behēold*, *sǣde*, and *wǣre* are the etymons of the modern verbs *brought*, *beheld*, *said*, and *were*. You can see in the verb *be* the singular past-tense inflection *-e* (*wǣre*) and the plural past-tense inflection *-on* (*wǣron*). Among other words that still exist today are *hwǣðer* 'whether,' *hū* 'how,' *crīsten* 'Christian,' and *hǣðen* 'heathen.' Not so transparent are a few others that can trigger a flash of recognition once the link is pointed out: *rihtlīce* 'rightly,' *cwæð* 'quoted,' *heofonum* 'heaven,' *engla* 'angel.'

Grammar: Syntax and Morphology in the Narrative

While there was a preference for SVO in main clauses, other orders also occurred. For example, the verb appeared in second position after an introductory adverb such as *þā* (*þā gesēah he*, line 4; note also lines 1 and 8). In subordinate clauses, the verb tended to occur in final position (*þæt hī hǣðene wǣron*, line 12, and 1, 7, 9, 13, 14, 17). As in Modern English, noun phrases had the order adjective-noun (*sumum sǣle* 'a certain time') or article-noun (*þǣre strǣt* 'the street'), and prepositional phrases had the order preposition-(article)-(adjective)-noun (*æt sumum sǣle*, *be þǣre strǣt*). There happen to be no negatives in the passage, but Old English had negative concord (double negative) as in *Nis nū cwicra nān* . . . , the example given above in the discussion of relative pronouns.

Text Structure of the Narrative

One striking characteristic of Old English prose was a strong preference for linking sentences with < ⅂ > 'and' and *þā* 'then,' much as in Modern English oral narratives. Subordinators that made explicit the relation between one clause and another (*because, whether, as, when*) existed in Old English but their frequent use in writing was a later development. More typically in Old English writing (as in Modern English conversation) clauses are introduced with 'and' or 'then' as in lines 1, 3, 4, 8, and 17. In addition to the relative clauses, the passage contains a few other examples of subordination: *swā swā* 'as' in line 1, *hwæðer* 'whether' in line 10, and *for ðan ðe* 'because' in line 16.

Middle English: 1100–1500

Middle English refers to a period of great variation and instability in the history of English.

The Norman Invasion

In the year 1066, William, Duke of Normandy, sailed across the Channel to claim the English throne. After winning the Battle of Hastings, he was crowned king of England in Westminster Abbey on Christmas Day, and with his coronation Anglo-Saxon England passed into history. Thus was a Norman kingdom established in England, and for generations the king of England and the duke of Normandy would be the same person. The Norman invasion would reshape England's institutions and exercise a profound effect on its language.

The Norman French spoken by the invaders quickly became the language of England's ruling class, while the lower classes continued to speak English. Following the invasion, English took a forced recess from many of its previous duties. In particular, it was relieved of many of its functions in the affairs of government, the court, the church, and education; such important activities were now conducted in French. Indeed, for two centuries after the conquest, the kings of England could not speak the language of many of their subjects, and monolingual English-speaking subjects could not understand their king. Richard the Lion-Hearted, the most famous king of the period, was in every way French and, during his 10-year reign (1189–1199), visited England only twice for a total of less than 10 months. Eventually the middle classes became bilingual, speaking English to peasants and French to the ruling classes.

After 1200 the situation began to change. In 1204 King John lost Normandy to King Philip of France, and on both sides of the Channel decrees were issued commanding that no one could own land in both England and France. Cut off from its Norman origins, the force that had sustained the use of French in England began to dissipate.

Middle English Vocabulary

A hundred years later, at the beginning of the fourteenth century, spoken English came to be known again by all of England's inhabitants. Not surprisingly, though, the English that emerged was strikingly different from the English used prior to the Norman invasion. For one thing, the vocabulary of Middle English was spiced by thousands of Norman French words as speakers learning English used French words for things whose English labels they no longer knew.

It has been reliably estimated that approximately 10,000 French words came into English during the Middle English period, and most remain in use today. Especially plentiful were words pertaining to religion, government, the courts, and the army and navy, although many borrowings relate to food, fashion, and education—arenas in which the Norman invaders and their successors had wielded great influence in England.

Once English had been reestablished as the language of the law, the residents of England found themselves without sufficient English terminology to carry on the activities that had been conducted for centuries in French. Hence a good many French legal terms were borrowed, including even the words *justice* and *court*. To discuss events in a courtroom today, the following words are used—all borrowed from French during the Middle English period: *judgment, plea, verdict, evidence, proof, prison,* and *jail*. The actors in a courtroom have French names: *bailiff, plaintiff, defendant, attorney, jury, juror,* and *judge,* as do certain crimes, including *felony, assault, arson, larceny, fraud, libel, slander,* and *perjury*. The word *crime* itself comes from French. We have cited examples only from the domain of law (a word that derives from Old English *lagu*). Extensive lists of French borrowings could also be provided for other arenas in which the French were socially and culturally influential.

Middle English Sounds

There was considerable change in some vowels and consonant patterns between Old English and the end of Middle English.

Vowels Most long vowels of Old English remained unchanged in Middle English. But the Old English long vowel /ɑ:/ in words like *bān, stān,* and *bāt* became long /ɔ:/ (and in Modern English /o/) as in *boon* 'bone,' *stoon* 'stone,' and *boot* 'boat.' Many diphthongs were simplified in late Old English and early Middle English. Thus the vowels of *sēon* 'see' and *bēon* 'be' were monophthongized to long /e:/, a sound that later became /i/ in Modern English.

Short vowels in unstressed syllables, which had been kept distinct at least in early West Saxon, tended to merge in schwa [ə], usually written <e>.

Consonants and Consonant Clusters The Old English initial consonant clusters /hl-/, /hn-/, /hr-/, and /kn-/ were simplified to /l/, /n/, and /r/, losing their initial /h/ or /k/: *hlāf* 'loaf,' *hlot* 'lot,' *hnecca* 'neck,' *hnacod* 'naked,' *hrōf* 'roof,' *hræfn* 'raven,' *hring* 'ring,' *cnif* 'knife,' *cnoll* 'knoll,' *cniht* 'boy, knight.' Of considerable consequence was the merging of word-final /m/ and /n/ in a single sound (/n/) when they occurred in unstressed syllables (*foxum > foxun*). Significantly, unstressed syllables included *all* the inflections on nouns, adjectives, and verbs. By the end of the Middle English period even this /n/ was dropped altogether (*foxun > foxen > foxe*), and the final -*e* was also eventually dropped.

Middle English Inflections

Three of the phonological changes just mentioned had a profound effect on the morphology of Middle English.

1. -m > -n
2. -n > Ø
3. a, o, u, e > e [ə] (when not stressed)

Figure 13.4 shows how, as a consequence of these few sound changes, certain sets of Old English inflections merged, becoming indistinguishable in Middle English and being further reduced or even dropped in early Modern English. As a result of these mergers, the Old English noun and adjective paradigms became greatly simplified in Middle English, and grammatical gender disappeared (see Table 13.7).

Nouns The frequently used subject and object noun phrase forms (nominative and accusative cases) established the nominative and accusative plural form *foxes* (and the *-es* inflection for other nouns in general) throughout the plural.

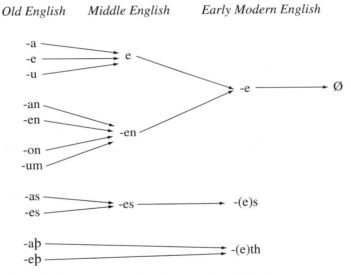

Figure 13.4 The Historical Reduction of English Inflections

Table 13.7 *Four Middle English Noun Declensions*

	'Fox'	'Lore'	'Animal'	'Foot'
Singular				
Nom./Acc.	fox	loor	deer	foot
Genitive	foxes	loor(e)	deeres	footes
Dative	fox(e)	loor(e)	deer(e)	foot
Plural				
Nom./Acc.	foxes	loor(e)	deer	feet
Genitive/Dative	foxes	loor(e)	deer(e)	foot(e)

They also established the nominative and accusative singular throughout the singular except that the genitive in -s was maintained. Thus the Middle English paradigm for a noun such as *fox* came to be what it is in Modern English: *fox* and *foxes* in the singular (*foxes* is now spelled *fox's*) and *foxes* throughout the plural (possessive *foxes'*).

In some other noun paradigms, damage to the morphological distinctions caused by the merging of unstressed vowels was even greater. Old English *dēor* was reduced to three forms (*deer/deeres/deere*), while *lār* was reduced to two (*loor* and *loore*), with a distinction that was then lost when final inflected -e vanished about 1500.

We have the Modern English forms of the word *deer* (*deer* and *deer's*) from the nominative and accusative singular inflection, which were extended throughout the singular (except that the ending in -s has been kept in the genitive). The parallel nominative and accusative plural form extended throughout the plural (except that by analogy with all other nouns the genitive plural adds -s to the form of the nominative plural). From the *foot* declension, the origin of the Modern English forms is clear: Middle English nominative and accusative *foot* was extended throughout the singular, with the -s of the genitive form *footes* maintained; the nominative and accusative plural *feet* was extended throughout the plural (and, as usual, the inflected genitive is formed by adding -s to the nominative).

Adjectives The merging of distinct inflections that collapsed the noun declensions also had a drastic effect on adjectives. The only indefinite forms to survive the phonological change from Old English were *goodne* (masculine accusative singular), *goodes* (masculine and neuter genitive singular), and *goodre* (feminine genitive, dative, and instrumental singular, and genitive plural). Then *good* became the universal form for the singular. In the plural, the nominative, accusative, and dative forms for all genders became *good*, and by analogy the genitive plural also became *good*. That left *good* as the only form in the singular and plural, which yielded Modern English *good* as the invariable form of the adjective (comparative and superlative forms aside).

In the definite declension, the only forms to survive were *good* and *goodre*. Then *goodre* was re-formed to *good* by analogy (whereby one form takes on the shape of other forms in the same or another paradigm), thus leaving only a single definite adjective form, which was the same as the indefinite. Astonishingly, a few simple phonological changes (and some analogical adaptations) reduced the complexity of Old English adjectives to the striking simplicity of today's.

Middle English Word Order

Much could be said about Middle English syntax, but the language changed so thoroughly during the four centuries of this period that a good deal of provision would have to be made for intermediate stages. Since we have described Old English and Modern English syntax, suffice it to say that Middle English was a transitional period, especially with respect to the change from relying on inflection to relying on word order for a considerable amount of information about grammatical relations. As the inflections of Old English disappeared, the word order of Middle English became increasingly fixed. The communicative work previously accomplished by inflectional morphology on nouns fell principally to prepositions and word order. We have already noted that Old English preferred SVO word order in main clauses and SOV in subordinate clauses. The exclusive use of the SVO pattern emerged in the twelfth century and remains characteristic to this day.

Where Men and Women Go All Naked: A Middle English Travel Fable

You can now see how some of these features of morphology and syntax came together in Middle English prose. Figure 13.5 is a passage from *The Travels of John Mandeville*. It's a translation of Mandeville's French work by an unknown English writer in the fifteenth century (about the time of Chaucer's death in 1400). In our passage, Mandeville describes a fabulous place called Lamary.

We analyze the passage with a view to how early fifteenth-century English differs from today's. The passage is intelligible, although you'll note a few marked differences (and some subtle ones) between it and today's English.

Vocabulary in the Fable

Not a single word in the passage will be unknown to you, although a few (such as *lond* 'land,' *hete* 'heat,' *ʒeer* 'year,' *byʒen* 'buy,' and *hem* 'them') may not be instantly recognizable. (The graph <ʒ>, called *yogh*, was pronounced [j], like <y> in *you*.) Not all the words borrowed from French during the Middle English period immediately took their current form, but most are nevertheless transparent: *custom, strange, clothed, nature, comoun, clos, contradiccioun, contree, habundant, marchauntes.*

Morphology in the Fable

In the fable, only a few inflections remain from Old English that have not survived into Modern English. For example, third-person singular present-tense verbs end in *-(e)th*: *holdeth, hath, lyketh, taketh,* and plural present-tense verbs end in *-n* or *-en*: *gon, scornen, seyn, ben, eten, bryngen, byʒen,* and others. This *-n* or *-en* is not the direct reflex of the Old English plural form *-aþ* but was apparently introduced from the subjunctive plural (see Table 13.6) so as to maintain a distinction between the singular and the plural, which otherwise would have been lost when the unstressed vowels of the singular *-eþ* and the plural *-aþ* merged to give Middle English *-eth* for both forms (see Figure 13.4). As shown in line 3 of Figure 13.5, Mandeville's translator alternates between the spellings *þei* and *thei* for the third-person plural subject pronoun, but the *þ/th* forms of the objective case do not yet appear in this passage, which instead shows the objective form *hem* (lines 19, 20, and 21). Otherwise, several of the Modern English inflections have their current form (after slight spelling adjustments): *goynge* 'going,' *clothed, godes* 'goods,' *þinges* 'things,' *marchauntes* 'merchants,' and

1. In þat lond is full gret hete,
   In that land is very great heat,

2. and the custom þere is such þat men and wommen gon all naked.
   and the custom there is such that men and women go all naked.

3. And þei scornen, whan thei seen ony strange folk goynge clothed.
   And they scorn, when they see any strange folk going clothed.

4. And þei seyn, þat god made Adam and Eue all naked
   And they say, that God made Adam and Eve all naked

5. and þat no man scholde schame him to schewen him such as god made him;
   and that no man should shame himself to show himself such as God made him;

6. for no thing is foul þat is of kyndely nature . . .
   for no thing is foul that is of natural nature . . .

7. And also all the lond is comoun; for all þat a man
   And also all the land is common; for all that a man

8. holdeth o ȝeer, another man hath it anoþer ȝeer,
   keeps one year, another man has it another year,

9. and euery man taketh what part þat him lyketh.
   and every man takes what part that him pleases.

10. And also all the godes of the lond ben comoun, cornes and all oþer þinges;
    And also all the goods of the land are common, grains and all other things;

11. for no þing þere is kept in clos, ne no þing þere is vndur lok,
    for no thing there is kept in a closet nor no thing there is under lock,

12. and euery man þere taketh what he wole, withouten ony contradiccioun.
    and every man there takes what he wants, without any contradiction.

13. And als riche is o man þere as is another.
    And as rich is one man there as is another.

14. But in þat contree þere is a cursed custom:
    But in that country there is a cursed custom:

15. for þei eten more gladly mannes flesch þan ony oþer flesch.
    for they eat more gladly man's flesh than any other flesh.

16. And ȝit is þat contree habundant of flesch, of fissch,
    And yet is that country abundant with flesh, with fish,

17. of cornes, of gold and syluer, and of all oþer godes.
    with grains, with gold and silver, and with all other goods.

18. Þider gon marchauntes and bryngen with hem children,
    Thither go merchants and bring with them children,

19. to selle to hem of the contree; and þei byȝen hem.
    to sell to them of the country; and they buy them.

20. And ȝif þei ben fatte, þei eten hem anon; and ȝif þei ben lene,
    And if they are fat, they eat them at once; and if they are lean,

21. þei feden hem till þei ben fatte, and þanne þei eten hem.
    they feed them until they are fat, and then they eat them.

22. And þei seyn, þat it is the best flesch and the swettest of all the world.
    And they say, that it is the best flesh and the sweetest of all the world.

Figure 13.5 A Travel Fable Written in Middle English Around the Year 1400

swettest 'sweetest.' Even certain words that had kept their exceptional forms from Old English are the same or nearly the same in 1400 and today: *men, wommen, folk, children,* and *best.* Being among the more common words, they were more likely to maintain their unusual forms than were less frequently used words.

Syntax in the Fable

A notable difference in syntax can be seen in the first line. Where Modern English requires a so-called "dummy subject" (one without a referent), Middle English did not require one: *In þat lond is . . . .* But it allowed a dummy subject, as with *þere* in line 14: *But in þat contree þere is . . . .* Another feature is negative concord, as in *ne no þing* 'nor nothing' in line 11, which remains widespread today in nonstandard usage.

There are marked word order differences. In line 13, compare this word-for-word equivalent with its current English version (following the slash): *And as rich is one man there as is another/And one man there is as rich as another.* Note, too, that the adverb phrase *more gladly* (line 15) follows its verb instead of preceding it as it would in Modern English. Finally, note the relic of Old English verb-second word order in line 18 (*Thither go merchants*) and the prepositional phrase *with hem* in the same line, which in Modern English would follow the direct object *children.*

Among subtler syntactic differences is the use of *scorn* as an intransitive verb (that is, a verb without a direct object) in line 3. In Modern English, *scorn* requires a direct object: you must scorn something or someone. Note, too, the use of the nonreflexive pronoun *him* in line 5. You can note another difference in line 9, where the object form *him* complements the verb *lyketh* (in a benefactive semantic role); *him lyketh* literally translates *to him (it) likes* 'it pleases him.' Since Old English times, this impersonal construction had not required a subject but a dative (or, later, objective) case form of the pronoun. It resembles the French *s'il vous plait* 'if it you pleases,' which may have influenced the now archaic formulation *if it please you* or *if it please the court.*

Because we are accustomed to finding relatively conservative syntax in such places as the King James Bible and certain formal prose styles such as legalese, it is easy to overlook some of the syntactic differences between late Middle English and current English. Still, this passage, now six centuries old, is obviously English and surprisingly transparent.

Modern English: 1500–Present

Chapters 2 through 6 of this book examined the structure of current English in detail, and there is no need to recapitulate that material here. This section focuses instead on what changes occurred in the earliest stages of Modern English to move the language from the forms of Middle English to those we know today.

Early and Late Modern English

As our analysis of Mandeville's travel fable shows, by the beginning of the fifteenth century Middle English had developed many of the principal syntactic patterns we know today. The complex inflectional system of Old English had been dramatically simplified; and today's system, with fewer than ten inflections, had emerged. Most nouns that had been inflected in Old English according to various patterns now conformed to the *fox* pattern. By the time of Shakespeare, third-person plural pronouns with *th-* (*they, their,* and *them*) instead of *h-* had been in general use for a century; Chaucer and the Mandeville translator had used *they* but still used the older possessive form *her* (not *their*) and objective form *hem* (not *them*). In addition, word order had become more fixed, essentially as it is in Modern English.

The language of the late 1400s is in most ways Modern English—although we should be mindful that a dramatic shift already under way in the pronunciation of vowels had a profound effect on English phonology sometime between 1450 and 1650, as we'll see. That phonological change is not apparent to the eye simply because the modern spelling of English vowels had essentially been established by the time of William Caxton, who founded his printing press in the vicinity of Westminster Abbey in 1476, before the shift had progressed very far and whose spellings disguise the fundamental alteration that subsequently affected the system of English vowels.

Phonology: The English Vowel Shift

In the Mandeville travel passage, certain words are easily recognized by their similar spellings to Modern English, as with *gret, hete, schame,* and *foul,* which are similar to their modern counterparts. The written similarity, however, disguises the fact that the words as *pronounced* in Chaucer's time would not likely be recognizable by a modern listener. Sometime during the centuries between 1450 and 1650, all the long vowels of Middle English underwent a systematic shift. Each long front vowel was raised and became pronounced like another vowel higher in the system, and each long back vowel was raised and pronounced like a vowel higher in the system. Thus /ɔ:/ came to be pronounced /o:/, /e:/ came to be pronounced /i:/, and so on. The two highest long vowels, /i:/ and /u:/, unable to be raised farther, became the diphthongs /aj/ and /aw/ respectively. Thus Middle English *I* /i:/ became /aj/, *hous* /hu:s/ became /haws/ 'house,' and so on. We can represent the situation as in Figure 13.6.

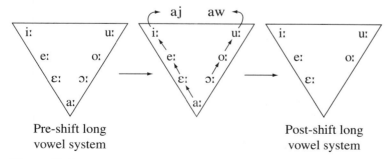

Pre-shift long vowel system

Post-shift long vowel system

Figure 13.6 The English Vowel Shift

Source: Adapted from Theodora Bynon, *Historical Linguistics* (Cambridge: Cambridge University Press, 1977), p. 82.

Try It Yourself Note that in becoming the diphthongs /aj/ and /aw/, the highest long vowels /iː/ and /uː/ have, in effect, moved from the highest positions in vowel space to the lowest, with /a/ being a low vowel. You'll recall from Chapter 11 that one of the hallmarks of Southern American English is a monophthongization of /aj/ in general. What similarities can you identify in the English Vowel Shift of Figure 13.6 and the Southern Shift as pictured in Figure 11.10 in "The Atlas of North American English" section of Chapter 11? What about between the English Vowel Shift and the Northern Cities Shift, as pictured in Figure 11.9?

Modern English Morphology

Verbs Of the hundreds of strong (irregular) verbs in Old English, relatively few survive in Modern English. Of those that do, many are now inflected as regular verbs. One tally suggests that of the 333 strong verbs of Old English, only 68 continue as irregular verbs in Modern English. Among those that have become regular over the centuries are *burned, brewed, climbed, flowed, helped,* and *walked.* By contrast, slightly more than a dozen weak verbs have become irregular in the history of English, including *dive,* which has developed a past-tense form *dove* alongside the historical form *dived.* You also likely have heard *drug* for *dragged* and *snuck* for *sneaked,* as they have become more frequent, even in formal written usage. Among other verbs that are now irregular but were formerly regular are *wear, spit,* and *dig,* with their newer past-tense forms being *wore, spat,* and *dug.*

Definite Article The initial consonant of *sē* and *sēo,* the Old English masculine and feminine nominative singular demonstrative, differed from all other forms, which began with [θ] (orthographic < þ >). *Sē* was reshaped, apparently by analogy with forms having initial [θ]. By Middle English, *þe* had become the only definite article in the north of England, and its use soon spread. Chaucer uses only *the,* pronounced [θə], not [ðə]. The voicing of the initial consonant as we know it today occurred because the customary lack of stress on *the* encouraged assimilation to the vowel nucleus, which is voiced.

Indefinite Article The history of the indefinite article *a/an* is also remarkable, for while Old English did not use an indefinite article, *a/an* is among the top ten most common words in English today. While *a* has been pronounced as [ə] and [e] (or [eɪ] or [ej]) for some time, with [e] being used for emphasis, its use seems to be on the rise even in neutral situations that don't call for emphasis.

Personal Pronouns Personal pronouns retain more of their Old English complexity than any other part of speech. Still, there have been some significant changes in pronouns over the centuries. Our comparison of Old English and

Ye Olde Booke Shoppe

In the early fourteenth century some English writers merged the runic letter <þ> and the Roman letter <y> in their manuscripts, setting the stage for readers to confuse the two graphs. In the fifteenth century, the use of <þ> decreased, but even Chaucer, who died in 1400, generally used <th> where earlier writers had used <þ>. Some writers and printers of the time used y^e, y^t, y^{ei}, y^m, y^u to represent the words *the, that, they, them,* and *thou,* and such abbreviations (or *compendia,* as they are called) continued in manuscripts into the eighteenth century. In books printed as late as the sixteenth century you can find y^e for *the* (sometimes with <e> superscripted directly above <y>) and y^t for *that* (also sometimes with <t> appearing directly above <y>). Among the citations listed in the *Oxford English Dictionary* are these from eighteenth-century letters: "I am to inform you yt ye Duchess continues as well as can be, and ye Babe too" and "He told y^m yt ye French was landing in the Marsh." Some of these shorthand forms continued into nineteenth-century correspondence as well. As for current use of <y> for <th>, the *OED* characterizes it as "pseudoarchaic" and gives as examples Lewis Carroll's "Ye Carpette Knighte" and shop signs like "Ye Olde Booke Shoppe."

Modern English pronouns in Table 13.4 shows that the dual number ('you two' and 'we two') was lost entirely (starting at the beginning of the Middle English period). During the early Modern English period, the distinction between the second-person singular and plural forms—between singular *thou* and *thee* (Old English *þū* and *þē*) and plural *ye* and *you* (Old English *gē* and *ēow*)—evaporated.

Under the apparent influence of French, speakers of English began using the plural forms *ye, your,* and *you* as a sign of respect or formality, much as happens with French *vous,* which is grammatically plural but is used to show respect and deference when addressing a solitary stranger, elder, or social superior. Among the upper social classes in England, the historical plural form *you* came to be used as a mutual sign of respect even in informal conversation between equals. In time, the singular forms all but disappeared, along with the distinction between the plural subject and object forms *ye* and *you.* Thus, from the sixfold distinction found in Old English and much of Middle English, Modern English has only a twofold distinction—between *you* and *yours.* (See Table 13.4 in the "Old English Vocabulary and Morphology" section above.)

Many Modern English speakers find it challenging to get along without a distinct second-person plural pronoun, and new plural forms have cropped up in some varieties. Some of these forms are regionally marked: *y'all* in the American South; *youse* (pronounced [juz], [jɪz], or [jəz]) in New York City and parts of Ireland and England; and *y'uns* (pronounced [jənz] or [jɪnz]) in western Pennsylvania and the northern Ohio valley; *you lot* in parts of England. Standard English no longer has a distinctive second-person plural pronoun, although one can say such things as *you two* or *all of you.* Increasingly heard as an informal plural, especially in American English, is *you guys,* and it is used for males and females alike.

Through the first three quarters of the twentieth century, forms of the masculine singular pronoun were commonly used not only in reference to males but also for females and males, as in *Everyone should give meaning to his life*. A notable recent development is a vigorous move away from such sexist pronoun use in favor of nonsexist practice. This move has led to the introduction of an occasional new and not highly successful written form, the most apparent of which is *s/he* (first recorded in the 1970s). More important, it has fostered thoughtful use of third-person pronouns generally and prompted much more frequent use of *he or she* (not *he* alone) following antecedent indefinite pronouns, as in *The coach has never told anyone that he or she didn't make the team*, and following noun phrases representing both males and females, as in *A doctor should tell everyone he or she treats what to expect with new medications*. Instead of *he or she*, which seems stilted to many users, the third-person *plural* pronouns are common, and they too have the virtue of being gender neutral. As a result, sentences like *Everyone should take their share of responsibility* and *Has anyone here ever told anybody they're a writer?* are common. Although widespread in speech in North America and in both speech and writing in Britain, some editors, teachers, and others object to the use of a plural pronoun in reference to a grammatically singular antecedent. This development in the use of third-person pronouns thus remains in flux and unsettled.

Modern English Word Order

Deprived of its earlier inflectional signposts to meaning, Modern English has become an analytical language—more like Chinese than Latin. With nouns inflected only for the possessive case (and for number), word order is now the chief signal of grammatical relations such as subject and object. Pronouns preserve more case distinctions than nouns, but even pronouns are subordinate to the grammatical relations that word order signals, so that *Him and me saw her at the party*, though not standard, is not confusing in any way as to subject and object.

Why English advanced farther than its Germanic cousins along the path to becoming an analytical language (rather than remaining an inflected one) is not altogether clear. Possible explanations may be found in the thoroughgoing contact between the Danes and the English after the ninth century, in the French ascendance over English for numerous secular and religious purposes in the early Middle English period, and in the preservation of the vernacular chiefly in folk speech and therefore without the conservationist brake of writing for several generations in the eleventh and twelfth centuries. The influence of the Danes is particularly important. When they invaded England in the eighth and ninth centuries, they spoke Germanic varieties that must have been quite similar to the dialects spoken in England, but the Danish varieties had different inflections. It's easy to imagine that children exposed to parents and friends using different inflectional suffixes might look for other means to signal the differences indicated by these competing inflections.

In any case, decades before the Norman Conquest in 1066, those inflectional reductions started that became apparent when English reemerged. Doubtless they had advanced further in speech than the written texts of the day indicate. Thus phonological reductions undermined the inflectional morphology, and, as inflection grew less able to signal grammatical relations and semantic roles, word order and the deployment of prepositions came to bear those communicative tasks less redundantly. Gradually, the freer word order of Old English yielded to the relatively fixed order of Modern English, in which linear arrangements of words are the chief marker of grammatical relations.

Spurred by an almost total absence of inflections on nouns, Modern English syntax has evolved to permit unusually free interplay among grammatical relations and semantic roles. With nouns marked only for possessive case and pronouns only for possessive and objective cases, Modern English exercises minimal inflectional constraint on subject noun phrases, which are consequently free to represent an exceptionally wide range of semantic roles (as illustrated in Chapter 6 in the "Semantic Roles and Grammatical Relations" section).

Modern English Vocabulary

As had earlier happened during the Middle English period, when English supplanted French and borrowed thousands of French words to do what had long been done using the French language, so in the course of the early Modern English period, as English came to be used for functions Latin had previously served, a great many words were borrowed from Latin (and through Latin from Greek). The borrowed words tend to be more learned words, reflecting the arenas in which Latin was used. Even with these borrowings, English needed still more words as it spread into every sphere of activity. The *Oxford English Dictionary* records loan words from about 50 different languages borrowed during the first century and a half of Modern English (1500–1650) when the vernacular replaced Latin in nearly every learned arena.

Among the Latin borrowings of this period are the following nouns (we limit ourselves to just a few beginning with the letter *a*):

allusion	appendix
anachronism	atmosphere
antipathy	autograph
antithesis	axis

Among the adjectives are *abject, agile,* and *appropriate*; among the verbs, *adapt, alienate,* and *assassinate*. Some of these, although introduced to English from Latin, came originally from Greek, but during the Renaissance some other words were borrowed directly from Greek, including these:

acme	idiosyncrasy
anonymous	lexicon
catastrophe	ostracize
criterion (and criteria)	polemic
tantalize	tonic

Not everyone in England appreciated borrowed words, and writers using these unfamiliar terms were criticized for their "inkhorn" words. Not every borrowed term survived.

Borrowing continued to this day, and French has remained the major contributor, but over the intervening centuries English has shown increasing reliance on native sources to expand its lexicon. In particular, late Modern English favors compounding, especially of nouns with nouns. Strings of nouns put together to create other nouns are abundant, as with these comprising two nouns: *chat room, car crash, news junkies, juice bar, brick wall, summer vacation, park sorcerers, fireworks display, coaster ride, school rules, highway bridge, tomb raider, assassination plot, video game, ad business, race relations, gender equality, reality show,* and *foot traffic.* Not quite as common are those with three nouns: *Florida theme park, family-vacation budget, theme-park eatery, thriller-movie division, industry newsletter, consumer book market, print sales figures, civil rights worker, community news summit, cell-phone call, cell-phone usage,* and *Internet-investigations unit.* Those with four are less common still: *hit 1998 space opera-strategy game, video-game-style showdown, daredevil stunt work,* and *cell-phone surveillance service.*

But by no means are compounds the only vital way of increasing the English wordstock. Blends are popular, as with *animatronic, infomercials, sexting, swellegant, podcast, walkathon, e-tailer* and *e-zine,* not all of which are destined for long life. Remaining productive are prefixing (<u>*pre*</u>*show,* <u>*post*</u>*ride,* <u>*off*</u>*-peak,* <u>*super*</u>*killers,* <u>*mini*</u>*dress,* <u>*e*</u>*-reader,* <u>*multi*</u>*player,* <u>*co*</u>*-workers,* <u>*non*</u>*obvious,* <u>*cyber*</u>*dissidents,* <u>*hyper*</u>*local,* <u>*under*</u>*reported,* <u>*over*</u>*crowded,* <u>*mega*</u>*-low*) and suffixing (*preposterous*<u>*ness*</u>*, limit*<u>*less*</u>*, Cheever*<u>*esque*</u>*, corporat*<u>*ize*</u>*, food*<u>*ies*</u>*, full-tim*<u>*er*</u>). Conversion, too, continues to make contributions, as in *a must-see, to monitor, to mushroom, to text, to fist-bump,* and *to deejay.* Shortenings are also numerous, and these few illustrate some of the patterns: *exes* (e.g., ex-boyfriends, ex-wives), *adman* (advertising man), *perps* (perpetrators), and *prep time* (preparation time). Phrasal verbs are also very popular, as in *to cheer someone on* 'encourage'; *to leave off* 'stop, quit'; *to move on; to grow up; to figure something/someone out; to sign on; to turn out* 'found to be'; *to wear off* 'diminish in effect.' All of these examples are taken from a single issue of *Time* magazine—and they could have been multiplied many times over from that source alone.

How Computers Track Change in English

A project of major importance for the study of the history of English is the digitizing of the *Oxford English Dictionary* (*OED*). The *OED* is a mammoth multivolume dictionary that records every word appearing in English printed materials since the Old English period. Or perhaps we should say *nearly* every word, for the *OED* was compiled during Victorian times and not *every* word of English was allowed access to its Victorian pages. Among words you won't find in the original *OED* are the infamous four-letter "Anglo-Saxonisms." The *OED* took half a century to complete, and by time the final volume was published in 1928, a good deal more had been learned about the words at the beginning of the alphabet, which had

appeared in the earliest volumes. That new information required a large supplemental volume. In the 1970s a further four-volume supplement was needed, so much had the language changed since the supplement of 1933. Then, in 1989, the original 12 volumes were digitized with the five supplemental volumes incorporated, creating a second edition of this grand dictionary, which appeared in 20 large volumes, weighing 137 pounds and taking up nearly four feet of shelf space. The second edition was made available on a compact disc, smaller, less expensive, and easier and more efficient to use. With access to the CD-ROM, you can readily search through a thousand years of

English language history and find citations for any word that interests you, along with information about the author, date, and source for each citation. You can determine the date of a word's first recorded use; you can limit your search to any time period or author. The CD-ROM makes it possible to discover all the words that entered the language in a specified time period or all the words borrowed from a particular language—say, Japanese or French or Hindi.

Several major historical corpora of English have been compiled in recent years. In the previous chapter, we described the Helsinki Corpus and ARCHER. Corpora such as these have made possible previously unknown information about the history of English, and accessibility to them has given researchers an opportunity to explore the history of particular structures or words. ■

Summary

- English belongs to the West Germanic group of the Germanic branch of the Indo-European language family. It is *not* descended from Latin, but both Latin and English are members of the Indo-European language family and are descended from Proto-Indo-European.
- In the course of its history, English has been enriched by thousands of loan words from more than 100 languages—most notably French, as the descendants of the Norman invaders started using English in the thirteenth century, and Latin, when the vernacular came to be used during the Renaissance in arenas previously reserved for the classical language.
- *Beowulf* is an epic poem of the Old English period (700–1100). Chaucer (1340–1400) wrote during the Middle English period (1100–1500). Shakespeare (1564–1616) wrote early in the Modern English period (1500–present).
- Old English was a highly inflected language, but sound changes subsequently eroded most of the inflectional morphology.
- As a result of the erosion of inflections in the Middle English period, Modern English is an analytical language, relying principally on word order to express grammatical relations that were formerly marked by inflections.

 ## What Do You Think? REVISITED

- *Ye Olde Coffee Shoppe.* The information in the menu is correct. *Ye* is a misinterpretation of the letter thorn Þ or its lowercase variant þ as it appeared in the word *the*. Far from being hogwash, this use of *Ye* underscores the tentative relationship between a sound and its representation in writing.
- *San Diego and Santa Monica.* Many cities in California and the Southwest carry names given to honor patron saints when Spaniards first established missions in those cities. In Spanish, *San* is the masculine form for 'saint' and *Santa* the feminine form. Niece Agnes may be interested to know that just north of Santa Barbara lies the Santa Ynez Valley, named in honor of Saint Agnes. Place-names often reveal something about the cultural background of earlier settlers in those places.

- *English and German inflections.* About 1,000 years ago, German and English had about the same number of inflections on nouns, and those inflections have remained relatively constant in the course of the history of German. In contrast, as English developed, a few sound changes in unstressed syllables led to the merging of various endings. Once that happened, their usefulness was greatly reduced and they faded from use.
- *Irregular English plurals.* In Old English, *sheep* and *deer* belonged to a group of nouns that had different endings (that is, they were declined differently) from those nouns that became the modern-day ones ending in *-s*.
- *Stodgy Stan.* A preference for gender-neutral pronouns responds to concerns that using masculine pronouns to refer to men and women is sexist and socially unacceptable. In Britain, *they* is a vigorous solution in speech and writing, even when referring to a grammatically singular antecedent (*the fraud victim*). In North America, *they* is a common solution in speech, but many teachers, editors, and others object to its use in writing on the grounds that *he or she* can do the job and doesn't violate traditional rules of number agreement. Usage in this matter remains unsettled (although *s/he* seems out of favor), but in either case the important social point is honored: *they* and *he or she* are both gender neutral. ■

Exercises

13-1. Any Modern English word that was borrowed from Latin or Greek does not show the influence of Grimm's law, which affected only the Germanic branch of Indo-European. For many such borrowed words, English also has a word that it inherited directly from Indo-European through Germanic. Of course, any such inherited word would have undergone the consonant shifts described by Grimm. For each *borrowed* word below, cite an English word that is related in meaning and whose pronunciation shows the result of the consonant shift. For this exercise, focus only on the initial consonant of each word.

Example: Given *pedal*, you would seek a word like *foot*, which has a related meaning and begins with [f] (because Indo-European [p] became [f] in Germanic).

cardiac	paternal	plenitude	cordial
dual	pentagon	dentist	canine
capital	piscatory	triangle	decade

13-2. This exercise is like the preceding one, except here you're given English words that have undergone the Germanic consonant shift. You must provide another English word that is likely to have been borrowed because it has a closely related meaning but does *not* show the results of Grimm's law. Bear in mind that Latin and Greek borrowings tend to be more learned or technical than the related ones inherited directly from Indo-European. Focus only on the boldfaced consonant.

Example: Given *foot*, you would seek a word that begins with [p] such as *podiatrist* 'foot doctor.'

tooth   li**p**   fire
ten   **h**ound   eat

13-3. You know that, by the effects of Grimm's law, Indo-European *[bʰ] became [b] and Indo-European *[gʰ] became [g] in Germanic. Not being a Germanic language, Latin did not undergo these consonant shifts. Instead, in Latin, Indo-European *[bʰ] became [f] and *[gʰ] became [h]. We represent these facts in the following correspondences:

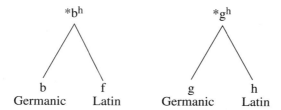

Given this information, provide an English word inherited directly from Indo-European for each of the following words, which are all borrowed from Latin, sometimes via French or another Romance language. Focus on the initial consonant, bearing in mind that other changes may have affected the remainder of the word.

fraternity   flame
fundamental   hospitable
fragile   fracture

13-4. Indicate which allophone of /f/, /θ/, or /s/ was pronounced in each of the following Old English words (use the description of the allophonic distribution given earlier to help you determine the correct answer): þæt, sēo, his, ūs, wæs, æðeling 'prince,' frēosan 'freeze,' dēmst 'judge,' līfes 'of life,' þā 'then,' drīfan 'drive,' wulfas 'wolves,' hræfn 'raven,' bosm 'bosom,' seofon 'seven,' bæþ 'bath,' sceaft 'shaft.'

13-5. a. Identify the grammatical gender of the following Old English nouns and give the genitive singular and nominative plural forms for each of them.
sē stān   'the stone'
þæt word   'the word'
sēo wund   'the wound'

b. For each of these Old English noun phrases, provide the Old English pronoun that would be used in the space given.

Sē stān, _____ is gōd.   'The stone, it is good.'
Ðæt word, _____ is gōd.   'The word, it is good.'
Sēo wund, _____ nis gōd.   'The wound, it isn't good.'

13-6. Compare the Old English passage with the Middle English passage and identify ways in which Middle English differs from Old English in orthography, vocabulary, morphology, and word order. Provide an example from the passages to illustrate each point.

13-7. Earlier in this chapter you saw several words whose meaning has changed from Old English to Modern English. One example is *dēor*, which meant 'animal' in Old English but has narrowed its meaning to 'deer' in Modern English. Among several other ways, words can change their meaning by becoming more specialized, as with *deer*, or by becoming more generalized. Examine the Old English words and meanings that follow and note what each word has become in Modern English. State whether each word's meaning has become more specialized or more generalized in the course of its development.

Old English	Modern English
steorfan 'die'	starve
berēafian 'deprive of'	bereave
hlāf 'bread'	loaf
spēdan 'prosper'	speed
spellian 'speak'	spell
hund 'dog'	hound
mete 'food'	meat
wīf 'woman'	wife
dōm 'judgment'	doom
sellan 'give'	sell
tīd 'time'	tide

13-8. Nearly all of the words listed below were borrowed into English from other languages. Keeping in mind the character of the word and what it signifies, make an educated guess as to the likely source language for each word and the approximate date of borrowing using half-century periods such as 1900–1950. Then, look up each word's origin in a good dictionary, noting for borrowed words the actual source language and the date of borrowing. For which words has no source been identified? (The source language will be identified in most good dictionaries; the date of borrowing may not be. *Merriam-Webster's Collegiate Dictionary*, eleventh edition, and some others do supply dates. It may be useful for different students or groups to tackle separate columns and compare their findings.)

barf	duffel	hummus	tandoori
zilch	mai tai	tortilla	ginseng
kibble	moped	nosh	glitch
bummer	jeans	ginger	schlock
dinosaur	disco	giraffe	kvetch
leviathan	dude	ciao	glasnost
tae kwon do	sphere	karate	kayak
piña colada	taffy	kimono	shtick
kerchief	dim sum	kung fu	moussaka
teriyaki	cadaver	paparazzi	whiskey
catsup	denim	taffeta	karma
hunk	algebra	falafel	caucus
honcho	alarm	mutton	caddie
macho	a la mode	klutz	goober

13-9. Go to a website at which you can find an image of the beginning of the original *Beowulf* poem (one such site is identified as "Hwæt we Gar-Dena" under "Other Resources" below). Carefully compare the beginning of the manuscript version with the transcription given earlier in this chapter. Then, on the basis of the correspondences between the Old English orthography and the Modern English transcription, provide the transcription for another three lines.

Other Resources

Internet

LISU Website: http://www.CengageBrain.com For users of this textbook. Provides updated Internet links as well as supplemental material for students and instructors. Here you will find interactive learning tools.

The English Companions: http://www.tha-engliscan-gesithas.org .uk/ This site represents a society for people interested in the history and culture of Anglo-Saxon England, including Old English. It has links to YouTube segments of people reciting Old English poetry and much else of interest. For members of the society there is an inexpensive correspondence course on Old English.

Hwæt we Gar-Dena: http://web.cn.edu/kwheeler/images/Beowulfpage .jpeg To see an Old English manuscript containing the words from *Beowulf* given in the "Thousand Years of Change" section at the beginning of this chapter, visit this site (or others that you can identify by doing a Google search for "Beowulf manuscript"). For an informative exercise, compare the manuscript version with what is printed in this chapter.

The Oxford English Dictionary Online: http://oed.com/ Many college and university libraries subscribe to the online *OED*, which can be accessed over the web. The online *OED* is continuously updated, so you can watch lexicographers endeavoring to keep pace with an evolving English lexicon.

Video and Audio

- **The Story of English** A video series hosted by Robert MacNeil. Two videos treat the development of English—"The Mother Tongue" and "A Muse of Fire." Available in libraries and through video rental outlets.
- **The Chaucer Studio** A good source for audiocassettes of Old and Middle English; some recordings available for downloading. Go to **http://creativeworks.byu.edu/chaucer/**.

Suggestions for Further Reading

- **John Algeo. 2010.** *The Origins and Development of the English Language,* **6th ed**. (Boston: Wadsworth/Cengage Learning). Based on an earlier work by Thomas Pyles, this time-tested and well-written chronological treatment artfully balances internal and external history.
- **Tim William Machan and Charles T. Scott, eds. 1992.** *English in its Social Contexts: Essays in Historical Sociolinguistics* (New York: Oxford University Press). Accessible essays aiming to contextualize changes in English within the social contexts of their times. Also contains chapters on the spread of English around the globe and British, American, and Australian English.
- **Richard Hogg and David Denison, eds. 2006.** *A History of the English Language.* (Cambridge, UK: Cambridge University Press). Organized topically (phonology, morphology, syntax, vocabulary) rather than by historical periods, this volume neatly complements many others and contains separate chapters on the history of British dialects, North American English, and English worldwide.

Advanced Reading

There are excellent general histories of the English language. Baugh and Cable (2001)—from which come our examples of French borrowings into Middle English, Latin and Greek borrowings into early Modern English, and regular and irregular verbs—is superb on the external history of the language. Millward and Hayes (2011) is also very good. Mugglestone (2006) comprises chapters written by experts on the various periods of English. Smith (1996) integrates internal and external history in systematically explanatory ways. Hughes (2000) focuses on the lexicon. Several of our Old English examples come from Quirk and Wrenn (1957). Especially valuable for Old English syntax is Mitchell and Robinson (2007). Burrow and Turville-Petre (2004) provides Middle English texts and discussion. For the early Modern English period, Barber (1997) is good on language structure, attitudes toward borrowing and correctness, and semantic change in the lexicon. Görlach (1991) is useful, especially on writing and spelling. Dillard (1992) treats American English.

Background information about Indo-European is conveniently found in Philip Baldi's "Indo-European Languages" and about Germanic in John A. Hawkins's "Germanic Languages," both in Comrie (2009). Two excellent sources about life in Anglo-Saxon Britain are Campbell et al. (1982) and Wood (1986), with photographs of artifacts, ruins, and manuscripts; Wood's book accompanied a BBC series. The lavishly illustrated Evans (1986) describes the treasures evacuated at the site of a burial ship for a seventh-century king of an Anglo-Saxon kingdom. Highly readable is Laing and Laing (1982), with a bias toward the archaeological.

Hogg (1992–2001) is a multivolume reference work that synthesizes what is known about the history of English. Designed for an educated general audience, instructors will find the work useful in providing additional insight into most matters related to historical English.

References

Barber, Charles. 1997. *Early Modern English* (Edinburgh: Edinburgh University Press).

Baugh, Albert C. & Thomas Cable. 2001. *A History of the English Language*, 5th ed. (Englewood Cliffs, NJ: Prentice-Hall).

Burrow, J. A. & Thorlac Turville-Petre, eds. 2004. *A Book of Middle English*, 3rd ed. (Malden, MA: Wiley-Blackwell).

Campbell, James, Eric John & Patrick Wormald. 1982. *The Anglo-Saxons* (Oxford: Phaidon).

Comrie, Bernard, ed. 2009. *The World's Major Languages*, 2nd ed. (London: Routledge).

Dillard, J. L. 1992. *A History of American English* (London: Longman).

Evans, Angela Care. 1986. *The Sutton Hoo Ship Burial* (London: British Museum Publications).

Görlach, Manfred. 1991. *Introduction to Early Modern English* (Cambridge, UK: Cambridge University Press).

Hogg, Richard M., ed. 1992–2001. *The Cambridge History of the English Language*, 6 vols. (Cambridge, UK: Cambridge University Press).

Hughes, Geoffrey. 2000. *A History of English Words* (Oxford: Blackwell).

Laing, Lloyd & Jennifer. 1982. *Anglo-Saxon England* (London: Paladin).

Millward, C. M. & Mary Hayes. 2011. *A Biography of the English Language*, 3rd ed. (Boston: Wadsworth/Cengage Learning).

Mitchell, Bruce & Fred C. Robinson. 2007. *A Guide to Old English*, 7th ed. (New York: Blackwell).

Mugglestone, Lynda, ed. 2006. *The Oxford History of English* (Oxford: Oxford University Press).

Quirk, Randolph & C. L. Wrenn. 1957. *An Old English Grammar* (New York: Holt).

Smith, Jeremy. 1996. *An Historical Study of English: Function, Form and Change* (New York: Routledge).

Wood, Michael. 1986. *Domesday: A Search for the Roots of England* (London: BBC Books).

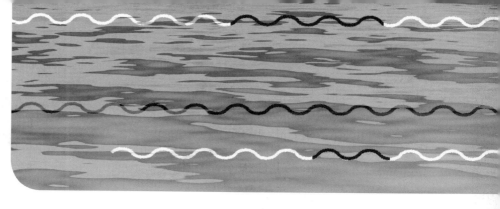

14

Acquiring First and Second Languages

What Do You Think?

- Brenda brags about her two-and-a-half-year-old daughter, DeeDee. "She doesn't use vocabulary she hasn't heard, but she's always uttering sentences she's never heard before." Brenda asks how that's possible. What do you tell her?
- At the nursery school where you work after class, a parent reports reading in the Sunday newspaper that *all* children acquire the grammatical parts of their language in approximately the same order. "But," she confides, "I don't believe it!" Who's right?
- At a family picnic, Brad notices that toddler Tricia consistently says "maked" and "breaked" and "runned" for *made, broke,* and *ran.* "Where do kids learn those words!" he exclaims. "They don't hear them from adults. Where do they get them?" What do you tell Brad?
- Friend Frank is having a tough time mastering Spanish and feels frustrated because it's obviously so easy for young kids to master it. He wants to know why it's so tough for him. What's the explanation?

Introduction

The language of children, even very young ones, is remarkably rich. Early in life children reveal mastery of the phonological, syntactic, and semantic systems described in earlier chapters, as well as a high degree of communicative competence in the appropriate use of language. To cite one example, as early as age five, children playing with hand puppets demonstrate productive control over a range of registers, including aspects of the characteristic talk between doctors and patients and between doctors and nurses. Language acquisition seems so natural and effortless that parents, elated with the addition of each successive word, take it for granted that children will acquire their native language without a hitch. It seems obvious to anyone who has interacted with children that the process of acquiring a first language is largely automatic, even if it is subject to some predictable missteps. Still, if the ease with which a child accomplishes this magnificent achievement tickles parents, it challenges researchers. In this chapter you'll see why language acquisition intrigues and puzzles linguists and psychologists and why not everyone agrees about the nature of a child's task.

For much of the twentieth century, it was widely thought that language learning was essentially a process of induction, much like other learned behavior. A child would generalize about linguistic patterns from the language samples it heard in its interactions with parents, siblings, and other caretakers. Rather than resembling such bodily systems as digestion and respiration (which do *not* require learning), language was thought to be different. Because languages vary from culture to culture, it was thought that children must *induce* the patterns of their language from the speech of those around them. In this respect, language learning appeared to resemble other forms of cultural behavior like brushing your teeth, tying your shoelaces, or doing addition and subtraction.

Try It Yourself "Children master the intricacies of their native language before they are able to tie a knot, jump rope, or draw a decent-looking circle," writes William O'Grady. Given what you know about the complexity of language systems as discussed earlier in this book, what is the likelihood that children could learn all they know about language by imitating what they hear when adults talk?

The view of first-language learning as similar to other forms of learning is now regarded as implausible, and in a dramatic shift of perceptions, language acquisition is viewed as an inductive process only in limited respects. Indeed, rather than focusing on differences in languages, some linguists and psychologists focus on the similarities across languages, linguistic universals like those described in Chapter 7, and explain their universality by positing structures of the human mind that are innate and do not depend on learning. Other linguists and psychologists view the similarities across languages as the result not so much of uniform mental *structures* as of uniform mental *strategies* or dispositions for analyzing and acquiring language. For decades there has been, and continues to be, intense interest in characterizing what some psycholinguists call the *language-making capacity* and some grammarians call the *language acquisition device*.

Acquiring a First Language

Acquiring a language entails more than learning the meaning of various expressions. A child acquiring a language must master an entire system that can generate countless sentences (surprisingly few of which have been heard before) and deploy them appropriately in conversations and other social interactions. Language acquisition also entails the ability to understand both new and familiar utterances of those around us and to interpret them appropriately in their social contexts.

Besides the words of their language and a range of meanings for them, children must master morphological, phonological, syntactic, semantic, and pragmatic patterns. A child must know when to speak and when to listen, when and how to interrupt, when and how to greet, when to tease and how to recognize teasing from its contextualization cues, and so on. All children must learn how to make utterances achieve their intended objective and how to understand under what circumstances a particular utterance serves different functions—for example, to offer food to someone (*Do you like chocolate? Have you ever tasted a kumquat?*) or request information (*Do you like chocolate? Have you ever tasted a kumquat?*). In other words, every child must learn the grammar of his or her language and the culturally appropriate use of its grammar in diverse social situations. Acquiring a language entails mastery of the full range of grammatical and communicative competence.

There is evidence to suggest that at least some (and perhaps a good deal) of what children know about language structure could not have been learned from the data surrounding them. To the extent that certain language structures cannot be inferred from the data available to children, it is reasonable to hypothesize that the human language capacity provides those structures at birth or in the course of natural development. The issue can be framed in terms of "nature" versus "nurture," what is inborn versus what must be learned, what is prewired into the brain at birth ("hardware") and what must be programmed by interaction with adult language ("software"). The challenge is to determine the nature and degree of the contributions made by biology and by socialization.

Alternatively, some psychologists and linguists suspect not so much that children share particular language structures as that they share strategies for analyzing language. In Chapter 4, we discussed how difficult it would be for a child to sort out the continuous string of sound in adult speech into the distinct sounds that constitute the phonological inventory of his or her language. Children appear to arrive at the task of language learning already in possession of the "knowledge" that language consists of distinct sounds. They are "preprogrammed" to analyze a continuous string of vocal sounds for its individual phonological segments. In the same way, they seem naturally endowed with strategies for analyzing other aspects of language, and it is this set of *operating principles* for analyzing language that would contribute to the similarity of acquisition patterns across languages. As illustrations of such operating principles, children are thought to pay attention to the order of words in utterances and the order of morphemes in words, with particular attention to the ends of words (where inflections occur), to focus on consistent relationships between form and content, and to look for generalizations.

Operating Principles in First-Language Acquisition

Pay attention to the order of words in utterances.

Pay attention to the order of morphemes in words.

Pay particular attention to word endings (inflections).

Focus on consistent relationships between expression and content.

Look for generalizations.

Many linguists and psychologists are convinced that language is not acquired by imitation—certainly not solely by imitation and probably not principally—although exposure to a particular language is, obviously, an essential ingredient in the process of its acquisition. Still, children have an undeniable capacity to be creative with language and certainly don't need to hear a particular sentence before saying it. They often utter sentences they haven't heard before and know intuitively which sentences are possible and which are not, although they go through periods when they make predictable mistakes. While they may say *He eated my candy* or *Oh! Hurt meself* or *Where did you found it?* they don't say "Mine is candy that" or "Candy my eated he" or countless other conceivable but nonoccurring sentences. In fact, the errors children make are of a very limited sort. English-speaking children can be heard overgeneralizing the past tense by adding an *-ed* ending to all verbs and making the other mistakes noted previously. Because adult native speakers of English don't say *eated* or *did you found* and because even children who lack contact with other children do say such things, errors such as these cannot arise from mimicry. Language acquisition is a robust process that goes beyond inducing the correct generalizations on the basis of forms that have been heard.

Principles of Language Acquisition

Two aspects of general maturation are crucial to a child's ability to acquire a language: *the ability to symbolize* and *the ability to use tools*.

Maturation and Symbolization As a system of symbols, language is an arbitrary representation of other things—other entities, experiences, feelings, thoughts, and so on. In order to acquire language, a child must first be able to hold in mind a symbolic realization of something else. Even if it is no more than a mental picture of an absent object, such symbolization is a prerequisite to language acquisition.

Using Tools The second ability—wider-ranging than its application to language—is the ability to use tools to accomplish goals. Language is a tool made up entirely of symbols, and among other characterizations it can be seen as a system of symbols that gets work done. From an early age, children routinely use language to get fed, changed, handed a toy, and all the other things they can't do for themselves. Such purposeful activity is called tool use, and language is an effective tool for accomplishing work of many sorts. Given their extremely limited ability to achieve their goals physically, children's motivation to develop this powerful symbolic tool must be extraordinarily strong (and may be influential in the evolution of the human species).

All Languages Are Equally Challenging Every child who is capable of acquiring a particular human language is capable of acquiring any human language. There is no biological basis—in the lips or the brain—that disposes some children to learn a particular language. Children find all languages about equally easy to acquire, although acquiring particular features of one language may require more time than acquiring equivalent aspects of a different language. For example, German definite articles have several different forms representing three genders, two numbers, and four cases (see Table 2.10). Children acquiring German need more time to master its definite articles than English-speaking children need to learn the form *the* that English uses for any gender, number, and case. (English speakers use *the* in the phrases *the boy*, *for the daughter*, and *to the lions*, whereas the German definite article would have different forms in those phrases, reflecting different cases and genders: *der*, *die*, and *den*, respectively). On balance, though, when considered in their entirety, all languages are about equally easy (or equally challenging) for a child to learn.

By the age of 6, barring severe mental or physical impairments, children the world over have acquired most of what they need to know to speak their language fluently. By the time a child arrives in school, perhaps 80 percent of the structures of his or her language and more than 90 percent of the sound system have been acquired. "Doubtless the greatest intellectual feat any one of us is ever required to perform," Leonard Bloomfield remarked of language acquisition. Fortunately, it is a feat that human beings are gifted at. This universal success has convinced linguists and psycholinguists that infants come to the task of acquiring a language with a genetic predisposition to do so and with certain analytical advantages that facilitate the process. There is little doubt that, at the very least, children are born with certain mechanisms or cognitive strategies that help in the task of language acquisition, and certain structures or kinds of structure may be innate as well.

Adult Input in Language Acquisition

Stating that language acquisition is not a process of imitation doesn't diminish the crucial importance of exposure to linguistic input in acquiring a language. Acquisition requires interaction with speakers of the language being acquired. As witness to the necessity of adult input, there is the case of Genie, a child who was not exposed to any language while she was growing up. Genie's parents locked her away for the first 13 years of her life and seldom spoke to her. When she was discovered, she was unable to speak. Deprived of linguistic input in the first few years of life, Genie's capacity for language acquisition had become impaired. Linguist Susan Curtiss tried teaching her English, but the attempts were not altogether successful.

On the other hand, parents do not generally teach language to young children directly and, in ordinary settings, rarely correct young children's grammatical mistakes, although they do correct utterances that are inaccurate or misleading. A child who says *Kitty's hands are pink* may be told *No. Kitty doesn't have hands: Kitty has PAWS.* But if a child asks, *Where Kitty go?* (for 'Where did Kitty go?'), adults are not likely to correct the utterance. To a great extent, then, children acquire the grammar of their language without direct instruction from adults.

Edward Finegan

Of course, certain aspects of language use *are* deliberately taught to children. In cultures around the world, children are engaged in conversation with adults almost from the start, as in the photograph of a mother and her 4-month old baby. In Western cultures, though not in all cultures, parents often treat baby noises as openings to conversations. From their first few months children are socialized into interactional routines of turn taking, where even their burps, hiccups, and sneezes are regarded as opening turns to which parents respond. Children are socialized so effectively that the turn-taking patterns of school-age children have been pretty much established since age 1. Later, when young children go trick-or-treating at Halloween (to take the example of a context in which politeness becomes a salient aspect of interaction), they may not produce the appropriate utterances unless prompted (*Say "thank you"! What do you say?*). So children need consciously to learn certain rules of language use, and adults typically provide instruction for these politeness rules.

Baby Talk: How Adults Talk to Children Even when adults are not explicitly teaching children the rules of language use, they frequently modify their speech, adapting it to what they think children will readily understand and acquire. You have probably witnessed parents and siblings using *baby talk* (also called "motherese" or "infant-directed speech") in addressing babies.

- Ooohh, what a biiig smiile! Is Baby smiling at Mommy?
- Baby is smiling at her Mommy? Yeess!
- Is Baby happy to see Mommy?
- Is Baby hungry? Yeess? Oopen wiiide . . .
- Hmmmm! Baby likes soup. Yeess!
- Wheere's the soup? All gone!

This example, uttered slowly and with exaggerated intonation, is typical of the kind of linguistic input that English-speaking parents and other caregivers provide to young children.

Baby talk differs from talk between adults in characteristic ways. When addressing babies, adults' voices frequently assume a higher pitch than usual. Adults also exaggerate their intonation and speak slowly and clearly. Repetitions and partial repetitions (*Is Baby smiling at Mommy? Baby is smiling at her Mommy?*) are frequent in baby talk. Sentences are short and simple, with few subordinate clauses and few modifiers. Personal names like *Baby* and *Mommy* are preferred over pronouns like *you* and *I*. Compared to adult talk to other adults, baby talk has more frequent content words (nouns, verbs, adjectives) and fewer function words (subordinators, determiners). Utterances addressed to very young children frequently include special baby-talk vocabulary—words such as *doggie*, *horsie*, *tummy*, and *din-din*, which are more easily perceived or pronounced but do not normally occur in adult talk—and the choice of baby-talk words is more restricted than in ordinary speech. Baby talk is typically concrete and refers to items and actions in the child's immediate environment and experience. It also includes a high proportion of questions, particularly for young children (*Is Baby hungry?*), and of imperatives (*Oopen wiiide*). These modifications may serve to hold a child's attention or to simplify the linguistic input he or she hears, possibly making utterances easier to perceive or analyze. Especially in repetitions and shorter expressions addressed to young children, adults chunk their speech by constituent structure, a practice that could provide useful syntactic insight to learners. Baby-talk features are summarized below.

Characteristics of Talk to Babies

Higher than usual pitch	Concrete, immediate referents
Frequent questions	Exaggerated intonation contours
Frequent repetitions	Slow and clear enunciations
Frequent imperatives	Baby-talk words (*doggie, tummy*)
Few modifiers	Frequent content words (nouns, verbs)
Few function words	Personal names instead of pronouns (*Mommy*, not *I*)
Few subordinate clauses	Chunking by constituent structure

At a somewhat more advanced stage, when children start producing utterances, parents and other caretakers have been observed to echo those utterances in a fuller form than the child offered. Sometimes the intonation of the caretaker's expansions confirms what the child has said; sometimes a questioning intonation seems to be seeking clarification. The following examples are illustrative.

Adult Expansions of Children's Utterances

CHILD	ADULT
Baby highchair	Baby is in the highchair.
Mommy eggnog	Mommy had her eggnog.
Eve lunch	Eve is having lunch.
Throw Daddy	Throw it to Daddy.

Expansions occur far less frequently when parents and other caretakers are alone with children than when other adults are present, and such expansions may be intended as "translations" of the baby's speech, more for the aid of the observer than for the benefit of the child.

Features of baby talk are found in cultures far and wide. When the Berbers of North Africa address babies, they simplify their language in some of the same ways that Americans do; the same is true of the Japanese. Not all cultures modify speech to children, but modification is widespread. Children themselves acquire baby talk very early in life, and 4-year-olds can be heard using features of this register when addressing younger children, while even 2-year-olds use it with younger siblings.

The extent to which baby talk helps children in acquiring language is difficult to assess, but in cultures where baby talk is absent (as it is in Samoa, parts of Papua New Guinea, and among the Kipsigis of Kenya, for example) children acquire their native language at the same rate as children exposed to baby talk. So baby talk is not essential to successful language acquisition.

Still, baby talk does serve some functions. First, it exposes small children to simple language, and simple language may be helpful in the task of unraveling constituent structures and certain grammatical operations. Since children have to figure out so many different grammatical features, selective input (fewer words, fewer complex sentences, and repetitions) facilitates their task. In addition, considering English, the unusually high percentage of questions that caregivers address to infants has the effect of exposing them to a greater number of auxiliaries (*Did Baby fall?*) than would the use of declarative sentences (*Baby fell*). Baby talk may also inculcate certain rules of language use, particularly the rules of conversation (see Chapter 9). By asking many questions of small children, adults help socialize them into the question-answer sequences and into the alternating turn-taking patterns of conversation. From the earliest stages, adults alternate their utterances with a baby's babblings, and the implicit message is to alternate one's utterances with one's interlocutor's. Interactional patterns between caregivers and children can thus provide a framework within which utterances can be situated and acquisition of grammar can take place.

Stages of Language Acquisition

Babbling Whatever the nature of the input they receive, children go through several stages in the process of acquiring their native language. At the babbling stage, which starts at about 6 months of age, children first utter a series of identical syllables such as *ba-ba-ba* or *ma-ma-ma*. A couple of months later, as the vocal apparatus matures, this reduplicated babbling blossoms into a wider range of syllable types such as *babbab* and *ab-ab*. These early babblings are similar the world over and occur with or without others present. When some babbled sounds stabilize for a child and are linked to a consistent referent or appear to be used with a consistent purpose (for example, to be handed something), they are called *vocables* or protowords. Children may use a vocable such as *baba* to indicate they do not want something while *mama* serves to indicate they do want something.

One-Word Stage Starting around a year old, when children take their first steps, they are also heard uttering words such as *mama*, *dada*, and *up*. These early words are of simple structure and typically refer to familiar people (mother and father), toys and pets (teddy bear and kitty), food and drink (cookie and juice), and social interaction (as in *bye-bye*). By this stage children already use vocal noises to get and hold attention socially and to achieve other objectives.

Often, the same word is used to refer to things that have a similar appearance, as when a child learns the word *doggie* for the family dog and then extends it to all dogs. Children are thus inclined to generalize word meanings and even to overgeneralize, as when *doggie* is applied to cats as well as dogs, or even to all animals.

Observation of utterances at the one-word stage suggests that children are not rehearsing simple words but expressing single words to convey whole propositions. A child uses the word *dada*, for example, to mean different things in different contexts: 'Here comes Daddy' (upon hearing a key in the door at the end of the day); 'This is for Daddy' (when handing Daddy a toy); 'That is where Daddy usually sits' (when looking at Daddy's empty chair at the kitchen table); or 'This shoe is Daddy's' (when touching a shoe belonging to Daddy).

One-Word Stage

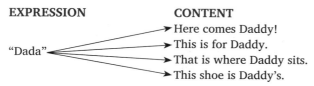

In different contexts, a child may give the same word different intonations. Holding a shoe and uttering *dada*, a child is not merely naming the object of its focus but is using a relatively simple expression to communicate relatively complex content.

Two-Word Stage From the one-word-utterance stage, children move on to utterances such as *Daddy come*, *Shoe mine*, and *Apple me*. The transition from the one-word stage to the two-word stage occurs at about 20 months of age, when the child has a vocabulary of about 50 words. At this stage, utterances show a preference for combining a nounlike element with a predicate-like element, and children tend to verbalize in propositions—to name something and then say something about it: *Daddy,* [*he is*] *com*[*ing*], *Shoe,* [*it's*] *mine*; *Apple,* [*give it to*] *me*. Other forms also occur, as in *More juice* and *There Daddy*, in which the predicate-like element precedes the noun. One striking fact about the two-word-utterance stage is that children from different cultures appear to express basically similar things in their propositions at this stage.

Two-Word Stage

EXPRESSION	CONTENT
"Daddy come"	Daddy, he is coming.
"Shoe mine"	The shoe, it's mine.
"Apple me"	The apple, give it to me.
"More juice"	I want more juice.
"There Daddy"	There is Daddy.

We don't know whether the disposition to verbalize in propositions is a tendency of the language process itself or is tied to aspects of perception. But from the start children seem to be trying to convey propositions, even when the expression is a mere word. If this interpretation is correct, children at the two-word stage are not attempting to communicate more content by using two words instead of one but to *express* more of the content than at the one-word stage. As children master their language system, they learn to balance *expression* and *context* so as to communicate *content* efficiently and effectively.

Beyond Two Words Beyond the two-word stage, distinct three-word and four-word stages are not recognized. Instead, progress is typically measured by the average number of morphemes (or sometimes words) in a child's utterances. Between about two years (2;0) and two-and-a-half years (2;6) of age, a child's expressions become considerably more complex. Utterances contain several words representing single clauses. Consider these single-clause utterances from a boy of 2 years and 5 months:

1. Mimo hurt me. [about a past action by his brother]
2. Yeah, that money Neina. ('Yeah, that money is Zeina's.')
3. Me put it back. ('I'll put it back.')
4. No do that again! [to an adult whispering in his ear]
5. Oh! hurt meself. [upon bumping his arm into a door]
6. That's mine, Uncle Ed. [showing a toy to an uncle]

Try It Yourself To make these utterances, the boy must have considerable knowledge of English, even if his knowledge does not exactly match the linguistic knowledge of an adult. Examine the six utterances and spell out in as much detail as possible just what linguistic knowledge the boy must have to say them in the contexts described.

To utter such sentences, the boy must have a good deal of information about English vocabulary, syntax, and pragmatics. Obviously, he knows such English words as *money, mine,* and *that's.* Saying those words entails knowing what sounds they contain and in what order. That the words are used in appropriate contexts indicates that he knows what the words refer to and in what situations they are appropriate. He knows the lexical categories (the parts of speech) of these words and how to combine them with other categories, both morphologically (*me, meself, mine*) and syntactically (*Mimo hurt me* and *Me put it back*). Possibly he knows which form of the copula BE agrees with the demonstrative subject *that* and how to contract *is* to *'s* and attach it to *that,* although *that's* may be an unanalyzed unit for him at this stage. The child has also mastered basic SVO word order, as in *Mimo hurt me* (although pronominal subjects are not yet obligatory, as a comparison between *Me put it back* and *Hurt meself* shows). He also shows knowledge of declarative and imperative sentence structures and of negative imperatives.

The phrase *that money* (in 2) indicates knowledge that *money* belongs to the category of nouns—the category that takes determiners such as *that* and *the.* Given the contexts in which the utterances occur, it is also apparent that the child is uttering propositions, although some are incompletely encoded or differ from adult formulations. More noteworthy than the matches between some of these utterances and those of an adult grammar, as with 1 and 6, is the fact that the child is using language in a systematic fashion. The structured utterances are governed by rules of grammar that stay constant from utterance to utterance: subjects precede verbs; verbs precede objects and other complements; and adverbs (*back* and *again*) follow objects.

Of course, there are many other forms of the adult grammar that the child has not yet fully mastered, including syntactic and morphological matters. Syntactically, no subject is expressed in 5, no verb in 2, and no auxiliary in 3, all of which would be required in well-formed adult utterances. Morphologically, the possessive marker is not fully mastered: it appears in *mine* but is lacking in *Neina;* the adult subject form of the first-person pronoun *I* and the adult reflexive form *myself* have not yet been acquired. By around 3 years of age, utterances containing multiple clauses appear, at first coordinating two clauses, as in *There's his face and he's Mister George Happy.* Later, children subordinate one clause to another with subordinators like *'cause, so,* and *if* in the early stages and then *why* and *what: Me don't know where box is now. Why did you give to her when her been flu?*

How Do Children Acquire Morphology and Grammar?

Interestingly, the morphemes and grammatical structures of language are generally acquired by children in a set order, with variation from child to child tending to be slight. This pattern suggests an internally regulated sequence for grammatical acquisition. Psychologist Roger Brown examined the order in which 14 morphemes were acquired by three English-speaking children and found that they were acquired in the order given below:

Acquisition Order for English Morphemes

1. Present progressive verb (with or without auxiliary): *(is) playing, (are) singing*

2-3. Prepositions *in* and *on*

4. Regular noun plural: *toys, cats, dishes*

5. Irregular past-tense verbs: *came, fell, saw, hurt*

6. Possessive noun: *Daddy's, doggie's*

7. Uncontractible copula: *Here I am, Who is it?*

8. Articles: *a* and *the*

9. Regular past-tense verbs: *played, washed, wanted*

10. Regular third-person singular present-tense verbs: *sees, wants, washes*

11. Irregular third-person singular present-tense verbs: *does, has*

12. Uncontractible auxiliary: *She isn't crying, He was eating*

13. Contractible copula: *That's mine, What's that?*

14. Contractible auxiliary: *He's crying*

The three children acquired these forms basically in the same *order*, but not *at the same speed.* Between acquisition of the present progressive (the earliest acquired) and the contractible auxiliary (the last), anywhere from 6 to 14 months elapsed. One child acquired the contractible auxiliary by 2;3, while another took until 3;6.

The order tracked among Brown's young "consultants" basically replicated the order other linguists and psychologists had tracked with other children, and the slight variations probably have to do with the criteria used for judging "acquisition." For example, Brown judged a feature to be acquired only when a child used it correctly in 90 percent of the required cases in three successive sampling sessions. Other researchers used different criteria, such as the first time that a correct use was observed.

What Determines Acquisition Order? As to what determines the order of acquisition, it would seem reasonable to suppose that the frequency with which a child hears a form from adults will influence the order of acquisition. In fact, however, Brown was unable to correlate frequency of parental use with the order of acquisition. The most frequent of the 14 morphemes in the parents' speech was the articles, which appeared eighth in the order of child acquisition. The prepositions, on the other hand, were acquired second by children although they were used relatively little by parents. In determining the order of acquisition, what seems more influential than frequency is relative complexity. Morphemes that encode several semantic notions and those that are syntactically more complex tend to be acquired later than those that encode a single semantic notion and are syntactically simpler.

Exceptions and Overgeneralizations No doubt you have observed that children tend to overgeneralize the patterns of inflectional morphology. You've heard kids say things like "eated" for *ate* and "foots" for *feet*. There are some sixty-odd irregular verbs in English, and among those that get overgeneralized are the ones listed below.

Overgeneralization of Past-Tense Verbs

eated	ate	doed	did
maked	made	speaked	spoke
finded	found	breaked	broke
hitted	hit	goed	went
falled	fell	runned	ran

English has far fewer nouns like *foot* that form their plurals irregularly; among those that children overgeneralize are those listed below.

Overgeneralization of Noun Plurals

foots	feet	mans	men
tooths	teeth	mouses	mice
childs	children	peoples	people

Evidence from several languages suggests that children tend naturally to overgeneralize or "overregularize" the morphological rules they acquire.

Sentence Structure The sentences of the 29-month-old (2;5) boy (in the "Beyond Two Words" section earlier) contain single clauses only. Before that boy was 5 years old, negative sentences were under control, as in *That isn't yours* and *That doesn't belong to you*, and sentences incorporating more than one clause were commonplace, including imperatives (*Guess who's visiting me*) and interrogatives (*Do you know what I did at school today?*). Even at age 5, though, relative clauses were not fully acquired, although certain kinds of relatives are understood by children as early as 3 years of age. When children first produce relative clauses, they attach them to object noun phrases, as in *You broke the one that I found*. Attaching relative clauses to subjects (as in *The one that I found is red*) represents a later stage of acquisition; attaching them to other grammatical relations comes later still.

Negation Every language has ways of expressing negation. At first, children express negation by the simple utterance *no*, either alone or preceding other expressions: *No. No want. No that. No do that*. At a somewhat later stage, by

3 years of age, more complex expressions incorporate negations, as in these: *Can't get it off. Don't know. It doesn't go that way. That not go in there.*

Questions Every language also has ways of asking questions. Some do so simply by adding a question word to the end of a statement. English has a relatively complex way of forming questions, and mastery of its question-formation rules takes time. In the early stages, interrogative utterances have the same syntax as declaratives, as in *That mine*. Sometimes the intonation of questions differs from that of statements. By 3 years of age, children have mastered most aspects of question formation, as in these questions from a 3-year-old girl named Sophie:

Information Questions	**Yes/No Questions**
What is he called?	Is this a box?
What goes in this hole?	Do it go this side?
Why didn't me get flu?	Can me put it in like that?
Why's he so small?	
Where are you Mummy?	

How Fast Do Children Acquire Vocabulary?

At the start of the two-word stage, around 20 months (1;8) of age, a child knows approximately 50 words. Mostly they are nouns referring to concrete, familiar objects (*shoe, clock, apple, baby, milk, nose*) or expressions for salient notions in the child's environment (*more, no, bye-bye, oh, walk, what's that*). By age 5, the child's vocabulary is increasing by about 15 or 20 words a day. Estimates of the number of basic words known by schoolchildren of age 6 run about 7,800, even counting a word set like *cat, cats, cat's, cats'* or *walk, walks, walked, walking* as a single word. If you count derived forms such as *dollhouse* as a third word besides *doll* and *house*, then 13,000 words would be a reliable figure. Astonishingly, two years later, by age 8, a child's vocabulary has increased to 17,600 basic words (or 28,300 words including derived forms). This represents an average increase *each day* of more than 13 basic words (or 21 words and derived forms). Of course, a full range of meanings for any word is generally acquired only by stages over a period of time. Indeed, this phenomenon, like the acquisition of vocabulary itself, continues well into adulthood, though at a drastically reduced rate.

How Do Children Acquire the Sounds of Language?

You have probably listened to a child uttering words and expressions that you could understand within their context even though the pronunciations did not match your own. "Neina" /nenɑ/ for *Zeina* /zenɑ/ in the speech from the boy of 2 years, 5 months is one illustration. Other examples might be "poon" or "bude" for *spoon*, "du" for *juice*, and "dis" or "di" [dɪ] for *this*. Such pronunciations suggest that a child masters certain aspects of a word before others. In these cases, the context indicates that the child knows the word's lexical category and certain semantic information (such as its referent); the child also knows some of its phonological content, although mastery of the pronunciation is incomplete. Here we examine certain patterns of phonological acquisition among English-speaking children and draw some cross-linguistic comparisons.

From as early as 2 months of age, infants react differently to different speech sounds, and they can recognize individual voices—their mother's, for example. (We know this from changes in the rate of sucking when voices alternate.) Prior to their production of recognizable utterances at about 12 months of age, infants go through a lengthy babbling stage, during which they appear to be rehearsing a wide range of sounds, extending beyond the sounds spoken around them and therefore beyond the phonological inventory needed for their own language.

Early babbling consists of simple syllable-like sequences of a consonant followed by a vowel: *ba-ba-ba*. Repetitions of CV syllables are then followed by sequences that juxtapose different CV syllables (*bamama*), first yielding CVCV patterns and then CVC patterns (such as *bam* and *mam*, which lack the vowel of the second CVCV syllable). These early babblings reveal a preference for voiced stops and nasals [b d g m n] and a dispreference for fricatives [f v θ ð s z] and liquids [l r]. Not surprisingly, sounds that are relatively rare among the world's languages tend to be acquired later than sounds that are common. By 8 or 9 months of age children are able to mimic adult intonation patterns to a striking degree. Unlike the sounds of babbling, these intonation patterns differ from language to language.

Consonant Sounds of Babbling

PREFERRED			DISPREFERRED		
b	d	g	v	ð	z
m	n		f	θ	s
			l/r		

Before the first recognizable words are produced around age 1, the list of speech sounds actually shrinks (and a few children even go through a silent period), after which the inventory of sounds belonging to the adult language is gradually and systematically acquired. Full phonological development takes several years, and the last sounds may not be acquired before age 6 or so.

Between 12 months and 18 months of age, a child learns to produce about 50 words (which is only about a fourth of those it can recognize). The range of sounds and of syllable types needed to give voice to so small a lexicon is relatively limited (5 vowels and 10 consonants would generate 50 monosyllabic words of CV type). At about 18 months of age, however, children typically experience a "word spurt," and for this larger lexicon the previous inventory of sounds and syllables is inadequate and must be expanded.

Try It Yourself What generalization can you make about the preferred sounds of babbling as compared to the dispreferred sounds? Think in terms of phonological features or natural classes.

Around 24 months (2;0) of age, an English-speaking child typically has acquired the following consonant sounds, although not all of them can be produced in all the positions within a word where adults produce them:

Inventory of English Consonants at Age Two

Nasals	m		n	
Stops	b		d	g
	p		t	k
Fricatives		f	s	h
Approximants	w			

A year later, at about 36 months (3;0), the child has added /j/ and /ŋ/ to its inventory, although [b], [d], [g], and [k] still remain elusive in word-final position. Consonant clusters (as in *spilled* [spɪld] or [spɪlt], *stopped* [stɑpt], and *asked* [æskt]) present children with particular challenges. In fact, of the wide range of clusters that adults use, the 3-year-old may have mastered only final /ŋk/, as in *pink* and *sink*.

By around 4 years of age, the inventory of consonants has expanded significantly and stands approximately as given here.

Inventory of English Consonants at Age Four

Nasals	m		n			ŋ
Stops	b		d			g
	p		t			k
Fricatives		f	s	ʃ		h
		v	z			
Affricates				tʃ		
				ʤ		
Approximants	w	l/r		j		

At this stage the voiced fricatives /v/ and /z/ may be present only in medial position (as in *over* and *dizzy*), but the child may not yet be able to produce them in word-final or word-initial position. Recall that the 29-month-old (2;5) boy whose utterances we analyzed earlier substituted the nasal [n] for initial [z] in the name *Zeina*, presumably influenced by anticipation of the [n] to follow, as commonly happens with children. The interdental fricative sounds /θ/ and /ð/ (as in *thin* and *then*) have yet to be added to the 4-year-old's inventory in any position, as has the relatively rare /ʒ/ (as in *measure*). Between the ages of 4 and 6, then, an English-speaking child may still lack /ʒ/, /v/, /θ/, /ð/, and /z/, at least in some positions. And still ahead lies mastery of the morphophonemic rules that account for variation between underlying forms and surface forms (as in the [t]/[ɾ] alternation of *late* [let] and *later* [leɾər] or the [d]/[ɾ] alternation of *dad* and *daddy*). Mastery of the more complex syllable structures and consonant clusters also lies ahead.

Substituting and Omitting Sounds Can you imagine that, until a child mastered the phonological inventory of his or her language, the child would skip the sounds not yet learned, producing pronunciations such as *oo* [u] for *shoe* and *juice*? As you know, that isn't what happens. Instead, children generally attempt to pronounce all the sounds in a word, although they manage it by various simplifications. The principal ones in early pronunciations involve substituting easier sounds for harder ones, as in these processes:

Stopping: fricatives and affricates pronounced as stops

Devoicing: final obstruents devoiced

Voicing: initial obstruents voiced before vowels

Fronting: velars and alveopalatals pronounced as alveolars

Gliding: liquids pronounced as approximants (i.e., as glides)

Vocalization: liquids replaced by vowels

Denasalization: nasals replaced by oral stops

Processes of Substitution in Child Language

Stopping	v → b	van → [bæn]
	ð → d, n	that → [dæt], there → [nɛr]
	ʤ → d	jack → [dæk], jam → [dæb]
	tʃ → d	check → [dɛk]
Devoicing	b → p	knob → [nɑp]
	-d → t	bad → [bæt]
	-g → t	dog → [dɑt]
	-v → f	stove → [duf]
Voicing	p- → b	pot → [bɑt]
	t- → d	toe → [du:]
	k- → d	kiss → [dɪ]
Fronting	k → t	duck → [dɑt]
	g → d	gate → [det]
	θ → f	thumb → [fʌm]
	ʃ → z	shoes → [zus]
	ʒ → z	rouge → [wu:z]
	tʃ → ts	match → [mæts]
	ʤ → dz	cabbage → [tæ:bədz]
Gliding	r → w	rock → [wɑt], sorry → [sɑwɑ]
Vocalization	l → u	table → [dubu]
Denasalization	m → p, b	lamb → [bæp], broom → [bub], jam → [dæb]

(After Ingram 1989, pp. 371–72)

Actually, besides the substitution processes described above, some omission also takes place. For example, as illustrated below, young children typically delete unstressed syllables from trisyllabic words (as in *nana* for *banana*) and sometimes the unstressed syllable of a disyllabic word; they sometimes omit final consonants; and they often reduce consonant clusters.

Processes of Omission in Child Language

Deletion of syllable	banana → [nænə], kitchen → [kɪtʃ], pocket → [bɑt]
Deletion of final consonant	doll → [dɑ], far → [fɑ]

Reduction of consonant clusters

stop + liquid → stop	glass → [dæs], bread → [but]
s- + stop → stop	star → [dɑ]
s- + nasal → nasal	snake → [nek]
nasal + voiced stop → nasal	hand → [hæn]

Determinants of Acquisition Order It isn't entirely clear what determines the order in which sounds are acquired. If it would seem reasonable to assume that the more frequently a child heard a particular sound, the sooner it would be acquired, the facts point elsewhere. Consider that the most frequent English consonant sounds are the fricatives [s], [d], [z], and [v]. Either [s] or [z] occurs in the plural form of most nouns, the possessive form of every noun, the third-person singular present-tense form of all verbs (*eats, does, is*), certain common pronouns and possessive determiners (*his, hers, yours*), and some other common words (*was* and *some*). In light of such frequency, it is not surprising that [s] is acquired relatively early (by about 24 months). But, perplexingly, [z] is not acquired until 4 years of age and then usually only in medial position. Consider also that [ð] is acquired very late although it occurs in extremely frequent words like *this, that,* and *the,* while [v], even at 4 years of age, is produced in medial position but not initially or finally, where it is common in such words as *very, have,* and *of*. Clearly, frequency of occurrence in adult speech is not the sole determinant in the order of acquisition.

More influential than frequency is the functional importance of a sound in its phonological system. A sound has a high functional load if it serves to differentiate many words (or words that are very frequent), and high functional load seems to promote early acquisition. Thus, the affricate /tʃ/ is acquired much later by children learning English than by Guatemalan children learning the Mayan language Quiché. The reason appears to be that /tʃ/ contrasts with other sounds in many more Quiché words than it does in English words, and the high functional load of the /tʃ/ sound in Quiché fosters early acquisition. By contrast, the low functional importance of /tʃ/ in English bumps it towards the end of the acquisition line.

Phonological Idioms Before acquiring all the sounds in the inventory of his or her language, a child may be able to produce some sounds as part of fixed phrases or phonological "idioms." In much the same way that adults have semantic idioms (*kick the bucket, bite the dust*) and syntactic idioms (*the sooner the better*), so children may produce unanalyzed words containing sounds that they do not yet have as separate units of their phonological inventory. They have learned to pronounce the word as a whole but haven't mastered all the individual sounds as such. The child can thus make a lexical contrast without yet having the contrasting sounds in its phonological inventory.

How Do Researchers Study Language Acquisition?

Studies of child language and language acquisition have most commonly been naturalistic, or observational, studies. At regular intervals researchers have tape-recorded ordinary interactions between adults and children or among children and transcribed those results for analysis. There have also been diary studies (carried out by parents who were themselves linguists or psychologists) that record a child's utterances, the age at which they occur, and the situational context surrounding them. Depending on the focus and goals of the observer, diary studies represent different degrees of detail, ranging from ordinary orthography to a narrow phonetic transcription. Quite naturally, observational studies of child language have focused on the *production* of words and sentences.

Receptive Competence and Productive Competence

So far we haven't said much about a child's *receptive* mastery, or understanding, nor drawn a distinction between what a child's *grammatical competence* might allow but its *production apparatus* be unable to utter. After all, a child could have the grammatical competence to generate adult pronunciations but remain unable to utter them because of physiological immaturity in the vocal apparatus.

"FIS" Phenomenon An oft-repeated story tells of a child who pronounced *fish* as *fis* [fɪs] but objected to an adult imitating the *fis* pronunciation. "This is your *fis*?" the adult asked. "No," said the child: "my *fis*." When the adult repeated the question, the child again rejected the *fis* pronunciation. When the adult eventually said, "Your *fish*?" the child concurred: "Yes, my *fis*"! The child could hear the distinction between *fish* and *fis* and recognized *fis* as an incorrect pronunciation. But in attempting to say *fish* the child produced a word that replicated the *fis* it knew to be wrong. We should be careful interpreting such data, however. It may seem that the child knows and recognizes the difference between [fɪʃ] and [fɪs] while being unable to pronounce [fɪʃ] because of limitations in the vocal apparatus, but there are other possible explanations. Consider the case of the child who consistently pronounced *puddle* as *puggle*: the obvious hypothesis that the vocal apparatus was not yet capable of pronouncing /d/ intervocalically was belied by the fact that the child systematically pronounced *puzzle* as *puddle*.

Big Bigs In saying a word like *pig* or *tug*, the voicing required in pronouncing the vowels is anticipated by adults in such a fashion that /p/ and /t/, though they begin without voicing, become voiced just preceding the onset of the vowel. It is almost as if the pronunciation were [pbɪg] and [tdʌg]. The key to an adult's distinguishing initial /p/ and /b/ before vowels is *how long* the voicing is delayed, not whether it is present or absent. A child may be perceived as failing to distinguish voiced from voiceless initial stops, pronouncing *tug* and *Doug* alike as [dʌg] or *pig* and *big* alike as [bɪg]. But laboratory analyses indicate that some children systematically distinguish initial /t/ from /d/ and initial /p/ from /b/ by delaying the voicing onset time for the voiceless stops (/t/ and /p/) for a longer period than they delay voicing for the voiced stops (/d/ and /b/). The delayed voicing is detectable by laboratory instruments but not by the human ear. This would indicate that the child has heard the voiceless and voiced stops and internalized the difference between them but has not yet learned to delay the onset of voicing long enough to be detected by adults.

There is general agreement that receptive mastery of language outpaces production, but it is not clear that this is so at all stages of language development and in all respects. Still, children generally seem able to understand more than they can produce—that is, their lexical and syntactic repertoire is greater than their production reveals. At about 18 months of age, as we mentioned above, a child understands about 200 words, although only about 50 appear in his or her speech. In attempts to analyze the language competence of children, then, naturalistic observation alone may offer an incomplete picture, so researchers have had to invent ingenious ways to get at receptive competence.

Wugs and Other Experimental Techniques

One experimental technique elicits utterances that children would not otherwise have occasion to say. In one study, children were shown drawings of an imaginary bird or animal and told, for example, "This is a wug." The next drawing would depict two such birds or animals, and the child would be suitably prompted to offer a plural form: "Now there is another one. There are two of them. There are two ___?" This technique can uncover how much morphophonemic variation of the plural morpheme (for example, [s] versus [z]) the child has mastered. Alternatively, pictures of people carrying out novel actions such as "ricking" can be used to elicit past tenses and progressive forms of verbs. With another technique, children using hand puppets speak in the voices of their puppets to another puppet voiced by the researcher. In a third technique, children are asked simply to repeat words or sentences (to display their progress for repetition of sounds, syllable structures, and grammatical forms). In a fourth technique, designed to gauge understanding, children playing with dolls are asked to act out such sentences as "The horse pushed the cow" and "The horse was pushed by the cow," which would test their understanding of the meaning of passives.

Although child language and first-language acquisition are important to many aspects of linguistic theory, a good deal about the processes of acquisition remains unclear or uninvestigated. The interaction between physiological and mental limitations, on the one hand, and the nature of the internalized grammar, on the other, makes interpreting child language data challenging. Given the complexities of interpreting child language data, the most reliable findings and theories will be those that emerge from using a variety of naturalistic and experimental methodologies.

Acquiring a Second Language

Besides your first language, you have probably acquired at least the rudiments of a second language, perhaps Russian, Spanish, German, French, Japanese—or English. The term *first language* refers to the language one acquires in infancy. A second language is *any* language that is acquired after one's first language; it may well be a third or fourth "second language." When we speak of second languages in this chapter, we focus on those acquired beyond childhood.

First and Second Languages

There are two common situations in which adults learn a second language. Some may study a foreign language in school or college. As with English taught abroad, such situations often provide relatively little opportunity for experience with the spoken language outside the classroom. In this sense, the study of French in the United States could be called "French as a foreign language," paralleling the "English as a foreign language" studied in Jiddah, Tokyo, Taipei, and elsewhere. It's useful to bear in mind that studying a foreign language typically involves activities that differ significantly from those surrounding first-language acquisition and the acquisition of a second language in a community where it is spoken natively and widely. When people acquire a language in a community in which it is spoken natively, they can participate in a range of communicative activities in the target language.

When populations of Poles, Italians, Germans, Norwegians, and others migrated to America in the nineteenth and early twentieth centuries, they settled in a land that was largely English speaking, although many immigrants initially lived in neighborhoods where their first language could be used with neighbors and shopkeepers as well as at home. The migrations of the present day, from Asia and Latin America, for example, represent a similar situation, although the communities in which immigrants now settle often have large enough immigrant populations to maintain the "foreign" language in newspapers and in radio and television broadcasting, as well as in shops, churches, and homes. In some metropolitan areas, dozens of locally broadcast "foreign" languages can be heard on the radio every day, and cable networks regularly broadcast news and entertainment in languages other than English. In Los Angeles, for example, television news is broadcast in Korean, Mandarin, Spanish, Persian, Tagalog, and several other languages every day, and there are soap operas and variety shows in these languages and others. Daily newspapers are also published locally in several languages and sold at newsstands side by side with English-language dailies. For elections, sample ballots in Los Angeles typically include a full-page notice informing registered voters that voter information pamphlets are available not only in English but in Chinese, Japanese, Korean, Vietnamese, Tagalog, and Spanish. (See the photo in Chapter 1.)

Staff members at many bank branches in Los Angeles are bilingual in English and another language spoken in the neighborhood, and many other commercial and professional establishments routinely provide bilingual service. As a result of such interwoven linguistic networks in some North American communities and communities around the globe, the distinction between second language and "foreign" language is not altogether tidy.

Comparing First- and Second-Language Acquisition

Typically there are significant differences between first- and second-language learning. To begin with (and by definition), first-language acquisition involves an initial linguistic experience, while a second language is mastered only by someone who already speaks another language. However blank the language slate may be at birth, it is certainly not blank after first-language acquisition is completed.

Additionally, a first language is usually acquired in a home environment by an infant in the care of parents and other caretakers, with many activities—linguistic and otherwise—jointly focused on the child. In such circumstances, language use is closely tied to the immediate surroundings and the context of language use. Caretakers use language in reference to objects in the immediate environment (objects that can be seen or heard by the infant), and language content reflects ongoing activity in which child and caretaker are participating as actors (as with eating or bathing) or as observers (of activities within sight or earshot). In contrast, second-language learning is seldom so context bound. Ordinarily an adult speaking a second language in a classroom is using it to discuss imaginary or decontextualized events removed from the learning situation.

A third difference has to do with the adaptability and malleability of learners as a consequence of age and of social identity. Infants have not yet developed strong social identities as to gender, ethnicity, or social status, factors that can be an important part of the social identity and self-awareness of adolescents and adults. Since language use reflects (and helps create) social identity, as you saw in Chapter 11, the social-psychological experiences of first- and second-language acquisition can differ greatly. For many second-language learners, the language variety being studied is emblematic of a different social status or different ethnicity from that represented by their first language, and for nearly all learners it represents new and different cultural values. For infants, this is not the case, of course, so such factors do not come into play in first-language acquisition. Ordinarily, acquisition of a first language and of a social identity go hand in hand and are inseparable.

A fourth difference is that second-language learners ordinarily have linguistic meta-knowledge that is lacking at least in the early stages of a first language. That is, with a second language, speakers may already possess a vocabulary for referring to language structures and language uses. They will certainly be aware that words and sounds differ from language to language, that some sounds are more difficult to make than others, that languages differ grammatically, and that speakers can be recognized as native or nonnative by their speech patterns. Naturally, such meta-knowledge is lacking for the first-language acquirer, who plays with language spontaneously and unselfconsciously.

Even when second-language learners haven't been exposed to such terms as *noun*, *verb*, and *sentence*, they are aware of certain linguistic phenomena—the existence of words, the notions of regional, social, and foreign accent, the existence of well-formed and ill-formed sentences, and so on. For many other second-language learners, phonological terms such as *consonant* and *vowel* and grammatical terms such as *verb* and *subject* are familiar. Just what influence knowledge of such categories may have on second-language acquisition is not known. Some investigators believe that conscious knowledge of grammar can facilitate acquisition for some learners, but to what degree and in what ways are not well understood.

The Role of Motivation in Second-Language Learning

Among the things that clearly affect mastery of a second language is the learner's motivation. People learn another language for many reasons, from preparing to vacation abroad, where one may need to seek directions in the local language, to preparing to take up permanent residence in a locale where it is the sole means of communication. For some students the principal reason for second-language study is to meet a graduation requirement. Motivations for second-language learning can be grouped under the headings of instrumental and integrative.

Instrumental Motivation An **instrumental motivation** is one in which knowledge of the target language will help achieve some other goal: reading scientific works, singing or understanding opera, conducting business. For such uses, only a narrow range of registers (or even a single register) is necessary, and little or no social integration of the learner into a community using the language is desired.

Integrative Motivation By contrast, when you take up residence in a community that uses the target language in its social interactions, **integrative motivation** encourages you to learn the new language as a way of integrating yourself socially into the community and becoming one of its members. Integrative motivation typically underlies successful acquisition of a wide range of registers and a nativelike pronunciation, achievements that usually elude learners with instrumental motivation.

The Role of Attitudes in Second-Language Learning

Language attitudes can have a profound effect on your ability to acquire a second language, especially beyond adolescence. *Studying* a foreign language is parallel to learning math or history; a body of information must be mastered, certainly including much vocabulary and perhaps including terms such as case, tense, (subjunctive) mood, and (subordinate) clause. This kind of foreign-language learning differs not only from first-language acquisition but also from second-language acquisition in immersion situations in which you can acquire a language in a fashion approximating (however inadequately) the environment normally surrounding first-language acquisition. Because the language variety you acquire becomes part of your social identity, the acquisition of a second language must be seen not just as an intellectual exercise but as an enterprise that affects or alters your social identity.

Your attitude toward the second language and your motivation can affect the success of acquisition. In acquiring a foreign language, your efforts are mediated by what linguist Stephen Krashen has called an affective filter—a psychological disposition that facilitates or inhibits your natural language-acquisition capacities. Krashen maintains that if there is sufficient comprehensible language use surrounding a learner, the acquisition of a second language, even by an adult, can proceed as effortlessly and efficiently as first-language acquisition, provided that the affective filter is not blocking the operation of these capacities.

The learning of a second language in school is increasingly viewed not as an intellectual or educational endeavor but as a social-psychological phenomenon. One social psychologist describes this perspective as follows:

> In the acquisition of a second language, the student is faced with the task not simply of learning new information . . . which is part of his *own* culture but rather of *acquiring* symbolic elements of a different ethnolinguistic community. The new words are not simply new words for old concepts, the new grammar is not simply a new way of ordering words, the new pronunciations are not merely 'different' ways of saying things. They are characteristics of another ethnolinguistic community. Furthermore, the student is not being asked to learn about them; he is being asked to acquire them, to make them part of his own language reservoir. This involves imposing elements of another culture into one's own lifespace. As a result, the student's harmony with his own cultural community and his willingness or ability to identify with other cultural communities become important considerations in the process of second language acquisition. (R. C. Gardner, "Social Psychological Aspects of Second Language Acquisition," in Howard Giles and Robert St. Clair, eds., *Language and Social Psychology* [Oxford: Blackwell, 1979], pp. 193–94.)

Teaching and Learning Foreign Languages

Among methods of foreign-language instruction, you are probably familiar with pattern drills, translation, composition, listening comprehension, and a few others. Some methods are grounded in the behaviorist assumption that language mastery is a matter of inducing the right habits, much as first-language acquisition was earlier assumed to be. Other methods, aiming to be more naturalistic, attempt to emulate the kinds of language experience children have when acquiring a first language. With naturalistic methods the emphasis is on interactional use, especially conversation, focused on matters close at hand; noninteractional use aims to provide abundant input that is nearly fully comprehensible to the learner because of its familiarity.

Contrastive Analysis For decades, learning a second language was viewed as a matter of knowing and practicing the well-formed utterances of the target language. Learning a second language was approached as a matter of drilling grammatical patterns, and drill focused on patterns that differ from those of the first language. To prepare teaching materials, researchers carried out a **contrastive analysis** of the phonological and grammatical structures of the native and target languages, producing a list of morphological, grammatical, and phonological features that might prove difficult for learners because they differed from those of the first language.

For various reasons, teaching materials based on contrastive analysis have not proven very effective. A number of problems have been uncovered, among them the recognition of an asymmetry between learners acquiring one another's language. Contrastive analysis predicts that when two languages contrast, the difference between them should prove equally challenging for speakers of both languages. In fact, however, difficulties typically prove asymmetrical. Rather than English and Chinese speakers having equivalent difficulties learning one another's language, there are great differences in various parts of the grammar. Mastering a distinction such as English makes between masculine and feminine singular pronouns (*he* versus *she*) proves difficult for speakers of Chinese, which makes no such distinction, whereas it is easy for English speakers to ignore the distinction in learning Chinese. Similarly, Chinese doesn't express the copula BE in many places where English requires it. It is relatively easy for English speakers to omit BE in such sentences but very challenging for Chinese speakers to express it in English when it is required. Likewise, English speakers find it tough to learn the Chinese tone system, while Chinese speakers find it easy to adapt to the absence of a tone system in English. Contrastive analysis also suggests that certain differences in structure should warrant considerable attention, whereas in practice learners may avoid the structure, substituting alternative means of expression in the target language.

Interlanguage Some researchers view second-language learners as developing a series of interlanguages in their progression toward mastery of the target language. An **interlanguage** is that form of the target language that a learner has internalized, and the interlanguage grammar underlies the spontaneous utterances of a learner in the target language. The grammar of an interlanguage can differ from the grammar of the target language by containing rules borrowed from the native language, by containing overgeneralizations, by lacking certain sounds of the target language, by inappropriately marking certain verbs in the lexicon as requiring (or not requiring) a preposition, by lacking certain rules altogether, and so on. A language learner can be viewed as progressing from one interlanguage to another, each one approximating more closely the target language.

Fossilizing For various reasons, often related to the kind of motivation a learner has, the language-learning process typically slows down or ceases at some point, and the existing interlanguage stabilizes, with negligible further acquisition except in vocabulary. When such stabilization occurs, the interlanguage may contain rules or other features that differ from those of the target language. This **fossilization** underlies the nonnative speech characteristics of someone who may have spoken the target language for some time but has stopped the process of learning. In other words, many second-language learners fossilize at a stage of acquisition that falls far short of nativelike speech.

Fossilization then is at the root of a foreign accent when, for instance, certain sounds have not been acquired or their allophonic distribution in the fossilized interlanguage does not match that of native speakers of the target language. The pronunciation of English *thin* and *then* as *sin* and *zen* by native speakers of French may reflect fossilization at a stage before the English sounds /θ/ and /ð/ (which do not occur in the French inventory) have been acquired. Likewise, the language of the English speaker who pronounces the French words *pain* 'bread' and *Pierre* with the aspirated [pʰ] that English has in word-initial position (instead of the unaspirated [p] of French) may have fossilized before the distribution of the French allophones was mastered.

Grammatical fossilization is manifest in expressions such as those below, spoken by a native speaker of Mandarin.

1. I want to see what can I buy.
2. Where I can buy them?
3. What you gonna do on Tuesday?
4. I will cold.
5. Where did you found it?
6. Why you buy it?
7. How you pronounce this word?
8. Oh! Look this.

Such sentences reflect the speaker's current interlanguage grammar; for a speaker whose acquisition of English has ceased to develop, the utterances would represent fossilization.

Language Teaching Practices Researchers have been investigating second-language learning and second-language teaching methods intensely for several decades, and a good deal is known now, but some of the findings and conclusions point in different directions. In part, of course, that reflects the very different circumstances in which second and foreign languages are acquired when compared to first languages. Reflecting on the research of past decades, Rod Ellis, a respected researcher himself, has recently compiled a set of recommended principles for teachers of second languages to help ensure the success of their students.

We list some of the principles below (the rest—and discussion of all of them—can be found under Ellis in the "References" section given at the end of this chapter):

1. Instruction needs to ensure that learners develop both a rich repertoire of formulaic expressions and a rule-based competence.

2. Instruction needs to ensure that learners focus predominantly on meaning.

3. Instruction needs to ensure that learners also focus on form.

4. Instruction needs to be predominantly directed at developing implicit knowledge of the L2 while not neglecting explicit knowledge.

5. Successful instructed language learning requires extensive L2 input.

6. Successful instructed language learning also requires opportunities for output.

7. The opportunity to interact in the L2 is central to developing L2 proficiency.

8. Instruction needs to take account of individual differences in learners.

From these principles, you should be able to infer several things about the state of the art in second-language teaching and the research that underlies it. For example, the first principle suggests that second languages are learned partly by rule and partly in whole chunks—one an analytic, the other a gestalt approach. The second and third principles, coupled with the fifth and seventh, underscore the fact that language can be represented as a triangle—as we saw in Chapter 1—with meaning, expression (or form), and interaction (or context) as its three sides and that second-language learning is best done with respect to all sides of the triangle. The eighth principle recognizes the fact that, unlike first-language acquisition, which despite differences around the globe is highly uniform in its motivation and outcomes, second-language acquisition differs greatly across situations and learners and that what may succeed with one student may not succeed with another.

COMPUTERS AND LANGUAGE LEARNING

In recent years, computers have played an increasingly important role in the study of first-language acquisition. The question of nature versus nurture—addressing the likelihood that language is either partly innate or entirely learned—has prompted researchers to create models of how language would be acquired given one set of assumptions or another. Computers have proven essential to such complicated modeling, and while little agreement exists about the facts of acquisition, computational modeling is a strong ally in addressing the question.

On another front, data collection and analysis have been the bedrock of many of the best studies of acquisition, so it isn't surprising that corpora of children's language have been compiled. Collecting copious data of children's language is challenging and time-consuming, as well as difficult and expensive to transcribe for research purposes. In order to pool resources and make available to a spectrum of researchers the data that have been collected, researchers at Carnegie Mellon University have spearheaded a project called CHILDES (Child Language Data Exchange System), which makes its database and software programs available to scholars worldwide. The child language data, transcribed to agreed-upon standards by researchers around the globe, is accompanied by a set of software programs nicknamed CLAN. With CLAN, researchers have explored the vast resources of the CHILDES database and have made a major impact on the ways in which research into first-language acquisition is carried out. (For more information about CHILDES or for access to the files, see the CHILDES website, cited in the "Other Resources" section at the end of this chapter.)

Corpora of second-language learners are also now being compiled. They, too, give promise of providing researchers with previously unimagined access to high-quality data in abundance. For example, the compilers of the *Longman Active Study Dictionary of English* relied on the "Longman Learner's Corpus of Students' English" to write over 250 new usage notes.

For decades computers have been used in language laboratories to support students studying foreign languages, and an entire field has sprung up that goes by the nickname of CALL, for computer-assisted language learning. You are doubtless familiar with some of the language teaching methods facilitated by CALL. Among the most familiar ways in which computers have assisted language learners are by making CD-ROMs available for listening to language lessons. Of course, in some sense CD-ROMs have simply replaced audiocassette recordings, but they enable much freer interaction with the foreign-language materials. They also enable multimedia language lessons, including audio and visual presentations. Programs on CD-ROM are sometimes accompanied by interactive teaching and testing.

Other uses of the computer are even more innovative, though not everyone is convinced of their efficacy. In one interesting application, CD-ROM audio programs are accompanied by voiceprints of native speakers and a microphone for use by the learner. Using a relatively advanced speech recognition technology, learners of Spanish, German, French, and English, for example, can practice their pronunciation until it matches the pronunciations of the native speaker voice.

There is no doubt that computers will enable researchers to test their hypotheses more efficiently and more definitively than has been possible before. There is also no doubt that microcomputer technologies are revolutionizing the way that learners can tackle a foreign language. What the future holds in these respects can hardly be imagined. ■

Summary

- Children do not acquire their native language through instruction by adults or through mere imitation of what they hear adults say.
- While a child must receive some linguistic input in order to acquire language, input is not the sole factor and may not be the chief factor that accounts for the development of grammatical competence and the ability to produce and understand language.
- There is considerable evidence that children are born with the mental capacity to acquire language, probably with a disposition to acquire certain kinds of structures, and perhaps with additional specifications as to the kinds of grammar that are eligible for acquisition.
- Various stages of language acquisition can be identified, distinguished by the amount of content a child is able to express in an utterance vis-à-vis an adult's expression in equivalent circumstances.
- Even before children utter their first interpretable words, they use language socially, for example, by engaging in turn-taking expressions with caregivers.

- Adopting a second-language variety—whether a standard variety of one's first language or a foreign language—is not merely an intellectual exercise but an experience fraught with emotional overtones.
- The study of a foreign language cannot be equated with the study of history or math because, more than understanding, it involves adapting to certain customs of a different social group.

What Do You Think? REVISITED

- *Bragging Brenda.* Kids learn vocabulary only by hearing it. But they intuit syntactic processes as abstract patterns that apply to broad categories and use those patterns to produce sentences they've never heard before.
- *Nursery school parent.* It's true. Although there's some variation, children acquire the grammatical parts of their language in approximately the same order.
- *Brad and Tricia.* Kids don't hear anyone say "maked," "breaked," or "runned" for *made, broke,* and *ran,* but they often overgeneralize the patterns they do hear for creating grammatical forms. The fact that they overgeneralize suggests that they don't imitate what they hear but apply intuited patterns, sometimes even to words that are exceptions.
- *Frustrated Frank.* Once a first language is acquired, it may "interfere" with acquisition of a second language and contribute to a "foreign accent." There's no interference acquiring a first language. In addition, Frank's social identity is intertwined with his first language, and acquiring a second language may require adaptation to the social identity represented by the other language. That's also something that's not true of first language acquisition. Much of the process of acquiring a first language is automatic and not consciously learned. Likewise, the process of acquiring a second language is not altogether a conscious activity and not altogether under one's conscious control. ■

Exercises

14-1. Make a list of baby-talk vocabulary in your first language. Identify the kinds of referents baby-talk vocabulary has, the lexical categories most frequently represented, and the phonological form of such vocabulary. If there are different first languages represented in your class, compare the characteristics of baby-talk terms cross-linguistically as to kinds of referents, lexical categories, and phonological form.

14-2. a. Explain in what ways the use of personal names such as *Baby* and *Mommy* could be easier for a young child to perceive and analyze than personal pronouns such as *I* and *you*.

b. Explain in what ways the use of content words (nouns, verbs, adjectives) could make baby talk easier for a child to analyze and understand than function words such as conjunctions and articles.

14-3. Tape-record a brief passage of talk between an adult or older child and a young child. Transcribe 30 seconds of the recorded talk and identify an example of each feature of baby talk discussed in this chapter. Organize your list into features of phonology, vocabulary, syntax, and discourse. (Television shows for children may provide access to such samples.)

14-4. On the basis of what you know about overgeneralizations of morphological rules, what forms would you predict children might use for each of the adult words below? In each case identify the rule that is being overgeneralized.

Verbs				**Nouns**	**Adjectives**	**Pronouns**
hurt	told	took	threw	geese	better	I
ate	came	bled	broke	sheep (pl.)	beautiful	myself

14-5. The utterances below (taken, slightly adapted, from Fletcher [1985]) were spoken by an English child named Sophie on three separate days over the course of about a year. Examine them closely and characterize the progress of Sophie's language acquisition across the three occasions with respect to the following features:

possessive determiners (*my, your*)	yes/no questions
the copula BE (*is, are*)	prepositions
adverbs (*down, there*)	interrogative word order
declarative word order	negative sentences
clauses per utterance	information questions
auxiliary DO	auxiliaries other than DO
contractible copula	regular noun plurals

Example: Personal pronouns—Based on this sample, Sophie, at 2;4, displays second-person *you* and first-person singular *me*; she uses *me* for both subject and oblique grammatical relations. At 3;0 she uses *her* for subject and oblique relations. At 3;5, the adult forms *I, you,* and *we* occur as subjects, *me* as object, and *it* as subject and object, but *her* appears as the subject form instead of *she*.

Age 2 Years, 4 Months

(1) Me want your tea.
(2) Where's the doll house?
(3) Mary come me.
(4) Me want Daddy come down.
(5) That your turn.
(6) That's a mess.
(7) You play "Snakes and Ladders" me?

Age 3 Years

(8) Shall me sit mon my legs?
(9) Can me put it in like that?
(10) That not go in there.
(11) Why did Hester be fast asleep?
(12) What this one called?
(13) What did her have wrong with her?
(14) What is that one called?
(15) Daddy didn't give me two in the end.

Age 3 Years, 5 Months

    (16) This isn't a piano book.

    (17) I don't know what to do.

    (18) Where my corder?

    (19) Can you take off my shoes?

    (20) How did that broke?

    (21) You won't let me play a guitar.

    (22) If you do it like this, it won't come down.

    (23) While Hester at school we can buy some sweets.

    (24) When her's at school I'll buy some sweeties.

    (25) I want to ring up somebody and her won't be there tomorrow.

14-6. Compare the nonnative adult English sentences in the section on "Fossilizing" with the native English sentences of the child Sophie given in Exercise 14-5. List as many features as you can that are shared by both sets of data and that belong only to one set or the other. Which features seem easier for the young Sophie to learn than for the adult nonnative speaker, and which seem easier for the nonnative speaker than for Sophie? What explanation can you offer for why certain features might be harder for Sophie or harder for the nonnative speaker to learn?

14-7. Cite four reasons that make it more difficult to gather language data from preschoolers than from schoolchildren and adults, and identify several technological advances (beginning with the tape recorder) that can help overcome those difficulties and increase the quantity or quality of data for research into first-language acquisition.

Especially for Educators and Future Teachers

14-8. Reflect on your experience in learning a second language. Were you generally successful at it? If so, what contributed to that success? If not, what made it difficult for you? Were there others—perhaps fellow students—who found it easier or harder than you to learn a second language? If you have learned more than one second language, were they equally easy or equally difficult? If not, what could account for the difference? Did your attitude toward the people whose language you were learning influence your success?

14-9. What implications for second-language teachers do you see in the discussion of identity and attitudes in this chapter?

14-10. A print ad for the language learning program Rosetta Stone asks, "What's the fastest way to learn a language?" and answers in big letters: ACT LIKE A BABY. Generally speaking, you wouldn't want your students acting like babies, so what does the ad mean? In what way does it make sense for a second-language learner to act like a baby?

Other Resources

Internet

 LISU Website: http://www.CengageBrain.com For users of this textbook. Provides updated Internet links as well as supplemental material for students and instructors. Here you will find interactive learning tools.

 CHILDES: http://childes.psy.cmu.edu/ A rich source of information about research in child language acquisition, this website also offers data and software.

Videos

- **Acquiring the Human Language: "Playing the Language Game"** Part of *The Human Language Series*, an award-winning set of four videos originally broadcast on PBS in 1995. This 55-minute video explores how children seem to acquire language spontaneously and without instruction. It asks, "Do people imitate those around them or is grammar inherited?" (available through Transit Media at **http://www.transitmedia.net/**).
- **The Human Language Evolves: "With and Without Words"** Part of the same series as the previous entry, this excellent 55-minute video explores the reasons human beings acquired language while chimpanzees and other species did not; includes fascinating discussion of animal and human gestures.
- **Baby Talk** An informative video about first-language acquisition beginning in the womb; produced by NOVA and first broadcast in 1985; available only on VHS cassette from libraries and video rental outlets; copies may be available from vendors at www.amazon.com.
- **Secret of the Wild Child** This Emmy-winning video in the NOVA series explores the troubled history of Genie. You can get NOVA videos from many video rental outlets. For information about purchasing NOVA videos, visit WGBH's website at **http://www.pbs.org/wgbh/nova/novastore.html**. To read an online transcript of this video, visit **http://www.pbs.org/wgbh/nova/transcripts/2112gchild.html**.
- **An English-Speaking World** From *The Story of English* series with host Robert MacNeil, this video discusses English around the world and offers insight into instrumental motivations for second-language acquisition; available only on VHS videocassettes from libraries and video rental outlets; copies may be available from vendors represented at **http://www.amazon.com**.

Suggestions for Further Reading

- **Gerry T. M. Altmann. 1999.** *The Ascent of Babel: An Exploration of Language, Mind, and Understanding* (Oxford: Oxford University Press). Written by a psychologist, this wide-ranging treatment of the cognitive aspects of first-language acquisition is written in nontechnical language but requires some worthwhile effort.
- **Roger Brown. 1973.** *A First Language: The Early Stages* (Cambridge, MA: Harvard University Press). An accessible classic. Our examples of adult expansions of children's utterances and the list of 14 morphemes ordered by acquisition sequence come from this book.
- **Eve V. Clark. 2009.** *First Language Acquisition*, **2nd ed.** (Cambridge, UK: Cambridge University Press). Another highly accessible follow-up to the present chapter.
- **Rod Ellis. 1997.** *Second Language Acquisition* (Oxford: Oxford University Press). An accessible textbook about how second languages are acquired.
- **Susan M. Gass & Larry Selinker. 2008.** *Second Language Acquisition: An Introductory Course*, **3rd ed.** (New York: Routledge). Well rehearsed over the years, this staple is highly recommended for beginning students.
- **Jean Berko Gleason & Nan Bernstein Ratner, eds. 2008.** *The Development of Language*, **7th ed.** (Boston: Allyn & Bacon). A good next step after the present chapter, with separate chapters on phonology, syntax, semantics, and pragmatics, as well as on atypical language and the neurological bases of language acquisition.
- **Patsy M. Lightbown & Nina Spada. 2006.** *How Languages Are Learned*, **3rd ed.** (Oxford: Oxford University Press). An excellent and time-tested blend of practical and theoretical approaches to second-language acquisition.

- **Lourdes Ortega. 2009.** *Understanding Second Language Acquisition* (London: Hodder Education). Written as an introductory textbook, this enthusiastic approach is recommended especially for graduate students approaching language acquisition as a new subject.
- **Robert E. Owens, Jr. 2007.** *Language Development: An Introduction,* **7th ed.** (Boston: Allyn and Bacon). A detailed, accessible treatment attending to social and psychological concerns and including a chapter on school-age literacy development.
- **Muriel Saville-Troike. 2005.** *Introducing Second Language Acquisition* (Cambridge, UK: Cambridge University Press). An excellent first book in SLA, covering the basics from psychological and social points of view and including discussion of pedagogy.
- **Virginia Yip & Stephen Matthews. 2007.** *The Bilingual Child: Early Development and Language Contact* (Cambridge, UK: Cambridge University Press). Winner of the Linguistic Society of America's Leonard Bloomfield Book Award in 2009, this richly detailed study traces the acquisition of English and Cantonese by the authors' two children.

Advanced Reading

Comprehensive treatments of first-language acquisition can be found in Bavin (2009) and Fletcher and MacWhinney (1995). In some instances, the chapters in the latter work may rely on more background than students who have read only the present textbook will possess, but they are useful overviews for instructors. Chapter 4 of Slobin (1979) is highly accessible. Goodluck (1991) provides a clear introduction to aspects of child language acquisition that bear closely on current grammatical theory. O'Grady (1997; 2005) are well-balanced treatments of syntactic development, offering analysis from various theoretical points of view.

Curtiss (1977) recounts the story of Genie, the child who received virtually no language input. Schieffelin and Ochs (1986) contains fascinating descriptions of socialization into linguistic and social roles in diverse cultures, including those of Samoa, Papua New Guinea, Lesotho (in southern Africa), and Japan. Andersen (1990) describes preschoolers' mastery over the registers associated with social roles such as father, mother, and child in middle-class American homes, as well as teacher and doctor. The socialization of children into gender roles is explored in Swann (1992). Gleason (1980) describes observations of adults teaching children politeness rules for Halloween trick-or-treating, an example of consciously prescriptive input. Slobin (1985) provides a wealth of information on language acquisition around the globe. Peters (1983) investigates the strategies that children use to analyze linguistic input and ways in which baby talk may help that process.

Wanner and Gleitman (1982) lays out the state of knowledge in language acquisition from diverse vantage points; we have relied for some of our discussion on the overview chapter by the editors and on Slobin's chapter, "Universal and Particular in the Acquisition of Language." Ingram (1989), on which we have relied for the stages of phonological acquisition, offers detailed discussion of the research on first-language acquisition. Fletcher (1985) contains four samples of Sophie's language at six-month intervals between 2;6 and 4;0; we have borrowed several examples from these transcriptions. Our discussion of vocabulary acquisition follows M. C. Templin's *Certain Language Skills,* as reported in Miller (1977).

For second-language acquisition, Krashen and Terrell (1983) presents an integrated approach, emphasizing naturalistic ways of experiencing comprehensible input. Ryan and Giles (1982) discusses the empirical study of language attitudes and address the role of attitudes in second-language acquisition. Gardner and Lambert (1972) discusses attitudes and motivation in second-language acquisition.

References

Andersen, Elaine Slosberg. 1990. *Speaking with Style: The Sociolinguistic Skills of Children* (London: Routledge).

Bavin, Edith L., ed. 2009. *The Cambridge Handbook of Child Language* (Cambridge, UK: Cambridge University Press.

Curtiss, Susan. 1977. *Genie: A Psycholinguistic Study of a Modern-day "Wild Child"* (New York: Academic).

Ellis, Rod. 2005. "Principles of Instructed Language Learning." *Asian EFL Journal* 7 (3): 9-24. [Available at: http://www.asian-efl-journal.com/September_2005_EBook_editions.pdf]

Fletcher, Paul. 1985. *A Child's Learning of English* (London: Blackwell).

Fletcher, Paul & Brian MacWhinney. 1995. *The Handbook of Child Language* (Malden, MA: Blackwell).

Gardner, Robert C. & Wallace E. Lambert. 1972. *Attitudes and Motivation in Second-Language Learning* (Rowley, MA: Newbury House).

Gleason, Jean Berko. 1980. "The Acquisition of Social Speech: Routines and Politeness Formulas," in Howard Giles, W. Peter Robinson & Philip M. Smith, eds., *Language: Social Psychological Perspectives* (New York: Academic).

Goodluck, Helen. 1991. *Language Acquisition: A Linguistic Introduction* (Oxford: Blackwell).

Ingram, David. 1989. *First Language Acquisition: Method, Description, and Explanation* (Cambridge, UK: Cambridge University Press).

Krashen, Stephen D. & Tracy D. Terrell. 1983. *The Natural Approach: Language Acquisition in the Classroom* (Hayward, CA: Alemany).

Miller, George A. 1977. *Spontaneous Apprentices: Children and Language* (New York: Seabury).

O'Grady, William. 1997. *Syntactic Development* (Chicago: University of Chicago Press).

———. 2005. *How Children Learn Language* (Cambridge, UK: Cambridge University Press).

Peters, Ann M. 1983. *The Units of Language Acquisition* (Cambridge, UK: Cambridge University Press).

Ryan, Ellen Bouchard & Howard Giles, eds. 1982. *Attitudes towards Language Variation: Social and Applied Contexts* (London: Edward Arnold).

Schieffelin, Bambi B. & Elinor Ochs, eds. 1986. *Language Socialization across Cultures* (Cambridge, UK: Cambridge University Press).

Slobin, Dan I. 1979. *Psycholinguistics*, 2nd ed. (Glenview, IL: Scott Foresman).

———. ed. 1985. *The Crosslinguistic Study of Language Acquisition*. 2 vols. (Hillsdale, NJ: Erlbaum).

Swann, Joan. 1992. *Girls, Boys and Language* (Oxford: Blackwell).

Wanner, Eric & Lila R. Gleitman, eds. 1982. *Language Acquisition: The State of the Art* (Cambridge, UK: Cambridge University Press).

Glossary

This glossary characterizes important terms used in this book. Typically, when first discussed in the text, such terms are printed in **boldface** to indicate their importance. Some terms, boldfaced only in headings, are included in the glossary as well because of their frequent use throughout the text. Within the glossary, *italicized* terms with an asterisk have their own entry. For further discussion of a term, consult the index.

A

absolute universal A linguistic pattern at play in all languages of the world without exception. Example: "Any language with voiced stops also has voiceless stops."

accent The pronunciation features of any spoken language *variety.

acronym An abbreviation formed by combining the initials of an expression into a pronounceable word. Examples: *NATO, SARS, radar, yuppy, scuba* (but not *USA, CNN, SUV, UN, BBC, ATM*, whose pronunciations merely voice the names of the letters, as in *C-N-N*).

adjacency pair A set of two consecutive, ordered turns that "go together" in a conversation, such as question/answer sequences and greeting/greeting exchanges.

adjective A lexical category of words that serve semantically to specify the attributes of *nouns (as in *tall ships*) and that can represent degrees of comparison morphologically (*taller*) or syntactically (*most beautiful*); adjectives may have attributive function (*those tall ships*) or predicative function (*those ships are tall*).

adverb A lexical class with wide-ranging functions and no inflections. Many English adverbs are derived from *adjectives with the *derivational morpheme -LY (as in *suddenly, quickly* from *sudden, quick*), but the most common adverbs have no distinguishing marks (*soon, very, today*).

affective meaning Information conveyed about the attitudes and emotions of language users toward the content or context of their expression; together with *social meaning, affective meaning is sometimes called *connotation*.

affix A *bound morpheme that attaches to a root or stem *morpheme (called the *root* or *stem*). *Prefixes and *suffixes are the most common types of affixes in the world's languages; less common are *infixes and *circumfixes.

affricate A sound produced when air is built up by a complete closure of the oral tract at some *place of articulation and then released and continued like a *fricative*; also called a *stop fricative*. Examples: English [tʃ] as in *chin* and [dʒ]) as in *gin*; German [ts] as in *Zeit* 'time.' In American practice, [tʃ] is sometimes represented by [č] and [dʒ] by [ĵ].

agreement The marking of a word (as with an *affix) to indicate its grammatical relationship to another word in the sentence. Thus, a verb that *agrees* with its *subject in *person and *number has a form that indicates that relationship; an adjective may agree with a noun in *gender, *number, and *case.

allomorph An alternate realization (i.e., phonological form) of a morpheme in a particular linguistic environment. For example, the English 'PLURAL' morpheme has three allomorphs: [əz] (as in *buses*), [z] (*twigs*), and [s] (*cats*).

allophone A phonetic realization (i.e., a pronunciation) of a *phoneme in a particular phonological environment. Example: In English, unaspirated [p] and *aspirated [pʰ] are allophones of the phoneme /p/, and they occur in *complementary distribution*.

alphabet A writing system in which, ideally, each graphic sign represents a distinctive sound (i.e., a *phoneme*) of the language.

alveolar A sound articulated at the alveolar ridge, the bony ridge just behind and above the upper teeth.

alveo-palatal A *place of articulation* in the oral cavity between the alveolar ridge and the palate. Example: The English sound [ʃ] (sometimes written [š]) represented by <sh> in *shoe* is articulated in the alveo-palatal region.

ambiguous Characterizes an expression that can be interpreted in more than one way as a consequence of having more than one *constituent structure* ([*french fries and cole slaw] or soup; french fries and [cole slaw or soup]*) or more than one *referential meaning* (*bank of a river, savings bank*).

antonymy In *lexical semantics*, denotes opposite meanings; word pairs with opposite meanings are said to be *antonymous*, as with *wet* and *dry; new* and *old*.

appropriateness conditions Conventions that regulate the interpretation under which an *utterance* serves as a particular *speech act*, such as a question, promise, or invitation.

approximant A sound produced when one articulator approaches another but the vocal tract is not sufficiently narrowed to create the audible friction that typically characterizes a *consonant* sound. Examples: [w], [j], [r], [l]. See *liquid*.

argot The specialized vocabulary of a group, often an occupational or recreational group; unlike *slang*, argot is not limited to situations of extreme informality.

aspect A grammatical category of the verb, marking the way in which a situation described by the verb takes place in time, for example, as continuous, repetitive, or instantaneous. The English progressive (as in *is walking* or *was walking*, as distinct from *walks* or *walked*) marks continuous aspect.

aspirated Sounds produced with an accompanying puff of air; represented in phonetic transcription by the *diacritic* raised [ʰ], as in [pʰ].

assimilation A phonological process whereby a sound becomes phonetically similar (or identical) to a neighboring sound. Examples: In Korean, underlying /p/ is pronounced as [b] between vowels; that is, /p/ assimilates to the voicing of the neighboring vowels.

auxiliary verb Used with (or instead of) the main verb to carry certain kinds of grammatical information, such as *tense* and *aspect*. In English, the auxiliary verb is inverted with the *subject* in yes/no questions (*Can Lou swim?*) and carries the negative element in contractions (*Lou can't swim*).

B

bilabial A *place of articulation* involving both lips; a sound produced there.

bilingualism The state of having *competence*, both grammatical and communicative, in more than one language.

bound morpheme A *morpheme* that cannot stand alone as a word. Examples: -MENT (as in *establishment*), -ER (*painter*), and 'PLURAL' (*zebras*). See *free morpheme*.

branch A line in a tree or tree diagram that descends from a *node*.

C

case A grammatical category associated with nouns and pronouns, indicating their grammatical relationship to other elements in the clause, often the verb. Example: The pronoun *I* is marked for common case, *me* for objective case, while *book* is said to be unmarked or to be marked for common case. In some languages, adjectives agree in case with nouns.

circumfix A discontinuous morpheme that combines a *prefix* and *suffix* in a single *morpheme* occurring on both ends of a root or stem.

clause A constituent unit of syntax consisting of a verb with its noun phrases; a clause can stand alone as a simple sentence or function as a *constituent* of another clause.

click A *stop* *consonant* defined by its *manner of articulation* and pronounced at various *places of articulation*; clicks such as the alveolar click used in English to express disapproval, as in *tsk-tsk* or *tut-tut*, function as phonemes in some Bantu languages, such as Zulu and Xhosa.

coda Any consonants that follow the *nucleus* in the *rhyme* of a *syllable*; for example, in the syllable [pɛn], [n] is the coda; in [spɛnt], [nt] is the coda.

code switching Alternating between two or more language *varieties* when speaking with others who share those varieties.

cognates Words or *morphemes* that have developed from a single, historically earlier source. Example: English *father*, German *Vater*, Spanish *padre*, and Gothic *fadar* are cognates because all of them have developed from the same reconstructed Proto-Indo-European word (*pəter*). Also said of languages that have a common historical ancestor, as with English, Russian, German, Persian, and the other *Indo-European* languages.

collocation Word pairs or sets that habitually co-occur (i.e., occur near one another) in *texts*.

communicative competence See *competence*.

comparative reconstruction A method used in historical linguistics to uncover vocabulary and structures of an ancestor language by drawing inferences from the evidence remaining in several daughter languages. See also *cognates* and *correspondence set*.

competence The ability to produce and assign meaning to grammatical sentences is called *grammatical competence*; the ability to produce and interpret utterances appropriate to their context of use is called *communicative competence*.

complementary distribution A pattern of distribution of two or more sounds that do not occur in the same position within words in a given language. Example: In English, [pʰ] does not occur where [p] occurs (and vice versa).

conditioned sound change A *regular sound change* that occurs only in a particular, specifiable sound environment but not in all environments in which the sound appears. Example: The merger of the vowels in *pin* and *pen* in Southern American English is a conditioned sound change because it occurs only before nasals; thus, *pit* and *pet* are not pronounced alike, but *him* and *hem* are homophonous.

conjugation See *paradigm*.

conjunction A closed class of words that serve to link clauses or phrases; *coordinating conjunctions* conjoin expressions of the same status, as with clauses (*She went but he stayed*) or noun phrases (*Alice and I*); *subordinating conjunctions* embed one clause into another (*Leave when you're ready*).

consonant sound A speech sound produced by partial or complete closure of part of the vocal tract, thus obstructing the airflow and creating audible friction. Consonants are described in terms of *voicing*, *place of articulation*, and *manner of articulation*. Abbreviated C.

constituent A syntactic unit that functions as part of a larger unit within a sentence; typical constituent types are verb phrase, noun phrase, prepositional phrase, and *clause*.

constituent structure The linear and hierarchical organization of the words of a sentence into syntactic units.

content word A word whose primary function is to describe entities, ideas, qualities, and states of being in the world; *nouns*, *verbs*, *adjectives*, and *adverbs* are content words; content words are contrasted with *function words*.

context One of three main elements (besides *expression and *meaning) in a speech situation. Context typically refers to those aspects of a speech situation that affect the expression and enable an interpretation.

contractions Spoken or written expressions that represent a fusion of two or more words in a single word. Examples: *can't/cannot*; *she'll/she will*; *could've/could have*; *wanna/want to*; *gonna/going to*.

contrastive In *semantics, a noun phrase that is marked as being in opposition to another noun phrase in the same *discourse.

contrastive analysis A method of analyzing languages for instructional purposes whereby a native language and target language are compared with a view to establishing points of difference likely to cause difficulties for learners.

converseness A reciprocal relationship between two words, as in *husband* and *wife* or *buy* and *sell*.

cooperative principle Four maxims that describe how language users cooperate in producing and understanding utterances in context: *quantity, quality, relevance, manner*.

coordinating conjunction A category of *function words that serve to conjoin expressions of the same status, such as *clause (He spoke <u>and</u> I wept), *adverb (slowly <u>but</u> surely), or noun (Thelma <u>and</u> Louise).

corpus A representative collection of texts, usually in machine-readable form and including information about the situation in which each text originated, such as the speaker or author, addressee, or audience.

corpus linguistics The activities involved in compiling and using a *corpus to investigate natural language use.

correspondence set A set of sounds in different languages, all of which derive from a single sound in a historically earlier language.

creole A contact language, a former *pidgin, that has "acquired" native speakers.

creolization The process a *pidgin undergoes once it acquires native speakers and develops into a full-blown language.

cuneiform A written sign developed by the Sumerians and Akkadians in the Middle East around 3000 B.C.; characterized by the wedgelike shape that results from its being written on wet clay with a stylus.

D

declension A noun *paradigm, as in English *woman, woman's, women, women's*.

definite A noun phrase that is marked to indicate that the speaker believes the addressee can identify its referent; contrast with *indefinite*. In English, definiteness and indefiniteness can be marked by the choice of determiner (e.g., *the* versus *a*).

deixis The marking of the orientation or position of entities and situations with respect to certain points of reference such as the place (*here/there*) and time (*now/then*) of utterance.

demonstrative pronouns *Pronouns that refer to things relatively near or relatively far away from the speaker or the focus of discussion, as with *this, that,* and *those*.

derivation In morphology designates a process whereby one lexical item is transformed into another one with a related meaning but belonging to a different lexical class. Example: The *adverb *slowly* is derived from the *adjective *slow* by suffixing the *derivational morpheme -LY.

derivational morpheme A *morpheme that serves to derive a word of one class or meaning from a word of another class or meaning. Examples: -MENT (as in *establishment*) derives the noun from the verb *establish*; RE- (*repaint*) changes the meaning of the verb *paint* to 'paint again.'

determiner Occurring as part of a noun phrase, a closed class of words including indefinite and definite articles (*a, the*) and several other kinds generally having the same distributional properties as articles: demonstratives, possessives (*my, our*), and interrogatives.

diacritic A mark attached to a phonetic character (or letter) to indicate a specific feature of the represented sound, such as aspiration [ʰ] or tone [ˇ].

dialect A language *variety* characteristic of a particular social group; dialects can be characteristic of regional, ethnic, socioeconomic, or gender groups.

diphthong A vowel sound whose production requires the tongue to start in one place and move to another. Examples: the vowels in *lied, loud*, and *Lloyd*. See also *glide*.

direct object A kind of grammatical relation; one of two kinds of objects; the noun phrase in a *clause* that, together with the verb, usually forms the verb phrase *constituent*; the object NP is immediately dominated by VP. Example: *She drove a truck*. See also *indirect object*.

discourse Spoken or written language use in particular social situations; discourse is a broader term than *text* in that it includes context and the intended and actual interpretations.

displacement The characteristic of languages whereby speakers are able to refer to events that are not temporally or spatially present in the *speech situation*.

E

etymon The linguistic form from which a word or *morpheme* is historically derived.

expression Any bit of spoken, written, or signed language; the audible or visible aspect of language use that conveys particular content in a given *context*.

F

family See *language family*.

flap A *manner of articulation* produced by quickly flapping the tip of the tongue against some *place of articulation* on the upper surface of the vocal tract, commonly the *alveolar ridge*, as for <t> in the American English pronunciation of *metal* [mɛɾəl]; also called a *tap*.

fossilization Refers to a final form of *interlanguage* that falls short of the target language; the stage of second-language acquisition where a learner has ceased making substantial progress toward the target language.

free morpheme A *morpheme* that can stand alone as a word. Examples: ZEBRA, PAINT, PRETTY, VERY. See *bound morpheme*.

free variation *Allophones* of a given *phoneme* that can occur in the same position in a word without altering the word's meaning, as in the final sound of the English word *step*, which can be released [p] or unreleased [p˺].

fricative A consonant sound made by passing a continuous stream of air through a narrowed passage in the vocal tract, thereby causing turbulence, such as that created between the lower lip and the upper teeth in the production of [f] and [v].

function words Words such as *determiners* and *conjunctions* whose primary role is to mark grammatical relationships between *content words* or structures such as *phrases* and *clauses*.

G

gender A system in which all the nouns of a language fall into distinct classes. Example: German has a gender system of three noun classes (masculine, feminine, and neuter) whose inflections and associated determiners and *adjectives* vary in form for *number* and *case* in *agreement* with the gender class of the noun.

given information Information already introduced into a *discourse and therefore presumed to be at the forefront of a hearer's mind; also called old information.

glide A transition from a vowel of one quality to a vowel of another quality. In [iᵊ], the superscript schwa represents a glide from the high front position of [i] to the mid central position of [ə]. Glides can be offglides, with the peak on the first element (as in [iᵊ]), or onglides, with the peak on the second element (as in certain pronunciations of *spoon* ['u]). See also *diphthong.

glottis A narrow aperture between two folds of muscle (the vocal cords) in the *larynx.

grammatical competence See *competence.

grammatical relation The syntactic role that a noun phrase plays in its *clause (for example, *subject or *direct object).

H

head The pivotal or central word in a phrase, giving the phrase its name and character, including its distributional and agreement properties, as with the noun in a noun phrase or the preposition in a prepositional phrase. Example: In a sentence like *A dozen pints of blood were donated*, the plural verb *were donated* agrees with *pints*, the head of the noun phrase subject, and not with *blood*.

homonymy The state of having identical expression but different meanings (*book a flight* and *buy a book*); *homophonous* is sometimes used with the related sense of 'sounding alike' but not necessarily having the same written form (*see* and *sea*) or meaning.

homophony In semantic analysis, refers to words that are pronounced alike but have different meanings, as in *two, to, too; see, sea.*

hyponym A term whose *referent is included in the referent of another term. Example: *Blue* is a hyponym of *color; sister* is a hyponym of *sibling.*

I

iconic sign See *representational sign.

illocution The intention that a speaker or writer has in producing a particular utterance. Example: The illocution of the utterance *Can you pass the salt?* is a request that the salt be passed and not (as the structure would indicate) an inquiry about the addressee's *ability* to pass the salt.

implicational universal A universal rule of the form "If condition P is satisfied, then conclusion Q holds."

indefinite See *definite.

indirect object One of two *grammatical relations known as objects, the other being a *direct object. Indirect objects usually occur in English before the direct object (*He gave the clerk a rose*).

indirect speech act An *utterance whose *locution (or literal meaning) and *illocution (or intended meaning) are different. Example: *Can you pass the salt?* is literally a yes/no question but is usually uttered as a request or polite directive for action.

Indo-European A *language family whose members are descendants of an ancestral language called Proto-Indo-European, spoken probably in Central Asia about 6,000 years ago.

infinitive The basic form of a verb, expressed in English sometimes with the particle *to*, as in *to see.*

infix A bound *morpheme that is inserted within another morpheme.

inflectional morpheme A *bound morpheme that creates variant forms of a word to mark its syntactic function in a sentence. Examples: The suffix *-s* added to a *verb (as in *paints*) marks the verb as agreeing with a third-person singular *subject; -er* (*taller*) marks *adjectives for comparative *degree.

information structure The level of structure at which certain elements in a sentence are highlighted or backgrounded according to their prominence in the discourse. See also *pragmatics.

instrumental motivation The kind of motivation one has in acquiring a second language so as to be able to use it for any purpose other than becoming a participating member of the social community that speaks the language.

integrative motivation The kind of motivation one has in acquiring a second language in order to become a socially functioning member of the community speaking that language.

interdental A *place of articulation* between the upper and lower teeth. Also used of sounds produced at that place. Examples of the sound: <th> as in English *thin* [θ] and *then* [ð].

interlanguage The form of a second language that a learner has internalized at any point in the acquisition process and which therefore underlies the learner's spontaneous utterances in the target language.

interrogative pronoun A kind of *pronoun* that serves to ask a question, as with *who, which,* and *whose.*

interweaving morpheme A discontinuous morpheme that is distributed across or within elements of another discontinuous morpheme, as various morphemes are distributed within the tri-literal Arabic root KTB (as in *kitaaba* and *iktataba*).

intransitive verb A verb that does not take a *direct object.* Examples: *She <u>smiled</u> graciously. Joyce <u>died</u> in Zurich.*

isogloss The geographical boundary marking the limit of the regional distribution of a particular word, pronunciation, or usage.

J

jargon Specialist terms, especially those used by occupational, recreational, or other specialist groups, such as with medical jargon or computer jargon.

L

language family A group of languages that have all developed from a single ancestral language.

language typology The classification of languages into types or kinds according to useful criteria such as word order or general phonological characteristics.

language universal See *universal.

larynx The part of the windpipe that houses the vocal cords; also called the voice box.

layered structure The levels of analysis in linguistic expression: expressions comprise *constituents* that are in turn made up of constituents that are in turn. . . . Example: *unalterable* has the two constituents *un* and *alterable*; *alterable* has the two constituents *alter* and *able*; this can be represented in the bracketing [un [alter + able]].

lexical category The category such as *noun, *verb, or *preposition* that a word belongs to based on its inflectional, distributional and collocational characteristics, and to a lesser extent its meaning. Also known as word class or part of speech.

lexical item A unit in the *lexicon*; the notion of lexical item includes all inflected forms; thus, *child, child's, children,* and *children's* constitute the lexical item CHILD.

lexical semantics The subfield of *semantics* that deals with word meaning.

lexicon The list of all words and *morphemes* stored in a native speaker's memory; this internalized dictionary includes all nonpredictable information about each *lexical item.

lingua franca A language *variety* used for communication among groups of people who do not otherwise share a common language. Example: English is the lingua franca of the international scientific community.

linguistic meaning The term used to cover sense meaning and referential meaning.

linguistic repertoire The set of language *varieties (including *registers and *dialects) used in the speaking and writing practices of a speech community; also called verbal repertoire.

liquid The name given to [r] and [l] in order to distinguish them from other *approximants.

locution The literal meaning of an *utterance. Example: The locution of the utterance *Can you close the window?* is a question about the hearer's ability to close the window.

logographic writing Writing in which each sign represents a word. Examples: <8> 'eight' and <$> 'dollar' are logographic signs, as are Chinese characters and Japanese kanji.

low back merger The result of a sound change in which the two formerly distinct vowels [ɑ] and [ɔ] came to be pronounced identically, such that in some North American English dialects the members of the pairs *hock* and *hawk* and *cot* and *caught* are not distinguished.

M

manner of articulation How the airstream is obstructed in the vocal tract in the production of a sound.

marked The elements of a *semantic field with less basic meaning. Usually, more marked elements have more precise meanings than less marked elements, can be described in terms of less marked elements, and are less frequent in natural speech. Example: *Cocker spaniel* is more marked than *dog*.

matrix clause A clause in which another clause is embedded, as in the underscored parts of *The film* that he rented *had been widely panned*.

meaning The term covers *linguistic meaning, *social meaning, and *affective meaning.

merger The historical process in which two distinct sounds evolve into a single sound, as exemplified in the *low back merger.

metaphor An extension of a word's use beyond its primary meaning to include referents that bear some similarity to the word's primary referent, as in *eye of a needle*.

minimal pair A pair of words that differ by only a single sound in the same position. Examples: *look/took*; *spill/still*; *keep/coop*.

modality A grammatical category of *verbs marking speakers' attitudes toward the status of their assertions as factual (indicative), hypothetical (subjunctive), and so on; also called *mood*. While some languages mark modality by inflection on the verb, English uses *modal* verbs (e.g., *must, may,* and *can,* as in *must begin, may arrive, can talk*), which lack typical morphological inflections such as *-s* and *-ing*.

modes Channels of linguistic expression: speaking, writing, and signing.

monomorphemic Said of a word comprising a single *morpheme, as with *tell, tall,* or the *tale*.

mood See *modality.

morpheme The smallest linguistic unit that carries meaning or serves a grammatical function. A morpheme can be realized as a word, as with *zebra* and *paint*, or part of a word, as in *zebras*, which contains two morphemes (ZEBRA and 'PLURAL') and *repainted*, containing three (-RE, PAINT, and 'PAST TENSE').

N

nasals A class of sounds (including the consonants [m] and [n]) produced by lowering the velum and allowing air to pass out of the vocal tract through the nasal cavity.

nativization The process through which a speech community adopts another speech community's language as its own and modifies the structure of that new language, thus developing a new dialect that becomes characteristic of the adopting community.

natural class A set of speech sounds that can all be characterized by one or a few phonological features and that includes all the sounds of a given language that are characterized by those phonological features. Example: /p t k/ form the natural class of voiceless stops in English because the class includes all the voiceless stops in the language and no other sounds.

negative concord The realization of negation on all of the elements of an expression that are able to carry such markers; also called *double negation* or *multiple negation*. Example: *She don't want none.*

neutralized The localized loss of a distinction between two *phonemes* that have identical *allophones* in a certain environment. Example: In American English, /t/ in *metal* and /d/ in *medal* are neutralized in that both are pronounced [ɾ] (intervocalically following a stressed syllable).

new information Information introduced into a *discourse* for the first time. See *given information*.

node The name given to a point in a tree diagram (or tree) from which at least one *branch* descends.

noun A *lexical category* of words that function syntactically as *heads* of noun phrases and semantically as *referring expressions*; nouns can be characterized morphologically by certain inflections and syntactically by their distribution in phrases and clauses; in traditional terms, a noun is defined semantically as the name of a person, place, or thing.

nucleus In a *syllable*, that part of the *rhyme* that is the peak; usually a *vowel*, but sometimes a *sonorant*; the nucleus is the sole essential element of a syllable. Example: In the English syllable [pɛn], [ɛ] is the nucleus.

number A grammatical category associated with *nouns* and *pronouns* and indicating something about the quantity of referents. Example: *Car* and *he* are marked for singular number, while *cars* and *they* are marked for plural number. Number can also be marked on verbs, usually in *agreement* with subjects, as in singular *He sleeps,* plural *They sleep.*

O

object See *direct object*.

oblique A noun phrase whose *grammatical relation* in a *clause* is other than *subject*, *direct object*, or *indirect object*; oblique usually marks semantic categories such as location or time and in English is usually expressed as the object of a preposition.

obstruent A cover term for *stops*, *fricatives*, and *affricates*, three classes of consonant sounds that impede or obstruct the airflow by constricting the vocal passage.

offglide See *glide*.

onset One or more consonants that precede the *rhyme* in a *syllable* constitute the onset; [p] is the onset in the syllable [pɛn]; [sp] in [spɛnt]; [str] in [strɛtʃ].

orthography A system of spelling used to achieve a match between the sound system of a language and the alphabet representing it.

P

paradigm The set of forms constituting the inflectional variants of a particular word; see also *declension* and *conjugation*.

participle Refers to -ING and -ED/-EN forms of the verb, as in *is walking, had kicked,* or *had been stolen.* (It does not refer to past-tense forms as in *they walked* or *she* *swam*); traditional terminology calls the -ING form the present or progressive participle and the -ED/-EN form the past or perfective or passive participle.

person A grammatical category associated principally with pronouns marking reference to the speaker (first person), the addressee (second person), a third party (third person), or a combination of these; verbs in a clause are sometimes marked for person *agreement*, usually with their *subject*.

personal pronoun A kind of *pronoun* that refers to another entity whose referent is clear from the linguistic or situational *context*; personal pronouns represent parties to an interaction and are typically marked for *person* (speaker: first person; addressee: second person; or entities spoken about: third person) and *number* (e.g., singular, dual, plural).

phoneme A distinctive structural element in the sound system of a language. A phoneme is an abstract element (defined by a set of phonological features) that can have alternative manifestations (called *allophones*) in different phonological environments. Example: The English phoneme /p/ has several allophones, including aspirated [pʰ], unreleased [p˺], and unaspirated [p].

phonetics The study of sounds made in the production of human speech.

phonological rule A rule that specifies the *allophones* of a *phoneme* and their distribution in a particular language and generally of the form A → B / C_D, meaning A is realized as B in the environment after C and before D.

phonotactic constraints Rules that specify the structure of *syllables* permitted in a particular language.

phrase Refers to syntactic *constituents* smaller than a *clause* and, usually but not always, larger than a word—as in noun phrase, adjective phrase, prepositional phrase.

phrase-structure rule A rule that describes the composition of *constituents* in *underlying structure*; also called rewrite rule or phrase-structure expansion rule. Example: S → NP VP is a phrase-structure rule stating that a sentence is made up of a noun phrase and a verb phrase in that order.

pictogram A symbolic drawing that represents an object or idea independently of the word that refers to that object or idea, such as highway signs that pictorially indicate dangerous curves or merging traffic without the use of words.

pidgin A contact language that develops in multilingual colonial situations, in which one language (commonly that of the colonizer) forms the base for a simple and usually unstable new *variety*; pidgins are restricted in use and not spoken natively by anyone.

place of articulation The location in the mouth cavity where the airstream is obstructed in the production of a sound. Example: *Alveolar* sounds such as [t] and [s] are produced by obstructing the airstream at the alveolar ridge.

polysemy Refers to multiple related meanings for a given word or sentence; a word with more than one meaning is said to be polysemic.

portmanteau word A word combining more than one *morpheme* in such a way that the morphemes cannot be separated into distinct sets of phonological segments. Examples: French *du*, comprising DE and LE; sometimes used to refer to a word combining parts of other words, as with *smog* (from *smoke* and *fog*).

possessor A *grammatical relation* between two nouns that are closely associated, often by virtue of having a possessive relationship. Examples: <u>Luke's</u> harp, the book's cover.

postposition A category of words that serve syntactically as *heads* of postpositional phrases and semantically to indicate a relationship between two entities; except that they follow their complements, postpositions are like *prepositions*. Examples: Japanese *Taroo <u>no</u>* 'of Taro' and *hasi <u>de</u>* 'with chopsticks.'

pragmatics The subfield of linguistics that studies language use, in particular the relationship among *syntax, *semantics, and interpretation in light of the *context of situation.

predication The part of a *clause that makes a statement about a particular entity. Example: In *Lou likes ice cream,* the predication made of Lou is *likes ice cream.*

prefix An *affix that attaches to the front of a word stem.

preposition A category of words that serve syntactically as *heads of prepositional phrases and semantically to indicate a relationship between two entities. Examples: <u>to</u> *school,* <u>with</u> *liberty,* <u>in</u> *the spring.* See also *postpositions.

productivity The ability to generate and comprehend an infinite number of sentences by relying on a language's ability to combine and recombine a relatively small number of structures into sentences.

pronoun Any of several closed categories of words, traditionally defined as taking the place of nouns (or more accurately noun phrases). *Personal pronouns (e.g., *she, they, you*) are the most familiar type; other types include *relative pronouns, *demonstrative pronouns, *interrogative pronouns, and *indefinite pronouns (e.g, *anyone, someone*).

prosody Refers to variations in the volume, pitch, rhythm, and speed of speech.

R

recursion The property of incorporating linguistic structures within other linguistic structures, as with embedding a *clause within another clause; saying *She said* [*she wanted one*] instead of *She said* [*something*].

redundancy Repeated information in a linguistic expression. Example: *Those books* expresses plurality of the noun phrase in both the *determiner and the *noun, as contrasted with *the books,* which represents it only on the noun.

reduplication A morphological process by which a *morpheme or part of a morpheme is repeated, creating a word with a different meaning or lexical category. Example: Mandarin Chinese *sànsànbu* 'to take a leisurely walk' is formed by reduplicating the first syllable of *sànbu* 'to walk.' Unlike reduplication, repetition (as in English *very, very tired*) does not create a new word.

reference A semantic category through which language provides information about the relationship between a noun phrase and its *referent.

referent The real-world entity (person, object, notion, situation) referred to by a linguistic expression.

referential Said of a noun phrase that refers to a particular entity; *a good piano teacher* is referential in *Tom knows a good piano teacher* but not in *Tom wants to find a good piano teacher.*

referential meaning The meaning that an *expression has by virtue of its ability to refer to an entity; referential meaning is contrasted with *social meaning and *affective meaning and is sometimes called denotation.

referring expression An *expression that refers to an entity or situation.

reflex In historical linguistics, a linguistic form that derives from an earlier form called its *etymon; reflexes of the same etymon are called *cognates.

register A language *variety associated with a particular situation of use. Examples: baby talk, legalese, telephone conversation.

regular sound change A sound change that affects all the words in which a particular sound occurs in a particular sound environment. Regular sound change may be *conditioned sound change or *unconditioned sound change. See *sporadic sound change.

relative clause A *clause syntactically embedded in a noun phrase and semantically serving to modify a noun. The modified noun is the *head of the relative clause.

Example: In *This is the book that I told you about*, the underscored relative clause modifies *book*.

relative pronoun Within a relative clause, a *pronoun* referring to an entity expressed in the *matrix clause*, as in *The book that I gave to Shirley disappointed her*.

repair A sequence of turns in a conversation during which a previous *utterance* is edited, corrected, or clarified.

repertoire See *linguistic repertoire*.

representational sign A sign that is basically arbitrary but nevertheless bears some resemblance to its referent or some feature of its referent. Example: *III* 'three'; *trickle, meow*.

rhyme That part of a *syllable* comprising the *nucleus* and the *coda*. Example: In the syllable [pɪn], [ɪn] is the rhyme; in [wɪʃt] 'wished,' [ɪʃt] is the rhyme.

S

segment An individual sound in a language, comprising a set of phonological features such as voiced alveolar stop for [d] or voiceless interdental fricative for [θ]. More accurately, a segment is a set of gestures comprising the combination of those features. As examples, the English words [θɪn] 'thin,' [nod] 'node,' [ʃɪp] 'ship,' [tʃɪp] 'chip,' and [ʤʌʤ] 'judge' have three segments each.

semantic field A set of words with an identifiable semantic affinity. Example: *angry, sad, happy, exuberant, depressed*.

semantic role The way in which the *referent* of a noun phrase is involved in the situation described or represented by the *clause*, for example as agent, patient, or cause.

semantics The systematic ways in which languages structure meaning, especially in words, phrases, and sentences; also used of the study of those ways.

sequence constraints See *phonotactic constraints*.

sibilant A member of a set of *fricative* sounds made by passing a continuous stream of air through a narrowed passage in the vocal tract, thereby causing hissing, such as that created between the blade of the tongue and the back of the *alveolar* ridge in the production of [s] and [ʃ], as in *sis* and *shush*.

sign An indicator of something else, for example of an object or event, as smoke is a sign of fire and <8> is a sign of the number 'eight.' See also *representational sign*.

simple sentence A sentence that contains only one *clause*.

slang Words and expressions used in situations of extreme informality, sometimes with rebellious undertones or an intention of distancing its users from certain mainstream social values.

social dialect A language *variety* characteristic of a social group, typically socioeconomic groups, gender groups, or ethnic groups, as distinct from regional groups.

social meaning Information that linguistic *expressions* convey about the social characteristics of their producers and of the situation in which they are produced; together with *affective meaning*, social meaning is sometimes called *connotation*.

sonorant A class of *consonant* sounds comprising *nasals* and *liquids*.

speech act An action carried out by the use of language in particular circumstances, as with promising, lying, and inviting.

speech event An event in which members of a community interact linguistically on one or more topics, for a particular purpose, with awareness of the social relations among the interlocutors.

speech situation Usually broader than a *speech event* but used in this book to represent the coming together of significant factors such as purpose, setting, and participants in the creation of a *discourse*.

split A historical development in which a single sound changes into two sounds, one of which may be the original sound. Example: Proto-Indo-European *p became /f/ in Germanic and /p/ in Romance.

sporadic sound change A sound change that affects individual words but not all words in which the sound occurs or even all those that share a particular linguistic environment. Example: The pronunciation of *nuclear* as "nu-ku-lar" is a sporadic sound change. See *regular sound change.

standard variety The language *variety that has been recorded in dictionaries and grammars and serves a speech community especially in its written and public functions.

stop A speech sound created when air is built up at a *place of articulation in the vocal tract and suddenly released through the mouth; called *oral stops* when nasals are excluded.

style See *register.

subcategorization Information about the types of clause structure that each *verb permits in the verb phrase. For example, a verb may permit one or two noun phrases, or none; as in *He burned the rice*, *She sold him the book*, and *He fell*, respectively.

subgroup A set of languages that belong to the same *language family and developed as a single language for a period of time after other subgroups had become separate languages. Examples: Romance and Germanic are subgroups of *Indo-European; West Germanic is the subgroup of Germanic to which English belongs; also called a *branch*.

subject A noun phrase immediately dominated by S in a phrase structure.

subordinating conjunction or subordinator A word that links clauses to one another in a noncoordinate role, thus marking the boundary between an embedded clause and its *matrix clause. Examples: *I think that he fell. She wondered whether he won.*

suffix An *affix that attaches to the end of a word stem.

surface form A word's actual pronunciation; generated by the application of the *phonological rules of a language to the *underlying form; sometimes also said of sentences (see *underlying structure).

surface structure The *constituent structure of a sentence after all applicable *syntactic operations (sometimes called *transformations*) have applied.

syllabic writing Writing in which each graphic *sign represents a *syllable rather than a word or a sound.

syllable A phonological unit consisting of one or more sounds, including a peak (or *nucleus) that is usually a *vowel or *diphthong; frequent syllable types in the world's languages are CV and CVC.

synonymous Used in *semantics to refer to words or sentences that mean the same thing.

syntactic operation A process (or rule) that alters a *constituent structure, transforming it into another constituent structure in a systematic way.

syntax The structure of sentences and the study of sentence structure.

T

tap See *flap.

tense A category of the *verb that marks time reference, for example past (*walked*) or present (*walk*).

text A unitary stretch of *expression created in a real-world social situation; usually but not always longer than a sentence (*Smoking Not Permitted*; *Closed*; *Gesundheit*); more commonly used in written than in spoken or signed expression but applicable to any mode; sometimes used for a piece of text rather than an entire text.

Examples: a novel, a personal letter, a classified advertisement, a screenplay, song lyrics, a scholarly or scientific article.

topic The main center of attention in a sentence; what the sentence is about.

transformation See *syntactic operation.*

transitive verb A verb that takes a *direct object,* as in She <u>found</u> the book.

trill A *manner of articulation* characterized by the rapid vibrating of one articulator against another articulator (but not including vocal cord vibration).

turn A basic term in the analysis of conversation, which comprises a series of turns among interlocutors.

typology A field of inquiry that seeks to classify the languages of the world into different types according to particular structural characteristics.

U

unconditioned sound change A *regular sound change* that affects every word in which the sound occurs. See *conditioned sound change.*

underlying form The form of a *morpheme* that is stored in the internalized *lexicon;* sometimes also said of sentences (see *underlying structure*).

underlying structure The abstract structure of a sentence before any *syntactic operation* has applied; sometimes called deep structure.

universal A linguistic pattern at play in most or all of the world's languages. See also *absolute universal* and *universal tendency.*

universal tendency A linguistic pattern at play in most, but not all, of the world's languages. Example: Most verb-final languages place adjectives before the nouns they modify.

utterance *Expression* produced in a particular context with a particular intention.

V

variety Any language, *dialect,* or *register.*

velar A *consonant* sound whose *place of articulation* is the velum, that is, a consonant produced by the tongue approaching or touching the roof of the mouth at the velum.

verb A category of words that syntactically determine the structure of a *clause,* especially with respect to noun phrases; that semantically express the action or state of being represented by a clause; and that can be marked morphologically for certain categories (not all of which are realized in English): *tense* (present: walk/past: walked), *mood,* *aspect* (walk/walking), *person* (first: walk/third: walks), and *number* (singular: walks/plural: walk). See also *auxiliary verb.*

voicing The vibration in the *larynx* caused by air from the lungs passing through the vocal cords when they are partly closed; speech sounds are said to be *voiced* or *voiceless.*

vowel sounds One of two major classes of sounds (the other being *consonants*), vowels are articulated without complete closure in the oral cavity and without sufficient narrowing to create the friction characteristic of consonants. Abbreviated V.

Index

NOTE: Separate indices for languages, internet sites and videos follow this general index. Terms followed by an asterisk * are defined in the Glossary. The abbreviation "ex" following a page number refers to an exercise.

Index of Languages

Index of Internet Sites, Films and Videos

Credits

This page constitutes an extension of the copyright page. We have made every effort to trace the ownership of all copyrighted material and to secure permission from copyright holders. In the event of any question arising as to the use of any material, we will be pleased to make the necessary corrections in future printings. Thanks are due to the follow authors, publishers, and agents for permission to use the material indicated.

Chapter 1: 19: Source: "Language in the USA" edited by Edward Finegan and John R. Rickford, p. 232 (Cambridge, UK: Cambridge University Press, 2004). 19: Source: "Language in the USA" edited by Edward Finegan and John R. Rickford, p. 233 (Cambridge, UK: Cambridge University Press, 2004).

Chapter 3: 88: From Ladefoged. "Course in Phonetics," 4E. © 2001 Heinle/Arts & Sciences, a part of Cengage Learning, Inc. Reproduced by permission. www .cengage.com/permissions

Chapter 8: 289: Source: D. Biber, S. Conrad, R. Reppen, "Corpus Linguistics." (Cambridge, UK: Cambridge University Press, 1998).

Chapter 10: 343: Source: "The Social Stratification of English in New York City" by William Labov (Washington, D.C.: Center for Applied Linguistics, 1966). 344: Source: B. Wald and T. Shopen, "A Researcher's Guide to the Sociolinguistic Variable (ING)" in "Style and Variables in English," ed. Timothy Shopen and Joseph Williams, p. 247 (Cambridge, MA: Winthrop, 1981). 344: Source: "Sociolinguistics: An Introduction to Language and Society," 4th ed., by Peter Trudgill (New York: Penguin, 2000). 345, 346: Source: Biber, D., "Variation across Speech and Writing" (Cambridge, UK: Cambridge University Press, 1988).

Chapter 11: 376: Source: From "American Regional Dialects: A Word Geography" by Craig M. Carver, p. 248 (Ann Arbor: University of Michigan Press, 1987). 378: From "A Word Geography of the Eastern United States" by Hans Kurath (Ann Arbor: University of Michigan Press, 1949). 379: Source: From "The Regional Vocabulary of Texas" by E. Bagby Atwood (Austin: University of Texas Press, 1962). Copyright © 1962. 379: Source: From "Linguistic Atlas of the Gulf States, Vol. I: Handbook for The Linguistic Atlas of the Gulf States" edited by Lee Pederson (Athens: University of Georgia Press, 1986). Reprinted by permission of The University of Georgia Press. 380: "Principal and Subsidiary Dialect Areas in the North-Central States" by Albert H. Marckwardt, 1957. 381: From Allen. "Linguistic Atlas of Upper Midwest, Vol. 1," 1E. © 1982 Gale, a part of Cengage Learning, Inc. Reproduced by permission. www.cengage.com/permissions. 383, 384: Reprinted by permission of the publisher from "Dictionary of American Regional English, Vol. 1 A–C," edited by Frederic G. Cassidy, Cambridge, Mass.: The Belknap Press of Harvard University Press, Copyright © 1985 by the President and Fellows of Harvard College. 386, 387, 388: Source: Labov, William, 1996. "The Organization of Dialect Diversity In America," available at http://www .ling.upenn.edu/phono_atlas/ICSLP4.html. 395, 396, 397: From: Labov,

William. 2006. "The Social Stratification of English in New York City," 2nd ed. (Cambridge, UK: Cambridge University Press). 398: From" Sociolinguistics: An Introduction to Language and Society," 4th ed., by Peter Trudgill (New York: Penguin, 2000). 399: Source: 'Some Results of a Sociolinguistic Study of Montreal French' by Gillian Sankoff and Henrietta Cedergren in "Linguistic Diversity in Canadian Society," edited by R. Darnell, pp. 61–87 (Edmonton: Linguistic Research, 1971). 400: Source: 'Diachronic Reconstruction by Dialect Comparison of Variable Constraints' by Tracy D. Terrell in "Variation Omnibus," edited by David Sankoff and Henrietta Cedergren, pp. 115–124 (Edmonton: Linguistic Research, 1981). 401: Source: 'Some Results of a Sociolinguistic Study of Montreal French' by Gillian Sankoff and Henrietta Cedergren in "Linguistic Diversity in Canadian Society," edited by R. Darnell, pp. 61–87 (Edmonton: Linguistic Research, 1971).

Chapter 12: 423: Source: "The Prehistory of Polynesia," Jennings, J. D., 1979. 432: Source: Terrell, 1986, "Prehistory in the Pacific Islands: A Study of Variation in Language, Customs, and Human Biology." 440: Source: "The Prehistory of Polynesia," Jennings, J. D., 1979. 444: Source: "Language in Africa: An Introductory Survey" by Edgar A. Gregersen (New York: Gordon & Breach, 1977). 453: Copyright © Grass Roots Comic Company Ltd. (bob.browne@ global.net.pg).

Chapter 13: 487: From "Historical Linguistics" by Theodora Bynon, p. 82 (Cambridge, MA: Cambridge University Press, 1977). Reprinted with the permission of Cambridge University Press.

Chapter 14: 514: After Ingram, David. 1989. "First Language Acquisition: Method, Description, and Explanation" (Cambridge: Cambridge University Press), pp. 371–72.